# THE COMPLETE ALIEN OMNIBUS

*Also by Alan Dean Foster*

# THE COMPLETE ALIEN OMNIBUS

# ALIEN

Novelization by Alan Dean Foster
Screenplay by Dan O'Bannon
Story by Dan O'Bannon and Ronald Shusett

# ALIENS

Novelization by Alan Dean Foster
Based on the screenplay by James Cameron

# ALIEN$^3$

Novelization by Alan Dean Foster
Based on a screenplay by David Giler
& Walter Hill and Larry Ferguson
Story by Vincent Ward

WARNER BOOKS

A *Warner* Book
*Alien* first published in Great Britain in 1979 by Futura Publications
TM & © 1979 by Twentieth Century Fox Film Corporation

*Aliens* first published in 1986 by Futura Publications
TM & © 1986 by Twentieth Century Fox Film Corporation

*Aliens*³ first published in Great Britain in 1992 by Warner Books,
by arrangement with Warner Books, Inc, New York
TM & © 1992 by Twentieth Century Fox Film Corporation

This omnibus edition published by Warner Books 1993
by arrangement with Warner Books, Inc, New York
TM & © 1993 Twentieth Century Fox Film Corporation

A CIP catalogue record for this book
is available from the British Library.

ISBN 0 7515 0667 2

Photoset in North Wales by
Derek Doyle & Associates, Mold, Clwyd.
Printed in England by Clays Ltd, St Ives plc

Warner Books
A Division of
Little, Brown and Company (UK) Limited
165 Great Dover Street
London SE1 4YA

# ALIEN

Screenplay by Dan O'Bannon
Story by Dan O'Bannon and
Ronald Shusett

For Jim McQuade
A good friend and fellow explorer
of extreme possibilities . . .

**I**

Seven dreamers.

You must understand that they were not professional dreamers. Professional dreamers are highly paid, respected, much sought-after talents. Like the majority of us, these seven dreamt without effort or discipline. Dreaming professionally, so that one's dreams can be recorded and played back for the entertainment of others, is a much more demanding proposition. It requires the ability to regulate semiconscious creative impulses and to stratify imagination, an extra-ordinarily difficult combination to achieve. A professional dreamer is simultaneously the most organized of all artists and the most spontaneous. A subtle weaver of speculation, not straightforward and clumsy like you or I. Or these certain seven sleepers.

Of them all, Ripley came closest to possessing that special potential. She had a little ingrained dream talent and more flexibility of imagination than her companions. But she lacked real inspiration and the powerful maturity of thought characteristic of the prodreamer.

She was very good at organizing stores and cargo, at pigeonholing carton A in storage chamber B or matching up manifests. It was in the warehouse of the mind that her filing system went awry. Hopes and fears, speculations and half creations slipped haphazardly from compartment to compartment.

1

Warrant officer Ripley needed more self-control. The raw rococo thoughts lay waiting to be tapped, just below the surface of realization. A little more effort, a greater intensity of self-recognition and she would have made a pretty good prodreamer. Or so she occasionally thought.

Captain Dallas now, he appeared lazy while being the best organized of all. Nor was he lacking in imagination. His beard was proof of that. Nobody took a beard into the freezers. Nobody except Dallas. It was a part of his personality, he'd explained to more than one curious shipmate. He'd no more part with the antique facial fuzz than he would with any other part of his anatomy. Captain of two ships Dallas was: the interstellar tug *Nostromo*, and his body. Both would remain intact in dreaming as well as when awake.

So he had the regulatory capability, and a modicum of imagination. But a professional dreamer requires a deal more than a modicum of the last, and that's a deficiency that can't be compensated for by a disproportionate quantity of the first. Dallas was no more realistic prodreamer material than Ripley.

Kane was less controlled in thought and action than was Dallas, and possessed far less imagination. He was a good executive officer. Never would he be a captain. That requires a certain drive coupled with the ability to command others, neither of which Kane had been blessed with. His dreams were translucent, formless shadows compared to those of Dallas, just as Kane was a thinner, less vibrant echo of the captain. That did not make him less likeable. But prodreaming requires a certain extra energy, and Kane had barely enough for day-to-day living.

Parker's dreams were not offensive, but they were less pastoral than Kane's. There was little imagination in them at all. They were too specialized, and dealt only rarely with human things. One could expect nothing else from a ship's engineer.

Direct they were, and occasionally ugly. In wakefulness this deeply buried offal rarely showed itself, when the engineer became irritated or angry. Most of the ooze and contempt fermenting at the bottom of his soul's cistern was kept well hidden. His shipmates never saw beyond the distilled Parker floating on top, never had a glimpse of what was bubbling and brewing deep inside.

Lambert was more the inspiration of dreamers than dreamer herself. In hypersleep her restless musings were filled with intersystem plottings and load factors cancelled out by fuel considerations. Occasionally imagination entered into such dream structures, but never in a fashion fit to stir the blood of others.

Parker and Brett often imagined their own systems interplotting with hers. They considered the question of load factors and spatial juxtapositions in a manner that would have infuriated Lambert had she been aware of them. Such unauthorized musings they kept to themselves, securely locked in daydreams and nightdreams, lest they make her mad. It would not do to upset Lambert. As the *Nostromo*'s navigator she was the one primarily responsible for seeing them safely home, and that was the most exciting and desirable cojoining any man could imagine.

Brett was only listed as an engineering technician. That was a fancy way of saying he was just as smart and knowledgeable as Parker but lacked seniority. The two men formed an odd pair, unequal and utterly different to outsiders. Yet they coexisted and functioned together smoothly. In large part their success as both friends and coworkers was due to Brett never intruding on Parker's mental ground. The tech was as solemn and phlegmatic in outlook and speech as Parker was voluble and volatile. Parker could rant for hours over the failure of a microchip circuit, damning its ancestry back to the soil from which its rare earth constituents were first mined. Brett would patiently comment, 'right'.

For Brett, that single word was much more than a mere statement of opinion. It was an affirmation of self. For him, silence was the cleanest form of communication. In loquacious-

**4**   ALAN DEAN FOSTER

ness lay insanity.

And then there was Ash. Ash was the science officer, but that wasn't what made his dreams so funny. Funny peculiar, not funny ha-ha. His dreams were the most professionally organized of all the crew's. Of them all, his came nearest to matching his awakened self. Ash's dreams held absolutely no delusions.

That wasn't surprising if you really knew Ash. None of his six crewmates did, though. Ash knew himself well. If asked, he could have told you why he could never become a prodreamer. None ever thought to ask, despite the fact that the science officer clearly found prodreaming more fascinating than any of them.

Oh, and there was the cat. Name of Jones. A very ordinary housecat, or, in this instance, shipcat. Jones was a large yellow tom of uncertain parentage and independent mien, long accustomed to the vagaries of ship travel and the idiosyncrasies of humans who travelled through space. It too slept the cold sleep, and dreamt simple dreams of warm, dark places and gravity-bound mice.

Of all the dreamers on board he was the only contented one, though he could not be called an innocent.

It was a shame none of them was qualified as prodreamers, since each had more time to dream in the course of their work than any dozen professionals, despite the slowing of their dream pace by the cold sleep. Necessity made dreaming their principal avocation. A deep-space crew can't do anything in the freezers *but* sleep and dream. They might remain forever amateurs, but they had long ago become very competent ones.

Seven of them there were. Seven quiet dreamers in search of a nightmare.

While it possessed a consciousness of a sort, the *Nostromo* did not dream. It did not need to, anymore than it needed the preserving effect of the freezers. If it did dream, such musings must have been brief and fleeting, since it never slept. It worked, and maintained, and made certain its hibernating human complement stayed always a step ahead of ever-ready death, which followed the cold sleep like a vast grey shark behind a ship at sea.

Evidence of the *Nostromo*'s unceasing mechanical vigilance was everywhere on the quiet ship, in soft hums and lights that formed the breath of instrumental sentience. It permeated the very fabric of the vessel, extended sensors to check every circuit and strut. It had sensors outside too, monitoring the pulse of the cosmos. Those sensors had fastened on to an electromagnetic anomaly.

One portion of the *Nostromo*'s brain was particularly adept at distilling sense out of anomalies. It had thoroughly chewed this one up, found the flavour puzzling, examined the results of analysis, and reached a decision. Slumbering instrumentalities were activated, dormant circuits again regulated the flow of electrons. In celebration of this decision, banks of brilliant lights winked on, life signs of stirring mechanical breath.

A distinctive beeping sounded, though as yet there were only artificial tympanums present to hear and acknowledge. It was a sound not heard on the *Nostromo* for some time, and it signified an infrequent happening.

Within this awakening bottle of clicks and flashes, of devices conversing with each other, lay a special room. Within this room of white metal lay seven cocoons of snow-coloured metal and plastic.

A new noise filled this chamber, an explosive exhalation that filled it with freshly scrubbed, breathable atmosphere. Mankind had willingly placed himself in this position, trusting in little tin gods like the *Nostromo* to provide him with the breath of life when he could not do so for himself.

Extensions of that half-sentient electronic being now tested the newly exuded air and pronounced it satisfactory for sustaining life in puny organics such as men. Additional lights flared, more linkages closed. Without fanfare, the lids on the seven chrysalises opened, and the caterpillar shapes within began to emerge once more into the light.

Seen shorn of their dreams, the seven members of the *Nostromo*'s crew were even less impressive than they'd been in hypersleep. For one thing, they were dripping wet from the preservative cryosleep fluid that had filled and surrounded their bodies. However analeptic, slime of any sort is not becoming.

For another, they were naked, and the liquid was a poor substitute for the slimming and shaping effects of the artificial skins called clothes.

'Jesus,' muttered Lambert, disgustedly wiping fluid from her shoulders and sides, 'am I cold!' She stepped out of the coffin that preserved life instead of death, began fumbling in a nearby compartment. Using the towel she found there, she commenced wiping the transparent syrup from her legs.

'Why the hell can't Mother warm the ship *before* breaking us out of storage?' She was working on her feet now, trying to remember where she'd dumped her clothes.

'You know why,' Parker was too busy with his own sticky, tired self to bother staring at the nude navigator. 'Company policy. Energy conservation, which translates as Company cheap. Why waste excess power warming the freezer section until the last possible second? Besides, it's always cold coming out of hypersleep. You know what the freezer takes your internal temperature down to.'

'Yeah, I know. But it's still cold.' She mumbled it, knowing Parker was perfectly correct but resenting having to admit it. She'd never cared much for the engineer.

Damn it, Mother, she thought, seeing the goosebumps on her forearm, let's have some *heat*!

Dallas was towelling himself off, dry-sponging away the last of the cryosleep gunk, and trying not to stare at something the others could not see. He'd noticed it even before rising from his freezer. The ship had arranged it so that he would.

'Work'll warm us all up fast enough.' Lambert muttered something unintelligible. 'Everybody to your stations. I assume you all remember what you're getting paid for. Besides sleeping away your troubles.'

No one smiled or bothered to comment. Parker glanced across to where his partner was sitting up in his freezer. 'Morning. Still with us, Brett?'

'Yo.'

'Lucky us.' That came from Ripley. She stretched, turning it into a more aesthetic movement than any of the others. 'Nice to know our prime conversationalist is as garrulous as ever.'

Brett just smiled, said nothing. He was as verbal as the machines he serviced, which was to say not at all, and it was a running joke within the septuple crew family. They were laughing with him at such times, not at him.

Dallas was doing side twists, elbows parallel to the floor, hands together in front of his sternum. He fancied he could hear his long-unused muscles squeak. The flashing yellow light, eloquent as any voice, monopolized his thoughts. That devilish little sun-hued cyclops was the ship's way of telling them they'd been awakened for something other than the end of their journey. He was already wondering why.

Ash sat up, looked around expressionlessly. For all the animation in his face, he might as well still have been in hypersleep. 'I feel dead.' He was watching Kane. The executive officer was yawning, still not fully awake. It was Ash's professional opinion that the exec actually enjoyed hypersleep and would spend his whole life as a narcoleptic if so permitted.

Unaware of the science officer's opinion, Parker glanced over at him, spoke pleasantly. 'You look dead.' He was aware that his own features probably looked no better. Hypersleep tired the skin as well as the muscles. His attention turned to Kane's coffin. The exec was finally sitting up.

'Nice to be back.' He blinked.

'Couldn't tell it to any of us, not by the time it takes you to wake up.'

Kane looked hurt. 'That's a damn slander, Parker. I'm just slower than the rest of you, that's all.'

'Yeah.' The engineer didn't press the point, turned to the

captain, who was absorbed in studying something out of the engineer's view. 'Before we dock, maybe we'd better go over the bonus situation again.'

Brett showed faint signs of enthusiasm, his first since awakening. 'Yeah.'

Parker continued, slipping on his boots. 'Brett and I think we deserve a full share. Full bonus for successful completion plus salary and interest.'

At least he knew deep sleep hadn't harmed his engineering staff, Dallas mused tiredly. Barely conscious for a couple of minutes, they were complaining already.

'You two will get what you contracted for. No more and no less. Just like everybody else.'

'Everybody gets more than us,' said Brett softly. For him, that constituted a major speech. It had no effect on the captain, however. Dallas had no time now for trivialities or half-serious wordplay. That blinking light commanded his full attention, and choreographed his thoughts to the exclusion of all else.

'Everybody else deserves more than you two. Complain to the Company disburser if you want. Now get below.'

'Complain to the Company.' Parker was muttering unhappily as he watched Brett swing out of his coffin, commence drying his legs. 'Might as well try complaining directly to God.'

'Same thing.' Brett was checking a weak service light on his own freezer compartment. Barely conscious, naked and dripping with liquid, he was already hard at work. He was the sort of person who could walk for days on a broken leg but was unable to ignore a malfunctioning toilet.

Dallas started for the central computer room, called back over a shoulder. 'One of you jokers get the cat.'

It was Ripley who lifted a limp yellowish form from one of the freezers. She wore a hurt expression. 'You needn't be so indifferent about it.' She stroked the soaked animal affectionately. 'It's not a piece of equipment. Jones is a member of the crew as much as any of us.'

'More than some.' Dallas was watching Parker and Brett,

fully dressed now, receding in the direction of engineering. 'He doesn't fill my few on-board waking hours with complaints about salary or bonuses.'

Ripley departed, the cat enveloped in a thick dry towel. Jones was purring unsteadily, licking himself with great dignity. It was not his first time out of hypersleep. For the present, he would tolerate the ignominy of being carried.

Dallas had finished drying himself. Now he touched a button set into the base of his coffin. A drawer slid silently outward on nearly frictionless bearings. It contained his clothing and few personal effects.

As he was dressing, Ash ambled over to stand nearby. The science officer kept his voice low, spoke as he finished seaming his clean shirt.

'Mother wants to talk to you?' As he whispered, he nodded in the direction of the yellow light flashing steadily on the suspended console nearby.

'I saw it right off.' Dallas slipped arms into shirt. 'Hard yellow. Security one, not warning. Don't tell the others. If anything's seriously wrong, they'll find out soon enough.' He slipped into an unpressed brown jacket, left it hanging open.

'It can't be too bad, whatever it is.' Ash sounded hopeful, gestured again at the steadily winking light. 'It's only yellow, not red.'

'For the moment.' Dallas was no optimist. 'I'd have preferred waking up to a nice, foresty green.' He shrugged, tried to sound as hopeful as Ash. 'Maybe the autochef's on the blink. That might be a blessing, considering what it calls food.'

He attempted a smile, failed. The *Nostromo* was not human. It did not play practical jokes on its crew, and it would not have awakened them from hypersleep with a yellow warning light without a perfectly good reason. A malfunctioning autochef did not qualify as a candidate for the latter.

Oh well. After several months of doing nothing but sleeping, he had no right to complain if a few hours' honest sweat was now required of him . . .

The central computer room was little different from the other awake rooms aboard the *Nostromo*. A disarming kaleidoscope of lights and screens, readouts and gauges, it conveyed the impression of a wild party inhabited by a dozen drunken Christmas trees.

Settling himself into a thickly padded contour seat, Dallas considered how to proceed. Ash took the seat opposite the Mind Bank, manipulated controls with more speed and ease than a man just out of hypersleep ought to have. The science officer's ability to handle machines was unmatched.

It was a special rapport Dallas often wished he possessed. Still groggy from the after-effects of hypersleep, he punched out a primary request. Distortion patterns chased each other across the screen, settled down to form recognizable words. Dallas checked his wording, found it standard.

ALERT OVERMONITORING FUNCTION FOR MATRIX DISPLAY AND INQUIRY.

The ship found it acceptable also, and Mother's reply was immediate. OVERMONITOR ADDRESS MATRIX. Columns of informational categorizations lined up for inspection beneath this terse legend.

Dallas examined the long list of fine print, located the section he wanted, and typed in, COMMAND PRIORITY ALERT.

OVERMONITOR FUNCTION READY FOR INQUIRY, Mother responded. Computer minds were not programmed for verbosity. Mother was no exception to the rule.

Which was fine with Dallas. He wasn't in a talkative mood. He typed briefly, WHAT'S THE STORY, MOTHER?, and waited . . .

You couldn't say that the bridge of the *Nostromo* was spacious. Rather, it was somewhat less claustrophobic than the ship's other rooms and chambers, but not by much. Five contour seats awaited their respective occupants. Lights flashed patiently on and off at multiple consoles, while numerous screens of varying shapes and sizes also awaited the arrival of humans who were prepared to tell them what to display. A large bridge would have been an expensive frivolity, since the crew spent most of its flight time motionless in the freezers. It was designed strictly for work, not for relaxation or entertainment. The people who worked there knew this as thoroughly as did the machines.

A seal door slid silently into a wall. Kane entered, followed closely by Ripley, Lambert and Ash. They made their way to their respective stations, settled behind consoles with the ease and familiarity of old friends greeting one another after a long time apart.

A fifth seat remained empty, would continue unoccupied until Dallas returned from his tête-à-tête with Mother, the *Nostromo*'s Mind Bank computer. The nickname was an accurate one, not given in jest. People grow very serious when speaking about the machinery responsible for keeping them alive. For its part, the machine accepted the designation with equal solemnity, if not the emotional overtones.

Their clothing was as relaxed as their bodies, casual travesties of crew-member uniforms. Each reflected the personality of the wearer. Shirts and slacks, all were rumpled and worn after years of storage. So were the bodies they encased.

The first sounds spoken on the bridge in many years summed up the feelings of all present, even though they couldn't understand them. Jones was meowing when Ripley set him on the deck. He changed that to a purr, sliding sensuously around her ankles as she snuggled herself into the high-backed seat.

'Plug us in.' Kane was checking out his own console, caressing the automatics with his eyes, hunting for contrasts and uncertainties as Ripley and Lambert commenced throwing necessary switches and thumbing requisite controls.

There was a flurry of visual excitement as new lights and colours migrated across readout panels and screens. It gave the feeling that the instruments were pleased by the reappearance of their organic counterparts and were anxious to display their talents at first opportunity.

Fresh numbers and words appeared on readouts in front of

him. Kane correlated them with well-remembered ones imprinted in his mind. 'Looks okay so far. Give us something to stare at.'

Lambert's fingers danced an arpeggio on a tightly clustered rank of controls. Viewscreens came alive all over the bridge, most suspended from the ceiling for easier inspection. The navigator examined the square eyes closest to her seat, frowned immediately. Much that she saw was expected. Too much was not. The most important thing, the anticipated shape that should be dominating their vision, was absent. So important was it that it negated the normality of everything else.

'Where's Earth?'

Examining his own screen carefully, Kane discerned blackness speckled with stars and little else. Granting the possibility that they'd emerged from hyperspace too soon, the home system at least should be clear on the screen. But Sol was as invisible as the expected Earth.

'You're the navigator, Lambert. You tell me.'

There *was* a central sun fixed squarely in the middle of the multiple screens. But it wasn't Sol. The colour was wrong, and the computer-enhanced dots orbiting it were worse than wrong. They were impossible, improper of shape, of size, of number.

'That's not our system,' Ripley observed numbly, giving voice to the obvious.

'Maybe the trouble's just our orientation, not that of the stars.' Kane didn't sound very convincing, even to himself. 'Ships have been known to come out of hyperspace ass-backward to their intended destinations. That could be Centauri, at top amplification. Sol might be behind us. Let's take a scan before we do any panicking.' He did not add that the system visible on the screens resembled that of Centauri about as much as it did that of Sol.

Sealed cameras on the battered skin of the *Nostromo* began to move silently in the vacuum of space, hunting through infinity for hints of a warm Earth. Secondary cameras on the *Nostromo*'s cargo, a monstrous aggregation of bulky forms and metal shapes, contributed their own line of sight. Inhabitants of an earlier age would have been astonished to learn that the *Nostromo* was towing a considerable quantity of crude oil through the void between the stars, encased in its own automatic, steadily functioning refinery.

That oil would be finished petrochemicals by the time the *Nostromo* arrived in orbit around Earth. Such methods were necessary. While mankind had long since developed marvellous, efficient substitutes for powering their civilization, they had done so only after greedy individuals had sucked the last drop of petroleum from a drained Earth.

Fusion and solar power ran all of man's machines. But they couldn't substitute for petrochemicals. A fusion engine could not produce plastics, for example. The modern worlds could exist without power sooner than they could without plastics. Hence the presence of the *Nostromo*'s commercially viable, if historically incongruous, cargo of machinery and the noisome black liquid it patiently processed.

The only system the cameras picked up was the one set neatly in the centre of the various screens, the one with the improper necklace of planets circling an off-colour star. There was no doubt now in Kane's mind and less than that in Lambert's that the *Nostromo* intended that system to be their immediate destination.

Still, it could be an error in time and not in space. Sol could be the system located in the distance just to this star's left or right. There was a sure way to find out.

'Contact traffic control.' Kane was chewing his lower lip. 'If we can pick up anything from them, we'll know we're in the right quadrant. If Sol's anywhere nearby, we'll receive a reply from one of the outsystem relay stations.'

Lambert's fingers nicked different controls. 'This is the deep-space commercial tug *Nostromo*, registration number one eight zero, two four six, *en route* to Earth with bulk cargo crude petroleum and appropriate refinery. Calling Antarctica traffic control. Do you read me? Over.'

Only the faint, steady hiss of distant suns replied over the speakers. Near Ripley's feet, Jones the cat purred in harmony with the stars.

Lambert tried again. 'Deep-space commercial tug *Nostromo* calling Sol/Antarctica traffic control. We are experiencing navigation-fix difficulties. This is a priority call; please respond.' Still only the nervous stellar sizzle-pop. Lambert looked worried. 'Mayday, mayday. Tug *Nostromo* calling Sol traffic control or any other vessel in listening range. Mayday. Respond.'

The unjustified distress call (Lambert knew they were not in any immediate danger) went unanswered and unchallenged. Discouraged, she shut off the transmitter, but left the receiver on all-channels open in case another broadcasting ship happened to pass close by.

'I knew we couldn't be near our system,' Ripley mumbled. 'I know the area.' She nodded towards the screen hanging above her own station. 'That's nowhere near Sol, and neither are we.'

'Keep trying,' Kane ordered her. He turned back to face Lambert. 'So then where are we? You got a reading yet?'

'Give me a minute, will you? This isn't easy. We're way out in the boondocks.'

'Keep trying.'

'Working on it.'

Several minutes of intense searching and computer co-operation produced a tight grin of satisfaction on her face. 'Found it . . . and us. We're just short of Zeta II Reticuli. We haven't even reached the outer populated ring yet. Too deep to grab onto a navigation beacon, let alone a Sol traffic relay.'

'So what the hell are we doing here?' Kane wondered aloud. 'If there's nothing wrong with the ship and we're not home, why did Mother defrost us?'

It was only coincidence and not a direct response to the exec's musing, but an attention-to-station horn began its loud and imperative beeping . . .

Near the stern of the *Nostromo* was a vast chamber mostly filled with complex, powerful machinery. The ship's heart lived there, the extensive propulsion system that enabled the vessel to distort space, ignore time, and thumb its metallic nose at Einstein . . . and only incidentally power the devices that kept her fragile human crew alive.

At the fore end of this massive, humming complex was a glass cubicle, a transparent pimple on the tip of the hyperdrive iceberg. Within, settled in contour seats, rested two men. They were responsible for the health and well-being of the ship's drive, a situation both were content with. They took care of it and it took care of them.

Most of the time it took perfectly good care of itself, which enabled them to spend their time on more enlightening, worthwhile projects such as drinking beer and swapping dirty stories. At the moment it was Parker's turn to ramble. He was reciting for the hundredth time the tale of the engineering apprentice and the free-fall cathouse. It was a good story, one that never failed to elicit a knowing snigger or two from the silent Brett and a belly laugh from the storyteller himself.

'. . . and so the madam busts in on me, all worried and mad at the same time,' the engineer was saying, 'and insists we come and rescue this poor sap. Guess he didn't know what he was getting into.' As usual, he roared at the pun.

'You remember that place. All four walls, floor and ceiling perfectly mirrored, with no bed. Just a velvet net suspended in the centre of the room to confine your activities and keep you from bouncing off the walls, and zero-gee.' He shook his head in disapproving remembrance.

'That's no place for amateurs to fool around, no sir! Guess this kid got embarrassed or cajoled into trying it by his crewmates.

'From what the girl involved told me later, as she was cleaning herself up, they got started off fine. But then they started to spin, and he panicked. Couldn't stop their tumbling. She tried, but it takes two to stop as well as start in free-fall.

What with the mirrors messing up his sense of position and all, plus the free tumbling, he couldn't stop throwing up.' Parker downed another mouthful of beer. 'Never saw such a mess in your natural life. Bet they're still working on those mirrors.'

'Yeah.' Brett smiled appreciatively.

Parker sat still, letting the last vestiges of the memory fade from his mind. They left a pleasantly lascivious residue behind. Absently, he flipped a key switch over his console. A gratifyingly green light appeared above it, held steady.

'How's your light?'

'Green,' admitted Brett, after repeating the switch-and-check procedure with his own instrumentation.

'Mine too.' Parker studied the bubbles within the beer. Several hours out of hypersleep and he was bored already. The engine room ran itself with quiet efficiency, wasted no time making him feel extraneous. There was no one to argue with except Brett, and you couldn't work up a really invigorating debate with a man who spoke in monosyllables and for whom a complete sentence constituted an exhausting ordeal.

'I still think Dallas is deliberately ignoring our complaints,' he ventured. 'Maybe he can't direct that we receive full bonuses, but he is the captain. If he wanted to, he could put in a request, or at least a decent word for the two of us. That'd be a big help.' He studied a readout. It displayed numbers marching off plus or minus to right and left. The fluorescent red line running down its centre rested precisely on zero, splitting the desired indication of neutrality neatly in two.

Parker would have continued his rambling, alternating stories and complaints had not the beeper above them abruptly commenced its monotonous call.

'Christ. What is it now? Can't let a guy get comfortable before somebody starts farting around.'

'Right.' Brett leaned forward to hear better as the speaker cleared a distant throat.

It was Ripley's voice. 'Report to the mess.'

'Can't be lunch, isn't supper.' Parker was confused. 'Either we're standing by to offload cargo, or . . .' He glanced questioningly at his companion.

'Find out soon,' said Brett.

As they made their way towards the mess, Parker surveyed the less than antiseptically clean walls of 'C' corridor with distaste. 'I'd like to know why they never come down here. This is where the real work is.'

'Same reason we have half a share to their one. Our time is their time. That's the way they see it.'

'Well, I'll tell you something. It stinks.' Parker's tone left no doubt he was referring to something other than the odour the corridor walls were impregnated with . . .

# II

Though far from comfortable, the mess was just large enough to hold the entire crew. Since they rarely ate their meals simultaneously (the always functional autochef indirectly encouraging individuality in eating habits), it hadn't been designed with comfortable seating for seven in mind. They shuffled from foot to foot, bumping and jostling each other and trying not to get on each other's nerves.

Parker and Brett weren't happy and took no pains to hide their displeasure. Their sole consolation was the knowledge that nothing was wrong with engineering and that whatever they'd been revived to deal with was the responsibility of persons other than themselves. Ripley had already filled them in on the disconcerting absence of their intended destination.

Parker considered that they would all have to re-enter hypersleep, a messy and uncomfortable process at its best, and cursed under his breath. He resented anything that kept him separated from his end-of-voyage paycheck.

'We know we haven't arrived at Sol, Captain.' Kane spoke for the others, who were all eyeing Dallas expectantly. 'We're nowhere near home and the ship has still seen fit to hustle us all out of hypersleep. Time we found out why.'

'Time you did,' Dallas agreed readily. 'As you all know,' he began importantly, 'Mother is programmed to interrupt our journey and bring us out of hyperdrive and sleep if certain specified conditions arise.' He paused for effect, said, 'They have.'

18

'It would have to be pretty serious.' Lambert was watching Jones the cat play with a blinking telltale. 'You know that. Bringing a full crew out of hypersleep isn't lightly done. There's always some risk involved.'

'Tell me about it.' Parker muttered it so softly only Brett could overhear.

'You'll all be happy to learn,' Dallas continued, 'that the emergency we've been awakened to deal with does not involve the *Nostromo*. Mother says we're in perfect shape.' A couple of heartfelt 'amens' sounded in the cramped mess.

'The emergency lies elsewhere – specifically, in the unlisted system we've recently entered. We should be closing on the particular planet concerned right now.' He glanced at Ash, who rewarded him with a confirming nod. 'We've picked up a transmission from another source. It's garbled and apparently took Mother some time to puzzle out, but it's definitely a distress signal.'

'Whoa, that doesn't make sense.' Lambert looked puzzled herself. 'Of all standard transmissions, emergency calls are the most straightforward and the least complex. Why would Mother have the slightest trouble interpreting one?'

'Mother speculates that this is anything but a "standard" transmission. It's an acoustic beacon signal, which repeats at intervals of twelve seconds. That much isn't unusual. However, she believes the signal is not of human origin.'

*That* provoked some startled muttering. When the first excitement had faded, he explained further. 'Mother's not positive. That's what *I* don't understand. I've never seen a computer show confusion before. Ignorance yes, but not confusion. This may be a first.

'What is important is that she's certain enough it's a distress signal to pull us out of hypersleep.'

'So what?' Brett appeared sublimely unconcerned.

Kane replied with just a hint of irritation. 'Come on, man. You know your manual. We're obliged under section B2 of Company in-transit directives to render whatever aid and

assistance we can in such situations. Whether the call is human
or otherwise.'

Parker kicked at the deck in disgust. 'Christ. I hate to say this,
but we're a commercial tug with a big, hard-to-handle cargo.
Not a damn rescue unit. This kind of duty's not in our contract.'
He brightened slightly. 'Of course, if there's some extra money
involved for such work . . .'

'You'd better read your own contract.' Ash recited as neatly as
the main computer he was so proud of. ' "Any systematic
transmission indicating possible intelligent origin must be
investigated." At penalty of full forfeiture of all pay and bonuses
due on journey's completion. Not a word about bonus money
for helping someone in distress.'

Parker gave the deck another kick, kept his mouth shut.
Neither he nor Brett considered himself the hero type. Anything that could force a ship down on a strange world might
treat them in an equally inconsiderate manner. Not that they
had any evidence that this unknown caller had been forced
down, but being a realist in a harsh universe, he was inclined to
be pessimistic.

Brett simply saw the detour in terms of his delayed paycheck.

'We're going in. That's all there is to it.' Dallas eyed them each
in turn. He was about fed up with the two of them. He no more
enjoyed this kind of detour than they did, and was as anxious to
be home and offloading their cargo as they were, but there were
times when letting off steam crossed over into disobedience.

'Right,' said Brett sardonically.

'Right, *what*?'

The engineering tech was no fool. The combination of
Dallas's tone combined with the expression on his face told Brett
it was time to ease up.

'Right . . . we're going in.' Dallas continued to stare at him and
he added with a smile, 'Sir.'

The captain turned a jaundiced eye on Parker, but that
worthy was now subdued.

'Can we land on it?' he asked Ash.

'Somebody did.'

'That's what I mean,' he said significantly. ' "Land" is a benign term. It implies a sequence of events successfully carried out, resulting in the gentle and safe touchdown of a ship on a hard surface. We're faced with a distress call. That implies events other than benign. Let's go find out what's going on . . . but let's go quietly, with boots in hand.'

There was an illuminated cartographic table on the bridge. Dallas, Kane, Ripley, and Ash stood at opposite points of its compass, while Lambert sat at her station.

'There it is.' Dallas fingered a glowing point on the table. He looked around the table. 'Something I want everyone to hear.'

They resumed their seats as he nodded to Lambert. Her fingers were poised over a particular switch. 'Okay, let's hear it. Watch the volume.'

The navigator flipped the switch. Static and hissing sounds filled the bridge. These cleared suddenly, were replaced by a sound that sent shivers up Kane's back and unholy crawling things down Ripley's. It lasted for twelve seconds, then was replaced by the static.

'Good God.' Kane's expression was drawn.

Lambert switched off the speakers. It was human on the bridge again.

'What the hell is it?' Ripley looked as though she'd just seen something dead on her lunch plate. 'It doesn't sound like any distress signal I ever heard.'

'That's what Mother calls it,' Dallas told them. 'Calling it "alien" turns out to have been something of an under-statement.'

'Maybe it's a voice.' Lambert paused, considered her just-uttered words, found the implications they raised unpleasant, and tried to pretend she hadn't said them.

'We'll know soon. Have you homed in on it?'

'I've found the section of planet.' Lambert turned gratefully to her console, relieved to be able to deal with mathematics instead of disquieting thoughts.

'We're close enough.'

'Mother wouldn't have pulled us out of hypersleep unless we were,' Ripley murmured.

'It's coming from ascension six minutes, twenty seconds; declination minus thirty-nine degrees, two seconds.'

'Show me the whole thing on a screen.'

The navigator hit a succession of buttons. One of the bridge viewscreens flickered, gifted them with a bright dot.

'High albedo. Can you get it a little closer?'

'No. You have to look at it from this distance. That's what I'm going to do.' Immediately the screen zoomed in tighter on the point of light, revealing an unspectacular, slightly oblate shape sitting in emptiness.

'Smart ass.' Dallas voiced it without malice. 'You sure that's it? It's a crowded system.'

'That's it, all right. Just a planetoid, really. Maybe twelve hundred kilometres, no more.'

'Any rotation?'

'Yeah. 'Bout two hours, working off the initial figures. Tell you better in ten minutes.'

'That's good enough for now. What's the gravity?'

Lambert studied different readouts. 'Point eight six. Must be pretty dense stuff.'

'Don't tell Parker and Brett,' said Ripley. 'They'll be thinking it's solid heavy metal and wander off somewhere prospecting before we can check out our unknown broadcaster.'

Ash's observation was more prosaic. 'You can walk on it.' They settled down to working out orbiting procedure . . .

The *Nostromo* edged close to the tiny world, trailing its vast cargo of tanks and refinery equipment.

'Approaching orbital apogee. Mark. Twenty seconds. Nineteen, eighteen . . .' Lambert continued to count down while her mates worked steadily around her.

'Roll ninety-two degrees starboard yaw,' announced Kane, thoroughly businesslike.

The tug and refinery rotated, performing a massive

pirouette in the vastness of space. Light appeared at the stern of the tug as her secondary engines fired briefly.

'Equatorial orbit nailed,' declared Ash. Below them, the miniature world rotated unconcernedly.

'Give me an EC pressure reading.'

Ash examined gauges, spoke without turning to face Dallas. 'Three point four five en slash em squared . . . about five psia, sir.'

'Shout if it changes.'

'You worried about redundancy management disabling CMGS control when we're busy elsewhere?'

'Yeah.'

'CMG control is inhibited via DAS/DCS. We'll augment with TACS and monitor through ATMDC and computer interface. Feel better now?'

'A lot.' Ash was a funny sort, kind of coldly friendly, but supremely competent. Nothing rattled him. Dallas felt confident with the science officer backing him up, watching his decisions. 'Prepare to disengage from platform.' He flipped a switch, addressed a small pickup. 'Engineering, preparing to disengage.'

'L alignment on port and starboard is green,' reported Parker, all hint of usual sarcasm absent.

'Green on spinal umbilicus severance,' added Brett.

'Crossing the terminator,' Lambert informed them all. 'Entering nightside.' Below, a dark line split thick clouds, leaving them brightly reflecting on one side, dark as the inside of a grave on the other.

'It's coming up. It's coming up. Stand by.' Lambert threw switches in sequence. 'Stand by. Fifteen seconds . . . ten . . . five . . . four. Three. Two. One. Lock.'

'Disengage,' ordered Dallas curtly.

Tiny puffs of gas showed between the *Nostromo* and the ponderous coasting bulk of the refinery platform. The two artificial structures, one tiny and inhabited, the other enormous and deserted, drifted slowly apart. Dallas watched the separation intently on number two screen.

'Umbilicus clear,' Ripley announced after a short pause.

'Precision corrected.' Kane leaned back, in his seat, relaxing for a few seconds. 'All clean and clear. Separation successful. No damage.'

'Check here,' added Lambert.

'And here,' said a relieved Ripley.

Dallas glanced over at his navigator. 'You sure we've left her in a steady orbit? I don't want the whole two billion tons dropping and burning up while we're poking around downstairs. Atmosphere's not thick enough to give us a safe umbrella.'

Lambert checked a readout. 'She'll stay up here for a year or so easy, sir.'

'All right. The money's safe and so's our skulls. Let's take it down. Prepare for atmospheric flight.' Five humans worked busily, each secure in his or her assigned task. Jones the cat sat on a port console and studied the approaching clouds.

'Dropping.' Lambert's attention was fixed on one particular gauge. 'Fifty thousand metres. Down. Down. Forty-nine thousand. Entering atmosphere.'

Dallas watched his own instrumentation, tried to evaluate and memorize the dozens of steadily shifting figures. Deep-space travel was a question of paying proper homage to one's instruments and letting Mother do the hard work. Atmospheric flight was another story entirely. For a change, it was pilot's work instead of a machine's.

Brown and grey clouds kissed the underside of the ship.

'Watch it. Looks nasty down there.'

How like Dallas, Ripley thought. Somewhere in the dun-hued hell below another ship was bleating a regular, inhuman, frightening distress call. The world itself was unlisted, which meant they'd begin from scratch where such matters as atmospheric peculiarities, terrain, and such were concerned. Yet to Dallas, it was no more or less than 'nasty'. She'd often wondered what a man as competent as their captain was doing squiring an unimportant tub like the *Nostromo* around the cosmos.

The answer, could she have read his mind, would have surprised her. He liked it.

'Vertical descent computed and entered. Correcting course slightly,' Lambert informed them. 'On course now, homing. Locked and we're headed in straight.'

'Check. How's our plotting going to square with secondary propulsion in this weather?'

'We're doing okay so far, sir. I can't say for sure until we get under these clouds. If we can get under them.'

'Good enough.' He frowned at a readout, touched a button. The reading changed to a more pleasing one. 'Let me know if you think we're going to lose it.'

'Will do.'

The tug struck an invisibility. Invisible to the eye, not to her instruments. She bounced once, twice, a third time, then settled more comfortably into the thick wad of dark cloud. The ease of the entry was a tribute to Lambert's skills in plotting and Dallas's as a pilot.

It did not last. Within the ocean of air, heavy currents swirled. They began buffeting the descending ship.

'Turbulence.' Ripley wrestled with her own controls.

'Give us navigation and landing lights.' Dallas tried to sort sense from the maelstrom obscuring the viewscreen. 'Maybe we can spot something visually.'

'No substitute for the instruments,' said Ash. 'Not in this.'

'No substitute for maximum input, either. Anyhow, I like to look.'

Powerful lights came on beneath the *Nostromo*. They pierced the cloud waves only weakly, did not provide the clear field of vision Dallas so badly desired. But they did illuminate the dark screens, thereby lightening both the bridge and the mental atmosphere thereon. Lambert felt less like they were flying through ink.

Parker and Brett couldn't see the cloud cover outside, but

they could feel it. The engine room gave a sudden shift, rocked
to the opposite side, shifted sharply again.

Parker swore under his breath. 'What was that? You hear
that?'

'Yeah.' Brett examined a readout nervously. 'Pressure drop
in intake number three. We must've lost a shield.' He punched
buttons. 'Yep, three's gone. Dust pouring through the intake.'

'Shut her down, shut her down.'

'What do you think I'm doing?'

'Great. So we've got a secondary full of dust.'

'No problem . . . I hope.' Brett adjusted a control. 'I'll bypass
number three and vent the stuff back out as it comes in.'

'Damage is done, though.' Parker didn't like to think what
the presence of wind-blown abrasives might've done to the
intake lining. 'What the hell are we flying through? Clouds or
rocks? If we don't crash, dollars to your aunt's cherry we get an
electrical fire somewhere in the relevant circuitry.'

Unaware of the steady cursing taking place back in
engineering, the five on the bridge went about the business of
trying to set the tug down intact and near to the signal source.

'Approaching point of origin.' Lambert studied a gauge.
'Closing at twenty-five kilometres. Twenty. Ten, five . . .'

'Slowing and turning.' Dallas leaned over on the manual
helm.

'Correct course three degrees, four minutes right.' He
complied with the directions. 'That's got it. Five kilometres to
centre of search circle and steady.'

'Tightening now.' Dallas fingered the helm once more.

'Three kiloms. Two.' Lambert sounded just a mite excited,
though whether from the danger or the nearness of the signal
source Dallas couldn't tell. 'We're practically circling above it
now.'

'Nice work, Lambert. Ripley, what's the terrain like? Find us
a landing spot.'

'Working, sir.' She tried several panels, her expression of
disgust growing deeper as unacceptable readings came back.

Dallas continued to make sure the ship held its target in the centre of its circling flightpath while Ripley fought to make sense of the unseen surface.

'Visual line of sight impossible.'

'We can see that,' Kane mumbled. 'Or rather, can't see it.' The rare half-glimpses the instruments had given him of the ground hadn't put him in a pleasant frame of mind. The occasional readings had hinted at extensive desolation, a hostile, barren desert of a world.

'Radar gives me noise.' Ripley wished electronics could react to imprecations as readily as people. 'Sonar gives me noise. Infra-red, noise. Hang on, I'm going to try ultra violet. Spectrum's high enough not to interfere.' A moment, followed by the appearance on a crucial readout of some gratifying lines at last, followed in turn by brightly lit words and a computer sketch.

'That did it.'

'And a place to land on it?'

Ripley looked fully relaxed now. 'As near as I can tell, we can set down anywhere you like. Readings say it's flat below us. Totally flat.'

Dallas's thoughts turned to visions of smooth lava, of a cool but deceptively thin crust barely concealing molten destruction. 'Yeah, but flat what? Water, pahoehoe, sand? Bounce something off, Kane. Get us a determination. I'll take her down low enough so that we lose most of this interference. If it's flat, I can get us close without too much trouble.'

Kane flipped switches. 'Monitoring. Analytics activated. Still getting noise.'

Carefully, Dallas eased the tug towards the surface.

'Still noisy, but starting to clear.'

Again, Dallas lost altitude. Lambert watched gauges. They were more than high enough for safe clearance, but at the speed they were travelling that could change rapidly if anything went wrong with the ship's engines, or if an other-worldly downdraft should materialize. Nor could they cut their speed further. In this wind, that would mean a critical loss of control.

'Clearing, clearing . . . that's got it!' He studied readouts and contour lines, provided by the ship's imaging scanner. 'It was molten once, but not anymore. Not for a long time, according to the analytics. It's mostly basalt, some rhyolite, with occasional lava overlays. Everything's cool and solid now. No sign of tectonic activity.' He utilized other instruments to probe deeper into the secrets of the tiny world's skin.

'No faults of consequence below us or in the immediate vicinity. Should be a nice place to set down.'

Dallas thought briefly. 'You're positive about that surface composition?'

'It's too old to be anything else.' The executive officer sounded a touch peeved. 'I know enough to check age data along with composition. Think I'd take any chances putting us down inside a volcano?'

'All right, all right. Sorry. Just checking. I haven't done a landing without charts and beacon since school training. I'm a bit nervous.'

'Ain't we all?' admitted Lambert readily.

'If we're set then?' No one objected. 'Let's take her down. I'm going to spiral in as best I can in this wind, try to get us as close as possible. But you keep a tight signal watch on, Lambert. I don't want us coming down on top of that calling ship. Warn me for distance if we get too close.' His tone was intense in the cramped room.

Adjustments were made, commands given and executed by faithful electronic servants. The *Nostromo* commenced to follow a steady spiralling path surfaceward, fighting cross-winds and protesting gusts of black air every metre of the way.

'Fifteen kilometres and descending,' announced Ripley evenly. 'Twelve . . . ten . . . eight.' Dallas touched a control. 'Slowing rate. Five . . . three . . . two. One kilometre.' The same control was further altered. 'Slowing. Activate landing engines.'

'Locked.' Kane was working confidently at his console. 'Descent now computer monitored.' A crisp, loud hum filled the bridge as Mother took over control of their drop, regulating the last metres of descent with more precision than the best human pilot could have managed.

'Descending on landers,' Kane told them.

'Kill engines.'

Dallas performed a final prelanding check, flipped several switches to OFF. 'Engines off. Lifter quads functioning properly.' A steady throbbing filled the bridge.

'Nine hundred metres and dropping.' Ripley watched her console. 'Eight hundred. Seven hundred. Six.' She continued to count off the rate of descent in hundreds of metres. Before long she was reciting it in tens.

At five metres the tug hesitated, hovering on its landers above the storm-racked, night-shrouded surface.

'Struts down.' Kane was already moving to execute the required action as Dallas was giving the order. A faint whine filled the bridge. Several thick metal legs unfolded beetle-like from the ship's belly, drifted tantalizingly close to the still unseen rock below them.

'Four metres . . . ufff!' Ripley stopped. So did the *Nostromo*, as landing struts contacted unyielding rock. Massive absorbers cushioned the contact.

'We're down.'

Something snapped. A minor circuit, probably, or perhaps an overload not properly compensated for, not handled fast enough. A terrific shock ran through the ship. The metal of the hull vibrated, producing an eerie, metallic moan throughout the ship.

'Lost it, lost it!' Kane was shouting as the lights on the bridge went out. Gauges screamed for attention as the failure snowballed back through the interdependent metal nerve ends of the *Nostromo*.

When the shock struck engineering, Parker and Brett were preparing to crack another set of beers. A line of ranked pipes set into the moulded ceiling promptly exploded. Three panels in the control cubicle burst into flame, while a nearby pressure valve swelled, then burst.

The lights went out and they fumbled for hand beams while Parker tried to find the button controlling the back-up generator, which provided power in the absence of direct service from the operating engines.

Controlled confusion reigned on the bridge. When the yells and questions had died down, it was Lambert who voiced the most common thought.

'Secondary generator should have kicked over by now.' She took a step, bumped a knee hard against a console.

'Wonder what's keeping it?' Kane moved to the wall, felt along it. Backup landing controls . . . here. He ran his fingers over several familiar knobs. Aft lock stud . . . there. Nearby ought to be . . . his hand fastened on an emergency lightbar, switched it on. A dim glow revealed several ghostly silhouettes.

With Kane's light serving as a guide, Dallas and Lambert located their own lightbars. The three beams combined to provide enough illumination to work by.

'What happened? Why hasn't the secondary taken over? And what caused the outage?'

Ripley thumbed the intercom. 'Engine room, what happened? What's our status?'

'Lousy.' Parker sounded busy, mad, and worried all at once. A distant buzzing, like the frantic wings of some colossal insect, formed a backdrop to his words. Those words rose and faded, as though the speaker were having trouble staying in range of the omni-directional intercom pickup.

'Goddamn dust in the engines, that's what happened. Caught it coming down. Guess we didn't close it off and clean it out in time. Got an electrical fire back here.'

'It's big,' was Brett's single addition to the conversation. He sounded weak with distance.

There was a pause, during which they could make out only the *whoosh* of chemical extinguishers over the speaker. 'The intakes got clogged,' Brett finally was able to tell the anxious knot of listeners. 'We overheated bad, burnt out a whole cell, I think. Christ, it's really breaking loose down here . . .'

Dallas glanced over at Ripley. 'Those two sound busy enough. Somebody give me the critical answer. Something went *bang*. I hope to hell it was only back in their department, but it could be worse. Has the hull been breached?' He took a deep breath. 'If so, where and how badly?'

Ripley performed a quick scan of the ship's emergency pressurization gauges, then made a rapid eye search via individual cabin diagrams before she felt confident in replying with certainty. 'I don't see anything. We still have full pressure in all compartments. If there is a hole, it's too small to show and the self-seal's already managed to plug it.'

Ash studied his own console. Along with the others, it was independently powered in the event of a massive energy failure such as they were presently experiencing. 'Air in all compartments shows no sign of contamination from outside atmosphere. I think we're still tight, sir.'

'Best news I've had in sixty seconds. Kane, hit the exterior screens that are still powered up.'

The executive officer adjusted a trio of toggles. There was a noticeable flickering, hints of faint geologic forms, then complete darkness.

'Nothing. We're blind outside as well as in here. Have to get secondary power at least before we can have a look at where we are. Batteries aren't enough for even minimal imaging.'

The audio sensors required less energy. They conveyed the voice of this world into the cabin. The storm-wind sounds rose and fell against the motionless receptors, filling the bridge with a hoo-click that sounded like fish arguing.

'Wish we'd come down in daylight.' Lambert gazed out a dark port. 'We'd be able to see without instruments.'

'What's the matter, Lambert?' Kane was teasing her. 'Afraid of the dark?'

She didn't smile back. 'I'm not afraid of the dark I know. It's the dark I don't that terrifies me. Especially when it's filled with noises like that distress call.' She turned her attention back to the dustswept port.

Her willingness to express their deepest fears did nothing to improve the mental atmosphere on the bridge. Cramped at the best of times, it grew suffocating in the near blackness, made worse by a continuing silence among them.

It was a relief when Ripley announced, 'We've got intercom to engineering again.' Dallas and the others watched her expectantly as she fiddled with the amp. 'That you, Parker?'

'Yeah, it's me.' From the sound of it, the engineer was too tired to snap in his usual acerbic manner.

'What's your status?' Dallas crossed mental fingers. 'What about the fire?'

'We finally got it knocked down.' He sighed, making it sound like the wind over the 'com. 'It got into some of that old lubrication lining the corridor walls down on C level. For a while I thought we'd get our lungs seared proper. The combustible stuff was thinner than I thought, though, and it burnt out fast before it ate up too much of our air. Scrubbers seem to be getting the carbon out okay.'

Dallas licked his lips. 'How about damage? Never mind the superficial stuff. Ship-efficiency function and performance hindrance are all I'm concerned about.'

'Let's see . . . four panel is totally shot.' Dallas could imagine the engineer ticking off items on his fingers as he reported back. 'The secondary-load sharing unit is out and at least three cellites on twelve module are gone. With all that implies.' He let that sink in, added, 'You want the little things? Give me about an hour and I'll have you a list.'

'Skip it. Hold on a second.' He turned to Ripley. 'Try the screens again.' She did so, with no effect. They remained as blank as a Company accountant's mind.

'We'll just have to do without a while longer,' he told her.

'You sure that's everything?' she said into the pickup. Ripley found herself feeling sympathy for Parker and Brett for the first time since they'd become part of the crew. Or since she had, as Parker preceded her in seniority as a member of the *Nostromo*'s complement . . .

'So far.' He coughed over the speaker. 'We're trying to get full ship power back right now. Twelve module going out screwed up everything back here. Let you know better about power when we've gone through everything the fire ate.'

'What about repairs? Can you manage?' Dallas was running over the engineer's brief report in his mind. They ought to be able to patch up the initial damage, but the cellite problem would take time. What might be wrong with module twelve he preferred not to think about.

'Couldn't fix it all out here no matter what,' Parker replied.

'I didn't think you could. Don't expect you to. What *can* you do?'

'We need to reroute a couple of these ducts and reline the damaged intakes. We'll have to work around the really bad damage. Can't fix those ducts properly without putting the ship in a full drydock. We'll have to fake it.'

'I understand. What else?'

'Told you. Module twelve. I'm giving it to you straight. We lost a main cell.'

'How? The dust?'

'Partly.' Parker paused, exchanged inaudible words with Brett, then was back at the pickup. 'Some fragments agglutinated inside the intakes, caked up, and caused the overheating that sparked the fire. You know how sensitive those drivers are. Went right through the shielding and blew the whole system.'

'Anything you can do with it?' Dallas asked. The system had to be repaired somehow. They couldn't replace it.

'I think so. Brett thinks so. We've got to clean it all out and revacuum, then see how well it holds. If it stays tight after it's been scoured, we should be fine. If it doesn't, we can try metalforming a patchseal. If it turns out that we've got a crack running the length of the duct, well . . .' His voice trailed away.

'Let's not talk about ultimate problems,' Dallas suggested. 'Let's stick with the immediate ones for now and hope they're all we have to deal with.'

'Okay by us.'

'Right,' added Brett, sounding as though he was working somewhere off to the engineer's left.

'Bridge out.'

'Engineering out. Keep the coffee warm.'

Ripley flipped off the intercom, looked expectantly at Dallas. He sat quietly, thinking.

'How long before we're functional, Ripley? Given that Parker's right about the damage and that he and Brett can do their jobs and the repairs hold?'

She studied readouts, thought for a moment. '*If* they can reroute those ducts and fix module twelve to the point where it'll carry its share of the power load again, I'd estimate fifteen to twenty hours.'

'Not too bad. I got eighteen.' He didn't smile, but he was feeling more hopeful. 'What about the auxiliaries? They'd better be ready to go when we get power back.'

'Working on it.' Lambert made adjustments to concealed instrumentation. 'We'll be ready here when they're finished back in engineering.'

Ten minutes later a tiny speaker at Kane's station let go with a series of sharp beeps. He studied a gauge, then flipped on the 'com. 'Bridge. Kane here.'

Sounding exhausted but pleased with himself, Parker spoke from the far end of the ship. 'I don't know how long it'll hold . . . some of the welds we had to make are pretty sloppy. If everything kicks over the way it ought to, we'll retrace more carefully and redo the seals for permanence. You ought to have power now.'

The exec thumbed an override. Lights returned to the bridge, dependent readouts flickered and lit up, and there were scattered grunts and murmurs of appreciation from the rest of the crew.

'We've got power and lights back,' Kane reported. 'Nice work, you two.'

'All our work is nice,' replied Parker.

'Right.' Brett must have been standing next to the intercom pickup back by the engines, judging from the steady hum that formed an elegant counterpoint to his standard monosyllabic response.

'Don't get too excited,' Parker was saying. 'The new links should hold, but I'm not making any promises. We just threw stuff together back here. Anything new up your way?'

Kane shook his head, reminded himself that Parker couldn't see the gesture. 'Not a damn thing.' He glanced out the nearest port. The bridge lights cast their faint glow over a patch of featureless, barren ground. Occasionally the storm raging outside would carry a large fragment of sand or bit of rock into view and there would be a brief flash produced by reflection. But that was all.

'Just bare rock. We can't see very far. For all I know we could be squatting five metres from the local oasis.'

'Dream on.' Parker shouted something to Brett, closed with a workmanlike, 'Be in touch if we have any trouble. Let us know the same.'

'Send you a postcard.' Kane switched off . . .

# III

It might have been better for everyone's peace of mind if the emergency had continued. With lights and power back and nothing to do save stare emptily at each other, the five people on the bridge grew increasingly restless. There was no room to stretch out and relax. A single floor pacer would have used all the available deck. So they moped at their stations, downed inordinate quantities of coffee spewed out by the autochef, and tried to think of something to do that would keep their damnably busy brains from concentrating on the present unpleasant situation. As to what lay outside the ship, possibly close by, they elected not to speculate aloud.

Of them all, only Ash seemed relatively content. His only concern at the moment was for the mental condition of his shipmates. There were no true recreation facilities on the ship for them to turn to. The *Nostromo* was a tug, a working vessel, not a pleasure craft. When not performing necessary tasks her crew was supposed to be spending its blank time in the comforting womb of hypersleep. It was only natural that unoccupied wake time would make them nervous under the best of circumstances, and the present circumstances were something less than the best.

Ash could run problems in theory through the computer over and over, without ever becoming bored. He found the awake time stimulating.

'Any response yet to our outcalls?' Dallas leaned out from his chair to eye the science officer.

'I've tried every type of response in the manual, plus free association. I've also let Mother try a strictly mechanalog code approach.' Ash shook his head and looked disappointed. 'Nothing but the same distress call, repeated at the usual intervals. All the other channels are blank, except for a faint, steady crackle on oh-point-three-three.' He jabbed upward with a thumb.

'Mother says that's the characteristic discharge of this world's central star. If anything, or anyone, is alive out there, it's unable to do more than call for help.'

Dallas made a rude noise. 'We've got full power back. Let's see where we are. Kick on the floods.'

Ripley threw a switch. A chain of powerful lights, bright pearls on the dark setting of the *Nostromo*, came to life outside the ports. Wind and dust were more evident now, sometimes forming small whirlpools in the air, sometimes blowing straight and with considerable force across their line of sight. Isolated rocks, rises and falls, were the only protrusions on the blasted landscape. There was no sign of anything living, not a patch of lichen, a bush, nothing. Only wind and dust swirling in an alien night.

'No oasis,' Kane whispered to himself. Blank and featureless, inhospitable.

Dallas rose, walked to a port, and stared out at the continuing storm, watched splinters of rock scud past the glass. He wondered if the air was ever still on this little world. For all they knew of local conditions, the *Nostromo* might have set down in the midst of a quiet summer's day. That was unlikely. This globe wasn't big enough to produce really violent weather, like on Jupiter, say. He drew some consolation from that, realizing that the weather outside probably couldn't get much worse.

The vagaries of the local climate formed the principal topic for discussion. 'We can't go anywhere in this,' Kane pointed out. 'Not in the dark, anyway.'

Ash looked up from his console. He hadn't moved, evidently content physically as well as mentally. Kane couldn't understand how the science officer could do it. If he hadn't left his own station occasionally to walk around, he'd be going crazy by now.

Ash noticed his stare, offered some hopeful information. 'Mother says the local sun's coming up in twenty minutes. Wherever we decide to go, it won't be in the dark.'

'That's something,' admitted Dallas, grasping at the least bit of encouragement. 'If our callers won't or can't talk further, we'll have to go looking for them. Or for it, if the signal's being produced by an automatic beacon. How far are we from the source of the transmission?'

Ash studied readouts, activated a ground-level plotter for confirmation. 'About three thousand metres, over mostly level terrain as near as the scanners can tell, roughly northeast of our present position.'

'Composition of terrain?'

'Seems to be the same as we determined on descent. Same hard stuff we're sitting on now. Solid basalt with minor variations, though I wouldn't rule out the possibility of encountering some large amygdaloidal pockets here and there.'

'We'll watch our step, then.'

Kane was comparing distance with suit time in his head. 'At least it's close enough to walk to.'

'Yeah.' Lambert looked pleased. 'I didn't fancy having to move the ship. A straight drop from orbit's easier to plot than a surface-to-surface shift in this kind of weather.'

'Okay. We know what we're going to be walking on. Let's find out what we're going to be walking through. Ash, give us a preliminary atmospheric.'

The science officer punched buttons. A tiny port opened on the skin of the *Nostromo*. It shoved a metal flask out into the wind, sucked in a minute portion of this world's air, and sank

The sample was ejected into a vacuum chamber. Sophisticated instruments proceeded to pick it to pieces. Very shortly these pieces of air appeared in the form of numbers and symbols on Ash's console.

He studied them briefly, requested a double check on one, then reported to his companions.

'It's almost a primordial mix. Plenty of inert nitrogen, some oxygen, a high concentration of free carbon dioxide. There's methane and ammonia, some of the latter existing in the frozen state . . . it's cold outside. I'm working on the trace constituents now, but I don't expect any surprises. It all looks pretty standard, and unbreathable.'

'Pressure?'

'Ten to the fourth dynes per square centimetre. Won't hold us back unless the wind really picks up.'

'What about moisture content?' Kane wanted to know. Images of an imaginary off-Earth oasis were rapidly fading from his mind.

'Ninety-eight double P. It may not smell good, but it's humid. Lot of water vapour. Weird mixture, that. Wouldn't think to find that much vapour coexisting with the methane. Oh well. I wouldn't advise drinking from any local water holes, if they exist. Probably not water.'

'Anything else we should know?' Dallas asked.

'Just the basalt surface, plenty of cold, hard lava. And cold air, well below the line,' Ash informed them. 'We'd need suits to handle the temperature even if the air were breathable. If there's anything alive out there, it's tough.'

Dallas looked resigned. 'I suppose it was unreasonable to expect anything else. Hope springs eternal. There's just enough of an atmosphere to make vision bad. I'd have preferred no air at all, but we didn't design this rock.'

'You never know.' Kane was being philosophical again. 'Might be something else's idea of paradise.'

'There's no point in cursing it,' Lambert advised them. 'It could've been a helluva lot worse.' She studied the storm outside. It was gradually growing lighter as dawn approached.

'I sure prefer this to trying to set down on some gas giant, where we'd have three-hundred kph winds in a calm period and ten or twenty gravities to cope with. At least we can walk around on this without generator support and stabilizers. You people don't know when you're well off.'

'Funny that I don't feel well off,' Ripley countered. 'I'd rather be back in hypersleep.' Something moved against her ankles and she reached down to stroke Jones's rump. The cat purred gratefully.

'Oasis or not,' Kane said brightly, 'I volunteer for first out. I'd like a chance for a close look at our mysterious caller. Never know what you might find.'

'Jewels and money?' Dallas couldn't repress a grin. Kane was a notorious rainbow chaser.

The exec shrugged. 'Why not?'

'I hear you. Okay.' It was accepted that Dallas would be a member of the little expedition. He glanced around the bridge for a candidate to complete the party. 'Lambert. You too.'

She didn't look happy. 'Swell. Why me?'

'Why not you? You're our designated direction finder. Let's see how good you are outside your seat.' He started for the corridor, paused, and said matter-of-factly, 'One more thing. We're probably faced with a dead derelict and a repeating beacon or we'd likely have heard from any survivors by now. But we still can't be sure what we'll run into. This world doesn't appear to be teeming with life, inimical or otherwise, but we won't take unnecessary risks. Let's get out some weapons.' He hesitated as Ripley moved to join them.

'Three is the maximum I can let off ship, Ripley. You'll have to wait your turn out.'

'I'm not going out,' she told him. 'I like it here. It's just that I've done everything I can here. Parker and Brett are going to need help with the fine work while they're trying to fix those ducts . . .'

It was entirely too hot back in the engine room, despite the best efforts of the tug's cooling unit. The trouble stemmed from the amount of welding Parker and Brett had to do and the cramped quarters they were forced to work in. The air near the thermostats would remain comparatively cool, while that around the weld itself could overheat rapidly.

The laser welder itself wasn't at fault. It generated a relatively cool beam. But where metal melted and flowed together to form a fresh seal, heat was generated as a by-product. Both men were working with shirts off and the sweat streamed down their naked torsos.

Nearby, Ripley leaned against a wall and used a peculiar tool to pop out a protective panel. Complex aggregations of coloured wire and tiny geometric shapes were exposed to the light. Two small sections were charred black. Using another took, she dug the damaged components out, searched in the loaded satchel slung over one shoulder for the proper replacements.

As she was snapping the first of them into place, Parker was shutting off the laser. He examined the current weld critically. 'Not bad, if I do say so.' He turned to look back at Ripley. Sweat was making her tunic stick to her chest.

'Hey Ripley . . . I got a question.'

She didn't glance back from her work. A second new module snapped neatly into place beside the first, like a tooth being replanted in its socket.

'Yeah? I'm listening.'

'Do we get to go out on the expedition or are we stuck in here until everything's fixed? We've already restored power. The rest of this stuff,' and he indicated the battered engine room with a sharp wave of one hand, 'is cosmetic. Nothing that can't wait for a few days.'

'You both know the answer to that.' She sat back, rubbed her hands as she looked over at him. 'The captain picked his pair, and that's that. Nobody else can go out until they come back and report. Three out, four on. That's the rules.' She paused at a sudden thought, eyed him knowingly.

'That's not what's bothering you, is it? You're worried about what they might find. Or have we all misjudged you and you're really a high-minded seeker after knowledge, a true devotee of pushing back the frontiers of the known universe?'

'Hell, no.' Parker didn't seem the least offended by Ripley's casual sarcasm. 'I'm a true devotee of pushing back the frontiers of my bank account. So . . . what about shares in case they find anything valuable?'

Ripley looked bored. 'Don't worry. You'll both get what's coming to you.' She started to hunt through the parts satchel for a certain solid-state module to fill the last remaining damaged section in the open square of wall.

'I'm not doing any more work,' Brett suddenly announced, 'unless we're guaranteed full shares.'

Ripley found the necessary part, moved to emplace it within the wall. 'You're each guaranteed by contract that you'll receive a share in anything we find. Both of you know that. Now knock it off and get back to work.' She turned away, began to check to make certain the newly installed modules were operating properly.

Parker stared hard at her, opened his mouth to say something, thought better of it. She was the ship's warrant officer. Antagonizing her would do them no good at all. He'd made his point and been rebuffed. Better to leave it at that, no matter how he felt inside. He could be logical when the situation demanded it.

Angrily, he snapped the laser back on, started to seal another section of ruptured duct.

Brett, handling the power and train for the welder, said to no one in particular, 'Right.'

Dallas, Kane and Lambert made their way down a narrow corridor. They now wore boots, jackets and gloves in addition to their insulated work pants. They carried laser pistols, miniature versions of the welder currently being used by Parket and Brett.

They stopped outside a massive door well marked with warning symbols and words.

MAIN AIRLOCK: AUTHORIZED PERSONNEL ONLY.
Dallas always found the admonition amusingly redundant,
since there could be no such thing as an unauthorized person
aboard the ship, and anyone authorized to be aboard was
authorized to use the airlock.

Kane touched a switch. A protective shield popped back,
revealed three buttons hidden beneath. He depressed them in
proper sequence. There was a whine and the door moved out
of their way. They entered.

Seven vacuum suits were arranged on the walls. They were
bulky, awkward, and absolutely necessary for this hike if Ash's
evaluations of the outside conditions were even half accurate.
They helped one another into the life-supporting artificial
skins, checked out each other's suit functions.

Then it was time to don helmets. This was done with proper
solemnity and care, everyone taking turns making certain his
neighbour's seal was tight.

Dallas checked out Kane's helmet, Kane checked Lambert,
and she performed the same service for the captain. They
executed this tripartite play with utmost seriousness, the
spacefarers' equivalent of three apes grooming one another.
Automatic regulators were engaged. Soon all three were
breathing the slightly stale but healthy air from their respective
tanks.

Dallas used a gloved hand, activated the helmet's internal
communicator. 'I'm sending. Do you hear me?'

'Receiving,' announced Kane, pausing to boost the power on
his own pickup. 'You read me back?' Dallas nodded, turned to
the still sullen Lambert.

'Come on, Lambert,' Dallas said, trying to cheer her. 'I chose
you for your abilities, not your sunny disposition.'

'Thanks for the flattery,' she replied drily, 'and thanks for
nothing. Why couldn't you have taken Ash or Parker? They'd
probably have loved the chance to go.'

'Ash has to remain on board. You know that. Parker has
work to do back in the engine room and couldn't navigate his ·

way out of a paper bag without instruments. I don't care if you curse me every metre of the way. Just make sure we find the source of that damned signal.'

'Yeah. Wonderful.'

'All right, we're set, then. Keep away from the weapons unless I say otherwise.'

'You expecting friendly company?' Kane looked dubious.

'Hope for the best rather than the worst.' He thumbed the communicator's exterior suit controls, opened another channel. 'Ash, you there?'

It was Ripley who responded. 'He's on his way down to the science blister. Give him a couple of minutes.'

'Check.' He turned to Kane. 'Close inner hatch.' The exec hit the necessary controls and the door slid shut behind them. 'Now open the outer.'

Kane repeated the procedure that had admitted them to the lock. After the last button had been depressed, he stood back with the others and waited. Unconsciously, Lambert pressed her suit back against the inner lock door, an instinctive reaction to the approaching unknown.

The outer hatch slid aside. Clouds of dust and steam drifted before the three humans. The predawn light was the colour of burnt orange. It wasn't the familiar, comforting yellow of Sol, but Dallas had hopes it might improve as the sun continued to rise. It gave them enough light to see by, though there was little enough to see in that dense, particle-thick air.

They stepped out onto the lift platform that ran between support struts. Kane touched another switch. The platform descended, sensors located on its underside telling it where the ground was. It computed distance, halted as its base kissed the highest point of dark stone.

With Dallas leading, more from habit than formal procedure, they made their careful way onto the surface itself. The lava was hard and unyielding under their suit boots. Gale-force winds buffeted them as they surveyed the windswept landscape. At the moment they could see nothing save what ran off beneath their boots into the orange-and-brown mist.

What an unrelievedly depressing place, Lambert thought. Not necessarily frightening, though the inability to see very far was disconcerting enough. It reminded her of a night dive in shark-infested waters. You could never tell what might suddenly come at you out of the darkness.

Maybe she was rendering a harsh decision too soon, but she didn't think so. In all that shrouded land there was not a single warm colour. Not a blue, not a green; only a steady seepage of yellow, sad orange, tired browns and greys. Nothing to warm the mind's eye, which in turn might ease one's thoughts. The atmosphere was the colour of a failed chemistry experiment, the ground that of compact ship excreta. She pitied anything that might have lived here. Despite lack of evidence either way, she had a gut feeling that nothing lived on this world now.

Perhaps Kane was right. Perhaps this was some unknown creature's concept of paradise. If that proved to be the case, she didn't think she cared for such a creature's company.

'Which way?'

'What?' The fog and clouds had misted over her thoughts. She shook them away.

'Which way, Lambert?' Dallas was staring at her.

'I'm okay. Too much thinking.' In her mind she was visualizing her station on board the *Nostromo*. That seat and its navigation instrumentation, so confining and stifling under normal conditions, now seemed like a small slice of heaven.

She checked a line on the screen of a small device attached to her belt. 'Over here. That way.' She pointed.

'You lead.' Dallas stepped in behind her.

Followed by the captain and Kane, she started off into the storm. As soon as they left the protective bulk of the *Nostromo*, the storm was able to surround them on all sides.

She stopped, disgusted, and operated suit instrumentation. 'Now I can't see a goddamn thing.'

Ash's voice sounded unexpectedly in her helmet. 'Turn on

the finder. It's tuned to the distress transmission. Let it lead you and don't mess with it. I've already set it myself.'

'It's on and tuned,' she shot back. 'You think I don't know my own job?'

'No offence,' the science officer responded. She grunted, stalked off into the mists.

Dallas spoke towards his own helmet pickup. 'Finder's working okay. You sure you're receiving us clear, Ash?'

Within the science blister on the lower skin of the ship, Ash switched his gaze from the dust-obscured figures moving slowly away to the brightly lit console in front of him. Three stylized images stood out sharp and clear on the screen. He touched a control and there was a slight whine as the science chair slid a notch on its rails, aligning him precisely with the glowing screen.

'See you right now out the bubble. Read you clear and loud. Good imaging on my board here. I don't think I'll lose you. Mist isn't thick enough and there doesn't seem to be as much interference down here on the surface. Distress signal is on a different frequency so there's no danger of overlap.'

'Sounds good.' Dallas's voice sounded unnatural over the blister speaker. 'We're all receiving you clearly. Let's make sure we keep the channel open. We don't want to get lost out here, not in this stuff.'

'Check. I'll be monitoring your every step. Won't bother you unless something comes up.'

'Check here. Dallas out.' He left the ship channel open, noticed Lambert watching him from behind her suit's dome. 'We're wasting suit time. Let's move.'

She turned wordlessly, her attention going back to the finder, and started off again into the dancing muck. The slightly lower gravity eliminated the burden of suits and tanks, though all still wondered at the composition of a world so small that could generate this much pull. Mentally, Dallas reserved time for a geological check in depth. Maybe that was Parker's influence, but the possibility of this world holding large deposits of valuable heavy metals couldn't be ignored.

The Company would of course claim any such discovery, since it was being made with Company equipment and on Company time. But it could mean some generous bonuses. Their unintentional stop here might turn out to be profitable after all.

Wind drove at them, hammering them with dirt and dust, a solid rain.

'Can't see more than three metres in any direction,' Lambert muttered.

'Quit griping.' That was Kane.

'I like griping.'

'Come on. Quit acting like a couple of kids. This isn't the place for it.'

'Wonderful little place, though.' Lambert wasn't intimidated. 'Totally unspoiled by man or nature. Great place to be . . . if you're a rock.'

'I said, that's enough.' She went quiet at that, but continued to complain under her breath. Dallas could order her to stop talking, but he couldn't keep her from grumbling.

Abruptly, her eyes brought information that momentarily took her thoughts away from their steady condemnation of this place. Something had disappeared from the screen of the finder.

'What's wrong?' Dallas asked.

'Hang on.' She made a slight adjustment to the device, made difficult because of the bulky gloves. The line that had vanished from the face of the finder reappeared.

'Lost it. I've got it again.'

'Any problems?' A distant voice sounded in their helmets. Ash was voicing concern.

'Nothing major,' Dallas informed him. He turned a slow circle, trying to locate something solid within the storm. 'Still a lot of dust and wind. Starting to get some fade on the finder beam. We lost the transmission for a second.'

'It's still strong back here.' Ash checked his own readouts. 'I don't think it's the storm. You might be entering some hilly terrain. That could block out the signal. Watch yourselves. If you lose it and can't regain, switch the finder to trace my channel back towards the ship until you can pick up the transmission again. Then I'll try to direct you from here.'

'We'll keep it in mind, but so far that's not necessary. We'll let you know if we run into that much trouble.'

'Check. Ash out.'

It was quiet again. They moved without talking through the dust-laden, orange limbo. After a while, Lambert stopped.

'Lose it again?' Kane asked.

'Nope. Change of direction.' She gestured off to their left. 'That way now.'

They continued on the new course, Lambert keeping all her attention on the finder's screen, Dallas and Kane keeping theirs on Lambert. Around them the storm grew momentarily wilder. Dust particles made insistent ticking noises as the wind drove them against the faceplates of their helmets, forming speech patterns within their brains.

Tick, tick . . . let us in . . . flick, pock . . . let us in, let us in . . .

Dallas shook himself. The silence, the cloud-enveloped desolation, the orange haze; all were beginning to get to him.

'It's close,' Lambert said. Suit monitors simultaneously informed the distant Ash of their suddenly increased pulse rate. 'Very close.'

They continued on. Something loomed ahead, high above them. Dallas's breath came in short gasps now, from excitement as much as exertion.

Disappointment . . . it was only a large rock formation, twisted and grotesque. Ash's guess about the possibility of them entering higher country was proven correct. They took temporary shelter beneath the stone monolith. At the same time, the line vanished from Lambert's finder.

'Lost it again,' she told them.

'Did we pass it?' Kane studied the rocks, tried to see over them, and could not.

'Not unless it's underground.' Dallas leaned back against the rock wall. 'Might be behind this stuff.' He tapped the stone with a suited fist. 'Or it might be just a fade due to the storm. Let's take a break and see.'

They waited there, resting with their backs to the scoured wall. Dust and mist howled around them.

'Now we're really blind,' said Kane.

'Should be dawn soon.' He adjusted his pickup. 'Ash, if you hear me. How long until daylight?'

The science officer's voice was faint, distorted with static. 'Sun's coming up in about ten minutes.'

'We should be able to see something then.'

'Or the other way around,' Lambert put in. She didn't try to hide her lack of enthusiasm. She was damn tired and they had yet to reach the source of the signal. Nor was it physical weakness. The desolation and eerie colouring were tiring her mind. She longed for the clean, bright familiarity of her console.

The increasing brightness didn't help. Instead of raising their spirits, the rising sun chilled them by turning the air from orange to blood. Maybe it would be less intimidating when the feeble star was completely up . . .

Ripley wiped a hand across her brow, let out a tired breath. She closed the last wall panel she'd been working behind after making certain the new components were functioning properly, put her tools back in the satchel's compartments.

'You ought to be able to handle the rest. I've finished the delicate stuff.'

'Don't worry. We'll manage,' Parker assured her, keeping his tone carefully neutral. He didn't look in her direction, continued to concentrate on his own job. He was still upset over the chance he and Brett might be left out of whatever find the expedition might make.

She started for the nearest up companionway. 'If you run into trouble and need help, I'll be on the bridge.'

'Right,' said Brett softly.

Parker watched her go now, saw her lithe form disappear upward. 'Bitch.'

Ash touched a control. A trio of moving shapes became sharp and regular, losing their fuzzy halos, as the enhancer did its job. He checked his other monitors. The three suit signals continued to come in strong.

'How's it going?' a voice wanted to know over the intercom.

Quickly he shut off the screen, hit his respond. 'All right so far.'

'Where are they?' Ripley asked.

'Getting close to the source. They've moved into some rocky terrain and the signal keeps fading on them, but they're so close I don't see how they can miss it. We ought to hear from them pretty soon.'

'Speaking of that signal, haven't we got anything fresh on it by this time?'

'Not yet.'

'Have you tried putting the transmission through ECIU for detailed analysis?' She sounded a touch impatient.

'Look, I want to know the details as badly as you do. But Mother hasn't identified it yet, so what's the point in my fooling with it?'

'Mind if I give it a shot?'

'Be my guest,' he told her. 'Can't do any harm, and it's something to do. Just let me know the instant you hit on anything, if you happen to get lucky.'

'Yeah. If I happen to get lucky.' She switched off.

She settled a little deeper into her chair on the bridge. It felt oddly spacious now, what with the rest of the bridge crew outside and Ash down in his blister. In fact, it was the first time she could recall being alone on the bridge. It felt strange and not altogether comfortable.

Well, if she was going to take the trouble to work her way through ECIU analysis, she ought to get started. A touch of a switch filled the bridge with that tormented alien wail. She hurriedly turned down the volume. It was disquieting enough to listen to when subdued.

She could easily conceive of it being a voice, as Lambert had suggested. That was a concept more fanciful than scientific, however. Get a grip on yourself, woman. See what the machine has to say and leave your emotional reactions out of it.

Aware of the unlikelihood of having any success where Mother had failed, she activated a little-used panel. But as Ash had said, it was something to do. She couldn't bear to sit and do nothing on the empty bridge. It gave her too much time to think. Better make-work than none at all . . .

# IV

As the hidden sun continued to rise, the bloody red colour of the atmosphere began to lighten. It was now a musty, dirty yellow instead of the familiar bright sunshine of Earth, but it was a vast improvement over what had been.

The storm had abated somewhat and the omnipresent dust had begun to settle. For the first time, the three footweary travellers could see more than a couple of metres ahead.

They'd been climbing for some time. The terrain continued hilly, but except for isolated pillars of basalt it was still composed of lava flows. There were few sharp projections, most having been ground down to gentle curves and wrinkles by untold aeons of steady wind and driven dust.

Kane was in the lead, slightly ahead of Lambert. Any minute now he expected her to announce they'd regained the signal. He topped a slight rise, glanced ahead expecting to see more of what they'd encountered thus far: smooth rock leading upward to another short climb.

Instead, his eyes caught something quite different, different enough to make them go wide behind the dirty, transparent face of the helmet, different enough to make him shout over the pickup.

'JESUS CHRIST!'

'What is it? What's the mat ...?' Lambert pulled up alongside him, followed by Dallas. Both were as shocked by the unexpected sight as Kane had been.

They'd assumed the distress signal was being generated by machinery of some sort, but no pictures of the transmitter source had formed in their minds. They'd been too occupied with the storm and the simple necessity of staying together. Confronted now with a real source, one considerably more impressive than any of them had dared consider, their scientific detachment had temporarily vanished.

It was a ship. Relatively intact it was, and more alien than any of them had imagined possible. Dallas would not have labelled it gruesome, but it was disturbing in a way hard technology should not have been. The lines of the massive derelict were clean but unnatural, imbuing the entire design with an unsettling abnormality.

It towered above them and the surrounding rocks on which it lay. From what they could see of it, they decided it had landed in the same manner as the *Nostromo*, belly down. Basically it was in the shape of an enormous metallic 'U', with the two horns of the U bent slightly in towards one another. One arm was slightly shorter than its counterpart and bent in more sharply. Whether this was due to damage or some alien conception of what constituted pleasing symmetry they had no way of knowing.

As they climbed closer they saw that the craft thickened somewhat at the base of the U, with a series of concentric mounds like thick plates rising to a final dome. Dallas formed the opinion that the two horns contained the ship's drive and engineering sections, while the thicker front end held living quarters, possibly cargo space and the bridge. For all they knew, he might have everything exactly reversed.

The vessel lay supine, displaying no indication of life or activity. This near, the regained transmission was deafening and all three hastened to lower the volume in their helmets.

Whatever metal the hull was composed of, it glistened in the increasing light in an oddly vitreous way that hinted at no alloy ever formed by the hand of man. Dallas couldn't even be sure it was metal. First inspection revealed nothing like a weld, joint, seal or any other recognizable method of cojoining separate plates or sections. The alien ship conveyed the impression of having been grown rather than manufactured.

That was bizarre, of course. Regardless of the method of construction, the important thing was that it was undeniably a ship.

So startled were they by the unexpected sight that none of them gave a thought to what the seemingly intact derelict might be worth in the form of bonuses or salvage.

All three were shouting at the same time into their helmet pickups. 'Some kind of ship, all right,' Kane kept repeating inanely; over and over.

Lambert studied the lustrous, almost wet shine of the curving sides, the absence of any familiar exterior features, and shook her head in wonder. 'Are you positive? Maybe it could be a local structure. It's weird . . .'

'Naw.' Kane's attention was on the twin, curving horns that formed the rear of the vessel. 'It's not fixed. Even allowing for alien architectural concepts, it's clear enough this isn't intended to be part of the landscape. It's a ship, for sure.'

'Ash, can you see this?' Dallas remembered that the science officer could see clearly via their respective suit video pickups, had probably noticed the wreck the moment Kane had topped the rise and given his shocked cry.

'Yeah, I can see it. Not clear, but enough to agree with Kane that it's a ship.' Ash's voice sounded excited in their helmets. At least it was as excited as the science officer ever sounded. 'Never seen anything like it. Hang on a minute.' They waited while Ash studied readouts, ran a couple of rapid queries through the ship's brain.

'Neither has Mother,' he reported. 'It's a completely unknown type, doesn't correlate with anything we've ever encountered before. Is it as big as it looks from here?'

'Bigger,' Dallas told him. 'Massive construction, no small details visible as yet. If it's constructed to the same scale as our ships, the builders must've been a damn sight bigger than us.'

Lambert let out a nervous giggle. 'We'll find out, if there are any of them left on board to give us a welcome.'

'We're close and in line,' Dallas said to Ash, ignoring the navigator's comment. 'You ought to be receiving a much clearer signal from us. What about the distress call? Any shift? We're too close to tell.'

'No. Whatever's producing the transmission is inside that. I'm sure of it. Got to be. If it was farther out, we'd never have picked it up through that mass of metal.'

'If it is metal.' Dallas continued to examine the alien hull. 'Almost looks like plastic.'

'Or bone,' a thoughtful Kane suggested.

'Assuming the transmission is coming from inside, what do we do now?' Lambert wondered.

The exec started forward. 'I'll go in and have a look, let you know.'

'Hold on, Kane. Don't be so damned adventurous. One of these days it's going to get you into trouble.'

'I'll settle for getting inside. Look, we've got to do something. We can't just stand around out here and wait for revelations to magically appear in the air above the ship.' Kane frowned at him. 'Are you seriously suggesting we don't go inside?'

'No, no. But there's no need to rush it.' He addressed the distant science officer. 'You still reading us, Ash?'

'Weaker now that you're on top of the transmitter,' came the reply. 'There's some unavoidable interference. But I'm still on you clear.'

'Okay. I don't see any lights or signs of life. No movement of any kind except this damn dust. Use us for a distance-and-line fix and try your sensors. See if you can see or find anything that we can't.'

There was a pause while Ash hastened to comply with the order. They continued to marvel at the elegantly distorted lines of the enormous vessel.

'I've tried everything,' the science officer finally reported. 'We're not equipped for this kind of thing. The *Nostromo*'s a commercial tug, not an exploration craft. I'd need a lot of expensive stuff we just don't carry to get a proper reading.'

'So . . . what can you tell me?'

'Nothing from here, sir. I can't get any results at all. It's putting out so much power I can't get any acceptable reading whatsoever. We just don't carry the right instrumentation.'

Dallas tried to conceal his disappointment from the others. 'I understand. It's not crucial anyway. But keep trying. Let me know the minute you do find anything, anything at all. Especially any indication of movement. Don't go into details. We'll handle any analysis at this end.'

'Check. Watch yourselves.'

What now, Captain? Dallas's gaze travelled the length of the huge ship, returned to discover Kane and Lambert watching him. The exec was right, of course. To know that this was the source of the signal was not sufficient. They had to trace it to the generator, try to discover the cause behind the signal and the presence of this ship on this tiny world. To have come this far and not explore the alien's innards was unthinkable.

Curiosity, after all, was what had driven mankind out from his isolated, unimportant world and across the gulf between the stars. It had also, he thoughtfully reminded himself, killed the figurative cat.

He came to a decision, the only logical one. 'It looks pretty dead from out here. We'll approach the base first. Then, if nothing shows itself . . .'

Lambert eyed him. 'Yeah.'

'Then . . . we'll see.'

They started towards the hull, the superfluous finder dangling from Lambert's belt.

'At this point,' Dallas was saying as they neared the overhanging curve of the hull, 'there's only one thing I can . . .'

Back aboard the Nostromo, Ash followed every word carefully. Without warning, Dallas's voice faded. It came back strong once more before disappearing completely. Simultaneously, Ash lost visual contact.

'Dallas!' Frantically, he jabbed buttons on the console, threw switches, demanded better resolution from the already overstrained pickups. 'Dallas, do you read me? I've lost you. Repeat, I've lost you . . .'

Only the constant thermonuclear hiss of the local sun sounded plantively over the multitude of speakers . . .

Up next to the hull, the colossal scale of the alien vessel was more evident than ever. It curved above them, rising into the dust-heavy air and looking more solid than the broken rock it rested upon.

'Still no sign of life,' Dallas murmured half to himself as he surveyed the hull. 'No lights, no movement.' He gestured towards the imagined bow of the ship. 'And no way in. Let's try up that way.'

As they strode carefully over shattered boulders and loose, shaly rock, Dallas was aware how small the alien ship made him feel. Not small physically, though the bulging, overbearing arc of the hull dwarfed the three humans, but insignificantly tiny on the cosmic scale. Humanity still knew very little of the universe, had explored a fraction of one corner.

It was exciting and intellectually gratifying to speculate on what might lie waiting in the black gulfs when one was behind the business end of a telescope, quite another to do so isolated on an unpleasant little speck of a world such as this, confronted by a ship of non-human manufacture that uncomfortably resembled a growth instead of a familiar device for manipulating and overcoming the neat laws of physics.

That, he admitted to himself, was what troubled him most about the derelict. Had it conformed to the familiar in its outlines and composition, then its non-human origin would not have seemed so threatening. He did not put his feelings down to simple xenophobia. Basically, he hadn't expected the alien to be so completely *alien*.

'Something's coming up.' He saw that Kane was pointing to the hull ahead of them. Time to set aside idle speculation, he told himself firmly, and treat with reality. This odd horn-shape was a spacecraft, differing only in superficial ways from the *Nostromo*. There was nothing malignant about the material it was formed of or ominous about its design. One was the result of a different technology, the latter possibly of aesthetic ideals as much as anything else. When viewed in that manner, the ship assumed a kind of exotic beauty. No doubt Ash was already raving over the vessel's unique design, wishing he were here among them.

Dallas noticed Lambert's unvaried expression and knew there was at least one member of the crew who'd trade places with the science officer without hesitation.

Kane had indicated a trio of dark blotches on the hull's flank. As they climbed nearer and slightly higher in the rocks, the blotches turned into oval openings, showed depth in addition to height and width.

They finally found themselves standing just below the three pockmarks in the metal (or plastic? or what?) hull. Narrower, still darker secondary gaps showed behind the exterior ovals. Wind whipped dust and pumice in and out of the openings, a sign that the gaps had remained open for some time.

'Looks like an entrance,' Kane surmised, hands on hips as he studied the gaps. 'Maybe somebody else's idea of an airlock. You see the inner hatch openings behind these?'

'If they're locks, why three of them so close to each other?' Lambert regarded the openings with suspicion. 'And why are they all standing open?'

'Maybe the builders liked to do things in threes.' Kane shrugged. 'If we can find one, I'll let you ask him.'

'Funny boy.' She didn't smile. 'I'll buy that, but what about leaving all three open?'

'We don't know that they're open.' Dallas found himself fascinated by the smooth-lipped ovals, so different from the *Nostromo*'s bulky, squarish lock entrances. These appeared moulded into the fabric of the hull instead of having been attached later in construction with awkward welds and seals.

'As to why they might be open, if they indeed are,' Dallas continued, 'maybe the crew wanted to get out in a hurry.'

'Why would they need three open locks to do that?'

Dallas snapped at her, irritated. 'How the hell am I supposed to know?' He added immediately after, 'Sorry ... that was uncalled for.'

'No it wasn't.' This time she did grin, slightly. 'It was a dumb question.'

'Time we got ourselves some answers.' Keeping his eyes on the ground and watching for loose rock, he started up the slight incline leading towards the openings. 'We've waited long enough. Let's move inside, if we can.'

'Might be someone's idea of a lock.' Kane studied the interior of the opening they now were entering. 'Not mine.'

Dallas was already inside. 'Surface is firm. Secondary door or hatch or whatever it was is open also.' A pause, then, 'There's a big chamber back here.'

'What about light?' Lambert fingered her own lightbar, slung at her waist opposite her pistol.

'Seems to be enough for now. Save power until we need it. Come on in.'

Kane and Lambert followed him through, down a short corridor. They emerged into a high-ceilinged room. If there were controls, gauges, or any kind of instrumentation in this section of the ship they were concealed behind grey walls. Looking remarkably like the inside of a human rib cage, rounded metal ribbings braced floor, roof and walls. Ghost light from outside danced on dust particles suspended in the nearly motionless air of the eerie chamber.

Dallas eyed his executive officer. 'What do you think?'

'I dunno. Cargo chamber, maybe? Or part of a complicated lock system? Yeah, that's it. We just passed through a double door and this here is the real lock.'

'Mighty big for just an airlock.' Lambert's voice sounded subdued in their helmets.

'Just guessing. If the inhabitants of this ship were to its scale what we are to the *Nostromo*, they'd likely need a lock this size. But I admit the cargo-hold idea makes more sense. Might even explain the need for three entryways.' He turned, saw Dallas leaning over a black hole in the floor.

'Hey, watch it, Dallas! No telling what might be down there, or how deep it goes.'

'The ship is standing open to the outside and nothing's taken notice of our entry. I don't think there's anything alive in here.' Dallas unclipped his lightbar, flipped it on and directed the brilliant beam downward.

'See anything?' Lambert asked.

'Yeah.' Kane smirked. 'Like a rabbit with a watch?' He sounded almost hopeful.

'Can't see a damn thing.' Dallas moved the light slowly from one side to the other. It was a narrow beam, but powerful. It would show anything lying a modest distance below them.

'What is it?' Lambert had walked over to stand alongside him, kept a careful distance from the abyss. 'Another cargo chamber?'

'No way of telling from here. It just goes down. Smooth walls as far as my light will reach. No indication of handholds, an elevator, ladder or any other means of descent. I can't see the bottom. Light won't reach. Must be an access shaft of some kind.' He turned off his light, moved a metre away from the hole and began unclipping gear from his belt and backpack. He laid it out on the floor, rose and glanced around the dimly illuminated, grey chamber.

'Whatever's downstairs will wait. Let's have a look around here first. I want to make sure there aren't any surprises. We might even find an easier way down.' He flicked his light on once more, played it over nearby walls. Despite their resemblance to a whale's insides, they remained gratifyingly motionless.

'Spread out . . . but not too far. Under no circumstances walk out of unlighted view of one another. This shouldn't take more than a couple of minutes.'

Kane and Lambert activated their own lightbars. Travelling in a line, they started to explore the vast room.

Fragments of some shattered grey material lay scattered about. Much of it was buried beneath the tiny dust dunes and finely ground pumice that had invaded the ship. Kane ignored the stuff. They were hunting for something intact.

Dallas's light fell unexpectedly on a shape that was not part of wall or floor. Moving closer, he used the light to trace its outlines. It appeared to be a smallish urn or vase, tan in colour, glossy in aspect. Moving closer, he tilted his head over the jagged, broken top, shone the light inside.

Empty.

Disappointed, he walked away, wondering that something seemingly so fragile had remained relatively undisturbed while other more durable substances had apparently withered and cracked. Though for all he knew, the composition of the urn might test the melting ability of his pistol.

He was almost ready to return to the shaft in the floor when his light fell on something complex and boldly mechanical. Within the semi-organic confines of the alien ship its reassuringly functional appearance was a great relief, though the design itself was utterly unfamiliar.

'Over here!'

'Something wrong?' That was Kane.

'Not a thing. I've found a mechanism.'

Lambert and Kane rushed to join him, their boots raising little puffs of animated dust. They added their own lights to Dallas's. All seemed quiet and dead, though Dallas had the impression of patient power functioning smoothly somewhere behind those strangely contoured panels. And evidence of mechanical life was provided by the sight of a single metal bar moving steadily back and forth on its grooved track, though it made, according to suit sensors, not a sound.

'Looks like it's still functioning. Wonder how long it's been running like this.' Kane examined the device, fascinated. 'Wonder what it does.'

'I can tell you that.' They turned to Lambert. She confirmed what Dallas had already guessed. She was holding her finder, the same instrument that had led them here from the *Nostromo*. 'It's the transmitter. Automatic distress call, just like we imagined it might be. It looks clean enough to be brand new, though it's likely been putting out that signal for years.' She shrugged. 'Maybe decades. Or longer.'

Dallas ran a small instrument over the surface of the alien device. 'Electrostatic repulsion. That explains the absence of dust. Too bad. There isn't much wind in here and the depth of the dust might give us a clue to how long the machine's been set up. It looks portable.' He turned the scanner off, slipped it back into its waist holder.

'Anyone else find anything?' They both shook their heads.

'Just ribbed walls and dust.' Kane sounded discouraged.

'No indication of another opening leading to a different part of the ship? No other floor gaps?' Again the double negative responses. 'That leaves us with the first shaft, or trying to bore a hole through the nearest wall. We'll try the first before we go slicing things up.' He noticed Kane's expression. 'Giving up?'

'Not yet. I will if we run through every centimetre of this big grey bastard and don't find anything besides blank walls and sealed machines.'

'That wouldn't bother me a bit,' said Lambert with feeling.

They retraced their steps, carefully positioned themselves close to the lip of the flush, circular opening in the deck. Dallas knelt, moving slowly in the suit, and felt as best he could of the shaft's rim.

'Can't tell much with these damned gloves on, but it feels regular. The shaft must be a normal part of the ship. I thought it might've been caused by an explosion. That is a distress call we're picking up.'

Lambert studied the hole. 'A shaped charge could make a smooth hole like that.'

'You'll do anything to make a guy feel good, won't you?' Dallas felt disappointed. 'But I still think it's a normal part of this ship. The sides are too regular, even for a shaped charge, no matter how powerful.'

'Just giving my opinion.'

'Either way, it's look down below, blow a hole in a wall, or go back outside and hunt for another entrance.' He looked across the shaft at Kane. 'This is your big chance.'

The exec looked indifferent. 'If you wish. Suits me. If I'm feeling generous, I'll even tell you about the diamonds.'

'What diamonds?'

'The ones I'm going to find spilling out of old alien crates down there.' He gestured at the blackness.

Lambert helped him secure the chest climbing unit, made certain the harness was firmly affixed to his shoulders and back. He touched the check stud, was rewarded by a faint beep over his helmet speaker. A green light winked on, then off, on the front of the unit.

'We've got power over here. I'm all set.' He eyed Dallas. 'You ready yet?'

'Another minute.' The captain had assembled a metal tripod from short lengths of metal. The resulting construction looked flimsy, too thin to support a man's weight. In actuality it could hold the three of them without so much as bending.

When it was locked, Dallas moved it so that its apex was positioned over the centre of the shaft. Braces secured the three legs to the deck. A small winch and spool arrangement attached to the apex held thin cable. Dallas manually unwound a metre or two of the gleaming lifeline, handed the end to Kane. The exec affixed the cable to the loop on his chest unit, double locked it tight and had Lambert check by pulling on it with all her weight. It held easily.

'Don't unhook yourself from the cable under any circumstances,' Dallas said sternly. 'Even if you see piles of diamonds sparkling just out of your reach.' He checked the cable unit for himself. Kane was a good officer. The gravity here was less than on Earth, but still more than adequate to make a mess of Kane if he fell. They had no idea how deep into the bowels of the ship the shaft went. Or the shaft might be a mining shaft, extending below the hull into the ground. That thought led to another, which made Dallas grin to himself. Maybe Kane would find his diamonds after all.

'Be out in less than ten minutes.' He spoke in his best no-nonsense tone. 'Read me?'

'Aye, aye.' Kane carefully sat down, swung his legs over the edge. Grasping the cable with both hands, he pushed off, hung by the cable in the middle of the opening. His lower body was cloaked in black air.

'If you're not out in ten minutes, I'll pull you out with the override,' Dallas warned him.

'Relax. I'll be a good boy. Besides, I can take care of myself.' He'd stopped swinging from side to side, now hung motionless in the gap.

'Do that. Keep us informed as you descend.'

'Check.' Kane activated the climbing unit. The cable unwound smoothly, lowering him into the shaft. He thrust out with his legs, contacted the smooth sides. Leaning back and bracing his feet against the vertical wall, he was able to walk downward.

Holding himself motionless, he switched on his lightbar, pointed it down. It showed him ten metres of dull-coloured metal before dissolving into nothingness.

'Hotter in here,' he reported, after a cursory inspection of his suit's sensory equipment. 'Must be warm air rising from below. Could be part of the engine complex, if that's still functioning. We know something's supplying power to that transmitter.'

Kicking away from the wall and playing out cable, he started down in earnest. After several minutes of rappelling his way down the shaft, he stopped to catch his breath. It *was* warmer, and growing more so the farther he dropped. The sudden changes put a burden on his suit's cooling system and he began to sweat, though the helmet's own unit kept his faceplate clear. His breathing sounded loud to him within the helmet and he worried because he knew Dallas and Lambert could hear. He didn't want to be called back up.

Leaning back, he glanced upward and saw the mouth of the shaft, a round circle of light set in a black frame. A dark blot appeared, obscured one round edge. Distant light glinted off something smooth and reflective.

'You okay down there?'

'Okay. Hot, though. I can still see you. Haven't hit bottom yet.' He sucked in a deep draught of air, then another, hyperventilating. The tank regulator whined in protest. 'This is real work. Can't talk anymore now.'

Bending his knees, he kicked away from the wall again, let out more cable. By now he'd gained some confidence with regard to his surroundings. The shaft continued steadily downward. So far it had displayed no inclination to narrow, or change direction. Widening he wasn't as concerned about.

He kicked off harder the next time, began taking longer and longer hops, falling steadily faster in the darkness. His lightbar continued to shine downward, continued to reveal nothing but the same monotonous, unvarying night beneath him.

Out of breath again he paused in his descent to run a check of his suit instrumentation. 'Interesting,' he said into his pickup. 'I'm below ground level.'

'Read you,' replied Dallas. Thinking of mine shafts, he asked, 'Any change in your surroundings? Still the same stuff walling the shaft?'

'Far as I can see. How am I doing on line?'

A brief pause while Dallas checked the cable remaining on the spool. 'Fine. Got over fifty metres left. If the shaft runs deeper than that we'll have to call this off until we can bring bigger stuff from the ship. I wouldn't think it'd go that far down, though.'

'What makes you think so?'

Dallas sounded thoughtful. 'Would make the ship all out of proportion.'

'Proportion to what? And to whose ideas of proportion?'

Dallas did not have a reply for that.

Ripley would have given up on the search if she'd had anything better to do. She did not. Playing at the ECIU board was better than wandering around an empty ship or staring at the vacant seats surrounding her.

Unexpectedly, a realignment of priorities in her querying jogged something within the ship's Brobdingnagian store of information. The resultant readout appeared on the screen so abruptly she almost erased it and continued with the next series before she realized she actually had received a sensible response. The trouble with computers, she thought, was that they had no intuitive senses. Only deductive ones. You had to ask the right question.

She studied the readout avidly, frowned, punched for elaboration. Sometimes Mother could be unintentionally evasive. You had to know how to weed out the confusing subtleties.

This time, however, the readout was clear enough, left no room for misunderstanding. She wished fervently that it had. She jabbed at the intercom. A voice answered promptly.

'Science blister. What is it, Ripley?'

'This is urgent, Ash.' She spoke in short, anxious gasps. 'I finally got something out of the Bank, via ECIU. It might have just come through, I don't know. That's not what matters.'

'Congratulations.'

'Never mind that,' she snapped worriedly. 'Mother has apparently deciphered part of the alien transmission. She's not positive about this, but from what I read I'm afraid that transmission may not be an SOS.'

That quieted Ash, but only for an instant. When he replied his voice was as controlled as ever, despite the import of Ripley's announcement. She marvelled at his self-control.

'If it's not a distress call, then what is it?' he asked quietly. 'And why the nervous tone? You are nervous, aren't you?'

'You bet your ass I'm nervous! Worse than that, if Mother's correct. Like I said, she's not positive. But she thinks that signal may be a warning.'

'What kind of warning?'

'What difference does it make, "what kind of warning"!'

'There is no reason to shout.'

Ripley took a couple of short breaths, counted to five. 'We have to get through to them. They've got to know about this right away.'

'I agree,' said Ash readily. 'But it's no use. Once they went inside the alien ship we lost them completely. I've had no contact with them for some time now. The combination of their proximity to the alien transmitter coupled with the peculiar composition of the vessel's hull has defeated every attempt of mine at re-establishing communication. And believe me, I've tried!' His next comment came off sounding like a challenge.

'You can try to raise them yourself, if you like. I'll help in any way I can.'

'Look, I'm not questioning your competence, Ash. If you say we can't contact them, we can't contact them. But damn it, we've got to let them *know*!'

'What do you suggest?'

She hesitated, then said firmly, 'I'm going out after them. I'll tell them in person.'

'I don't think so.'

'Is that an order, Ash?' She knew that in an emergency situation of this kind the science officer outranked her.

'No, it's common sense. Can you see that? Use your head, Ripley,' he urged her. 'I know you don't like me much, but try to view this rationally.

'We simply can't spare the personnel. With you and me, plus Parker and Brett, we've got minimum takeoff capability right now. Three off, four on. That's the rules. That's why Dallas left us all on board. If you go running after them, for whatever reason, we're stuck here until someone comes back. If they don't come back, no one will know what's happened here.' He paused, added, 'Besides, we've no reason to assume anything. They're probably fine.'

'All right.' She admitted it grudgingly. 'I concede your point. But this is a special situation. I still think someone should go after them.'

She'd never heard Ash sigh and he didn't do so now, but he gave her the impression of a man resigned to handling a Hobson's choice.

'What's the point?' He said it evenly, as though it were the most obvious thing in the world. 'In the time it would take one of us to get there, they'll know if it's an operative warning. Am I wrong or am I right?'

Ripley didn't reply, simply sat staring dully at Ash on the monitor. The science officer gazed steadily back at her. What she couldn't see was the diagram on his console monitor. She would have found it very interesting . . .

# V

Refreshed by the brief rest, Kane kicked away from the smooth wall of the shaft and continued downward. He kicked off a second time, waited for the impact of his booted feet contacting the hard side. They did not, sailed off into emptiness. The walls of the shaft had vanished. He was swinging in emptiness, hanging from the end of the cable.

Some kind of room, maybe another chamber like the big one above, he thought. Whatever it was, he'd emerged from the bottom of the shaft into it. He was breathing hard from the exertion of the descent and the increased warmth.

Funny, but the darkness seemed to press more tightly about him now that he was out of the shaft than it had when he'd been dropping within its narrow confines. He thought about what lay below him, how far away it might be, and what could happen to him if the cable broke now.

Easy, Kane, he told himself. Keep thinking of diamonds. Bright, many-faceted big ones, clear and flawless and fat with carats. Not of this foglike blackness you're twirling through, redolent of alien ghosts and memories and . . .

Damn, he was doing it again.

'See anything?'

Startled, he gave a reflexive jerk on the cable and started swinging again. He used the mechanism to steady himself, cleared his throat before replying. He had to remind himself that he wasn't alone down here. Dallas and Lambert waited just above, not that far distant. A modest hike southwest of the derelict lay the *Nostromo*, full of coffee, familiar sweat smells, and the patient comforts of deep sleep.

For an instant he found himself wishing desperately that he was back aboard her. Then he told himself that there were no diamonds aboard the tug, and certainly no glory. Both might still be found here.

'No, nothing. There's a cave or room below me. I've slipped clear of the shaft.'

'Cave? Keep a hold of yourself, Kane. You're still in the ship.'

'Am I? Remember what was said about shafts? Maybe that's right after all.'

'Then you ought to be swimming in your goddamn diamonds any minute now.'

Both men chuckled, Dallas's sounding hollow and distorted over the helmet speakers. Kane tried to shake some of the sweat from his forehead. That was the trouble with suits. When they kept you cool they were great, but when you started sweating you couldn't wipe a thing except your faceplate.

'Okay, so it's not a cave. But it feels like the tropics down here.' Leaning over slightly, he checked his waist instruments. He was far enough below the surface to be in a cave, but so far he'd found nothing to indicate he was anywhere but inside the bowels of the alien ship.

There was one way to find out. Locate the bottom.

'What's the air like down there? Besides hot.'

Another check, different readouts this time. 'Pretty much the same as outside. High nitrogen content, little to no oxy. Water vapour concentration's even higher down here, thanks to the temperature rise. I'll take a sample if you want. Ash can have fun playing with it.'

'Never mind that now. Keep going.'

Kane thumbed a switch. His belt recorded the approximate atmospheric composition at his present level. That should make Ash happy, though a sample would have been better. Still puffing, Kane activated the unit on his chest. With a confident hum, it resumed lowering him slowly.

It was lonelier than falling through space. Spinning slowly as the wire unwound, he dropped through total darkness, not a star or nebula in sight.

So completely had the peaceful blackness relaxed him that it was a shock when his boots struck a solid surface. He grunted in surprise, almost lost his balance. Steadying himself, he stood straight and deactivated the climber unit.

He was preparing to unhook the restraining cable when he recalled Dallas's directive. It was going to be awkward, exploring while trailing the constraining tie-line, but Dallas would have a fit if he discovered that Kane had released himself. So he'd have to manage as best he could and pray the trailing line didn't get itself entangled in something overhead.

Breathing more easily now, he flashed his lightbar and suit lights in an effort to make something out of his surroundings. It was instantly clear that his guess about being in a cave was as inaccurate as it had been emotional. This was obviously another chamber in the alien ship.

From the appearance of it, bare-walled and high-ceilinged, he supposed it to be a cargo hold. The light travelled across odd shapes and formations that were either an integral part of the hold wall or else had somehow been attached to it. They had a soft, almost flexible look, as opposed to the solid appearance of the bone ribs that reinforced corridor and chamber walls. They lined the walls from floor to ceiling, neat and orderly.

Yet somehow they didn't give him the impression of having been stowed. There was too much wasted space in the vaulted chamber. Of course, until they had some idea of what the protrusions were, it was absurd to speculate on the rationale behind alien methods of storing cargo.

'You all right down there, Kane?' Dallas's voice.

'Yeah. You ought to see this.'

'See what? What've you found?'

'I'm not sure. But it's weird.'

'What are you talking about?' There was a pause, then, 'Kane, could you be a little more specific? "Weird" doesn't tell us much. This whole ship is weird, but that's not how it's going to be described in the official report.'

'Okay. I'm in another big chamber like the one above. There's something all over the walls.'

Holding his lightbar extended in front of him in an unconsciously weaponlike pose, he walked over to the nearest wall and examined the protrusions. Up close, he was able to decide that they weren't part of the hull structure. Not only that, they looked more organic than ever.

Above, Dallas glanced over at Lambert.

'How long until sunset?'

She studied her instruments, touched a control on one briefly. 'Twenty minutes.' She accompanied the announcement with a meaningful stare. Dallas didn't comment, turned his attention back to the black circle of the shaft, continued to stare downward although he couldn't see a thing.

A flash of Kane's lightbar revealed still more of the peculiar objects attached to the floor of the chamber, in the centre of the room. He moved towards them, circled them while examining individual specimens in turn. Each was roughly a third of a metre high, oval in shape, and leathery in appearance. Choosing one at random, he turned his light on it, kept it focused there. The steady illumination revealed nothing new, nor did it seem to have any effect on the ovoid.

'It's like some kind of storage area, for sure.' There was no response from his helmet speakers. 'I said it's definitely a storage area. Anybody read me?'

'Loud and clear,' Dallas said quickly. 'We were listening, that's all. You say you're pretty sure it's a storage room?'

'That's right.'

'Anything to support that premise besides its size and shape?'

'Sure is. Those protrusions on the wall are also on the floor, and they're not part of the ship. This whole place is stocked with 'em. Leathery things. Matter of fact, they kind of resemble that urn you found above, only these are much softer looking. And these seem to be sealed, where yours was empty. They're all arranged according to somebody's concept of order, though there seems to be a lot of wasted space.'

'Funny-sounding kind of cargo, if that's what it is. Can you see if anything's in them?' Dallas was remembering the hollow urn shape he'd found.

'Hang on. I'll give it a closer look.' Leaving the lightbar on, he approached the particular specimen he'd been studying, reached out a gloved hand and touched it. Nothing happened. Leaning over he tugged at the sides, then the top. There was nothing resembling a catch or break on the smooth surface.

'Got a funny feel to it, even through the gloves.'

Dallas sounded suddenly concerned. 'I just asked if you could see what was in it. Don't try to open it. You don't know what it might hold.'

Kane peered close at the object. It hadn't changed and showed no effect from his pulling and tugging. 'Whatever it contains, it's sealed in tight.' Turning away, he played his light over the rows of ovoids. 'Maybe I can find one that's cracked or has split a little.'

In the faint backwash of his suit lights, a small bump appeared silently on the taut surface of the ovoid he'd touched. A second eruption appeared, then others, until there were raised spots across the smooth top.

'All the same,' he reported to Dallas and Lambert. 'Not a seam or break in any of them.' He turned his light absently back to the one he'd experimented with, leaned forward and squinted uncertainly at what he saw.

The opaque surface of the ovoid had become translucent. As he continued to stare, eyes widening, the surface continued to clear, becoming transparent as glass. Moving closer, he shone his light on the base of the object, stared hard, barely breathing as a shape within the oval container became visible.

'Jesus . . .'

'What? Kane, what's going on down there?' Dallas forced

himself not to shout.

A tiny nightmare was now clearly visible within the ovoid. It lay neatly coiled and folded about itself, compact and delicate and all made of a rubbery, filigreed flesh. It looked to Kane like a fraction of someone's delirium tremens plucked from the mind and given solidity and shape.

The thing was basically in the shape of a hand, many-fingered, with the long, bony fingers curled into the palm. It looked very much like the hand of a skeleton, save for the extra fingers. Something protruded from the centre of the palm, a short tube of some kind. A muscular tail was coiled beneath the base of the hand. On its back he could just make out a dim, convex shape that looked like a glazed-over eye.

That eye . . . if it was an eye and not simply some shiny excrescence . . . deserved a closer look. Despite the feeling of repugnance churning in his belly, he moved still closer and raised the light for a better view.

The eye moved and looked at him.

The ovoid exploded. Propelled outward by the sudden release of energy contained in the coiled tail, the hand opened and leaped at him. He raised an arm to ward it off, too late. It fixed itself to his faceplate. He had a horribly close glimpse of the weaving tube in the centre of the palm stroking the front of the glass, centimetres from his nose. Something started to sizzle and the material of the faceplace began to deliquesce. He panicked, tried to tear the creature away.

It was through the plate. Alien atmosphere, cold and harsh, mixed with breathable air. He felt faint, continued to pull weakly at the hand. Something was pushing insistently at his lips.

Beyond all horror now, he staggered about the chamber, trying to wrench the abomination from him. The long, sensitive fingers had slipped through the open faceplate. They reached over his skull and around the sides of his head, while the thick tail slid inside to wrap itself snake-like around his neck.

Barely getting air, the awful tube feeling like a fat worm sliding down his throat, he stumbled over his own feet, tripped and fell over backward.

'Kane . . . Kane, can you hear me?' Dallas was sweating inside his suit. 'Kane, answer me!' Silence. He thought a moment. 'If you can't use your communicator, give me two beeps off your tracking unit.' He looked to Lambert, who could receive the signal. She waited a proper interval, waited longer before shaking her head slowly.

'What do you think's the matter?' she asked.

'I don't know, I don't know. Maybe he's fallen and damaged his power cells.' He hesitated. 'He can't or won't answer. I think we'd better haul him out.'

'Isn't that a bit premature? I'm concerned too, but . . .'

Dallas had a slightly wild look in his eyes. When he caught Lambert staring at him he calmed himself.

'I'm okay. I'm okay. This place,' and he gestured at the cold walls, 'got to me for a moment, that's all. I still say we bring him up.'

'It'll yank him right off his feet if he's not expecting it. Could hurt him, especially if he has fallen and he's lying in a twisted position. If there's nothing really wrong you'll never hear the end of it.'

'Try him again.'

Lambert thumbed her own communicator. 'Kane . . . Kane. Goddamn it, answer us!'

'Keep trying.' While Lambert continued to call, alternately pleading and threatening, Dallas reached across the shaft opening and examined the cable. It moved easily in his hand. Too easily. He tugged, and a metre of line came up in his grasp without the expected resistance.

'Line's slack.' He glanced back at her.

'He still doesn't answer. Can't or won't. Do you think he could have gone and unhooked himself? I know what you told him, but you know how he is. Probably thought we wouldn't notice a temporary reduction in cable tension. If he spotted something and was afraid of the cable getting snagged or not reaching, I wouldn't put it past him to go and unlatch.'

'I don't care what he might've found. I do care that he doesn't answer.' Dallas adjusted the winch motor, switched it on. 'Too bad if it upsets him. If there's nothing wrong with him or his equipment, I'll make him wish he *had* unhooked.'

A flip of another switch and the winch began to reel in cable. Dallas watched it intently, relaxed a little when he saw the line snap taut after a couple of metres had been rewound. As expected, the cable slowed.

'There's weight on the end. It caught.'

'Is it hooked on something?'

'Can't be. It's still coming up, only slightly different speed. If it had gotten caught and was dragging something beside Kane, the different weight would make it rise slower or faster. I think he's still there, even if he can't answer.'

'What if he objects and tries to use his chest unit to try to descend?'

Dallas shook his head curtly. 'He can't do it.' He nodded towards the winch. 'The cable override's on the unit there, not the portable he's wearing. He'll come up whether he likes the idea or not.'

Lambert gazed expectantly down the shaft. 'I still can't see anything.'

A lightbar illuminated a portion of the hole. Dallas played it across smooth walls. 'Neither can I. But the line's still coming up.'

It continued its steady rise, both suited figures waiting anxiously for something to appear in the waiting circle of Dallas's light. It was several minutes before the cone of illumination was interrupted by something rising from below.

'Here he comes.'

'He's not moving.' Lambert searched nervously for a gesture of some kind from the nearing shape. An obscenity, anything . . . but Kane did not move.

The tripod bent slightly downward as the last few metres of

cable were reeled in.

'Get ready to grab him if he swings your way.' Lambert readied herself on the opposite side of the shaft.

Kane's body appeared, swinging slowly on the end of the cable. It hung limp in the dim light.

Dallas reached across the gap, intending to grab the motionless executive officer by his chest harness. His hand had almost made contact when he noticed the grey, equally motionless creature inside the helmet, enveloping Kane's head. He pulled back his groping hand as if burnt.

'What's the matter?' wondered Lambert.

'Watch out. There's something on his face, inside his helmet.'

She walked around the gap. 'What is . . .,' then she got her first glimpse of the creature, neatly snugged inside the helmet like a mollusc in its shell. 'Oh, Jesus!'

'Don't touch it.' Dallas studied the limp form of his shipmate. Experimentally, he waved a hand at the thing attached to Kane's face. It didn't budge. Bracing himself, ready to jerk back and run, he reached towards it. His hand moved close to the base, then towards the eye bulge on its back. The beast took no notice of him, exhibited no sigh of life except a slow pulsing.

'Is it alive?' Lambert's stomach was turning slowly. She felt as though she'd just swallowed a litre of the *Nostromo*'s half-recycled wastes.

'It's not moving, but I think it is. Get his arms, I'll take his legs. Maybe we can dump it off him.'

Lambert hurried to comply, paused, and looked back at him uncertainly. 'How come I get the arms?'

'Oh, hell. You want to switch?'

'Yeah.'

Dallas moved to trade places with her. As he did so he thought he saw one finger of the hand move, ever so slightly, but he couldn't be sure.

He started to lift under Kane's arms, felt the dead weight, hesitated. 'We'll never get him back to the ship this way. You take one side and I'll take the other.'

'Fair enough.'

They carefully turned the body of the exec onto his side. The creature did not fall off. It remained affixed to Kane's face as securely as it had been when the latter had been lying untouched on his back.

'No good. Wishful thinking. I didn't think it would fall off. Let's get him back to the ship.'

He slipped an arm behind Kane's back and raised him in a sitting position, then got one of the exec's arms across his shoulders. Lambert did the same on the other side.

'Ready now?' She nodded. 'Keep an eye on the creature. If it looks like it's fixing to fall away, drop your side and get the hell clear.' She nodded again. 'Let's go.'

They stopped just inside the entrance to the alien ship. Both were breathing heavily. 'Let him down,' Dallas told her. Lambert did so, gladly. 'This won't work. His feet will catch on every rock, every crevice. Stay with him. I'm going to try to make a travois.'

'Out of what?' But Dallas was already headed back into the ship, moving towards the chamber they'd just left.

'The winch tripod,' she heard him say in her helmet. 'It's strong enough.'

While waiting for Dallas to return, Lambert sat as far away from Kane as she could. Wind howled outside the derelict's hull, heralding the approaching nightfall. She found herself unable to keep her gaze from the tiny monster attached to Kane, unable to keep from speculating on what had happened.

She *was* able to prevent herself from thinking about what it might be doing to him. She had to, because hysteria lay down that particular mental path.

Dallas returned, sections of the disassembled tripod under his right arm. Spreading the pieces out on the deck, he began to rig a crude platform on which to drag Kane. Fear lent speed to his gloved fingers.

Once the device was finished, he lowered it gingerly to the surface outside. It fell the last couple of metres but did not break. He decided it would hold the unconscious exec until they could reach the *Nostromo*.

The short day was rapidly rushing to an end, the atmosphere once more turning the colour of blood, the wind rising mournfully. Not that they couldn't haul Kane back or find the tug in the dark, but Dallas now had less desire than ever to be abroad on this windswept world at night. Something grotesque beyond imagining had risen from the depths of the derelict to imprint itself on Kane's face and their minds. Worse terrors might even now be gathering in the dust-impregnated dusk. He longed desperately for the secure metal walls of the *Nostromo*.

As the sun fell behind rising clouds the ring of floodlights lining the underside of the tug winked on. They did not make the landscape around the ship cheerful, merely served to brighten the dismal contours of the igneous rock on which it rested. Occasional clots of thicker dust would swirl in front of them, temporarily obliterating even that feeble attempt to keep back the cloying darkness.

On the bridge, Ripley waited resignedly for some word from the silent exploration party. The first feelings of helplessness and ignorance had faded by now. They had been replaced by a vague numbness in body and soul. She could not bring herself to look out a port. She could only sit quietly, take an occasional sip of tepid coffee, and stare blankly at her slowly changing readouts.

Jones the cat was sitting in front of a port. He found the storm exhilarating and had evolved a frenetic game of swatting at the larger particles of dust whenever one struck the port's exterior. Jones knew he could never actually catch one of the flying motes. He understood the underlying physical laws behind the fact of a solid transparency. That lessened the delight of the game but did not obviate it. Besides, he could pretend that the dark fragments of stone were birds, though he'd never seen a bird. But he instinctively understood that concept, too.

Other monitors besides Ripley's were being watched, other gauges regularly evaluated. Being the only non-coffee drinker on the *Nostromo*, Ash did his work without liquid stimulation. His interest was perked only by new information.

Two gauges that had been motionless for some time suddenly came to life, the fresh numbers affecting the science officer's system as powerfully as any narcotic. He cut in amplifiers and thoroughly checked them out before opening the intercom to the bridge and announcing their reception.

'Ripley? You there, Ripley?'

'Yo.' She noted the intensity in his tone, sat up in her seat. 'Good news?'

'I think so. Just picked up their suit signals again. And their suit images are back on the screens.'

She took a deep breath, asked the frightening but necessary question: 'How many?'

'All of them. Three blips, steady signals.'

'Where are they?'

'Close ... very close. Someone must've thought to switch back on so we could pick them up. They're heading this way at a steady pace. Slow, but they keep moving. It looks good.'

Don't count on it, she thought to herself as she activated her station transmitter. 'Dallas ... Dallas, can you hear me?' A hurricane of static replied, and she fine-tuned. 'Dallas, this is Ripley. Acknowledge.'

'Easy, Ripley. We hear you. We're almost back.'

'What happened? We lost you on the screen, lost suit signals as well when you went inside the derelict. I've seen Ash's tapes. Have you ...?'

'Kane's hurt.' Dallas sounded exhausted and angry. 'We'll need some help getting him in. He's unconscious. Someone will have to give us a hand getting him out of the lock.'

A quick response sounded over the speakers. 'I'll go.' That was Ash.

Back in engineering, Parker and Brett were listening intently to the conversation.

'Unconscious,' repeated Parker. 'Always knew Kane would get himself in trouble some day.'

'Right.' Brett sounded worried.

'Not a bad guy, though, for a ship's officer. Like him better than Dallas. Not so fast with an order. I wonder what the hell happened to them out there?'

'Don't know. We'll find out soon enough.'

'Maybe,' Parker went on, 'he just fell down and knocked himself out.'

The explanation was as unconvincing to Parker as it was to Brett. Both men went quiet, their attention on the busy, crackling speaker.

'There she is.' Dallas had enough strength left to gesture with his head. Several dim, treelike shapes loomed up out of the almost night. They supported a larger amorphous shape: the hull of the *Nostromo*.

They had almost reached the ship when Ash reached the inner lock door. He stopped there, made sure the hatch was ready to be opened, and touched the stud of the nearest 'com.

'Ripley . . . I'm by the inner hatch.' He left the channel open, moved to stand next to a small port nearby. 'No sign of them yet. It's nearly full night outside, but when they reach the lift I ought to be able to make out their suit lights.'

'Okay.' She was thinking furiously, and some of her current thoughts would have surprised the waiting science officer. They were surprising to herself.

'Which way?' Dallas squinted into the dust, trying to make out shipmarks by the light from the floods.

Lambert gestured to their left. 'Over that way, I think. By that first strut. Lift should be just beyond.' They continued on in that direction until they almost tripped over the rim of the lift, firmly emplaced on hard ground. Despite their fatigue, they wrestled Kane's motionless form off the travois and onto the elevator, keeping the exec supported between them.

'Think you can keep him up? Be easier if we don't have to lift him again.'

She took a breath. 'Yeah, I think so. So long as someone will help us once we get outside the lock.'

'Ripley, are you there?'

'Right here, Dallas.'

'We're coming up.' He glanced over at Lambert. 'Ready?' She nodded.

He pressed a stud. There was a jerk, then the lift rose smoothly upward, stopped even with the lock egress. Dallas leaned slightly, hit a switch. The outer hatch slid aside and they entered the lock.

'Pressurize?' Lambert asked him.

'Never mind. We can spare a lockful of air. We'll be inside in a minute and then we can get out of these damn suits.' They closed the outer hatch, waited for the inner door to open.

'What happened to Kane?' Ripley again. Dallas was too tired to take notice of something in her voice besides the usual concern. He shifted Kane a little higher on his shoulder, not worrying so much about the creature now. It hadn't moved a centimetre on the trek back to the ship and he didn't expect it would suddenly move itself now.

'Some kind of organism,' he told her, the faint echo of his own voice reassuring in the confines of the helmet. 'We don't know how it happened or where it came from. It's attached itself to him. Never saw anything like it. It's not moving now, hasn't altered its position at all on the way back. We've got to get him into the infirmary.'

'I need a clear definition,' she told them quietly.

'Clear definition, hell!' Dallas tried to sound as rational as possible, keep the frustrated fury he was feeling out of his words. 'Look, Ripley, we didn't see what happened. He was down a shaft of some kind, below us. We didn't know anything was wrong until we hauled him out. Is that a clear enough definition?' There was silence from the other end of the channel.

'Look, just open the hatch.'

'Wait a minute.' She chose her words carefully. 'If we let it in, the entire ship could be infected.'

'Damn it, this isn't a germ! It's bigger than my hand, and plenty solid-looking.'

'You know quarantine procedure.' Her voice exhibited a determination she didn't feel. 'Twenty-four hours for decontamination. You've both got more than enough suit air remaining to handle that, and we can feed you extra tanks as necessary. Twenty-four hours won't prove conclusively that the thing's no longer dangerous either, but that's not my responsibility. I just have to enforce the rules. You know them as well as I do.'

'I know of exceptions, too. And I'm the one holding up what's left of a good friend, not you. In twenty-four hours he could be dead, if he isn't already. Open the hatch.'

'Listen to me,' she implored him. 'If I break quarantine we may all die.'

'Open the goddamn hatch!' Lambert screamed. 'To hell with Company rules. We have to get him into the infirmary where the autodoc can work on him.'

'I *can't.* If you were in my position, with the same responsibility, you'd do the same.'

'Ripley,' Dallas said slowly, 'do you hear me?'

'I hear you loud and clear.' Her voice was full of tension. 'The answer is still negative. Twenty-four hours decon, then you can bring him in.'

Within the ship, someone else came to a decision. Ash hit the emergency override stud outside the lock. A red light came on, accompanied by a loud, distinctive whine.

Dallas and Lambert stared as the inner door began to move steadily aside.

Ripley's console flashed, lit up with unbelievable words. INNER HATCH OPEN, OUTER HATCH CLOSED. She stared dumbly at the legend, not believing. Her instruments confirmed the incredible pronouncement.

Their heavy burden sagging between them, Dallas and Lambert staggered out of the lock into the corridor as soon as the inner hatch had swung aside enough to give them clearance. At the same time, Parker and Brett arrived.

Ash moved to help with the body, was waved back by Dallas. 'Stay clear.' They set Kane's body down, removed their helmets.

Keeping a respectful distance away, Ash walked around the crumpled form of the exec, until he caught sight of the thing on his head.

'God,' he murmured.

'Is it alive?' Parker studied the alien, admired the symmetry of it. That did not make it appear less loathsome in his eyes.

'I don't know, but don't touch it.' Lambert spoke as she slipped off her boots.

'Don't worry about that.' Parker leaned forward, trying to make out details of the creature where it was contacting Kane. 'What's it doing to him?'

'Don't know. Let's take him to the infirmary and find out.'

'Right,' agreed Brett readily. 'You two okay?'

Dallas nodded slowly. 'Yeah. Just tired. It hasn't moved, but keep an eye on it.'

'Will do.' The two engineers took the burden from the floor, slipping carefully beneath Kane's arms, Ash moving to help as best he could . . .

# VI

In the infirmary, they placed Kane gently on the extended medical platform. A complex of instruments and controls, different from any others aboard the ship, decorated the wall behind the unconscious exec's head. The table protruded from the wall, extending out from an opening about a metre square.

Dallas touched controls, activated the autodoc. He walked to a drawer, removed a tiny tube of gleaming metal from inside. After checking to make sure it was fully charged, he returned to stand next to Kane's body. Ash stood nearby, ready to help, while Lambert, Parker and Brett watched from the corridor behind a thick window.

A touch on the side of the tube produced a short, intense beam of light from its far end. Dallas adjusted the beam until it was as narrow and short as he could make it without reducing power. Carefully, he touched the end of the beam to the base of Kane's helmet. Metal began to separate.

He drew the cutter slowly across the side of the helmet, over the top and down the other side. He reached the base of the helmet on the other side, drew the beam through the thick seal. The helmet separated neatly. He and Ash each took a side as Dallas shut off the beam, removed the helmet.

Except for a slow, steady pulsing, the creature showed no sign of life, and no reaction to the removal of the helmet and its subsequent exposure to their full view.

Dallas hesitated, reached out and touched the creature,

85

hurriedly drew his hand back. It continued to pulse, did not react to the touch of his fingers. He reached down again, let his palm rest on the creature's back. It was dry and cold. The slow heaving made him slightly ill and he almost pulled his hand away again. When the creature still showed no inclination to object, he got the best grip he could on the rubbery tissue and pulled as hard as he could.

Not surprisingly, this had no effect. The thing neither moved nor relinquished its hold.

'Let me try.' Ash stood near a rack of nonmedical tools. He selected a pair of thick pliers, moved to the table. Carefully getting a grip on the creature, he leaned back.

'Still nothing. Try harder,' Dallas suggested hopefully. Ash adjusted the pliers for a thicker hold, pulled and leaned back at the same time.

Dallas raised a hand, noticing a trickle of blood running down Kane's cheek.

'Hold it. You're tearing the skin.'

Ash relaxed. 'Not me. The creature.'

Dallas looked sick. 'This isn't going to work. It's not going to come off without pulling his whole face away at the same time.'

'I agree. Let the machine work on him. Maybe it will have better luck.'

'It'd better.'

Ash touched several switches in sequence. The autodoc hummed and the opening at the far end of the platform lit up. Then the platform slid silently into the wall. A glass plate descended, sealing Kane tightly inside. Lights flashed on within the wall, Kane's body clearly visible behind the glass. On a nearby console, a pair of video monitors flickered to life. Ash moved to study their readouts. He was the closest thing to a human physician on the *Nostromo*, was aware of both the fact and the responsibility and was intensely anxious to learn anything the machine could tell him about Kane's present condition. Not to mention that of the alien.

A new figure appeared in the corridor, approached the

three onlookers. Lambert gave Ripley a long, hard look.

'You were going to leave us out there. You were going to leave Kane out there. Twenty-four hours you were going to make us sit around with that thing on his face and the night just beginning.' Her expression told her feelings far more clearly than did her words.

Parker, perhaps the last member of the crew one would expect to come to the warrant officer's defence, looked belligerently at the navigator.

'Maybe she should have. She was only following the rules.' He gestured towards the flashing interior of the autodoc and its motionless patient.

'Who the hell knows what it is or what it can do? Kane's a little impulsive, sure, but he's no dummy, and he couldn't avoid it. Maybe one of us'll be next.'

'Right,' agreed Brett.

Ripley's attention remained on Lambert. The navigator hadn't moved, stared back at her. 'Maybe I made a mistake. Maybe not. I hope I did. In any case, I was just trying to do my job. Let's leave it at that.'

Lambert hesitated, searching Ripley's face. Then she gave her a curt nod.

Ripley sighed, relaxing slightly. 'What happened out there?'

'We went into the derelict,' Lambert told her, watching the two men working with the autodoc inside. 'There were no signs of life. That transmission must have been going for centuries. We think we found the transmitter.'

'What about the derelict's crew?'

'No sign of them.'

'And Kane . . .?'

'He volunteered to search the lower level alone.' Her expression twisted. 'He was looking for diamonds. Instead, he apparently found some kind of eggs. We told him not to touch them. Probably too late. Something happened down there, where we couldn't see what was going on. When we pulled him out, it was on his face. Somehow it melted right through his helmet faceplate, and you know how strong that stuff is.'

'I wonder where it's from originally?' Ripley spoke without looking away from the infirmary interior. 'As dead as this planetoid seems to be, I'd guess it came in with the alien ship.'

'Christ knows,' said Parker softly. 'I'd like to know where it's from, too.'

'Why?' Ripley hardly glanced at him.

'So I'd know one more place to avoid.'

'Amen,' said Brett.

'What I want to know,' said Dallas questioningly, 'is how the hell is he breathing? Or is he?'

Ash studied readouts. 'Physically, he appears to be doing fine. Not only is he alive, despite having gone without normal air all the way back to the ship, but also all his vital signs are steady. Breathing all that nitrogen and methane should have killed him instantly, back on the derelict. According to the 'doc he's in a coma, but internally he's normal. A damn sight healthier than he has any right to be.

'As to how he's breathing, I can't say yet, but his blood's thoroughly oxygenated.'

'But how?' Dallas leaned over, tried to see up inside the autodoc. 'I checked that thing out pretty closely. His mouth and nose seemed to be completely blocked.'

Ash punched a trio of buttons. 'We know what's going on outside. We'd better have a look inside him.'

A large screen cleared, focused. It displayed a colour X-ray image of Kane's head and upper torso. Finer resolution could show blood flowing steadily through his arteries and veins, lungs pulsing, heart beating. At the moment the onlookers were more interested in the internal schematic of the small rounded shape covering the exec's face.

'I'm no biologist,' Ash said softly, 'but that's the damnedest maze of stuff I've ever seen inside another animal.' He gazed in amazement at the intricate network of forms and tubes. 'I don't have any idea what half of it's supposed to do.'

'Doesn't look any nicer from the inside than the out,' was

Dallas's only comment.

'Look at the musculature in those fingers, that tail,' Ash insisted. 'It may look fragile, but it's anything but. No wonder we couldn't pull it off him. No wonder *he* couldn't pull it off. I'm assuming he had time to try before he blanked out.'

It was clear what the creature was doing to Kane, if not why. The exec's jaws had been forced apart. A long, flexible tube extended from the palm of the hand-creature down his throat. It terminated at the end of his oesophagus. The tube was not moving, merely sitting there.

More than anything else, this part of the internal view made Dallas feel sick.

'It's got something down his goddamn throat.' His hands clenched, unclenched with murderous regularity. 'What the hell kind of thing is that to do to a person? It's not a fair way to fight. Damn it, Ash, it's not . . . *clean*.'

'We don't know that it's fighting with him, or even harming him.' Ash confessed to being confused by the whole situation. 'According to the medical monitors, he's fine. Merely unable to react to us. I know this sounds silly right now, but think a minute. Maybe the creature's a benign symbiote of some kind. Perhaps, in its own particular, confused way, it's done this to try to help him.'

Dallas laughed humourlessly. 'It's fond of him, all right. It won't let go.'

'That tube or whatever must be how it's supplying oxygen to him.' The science officer adjusted a control, switched to a tighter view and finer resolution. The screen showed Kane's lungs working steadily, at a normal pace, and seemingly without effort despite the obstruction in his throat. Ash switched back to the first view.

'What oxygen?' Dallas wanted to know. 'He came all the way back to the ship with a busted faceplate. The creature's not attached to his suit tanks so all his suit air must have bled out through the open regulator in the first couple of minutes.'

Ash looked thoughtful. 'I can imagine some possibilities.

There's a little free oxygen in the atmosphere here. Not much, but some. And a lot more tied up with the nitrogen in various oxides. I suspect the creature possesses the ability to break down those oxides and extract the oxygen. Certainly it has the capability to pass it on to Kane, perhaps also for itself. A good symbiote would be able to determine quickly what requirements its partner would have. Certain plants have the same oxygen-extracting ability; others prefer different gases. It's not an impossibility.' He turned back to the screens.

'Perhaps it's our terrestrial prejudices at work and it's really a plant and not an animal. Or maybe it possesses characteristics and abilities common to both.'

'It doesn't make sense.'

Ash glanced at him. 'What doesn't?'

'It paralyzes him, puts him into a coma, then works like mad to keep him alive.' He glanced up at the screen. 'I thought it would be, well, feeding on him somehow. The posture and position it's in right now is typical of feeding. But as the instruments say, it's doing exactly the opposite. I can't figure it.

'In any case, we can't leave the damn thing on him. It might be doing all kinds of things to him, maybe good, maybe bad. We can be sure of one thing, though. None of them are natural to the human system.'

Ash looked doubtful. 'I don't know if that's really such a good idea.'

'Why not?' Dallas eyed his science officer questioningly.

'At the moment,' Ash explained, not offended by the slight challenge in Dallas's voice, 'the creature is keeping him alive. If we remove it we risk losing Kane.'

'We have to take that chance.'

'What do you propose to do? It won't pull off.'

'We'll have to try cutting it off. The sooner we remove it, the better it's likely to be for Kane.'

Ash appeared ready to argue further, then apparently changed his mind. 'I don't like it, but I see your point. You'll take the responsibility? This is a science decision and you're taking it out of my hands.'

'Yeah, I'll take the responsibility.'

He was already pulling on a pair of disposable surgical gloves. A quick check indicated that the autodoc wasn't attached in any way to the body, wasn't doing anything to it that could result in harm if it was temporarily removed. A touch of a button and Kane slid back out of the machine.

A cursory inspection was enough to show that the creature still hadn't moved or released its grasp on Kane's face.

'The cutter?' Ash indicated the laser device Dallas had used to remove Kane's helmet.

'No. I'm going to proceed as slowly as possible. See if you can find me a manual blade.'

Ash moved to an instrument case, searched through it briefly. He returned with a thinner version of the cutter and handed it carefully to Dallas.

He inspected the tiny device, shifted it in his hand until he had a firm, comfortable grip on the slim pencil. Then he switched it on. A miniature version of the beam the heavy-duty cutter had generated appeared, shining coherently at the far end of the surgical knife.

Dallas moved to stand opposite Kane's head. Working with as much control as he could muster, he moved the light-blade towards the creature. He had to be prepared to pull away fast and carefully if it reacted. A wrong move and he could sever Kane's head from his shoulders as easily as a bad report could cut a man's pension.

The creature didn't move. Dallas touched the beam to grey skin, moved it a millimetre or two downward until he was sure he was actually cutting flesh. The beam travelled effortlessly down the creature's back.

Still the subject of this preliminary biopsy did not move, nor did it show any sign of pain from the continuing cut. At the top of the wound a yellowish fluid began to drip, flow down the smooth side.

'Starting to bleed,' Ash noted professionally.

The liquid flowed onto the bedding next to Kane's head. A small wisp of what Dallas first thought might be steam rose from the pallet. The dark gas was not familiar. The hissing noise that began to issue from the bedding was.

He stopped, removed the blade, and stared at the sizzling spot. The hissing grew louder, deeper. He looked downward.

The liquid had already eaten through the bedding and the metal medical platform. It was pooling and sizzling, a miniature hell, near his feet as it began to eat into the deck. Metal bubbled steadily. Gas produced as a by-product started to fill the infirmary. It seared Dallas's throat, reminding him of police control-gas, which was only mildly painful but impossible to stomach. He panicked at the thought of what this stuff might be doing to his own lungs.

Eyes filling with sharp tears, nose running, he tried frantically to close the wound by squeezing together the two sides of the cut with his hands. In the process, some of the still-flowing liquid leaked on to his gloves. They began to smoke.

As he staggered towards the corridor, he fought to pull them off before the tough material was eaten through and the liquid started on his skin. He threw them on the deck. The still-active droplets fell from the gloves and commenced dissolving additional pits in the metal.

Brett was looking mad and more than a little scared. 'Shit. It's going to eat through the decks and out the hull.' He turned, ran for the nearest companionway. Dallas yanked an emergency lamp from its holding socket and followed the engineering tech, the others crowding close behind.

The B deck corridor below was lined with instruments and conduits. Brett was already searching the ceiling below the infirmary. The liquid still had several intervening levels of alloy to penetrate.

Dallas turned the light on the roof, hunted, then held it steady. 'There.'

Above them, smoke began to appear. A smudge of yellow

fluid appeared, metal sizzling around it. It oozed downward, formed a drop, and fell. It immediately began to bubble on the deck. Dallas and Brett watched helplessly as the tiny pool increased in size and ate its way through the bulkhead.

'What's below us?'

'C corridor,' announced Parker. 'Not instrumentation.' He and Ripley rushed for the next down companionway while the others remained staring at the widening hole in the deck.

'What can we put under it?' Ash was considering the problem with his usual detachment, though fully aware that in a few minutes the *Nostromo* might be hulled. That would mean sealing all compartments until the destruction could be repaired. And it could be worse. A large amount of critical hyperdrive circuitry ran through the main hull. If the liquid ruined it, it was quite possible the resulting damage might be beyond the meagre capability of the ship's engineering staff to repair. Much of that circuitry was integral to the ship's construction and not designed to be worked on outside of a major zero-gee shipyard.

No one offered any suggestions as to what they might employ to catch the steady leak.

Below, Parker and Ripley moved cautiously along the narrower, darker confines of C corridor. Their attention remained fixed to the ceiling.

'Don't get under it,' Parker warned. 'If it can eat through deck alloy like that, I don't care to think what it could do to your pretty face.'

'Don't worry. I'll take good care of my pretty face. You watch out for your own.'

'Seems to be losing some activity.' Dallas peered at the hole in the floor, hardly daring to hope.

Brett and Ash stood opposite, crouching over the dark depression in the deck. Ash fished a stylus from one of his tunic pockets, probed the hole. The outer metal lining of the writing instrument bubbled weakly, looking like carbonated quicksilver. The bubbling stopped, petering out after barely marring the shiny finish. The science officer continued to poke at the hole. Instead of slipping through, the stylus met resistance.

'It's not passing more than three centimetres in. The liquid's stopped penetrating.'

Below, Parker glanced over at Ripley in the dim light. 'See anything?'

They continued to scan the ceiling. Beneath their feet lay a small service crawlway, and beyond that, the *Nostromo*'s primary hull. After that, there was only the atmosphere of an unknown planet.

'Nothing,' she finally replied. 'Keep an eye out. I'll go see what's happening above.' She turned, sprinted down the corridor towards the stairs.

Her first sight was of the others all crouching over the hole in the deck. 'What's going on? It hasn't come through yet.'

'I think it's lost steam.' Ash knelt over the pitted metal. 'Either the continuous reactions with the alloys have diluted its strength, or else it simply loses its caustic potential after a certain period of time. In any case, it no longer seems to be active.'

Ripley moved to check the still-smoking hole in the deck for herself. 'Could the alloy be stronger inside this deck than above? Maybe the stuff's corroding the deck horizontally now, looking for another weak place where it can eat downward.'

Ash shook his head. 'I don't think so. From what little I remember about ship construction, the principal decks and hull of the *Nostromo* are all composed of the same material. No, I think it's reasonable to assume the fluid is no longer dangerous.'

He started to put his stylus back in his pocket, still holding it by the unmarred end. At the last moment, he thought better of the idea, continued to let it dangle loosely from one hand.

Ripley noticed the hesitation, smirked at him. 'If it's no longer dangerous, why not put it back in your shirt?'

'There's no need to act recklessly. Plenty of time after I've run tests and made certain the substance is truly no longer active. Just because it can't eat through deck alloy any more doesn't mean it couldn't give you a helluva burn.'

'What do you think the stuff is?' Dallas's gaze travelled from the tiny crater in the deck to the hole in the ceiling overhead. 'I've never seen anything that could cut through hull alloy like that. Not with that kind of speed.'

'I've never seen anything like it myself,' the science officer confessed. 'Certainly highly refined varieties of molecular acid are tremendously powerful, but they generally will act only on certain specific materials. They have restricted general applications.

'On the other hand, this stuff appears to be a universal corrosive. We've already watched it demonstrate its ability to eat through several very different substances with equal facility. Or indifference, if you prefer. Hull alloy, surgical gloves, the medical pallet, infirmary bedding; it went through all of them with equal ease.'

'And that damned thing uses it for blood. One tough son-of-a-bitch little monster.' Brett spoke of the hand-shaped alien with respect, despite his feeling towards it.

'We don't know for a fact that it uses it for blood.' Ash's mind was functioning overtime under the pressure of the situation. 'It might be a component of a separate circulatory system, designed to lubricate the creature's insides. Or it might comprise part of a protective inner layer, a sort of liquid, defensive endothelium. It might be no more than the creature's counterpart of our own lymph fluid.'

'Wonderful defensive mechanism, though,' Dallas observed. 'You don't dare kill it.'

'Not on board a sealed ship, anyway.' Ripley made the interesting point quietly.

'That's so,' Ash conceded. 'We could take Kane outside, where the creature's fluids couldn't damage the *Nostromo*, and try cutting it off, except that we're fairly certain it's the only thing keeping him alive.'

'Once we cut it off him and got that tube out of his throat, we could feed him oxygen.' Ripley pressed the thought. 'A thermal wrap would keep him warm. For that matter, we could set up an air tent with a ground seal. Let the liquid drip onto the ground below it.'

'Not a bad idea,' admitted Ash, 'save for two things.' Ripley waited impatiently. 'First, as we've already discussed, removing the creature forcibly might result in a fatal interruption of life-sustaining action. The shock alone could kill Kane.

'Second, we have no guarantee that, upon being sufficiently injured, the creature might not react by spraying that liquid all over itself and everything else in sight. That would be a defensive reaction fully in keeping with the fluid's destructive and protective qualities.' He paused long enough to let the image dominate everyone's mind.

'Even if whoever was doing the actual cutting could somehow escape serious injury from the flying liquid, I would not care to be the one responsible for what would be left of Kane's face. Or head.'

'All right.' Ripley sounded a bit resentful. 'So maybe it wasn't such a brilliant idea. What do you suggest instead?' She jerked a thumb towards the infirmary above. 'Trying to haul him all the way home with that thing sitting on his skull?'

'I see no danger in that.' Ash was unimpressed by her sarcasm. 'As long as his vital signs remain stable, I consider that a viable alternative. If they show signs of failing, naturally we'll have to try something else. But at this time I have to say that I think removing the creature forcibly presents greater potential for injury to Kane than it does improvement.'

A new face appeared at the top of the nearby companionway. 'Still no sign of the stuff. It's stopped bleeding?' Parker switched his gaze from the sullen Ripley to Dallas.

'Yeah. After it ate through two levels.' He was still a bit stunned by the potency of the alien fluid.

Ripley came to life, looked around. 'We're all down here. What about Kane? No one's watching him . . . or the alien.'

There was a concerted rush for the stairs.

Dallas was the first one back at the infirmary. A quick glance inside showed him that nothing had changed. Kane still lay as they'd left him, immobile on the platform, the alien secured to his face.

Dallas was angry at himself. He'd acted like a damn kid. The liquid had demonstrated unexpected and dangerous properties, sure, but hardly enough to justify the total panic that had ensued. He should first have delegated one or two members of the crew to remain behind and keep an eye on the creature.

Fortunately, nothing had changed during their absence. The thing hadn't moved, nor, from the looks of it, had Kane. From now on, regardless of any problem that might arise elsewhere, there would be someone assigned to the infirmary at all times. The situation was serious enough without offering the alien the opportunity to do things unobserved.

'Any of the acid get on him?' Parker was at the portal, straining to see Kane.

Dallas walked over and stood next to the platform. He inspected the exec's head carefully. 'I don't think so. He looks okay. The fluid ran down the outside of the creature without contacting his skin.'

Brett crowded into the doorway. 'Is it still dripping that crap? We've got some ceramics down in engineering supply that'll hold just about anything. I don't know about this stuff, but we can give it a try if we have to. I can jury-rig a container out of scraps.'

'Don't bother,' Dallas told him. 'It's stopped bleeding.'

Ash was examining the section cut by the laser knife. 'Healed over. No sign of the wound. Remarkable regenerative abilities. You'd never know it had been touched.'

'There must be some way we can get it off.' Lambert shivered. 'It makes me sick to see it resting there like that, that tube or whatever it is down his throat.'

'You'd be a lot sicker if it was on you,' Ripley taunted her.

Lambert kept her distance. 'You're not being funny.'

'I'll say again, sir, I don't think it would be a good idea to try removing the creature.' Ash wasn't looking at him. 'It didn't work out too well the last time.'

Dallas glanced sharply at his science officer, then relaxed. As usual, Ash was only being objective. It wasn't in his nature to be sarcastic.

'So what do we do?' Lambert wanted to know.

'We do nothing,' Dallas finally said. 'We can't do anything. We tried and, as Ash noted, it nearly cost us a hulled ship. So . . . we feed him back to the autodoc and hope it can come up with a better idea.'

He touched a control. There was a soft hum as Kane's platform slid back into the machine. Dallas threw additional switches, was again provided with internal views of the comatose exec, plus related schematics and diagrams. They offered no new information, and no solutions.

Ash was correlating several readouts. 'His bodily functions continue normal, but there's some fresh indication of tissue degeneracy and breakdown.'

'Then it *is* hurting him,' Lambert said.

'Not necessarily. He's gone without food and water for some time. These readings might reflect a natural reduction in weight. There's no indication he's being drastically weakened, either by the creature or circumstances.

'Nevertheless, we want to keep him in the best condition possible. I'd better get some intravenous feeding started, until I can determine for sure whether the alien's absorbing protein from his system.' He activated a block of controls. New sounds echoed through the infirmary as the autodoc began to efficiently assume the job of feeding the helpless Kane and processing the resultant waste products.

'What's that thing?' Ripley was pointing at a portion of the slowly shifting internal scan. 'The stain on his lungs?'

'I don't see any "stain".'

Dallas studied the view. 'I think I see what she means. Increase magnification on the respiratory system, Ash.'

The science officer complied. Now the small blot that had caught Ripley's attention stood out clearly, a dark irregular patch overlying Kane's chest cavity. It was completely opaque.

'We don't know that it's on his lungs.' Ash fiddled with controls. 'It could just as readily be a scanner malfunction, or a radiation-damaged section of the scanner lens. Happens all the time.'

'Try more power,' Dallas demanded. 'Let's see if we can't improve the resolution.'

Ash adjusted instrumentation, but despite his best efforts the dark blot remained just that: an unresolved splotch of blackness.

'I can't raise the intensity any further or he'll begin to suffer radiation damage.'

'I know.' Dallas stared at the enigmatic blot. 'If we lose scanning capability now we won't know what the hell's happening inside him.'

'I'll handle it, sir,' the science officer assured him. 'I think I can clean up the lens. It's just a question of some slight repolishing.'

'But that'll leave us blind.'

Ash looked apologetic. 'I can't remove the blot without dismantling the scanner.'

'Skip it, then. As long as it doesn't grow to the point where it obscures our vision.'

'As you wish, sir.' Ash turned back to his readouts.

Brett looked confused, sounded frustrated. 'What happens now, huh? We just sit and wait?'

'No,' Dallas responded, remembering that he had a ship to run in addition to caring for Kane. '*We* sit and wait. You two go back to work . . .

# VII

'What do you think?'

Parker was leaning as close as he could, sweating along with Brett as the latter attempted to seal the delicate last connections within the cramped confines of twelve module. They were trying to perform work that normally employed the services of a remote automatic tracer and the facilities of a computerized tool runner. Since they possessed neither runner nor tracer they were forced to cope with the trouble utilizing instruments not designed for the purpose.

Wrong tools for the wrong job, Parker thought angrily. Somehow, they would have to manage. Unless twelve module was properly repaired and made operative once more they'd have one hell of a time trying to lift off. To get away from this world, Parker would have made the necessary internal replacements with his teeth.

Right now, though, it was Brett's turn to fight with the recalcitrant components. Like every other instrument aboard the *Nostromo*, the module used snap-in, factory-sealed replacement parts. The trick was to remove the ruined garbage without interrupting other critical functions or damaging still more delicate portions of the ship's drive. The new parts would fit in easily, if they could only get rid of the carbonized junk.

'I think I've got it,' his companion finally said. 'Give it a try.'

Parker stepped back, touched two buttons set into the overhead console, then glanced hopefully at a neighbouring

100

portable monitor. He tried the buttons a second time, without success. The monitor remained blissfully silent.

'Nothing.'

'Damn. I was sure that was it.'

'Well, it isn't. Try the next one. I know they all look okay, except for that number forty-three, and we've already replaced that. That's the trouble with these damn particle cells. If the regulator overloads and burns some of them out, you have to go inside and find the ones that have vacuum-failed.' He paused, added, 'Wish we had a tracer.'

'You and me both.' Soft sounds of metal scratching on plastic sounded from inside the unit.

'It's got to be the next one.' Parker tried to sound optimistic. 'We don't have to hand-check every single cell. Mother narrowed it down this far. Be thankful for small favours.'

'I'll be thankful,' Brett responded. 'I'll be thankful when we're off this rock and back in hypersleep.'

'Stop thinking about Kane.' He touched the two buttons, cursed silently. 'Another blank. Try the next one, Brett.'

'Right.' He moved to do so, replaced the cell he'd just checked in its proper place. Parker adjusted several overhead toggles. Maybe they could narrow down the injured line a little farther. Twelve module contained one hundred of the tiny particle acceleration cell chambers. The thought of manually checking every one of them to find a single one that had failed made him more than ready to break things.

At precisely the wrong moment, a voice called from a nearby 'com speaker. 'What's happening?'

Oh, hell, Parker thought. Ripley. That damn woman. I'll tell her what's happening. 'My Johnson is happening,' he informed her curtly, adding several things pitched just below the effective range of the omni pickup.

'Keep working,' he told his companion.

'Right.'

'What's that?' she said. 'I didn't catch that.'

He moved away from the module. A stab activated the 'com

amp. 'You want to know what's happening? A lot of hard work is what's happening. Real work. You ought to come back here and give it a try sometime.'

Her reply was instant, composed. 'I've got the toughest job on this ship.' Parker laughed derisively. 'I have to listen to your bullshit.'

'Get off my back.'

'I'll get off your back when module twelve is fixed, not before. You can count on that.' There was a click at the other end before Parker could offer his ready comment.

'What's up?' Brett leaned out of the module. 'You two fighting again?'

'Naw. Smart-mouthed broad, that's all.'

Brett hesitated, paused to examine the currently opened cell. 'Right. Let's try it again.'

Parker pushed the buttons, examined the monitor, thought of putting his fist through it while imagining it to be a certain warrant officer's face. He wouldn't do anything nearly so melodramatic, of course. Though short-tempered, he was sensible enough to realise how badly he needed the monitor.

And Ripley.

Ash was running a new battery of tests on Kane's comatose form. They provided additional information about his condition. None of it was particularly useful, but the science officer found it all fascinating.

Kane's insides were immediately visible to anyone who cared to enter the infirmary and have a look at the main medical viewscreen. Kane himself was in no position to object to this particularly intimate invasion of privacy.

Ripley walked in, took note of the readouts. His condition hadn't changed since she'd last seen him. She hadn't expected it to. The alien remained affixed to his face.

She studied the smaller readouts, then took the empty seat next to Ash. He acknowledged her arrival with a slight smile and did not turn from his console.

'Making some different tests on him,' he informed her. 'Just in case anything happens.'

'Like what?'

'I haven't the vaguest idea. But if anything does, I'll want to know about it as soon as it starts.'

'Anything new?'

'With Kane?' Ash considered, marshalling his thoughts. 'Still the same. He's holding steady. No, better than that. He's holding strong. No changes for the worse.'

'What about the creature? We know now it can leak acid and heal itself fast. Anything else we know?'

Ash sounded pleased with himself when he replied. 'Like I told you, I've been running tests. Since we can't do anything for Kane, I thought it sensible to try to learn as much as we can about the creature. You never know what seemingly insignificant discovery might lead to its eventual removal.'

'I know that.' She shifted impatiently in her chair. 'What have you found out?'

'It's got an outer layer of what appears to be protein polysaccharides. At least, that's my best guess. Hard to tell without a piece for detailed analysis, and attempting to remove even a sample might cause it to drain fluid again. We can't risk it dissolving part of the autodoc.'

'Not hardly,' she said drily. 'Right now that machine's the only chance Kane's got.'

'Exactly. What's more interesting than that is that it's constantly sloughing off cells within a secondary, internal dermis and replacing them with polarized organic silicates. It appears to have a double skin, with that acid flowing between the two layers. Also, the acid seems to be flowing under high pressure.

'It's a good thing Dallas didn't cut too deeply with the knife or I think it would have sprayed the entire infirmary.'

Ripley looked properly impressed.

'The silicate layer demonstrates a unique, very dense molecular structure under the scope. It might even be capable of resisting the laser. I know, I know,' he said in response to her look of disbelief, 'that sounds crazy. But this is the toughest chunk of organic material I've ever seen. The combination of the way those cells are aligned with what they're composed of adds up to something that defies all the rules of standard biology.

'Those silicated cells, for example. They're metal-bonded. The result is what gives the creature such resistance to adverse environmental conditions.'

'Anything new besides the silicates and the double dermis?'

'Well, I still have no idea what it breathes, or even if it breathes the way we think of standard respiration. It does seem to be altering the atmosphere around it, perhaps absorbing whatever gases it requires through numerous surface pores. There's certainly nothing resembling a nostril. As a living chemical factory it surpasses in efficiency anything I've ever heard of. Some of its internal organs don't seem to function at all, while other are doing things I can't begin to guess at.

'It's possible the visually quiescent organs have defensive functions. We'll find out if we ever have to provoke it further.' He cocked an expectant eye at her. 'That enough for you?'

'Plenty.' Kane shouldn't have been brought back on board, she mused. They should have left him and the creature outside. Ash was the one responsible for them being here.

She studied the science officer unobtrusively, watching him work his instruments, store pleasing results and discard those he had no use for. Ash was the last member of the crew she'd have suspected of being capable of a dramatic gesture, yet he was the one who'd made the sudden decision to let the explorers back aboard, going against all accepted procedure.

She had to correct herself. In addition to Ash, Dallas and Lambert had also gone against procedure in demanding admittance. And Kane's life had been at stake. Suppose Ash had obeyed her directive and left the three outside? Would Kane still be alive? Or would he now be just a statistic in the log? That would have simplified one thing, though: She wouldn't have to face Kane when he recovered and have to explain why she'd tried to refuse him and the others admittance.

Ash noticed her expression, looked concerned. 'Something the matter?'

'No.' She sat up straighter. 'Sum it all up for me. Pretend I'm as dumb as I sometimes feel. What's it all mean? Where do we stand with it?'

'Interesting combination of elements and structure make it practically invulnerable given our present situation and resources.'

She nodded. 'That's exactly how I read it, if your results are accurate.' He looked pained. 'Sorry. Okay, so it's invulnerable.' She was watching him closely. 'Is that why you went ahead and let it in?'

As always, the science officer refused to be baited. He showed nothing in the way of resentment when he replied. 'I was following a direct order from the captain. Remember?'

She forced herself to keep from raising her voice, knowing that Ash respected only reason. 'When Dallas and Kane are off the ship, I'm senior officer. I'm acting commander until one or the other actually sets foot back inside.'

'Yes, of course. I forgot, that's all. The emotions of the moment.'

'Like hell.' His attention remained fixed to various readouts. 'Emotions never made you forget anything.'

That made him turn to her. 'You think you know all about me. All of you. You're so sure you know exactly what kind of person I am. Let me tell you something, Ripley. When I opened the inner hatch I was aware of what I was doing, yes. But that business about who is in charge when, well, I'm capable of forgetfulness just like anyone else. My memory's very good, but it's subject to failure like anyone's. Even a mechanical memory like Mother's can lose track of information.'

Failure, sure, she thought. Selective failure. Still, the science officer could be telling the truth. She'd better watch out how many of her shipmates she insulted. Parker and Brett already felt something less than love for her, and now she was on the verge of making an enemy of Ash.

But she couldn't still the suspicions. She almost wished Ash would get mad at her.

'You also managed to forget the science division's own basic quarantine law, something that's drilled into every ship's officer early in flight school.'

'No.' At last, she thought. A statement she could believe. 'That I didn't forget.'

'I see. You didn't forget.' She paused for emphasis. 'You just went ahead and broke it.'

'You think I did it lightly. That I didn't consider the possible consequences of my action.'

'No, Ash. I'd never think that.' Again, he didn't react to provocation.

'I didn't like having to do it, but I saw myself as having no choice,' he explained softly. 'What would you have done with Kane? His only chance to stay alive seemed to rest with getting him into the infirmary, where the autodoc could work on him as soon as possible. His condition has been stabilized. I'm inclined to give credit for that to the machine and its rapid treatment, the early application of antisepsis and intravenous feeding.'

'You're contradicting yourself, Ash. A minute ago you said it was the creature who was keeping him alive, not the autodoc.'

'The creature does seem to be making a contribution, but it's doing so in Kane's atmosphere and environment. We've no way of knowing what it might have done if left alone with him outside. Here we can keep a close watch on his system and be ready to compensate if the creature shows signs of acting inimically towards him. We couldn't do that if he were still outside.' He paused long enough to throw a switch, check a reading. 'Besides, it was a direct order.'

'Meaning you'll listen to Dallas over me no matter what the situation?'

'Meaning the captain's the captain, and the fact that he was one metre outside the corridor instead of inside isn't reason enough for me to start ignoring his decisions.'

She looked away, furious with him and with herself. 'By breaking quarantine procedure you risk everybody's life, not just Kane's.'

Ash moved smoothly to punch out a request on the computer board, stared solemnly at the information provided. He spoke without facing the insistent Ripley.

'You think it was an easy decision for me to make? I'm aware of the rules regarding quarantine and alien life forms, probably more so than you. I had to balance them against a man's life.

'Maybe I should have let him die out there. Maybe I have jeopardized the rest of us. But I know one thing: Rule makers always draw up their precious rules and regulations in safety and comfort, not out in the field, where those same absolutes are supposed to be applied. At those times we have to rely on our own minds and feelings. That's what I did.

'So far the creature hasn't made a threatening gesture towards any of the rest of us. It may do so later on, in which case it will be facing an alarmed and ready group of six instead of an unprepared single man stumbling through the dark hold of an unfamiliar vessel. I'll balance that risk against Kane's life.' His fingers danced over the console.

'I don't dispute your personal feelings.' Ripley shifted her weight to her left, rose. 'I'm simply saying you have no right or authority to impose them on the rest of us. Maybe we don't feel like taking the same risk.'

'It doesn't matter now. Kane's aboard . . . and alive. Events will proceed from that reality, not from past alternatives. It's a waste of time discussing them.'

'This is your official position, then, as a science officer? Not exactly right out of the manual.'

'You are being repetitive, Ripley. Why? To provoke me? I have already voluntarily entered my actions in the official log, and will subject myself to whatever decision the Company may make in the matter. Yes, it's my official position. Remember that the prime consideration of science is the protection and betterment of human life. I would never contravene that.'

'No, but your idea of what betters human life might differ from someone else's.'

For some reason that caused him to turn and stare sharply at her, when her other, more direct probes had produced no response. 'I take my responsibility as science officer as seriously as you do that of warrant officer. That should be sufficient for you. I'm tired of this. If you have a specific accusation to make, lodge it with Dallas. If not,' and he turned back to his precious instrumentation, 'you do your job and I'll do mine.'

She nodded once. 'Fair enough.' Turning, she headed for the corridor . . . still unsatisfied but unsure why. Ash's answers had the veneer of validity, were hard to argue with. That wasn't what was troubling her.

It was the fact that his action in popping the lock to let the exploration team inside went against much more than the rules. It went against every facet of the science officer's personality, directly contradicted his demonstrated profession-alism in other matters. She hadn't known him that long, but until this incident he'd given her and everyone else aboard the impression that for him nothing ranked above the official science manual.

Ash claimed he'd done what he'd done only to save a man's life. She'd taken the official side. Was she wrong? Would Kane have agreed with her?

She headed for the bridge, much troubled in mind. Little bits of coincidence swam in her head, nagging at her thoughts. The mind glue to bring them together remained missing . . .

There was nothing to do on the *Nostromo* now but wait. Wait for Parker and Brett to complete their work, wait for a change in Kane's condition.

On the bridge, Lambert was amusing Jones the cat with some string. The string supposedly was on board solely for Jones's enjoyment, but the cat knew better. It was occasionally incumbent on him to entertain the humans. They seemed to derive considerable pleasure from his poking and swatting at the white cord as they manipulated it in their clumsy great paws.

Lambert called the game cat's cradle. Jones called it people's cradle. He was a very conscientious cat and did his best to keep the navigator smiling. They were so solemn sometimes. It was a difficult job for a cat. But Jones was conscientious. He continued to work at pleasing the human, thinking of food and warm, fat mice.

'What do you think?' Brett glanced out from beneath the overhang, eyed his colleague.

Parker adjusted a control, wiped sweat from his forehead. 'Almost. Another half a degree and we'll be finished. Maybe that'll satisfy Ripley.'

The engineering tech made a rude noise. 'Didn't you know? Ripley can't be satisfied.' Pinging sounds came from behind the intake screen he was working on.

Parker glanced at the silent intercom speaker and grunted a reply. 'If we don't get full shares after this, I'll lodge a complaint. We've earned double pay. Probably qualified for hazard as well. This time the Company had better make it worth our while or we'll go to the Guild. No messing around anymore.'

'Right,' snapped Brett. A hand extended outward from inside the tube where the screen was secured. 'Number three sealer ought to do it.'

Parker fished around in a neatly labelled but filthy plastic case, handed up a tiny grey square stencilled over in green and red, and glared at the inoffensive intercom . . .

The rhythm was primitive, unsophisticated and the recording had lost brilliance with age and much use, but Dallas lay back and absorbed the music as though he were present at the ancient recording session. One foot tapped silently, in unthinking podal counterpoint to the melody.

The communicator beeped for attention. It did so three times before catching the captain's notice. Letting out a resigned sigh, he reached out and shut off the music, then flipped the acknowledge switch for the 'com.

'Dallas here.'

'Ash. I think you should have a look at Kane. Something's happened.

Dallas swung his legs off the lounge, sat up quickly. Ash didn't sound worried, which was encouraging. He did sound confused, which was not.

'Serious?'

'Interesting.'

'I'll be right there.'

He stood and threw the final cutoff on the tape machine, reluctantly saw the green light on its flank wink out. Ash had said 'interesting'. That could mean a host of things, not necessarily good, had occurred. He found some relief in the knowledge that Ash would have said something very different if Kane had already expired.

Which meant that the exec was still alive ... but in an 'interesting' condition.

As it turned out, Ash wasn't even referring to Kane. His call had been prompted by the condition of something else.

Dallas found the science officer in the corridor outside the infirmary, his nose pressed to the glass. He was staring in, looking around as the captain approached.

'What's going on?' Ripley had suddenly appeared at the other end of the corridor. Her gaze switched rapidly from Ash to Dallas, back again. 'I heard over an open monitor.'

'Listening in?' Dallas eyed her curiously.

She made a face. 'Nothing else to do on this boat. Why? You object?'

'No. Just curious.' He looked through the thick glass into the infirmary, spoke to Ash when no great revelation manifested itself.

'Well?'

'Kane.' The science officer pointed. 'Look closely at him. All of him.'

Dallas stared, squinted, then noticed what Ash was talking about. Or rather, he didn't notice it.

'It's gone.' A fast inspection of the infirmary showed no sign of the alien. Kane remained motionless on the medical platform. His chest rose and fell steadily. He seemed to be breathing normally and without effort despite the absence of the alien. Lingering inspection showed what looked to be tiny black dots scattered around the rim of his face.

'Has it planted something on him?' Dallas tried to shy away from the repulsive thought.

'No.' Ash spoke positively, and Dallas was willing to believe him. He had to believe him. Anyway, the personnel dossiers said that the science officer's vision was the sharpest on board.

'They're indentations, not rises. I'd guess they're sucker marks.' Ash paused, added, 'Those aside, Kane appears undamaged by the experience.'

'Which may not be over yet,' Ripley put in. 'The door is seal-tight. It must still be in there.' She sounded confident, but it was a cover for her real feelings. The thought of the spidery hand-shape with its glazed, unblinking eye scrabbling about underfoot frightened her more than she dared show.

'We can't open the door,' Ash said thoughtfully. 'We don't want to let it out. The last thing we want to do is give it the run of the ship.'

'I couldn't agree more.' Ripley was scanning the infirmary floor, saw only bright metal and paint. 'We can't grab it or kill it from a distance. So where does that leave us?'

'When we tried to remove it from Kane's face,' Dallas said, 'we cut it, injured it. Maybe if we didn't threaten it too overtly, it wouldn't offer resistance. Maybe we can just pick it up.' Visions of spectacular Company commendations, perhaps a promotion, certainly a bonus, swirled through his head. Then he again noticed the unconscious form of Kane and felt guilty.

Ripley was still shuddering at the thought. 'You can try

picking it up. I'll watch the door.'

'I think it's a worthwhile idea.' Ash was moving away from the glass. 'It's an invaluable specimen. We should certainly make an attempt to capture it alive and intact.'

He touched the switch controlling the door. The infirmary was a good place to try to hunt down the intruder. It was double-walled, and save for the airlocks, it was the tightest compartment on the *Nostromo*.

The door slid back slightly. Ash looked to Dallas, who nodded. Again the control was touched and the door moved another few centimetres. Now it was open enough for a man to slip through. Dallas went in first, followed cautiously by Ripley. Ash entered last, quickly hit the stud, shutting the door behind them.

They stood close together in front of the door, scanning the room. Still no sign of the alien. Dallas pursed his lips, blew a sharp whistle. That failed to stir the creature, but it did make Ripley giggle a bit unsteadily.

Keeping his eyes on the hidden places, Dallas started towards an open cabinet. It would made an excellent hiding place. But close inspection of the interior showed only medical supplies, neatly arranged and undisturbed.

If they were going to try to trap the creature with something other than their hands, they needed something solid. Dallas chose the first suitably sized object he saw, a stainless-steel alloy tray. As he turned to continue the stalk, he was quite aware that if the creature felt sufficiently threatened, it could melt its way through the tray as easily and effortlessly as it could Dallas's hands. But the weight was comforting.

Ash was inspecting the far corner of the infirmary. Ripley grew bored standing next to the door. She walked in and looked beneath the platform holding Kane, thinking the creature might have attached itself to the underside. Every muscle in her body tensed, ready to throw her clear at the first sight of the tiny invader. She wasn't disappointed when the underside of the platform proved to be unoccupied.

Straightening, she considered where to search next. She brushed against a bulkhead. Something solid and unyielding landed on her shoulder. Her head jerked around and she found herself staring at long skeletal fingers and a dull grey cabochon of an eye.

Somehow she got out a single scream. Her muscles spasmed and she twisted awkwardly. As she did so, the creature tumbled heavily to the deck. It lay motionless.

Dallas and Ash had come running at her scream. Now the three of them stood gazing at the motionless shape lying among them. The fingers were clenched tight, uncannily like the hand of a dead man, which it still resembled more closely than anything else. Only the extra fingers, the tail, and the dull, lidless eye broke the illusion.

Ripley's right hand rested on the shoulder where the thing had landed. She was gulping air rather than inhaling it, the adrenalin slowly leaking from her system. She could still feel the alien weight on her.

She extended a booted foot, prodded the hand-shape. It didn't move or resist. In addition to the dullness of the single eye, its leathery skin looked shrunken and dry. She nudged it with her foot again, turning it over. The tube lay limply against the palm, almost completely retracted.

'I think it's dead.' Dallas studied the unanticipated corpse a moment longer, then glanced at Ripley. 'You okay?'

Tongue and larynx were forced into action. 'Yeah. It didn't do anything. I think it was long dead before it fell on me.'

She walked to the open cabinet and selected a long metal forceps. A touch on the curled fingers failed to elicit any reaction, as did a poke at the eye. Dallas held out the tray. Using the forceps, she manoeuvred the petrified alien into it, quickly flipped shut the gleaming lid.

They moved to a nearby table. The alien was carefully removed from the tray and placed on the flat surface. Ash turned a bright light on it. The illumination intensified the ghastly pallor of the thing. He chose a small probe, pushed and prodded the unresisting form.

'Look at those suckers.' He used the probe to indicate the series of small, deep holes lining the inside of the creature's 'palm'. They extended completely around it. 'No wonder we couldn't get it off him, between these, the fingers and that tail it wrapped around his neck.'

'Where's its mouth?' Dallas had to force his gaze away from the single eye. Even in death, the dull orb possessed a sort of hypnotic attraction.

'Must be this tubelike organ, up in here. The thing it had down his throat. But it never showed any sign of feeding.' Ash used the probe to turn the corpse over on its back. He got a grip on the tube with the forceps, partly pulled it out of the palm. As he extracted more of the tube, it changed colour to match the rest of the body.

'It's hardening as soon as it contacts the air.' Ash moved the tiny form over to a scanner, slipped it underneath the lens and adjusted controls. Numbers and words appeared on tiny screens when he depressed a certain button.

'That's all,' he finally informed them. 'It's over. It's dead. No life signs whatever. We may not know much about it, but it's not so alien you can't determine whether it's alive or not.'

Ripley's shoulder tingled. 'Good. Let's get rid of it.'

Ash looked at her in disbelief. 'You're joking, of course. Very funny.'

She shook her head. 'Like hell I am.'

'But . . . this has to go back.' Ash sounded almost excited. 'This is the first contact with a creature like this. There's nothing like it on any of the tapes, not even the hypotheticals. All kinds of tests should be run on it.'

'Fine,' she said. 'So run your tests, and then we'll get rid of it.'

'No, no. It requires the facilities of a completely equipped biology lab. I can only record the slightest details of construction and composition. I can't begin to guess at such critical things as its evolutionary history.

'We can't dump one of the greatest xenological discoveries of the past decade out the lock like a piece of common garbage! I protest, personally and in my capacity as science officer. Kane would do the same.'

'That thing bled acid, nearly bored a hole right through the ship.' She nodded towards it. 'God knows what it might do now that it's dead.'

'It hasn't done anything,' Ash countered. 'The acidic fluid is probably absorbed into the dead cells and has been rendered inert. It hasn't done a thing.'

'Not yet.'

Ash turned an imploring gaze on Dallas. 'It has not moved, nor resisted in any way when we prodded it all over, even in its eye. The scanner insists it's dead and I think it's safe to assume it's not a zombie. Dallas, we have to keep this specimen.'

When Dallas didn't respond, Ash continued. 'For one thing, if we can't pull Kane out of his coma, the medical team that treats him will need to have the creature that induced the condition. Throw it away and we might be throwing away the secret to reviving Kane.'

Dallas finally spoke. 'You're the science officer. It's your department, your decision.'

'Then it's made.' Ash bestowed a fond look on his acquisition. 'I'll seal it in a stasis tube. That'll arrest any possibility of revivication. We can handle it.'

'That's what Kane probably thought,' Ripley muttered. Dallas glared at her and she looked away. 'That takes care of the monster's future, I guess.' She gestured at the medical platform. 'What about Kane?'

Ash turned to face the pallet. After a brief examination of the exec and careful study of his sucker-marked face, the science officer activated several instruments on the medical console. The autodoc made noises, and readouts began to appear.

'He's running a fever.'

'Bad?'

'No. Nothing his system can't handle. The machine will bring his temperature down. He's still unconscious.'

'We can see that.'

Ash glanced back at the bitter Ripley. 'Not necessarily. He could be sleeping, which would be different.'

Ripley started to reply, was cut off by an angry Dallas. 'You two stop your bickering.' As if he didn't have enough to worry about, now he had to deal with tension between crewmates. Considering the mental pressure they'd all been under recently, such conflicts were to be expected, but he'd tolerate only the minimum necessary to relieve it. Open antagonism was something to be avoided at all costs. He had no time to deal with congealing cliques.

To get Ripley's mind off Ash and vice versa, he turned the conversation back to Kane. 'Unconscious and a slight fever. Anything else?'

Ash studied readouts. 'Nothing that shows here. His vital signs continue strong.'

'Long-term prognosis?'

The science officer looked hesitant. 'I'm not a medical officer. The *Nostromo* isn't big enough to rate one.'

'Or important enough. I know that. But you're the closest thing we've got. I just want your opinion. It's not going into the log and I certainly won't hold you to it. Hell, I can't hold you to it.' His gaze travelled back down to Kane, shipmate and friend.

'I don't want to appear unduly optimistic,' Ash said slowly, 'but based on his present condition and on what the monitors tell me, I'd say he may make it.'

Dallas grinned, nodded slowly. 'Good enough. Can't ask for more than that.'

'I hope you're right,' Ripley added. 'We disagree on some things, but this time I pray to God you're right.'

Ash shrugged. 'I wish I could do more for him, but as I said, I'm not trained for it. It's up to the autodoc. Right now I'm getting back some mighty peculiar readings, but there's no precedent for the machine to attack from. All we can do is wait until it figures out what the alien did to him. Then it can prescribe and commence treatment.' He looked suddenly disappointed.

'I wish I *was* medically qualified. I don't like waiting on machines.'

Ripley looked surprised. 'That's the first time I ever heard you say anything disparaging about a machine, Ash.'

'No machine is perfect. They ought to be more flexible. We need a complete hospital in here, not just this little autodoc. It's not designed to cope with anything this . . . well, this alien. The problem may be beyond its capability. Like any machine, it's only as effective as the information programmed into it. I just wish I knew more medicine.'

'This is also,' Ripley went on, 'the first time I've ever heard you express feelings of inadequacy.'

'If you know less than everything, you always feel inadequate. I don't see how you can feel otherwise.' He looked back down at Kane. 'That feeling is magnified when the universe confronts you with something utterly beyond your experience. I don't have the knowledge to cope properly, and it makes me feel helpless.'

Handling the forceps carefully, he lifted the alien by two of its fingers and transferred it to a large, transparent vial. He touched a control set into the vial's stopper, sealed the vial shut. A yellow glow filled the tube.

Ripley had watched the procedure intently. She half expected the creature to suddenly melt its way out of the stasis tube and come clutching for them all. Finally convinced that it could no longer threaten her, except in nightmares, she turned and headed for the infirmary exit.

'I don't know about the rest of you,' she said back over a shoulder, 'but I could do with some coffee.'

'Good thought.' Dallas glanced at Ash. 'You be okay in here by yourself?'

'You mean, alone with that?' He jerked a thumb in the direction of the sealed container, grinned. 'I'm a scientist. Things like that heighten my curiosity, not my pulse rate. I'll be fine, thanks. If anything develops or if Kane's condition shows hints of changing, I'll buzz you immediately.'

'Deal.' He looked back to the waiting Ripley. 'Let's go find that coffee.'

The infirmary door slid tightly shut behind them and they started back towards the bridge, leaving the autodoc to work on Kane, and Ash to work on the autodoc . . .

# VIII

The coffee soothed their stomachs if not their brains. Around them the *Nostromo* functioned smoothly, uninterested in the deceased alien stasised in the infirmary. Familiar hums and smells filled the bridge.

Dallas recognized some of the odours as issuing from various members of the crew. He took no offence at them, merely sniffed once or twice in recognition. Such fineries as deodorant were neither missed nor taken exception to on a ship the size of the *Nostromo*. Imprisoned in a metal bottle light-years from warm worlds and sanitized atmospheres, the crew's wakened minds were occupied by more important matters than the effluvia of one's neighbour.

Ripley looked troubled still.

'What's eating you? Still simmering over Ash's decision to open the lock and let us back in?'

Her voice was tight with frustration. 'How *could* you leave that kind of decision to him?'

'I told you,' he explained patiently. 'It was my decision to bring Kane in, not . . . oh, you mean about keeping the corpse of the alien?'

She nodded. 'Yeah. It's too late to argue about the lock. I might've been wrong on that. But keeping that thing on board, dead or not, after what it's done to Kane.'

He tried to mollify her. 'We don't know for sure that it's done anything to Kane except knock him out. According to the

119

readouts there's nothing else wrong with him.

'As to retaining it on board, I just run this ship. I'm only a pilot.'

'You're the captain.'

'A title of last resort, one that means nothing in specified situations. Parker can overrule me on a point of engineering. On anything that has to do with the science division, Ash has the final word.'

'And how does that happen?' She sounded more curious than bitter, now.

'Same way that everything else happens. On orders from the Company. Read your own directory.'

'Since when is it standard procedure?'

He was getting a touch exasperated. 'Come on, Ripley. This isn't a military vessel. You know as well as I that standard procedure is what they tell you to do. That principle includes the independence of different departments, like science. If I believed otherwise, I'm not sure I would've set down here.'

'What's the matter? Visions of discovery bonuses fading before the spectre of a dead man?'

'You know better than that,' he said sharply. 'There isn't a bonus large enough to trade for Kane's good health. Too late for that, now. We're here, and it's happened.

'Look, ease up on me, will you? I just haul cargo for a living. If I wanted to be a real explorer and go gallivanting off after discovery bonuses, I would've joined the Rim Corps. Gotten my head torn off at least half a dozen times by now. Glory . . . no thanks. Not for me. I'll settle for having my executive officer back again.'

She didn't reply this time, sat silently for several minutes. When she spoke the next time, the bitterness was gone. 'You and Kane been together on many flights?'

'Enough to know each other.' Dallas kept his voice level, eyes on his console.

'What about Ash?'

'You going to start in on that again?' He sighed. There was

nowhere to run. 'What about him?'

'Same thing. You say you know Kane. Do you know Ash? Have you ever shipped with him before?'

'No.' The thought didn't bother Dallas in the least. 'This is the first time. I went five hauls, long and short, various cargos, with another science officer. Then two days before we left Thedus, they replaced him with Ash.'

She stared at him significantly.

'So what?' he snapped at her. 'They also replaced my old warrant officer with you.'

'I don't trust him.'

'Sound attitude. Now me . . . I don't trust anyone.' Time, he thought, to change the subject. From what he'd seen so far, Ash was a fine officer, if a bit stiff when it came to being one of the gang. But personal intimacy wasn't a necessity on voyages where you spent most of your time, except arriving and departing, in the narcosis of hypersleep. As long as the man did his job, Dallas didn't give a damn about his personality. Thus far, there'd been no reason to question Ash's competency.

'What's holding up repairs?' he asked her.

She glanced at her chronometer, did some quick figuring. 'They ought to be pretty much finished by now. Shouldn't have to do more than fine-check.'

'Why didn't you say so?'

'There are still some things left to do, I'm sure, or they would've said something. Listen, you think I'm stalling for Parker, of all people?'

'No. What's left to do?'

She ran a fast request through her board. 'We're still blind on B and C decks. Scanners blew and need to be completely replaced there.'

'I don't give a damn about seeing B and C decks. I know what they look like. Anything else?'

'Reserve power systems blew just after we touched down. Remember the trouble with the secondaries?'

'But the main drivers are fixed?' She nodded. 'Then that

stuff about the reserves is crap. We can take off without them, get back into hypersleep and do some real travelling instead of hanging around here.'

'Is that a good idea? About taking off without having the secondaries fixed, I mean.'

'Maybe not. But I want out of here, and I want out now. We've investigated that signal all we're going to and there's nobody here to rescue except Kane. Let some properly equipped Company expedition set down and go digging around that derelict. That's not what we're paid for. We've complied with the directives. Now I've had enough. Let's get this turkey off the ground.'

They settled into their roles on the bridge. Kane and the dead alien were forgotten. Everything was forgotten, except take-off procedure. They were a unit now. Personal animosities and opinions were submerged in the desire to get the tug off the ground and back into clean, open space.

'Primary drive activated,' Ash reported, up from the infirmary and back at his regular station.

'Check.' This from Lambert.

'Secondaries still not functioning, sir.' Ripley frowned at the crimson readout on her overhead console.

'Yeah, I know. Navigator, are we set?'

Lambert studied her board. 'Orbital re-entry computed and entered. I'm matching up positions with the refinery now. Have it in a second. There.' She hit a series of buttons in sequence. Numbers flashed above Dallas's head.

'Good enough. We'll correct when we're up, if necessary. Stand by for lift-off.'

Swathed in roiling dust, the *Nostromo* began to vibrate. A roaring rose over the howl of the storm, a man-made thunder that echoed across lava hillocks and shattered hexagonal basalt columns.

'Standing by,' said Ripley.

Dallas glanced across at Ash. 'How's she holding?'

The science officer studied his gauges. 'Everything's

working. For how long, I can't say.'

'Just long enough to get us up.' Dallas flipped on the intercom. 'Parker, how do we look from down there? Can we make it out without engaging the deep drive?'

If they couldn't break gravity on the primary drive, Dallas knew, they'd have to cut in the hyper to get them out. But a second or two of hyperdrive would throw them completely out of this system. That would mean relocating it and using precious wake time to link up once more with their cargo. And wake time translated as air. Minutes equalled litres. The *Nostromo* could continue to recycle their meagre supply of breathing material only so long. When their lungs started rejecting it, they'd have to go back into the freezers whether they'd found the refinery or not.

Dallas thought of the gigantic floating factory, tried to imagine how long it would take for them to pay for it on their various modest salaries.

Parker's reply was hopeful, if not exactly encouraging. 'Okay. But remember, this is just a patch job. Need shipyard equipment to make proper repairs.'

'Will she hold together?'

'Ought to, unless we hit too much turbulence going up. That might blow the new cells . . . and that's all she said. No way we could fix them again.'

'So take it easy,' Brett added from his seat in the engineering cubicle.

'I hear you. We'll watch it. All we have to do is reach zero-gee and we can go hyper all the way into Sol. Then the damn cells can go like popcorn if they want to. But until we're up and out, you keep them intact if you have to hold them steady with your bare hands.'

'Do our best,' said Parker.

'Check. Bridge out.' Dallas turned to face the *Nostromo*'s warrant officer. Ripley was presently doubling duty for the incapacitated Kane. 'Take us up a hundred metres and bring in the landing struts.' He turned his attention to his own console. 'I'll keep her steady.'

'Up a hundred,' Ripley touched controls.

The thunder intensified outside as the tug lifted from the parched, dust-blasted surface. The ship hovered a hundred metres above the ground, dust racing confusedly beneath it. Massive leglike pillars that had supported the *Nostromo* now folded neatly into her metal belly.

A slight thump sounded on the bridge, confirming computer telltales. 'Struts retracted,' Ripley announced. 'Closing shields.' Metal plates slid tightly shut over the strut housings, sealing out dust particles and alien atmosphere.

'Standing by,' declared Ash.

'Okay. Ripley, Kane's not here, so it's all yours. Take us up.'

She nudged a double lever on the exec's console. The roaring outside was deafening now, though there was nothing to hear and be suitably impressed by the cleverness of mankind. Inclined slightly upward, the *Nostromo* began to move forward.

'Rolling up the G's,' she said, hitting several additional buttons. 'And here we go.'

Moving sharply skyward and accelerating steadily, the tug suddenly leaped ahead. Powerful winds clutched at the tough, alloyed skin, neither slowed the starship nor altered its course.

Lambert's attention was fixed on one particular gauge. 'One kilometre and ascending. On course, Orbital insertion in five point three two minutes.' If, she added silently to herself, we hold together that long.

'Sounding good,' Dallas murmured, watching two lines overlap pleasingly on his console. 'Engage artificial gravity.'

Lambert threw a switch. The ship seemed to stumble. Dallas's stomach protested as the fading gravity of the little world receding behind them was replaced by a full, unforgiving pull.

'Engaged,' Lambert reported, as her own insides finished realigning themselves.

Ripley's gaze danced from one readout to another. A slight

discrepancy appeared and she hurried to correct for it. 'Unequal thrust reading. I'm altering the vector now.' She nudged a switch, watched with satisfaction as a liquid needle crawled back to where it belonged. 'Compensation effected. Holding steady now. We're set.'

Dallas was beginning to believe they'd make it without any trouble when a violent tremor ran through the bridge. It sent personal possessions and frantic thoughts of the crew flying. The tremor lasted only an instant, wasn't repeated.

'What the hell was that?' Dallas wondered aloud. By way of reply, the 'com beeped for attention.

'That you, Parker?'

'Yea. We had some trouble back here.'

'Serious?'

'Starboard quad's overheating. Judge for yourself.'

'Can you fix it?'

'Are you kidding? I'm shutting it down.'

'Compensating again for unequal thrust,' Ripley announced solemnly.

'Just hold us together until we're beyond double zero,' Dallas asked the pickup.

'What do you think we're trying to do back here?' The intercom clicked off.

A slight change in the roaring of the engines became audible on the bridge. No one looked at their neighbour, for fear of seeing their own worries reflected there.

Moving a little more slowly but still slicing effortlessly through boiling clouds, the *Nostromo* continued to power spaceward, on course to meet with the drifting refinery.

In contrast to the comparative calm on the bridge, the engine room was the scene of frenzied activity. Brett was scooched up inside a tube again, sweating and wishing he was elsewhere.

'Got it figured?' asked Parker from outside.

'Yeah. I think so. Dust is clogging the damn intakes again. Number two's overheating now.'

'I thought we shut that junk out.'

'So did I. Must've slipped a screen again. Damn engines are too sensitive.'

'They weren't designed to fly through particulate hurricanes,' Parker reminded his associate. 'Spit on it for two more minutes and we'll be clear.'

A second tremor rattled the bridge. Everyone's attention stayed glued to their respective consoles. Dallas thought of querying engineering, then thought better of it and decided not to. If Parker had anything to report, he'd do so.

Come on, come on, he urged silently. Get it *up*. He promised himself that if Parker and Brett could keep the primaries functioning for another couple of minutes, he'd put them in for the bonuses they were constantly harping about. A gauge on his board showed that gravitational pull was fading rapidly. Another minute, he pleaded, one hand unconsciously caressing the nearby wall. Another lousy minute.

Erupting from the crown of clouds, the *Nostromo* burst into open space. One minute, fifty seconds later, the surface-gravity indicator on Dallas's console fell to zero.

That was the signal for some unprofessional but heartfelt cheering on the bridge.

'We made it.' Ripley lay exhausted against the padded back of her flight seat. 'Damn. We made it.'

'When the first tremor hit and we started velocity slide, I didn't think we were going to,' Dallas husked. 'I saw us splattering ourselves all over the nearest hillside. We might as well have done that if we'd had to go hyper and lost the refinery.'

'Nothing to worry about.' Lambert wasn't smiling. 'We could have landed again and stayed there. Then *our* automatic distress beacon would've come on. We could've relaxed in hypersleep while some other lucky crew got itself kicked out of the freezers to come and rescue *us*.'

Don't mention anything about bonuses yet, Dallas was telling himself. Surprise them with it when you wake up in Earth orbit. But for now, the engineering team was at least entitled to some verbal commendation. He addressed the 'com.

'Nice work, you two. How's she holding?'

'Now that we're out of that dust, she's purring like Jones.' A sharp crackling noise sounded over the speaker. Dallas frowned for a second, unable to place it. Then he realized that Parker had probably opened a beer while inadvertently holding it within range of the pickup.

'It was a walk in the park,' the engineer continued pridefully. 'When we fix something it stays fixed.' A gurgling sound filled the speaker, as if Parker were submerging.

'Sure it was. A good job,' Dallas assured him. 'Take a break. You've both earned it. And Parker?'

'Yo?'

'When we raise Earthside and you're co-ordinating your department with engineering control, keep your beer away from the mike.' The gurgling noise receded.

Satisfied, Dallas switched off and said to no one in particular, 'Let's pick up the money and go home. Put her in the garage, Lambert.'

The *Nostromo*'s angle of ascent began to flatten. Several minutes passed before a steady beeping began to sound from a telltale above the navigator's station.

'Here she comes,' she informed her companions. 'Right where she's supposed to be.'

'Okay.' Dallas was thumbing controls. 'Line us up and stand by to dock.' Instrumentation hummed as the tug adjusted its attitude with respect to the mountain of metal and plastic. Ripley threw a switch, and the tug locked itself in position backside first to the dull mass of the refinery.

'Positioned,' she said.

'Bring us in.' Dallas watched a certain readout intently, fingers poised over a rank of red buttons.

'We're moving.' Ripley's attention was focused on two screens at once. 'Distance shrinking. Twenty . . . fifteen . . . set.' She hit a switch.

Dallas depressed the red controls. 'Engines cut and primaries compensated for. We have inertial stability. Activate the hyperdrive lock.'

'Activated,' Ripley informed him. 'We're tied together.' When activated now, the *Nostromo* would generate a hyperdrive field of sufficient size to include the refinery. It would travel with them, enveloped in that mysterious manifestation of nonreality that enabled ships and men to travel faster than light.

'Set course for Earth,' Dallas ordered crisply. 'Then fire up the big one and get us up to light plus four, Ripley.'

'With pleasure.'

'Course computed and locked in,' said Lambert a moment later. 'Time to go home.' Then, to herself, 'Feets, get me out of here.'

Ripley touched a major control. The tiny world and its imprisoned alien ship vanished as though it had never existed. The *Nostromo* achieved, exceeded the speed of light. A corona effect materialized around the ship and refinery. Stars ahead of them became blue, those behind shifted to red.

Six crew members raced relievedly for home. Six crew members and something else named Kane . . .

They sat around the mess table and sipped coffee, tea or other warm liquid stimulants according to taste and habit. Their relaxed postures reflected their current state of mind, which until recently had been stiff as glass and twice as fragile. Now legs sprawled unconcernedly over chair arms, and backs slumped against cushions.

Lambert was still up on the bridge, making final course checks before she'd permit herself the luxury of collapsing. Ash was down in the infirmary, keeping watch over Kane. The executive officer and his condition were the principal topics of conversation.

Parker downed steaming tea, smacked his lips indelicately and proposed with his usual confidence, 'The best thing to do is just freeze him. Arrest the goddamn disease.'

'We don't know that freezing will alter his condition in any way,' Dallas argued. 'It might make him worse. What affects Earthside diseases might only intensify whatever this is that has a hold on him.'

'It's a damn sight better than doing nothing.' Parker waved the cup like a baton. 'And that's what the autodoc's done for him so far: nothing. Whatever he's got is beyond its capability to handle, just like Ash said. That medical computer's set up to handle things like zero-gee sickness and broken bones, not something like this. We all agree Kane needs specialized help.'

'Which you just admitted we can't offer him.'

'Right.' Parker leaned back in his chair. 'Exactly. So I say freeze him until we get back home and a doc specializing in alien diseases can run over him.'

'Right,' added Brett.

Ripley shook her head, looked put upon. 'Whenever he says anything, you say "right". You know that, Brett?'

He grinned. 'Right.'

She turned to face the engineer. 'What do you think about that, Parker? Your staff just follows you around and says "right". Like regular parrots.'

Parker turned to his colleague. 'Yeah. Shape up. What are you, some kind of parrot?'

'Right.'

'Oh, knock it off.' Dallas was sorry for the unthinking comment. A little levity would do them some good, and he had to up and step on it. Why did he have to be like that? The relationships among the members of the tug's crew were more informal ones among equals than a boss-and-employee type of chain of command. So, why did he all of a sudden feel compelled to play captain?

Perhaps because they were in a crisis situation of sorts and someone had to officially be 'in charge'. He was stuck with the responsibility. Lousy job. Right now he'd much rather have Ripley's, or Parker's. Especially Parker's. The two engineers could squat back in their private cubicle and blithely ignore

everything that didn't directly affect them. So long as they kept
the engines and ship's systems functioning, they were
answerable to no one save each other.

It occurred to Dallas that he didn't particularly like making
decisions. Maybe that was why he was commanding an old tug
instead of a liner. More revealingly, maybe that was why he
never complained about it. As tug captain he could spend most
of his ship time in hypersleep, doing nothing but dreaming
and collecting his salary. He didn't have to make decisions in
hypersleep.

Soon, he assured himself. Soon they could all return to the
private comforts of their individual coffins. The needles would
come down, the soporifics would enter their veins and numb
their brains, and they would drift pleasantly away, away to the
land where decisions no longer had to be made and the
unpleasant surprises of a hostile universe could not intrude.

As soon as they finished their coffee.

'Kane will have to go into quarantine,' he said absently,
sipping at his mug.

'Yeah, and so will we.' Ripley looked dismayed at the
thought. That was understandable. They would travel all the
way back to Earth, only to spend weeks in isolation until the
medics were convinced none of them harboured anything
similar to what had flattened Kane. Visions of green grass
underfoot and blue skies filled her mind. She saw a beach and
a blissfully groundbound little town on the coast of El Salvador.
It was painful to have to force them out.

Eyes turned as a new figure joined them. Lambert looked
tired and depressed.

'How about a little something to lower your spirits?' she told
them.

'Thrill me.' Dallas tried to prepare himself mentally for what
he suspected was coming. He knew what the navigator had
remained on the bridge to work out.

'According to my calculations, based on the time spent
getting to and from that unscheduled stop we made, the

amount of time spent making the detour . . .'

'Give me the short version,' Dallas said, interrupting her. 'We know we went off course to trace that signal. How long to Earth?'

She finished drawing a cup of coffee for herself, slumped into a chair, and said sadly, 'Ten months.'

'Christ.' Ripley stared at the bottom of her cup. Clouds and grass and beach receded farther in her mind, blended into a pale blue-green haze well out of reach. True, ten months in hypersleep was little different from a month. But their minds worked with real time. Ripley would rather have heard six months instead of the projected ten.

The intercom beeped for attention and Dallas acknowledged. 'What's up, Ash?'

'Come see Kane right away.' The request was urgently phrased, yet with a curious hesitancy to it.

Dallas sat up straight, as did the others at the table. 'Some change in his condition? Serious?'

'It's simpler if you just come see him.'

There was a concerned rush for the corridor. Coffee remained steaming on the deserted table.

Horrible visions clouded Dallas's thoughts as he made his way down to the infirmary with the others trailing behind. What gruesome after-effects had the alien disease produced in the exec? Dallas imagined a swarm of tiny grey hands, their single eyes shining wetly, crawling possessively over the infirmary walls, or some leprous fungus enveloping the rotting corpse of the luckless Kane.

They reached the infirmary, panting from the effort of running down corridor and companionways. There was no cluster of replicated alien hands crawling on the walls. No alien growth, fungoid or otherwise, decorated the body of the executive officer. Ash had greatly understated the matter when he'd reported a change in Kane's condition.

The exec was sitting up on the medical platform. His eyes were open and clear, functioning in proper concert with his brain. Those eyes turned to take in the knot of gaping arrivals.

'Kane?' Lambert couldn't believe it. 'Are you all right?' He looks fine, she thought dazedly. As though nothing had ever happened.

'You want anything?' asked Ripley, when he did not respond to Lambert's query.

'Mouth's dry.' Dallas abruptly remembered what Kane, in his present state, reminded him of: a man just coming out of amnesia. The exec looked alert and fit, but puzzled for no particular reason, as though he were still trying to organize his thoughts. 'Can I have some water?'

Ash moved quickly to a dispenser, drew a plastic cupful and handed it to Kane. The exec downed it in a single long swallow. Dallas noted absently that muscular co-ordination seemed normal. The hand-to-mouth drinking movements had been performed instinctively, without forethought.

While enormously gratifying, the situation was ridiculous. There had to be *something* wrong with him.

'More,' was all Kane said, continuing to act like a man in complete control of himself. Ripley found a large container, filled it brim full and handed it to him. He downed the contents like a man who'd just spent ten years wandering the deserts of Piolin, then sagged back on the padded platform, panting.

'How do you feel?' asked Dallas.

'Terrible. What happened to me?'

'You don't remember?' Ash said.

So, Dallas told himself with satisfaction, the amnesia analogy was nearer the mark than he'd suspected.

Kane winced slightly, more from muscles cramping from disuse than anything else, and took a deep breath. 'I don't remember a thing. I can barely remember my name.'

'Just for the record . . . and the medical report,' asked Ash professionally, 'what is your name?'

'Kane. Thomas Kane.'

'That's all you remember?'

'For the moment.' He let his gaze travel slowly over the

assembly of anxious faces. 'I remember all of you, though I can't put names to you yet.'

'You will,' Ash assured him confidently. 'You recall your own name and you remember faces. That's a good start. Also a sign that your loss of memory isn't absolute.'

'Do you hurt?' Surprisingly, it was the stoic Parker who asked the first sensitive question.

'All over. Feel like somebody's been beating me with a stick for about six years.' He sat up on the pallet again, swung his legs over the side and smiled. 'God, am I hungry. How long was I out?'

Dallas continued to stare at the apparently unharmed man in disbelief. 'Couple of days. You sure you don't have any recollection of what happened to you?'

'Nope. Not a thing.'

'What's the last thing you remember?' Ripley asked him.

'I don't know.'

'You were with Dallas and me on a strange planet, exploring. Do you remember what happened there?'

Kane's forehead wrinkled as he tried to battle through the mists obscuring his memories. Real remembrances remained tantalizingly out of reach, realization a painful, incomplete process.

'Just some horrible dream about smothering. Where are we now? Still on the planet?'

Ripley shook her head. 'No, I'm delighted to say. We're in hyperspace, on our way home.'

'Getting ready to go back in the freezers,' Brett added feelingly. He was as anxious as the others to repair to the mindless protection of hypersleep. Anxious for the nightmare that had forced itself on them to be put in suspension along with their bodies.

Though looking at the revitalized Kane made it hard to reconcile their memories with the image of the alien horror he'd brought aboard, the petrified creature was there for anyone to inspect, motionless in its stasis tube.

'I'm all for that,' Kane said readily. 'Feel dizzy and tired enough to go into deep sleep without the freezers.' He looked around the infirmary wildly. 'Right now, though, I'm starving. I want some food before we go under.'

'I'm pretty hungry myself.' Parker's stomach growled indelicately. 'It's tough enough coming out of hypersleep without your belly rumbling. Better if you go under with a full stomach. Makes it easier coming out.'

'I won't argue that.' Dallas felt some sort of celebration was in order. In the absence of partying material, a final presleep feast would have to do. 'We could all use some food. One meal before bed . . .'

# IX

Coffee and tea had been joined on the mess table by individual servings of food. Everyone ate slowly, their enthusiasm coming from the fact they were a whole crew again rather than from the bland offerings of the autochef.

Only Kane ate differently, wolfing down huge portions of the artificial meats and vegetables. He'd already finished two normal helpings and was starting in on a third with no sign of slowing down. Unmindful of nearby displays of human gluttony, Jones the cat ate delicately from a dish in the centre of the table.

Kane looked up and waved a spoon at them, spoke with his mouth full. 'First thing I'm going to do when we get back is eat some decent food. I'm sick of artificials. I don't care what the Company manuals say, it still tastes of recycling. There's a twang to artificials that no amount of spicing or seasoning can eliminate.'

'I've had worse than this,' Parker commented thoughtfully, 'but I've had better, too.'

Lambert frowned at the engineer, a spoonful of steak-that-wasn't suspended halfway between plate and lips. 'For somebody who doesn't like the stuff, you're pounding it down like there's no tomorrow.'

'I mean, I like it,' Parker explained, shovelling down another spoonful.

'No kidding?' Kane didn't pause in his eating, but did throw

Parker a look of suspicion, as though he thought the engineer might not be entirely right in the head.

Parker tried not to sound defensive. 'So I like it. It sort of grows on you.'

'It should,' Kane shot back. 'You know what this stuff is made out of.'

'I know what it's made out of,' Parker replied. 'So what? It's food now. You're hardly the one to talk, the way you're gulping it down.'

'I've got an excuse.' Kane stuffed another huge forkful in his mouth. 'I'm starving.' He glanced around the table. 'Anyone know if amnesia affects the appetite?'

'Appetite, hell.' Dallas picked at the remnants of his single serving. 'You had nothing in you but liquids all the time you were in the autodoc. Sucrose, dextrose and the like keep you alive but don't exactly satisfy. No wonder you're starving.'

'Yeah.' Kane swallowed another double mouthful. 'It's almost like I . . . like I . . .' He broke off, grimaced, then looked confused and a little frightened.

Ripley leaned towards him. 'What is it . . . what's wrong? Something in the food?'

'No . . . I don't think so. It tasted all right. I don't think . . .' He stopped in mid-sentence again. His expression was strained and he was grunting steadily.

'What's the matter then?' wondered a worried Lambert.

'I don't know.' He made another twisted face, looking like a fighter who'd just taken a solid punch in the gut. 'I'm getting cramps . . . getting worse.'

Nervous faces watched the exec's twist in pain and confusion. Abruptly, he let out a loud, deep-toned groan and clutched at the edge of the table with both hands. His knuckles paled and the tendons stood out in his arms. His whole body was trembling uncontrollably, as if he were freezing, though it was pleasantly warm in the mess room.

'Breathe deeply, work at it,' Ash advised, when no one else offered any suggestions.

Kane tried. The deep breath turned into a scream.

'Oh, God, it hurts so bad. It hurts. It hurts.' He stood unsteadily, still shaking, hands digging into the table as if afraid to let go. 'Ohhhh!'

'What is it?' Brett asked helplessly. 'What hurts? Something in. . .?'

The look of agony that took over Kane's face at that moment cut off Brett's questioning more effectively than any shout. The exec tried to rise from the table, failed and fell back. He could no longer control his body. His eyes bulged and he let out a lingering, nerve-chilling shriek. It echoed around the mess, sparing none of the onlookers, refusing to fade.

'His shirt . . .' Ripley murmured, as thoroughly paralyzed as Kane, though from a different cause. She was pointing at the slumping officer's chest.

A red stain had appeared on Kane's tunic. It spread rapidly, became a broad, uneven bloody smear across his lower chest. There followed the sound of fabric tearing, ugly and intimate in the cramped room. His shirt split like the skin of a melon, peeled back on both sides as a small head the size of a man's fist punched outward. It writhed and twisted like a snake's. The tiny skull was mostly all teeth, sharp and red-stained. Its skin was a pale, sickly white, darkened now by a crimson slime. It displayed no external organs, not even eyes. A nauseating odour, fetid and rank, reached the nostrils of the crew.

There were screams from others besides Kane now, shouts of panic and terror as the crew reflexively stumbled away from the table. They were preceded in instinctive retreat by the cat. Tail bottled, hair standing on end, it spat ferociously and cleared the table and the room in two muscle-straining leaps.

Convulsively, the toothed skull lunged outward. All of a sudden it seemed to fairly spurt from Kane's torso. The head and neck were attached to a thick, compact body covered in the same white flesh. Clawed arms and legs propelled it outward with unexpected speed. It landed messily among the dishes and food on the table, trailing pieces of Kane's insides. Fluid and blood formed an unclean wake behind it. It reminded Dallas of a butchered turkey with teeth protruding from the stump of a neck.

Before anyone could regain their senses and act, the alien had wriggled off the table with the speed of a lizard and vanished down the open corridor.

Much heavy breathing but little movement filled the mess. Kane remained slumped in his chair, his head thrown back, mouth agape. Dallas was grateful for that. It meant that neither he nor anyone else had to look at Kane's open eyes.

There was a huge, ragged hole in the executive officer's exploded chest. Even from a distance Dallas could see how internal organs had been pushed aside without being damaged, to provide a cavity large enough for the creature. Dishes lay scattered on table and floor. Much of the uneaten food was covered with a slick layer of blood.

'No, no, no, no. . .!' Lambert was repeating, over and over, staring blankly at the table.

'What was that?' Brett murmured, gazing fixedly at Kane's corpse. 'What the Christ was that?'

Parker felt sick, did not even think of taunting Ripley when she turned away from them all to retch. 'It was growing in him the whole time and he didn't even know it.'

'It used him for an incubator,' Ash theorized softly. 'Like certain wasps do with spiders on Earth. They paralyze the spider first, then lay their eggs on the body. When the larvae hatch, they begin to feed on . . .'

'For God's sake!' yelled Lambert, snapping out of her trance, 'Shut up, can't you?'

Ash looked hurt. 'I was only . . .' Then he caught a look from Dallas, nodded almost imperceptibly and changed the subject. 'It's self-evident what happened.'

'That dark stain on the medical monitors.' Dallas didn't feel too good himself. He wondered if he looked as shaky as his companions. 'It wasn't on the lens after all. It was inside him. Why didn't the scanners tell us that?'

'There was no reason, no reason at all, to suspect anything like this,' Ash was quick to point out. 'When we were monitoring him internally the stain was too small to take seriously. And it looked like it *was* a lens defect. In fact, it could have been a matching blot on the lens.'

'I don't follow you.'

'It's possible this stage of the creature generates a natural field capable of intercepting and blocking the scanning radiation. Unlike the first form, the "hand" shape, which we were easily able to see into. Other creatures have been known to produce similar fields. It suggests biological requirements we can't begin to guess at, or else a deliberately produced defence evolved to meet requirements so advanced I prefer *not* to guess at it.'

'What it boils down to,' observed Ripley, wiping her mouth with an unstained napkin, 'is that we've got another alien. Probably equally hostile and twice as dangerous.' She glared challengingly at Ash, but this time the science officer couldn't or wouldn't dispute her.

'Yeah. And it's loose on the ship.' Dallas moved unwillingly over to stand by Kane's body. The others slowly joined him. The inspection was necessary, no matter how unpleasant they found it. Eloquent glances passed from Parker to Lambert, Lambert to Ash and around the little circle. Outside, the universe, vast and threatening, pressed tight around the *Nostromo*, while the thick, ripe smell of death filled the corridors leading into the crowded mess . . .

Parker and Brett descended the companionway leading from the service deck above, joined the rest of a tired, discouraged group of hunters.

'Any signs?' Dallas asked the assemblage. 'Any strange smells, blood,' he hesitated momentarily, finished, 'pieces of Kane?'

'Nothing,' Lambert told him.

'Nothing,' echoed Ash, with obvious disappointment.

Parker brushed dust from his arms. 'Didn't see a goddamn thing. It knows how to hide.'

'Didn't see anything,' Brett confirmed. 'Can't imagine where it's got to. Though there's parts of the ship it could reach that we can't. I wouldn't think anything could survive in some of those heated ducts, though.'

'Don't forget the kind of environment its, uh. . .,' Dallas looked at Ash, 'what would you call its first stage?'

'Prelarval. Just giving it a name. I can't imagine its stages of development.'

'Yeah. Well, let's not forget what it was living in through its first incarnation. We know it's plenty tough, and adaptable as hell. Wouldn't surprise me if we found it nesting on top of the reaction chambers.'

'If that's where it's got to, we won't be able to get near it,' Parker pointed out.

'Then let's hope it's travelled in a different direction. Somewhere we can go after it.'

'We've got to find it.' Ripley's expression reflected a universal concern.

'Why not just go into hypersleep?' Brett suggested. 'Pump the air back into the tanks and suffocate it?'

'In the first place, we don't know how long this form can survive without air,' the warrant officer argued heatedly. 'It may not even need air. We only saw a mouth, not nostrils.'

'Nothing can exist without some kind of atmosphere.' Brett still sounded positive, though less so.

She cocked an eye at him. 'Want to bet your life on it?' He didn't respond. 'Besides, it only has to live without air for a little while. Maybe it can take up whatever gases it requires from its . . . food. We'd be sitting . . . no, we'd be sleeping ducks in the freezers. Remember how easily the first form melted through the faceplate of Kane's helmet? Who's to promise that this version can't do the same to our freezers?'

She shook her head resignedly. 'No way I'm going under until we've found the thing and killed it.'

'But we can't kill it.' Lambert kicked at the deck in frustration. 'As far as its internal composition, it's probably identical to the first version. If it is and we try to laser it, it's liable to spill or squirt acidic body fluids all over the place. It's a lot bigger than that "hand" was. If it leaks the same stuff, it might eat a hole larger than we could patch. You all know how critical hull integrity is during faster-than-light, not to mention how delicate the circuitry running through the primary hull is.'

'Son-of-a-bitch,' muttered Brett. 'If we can't kill it, what do we do with it when we find it?'

'Somehow,' Ripley said, 'we have to track it down, catch it and eject it from the ship.' She looked to Dallas for confirmation of the proposal.

He thought a moment. 'I don't see anything else but to try it.'

'Much more talking and not searching and it won't matter what we decide to do,' Ash informed them. 'Our supplies are based on us spending a limited amount of time out of hypersleep. Strictly limited. I strongly suggest we get started immediately on some kind of organized search.'

'Right,' agreed Ripley quickly. 'The first thing we have to do is find it.'

'No,' said Dallas in a funny kind of voice. They all looked at him. 'First we've got something else to do.' He looked back down the corridor, to where the body of Kane remained just visible through the mess doorway.

Miscellaneous supplies yielded just enough material to make a crude shroud, which Parker laser-sealed in the absence of thread. It was amateurishly rough and the informality of it as they walked away from the main lock bothered everyone. But they had the consolation of knowing they were doing as much as they could.

They could have frozen the body for more substantial burial back on Earth, but the transparent canopy of the freezer compartment would leave Kane's gutted body exposed for them all to see immediately on reawakening. Better to dispose of it here, quick and clean, where it could be forgotten as fast as possible.

Back on the bridge, they resumed their stations, depression making the air seem thick as Vaseline. Dallas checked readouts, said morosely, 'Inner hatch sealed.'

Riply nodded confirmation.

'Lock still pressurized?' Another nod. He hesitated, looked from one sombre face to the next. None returned his gaze. 'Anybody want to say anything?'

Naturally, there was nothing to say. Kane was dead. He'd been alive, now he was not alive. None of the crew were particularly strong with words.

Only Lambert spoke up. 'Get it over with.' Dallas thought that wasn't much of an epitaph, but he couldn't think of anything else except that they were wasting time. He made a sign to the watching Ripley.

She touched a stud. The outer cover on the lock popped. Air remaining in the lock propelled Kane's body out into the soil of nothingness.

It was a mercifully fast burial (Dallas couldn't bring himself to think of 'disposal'). Kane had received a neater departure than he had a death. His last, tormented scream still rattled around in Dallas's brain, like a pebble in a shoe.

They reassembled in the mess. It was easier to discuss things when everyone could see everyone else without straining. Also, it gave him an excuse to get everyone back there to help clean up the awful mess.

'I've checked on supplies,' Ripley told them. 'With stimulants we can keep going for about a week. Maybe a day longer, but no more than that.'

'Then what?' Brett picked at his chin.

'We run out of food and oxygen. Food we can do without, oxygen we can't. That last factor makes the interesting question of whether or not we could live off unrecycled artificials a moot point.'

Lambert made a face at the unappetizing prospect. 'Thanks, I think I'd rather die first.'

'All right.' Dallas tried to sound confident. 'That's what we've got, then. A week of full activity. That's plenty of time. More than enough to find one small alien.'

Brett looked at the floor. 'I still say we ought to try exhausting the air. That might kill it. Seems the safest way to me. Avoids the need to confront it directly. We don't know what individual kinds of nastiness this version can dish out.'

'We went through that, remember?' Ripley reminded him.

'That assumed we'd spend the airless time in the freezers. Suppose we put our pressure suits on instead, then bleed the air? It can't sneak up on us if we're awake in our suits.'

'What a swell idea.' Lambert's tone indicated that she considered it anything but.

'What's wrong with it?'

'We've got forty-eight hours of air in our pressure suits and it takes ten months to get home,' Ash explained. 'If the creature can go forty-nine without air, we're right back where we started, except we've lost two days' suit time.'

'Other than that,' said Lambert, 'a swell idea. Come on, Parker, think of something new, you two.'

The engineers had no intention of giving up on the idea so easily. 'Maybe we could run some kind of special lines from the suit tanks to the main ones. Brett and I are pretty good practical engineers. The valve connections would be tricky, but I'm sure we could do it. We got us back up, you know.'

'All by your little old selves.' Ripley didn't try to moderate her sarcasm.

'It's not practical.' Ash spoke sympathetically to the two men. 'You'll recall that we discussed the definite possibility this creature may be able to survive without air. The problem is more extensive than that.

'We can't remain hooked to the main tanks by umbilicals and simultaneously hunt the creature down. Even if your idea works, we'll have used so much air in the suits that there'll be none left to meet us when we emerge from hypersleep. The freezers will open automatically . . . to vacuum.'

'How about leaving some kind of message, or broadcasting ahead so they can meet us and fill us with fresh air as soon as we dock?' Parker wondered.

Ash looked doubtful. 'Too chancy. First, our broadcast won't arrive more than a minute or two before we do. For an emergency team to meet us the moment we slip out of hyperspace, link up from outside, fill us with air without damaging the integrity of the ship . . . no, I don't think it could be done.

'Even if it could, I concur with Ripley on one critical point. We can't risk re-entering the freezers until we're sure the creature is dead or under control. And we can't make sure it's dead if we spend a couple of days in our suits and then run for the freezers.'

Parker snorted. 'I still think it's a good idea.'

'Let's get to the real problem,' Ripley said impatiently. 'How do we find it? We can try a dozen ways of killing it, but only after we know where it is. There's no visual scan on B and C decks. All the screens are out, remember?'

'So we'll have to flush it out.' Dallas was surprised how easy the terrifying but obvious choice was to make. Once stated, he found himself resigned to it.

'Sounds reasonable,' admitted Ash. 'Easier said than done, however. How do you suggest we proceed?'

Dallas saw them wishing he wouldn't follow the inevitable to its end. But it was the only way. 'No easy way is right. There's only one way we can be sure not to miss it and still maximize our air time. We'll have to hunt for it room by room, corridor by corridor.'

'Maybe we can rig up some kind of portable freezer,' Ripley suggested halfheartedly. 'Freeze each room and corridor from a dis . . .' She broke off, seeing Dallas shaking his head sadly. She looked away. 'Not that I'm all that scared, you understand. Just trying to be practical. Like Parker, I think it would be a good idea to try to avoid a direct confrontation.'

'Knock it off, Ripley.' Dallas touched his chest with a thumb. 'I'm scared shitless. We all are. We haven't got the time to screw around with making up something that complicated. We fooled around too long by letting a machine try to help Kane.

Time we helped ourselves. That's what we're doing on board this bigger machine in the first place, remember? When the machines can't handle a problem, it becomes our job.

'Besides, I want the pleasure of watching the little monster explode when we blow it out the lock.'

It was not exactly an inspirational speech. Certainly nothing was farther from Dallas's mind. But it had a revivifying effect on the crew. They found themselves able to look at each other again, instead of at walls or floor, and there were mutters of determination.

'Fine,' said Lambert. 'We root it out of wherever it's hiding, then blow it out the lock. What I want to know is: How do we get from point A to point C?'

'Trap it somehow.' Ripley was turning various ideas over in her head. The alien's ability to bleed acid made all of them worse than useless.

'There might be substances other than metal it couldn't eat through so quickly,' Brett thought aloud, showing that his ideas were travelling along the same lines as Ripley's. 'Trylon cord, for example. If we had a net made out of the stuff, we could bag it without damaging it. It might not feel terribly threatened by a thin net the way it would by, say, a solid metal crate.' He looked around the circle.

'I could put something together, weld it real quick.'

'He thinks we're going butterfly hunting,' Lambert sneered.

'How would we get it into the net?' Dallas asked quietly.

Brett considered. 'Have to use something that wouldn't make it bleed, of course. Knives and sharp probes of any kind are out. Same goes for pistols. I could make up a batch of long metal tubes with batteries in them. We've plenty of both somewhere back in stores. Only take a few hours.'

'For the rods and the net?'

'Sure. Nothing fancy involved.'

Lambert couldn't stand it. 'First butterflies, now cattle prods. Why do we listen to this meathead?'

Dallas turned the idea over in his head, visualizing it from the optimum. The alien cornered, threatening with teeth and claws. Electric jolts from one side, strong enough to irritate but not injure. Two of them driving it into the net, then keeping it occupied while the rest of them dragged it towards the main lock. Maybe the alien burning its way through the net, maybe not. Second and third nets standing by in case it did.

Tossing the sacked monster into the lock, sealing the hatch and blowing the emergency. Goodbye, alien, off to Arcturus. Goodbye, nightmare. Hello, Earth and sanity.

He recalled Lambert's last disparaging comment, said to no one in particular. 'We listen to him because this time he just might be right . . .'

The *Nostromo*, oblivious to the frantic activity of some of its passengers, equally indifferent to the resigned waiting of its others, continued racing towards Earth at a multiple of the speed of light. Brett had requested several hours to complete the net and shock tubes, but he and Parker worked as if they had only minutes. Parker found himself wishing the work at hand was actually more complex. It might have kept him from having so much time to glance nervously at ledges, cabinets and dark corridors.

Meanwhile, the rest of the crew could only focus their attention elsewhere and wait for the completion of their hunting gear. In several minds, the initial thought of 'Where has the alien gone?' was beginning to be replaced by ticking little thoughts like 'What is the alien doing?'

Only one member of the crew was otherwise mentally occupied. He'd held onto the thought for some time now, until it had swollen to the bursting point. Now he had two choices. He could discuss it with the entire crew, or discuss it alone with its cause. If he chose to do the first and found himself proven wrong, as he desperately wished to be, he might do irreparable damage to crew morale. Not to mention exposing himself to an eventual crew-member-captain lawsuit.

If he was right in his thinking, the others would find out about it soon enough.

Ash was seated at the central readout console of the infirmary, asking questions of the medical computer and occasionally getting an answer or two. He glanced up and smiled amiably at Dallas's entrance, then turned back to his work.

Dallas stood quietly alongside, his eyes switching from the sometimes incomprehensible readouts back to his science officer. The numbers and words and diagrams that flashed on the screens were easier to read than the man.

'Working or playing?'

'No time for play,' Ash replied with a straight face. He touched a button, was shown a long list of molecular chains for a particular hypothetical amino acid. A touch on another button caused two of the selected chains to commence a slow rotation in three dimensions.

'I scraped some samples from the sides of the first hole the hand alien ate through the deck.' He gestured back towards the tiny crater on the right side of the medical platform where the creature had bled.

'I think there was enough acid residue left to get a grip on, chemically speaking. If I can break down the structure, Mother might be able to suggest a formula for a nullifying reagent. Then our new visitor can bleed all over the place if we chose to blast him, and we can neutralize any acid it might leak.'

'Sounds great,' Dallas admitted, watching Ash closely. 'If anyone aboard can do it, you can.'

Ash shrugged indifferently. 'It's my job.'

Several minutes of silence passed. Ash saw no reason to resume the conversation. Dallas continued to study the readouts, finally said evenly, 'I want to talk.'

'I'll let you know the minute I find anything,' Ash assured him.

'That's not what I want to talk about.'

Ash looked up at him curiously, then turned back to his instrumentation as new information lit up two small screens. 'I think breaking down the structure of this acid is critical. I should think you would, too. Let's talk later. I'm pretty busy right now.'

Dallas paused before replying, said softly but firmly, 'I don't care. I want to talk *now*.'

Ash flipped several switches, watched gauges go dead and looked up at the captain. 'It's your neck I'm trying to save, too. But if it's that important, go ahead.'

'Why did you let the alien survive inside Kane?'

The science officer scowled. 'I'm not sure you're getting through to me. Nobody "let" anything survive inside anybody. It just happened.'

'Bullshit.'

Ash said drily, unimpressed, 'That's hardly a rational evaluation of the situation, one way or the other.'

'You know what I'm talking about. Mother was monitoring his body. You were monitoring Mother. That was proper, since you're the best-qualified to do so. You must've had some idea of what was going on.'

'Look, you saw the black stain on the monitor screen same time as I did.'

'You expect me to believe the autodoc didn't have enough power to penetrate that?'

'It's not a question of power but of wavelength. The alien was able to screen out those utilized by the autodoc's scanners. We've already discussed how and why that might be done.'

'Assuming I buy that business about the alien being able to generate a defensive field that would prevent scanning . . . and I'm not saying I do . . . Mother would find other indications of what was happening. Before he was killed, Kane complained of being ravenous. He proved it at the mess table. Isn't the reason for his fantastic appetite obvious?'

'Is it?'

'The new alien was drawing on Kane's supply of protein, nutrients and body fat to build its own body. It didn't grow to that size by metabolizing air.'

'I agree. That is obvious.'

'That kind of metabolic activity would generate proportionate readings on the autodoc's gauges, from simple reduction of Kane's body weight to other things.'

'As for a possible reduction of weight,' Ash replied calmly, 'no such reading would appear. Kane's weight was simply transferred into the alien. The autodoc scanner would register it all as Kane's. What "other things" are you referring to?'

Dallas tried to keep his frustration from showing, succeeded only partly. 'I don't know, I can't give you specifics. I'm only a pilot. Medical analysis isn't my department.'

'No,' said Ash significantly, 'it's mine.'

'I'm not a total idiot, either,' Dallas snapped back. 'Maybe I don't know the right words to say what I mean, but I'm not blind. I can see what's going on.'

Ash crossed his arms, kicked away from the console and stared hard at Dallas. 'What exactly are you trying to say?'

Dallas plunged ahead. 'You want the alien to stay alive. Badly enough to let it kill Kane. I figure you must have a reason. I've only known you a short time, Ash, but so far you've never done anything without a reason. I don't see you starting now.'

'You say I have a reason for this postulated insanity you're accusing me of. Name one.'

'Look, we both work for the same Company.' He changed his approach. Since accusation hadn't worked, he'd try playing on Ash's sense of sympathy. It occurred to Dallas that he might be coming off as just a touch paranoid there in the infirmary. It was easy to put the problem off on someone he could handle, like Ash, instead of where it belonged, on the alien.

Ash was a funny guy, but he wasn't acting like a murderer.

'I just want to know,' he concluded imploringly, 'what's going on.'

The science officer unfolded his arms, glanced momentarily back at his console before replying. 'I don't know what the hell you're talking about. And I don't care for any of the insinuations. The alien is a dangerous form of life. Admirable in many ways, sure. I won't deny that. As a scientist I find it fascinating. But after what it's done I don't want it to stay alive any more than you do.'

'You sure?'

'Yeah, I'm sure.' He sounded thoroughly disgusted. 'If you hadn't been under so much pressure here lately, you would be too. Forget it. I will.'

'Yeah.' Dallas turned sharply, exited out the open door and headed up the corridor towards the bridge. Ash watched him go, watched for long moments thinking concerned thoughts of his own. Then he turned his attention back to the patient, more easily understandable instrumentation.

Working too hard, too hard, Dallas told himself, his head throbbing. Ash was probably right that he'd been operating under too much pressure. It was true he was worrying about everyone else in addition to the problem of the alien. How much longer could he carry this kind of mental burden? How much longer should he try to? He was only a pilot.

Kane would make a better captain, he thought. Kane handled this kind of worry more easily, didn't ever let it get too deep inside him. But Kane wasn't around to help.

He thumbed a corridor intercom. A voice answered promptly.

'Engineering.'

'Dallas. How are you guys coming?'

Parker sounded noncommittal. 'We're coming.'

'Damn it, don't be flip! Be specific!'

'Hey, take it easy, Dallas. Sir. We're working as fast as we can. Brett can only complete circuits so fast. You want to corner that thing and touch it with a plain metal tube or with a couple hundred volts?'

'Sorry.' He meant it. 'Do your best.'

'Doing it for everybody. Engineering out.' The intercom went blank.

That had been thoroughly unnecessary, he told himself furiously. Embarrassing as well. If he didn't hold together, how could he expect any of the others to?

Right now he didn't feel like facing anybody, not after that disturbing and inconclusive encounter with Ash. He still had to decide in his own mind whether he was right about the science officer or whether he was a damn fool. Given the lack of a motive, he irritably suspected the latter. If Ash was lying, he was doing so superbly. Dallas had never seen a man so in control of his emotions.

There was one place on the *Nostromo* where Dallas could occasionally snatch a few moments of complete privacy and feel reasonably secure at the same time. Sort of a surrogate womb. He turned up B corridor, not so preoccupied with his own thoughts that he neglected to search constantly for small, sly movements in dark corners. But nothing showed itself.

Eventually he came to a place where the hull bulged slightly outward. There was a small hatch set there. He pressed the nearby switch, waited while the hatch slid aside. The inner hatch of the shuttlecraft was open. It was too small to possess a lock. He climbed in and sat down.

His hand covered another red stud on the shuttle's control panel, moved away without touching it. Activating the corridor hatch would already have registered on the bridge. That wouldn't alarm anyone who happened to notice it, but closing the shuttle's own hatch might. So he left it open to the corridor, feeling a small but comforting touch apart from the *Nostromo* and its resident horror and uncertainties . . .

# X

He was studying the remaining oxygen for the last time, hoping some unnoticed miracle would have added another zero to the remorseless number on the gauge. As he watched the counter conclude its work, the last digit in line blinked from nine to eight. There was a thumping sound from the entryway and he spun, relaxed when he saw it was Parker and Brett.

Parker dumped an armload of metal tubes onto the floor. Each was about twice the diameter of a man's thumb. They clattered hollowly, sounding and looking very little like weapons. Brett untangled himself from several metres of netting, looking pleased with himself.

'Here's the stuff. All tested and ready to go.'

Dallas nodded. 'I'll call the others.' He sounded general call to bridge, passed the time waiting for the rest of the crew to arrive in inspecting the collection of tubes doubtfully. Ash was the last to arrive, having the farthest to come.

'We're going to try to coerce that thing with *those*?' Lambert was pointing at the tubes, her tone leaving little doubt as to her opinion of their effectiveness.

'Give them a chance,' Dallas said. 'Everybody take one.' They lined up and Brett passed out the units. Each was about a metre and a half long. One end bulged with compact intrumentation and formed a crude handhold. Dallas swung the tube around like a sabre, getting the feel of it. It wasn't heavy, which made him feel better about it. He wanted something he could get between himself and the alien in a hurry, acidic expectorations or other unimaginable forms of defence notwithstanding. There is something illogical and primitive, but very comforting, about the feel of a club.

'I put oh-three-three portable chargers in each of these,' Brett said. 'The batteries will deliver a pretty substantial jolt. They won't require recharging unless you hold the discharge button down for a long time, and I mean a *long* time.' He indicated the handle of his own tube. 'So don't be afraid to use 'em.

'They're fully insulated up here at the grip and partway down the tube. Touching the tube will make you drop it quick if you've got it switched on, but there's another tube inside that's supercool conductive. That's where most of the charge will be carried. It'll deliver almost one hundred per cent of the discharged power to the far tip. So be goddamn careful not to get your hand on the end.'

'How about a demonstration?' asked Ripley.

'Yeah, sure.' The engineering tech touched the end of his tube to a conduit running across the nearest wall. A blue spark leaped from tube to duct, there was a satisfying loud *crack*, and a faint smell of ozone. Brett smiled.

'Yours have all been tested. They all work. You've got plenty of juice in those tubes.'

'Any way to modulate the voltage?' Dallas wondered.

Parker shook his head. 'We tried to approximate something punishing but not lethal. We don't know anything about this variety of the creature, and we didn't have time for installing niceties like current regulators, anyway. Each tube generates a single, unvariable charge. We're not miracle workers, you know.'

'First time I ever heard you admit it,' said Ripley. Parker threw her a sour look.

'It won't damage the little bastard unless its nervous system is a lot more sensitive than ours,' Brett told them. 'We're as sure

of that as we can be. Its parent was smaller and plenty tough.' He
hefted the tube, looking like an ancient gladiator about to enter
the arena. 'This'll just give it a little incentive. Of course, it won't
break my heart if we succeed in electrocuting the little darling.'

'Maybe it will work,' Lambert conceded. 'So that's our possible
solution to problem one. What about problem number two:
finding it?'

'I've taken care of that.' Everyone turned in surprise to see
Ash holding a small, communicator-sized device. Ash was
watching only Dallas, however. Unable to meet the science
officer's eyes, Dallas kept his attention single-mindedly focused
on the tiny device.

'Since it's imperative to locate the creature as soon as possible,
I've done some tinkering of my own. Brett and Parker have
done an admirable job in concocting a means for manipulating
the creature. Here is the means for finding it.'

'A portable tracker?' Ripley admired the compact instrument.
It looked as if it had been assembled in a factory, instead of
something hastily cobbled together in a commercial tug's science
lab.

Ash nodded once. 'You set it to search for a moving object. It
hasn't much range, but when you get within a certain distance it
starts beeping, and the volume increases proportionate to
decreasing distance from the target.'

Ripley took the tracker from the science officer's hand,
turned it over, and examined it with a professional eye. 'What
does it key on? How do we tell alien from fellow bitcher?'

'Two ways,' Ash explained proudly. 'As I mentioned, its range
is short. That could be considered a shortcoming, but in this
instance it works to our advantage, since it permits two parties to
search close by one another without the tracker picking up the
other group.

'More importantly, it incorporates a sensitive air-density
monitor. Any moving object will affect that. You can tell from
the reading which direction the object is moving. Just keep it
pointed ahead of you.

'It's not nearly as sophisticated an instrument as I wished to have, but it's the best I could come up with in the limited time available.'

'You did great, Ash,' Dallas had to admit. He took the proffered tracker from Ripley. 'This should be more than sufficient. How many did you make up?' By way of reply, Ash produced one duplicate of the device in the captain's palm.

'That means we can work two teams. Good. I don't have anything fancy to offer as far as instructions. You all know what to do as well as I. Whoever finds it first nets it, somehow gets it into the lock, and blows it towards Rigel as fast as the hatches will function. I don't care if you feel like using the explosive bolts on the outer door. We'll walk out in our suits if we have to.'

He started for the corridor, paused to look around the cramped, instrument-packed room. It seemed impossible that anything could have slipped in there without being noticed, but if they were going to make a thorough search, they'd do well not to make exceptions.

'For starters, let's make sure the bridge is clean.'

Parker held one of the trackers. He turned it on, swept it around the bridge, keeping his attention on the crudely marked gauge set into the unit's face.

'Six displacements,' he announced when the sweep had been completed. 'All positioned approximately where each of us is standing. We seem to be clean in here . . . if this damn thing works.'

Ash spoke without taking offence. 'It works. As you've just demonstrated.'

Additional equipment was passed around. Dallas surveyed the waiting men and women. 'Everybody ready?' There were a couple of whispered, sullen 'nos', and everyone smiled. Kane's grisly passing had already faded somewhat from their memories. This time they were prepared for the alien and, hopefully, armed with the right tools for the task.

'Channels are open on all decks.' Dallas started purposefully for the corridor. 'We'll keep in constant touch. Ash and I will go with Lambert and one tracker. Brett and Parker will make the second team. Ripley, you take charge of it and the other tracker.

'At the first sign of the creature, your priority is to capture it and get it to the lock. Notifying the other team is a secondary consideration. Let's do it.'

They filed out of the bridge.

The corridors on A level had never seemed quite so long or so dark before. They were as familiar to Dallas as the back of his hand, yet the knowledge that something deadly might be hiding back in the corners and storage chambers caused him to tread softly where he would otherwise have walked confidently with his eyes closed.

The lights were on, all of them. That did not brighten the corridor. They were service lights, for occasional use only. Why waste power to light up every corner of a working vessel like the *Nostromo* when its crew spent so little time awake? Enough light to see by during departure and arrival and during an occasional in-flight emergency had been provided. Dallas was grateful for the lumens he had, but that didn't keep him from lamenting the floodlights that weren't.

Lambert held the other side of the net, across from Dallas. The web stretched from one side of the corridor to the other. He clenched his own end a bit tighter and gave a sharp pull. Her head turned towards him, wide-eyed. Then she relaxed, nodded at him and turned her attention back down the corridor. She'd been dreaming, sinking into a sort of self-hypnosis, her mind so full of awful possibilities she'd forgotten completely the business at hand. She should be hunting through corners and niches of the ship, not her imagination. The alert look returned to her face, and Dallas turned his own full attention back to the nearing bend in the corridor.

Ash followed close behind them, his eyes on the tracker screen. In his hands it moved slowly from side to side, scanning from wall to wall. The instrument was silent, except when the science officer swung it a bit too far to left or right and it detected Lambert or Dallas. Then it beeped querulously until Ash touched a control and silenced it.

They paused by a down-spiralling companionway. Lambert leaned over, called out. 'Anything down there? We're as clean as your mother's reputation up here.'

Brett and Parker reset their grips on the net while Ripley paused ahead of them, took her gaze from the tracker and shouted upward. 'Nothing here either.'

Above, Lambert and Dallas moved on, Ash following. Their attention was completely on the approaching turn in the corridor. They didn't like those bends. They provided places of concealment. Turning one and discovering only empty corridor stretching bleakly beyond was to Lambert like finding the Holy Grail.

The tracker was growing heavy in Ripley's hands when a tiny light suddenly winked red below the main screen. She saw the gauge needle quiver. She was certain it was in the needle, not her hands. Then the needle gave a definite twitch, moved just a hair away from the zero end of the indicator scale.

She made sure the tracker wasn't picking up either Parker or Brett before saying anything. 'Hold it. I've got something.' She moved a few paces ahead.

The needle jumped clear across the scale and the red light came on and stayed on. She stood watching it, but it showed no sign of movement save for the slight changes in its chosen location. The red light remained strong.

Brett and Parker were staring down the corridor, inspecting walls, roof and floor. Everyone remembered how the first alien, though dead, had dropped onto Ripley. No one was willing to take the chance that this version couldn't also climb. So they kept their eyes constantly on ceiling as well as deck.

'Where's it coming from?' Brett asked quietly.

Ripley was frowning at the tracker. The indicator needle had suddenly commenced bouncing all over the scale. Unless the creature was travelling through solid walls, the needle's behaviour didn't square with the movements of anything living. She shook it firmly. It continued its bizarre behaviour. And the red light remained on.

'I don't know. The machine's screwed up. Needle's spinning all over the scale.'

Brett kicked at the net, cursed. 'Goddamn. We can't afford any malfunctions. I'll wring Ash's . . .'

'Hang on,' she urged him. She'd turned the device on its end. The needle stabilized immediately. 'It's working properly. It's just confused. Or rather, I was. The signal's coming from below us.' They looked down at their feet. Nothing erupted through the decking to attack them.

'That's C level,' Parker grumbled. 'Strictly maintenance. It's going to be a messy place to search.'

'Want to ignore it?'

He glared at her, but with no real anger this time. 'That's not funny.'

'No. No, it's not.' She spoke contritely. 'Lead on. You two know that level better than I.'

Parker and Brett, carefully holding the net ready between them, preceded her down the little-used companionway. C level was poorly illuminated even by the *Nostromo*'s sparse standards. They paused at the base of the companionway to let their eyes adjust to the near darkness.

Ripley touched a wall accidentally, pulled her hand away in disgust. It was coated with a thick, viscous slime. Old lubricants, she mused. A liner would've been shut down if an inspector had discovered such conditions on it. But nobody fooled with such leaks on a ship like the *Nostromo*. The lubricants couldn't bother anyone important. What was a little rarely encountered mess to a tug crew?

When they'd finished this run she promised herself she'd request and hold out for a transfer to a liner or else get out of the service. She knew she'd made the same promise twice a dozen times before. This time she'd stick to it.

She pointed the tracker down the corridor. Nothing. When she turned it to face up the corridor, the red light winked back on. The illuminated needle registered a clear reading.

'Okay, let's go.' She started off, having confidence in the little needle because she knew Ash did solid work, because the device had functioned well thus far, and because she had no choice.

'We'll hit a split pretty soon,' Brett cautioned her.

Several minutes passed. The corridor became two. She used the tracker, started down the right-hand passage. The red light began to fade. She turned, headed down the other corridor. 'Back this way.'

The lights were scarcer still in this section of the ship. Deep shadows pressed tightly around them, suffocating despite the fact that no one trained to ship in deep space is subject to claustrophobia. Their steps clanged on the metal decking, were muffled only when they waded through slick pools of accumulated fluid.

'Dallas ought to demand an inspection,' Parker muttered disgustedly. 'They'd condemn forty per cent of the ship and then the Company would *have* to pay to clean it up.'

Ripley shook her head, threw the engineer a sceptical look. 'Want to bet? Be cheaper and easier for the Company to buy off the inspector.'

Parker fought to hide his disappointment. Another of his seemingly brilliant ideas shot down. The worst part of it was, Ripley's logic was usually unassailable. His resentment and admiration for her grew in proportion to one another.

'Speaking of fixing and cleaning up,' she continued, 'what's wrong with the lights? I said I wasn't familiar with this part of the ship, but you can hardly see your own nose here. I thought you guys fixed twelve module. We should have better illumination than this, even down here.'

'We did fix it,' Brett protested.

Parker moved to squint at a nearby panel. 'Delivery system must be acting cautious. Some of the circuits haven't been receiving their usual steady current, you know. It was tough enough to restore power without blowing every conductor on the ship. When things get tricky, affected systems restrict their acceptance of power to prevent overloads. This one's overdoing it, though. We can fix it.'

He touched a switch on the panel, cut in an override. The light in the corridor grew brighter.

They travelled further before Ripley abruptly halted and threw up a cautionary hand. 'Wait.'

Parker nearly fell in his haste to obey, and Brett almost stumbled in the netting. Nobody laughed or came near to doing so.

'We're close?' Parker whispered the question, straining with inadequate eyes to penetrate the blackness ahead.

Ripley checked the needle, matched it to Ash's hand-engraved scale etched into the metal alongside the illuminated screen. 'According to this it's within fifteen metres.'

Parker and Brett tightened their hold on the net without being told to. Ripley hefted her tube, switched it on. She moved slowly forward with the tube in her right hand and the tracker in the other. It was hard, oh, impossibly hard, to imagine any three people making less noise than Ripley, Parker and Brett were making in that corridor. Even the previous steady pantings of their lungs were muted.

They covered five metres, then ten. A muscle in Ripley's left calf jumped like a grasshopper, hurting her. She ignored it. They continued on, the distance as computed by the tracker shrinking irrevocably.

Now she was walking in a half crouch, ready to spring backward the instant any fragment of the darkness gave hint of movement. The tracker, its beeper now intentionally turned off, brought her to a halt at the end of fifteen point two metres. The light here was still dim, but sufficient to show them that nothing cowered in the malodorous corridor.

Slowly turning the tracker, she tried to watch both it and the far end of the passage. The needle shifted minutely on the dial.

She raised her gaze, noticed a small hatch set into the corridor wall. It was slightly ajar.

Parker and Brett noted where her attention was concentrated. They positioned themselves to cover as much of the deck in front of the hatch as possible. Ripley nodded at them when they were set, trying to shake some of the dripping perspiration from her face. She took a deep breath and set the tracker on the floor. With her free hand she grasped the hatch handle. It was cold and clammy against her already damp palm.

Raising the prod, she depressed the button on its handle end, slammed herself against the corridor wall, and jammed the metal tube inside the locker. A horrible squealing sounded loudly in the corridor. A small creature that was all bulging eyes and flashing claws exploded from the locker. It landed neatly in the middle of the net as a frantic pair of engineers fought to envelop it in as many layers of the rough strands as possible.

'Hang on, hang on!' Parker was shouting triumphantly. 'We got the little bastard, we. . .!'

Ripley was peering into the net. A great surge of disappointment went through her. She turned off the tube, picked up the tracker again.

'Goddman it,' she muttered tiredly. 'Relax, you two. Look at it.'

Parker let go of the net at the same time as Brett. Both had seen what they'd caught and were mumbling angrily. A very annoyed cat shot out of the entangling webwork, ran hissing and spitting back up the corridor before Ripley could protest.

'No, no.' She tried, too late, to instruct them. 'Don't let it get away.'

A faint flicker of orange fur vanished into the distance.

'Yeah, you're right,' agreed Parker. 'We should have killed it. Now we might pick it up on the tracker again.'

Ripley glanced sharply at him, said nothing. Then she turned her attention to the less homicidally inclined Brett. 'You go get him. We can debate what to do with him later, but it would be a good idea to keep him around or penned up in his box so he can't confuse the machine . . . or us.'

Brett nodded. 'Right.'

He turned and trotted back up the passageway after the cat. Ripley and Parker continued slowly in the opposite direction, Ripley trying to handle tracker and tube and help Parker with the net at the same time.

An open door led into a large equipment maintenance bay. Brett took a last look up and down the corridor, saw no sign of the cat. On the other hand, the loosely stocked chamber was full of ideal cat hiding places. If the cat wasn't inside, he'd rejoin the others, he decided. It could be anywhere on the ship by now. But the equipment bay was a logical place for it to take refuge.

There was light inside, though no brighter than in the corridor. Brett ignored the rows of stacked instrument pods, the carelessly bundled containers of solid-state replacement modules and dirty tools. Luminescent panels identified contents.

It occurred to him that by now his two companions were probably out of earshot. The thought made him jittery. The sooner he got his hands on that damned cat, the better.

'Jones . . . here, kitty, kitty. Jones cat. Come to Brett, kitty, kitty.' he bent to peer into a dark crevice between two huge crates. The slit was deserted. Rising, he wiped sweat from his eyes, first the left, then the right. 'Goddamn it, Jones,' he muttered softly, 'where the hell are you hiding?'

Scratching noises, deeper in the bay. They were followed by an uncertain but reassuring yowl that was unmistakably feline in origin. He let out a relieved breath and started for the source of the cry.

Ripley halted, looked tiredly at the tracker screen. The red light had gone out, the needle again rested on zero, and the beeper hadn't sounded in a long time. As she stared, the needle quivered once, then lay still.

'Nothing here,' she told her remaining retiarius. 'If there ever was anything here besides us and Jones.' She looked at Parker. 'I'm open to suggestions.'

'Let's go back. The least we can do is help Brett run down that friggin' cat.'

'Don't pick on Jones.' Ripley automatically defended the animal. 'He's as frightened as the rest of us.'

They turned and headed back up the stinking corridor. Ripley left the tracker on, just in case.

Brett had worked his way behind the stacks of equipment. He couldn't go much further. Struts and supports for the upper superstructure of the *Nostromo* formed an intricate criss-cross of metal around him.

He was getting discouraged all over again when another familiar yowl reached him. Turning a metal pylon, he saw two small yellow eyes shining in the dark. For an instant he hesitated. Jones was about the size of the thing that had burst from poor Kane's chest. Another miaow made him feel better. Only an ordinary tomcat would produce a noise like that.

As he worked his way nearer he bent to clear a beam and had a glimpse of fur and whiskers: Jones.

'Here kitty . . . good to see you, you furry little bastard.' He reached for the cat. It hissed threateningly at him and backed farther into its corner. 'Come on, Jones. Come to Brett. No time to fool around now.'

Something not quite as thick as the beam the engineering tech had passed under reached downward. It descended in utter silence and conveyed a feeling of tremendous power held in check. Fingers spread, clutched, wrapped completely around the engineer's throat and crossed over themselves. Brett shrieked, both hands going reflexively to his neck. For all the effect his hands had on them, those gripping fingers might as well have been welded together. He went up in that hand, legs dancing in empty air. Jones bolted beneath him.

The cat shot past Ripley and Parker, who'd just arrived. They plunged unthinking into the equipment bay. Soon they were standing where they'd seen Brett's legs flailing moments before. Staring up into blackness, they had a last brief glimpse of dangling feet and twisting torso receding upward. Above the helpless figure of the engineer was a faint outline, something man-shaped but definitely not a man. Something huge and malevolent. There was a split-second's sight of light reflecting off eyes far too big for even a huge head. Then both alien and engineer had vanished into the upper reaches of the *Nostromo*.

'Jesus,' Parker whispered.

'It grew.' Ripley looked blankly at her shock tube, considered it in relation to the hulking mass far above. 'It grew *fast*. All the time we were hunting for something Jones's size, it had turned into *that*.' She suddenly grew aware of their restricted space, of the darkness and massive crates pressing tight around them, of the numerous passages between crates and thick metal supports.

'What are we doing standing here? It may come back.' She hefted the toylike tube, aware of how little effect it would be likely to have on a creature that size.

They hurried from the bay. Try as they would, the memory of that last fading scream stayed with them, glued to their minds. Parker had known Brett a long time, but that final shriek induced him to run as fast as Ripley . . .

# XI

There was less confidence in the faces of those assembled in the mess room than last time. No one tried to hide it, least of all Parker and Ripley. Having seen what they were now confronted by, they retained very little in the way of confidence at all.

Dallas was examining a recently printed schematic of the *Nostromo*. Parker stood by the door, occasionally glancing nervously down the corridor.

'Whatever it was,' the engineer said into the silence, 'it was big. Swung down on him like a giant fucking bat.'

Dallas looked up from the layout. 'You're absolutely sure it dragged Brett into a vent.'

'It disappeared into one of the cooling ducts.' Ripley was scratching the back of one hand with the other. 'I'm sure I saw it go in. Anyway, there was nowhere else for it to go.'

'No question about it,' Parker added. 'It's using the air shafts to move around. That's why we never ran it down with the tracker.'

'The air shafts.' Dallas looked convinced. 'Makes sense. Jones does the same thing.'

Lambert played with her coffee, stirring the dark liquid with an idle finger. 'Brett could still be alive.'

'Not a chance.' Ripley wasn't being fatalistic, only logical. 'It snapped him up like a rag doll.'

'What does it want him for, anyway?' Lambert wanted to

know. 'Why take him instead of killing him on the spot?'

'Perhaps it requires an incubator, the way the first form used Kane,' Ash suggested.

'Or food,' said Ripley tightly. She shivered.

Lambert put down her coffee. 'Either way, it's two down and five to go, from the alien's standpoint.'

Parker had been turning his shock tube over and over in his hands, now he turned and threw it hard against a wall. It bent, fell to the deck and crackled a couple of times before lying still.

'I say we blast the rotten bastard with a laser and take our chances.'

Dallas tried to sound sympathetic. 'I know how you feel, Parker. We all liked Brett. But we've got to keep our heads. If the creature's now as big as you say, it's holding enough acid to burn a hole in the ship as big as this room. Not to mention what it would do to circuitry and controls running through the decks. No way can we chance that. Not yet.'

'Not yet?' Parker's sense of helplessness cancelled out much of his fury. 'How many have to die besides Brett before you can see that's the way to handle that thing?'

'It wouldn't work anyway, Parker.'

The engineer turned to face Ash, frowned at him. 'What do you mean?'

'I mean you'd have to hit a vital organ with a laser on your first shot. From your description of the creature it's now extremely fast as well as large and powerful. I think it's reasonable to assume it retains the same capacity for rapid regeneration as its first "hand" form. That means you'd have to kill it instantly or it would be all over you.

'Not only would that be difficult to do if your opponent were a mere man, it's also virtually impossible to do with this alien because we have no idea where its vital point is. We don't even know that it has a vital point. Don't you see?' He was trying to be understanding, like Dallas had been. Everyone knew how close the two engineers had been.

'Can't you envision what would happen? Let's say a couple of us succeeded in confronting the creature in an open area where we can get a clear shot at it, which is by no means a certainty. We laser it, oh, half a dozen times before it tears us all to pieces. All six wounds heal fast enough to preserve the alien's life, but not before it's bled enough acid to eat numerous holes in the ship. Maybe some of the stuff burns through the circuitry monitoring our air supply, or cuts the power to the ship's lights.

'I don't consider that an unreasonable scenario, given what we know about the creature. And what's the result? We've lost two or more people and shipwise we're worse off than we were before we confronted it.'

Parker didn't reply, looked sullen. Finally he mumbled, 'Then what the hell are we going to do?'

'The only plan that stands a chance of working is the one we had before,' Dallas told him. He tapped the schematic. 'Find which shaft it's in, then drive it from there into an air lock and blast it into space.'

'Drive it?' Parker laughed hollowly. 'I'm telling you the son-of-a-bitch is *huge*.' He spat contemptuously at his bent shock tube. 'We aren't driving that thing anywhere with those.'

'For once he has a point,' said Lambert. 'We have to get it to a lock. How *do* we drive it?'

Ripley's gaze travelled around the little cluster of humanity. 'I think it's time the science department brought us up to date on our visitor. Haven't you got any ideas, Ash?'

The science officer considered. 'Well, it seems to have adapted well to an oxygen-rich atmosphere. That may have something to do with its spectacularly rapid growth in this stage.'

'This "stage"?' Lambert echoed questioningly. 'You mean it might turn into something else again?'

Ash spread his hands. 'We know so little about it. We should be prepared for anything. It has already metamorphosed three times; egg to hand-shape, hand to the thing that came out of Kane, and that into this much larger bipedal form. We have no reason to assume that this form is the final stage in the chain of development.' He paused, added, 'The next form it assumes could conceivably be even larger and more powerful.'

'That's encouraging,' murmured Ripley. 'What else?'

'In addition to its new atmosphere, it's certainly adapted well for its nutritional requirements. So we know it can exist on very little, in various atmospheres, and possibly in none at all for an unspecified period of time.

'About the only thing we don't know is its ability to handle drastic changes in temperature. It's comfortably warm aboard the *Nostromo*. Considering the mean temperature on the world where we discovered it, I think we can reasonably rule out bitter cold as a potential deterrent, though the early egg form may have been tougher in that respect than the present one. There is precedent for that.'

'All right,' asked Ripley, 'what about the temperature? What happens if we raise it?'

'Let's give it a try,' said Ash. 'We can't raise the temperature of the entire ship for the same reasons we couldn't exhaust all the air. Not enough air time in our suits, limited mobility, helplessness while confined in the freezers and so on. But most creatures retreat from fire. It's not necessary to heat the whole ship.'

'We could string a high-voltage wire across a few corridors and lure it into one. That would fry it good,' Lambert suggested.

'This isn't an animal we're dealing with. Or if it is,' Ash told her, 'it's a supremely skilful one. It's not going to charge blindly into a cord or anything else blocking an obvious transit way like a corridor. It's already demonstrated that by choosing the air shafts to travel about in, instead of the corridors.

'Besides, certain primitive organisms like the shark are sensitive to electric fields. On balance, not a good idea.'

'Maybe it can detect the electrical fields our own bodies generate,' said Ripley gloomily. 'Maybe that's how it tracks.'

Parker looked doubtful. 'I wouldn't bet that it didn't depend on its eyes. If that's what those things are.'

'They aren't,' said Ripley.

'A creature so obviously resourceful probably utilizes many senses in tracking,' Ash added.

'I don't like the cord idea anyway.' Parker's face was flushed. 'I don't like tricking around. When it goes out the lock, I want to be there. I want to see it die.' He went quiet for a bit, added less emotionally, 'I want to hear it scream like Brett.'

'How long to hook up three or four incinerating units?' Dallas wanted to know.

'Give me twenty minutes. The basic units are already there, in storage. It's just a question of modifying them for hand-held use.'

'Can you make them powerful enough? We don't want to run into the kind of situation Ash described, if we were using lasers. We want something that'll stop it in its tracks.'

'Don't worry.' Parker's voice was cold, cold. 'I'll fix them so they'll cook anything they touch on contact.'

'Seems like our best chance, then.' The captain glanced around the table. 'Anyone got any better ideas?'

No one had.

'Okay.' Dallas pushed away from the table, rose. 'When Parker's ready with his flamethrowers, we'll start from here and work our way back down to C level and the bay where it took Brett. Then we'll try to trace it from there.'

Parker sounded dubious. 'It went up with him through the hull bracing before it entered the air shaft. Be hell trying to follow it up there. I'm no ape.' He stared warningly at Ripley, but she didn't comment.

'You rather sit here and wait until it's ready to come looking for you?' Dallas asked. 'The longer we can keep it on the defensive, the better it'll be for us.'

'Except for one thing,' Ripley said.

'What's that?'

'We're not sure it's ever been on the defensive.' She met his gaze squarely . . .

The flamethrowers were bulkier than the shock tubes and looked less effective. But the tubes had functioned as they were supposed to, and Parker had assured them all the incinerators would too. He declined to give them a demonstration this time because, he explained, the flamers were powerful enough to sear the decking.

The fact that he was trusting his own life to the devices was proof enough anyway, for everyone except Ripley. She was beginning to be suspicious of everyone and everything. She'd always been a little paranoid. Current events were making it worse. She began to worry as much over what was happening to her mind as she was about the alien.

Of course, as soon as they found and killed the alien, the mental problems would vanish. Wouldn't they?

The tight knot of edgy humanity worked its cautious way down from the mess to B level. They were heading for the next companionway when both tracking devices commenced a frantic beeping. Ash and Ripley quickly shut off the beepers. They had to follow the shifting needles only a dozen metres before a louder, different sound became audible, metal tearing.

'Easy.' Dallas cradled his flamethrower, turned the corner in the corridor. Loud rending noises continued, more clearly now. He knew where they were originating. 'The food locker,' he whispered back to them. 'It's inside.'

'Listen to that,' Lambert murmured in awe. 'Jesus, it must be big.'

'Big enough,' agreed Parker softly. 'I saw it, remember. And strong. It carried Brett like . . .' He cut off in mid-sentence, thoughts of Brett choking off any desire for conversation.

Dallas raised the nozzle of his flamethrower. 'There's a duct opening into the back of the locker. That's how it got here.' He glanced over at Brett. 'You sure these things are working?'

'I made them, didn't I?'

'That's what worries us,' said Ripley.

They moved forward. The tearing sounds continued. When they were positioned just outside the locker, Dallas glanced from Parker to the door handle. The engineer reluctantly got a grip on the heavy protrusion. Dallas stood back a couple of steps, readied the flamethrower.

'Now!'

Parker wrenched open the door, jumped back out of the way. Dallas thumbed the firing stud on the clumsy weapon. A startlingly wide fan of orange fire filled the entrance to the food locker, causing everyone to draw away from the intense heat. Dallas moved forward quickly, ignoring the lingering heat that burned his throat, and fired another blast inside. Then a third. He was over the raised base now and had to twist himself so he could fire sideways.

Several minutes were spent nervously waiting outside for the locker's interior to cool enough for them to enter. Despite the wait, the heat radiating from the smouldering garbage inside was so intense they had to walk carefully lest they bump into any of the oven-hot crates or the locker walls.

The locker itself was a total loss. What the alien had begun, Dallas's flamethrower had finished. Deep black streaks showed on the walls, testimony to the concentrated power of the incinerator. The stench of charred artificial-food components mixed with carbonized packaging was overpowering in the confined space.

Despite the havoc wrought by the flamethrower, not everything within the locker had been destroyed. Ample evidence of the alien's handiwork lay scattered about, untouched by the flames. Packages of every size were strewn about the floor, opened in ways and by means their manufacturers had never envisioned.

Solid-metal storage 'tins' (so called because of tradition and not their metallurgical make-up) had been peeled apart like fruit. From what they could see, the alien hadn't left much intact for the flamethrower to finish off.

Keeping trackers and incinerators handy, they poked through the debris. Pungent smoke drifted upward and burned their eyes.

Careful inspection of every sizeable pile of ruined supplies failed to produce the hoped-for discovery.

Since all the food stocked aboard the *Nostromo* was artificial and homogenous in composition, the only bones they would find would belong to the alien. But the closest thing they found to bones were the reinforcing bands from several large crates.

Ripley and Lambert started to relax against a still-hot wall, remembered not to. 'We didn't get it,' the warrant officer muttered disappointedly.

'Then where the hell is it?' Lambert asked her.

'Over here.'

They all turned to see Dallas standing near the back wall, behind a pile of melted black plastic. His flamethrower was pointing at the wall. 'This is where it went.'

Moving over, Ripley and the others saw that Dallas's frame was blocking the expected ventilator opening. The protective grille that normally covered the gap was lying on the floor below it, in pieces.

Dallas removed the lightbar from his belt, directed the beam into the shaft. It revealed only smooth metal twisting off into the distance. When he spoke he sounded excited.

'About time we got a break.'

'What are you talking about?' Lambert asked.

He looked back at them. 'Don't you see? This could end up working for us. This duct comes out at the main air-lock. There's only one other opening large enough along the way for the creature to escape through, and we can cover that. Then we drive it into the lock with the flamethrowers and blast it into space.'

'Yeah.' Lambert's tone indicated she didn't share the captain's enthusiasm for the project. 'Nothing to it. All you have to do is crawl into the vent after it, find your way through the maze until you're staring it in the face, and then pray it's afraid of fire.'

Dallas's smile waned. 'The addition of the human element sort of kills the simplicity of it, doesn't it? But it should work, given that it's fearful of fire. It's our best chance. This way we don't have to back it into a corner and hope the flames will kill it in time. It can keep on retreating ... right towards the waiting lock.'

'That's all fine and good,' agreed Lambert. 'The problem is: Who goes in after it?'

Dallas searched the group, hunting for a prospect to engage in the lethal game of tag. Ash had the coolest nerves of the lot, but Dallas still harboured suspicions about the science officer. Anyway, Ash's project to find a nullifier for the creature's acid ruled him out as a candidate for the chase.

Lambert put up a tough front, but was more likely to go to pieces under stress than any of the others. As for Ripley, she'd be fine up to the moment of actual confrontation. He wasn't sure whether she'd freeze or not. He didn't think that she would . . . but could he risk her life on that?

Parker ... Parker'd always pretended to be a tough son-of-a-bitch. He complained a lot, but he could do a rough job and do it right when he had to. Witness the shock tubes and now the flamethrowers. Besides, it was his friend who'd been taken by the alien. And he knew the quirks of the flamethrowers better than any of them.

'Well, Parker, you always wanted a full share and a trip's-end bonus.'

'Yeah?' The engineer sounded wary.

'Get in the pipe.'

'Why me?'

Dallas thought of giving his several reasons, decided to keep it simple instead. 'I just want to see you earn your full share, that's all.'

Parker shook his head, took a step backward. 'No way. You can have my share. You can have my whole salary for the trip.' He jerked his head in the direction of the shaft opening. 'I'm not going in there.'

'I'll go.' Dallas eyed Ripley. She figured to volunteer sooner or later. Funny lady. He'd always underestimated her. Everyone did.

'Forget it.'

'Why?' She looked resentful.

'Yeah, why?' put in Parker. 'If she's ready to go, why not let her go?'

'My decison,' he explained tersely. He looked at her, saw the mixture of resentment and confusion. She didn't understand why he'd turned her down. Well, no matter. Someday maybe he'd explain. If he could explain it to himself.

'You take the air lock,' he directed her. 'Ash, you'll stay here and cover this end in case it gets behind me somehow, or through me. Parker, you and Lambert cover the one side exit I told you about.'

They all regarded him with various looks of understanding. There was no doubt who was going into the vent.

Panting, Ripley reached the vestibule by the starboard lock. A glance at her tracker showed no movement in the area. She touched a nearby red switch. A soft hum filled that section of corridor. The massive lock door moved aside. When it was clear and the hum had died she thumbed the intercom.

'Ready starboard airlock.'

Parker and Lambert reached the section of corridor specified by Dallas, halted. The vent opening, grille-covered and innocent-looking, showed in the wall three quarters of the way up.

'That's where it'll be coming out, if it tries this way,' Parker observed. Lambert nodded, moved to the nearby 'com pickup to report that they were in position.

Back in the food locker, Dallas listened intently as Lambert's report followed Ripley's. Dallas asked a couple of questions, acknowledged the answers and switched off. Ash handed him his flamethrower. Dallas adjusted the nozzle and fired a couple of quick, short bursts.

'It's still working. Parker's a better applied machinist than even he thinks he is.' He noticed the expression on Ash's face. 'Something the matter?'

'You've made your decision. It's not my place to comment.'

'You're the science officer. Go ahead and comment.'

'This has nothing to do with science.'

'This is no time to hedge. Say what's on your mind.'

Ash eyed him with genuine curiosity. 'Why do you have to be the one to go? Why didn't you send Ripley? She was willing, and she's competent enough.'

'I shouldn't even have suggested anyone but myself.' He was checking the fluid level on the flamethrower. 'That was a mistake. It's my responsibility. I let Kane go down into the alien ship. Now it's my turn. I've delegated enough risk without taking any on myself. It's time I did.'

'You're the captain,' Ash argued. 'This is a time to be practical, not heroic. You did the proper thing in sending Kane. Why change now?'

Dallas grinned at him. It wasn't often you could catch Ash in a contradiction. 'You're hardly the one to be talking about proper procedure. You opened the lock and let us back into the ship, remember?' The science officer didn't reply. 'So don't lecture me on what's proper.'

'It'll be harder on the rest of us if we lose you. Especially now.'

'You just mentioned that you thought Ripley was competent. I concur. She's next in line of command. If I don't make it back, there's nothing I do that she can't.'

'I don't agree.'

They were wasting time. No telling how far ahead of him the creature was by now. Dallas was tired of arguing. 'Tough. That's my decision, and it's final.' He turned, put his right foot into the shaft opening, then slid the flamethrower in ahead of him, making sure it didn't slide on the slightly downward-inclining surface.

'Won't work like that,' he grumbled, peering in. 'Not enough room to crouch.' He removed his leg. 'Have to crawl it.' He ducked his head and wriggled into the opening.

There was less room in the shaft than he'd hoped. How something of the size Parker and Ripley had described had squirmed through the tiny crawlspace he couldn't imagine. Well, good! Dallas hoped the shaft would continue to narrow. Maybe the creature, in its haste to escape, would get itself wedged good and tight. That would make things simpler.

'How is it?' a voice called from behind him.

'Not too good,' he informed Ash, his voice reverberating around him. Dallas struggled into a crawling posture. 'It's just big enough to be uncomfortable.'

He switched on his lightbar, fumbled anxiously for a moment before locating the throat mike he'd slipped on. The light showed dark, empty shaft ahead of him, travelling in a straight metallic line with a slight downward curve. The incline would increase, he knew. He had a full deck level to descend before emerging behind the creature outside the starboard lock.

'Ripley, Parker, Lambert . . . are you receiving me? I'm in the shaft now, preparing to descend.'

Below, Lambert addressed the wall 'com, 'We read you. I'll try to pick you up as soon as you come within range of our tracker.' Next to her, Parker hefted his flamethower and glared at the grille covering the duct.

'Parker,' Dallas instructed the engineer, 'if it tries to come out by you two, make sure you drive it back in. I'll keep pushing it forward.'

'Right.'

'Ready by the lock,' Ripley reported. 'She's standing open and waiting for company.'

'It's on its way.' Dallas started crawling, his eyes on the tunnel ahead, fingers on the controls of the incinerator. The shaft here was less than a metre wide. Metal rubbed insistently at his knees and he wished he'd donned an extra pair of overalls. Too late for that now, he mused. Everyone was ready and prepared. He wasn't going back.

'How you doing?' a voice sounded over his mike speaker.

'Okay, Ash,' he told the anxious science officer. 'Don't worry about me. Keep your eyes on that opening in case it's slipped behind me somehow.'

He turned his first bend in the shaft, fighting to see in his head the exact layout of the ship's ventilating system. The printed schematic back in the mess was fuzzy and indistinct in his memory. The vents were hardly among the ship's critical systems. It was too late to wish that he'd taken more time to study them.

Several more tight turns showed in the shaft ahead of him. He paused, breathing heavily, and raised the tip of the flamethrower. There was nothing to indicate that anything lay hiding behind those bends, but it was better not to take chances. The incinerator's fuel level read almost full. It wouldn't hurt to let the creature know what was following close behind it, maybe drive it forward without having to face it.

A touch on the red button sent a gout of flame down the tunnel. The roar was loud in the constricted shaft, and heat rushed back across his protesting skin. He started forward again, taking care to keep his ungloved hands off the now hot metal he was crawling over. A little heat even penetrated the tough fabric of his pants. He didn't feel it. His senses were all concentrated forward, searching for movement and smell.

In the equipment area, Lambert thoughtfully regarded the tightly screened opening. She reached back, threw a switch. There was a hum and the metal grille slid out of sight, leaving a gaping hole in the wall.

'Are you crazy?' Parker eyed her uncertainly.

'That's the one it's got to come out of if it leaves the main shaft,' she told him. 'Let's keep it open. It's too dark behind the grille. I'd like to know if anything's coming.'

Parker thought to argue, decided his energy would be better spent keeping an eye on the opening, grilled or unblocked. Anyway, Lambert outranked him.

Sweat was seeping into his eyes, persistent as ants, and Dallas had to stop to wipe it away. Salt burned, impairing his sight. Ahead, the shaft turned steeply downward. He'd been expecting the downturn about now, but the satisfaction of having his memory confirmed gave him little pleasure. Now he'd have to watch his speed and balance in addition to the shaft itself.

Crawling to the drop, he pointed the flamethrower downward and let loose another fiery discharge. No screams, no aroma of seared flesh drifted back up to him. The creature was still far ahead. He wondered if it were crawling, perhaps angrily, perhaps fearfully, in search of the exit. Or maybe it was waiting, turned to confront its persistent pursuer with unconceivable methods of alien defence.

It was hot in the shaft, and he was growing tired. There was another possibility, he mused. What if the creature had somehow discovered another way to leave the shaft? In that event he'd have made the tense, agonizing crawl for nothing. There was still only one way to resolve all the questions. He started down the steep slide head first, keeping the flamethrower balanced and pointing forward.

It was Lambert who first noticed the movement of the tracker needle. She had a nervous minute until some hasty figuring matched the reading with a known quantity.

'Beginning to get a reading on you,' she informed the distant Dallas.

Okay.' He felt better, knowing that others knew exactly where he was. 'Stay on me.'

The shaft made another turn. He didn't recall there being quite so many twists and sharp bends, but he was positive he was still in the main shaft. He hadn't passed a single side tunnel wide enough to admit anything larger than Jones. Despite the alien's demonstrated aptitude for squeezing into small spaces, Dallas didn't think it could shrink its bulk enough to fit into a secondary vent pipe only a dozen or so centimetres across.

The present turn confronting him proved especially difficult to negotiate. The long, inflexible barrel of the flamethrower didn't make it any easier. Panting, he lay there and considered how to proceed.

'Ripley.'

She jerked at the sharpness in his voice, spoke hurriedly into the 'com pickup. 'I'm here. Reading you clearly. Anything wrong? You sound . . .' she caught herself. How else should Dallas sound except nervous?

'I'm okay,' he told her. 'Just tired. Out of shape. Too many weeks in hypersleep, you lose your muscle tone no matter what the freezers do for you.' He wriggled into a new position, gained a better view ahead.

'I don't think this shaft goes much further. It's getting hot in here.' That was to be expected, he told himself. The accumulated effect of multiple blasts from his flamethrower would tax the internal cooking capacity of the shaft's thermostats.

'Continuing on now. Stay ready.'

An onlooker could easily have read the relief in Dallas's face when he finally emerged from the cramped tunnel. It opened into one of the *Nostromo*'s main air ducts, a two-tiered tunnel split by a catwalk. He crawled out of the shaft and stood on the railless walkway, stretched gratefully.

A careful inspection of the larger passage proved negative. The only sound he heard was the patient throbbing of cooling machinery. There was a repair junction part-way down the walk and he strolled out to it, repeated his inspection there. As far as he could see, the huge chamber was empty.

Nothing could sneak up on him here, not while he was standing in the centre of the room. It would be a good place to grab a couple of minutes of much-needed rest. He sat down on the catwalk, casually examining the level floor below the junction, and spoke towards the throat mike.

'Lambert, what kind of reading are you getting? I'm in one of the central mixing chambers, at the repair station in the centre. Nothing here but me.'

The navigator glanced at her tracker, looked suddenly puzzled. She glanced worriedly at Parker, thrust the device under his gaze. 'Can you make any sense out of this?'

Parker studied the needle and readout. 'Not me. That's not my toy, it's Ash's. Confusing, though.'

'Lambert?' Dallas again.

'Here. I'm not sure.' She jiggled the tracker. The reading remained as incomprehensible as before. 'There seems to be some kind of double signal.'

'That's crazy. Are you getting two separate, distinct readings for me?'

'No. Just one impossible one.'

'It may be interference,' he told her. 'The way the air's shifting around in here, it could confuse the hell out of a jury-rigged machine designed to read air density. I'll push on ahead. It'll probably clear up as soon as I move.'

He rose, not seeing the massive, clawed hand rising slowly from the catwalk under him. The groping paw just missed his left foot as he continued onward. It drifted back beneath the walkway as silently as it had appeared.

Dallas had walked halfway to the end of the chamber. Now he stopped. 'Is that better, Lambert? I've moved. Am I registering any clearer now?'

'It's clear, all right.' Her voice was strained. 'But I'm still getting a double signal, and I think they're distinct. I'm not sure which one is which.'

Dallas whirled, his eyes darting around the tunnel, canvassing ceiling, floor, walls and the large shaft opening he'd just emerged from. Then he looked back down the catwalk to the repair junction, his gaze settling on the spot where he'd been sitting just seconds ago.

He lowered the nose of the flamethrower. If he was now the front signal, having moved down the catwalk, then the cause of the double signal ought to be . . . his finger started to tense on the incinerator's trigger.

A hand reached up from below and behind, toward his ankle.

The alien was the front signal.

Ripley stood alone by the duct, watching it and thinking of the open airlock standing ready nearby. There was a distant ringing sound. At first she thought it was inside her head, where funny noises often originated. Then it was repeated, louder, and followed by an echo this time. It seemed to be coming from deep within the shaft. Her hands tensed on the flamethrower.

The ringing ceased. Against her better judgement she moved a little closer to the opening, keeping the nozzle of the flamethrower focused on it.

There came a recognizable sound. A scream. She recognized the voice.

Forgetting all carefully laid plans, all sensible procedure, she ran the rest of the way to the opening. 'Dallas . . . Dallas!'

There were no more screams after the first. Only a soft, far-off thumping, which rapidly faded away. She checked her tracker. It displayed a single blip, the red colour also fading fast. Just like the scream.

'Oh my God. Parker, Lambert!' She rushed towards the pickup, yelled into the grid.

'Here, Ripley,' responded Lambert. 'What's going on? I just lost my signal.'

She started to say something, had it die in her throat. She suddenly remembered her new responsibilities, firmed her voice, straightened though there was no one around to see. 'We just lost Dallas . . .'

# XII

The four surviving members of the *Nostromo*'s crew reassembled in the mess. It was no longer cramped, confining. It had acquired a spaciousness the four loathed, and held memories they struggled to put aside.

Parker held two flamethrowers, dumped one onto the bare tabletop.

Ripley gazed sadly at him. 'Where was it?'

'We just found it lying there, on the floor of the mixing chamber below the walkway,' the engineer said dully. 'No sign of him. No blood. Nothing.'

'What about the alien?'

'The same. Nothing. Only a hole torn through to the central cooling complex. Right through the metal. I didn't think it was that strong.'

'None of us did. Dallas didn't either. We've been two steps behind this creature since we first brought the handstage aboard. That's got to change. From now on, we assume it's capable of anything, including invisibility.'

'No known creature is a natural invisible,' Ash insisted.

She glared back at him. 'No known creature can peel back three-centimetre-thick ship plating, either.' Ash offered no response to that. 'It's about time we all realized what we're up against.' There was silence in the mess.

'Ripley, this puts you in command.' Parker looked straight at her. 'It's okay with me.'

'Okay.' She studied him, but both his words and attitude were devoid of sarcasm. For once he'd dropped his omnipresent bullshit.

What now, Ripley, she asked herself? Three faces watched hers expectantly, waited for instructions. She searched her mind frantically for brilliance, found only uncertainty, fear and confusion—precisely the same feelings her companions were no doubt experiencing. She began to understand Dallas a little better, and now it didn't matter.

'That's settled, then. Unless someone's got a better idea about how to deal with the alien, we'll proceed with the same plan as before.'

'And wind up the same way.' Lambert shook her head. 'No thanks.'

'You've got a better idea, then?'

'Yes. Abandon ship. Take the shuttlecraft and get the hell out of here. Take our chances on making Earth orbit and getting picked up. Once we get back in well-travelled space someone's bound to hear our SOS.'

Ash spoke softly, words better left unsaid. Lambert had forced them out of him now. 'You are forgetting something: Dallas and Brett may not be dead. It's a ghastly probability, I'll grant you, but it's not a certainty. We can't abandon ship until we're sure one way or the other.'

'Ash is right,' agreed Ripley. 'We've got to give it another try. We know it's using the air shafts. Let's take it level by level. This time we'll laser-seal every bulkhead and vent behind us until we corner it.'

'I'll go along with that.' Parker glanced over at Lambert. She said nothing, looked downcast.

'How are our weapons?' Ripley asked him.

The engineer took a moment to check levels and feedlines on the flamethrowers. 'The lines and nozzles are still plenty clean. From what I can see they're working fine.' He gestured at Dallas's incinerator on the table. 'We could use more fuel for that one.' He turned sombre. 'A fair amount's been used.'

'Then you better go get some to replace it. Ash, you go with him.'

Parker looked at the science officer. His expression was unreadable. 'I can manage.' Ash nodded. The engineer cradled his own weapon, turned and left.

The rest of them stood morosely around the table, awaiting Parker's return. Unable to stand the silence, Ripley turned to face the science officer.

'Any other thoughts? Fresh ideas, suggestions, hints? From you or Mother.'

He shrugged, looking apologetic. 'Nothing new. Still collating information.'

She stared hard at him. 'I can't believe that. Are you telling me that with everything we've got on board this ship in the way of recorded information we can't come up with something better to use against this thing?'

'That's the way it looks, doesn't it? Keep in mind this is not your average, predictable feral we're dealing with. You said yourself it might be capable of anything.

'It possesses a certain amount of mental ammunition, at least as much as a dog and probably more than a chimpanzee. It has also demonstrated an ability to learn. As a complete stranger to the *Nostromo*, it has succeeded in quickly learning how to travel about the ship largely undetected. It is swift, powerful and cunning. A predator the likes of which we've never encountered before. It is not so surprising our efforts to deal with it have met with failure.'

'You sound like you're ready to give up.'

'I am only restating the obvious.'

'This is a modern, well-equipped ship, able to travel through hyperspace and execute a variety of complex functions. You're telling me that all its resources are inadequate to cope with a single large animal?'

'I'm sorry, captain. I've given you my evaluation of the situation as I see it. Wishing otherwise will not alter facts. A man with a gun may hunt a tiger during the day with some expectation of success. Turn out his light, put the man in the jungle at night, surround him with the unknown and all his primitive fears return. Advantage to the tiger.

'We are operating in the darkness of ignorance.'

'Very poetic, but not very useful.'

'I'm sorry.' He did not appear to care one way or the other. 'What do you want me to do?'

'Try and alter some of those "facts" you're so positive about. Go back to Mother,' she ordered him, 'and keep asking questions until you get some better answers.'

'All right. I'll try. Though I don't know what you expect. Mother can't hide information.'

'Try different questions. If you'll remember, I had some luck working through ECIU. The distress signal that wasn't?'

'I remember.' Ash regarded her with respect. 'Maybe you're right.' He left.

Lambert had taken a seat. Ripley moved and sat down next to her.

'Try to hang on. You know Dallas would have done the same for us. No way he would've left the ship without making sure whether or not we were alive.'

Lambert didn't look mollified. 'All I know is that you're asking us to stay and get picked off one by one.'

'I promise you. If it looks like it won't work out, I'll bail us out of here fast. I'll be the first one on the boat.'

She had a sudden thought. It was a peculiar one, oddly out of place and yet strangely relevant in some inexplicable way to all her present concerns. She glanced over at Lambert. Her companion had to answer truthfully or there'd be no point in asking the question. She decided that while Lambert might be queasy where other matters were involved, on this particular subject Ripley could trust her reply.

Of course, an answer one way or another probably wouldn't mean a thing. It was just a perverse little mind bubble that would grow and continue to dominate her thoughts until she popped it. No real meaning.

'Lambert, did you ever sleep with Ash?'

'No.' Her reply was immediate, leaving no room for hesitation or second thoughts. 'What about you?'

'No.' Both went quiet for a few minutes before Lambert spoke up voluntarily.

'I never got the impression,' she said casually, 'he was particularly interested.'

That was the end of it as far as the navigator was concerned. It was almost the end of it as far as Ripley was concerned. She could not have said why she continued to mull over the thought. But it hung maddeningly in her mind, tormenting her, and for her life's blood she couldn't imagine why.

Parker checked the level on the first methane cylinder, made sure the bottle of highly compressed gas was full. He did the same with a second, resting nearby. Then he hefted the two heavy containers and started back up the companionway.

It was as lonely on B deck as it had been below. The sooner he rejoined the others, the better he'd feel. In fact, he wished now he'd let Ash accompany him. He'd been an idiot to run off for the cylinders by himself. Everyone who'd been taken by the alien had been alone. He tried to jog a little faster, despite the awkward weight of the bottles.

He turned a bend in the corridor, stopped, nearly dropping one of the containers. Ahead lay the main airlock. Beyond it, but not far beyond, something had moved. Or had it? It was time for imagining things and he blinked, trying to clear mind and eyes.

He'd almost started ahead again when the shadow movement was repeated. There was a vague suggestion of something tall and heavy. Looking around, he located one of the ubiquitous wall 'coms. Ripley and Lambert should still be on the bridge. He thumbed the switch beneath the grid.

Something indecipherable drifted out from the speaker set in Ripley's console. At first she thought it was only localized static, then decided she recognized a word or two.

'Ripley here.'

'Keep it down!' the engineer whispered urgently into the pickup. Ahead of him, the movement in the corridor had suddenly ceased. If the creature had heard him . . .

'I can't hear you.' Ripley exchanged a puzzled look with Lambert, who looked blank. But when she spoke into her pickup again, she kept her voice down as requested. 'Repeat . . . why the need for quiet?'

'The alien.' Parker whispered it, not daring to raise his voice. 'It's outside the starboard lock. Yes, right now! Open the door slowly. When I give the word, close it fast and blow the outer hatch.'

'Are you sure. . .?'

He interrupted her quickly. 'I tell you, we've got it! Just do as I tell you.' He forced himself to calm down. 'Now open it. Slowly.'

Ripley hesitated, started to say something, then saw Lambert nodding vigorously. If Parker was wrong, they had nothing to lose but a minuscule amount of air. If he knew what he was doing, on the other hand . . . She threw a switch.

Below, Parker tried to become part of the corridor wall as a low whine sounded. The inner airlock door moved towards it. Several lights were flashing inside the lock. One was an especially bright emerald green. The alien regarded it with interest, moved to stand on the threshold of the lock.

Come on, damn you, the engineer thought frantically. Look at the pretty green light. That's right. Wouldn't you like to have the pretty green light all to yourself? Sure you would. Just step inside and take the beautiful greenness. Just a couple of steps inside and it can be yours forever. Just a couple of steps, God, just a couple of steps.

Fascinated by the steadily pulsing indicator, the alien stepped into the lock. It was completely inside. Not by much, but who could tell when it might suddenly grow bored, or suspicious?

'Now,' he husked into the pickup, '*now*.'

Ripley prepared to throw the emergency close. Her hand was

halfway to the toggle when the *Nostromo*'s emergency Klaxon wailed for attention. She and Lambert froze. Each looked to the other, saw only her own personal shock mirrored in her companion's face. Ripley threw the toggle over.

The alien heard the Klaxon too. Muscles contracted and it sprang backward, clearing the threshold of the lock in a single incredible leap. The hatch door slammed about just a fraction faster. One appendage was pinned between wall and door.

Liquid boiled out of the crushed member. The alien made a noise, like a moan or bellow made underwater. It wrenched itself backward, leaving the trapped limb pinned between metal. Then it turned and rushed down the corridor, blind with pain, hardly seeing the paralyzed engineer as it lifted and threw him aside before vanishing around the nearest corner. Above the crumpled Parker a green light was flashing and the words INNER HATCH CLOSED showed on a readout.

The metal of the lock continued to bubble and melt as the outer hatch swung open. A puff of frozen air appeared outside the lock as the atmosphere that had been contained within rushed into space.

'Parker?' Ripley spoke anxiously into the pickup, jabbed a switch, adjusted a slide. 'Parker? What's happening down there?' Her attention was caught by a green light winking steadily on her console.

'What's going on?' Lambert leaned out of her seat. 'Did it work?'

'I'm not sure. The inner hatch is sealed and the outer hatch has been popped.'

'That should do it. But what about Parker?'

'I don't know. I can't get a response out of him. If it worked, he should be screaming fit to bust the speakers.' She made a decision. 'I'm going down to see. Take over.' She slipped out of her chair, raced for B corridor.

She nearly fell a couple of times. Once she stumbled into a bulkhead and nearly knocked herself out. Somehow she kept her balance and staggered on. The alien was not uppermost in her mind. It was Parker, another human being. A rare enough commodity on board the *Nostromo* now.

She raced down the companionway onto B corridor, headed up towards the airlock. It was empty, except for a limp form sprawled across the deck: Parker.

She bent over him. He was groggy and half conscious. 'What happened? You look like hell. Did. . .?'

The engineer was trying to form words, had to settle for gesturing feebly towards the airlock. Ripley shut up, looked in the indicated direction, saw the bubbling hole in the lock door. The outer hatch was still open, ostensibly after blowing the alien out into nothingness. She started to rise.

The acid ate completely through.

There was a *bang* of departing air, and a small hurricane enveloped them. Air screamed as it was sucked into vacuum. A flashing red sign appeared in several recesses in the corridor walls.

CRITICAL DEPRESSURIZATION.

The Klaxon was sounding again, more hysterically now and with better reason. Emergency doors slammed shut all over the ship, beginning with the breached section. Parker and Ripley should have been safely sealed in a section of corridor . . . except that the airtight door separating them from the airlock vestibule had jammed on one of the methane cylinders.

Wind continued to tear at her as she hunted for something, anything, to fight with. There was only the remaining tank. She raised it, used it to hammer at the jammed cylinder. If either of them cracked, a slight spark from metal banging on metal could set off the contents of both bottles. But if she didn't knock it free, quickly, the complete depressurization would kill them anyway.

Lack of air was already weakening her. Blood frothed at her nose and ears. The fall in pressure made Parker's existing wounds bleed afresh.

She heaved the bottle at the trapped cylinder a last time. It popped free as easily as a clean birth. The door slammed the rest of the way shut behind it, and the howl of disappearing wind vanished. Confused air continued to swirl around them for several minutes more.

On the bridge, Lambert had seen the ominous readouts appear on her console: HULL BREACHED—EMERGENCY BULKHEADS CLOSED. She hit the 'com.

'Ash, get some oxygen. Meet me at the main lock by the last of the sealed doors.'

'Check. Be right there.'

Ripley staggered to her feet, fighting for every breath in the atmosphere-depleted chamber. She headed for the emergency release set inside every bulkhead door. There was a stud there that would slide the door back, opening onto the next sealed section and fresh air.

At the last instant, as she was about to depress the red button, she saw to her horror that she was fumbling against the door leading not down B corridor, but to the empty vestibule outside the lock. She turned, tried to aim herself, and fell as much as walked to the opposite door. It took precious minutes to locate the panel on it. Thoughts swam in her brain, broke apart like oil on water. The air around her was turning foggy, full of the smell of roses and lilac.

She thumbed the stud. The door didn't move. Then she saw she was pushing the wrong control. Sagging against the door for support, trying to give her rubbery legs some badly needed assistance, she fought to gather her strength for another try. There wasn't much air left worth breathing.

A face appeared at the port set in the door. It was distorted, bloated, yet somehow familiar. It seemed that she knew that face from sometime long ago. Someone named Lambert lived behind that face. She was very tired and started to slide slowly down the door.

She thought distant, angry thoughts as her last support was taken away. The door slid into the roof and her head struck the deck. A rush of clean air, ineffably sweet and refreshing, swept over her face. The mist began to fade from her eyes, though not yet from her starved brain.

A horn sounded the return of full internal pressurization as Lambert and Ash joined them. The science officer hurried to administer to Parker, who had collapsed again from lack of oxygen and was only now beginning to regain consciousness.

Ripley's eyes were open and working, but the rest of her body was dysfunctional. Hands and feet, legs and arms were sprawled in ungainly positions across her body and the deck, like the limbs of a slim, not particularly well-crafted doll. Her breath came in laboured, shallow gasps.

Lambert set one of the oxygen tanks down next to her friend. She placed the transparent mask over Ripley's mouth and nose, opened the valve. Ripley inhaled. A wonderful perfume filled her lungs. Her eyes closed from sheer pleasure. She stayed that way, unmoving, sucking in long, deep draughts of pure oxygen. The only shock to her system was of delight.

Finally she moved the respirator aside, lay for a moment breathing normally. Full pressure had been restored, she noted. The bulkhead doors had automatically retracted with the return of standard atmosphere.

To replenish that atmosphere, she knew, the ship had been forced to bleed their storage tanks. They'd deal with that new problem when they were forced to, she thought.

'Are you all right?' Ash was querying Parker. 'What finally happened here?'

Parker wiped a crust of dried blood from his upper mouth, tried to shake the webs from his brain. 'I'll live.' For the moment, he ignored the science officer's last question.

'What about the alien?' Ash tried again.

Parker shook his head, wincing at some sudden pain. 'We didn't get it. The warning Klaxon went off and it jumped back into the corridor. It caught an arm, or whatever you'd like to call it, in the closing inner door. Just pulled itself free like a lizard shedding its tail.'

'Why not,' commented Ash, 'with its inbuilt talent for regeneration?'

The engineer continued, sounding every bit as disappointed as he felt. 'We had the bastard. We *had* him.' He paused, added, 'When it pulled free of its limb, it bled all over the place. The limb did. I guess the stump healed over fast, lucky for us. The acid ate right through the hatch. That's what caused the depressurization.' He pointed shakily towards the door sealing off the airlock vestibule from the rest of the corridor.

'You can probably see the hole in the hatch from here.'

'Never mind that now.' Ash looked up curiously. 'Who hit the warning siren?'

Ripley was staring over at him. 'You tell me.'

'What does that mean?'

She wiped blood from her nose, sniffed. 'I guess the alarm went off by itself. That would be the logical explanation, wouldn't it? Just a temporary, slightly coincidental malfunction?'

The science officer rose, looked at her from beneath lowered lids. She'd made certain the remaining methane cylinder was within reach before she'd spoken. But Ash made no move towards her. She still couldn't figure him.

If he was guilty, he ought to jump her while she was weakened and Parker was worse. If he was innocent, he ought to be mad enough to do the same. He was doing nothing, which she hadn't prepared for.

At least his first words in response were predictable. He did sound angrier than usual. 'If you've got something to say, say it. I'm getting sick of these constant, coy insinuations. Of being accused.'

'Nobody's accusing you.'

'Like hell.' He lapsed into sullen silence. Ripley said nothing for a long moment, then gestured at Parker. 'Take him to the infirmary and get him patched up. Leastwise we know the autodoc can handle that.'

Ash gave the engineer a hand up, slipped Parker's right arm over his shoulders and helped him down the corridor. Ash walked past Ripley without looking back at her.

When he and his burden had disappeared around the first turn, Ripley reached up with a hand. Lambert took it, leaned back and watched with concern as Ripley swayed a little on her feet. Ripley smiled, released the steadying hand.

'I'll be okay.' She brushed fitfully at the stains on her pants. 'How much oxygen did that little episode cost us? I'll need an exact reading.' Lambert didn't reply, continued to stare speculatively at her.

'Something wrong with that? Why are you looking at me that way? Oxygen readings no longer for public consumption?'

'Don't bite my head off,' Lambert replied, without rancour. Her tone was disbelieving. 'You were accusing him. You actually accused him of sounding the alarm to save the alien.' She shook her head slowly. 'Why?'

'Because I think he's lying. And if I can get into the tape records, I'll prove it.'

'Prove what? Even if you could somehow prove that he was responsible for the alarm going off, you can't prove that it wasn't an accident.'

'Mighty funny time for that sort of accident, wouldn't you say?' Ripley was silent for a bit, then asked softly, 'You still think I'm wrong, don't you?'

'I don't know.' Lambert looked more tired than argumentative. 'I don't know anything any more. Yeah, I guess I have to say I think you're wrong. Wrong or crazy. Why would Ash, or anyone, want to protect the alien? It'll kill him as dead as it did Dallas and Brett. If they are dead.'

'Thanks. Always like to know who I can depend on.' Ripley turned away from the navigator, strode purposefully down the corridor towards the companionway.

Lambert watched her go, shrugged and started gathering up the cylinders. She handled the methane with as much care as the oxygen. It was equally vital to their survival . . .

'Ash, you in there? Parker?' When no response was forthcoming, Ripley cautiously entered the central computer annex. For an indeterminate time, she had the mind of the

*Nostromo* completely to herself.

Taking a seat in front of the main console, she activated the board, rammed a thumb insistently against the identification plate. Data screens flickered to life.

So far it had been easy. Now she had to work. She thought for a moment, tapped out a five-digit code she thought would generate the response she needed. The screens remained blank, waiting for the proper query. She tried a second, little-used combination, with equal lack of success.

She swore with frustration. If she was reduced to trying random combinations she'd be working in the annex until doomsday. Which, at the rate the alien was reducing the crew, would not be far in the future.

She tried a tertiary combination instead of a primary and was stunned when the screen promptly cleared, ready to receive and disseminate. But it didn't print out a request for input. That meant the code had been only half successful. What to do?

She glanced over at the secondary keyboard. It was accessible to any member of the crew, but not privy to confidential comment and information. If she could remember the interlock combination she could use the second keyboard to place questions with the main bank.

Quickly she changed seats, entered the hopefully correct interlock code and typed out the first question. The key would be whether or not the interlock was accepted without question. Acceptability would be signified by the appearance of her question on the screen.

Colours chased one another for a second. The screen cleared.

WHO TURNED ON AIRLOCK 2 WARNING SYSTEM?

The response was flashed below.

ASH.

She sat digesting that. It was the reply she'd expected, but having it printed out coldly for anyone to read brought the real import of it down on her heavily. So it had been Ash. The critical question now was: had it been Ash all the time? She entered the follow-up query:

IS ASH PROTECTING THE ALIEN?

This seemed to be Mother's day for brief responses.

YES.

She could be brief in turn. Her fingers moved on the keys.

WHY?

She leaned forward tensely. If the computer chose not to reveal further information, she knew of no additional codes that could pry answers free. There was also the possibility that the computer truly had no explanation for the science officer's bizarre actions.

It did, though.

SPECIAL ORDER 937 SCIENCE PERSONNEL EYES ONLY RESTRICTED INFORMATION.

Well, she'd managed this long. She could work around those restrictions. She was starting to when a hand slammed down next to her, sinking up to the elbow in the computer terminal.

Spinning in the chair, her heart missing a beat, she saw, not the creature, but a form and face now become equally alien to her.

Ash smiled slightly. There was no humour in that upturning of lips. 'Command seems a bit too much for you to handle. But then, proper leadership is always difficult under these circumstances. I guess you can't be blamed.'

Ripley slowly backed out of her chair, carefully keeping it between them. Ash's words might be conciliatory, even sympathetic. His actions were not.

'The problem's not leadership, Ash. It's loyalty.' She kept the wall at her back, started circling towards the doorway. Still grinning, he turned to face her.

'Loyalty? I see no lack of that.' He was all charm now, she thought. 'I think we've all been doing our best. Lambert's getting a little pessimistic, but we've always known she's on the emotional side. She's very good at plotting the course of the ship, not so good at planning her own.,'

Ripley continued to edge around him, forcing herself to smile back. 'I'm not worried about Lambert right now. I'm worried about you.' She started to turn to face the open doorway, feeling her stomach muscles tightening in anticipation.

'All that paranoia coming up again,' he said sadly. 'You just need to rest a little.' He took a step towards her, reached out helpfully.

She bolted, ducking just beneath his clutching fingers. Then she was out in the corridor, sprinting for the bridge. She was too busy to scream for help, and she needed the wind.

There was no one on the bridge. Somehow she got around him again, throwing emergency switches as she ran. Bulkhead doors responded by dropping shut behind her, each one just a second too late to cut him off.

He finally caught her in the mess chamber. Parker and Lambert arrived seconds later. The signals set off by the closing bulkhead doors had alerted them that something was wrong in the vicinity of the bridge, and they'd been on their way there when they encountered pursuer and pursued.

While it was not the type of emergency they'd expected to find, they reacted well. Lambert was first in. She jumped on Ash's back. Annoyed, he let go of Ripley, grabbed the navigator and threw her across the room, then returned to what he'd been doing a moment before, trying to squeeze the life out of Ripley.

Parker's reaction was less immediate but better thought out. Ash would have appreciated the engineer's reasoning. Parker hefted one of the compact trackers and stepped behind Ash, who single-mindedly continued to choke Ripley. The engineer swung the tracker with all his strength.

There was a dull *thunk*. The tracker continued through its arc while Ash's head went a different way.

There was no blood. Only multihued wires and printed circuits showed, protruding from the terminated stump of the science officer's neck.

Ash released Ripley. She collapsed on the floor, choking and holding her throat. His hands performed a macabre pantomime above his shoulders while hunting for the missing skull. Then he, or more properly, it, stumbled backward, regained its balance and commenced searching the deck for the separated head . . .

# XIII

'A robot . . . a goddamn robot!' Parker muttered. The tracker hung limp and unbloodied in one hand.

Apparently there were audio sensors located in the torso as well as the skull, because the powerful form turned immediately at the sound of Parker's voice and began to advance on him. Raising the tracker, the engineer wanged it down on Ash's shoulder, then again, and again . . . to no effect. Groping arms swung close, embraced Parker in a hug that was anything but affectionate. The hands climbed upward, locked around his neck and contracted with inhuman strength.

Ripley had recovered, now searched frantically until she spotted one of the old shock tubes they'd first planned to drive the alien with. She snatched it up, noting that it still carried a full charge.

Lambert was pulling at Ash's legs, trying to upend the rampaging machine. Naked wiring and contacts showed from the open neck. Ripley dug at them. Parker's eyes were glazing over, and faint wheezing sounds were coming from his constricted throat.

Finding a knot thick with circuitry, Ripley jabbed the prod inward and depressed the trigger. Ash's grip on the engineer appeared to weaken slightly. She withdrew the prod, aligned it differently and stabbed downward a second time.

Blue sparks flew from the stump. She jabbed again, crying inside, holding the trigger down. There was a bright flash and the smell of burnt insulation.

Ash collapsed. Chest rising and falling as he struggled to regain his wind, Parker rolled over, coughed a couple of times, spat phlegm on to the deck.

He blinked a few times, glared at the motionless hulk of the machine. 'Damn you. Goddamn Company machine.' He climbed to his feet, kicked at the metal. It did not react, lay supine and innocent on the deck.

Lambert looked uncertainly from Parker to Ripley. 'Will somebody please tell me what the hell's going on?'

'There's only one way to find out.' Ripley carefully set the shock tube aside, making certain it was within easy reach in case they needed it quickly, and approached the body.

'What's that?' Lambert asked.

Ripley looked over at Parker, who was massaging his throat. 'Wire the head back up. I think I burnt out the locomotor system in the torso, but the head and memory ought to be functional when powered up.

'He's been protecting the alien from the beginning. I tried to tell you.' She gestured at the corpse. It was hard to start thinking of fellow crew member Ash as just another piece of equipment. 'He let it on board, remember, against regulations.' Her expression twisted as she remembered.

'He was using Kane's life as an excuse, but he was never interested in Kane. He let that thing grow inside him, knew what was happening all the time. And he set off the emergency airlock Klaxon to save it.'

'But why?' Lambert was struggling, still couldn't put it all together.

'I'm only guessing, but the only reason I can come up with for putting a robot crew member on board with the rest of us and not letting us know about it at the time is that someone wanted a slave observer to report developments back to them.' She glanced up at Lambert. 'Who assigns personnel to the ships, makes last-minute changes like trading science officers and would be the only entity capable of secretly slipping a robot on board? For whatever purpose?'

Lambert no longer looked confused. 'The Company.'

'Sure.' Ripley smiled humourlessly. 'The Company's drone probes must have picked up the transmission from the derelict. The *Nostromo* happened to be the next Company vessel scheduled to pass through this spatial quadrant. They put Ash on board to monitor things for them and to make sure we followed something Mother calls Special Order 937.

'If the follow-up on the transmission turns out to be worthless, Ash can report that back to them without us ever knowing what was going on. If worthwhile, then the Company learns what it needs to know before it goes to the trouble of sending out an expensively equipped exploration team. Simple, matter of maximizing profit, minimizing loss. Their profit, our loss.'

'Great,' Parker snorted. 'You got it all figured out so far. Now tell me why we've got to put this son-of-a-bitch back together.' He spat at Ash's body.

Ripley already had Ash's head set up on a counter, was running a power line from a wall outlet near the autochef back to the quiescent skull. 'We have to find out what else they might be holding back. Agreed?'

Parker nodded reluctantly. 'Agreed.' He started forward. 'Here, let me do that.'

The engineer fooled with the wires and the connections located in the back of Ash's head, beneath the artificial hair. When the science officer's eyelids began to flicker, Parker grunted in satisfaction and stepped clear.   Ripley leaned close. 'Ash, can you hear me?' No response. She looked back at Parker. . 'The hookup's clean. Power level is self-adjusting. Unless some critical circuits were interrupted when the head hit the deck, he ought to reply. Memory cells and verbal-visual components are packed pretty tight in these sophisticated models. I'd expect it to talk.'

She tried again. 'Can you hear me, Ash?'

A familiar voice, not distant at all, sounded in the mess. 'Yes, I can hear you.'

It was hard for her to address the disembodied head, for all that she knew it was only part of a machine, like the shock tube or the tracker. She'd served too many hours with Ash.

'What . . . what was Special Order 937?'

'That's against regulations and my internal programming. You know I can't tell you.'

She stood back. 'Then there's no point in talking. Parker, pull the plug.'

The engineer reached for the wires and Ash reacted with sufficient speed to show that his cognitive circuits were indeed intact. 'In essence, my orders were as follows.' Parker's hand hovered threateningly over the power line.

'I was directed to reroute the *Nostromo* or make sure that this crew rerouted it from its assigned course so that it would pick up the signal, program Mother to bring you out of hypersleep and program her memory to feed you the story about the emergency call. Company specialists already knew that the transmission was a warning and not a distress signal.'

Parker's hands clenched into fists.

'At the source of the signal,' Ash continued, 'we were to investigate a life form, almost certainly hostile according to what the Company experts distilled from the transmission, and bring it back for observation and Company evaluation of any potential commercial applications. Using discretion, of course.'

'Of course,' agreed Ripley, mimicking the machine's indifferent tone. 'That explains a lot about why we were chosen, beyond the expense of sending a valuable exploration team in first.' She looked coldly pleased at having traced the reasoning behind Ash's words.

'Importation to any inhabited world, let alone Earth, of a dangerous alien life form is strictly prohibited. By making it look like we simple tug jockeys had accidentally stumbled onto it, the Company had a way of seeing it arrive at Earth "unintentionally". While we maybe got ourselves thrown in jail, something would have to be done with the creature. Naturally, Company specialists would magnanimously be standing ready to take this dangerous arrival off the hands of the customs officers, with a few judicious bribes prepaid just to smooth the transition.

'And if we were lucky, the Company would bail us out and take proper care of us as soon as the authorities determined we were honestly as stupid as we appeared. Which we've been.'

'Why?' Lambert wanted to know. 'Why didn't you warn us? Why couldn't we have been told what we were getting ourselves into?'

'Because you might not have gone along,' Ash explained with cold logic. 'Company policy required your unknowing co-operation. What Ripley said about your honest ignorance fooling customs was quite correct.'

'You and the damn Company,' Parker growled. 'What about our lives, man?'

'Not man.' Ash made the correction without anger. 'As to your lives, I'm afraid the Company considered them expendable. It was the alien life form they were principally concerned with. It was hoped you could contain it and survive to collect your shares, but that was, I must admit, a secondary consideration. It wasn't personal on the Company's part. Just the luck of the draw.'

'How comforting,' sneered Ripley. She thought a moment, said, 'You've already told us that our purpose in being sent to that world was to "investigate a life form, almost certainly hostile". And that Company experts knew all along the transmission was a warning and not a distress signal.'

'Yes,' Ash replied. 'It was much too late, according to what the translators determined, for a distress signal to do the senders any good. The signal itself was frighteningly specific, very detailed.

'The derelict spacecraft we found had landed on the planet, apparently in the course of normal exploration. Like Kane, they encountered one or more of the alien spore pods. The transmission did not say whether the explorers had time to determine if the spores originated on that particular world or if they had migrated there from somewhere else.

'Before they all were overcome, they managed to set up the warning, to keep the inhabitants of other ships that might consider setting down on that world from suffering the same fate. Wherever they came from, they were a noble people. Hopefully mankind will encounter them again, under more pleasant circumstances.'

'They were a better people than some I can think of,' Ripley said tightly. 'The alien that's aboard: How do we kill it?'

'The explorers who crewed the derelict ship were larger and possibly more intelligent than humankind. I don't think that you can kill it. But I might be able to. As I'm not organic in composition, the alien does not regard me as potential danger. Nor as a source of food. I am considerably stronger than any of you. I might be able to match the alien.

'However, I am not exactly at my best at the moment. If you would simply replace . . .'

'Nice try, Ash,' Ripley interrupted him, shaking her head from side to side, 'but no way.'

'You idiots! You still don't realize what you're dealing with. The alien is a perfectly organized organism. Superbly structured, cunning, quintessentially violent. With your limited capabilities you have no chance against it.'

'My God.' Lambert stared dully at the head. 'You admire the damned thing.'

'How can you not admire the simple symmetry it presents? An interspecies parasite, capable of preying on any life form that breathes, regardless of the atmospheric composition involved. One capable of lying dormant for indefinite periods under the most inhospitable conditions. Its sole purpose to reproduce its own kind, a task it pursues with supreme efficiency. There is nothing in mankind's experience to compare with it.

'The parasites men are used to combating are mosquitoes and minute arthropods and their ilk. This creature is to them in savagery and efficiency as man is to the worm in intelligence. You cannot even begin to imagine how to deal with it.'

'I've heard enough of this shit.' Parker's hand dropped towards the power line. Ripley put up a restraining hand, stared at the head.

'You're supposed to be part of our complement, Ash. You're our science officer as well as a Company tool.'

'You gave me intelligence. With intellect comes the inevitability of choice. I am loyal only to discovering the truth. A scientific truth demands beauty, harmony and, above all, simplicity. The problem of you versus the alien will produce a simple and elegant solution. Only one of you will survive.'

'I guess that puts us poor humans in our place, doesn't it? Tell me something, Ash. The Company expected the *Nostromo* to arrive at Earth station with only you and the alien alive all along, didn't it?'

'No. It was honestly hoped you would survive and contain the alien. The Company officials simply had no idea how dangerous and efficient the alien was.'

'What do you think's going to happen when the ship arrives, assuming we're all dead and the alien, instead of being properly restrained, has the run of the ship?'

'I cannot say. There is a distinct possibility the alien will successfully infect the boarding party and any others it comes in contact with before they realize the magnitude of the danger it presents and can take steps to combat it. By then it may be too late.

'Thousands of years of effort have not enabled man to eradicate other parasites. He has never before encountered one this advanced. Try to imagine several billion mosquitoes functioning in intelligent consort with one another. Would mankind have a chance?

'Of course, if I am present and functional when the *Nostromo* arrives, I can inform the boarding party of what they may expect and how to proceed safely against it. By destroying me, you risk loosing a terrible plague on mankind.'

There was silence in the mess, but not for long. Parker spoke first.

'Mankind, in the person of the Company, doesn't seem to give a damn about us. We'll take our chances against the alien. At least we know where *it* stands.' He glanced over at Ripley. 'No plague's going to bother me if I'm not around to worry about it. I say pull the plug.'

'I agree,' said Lambert.

Ripley moved around the table, started to disconnect the power cord.

'A last word,' Ash said quickly. 'A legacy, if you will.'

Ripley hesitated. 'Well?'

'Maybe it is truly intelligent. Maybe you should try to communicate with it.'

'Did you?'

'Please let my grave hold some secrets.'

Ripley pulled the wire from the socket. 'Good-bye, Ash.' She turned her attention from the silent head to her companions. 'When it comes to choosing between parasites, I'd rather take my chances with the one that doesn't lie. Besides, if we can't beat that thing we can die happy knowing that it's likely to get its hooks into a few Company experts . . .'

She was seated before the central computer console in the main annex when Parker and Lambert rejoined her. She spoke dejectedly. 'He was right about one thing, Ash was. We haven't got much of a chance.' She indicated a flashing readout. 'We've got less than twelve hours of oxygen left.'

'Then it's all over.' Parker looked at the deck. 'Reconnecting Ash would be a faster form of suicide. Oh, I'm sure he'd try to take care of the alien, all right. But he wouldn't leave us alive. That's one Company order he couldn't tell us. Because having told us everything else, he couldn't leave us around to tell the port authorities what the Company's been up to.' He grinned. 'Ash was a loyal Company machine.'

'I don't know about the rest of you,' said the unsmiling Lambert, 'but I think I prefer a painless, peaceful death to any of the alternatives on offer.'

'We're not there yet.'

Lambert held up a small card of capsules. Ripley recognized the suicide pills by their red colour and the miniature skull and crossbones imprinted on each. 'We're not. Huh.'

Ripley swung around in the chair. 'I'm saying we're not. You let Ash convince you. He said he was the only one with a chance to handle the alien, but he's the one lying in the mess disconnected, not us.

'We've got another choice. I think we should blow up the ship.'

'That's your alternative?' Lambert spoke softly. 'I'll stick with chemicals if you don't mind.'

'No, no. Remember what you proposed before, Lambert? *We* leave in the shuttle and then let the ship blow. Take the remaining air in portable tanks. The shuttle's got its own air supply. With the extra, there's a chance we might make it back to well-travelled space and get ourselves picked up. We may be breathing our own waste by that time, but it's a chance. And it'll take care of the alien.'

They went quiet, thinking. Parker looked up at Ripley, nodded. 'I like that better than chemicals. Besides, I'll enjoy watching some Company property go up in pieces.' He turned to leave. 'We'll get started bleeding the air into bottles.'

The engineer supervised the transfer of compressed air from the *Nostromo*'s main tanks into smaller, portable canisters they could lug on to the shuttle.

'That's everything?' Ripley asked when Parker leaned tiredly back against the hatchjamb.

'Everything we can carry.' He gestured at the ranked canisters. 'It may not look like much, but that stuff's really under pressure. Enough extra air to give us some breathing space.' He grinned.

'Great. Let's get some bulk artificial food, set the engines and get the hell out of here.' She stopped at a sudden thought: 'Jones. Where's Jones?'

'Who knows?' Parker clearly wasn't interested in the whereabouts of the ship's cat.

'Last I saw of him he was slinking around the mess, sniffing at Ash's body,' said Lambert.

'Go look. We don't want to leave him. We still have enough humanity in us for that.'

Lambert eyed her companion warily. 'No deal. I don't want to go anywhere on this ship by myself.'

'Always disliked that damn uppity cat,' Parker grumbled.

'Never mind,' Ripley told them. 'I'll go. You two load up the air and food.'

'Fair enough,' Lambert agreed. She and Parker loaded up oxygen canisters, headed for the shuttle. Ripley jogged towards the mess.

She didn't have to hunt long for the cat. After searching the mess and making certain she didn't touch Ash's decapitated form, she headed for the bridge. She found Jones immediately. He was lying on Dallas's console, preening himself and looking bored.

She smiled at him. 'Jones, you're in luck.'

Apparently the cat disagreed. When she reached for him he jumped lithely off the console and walked away, licking himself. She bent, followed him, coaxing with hands and voice.

'Come on, Jones. Don't play hard to get. Not now. The others won't wait for you.'

'How much do you think we'll need?' Lambert stopped stacking boxes, looked over at Parker and wiped a hair from her face.

'All we can carry. We don't want to make two trips.'

'For sure.' She turned to rearrange her assembled stack. A voice sounded over the open communicator.

'Goddamn it, Jones, come here. Here kitty . . . come to mama, kitty.' Ripley's tone was gentle and reassuring, but Lambert could detect the exasperation beneath.

Parker staggered out of Food Locker 2, hidden behind a double armload of food. Lambert continued to sort her boxes, occasionally trading one for another. The thought of eating raw, unpreprocessed artifical food was daunting at best. There was no autochef on the tiny shuttle. The raw bulk would keep them alive, but that was all. She wanted the tastiest selection possible.

She didn't notice the faint red light on the tracker lying nearby.

'Gotcha!' An indignant Jones resisted, but Ripley had him firmly by the nape of the neck. Nor did bracing his feet keep him from being shoved unceremoniously into his pressurized travelling case.

Ripley switched it on. 'There. Breathe your own recycled smell for a while.'

The two flamethrowers were lying outside the food locker. Parker knelt carefully and tried to pick up his. He overbalanced and a fair portion of the neatly aligned boxes tumbled from his arms.

'Goddamn.'

Lambert stopped her rearranging, tried to see around the locker doors. 'What's the matter?'

'Nothing. I was trying to carry too much at once, that's all. Just hurry it up.'

'I'm coming. Keep your head on.'

The red light on the tracker suddenly turned bright crimson, the beeper chirping simultaneously. Parker dropped his packages, stared at it and picked up his flamethrower. He called back in to Lambert.

'Let's get out of here.'

She'd heard the noise too. 'Right now.'

Something made a different sound behind her. She turned, screamed as the hand clutched at her. The alien was still unfolding its bulk from the airshaft.

Ripley heard the shriek over the open 'com speaker on the bridge and froze.

Parker looked back into the locker, went a little crazy when he saw what the alien was doing. Parker couldn't use the flamethrower without hitting Lambert. Swinging the incinerator like a club, he charged into the locker.

'Goddamn you!'

The alien dropped Lambert. She fell motionless to the deck as Parker landed a solid blow with the flamethrower. It had no effect on the alien. The engineer might as well have been trying to fracture the wall.

He tried to duck, failed. The single blow broke his neck, killing him instantly. The alien turned its attention back to Lambert.

Ripley still hadn't moved. Faint shrieks reached her over the 'com. The screams were Lambert's and they faded with merciful speed. Then it was quiet again.

She spoke towards the pickup. 'Parker . . . Lambert?'

She waited for a response, expecting none. Her expectations were fulfilled. The import of the continuing silence took only a moment to settle in.

She was alone. There were probably three living things left on the ship: the alien, Jones, and herself. But she had to be sure.

It meant leaving Jones behind. She didn't want to, but the cat had heard the screams and was meowing frantically. He was making too much noise.

She reached B deck unopposed, her flamethrower held tightly in both hands. The food locker lay just ahead. There was an outside chance the alien had left someone behind, being unable to manoeuvre itself and two bodies through the narrow ducts. A chance that someone might still be alive.

She peered around the jamb of the locker entrance. What remained showed her how the alien had succeeded in squeezing both victims into the airshaft.

Then she was running, running. Blindly, a little madly, neither thinking or caring. Walls reached out to stun her and slow her down, but nothing halted her crazed flight. She ran until her lungs hurt. They reminded her of Kane and the creature that had matured inside him, next to his lungs. That in turn reminded her of the alien.

All that thinking brought her back to her senses. Gulping for breath, she slowed and took stock of her surroundings. She'd run the length of the ship. Now she found herself standing alone in the middle of the engine room.

She heard something and stopped breathing. It was repeated, and she let out a cautious sigh. The sound was familiar, human. It was the sound of weeping.

Still cradling the flamethrower, she walked slowly around the room until the source of the noise lay directly below her. She found she was standing on a companionway cover, a round metal disc. Keeping half her attention on the well-lit chamber surrounding her, she knelt and removed the disc. A ladder descended into the near darkness.

She felt her way down the ladder until she reached solid footing. Then she activated her lightbar. She was in a small maintenance chamber. The light picked out plastic crates, rarely used tools. It also fell on bones with shreds of flesh still attached. Her skin crawled as the light moved over fragments of clothing, dried blood, a ruined boot. Bizarre extrusions lined the walls.

Something moved fitfully in the darkness. She spun, raising the nozzle of the flamethrower as her light sought out the cause of the movement.

A huge cocoon hung from the ceiling, off to her right. It looked like an enclosed, translucent hammock, woven from fine white silky material. It twitched.

Her finger tense on the trigger of the flamethrower, she walked nearer. The beam from her lightbar made the cocoon slightly transparent. There was a body inside . . . Dallas.

Quite unexpectedly the eyes opened and focused on Ripley. Lips parted, moved to form words. She moved closer, simultaneously fascinated and repelled.

'Kill me,' the whisper pleaded with her.

'What . . . what did it do to you?'

Dallas tried to speak again, failed. His head turned a little to the right. Ripley swung her light, turned it upward slightly. A second cocoon hung there, different in texture and colour from the first. It was smaller and darker, the silk having formed a hard, shining shell. It looked, although Ripley couldn't know it, like the broken, empty urn on the derelict ship.

'That was Brett.' Her light turned back to focus on the speaker again.

'I'll get you out of here.' She was crying. 'We'll crank up the autodoc, get you . . .'

She broke off, unable to talk. She was remembering Ash's analogy of the spider, the wasp. The live young feeding on the paralyzed body of the spider, growing, the spider aware of what was happening but . . .

Somehow she managed to shut off the horrid line of thought. Madness lay that way. 'What can I do?'

The same agonized whisper. 'Kill me.'

She stared at him. Mercifully, his eyes had closed. But his lips were trembling, as if he were readying a scream. She didn't think she could stand to hear that scream.

The nozzle of the flamethrower rose and she convulsively depressed the trigger. A molten blast enveloped the cocoon and the thing that had been Dallas. It and he burned without a sound. Then she swung the fire around the lair. The entire compartment burst into flames. She was already scrambling back up the ladder, heat licking at her legs.

She stuck her head out into the engine room. It was still deserted. Smoke curled up around her, making her cough. She climbed out, kicked the disc back into place, leaving enough of a gap for air to reach the fire. Then she strode resolutely towards the engine-room control cubicle.

Gauges and controls functioned patiently within, waiting to be told what to do. There was one particular board whose switches were outlined in red. She studied it a moment, recalling sequences, then began to close the switches one at a time.

One double switch lay protected beneath a locked cover. She pried at it a moment, then stepped back and hammered it loose with the butt end of the flamethrower, moved up and threw the dual control.

She waited an eternity. Sirens began to wail. A voice called from the intercom and she jumped, startled, until she recognized it as Mother's.

'Attention. Attention. The cooling units for the hyperdrive engines are not functioning. Overrides are not functioning. Engines will overload in four minutes, fifty seconds: four minutes, fifty seconds.'

She was halfway down B corridor when she remembered Jones.

She found him meowing steadily through the speaker, but undisturbed, alone in his pressurized box leading from the bridge to B level. Then his case was banging against her legs as she ran for the shuttle, the flamethrower tucked securely under her other arm.

They turned the last bend leading towards the shuttle. Jones suddenly hissed within the box, his back fur arching. Ripley came to a halt, stared dazedly at the open lock. Thrashing sounds drifted back to her.

The alien was inside the shuttle.

Leaving Jones safe on the B level companionway, she sprinted back towards the engine room. The cat protested mightily at being abandoned again.

As she dashed for the engine cubicle a patient, unconcerned voice filled the room. 'Attention. Engines will overload in three minutes, twenty seconds.'

A wall of heat hit her when she entered the cubicle. Smoke made it difficult to see. Machinery was whining, complaining loudly around her as she pushed at the perspiration beading on her face. Somehow she located the control board through the smoke, forced herself to remember proper sequencing as she reclosed the switches she'd opened only moments ago. The sirens continued their steady lament.

'Attention. Engines will overload in three minutes. Engines will overload in three minutes.'

Gasping for breath, she leaned against the hot wall as she jabbed a button. 'Mother, I've turned all the cooling units back on full!'

'Too late for remedial action. The drive core has begun to melt. Reaction irreversible at this point. Implosion incipient, followed by uncontainable overload and subsequent detonation. Engines will overload in two minutes, fifty-five seconds.'

Mother had always sounded comforting to Ripley. Now the computer voice was devoid of anthropomorphisms, remorseless as the time it was marking off.

Choking, her throat burning, she stumbled from the cubicle, the sirens giggling hysterically in her brain. 'Attention. Engines will overload in two minutes,' Mother announced via a wall speaker.

Jones was waiting for her on the companionway. He was quiet now, meowed out. She staggered back down towards the shuttle, half dragging the catbox, somehow keeping the flamethrower ready. Once she thought a shadow moved behind her and she whirled, but this time it was a shadow and nothing more.

She hesitated in the corridor, undecided what to do and desperately tired. A voice refused to let her rest. 'Attention. Engines will explode in ninety seconds.'

Putting down Jones's box, she gripped the flamethrower in both hands and rushed the shuttle lock.

It was empty.

She spun, charged back into the corridor, and grabbed at the catbox. Nothing materialized to challenge her.

'Attention. The engines will explode in sixty seconds,' said Mother calmly.

An unlucky Jones found himself dumped near the main console as Ripley threw herself into the pilot's seat. There was no time to plot niceties like trajectory or angle of release. She concentrated on hitting a single button that had one red word engraved beneath it.

LAUNCH.

Retainer bolts blew away with tiny, comical explosions. There was a blast of secondary engines as the shuttle fell away from the *Nostromo*.

G-forces tore at Ripley as she fought to strap herself in. The G-force would fade soon, the result of the shuttle leaving the *Nostromo*'s hyperdrive field and slanting off on its own path through space.

She finished strapping herself down, then allowed herself to breathe deeply of the shuttle's clean air. Howling sounds penetrated her exhausted brain. From her position she could just reach the catbox. Her head bent over the container and tears squeezed from her smoke-reddened eyes as she hugged it to her chest.

Her gaze rose to the rear-facing screen. A small point of light silently turned into a majestic, expanding fireball sending out tentacles of torn metal and shredded plastic. It faded, was followed up by a much larger fireball as the refinery went up. Two billion tons of gas and vaporized machinery filled the cosmos, obscured her vision until it, too, began to fade.

The shock struck the shuttlecraft soon after as the expanding superheated gas raced past. When the craft had settled she unstrapped, walked to the back of the little cabin and looked out a rear port. Her face was bathed in orange light as the last of the boiling fire globe vanished.

She finally turned away. The *Nostromo*, her shipmates, all had ceased to exist. They Were No More. It hit her harder in that quiet, isolated moment than she'd thought it would. It was the utter finality of it that was so difficult to accept, the knowledge that they no longer existed as components, however insignificant, of a greater universe. Not even as corpses. They simply had become not.

She did not see the massive hand reaching out for her from the concealment of deep shadow. But Jones did. He yowled.

Ripley spun, found herself facing the creature. It had been in the shuttle all the time.

Her first thought was for the flamethrower. It lay on the deck next to the crouching alien. She hunted wildly for a place to retreat to. There was a small locker nearby. Its door had popped open from the shock of the expanding gas. She started to edge towards it.

The creature started to rise as soon as she began to move. She leaped for the locker and threw herself inside, one hand diving for the handle. As she fell in, her weight pulled the door shut behind her with a slam.

There was a port in the upper part of the door. Ripley found herself practically nose-up against it in the shallow locker. Outside, the alien put its own head up next to the window, peered in at her almost curiously, as though she were an exhibit in a cage. She tried to scream and couldn't. It died in her throat. All she could do was stare wide-eyed at the apparition glaring back at her.

The locker was not airtight. A distinctive moaning reached her from outside. Distracted, the alien left the port to inspect the source of the strange noise. It bent, lifted the sealed catbox, causing Jones to howl more loudly.

Ripley knocked on the glass, trying to draw the creature's attention away from the helpless animal. It worked. The alien was back at the glass in a second. She froze, and it returned to its leisurely inspection of the catbox.

Ripley began a frantic search of the confined chamber. There was little inside except the single pressure suit. Working rapidly despite her inability to keep her hands from trembling, she slipped into it.

Outside the alien was shaking the catbox experimentally. Jones yowled through the box diaphragm. Ripley was halfway into the pressure suit when the alien threw the box down. It bounced but did not break open. Picking it up again, the alien hammered it against a wall. Jones was beyond sense, screamed steadily. The alien jammed the box into a crevice between two exposed conduits, began pounding the container into the opening while Jones fought to escape, hissing and spitting.

Pulling on the helmet, Ripley latched it tight. There was no one around to double-check for her. If the seals were improperly set she'd find out soon enough. A touch activated the respirator and the suit filled with bottled life.

She struggled to make a last search of the locker. There was nothing like a laser, which she couldn't have used in any case. But a long metal rod revealed a sharp tip when its protective rubber end was removed. It wasn't much of a weapon, but it gave her a little confidence, which was more important.

Taking a deep breath, she slowly unlatched the door, then kicked it open.

The alien turned to face the locker, caught the steel shaft through its mid-section. Ripley had run with all her weight behind it, and it penetrated deeply. The alien grabbed at the shaft as yellow fluid began to spill outward, hissing violently where it contacted the metal.

Ripley fell back, grabbed a strut support while her other hand flailed at and contacted an emergency release. That blew the rear hatch. Instantly, all the air in the shuttle and anything not secured by bolt or strap or arm was sucked out into space. The alien shot past her. With inhuman reflexes it reached out an appendage . . . and caught hold of her trailing leg, just above the ankle.

She found herself dangling partway out the hatch as she kicked desperately at the limb locked around her leg. It wouldn't let go. There was a lever next to the emergency release and she threw it over. The hatch slammed shut, closing her in, leaving the alien outside.

Acid began to foam along the hatch lining, leaking from the crushed member once wrapped around her ankle. Stumbling forward, she scanned the console, found the switches that activated the secondary engines. She pressed several of the buttons.

Near the stern of the shuttle, colourless energy belched outward. Incinerated, the alien fell away from the ship. The moment it was cut free, the acid stopped flowing.

She watched nervously as it continued to bubble, but there had been little bleeding. It finally stopped. She punched the small computer keyboard, waited dumbly for the readout.

REAR HATCH DAMAGE: QUERY.

ANALYSIS: MINOR REDUCTION OF HULL.

SHIP INTEGRITY NOT COMPROMISED. ATMOS-PHERIC HOLDING CAPACITY UNIMPAIRED. SUFFI-CIENT SEALANT TO COMPENSATE.

OBSERVATION: REPAIR DAMAGED SECTION AS SOON AS DESTINATION ACHIEVED. PRESENT HULL WILL FAIL INSPECTION.

She let out a yell, then moved back to peer out the rear port. A writhing, smoking shape was tumbling slowly away from the ship. Bits and pieces of charred flesh fell from it. Then the incredibly tough organism finally succumbed to the laws of differential pressure and the alien exploded, swelling up and then bursting, sending particles of itself in all directions. Harmless now, the smouldering fragments dwindled from sight.

It couldn't be said she was cheerful. There were lines in her face and a raped place in her brain that mitigated any such possibility. But she was composed enough to relax her body and lean back in the pilot's seat.

A touch on several buttons repressurized the cabin. She opened the catbox. With that wonderful facility common to all cats, the tom had already forgotten the attack. It curled up in her lap as she sat down again, a tawny curlicue of contentment, and started to purr. She stroked it as she dictated into the ship's recorder.

'I should reach the frontier in another four months or so. With a little luck the beacon network will pick up my SOS and put out the word. I'll have a statement ready to recite to the media and will secure a duplicate copy of it in this log, including a few comments of some interest to the authorities concerning certain policies of the Company.

'This is Ripley, ident number W5645022460H, warrant-officer, last survivor of the commercial starship *Nostromo*, signing off this entry.'

She thumbed the stop. It was quiet in the cabin, the first quiet of many days. She thought it barely possible she might rest now. She could only hope not to dream.

A hand caressed orange-yellow fur. She smiled. 'Come on, cat . . . Let's go to sleep . . .'

# ALIENS

Novelization by Alan Dean Foster
Based on the screenplay by James Cameron

For H.R. Giger
Master of the sinister airbrush.
Who reveals more about us than we wish to know.
From ADF and points west.

I

Two dreamers.

Not so very much difference between them despite the more obvious distinctions. One was of modest size, the other larger. One was female, the other male. The mouth of the first contained a mixture of sharp and flat teeth, a clear indication that it was omnivorous, while the maxillary cutlery of the other was intended solely for slicing and penetrating. Both were the scions of a race of killers. This was a genetic tendency the first dreamer's kind had learned to moderate. The other dreamer remained wholly feral.

More differences were apparent in their dreams than in their appearance. The first dreamer slept uneasily, memories of unmentionable terrors recently experienced oozing up from the depths of her subconscious to disrupt the normally placid stasis of hypersleep. She would have tossed and turned dangerously if not for the capsule that contained and restrained her movements—that and the fact that in deep sleep, muscular activity is reduced to a minimum. So she tossed and turned mentally. She was not aware of this. During hypersleep one is aware of nothing.

Every so often, though, a dark and vile memory would rise to the fore, like sewage seeping up beneath a city street. Temporarily it would overwhelm her rest. Then she would moan within the capsule. Her heartbeat would increase. The computer that watched over her like an electronic angel would note the accelerated activity and respond by lowering her body temperature another degree while increasing the flow of stabilizing drugs to her system. The moaning would stop. The dreamer would quiet and sink back into her cushions. It would take time for the nightmare to return.

Next to her the small killer would react to these isolated episodes by twitching as if in response to the larger sleeper's distress. Then it, too, would relax again, dreaming of small, warm bodies and the flow of hot blood, of the comfort to be found in the company of its own kind, and the assurance that this would come again. Somehow it knew that both dreamers would awaken together or not at all.

The last possibility did not unsettle its rest. It was possessed of more patience than its companion in hypersleep, and a more realistic perception of its position in the cosmos. It was content to sleep and wait, knowing that if and when consciousness returned, it would be ready to stalk and kill again. Meanwhile it rested.

Time passes. Horror does not.

In the infinity that is space, suns are but grains of sand. A white dwarf is barely worthy of notice. A small spacecraft like the lifeboat of the vanished vessel *Nostromo* is almost too tiny to exist in such emptiness. It drifted through the great nothing like a freed electron broken loose from its atomic orbit.

Yet even a freed electron can attract attention, if others equipped with appropriate detection instruments happen to chance across it. So it was that the lifeboat's course took it close by a familiar star. Even so, it was a stroke of luck that it was not permanently overlooked. It passed very near another ship; in space, 'very near' being anything less than a light-year. It appeared on the fringe of a range spanner's screen.

Some who saw the blip argued for ignoring it. It was too small to be a ship, they insisted. It didn't belong where it was. And ships talked back. This one was as quiet as the dead. More likely it was only an errant asteroid, a renegade chunk of nickel-iron off to see the universe. If it was a ship, at the very least it would have been blaring to anything within hearing range with an emergency beacon.

But the captain of the ranging vessel was a curious fellow. A minor deviation in their course would give them a chance to check out the silent wanderer, and a little clever bookkeeping would be sufficient to justify the detour's cost to the owners. Orders were given, and computers worked to adjust trajectory. The captain's judgment was confirmed when they drew alongside the stranger: it was a ship's lifeboat.

Still no sign of life, no response to polite inquiries. Even the running lights were out. But the ship was not completely dead. Like a body in frigid weather, the craft had withdrawn power from its extremities to protect something vital deep within.

The captain selected three men to board the drifter. Gently as an eagle mating with a lost feather, the larger craft sidled close to the *Narcissus*. Metal kissed metal. Grapples were applied. The sounds of the locking procedure echoed through both vessels.

Wearing full pressure suits, the three boarders entered their airlock. They carried portable lights and other equipment. Air being too precious to abandon to vacuum, they waited patiently while the oxygen was inhaled by their ship. Then the outer-lock door slid aside.

Their first sight of the lifeboat was disappointing: no internal lights visible through the port in the door, no sign of life within. The door refused to respond when the external controls were pressed. It had been jammed shut from inside. After the men made sure there was no air in the lifeboat's cabin, a robot welder was put to work on the door. Twin torches flared brightly in the darkness, slicing into the door from two sides. The flames met at the bottom of the barrier. Two men braced the third, who kicked the metal aside. The way was open.

The lifeboat's interior was as dark and still as a tomb. A section of portable grappling cable snaked along the floor. Its torn and frayed tip ended near the exterior door. Up close to the cockpit a faint light was visible. The men moved towards it.

The familiar dome of a hypersleep capsule glowed from within. The intruders exchanged a glance before approaching. Two of them leaned over the thick glass cover of the transparent sarcophagus. Behind them, their companion was studying his instrumentation and muttered aloud.

'Internal pressure positive. Assuming nominal hull and systems integrity. Nothing appears busted; just shut down to conserve energy. Capsule pressure steady. There's power feeding through, though I bet the batteries have about had it. Look how dim the internal readouts are. Ever see a hypersleep capsule like this one?'

'Late twenties.' The speaker leaned over the glass and murmured into his suit pickup. 'Good-lookin' dame.'

'Good-lookin', my eye.' His companion sounded disappointed. 'Life function diodes are all green. That means she's alive. There goes our salvage profit, guys.'

The other inspector gestured in surprise. 'Hey, there's something in there with her. Nonhuman. Looks like it's alive too. Can't see too clearly. Part of it's under her hair. It's orangish.'

'Orange?' The leader of the trio pushed past both of them and rested the faceplate of his helmet against the transparent barrier. 'Got claws, whatever it is.'

'Hey.' One of the men nudged his companion. 'Maybe it's an alien life-form, huh? That'd be worth some bucks.'

Ripley chose that moment to move ever so slightly. A few strands of hair drifted down the pillow beneath her head, more fully revealing the creature that slept tight against her. The leader of the boarders straightened and shook his head disgustedly.

'No such luck. It's just a cat.'

Listening was a struggle. Sight was out of the question. Her throat was a seam of anthracite inside the lighter pumice of her skull; black, dry, and with a faintly resinous taste. Her tongue moved loosely over territory long forgotten. She tried to remember what speech was like. Her lips parted. Air came rushing up from her lungs, and those long-dormant bellows ached with the exertion. The result of this strenuous interplay between lips, tongue, palate, and lungs was a small triumph of one word. It drifted through the room.

'Thirsty.'

Something smooth and cool slid between her lips. The shock of dampness almost overwhelmed her. Memory nearly caused her to reject the water tube. In another time and place that kind of insertion was a prelude to a particularly unique and loathsome demise. Only water flowed from this tube, however. It was accompanied by a calm voice intoning advice.

'Don't swallow. Sip slowly.'

She obeyed, though a part of her mind screamed at her to suck the restoring liquid as fast as possible. Oddly enough, she did not feel dehydrated, only terribly thirsty.

'Good,' she whispered huskily. 'Got anything more substantial?'

'It's too soon,' said the voice.

'The heck it is. How about some fruit juice?'

'Citric acid will tear you up.' The voice hesitated, considering, then said, 'Try this.'

Once again the gleaming metal tube slipped smoothly into her mouth. She sucked at it pleasurably. Sugared iced tea cascaded down her throat, soothing both thirst and her first cravings for food. When she'd had enough, she said so, and the tube was withdrawn. A new sound assailed her ears: the trill of some exotic bird.

She could hear and taste; now it was time to see. Her eyes opened to a view of pristine rain forest. Trees lifted bushy green crowns heavenward. Bright iridescent winged creatures buzzed as they flitted from branch to branch. Birds trailed long tail feathers like jet contrails behind them as they dipped and soared in pursuit of the insects. A quetzal peered out at her from its home in the trunk of a climbing fig.

Orchids bloomed mightily, and beetles scurried among leaves and fallen branches like ambulatory jewels. An agouti appeared, saw her, and bolted back into the undergrowth. From the stately hardwood off to the left, a howler monkey dangled, crooning softly to its infant.

The sensory overload was too much. She closed her eyes against the chattering profusion of life.

Later (another hour? another day?) a crack appeared in the middle of the big tree's buttressing roots. The split widened to obliterate the torso of a gambolling marmoset. A woman emerged from the gap and closed it behind her, sealing the temporary bloodless wound in tree and animal. She touched a hidden wall switch, and the rain forest went away.

It was very good for a solido, but now that it had been shut off, Ripley could see the complex medical equipment the rain forest imagery had camouflaged. To her immediate left was the medved that had responded so considerately to her request for first water and then cold tea. The machine hung motionless and ready from the wall, aware of everything that was happening inside her body, ready to adjust medication, provide food and drink, or summon human help should the need arise.

The newcomer smiled at the patient and used a remote control attached to her breast pocket to raise the backrest of Ripley's bed. The patch on her shirt, which identified her as a senior medical technician, was bright with colour against the background of white uniform. Ripley eyed her warily, unable to tell if the woman's smile was genuine or routine. Her voice was pleasant and maternal without being cloying.

'Sedation's wearing off. I don't think you need any more. Can you understand me?' Ripley nodded. The medtech considered her patient's appearance and reached a decision. 'Let's try something new. Why don't I open the window?'

'I give up. Why don't you?'

The smile weakened at the corners, was promptly recharged.

Professional and practiced, then; not heartfelt. And why should it be? The medtech didn't know Ripley, and Ripley didn't know her. So what. The woman pointed her remote towards the wall across from the foot of the bed.

'Watch your eyes.'

Now there's a choice non sequitur for you, Ripley thought. Nevertheless, she squinted against the implied glare.

A motor hummed softly, and the motorized wall plate slid into the ceiling. Harsh light filled the room. Though filtered and softened, it was still a shock to Ripley's tired system.

Outside the port lay a vast sweep of nothingness. Beyond the nothingness was everything. A few of Gateway Station's modular habitats formed a loop off to the left, the plastic cells strung together like children's blocks. A couple of communications antennae peeped into the view from below. Dominating the scene was the bright curve of the Earth. Africa was a brown, white-streaked smear swimming in an ocean blue, the Mediterranean a sapphire tiara crowning the Sahara.

Ripley had seen it all before, in school and then in person. She was not particularly thrilled by the view so much as she was just glad it was still there. Events of recent memory suggested it might not be, that nightmare was reality and this soft, inviting globe only mocking illusion. It was comforting, familiar, reassuring, like a worn-down teddy bear. The scene was completed by the bleak orb of the moon drifting in the background like a vagrant exclamation point: planetary system as security blanket.

'And how are we today?' She grew aware that the medtech was talking to her instead of at her.

'Terrible.' Someone or two had told her once upon a time that she had a lovely and unique voice. Eventually she should get it back. For the moment no part of her body was functioning at optimum efficiency. She wondered if it ever would again, because she was very different from the person she'd been before. That Ripley had set out on a routine cargo run in a now vanished spacecraft. A different Ripley had returned, and lay in the hospital bed regarding her nurse.

'Just terrible?' You had to admire the medtech, she mused. A woman not easily discouraged. 'That's better than yesterday, at least. I'd call "terrible" a quantum jump up from atrocious.'

Ripley squeezed her eyelids shut, opened them slowly. The Earth was still there. Time, which heretofore she hadn't given a hoot about, suddenly acquired new importance.

'How long have I been on Gateway Station?'

'Just a couple of days.' Still smiling.

'Feels longer.'

The medtech turned her face away, and Ripley wondered whether she found the terse observation boring or disturbing. 'Do you feel up to a visitor?'

'Do I have a choice?'

'Of course you have a choice. You're the patient. After the doctors you know best. You want to be left alone, you get left alone.'

Ripley shrugged, mildly surprised to discover that her shoulder muscles were up to the gesture. 'I've been alone long enough. Whattheheck. Who is it?'

The medtech walked to the door. 'There are two of them, actually.' Ripley could see that she was smiling again.

A man entered, carrying something. Ripley didn't know him, but she knew his fat, orange, bored-looking burden.

'Jones!' She sat up straight, not needing the bed support now. The man gratefully relinquished possession of the big tomcat. Ripley cuddled it to her. 'Come here, Jonesey, you ugly old moose, you sweet ball of fluff, you!'

The cat patiently endured this embarrassing display, so typical of humans, with all the dignity his kind was heir to. In so doing, Jones displayed the usual tolerance felines have for human beings. Any extraterrestrial observer privy to the byplay would not have doubted for an instant which of the two creatures on the bed was the superior intelligence.

The man who'd brought the good orange news with him pulled a chair close to the bed and patiently waited for Ripley to take notice of him. He was in his thirties, good-looking without being flashy, and dressed in a nondescript business suit. His smile was no more or less real than the medtech's, even though it had been practised longer. Ripley eventually acknowledged his presence with a nod but continued to reserve her conversation for the cat. It occurred to her visitor that if he was going to be taken for anything more than a delivery man, it was up to him to make the first move.

'Nice room,' he said without really meaning it. He looked like a country boy, but he didn't talk like one, Ripley thought as he edged the chair a little closer to her. 'I'm Burke. Carter Burke. I work for the Company, but other than that, I'm an okay guy. Glad to see you're feeling better.' The last at least sounded as though he meant it.

'Who says I'm feeling better?' She stroked Jones, who purred contentedly and continued to shed cat hair all over the sterile bed.

'Your doctors and machines. I'm told the weakness and disorientation should pass soon, though you don't look particularly disoriented to me. Side effects of the unusually long hypersleep, or something like that. Biology wasn't my favourite subject. I was better at figures. For example, yours seems to have come through in pretty good shape.' He nodded towards the bed covers.

'I hope I look better than I feel, because I feel like the inside of an Egyptian mummy. You said "unusually long hypersleep". How long was I out there?' She gestured towards the watching medtech. 'They won't tell me anything.'

Burke's tone was soothing, paternal. 'Well, maybe you shouldn't worry about that just yet.'

Ripley's hand shot from beneath the covers to grab his arm. The speed of her reaction and the strength of her grip clearly surprised him. 'No. I'm conscious, and I don't need any more coddling. How *long*?'

He glanced over at the medtech. She shrugged and turned away to attend to the needs of some incomprehensible tangle of lights and tubes. When he looked back at the woman lying in the bed, he found he was unable to shift his eyes away from hers.

'All right. It's not my job to tell you, but my instincts say you're strong enough to handle it. Fifty-seven years.'

The number hit her like a hammer. Fifty-seven too many hammers. Hit her harder than waking up, harder than her first sight of the home world. She seemed to deflate, to lose strength and colour simultaneously as she sank back into the mattress. Suddenly the artificial gravity of the station seemed thrice Earth-normal, pressing her down and back. The air-filled pad on which she rested was ballooning around her, threatening to stifle and smother. The medtech glanced at her warning lights, but all of them stayed silent.

Fifty-seven years. In the more than half century she'd been dreaming in deepsleep, friends left behind had grown old and died, family had matured and faded, the world she'd left behind had metamorphosed into who knew what. Governments had risen and fallen; inventions had hit the market and been outmoded and discarded. No one had ever survived more than sixty-five years in hypersleep. Longer than that and the body begins to fail beyond the ability of the capsules to sustain life. She'd barely survived; she'd pushed the limits of the physiologically possible, only to find that she'd outlived life.

'Fifty-seven!'

'You drifted right through the core systems,' Burke was telling her. 'Your beacon failed. It was blind luck that that deep salvage team caught you when they . . .' he hesitated. She'd suddenly turned pale, her eyes widening. 'Are you all right?'

She coughed once, a second time harder. There was a pressure—her expression changed from one of concern to dawning horror. Burke tried to hand her a glass of water from the nightstand, only to have her slap it away. It struck the floor and shattered. Jones's fur was standing on end as the cat leapt to the floor, yowling and spitting. His claws made rapid scratching sounds on the smooth plastic as he scrambled away from the bed. Ripley grabbed at her chest, her back arching as the convulsions began. She looked as if she were strangling.

The medtech was shouting at the omnidirectional pickup. 'Code Blue to Four Fifteen! Code Blue, Four One Five!'

She and Burke clutched Ripley's shoulders as the patient began bouncing against the mattress. They held on as a doctor and two more techs came pounding into the room.

It couldn't be happening. It couldn't!

'No—noooooo!'

The techs were trying to slap restraints on her arms and legs as she thrashed wildly. Covers went flying. One foot sent a medtech sprawling while the other smashed a hole in the soulless glass eye on a monitoring unit. From beneath a cabinet Jones glared out at his mistress and hissed.

'Hold her,' the doctor was yelling. 'Get me an airway, stat! And fifteen cc's of—!'

An explosion of blood suddenly stained the top sheet crimson, and the linens began to pyramid as something unseen rose beneath them. Stunned, the doctor and the techs backed off. The sheet continued to rise.

Ripley saw clearly as the sheet slid away. The medtech fainted. The doctor made gagging sounds as the eyeless, toothed worm emerged from the patient's shattered rib cage. It turned slowly until its fanged mouth was only a foot from its host's face, and screeched. The sound drowned out everything human in the room, filling Ripley's ears, overloading her numbed cortex, echoing, reverberating through her entire being as she . . .

. . . sat up screaming, her body snapping into an upright position in the bed. She was alone in the darkened hospital room. Coloured light shone from the insectlike dots of glowing LEDs. Clutching pathetically at her chest she fought to regain the breath the nightmare had stolen.

Her body was intact: sternum, muscles, tendons, and ligaments all in place and functional. There was no demented horror ripping itself out of her torso, no obscene birth in progress. Her eyes moved jerkily in their sockets as she scanned the room. Nothing lying in ambush on the floor, nothing hiding behind the cabinets waiting for her to let down her guard. Only silent machines monitoring her life and the comfortable bed maintaining it. The sweat was pouring off her even though the room was pleasantly cool. She held one fist protectively against her sternum, as if to reassure herself constantly of its continued inviolability.

She jumped slightly as the video monitor suspended over the bed came to life. An older woman gazed anxiously down at her. Night-duty medtech. Her face was full of honest, not merely professional, concern.

'Bad dreams again? Do you want something to help you sleep?' A robot arm whirred to life left of Ripley's arm. She regarded it with distaste.

'No. I've slept enough.'

'Okay. You know best. If you change your mind, just use your bed buzzer.' She switched off. The screen darkened.

Ripley slowly leaned back against the raised upper section of mattress and touched one of the numerous buttons set in the side of her nightstand. Once more the window screen that covered the far wall slid into the ceiling. She could see out again. There was the portion of Gateway, now brilliantly lit by nighttime lights and, beyond it, the night-shrouded globe of the Earth. Wisps of cloud masked distant pinpoints of light. Cities—alive with happy people blissfully ignorant of the stark reality that was an indifferent cosmos.

Something landed on the bed next to her, but this time she didn't jump. It was a familiar, demanding shape, and she hugged it tightly to her, ignoring the casual *meowrr* of protest.

'It's okay, Jones. We made it, we're safe. I'm sorry I scared you. It'll be all right now. It's going to be all right.'

All right, yes, save that she was going to have to learn how to sleep all over again.

Sunlight streamed through the stand of poplars. A meadow was visible beyond the trees, green stalks splattered with the brightness of bluebells, daisies, and phlox. A robin pranced near the base of one tree, searching for insects. It did not see

the sinewy predator stalking it, eyes intent, muscles taut. The
bird turned its back, and the stalker sprang.

Jones slammed into the solido of the robin, neither acquiring
prey nor disturbing the image, which continued its blithe quest
for imaged insects. Shaking his head violently, the tomcat
staggered away from the wall.

Ripley sat on a nearby bench regarding this cat-play. 'Dumb
cat. Don't you know a solido by now when you see one?'
Although maybe she shouldn't be too hard on the cat. Solido
design had improved during the last fifty-seven years.
Everything had been improved during the last fifty-seven
years. Except for her and Jones.

Glass doors sealed the atrium off from the rest of Gateway
Station. The expensive solido of a North American temperate
forest was set off by potted plants and sickly grass underfoot.
The solido looked more real than the real plants, but at least
the latter had an honest smell. She leaned slightly towards one
pot. Dirt and moisture and growing things. Of cabbages and
kings, she mused dourly. Horsepucky. She wanted off
Gateway. Earth was temptingly near, and she longed to put
blue sky between herself and the malign emptiness of space.

Two of the glass doors that sealed off the atrium parted to
admit Carter Burke. For a moment she found herself
regarding him as a man and not just a company cipher. Maybe
that was a sign that she was returning to normal. Her appraisal
of him was mitigated by the knowledge that when the *Nostromo*
had departed on its ill-fated voyage, he was two decades short
of being born. It shouldn't have made any difference. They
were approximately the same physical age.

'Sorry.' Always the cheery smile. 'I've been running behind
all morning. Finally managed to get away.'

Ripley never had been one for small talk. Now more than
ever, life seemed too precious to waste on inconsequential
banter. Why couldn't people just say what they had to say
instead of dancing for five minutes around the subject?

'Have they located my daughter yet?'

Burke looked uncomfortable. 'Well, I was going to wait until after the inquest.'

'I've waited fifty-seven years. I'm impatient. So humour me.'

He nodded, set down his carrying case, and popped the lid. He fumbled a minute with the contents before producing several sheets of thin plastic.

'Is she . . .?'

Burke spoke as he read from one of the sheets. 'Amanda Ripley-McClaren. Married name, I guess. Age sixty-six at . . . time of death. That was two years ago. There's a whole history here. Nothing spectacular or notable. Details of a pleasant, ordinary life. Like the kind most of us lead, I expect. I'm sorry.' He passed over the sheets, studied Ripley's face as she scanned the printouts. 'Guess this is my morning for being sorry.'

Ripley studied the holographic image imprinted on one of the sheets. It showed a rotund, slightly pale woman in her mid-sixties. Could have been anyone's aunt. There was nothing distinctive about the face, nothing that leapt out and shouted with familiarity. It was impossible to reconcile the picture of this older woman with the memory of the little girl she'd left behind.

'Amy,' she whispered.

Burke still held a couple of sheets, read quietly as she continued to stare at the hologram. 'Cancer. Hmmm. They still haven't licked all varieties of that one. Body was cremated. Interred Westlake Repository, Little Chute, Wisconsin. No children.'

Ripley looked past him, towards the forest solido but not at it. She was staring at the invisible landscape of the past.

'I promised her I'd be home for her birthday. Her eleventh birthday. I sure missed that one.' She glanced again at the picture. 'Well, she'd already learned to take my promises with a grain of salt. When it came to flight schedules, anyway.'

Burke nodded, trying to be sympathetic. That was difficult for him under ordinary circumstances, much more so this morning. At least he had the sense to keep his mouth shut instead of muttering the usual polite inanities.

'You always think you can make it up to somebody—later, you know.' She took a deep breath. 'But now I never can. I never can.' The tears came then, long overdue. Fifty-seven years overdue. She sat there on the bench and sobbed softly to herself, alone now in a different kind of space.

Finally Burke patted her reassuringly on her shoulder, uncomfortable at the display and trying hard not to show it. 'The hearing convenes at oh-nine-thirty. You don't want to be late. It wouldn't make a good first impression.'

She nodded, rose. 'Jones. Jonesey, c'mere.' Meowing, the cat sauntered over and allowed her to pick him up. She wiped self-consciously at her eyes. 'I've got to change. Won't take long.' She rubbed her nose against the cat's back, a small outrage it suffered in silence.

'Want me to walk you back to your room?'

'Sure, why not?'

He turned and started for the proper corridor. The doors parted to permit them egress from the atrium. 'You know, that cat's something of a special privilege. They don't allow pets on Gateway.'

'Jones isn't a pet.' She scratched the tom behind the ears. 'He's a survivor.'

As Ripley promised, she was ready in plenty of time. Burke elected to wait outside her private room, studying his own reports, until she emerged. The transformation was impressive. Gone was the pale, waxy skin; gone the bitterness of expression and the uncertain stride. Determination? he wondered as they headed for the central corridor. Or just clever makeup?

Neither of them said anything until they neared the sub-level where the hearing room was located. 'What are you going to tell them?' he finally asked her.

'What's to tell that hasn't already been told? You read my deposition. It's complete and accurate. No embellishments. It didn't need any embellishments.'

'Look, *I* believe you, but there are going to be some

heavyweights in there, and every one of them is going to try to pick holes in your story. You got feds, you got Interstellar Commerce Commission, you got Colonial Administration, insurance company guys—'

'I get the picture.'

'Just tell them what happened. The important thing is to stay cool and unemotional.'

Sure, she thought. All of her friends and shipmates and relatives were dead, and she'd lost fifty-seven years of reality to an unrestoring sleep. Cool and unemotional. Sure.

Despite her determination, by midday she was anything but cool and collected. Repetition of the same questions, the same idiotic disputations of the facts as she'd reported them, the same exhaustive examination of minor points that left the major ones untouched—all combined to render her frustrated and angry.

As she spoke to the sombre inquisitors the large videoscreen behind her was printing out mug shots and dossiers. She was glad it was behind her, because the faces were those of the *Nostromo*'s crew. There was Parker, grinning like a goon. And Brett, placid and bored as the camera did its duty. Kane was there, too, and Lambert. Ash the traitor, his soulless face enriched with programmed false piety. Dallas . . .

Dallas. Better the picture behind her, like the memories.

'Do you have earwax or what?' she finally snapped. 'We've been here three hours. How many different ways do you want me to tell the same story? You think it'll sound better in Swahili, get me a translator and we'll do it in Swahili. I'd try Japanese, but I'm out of practice. Also out of patience. How long does it take you to make up your collective mind?'

Van Leuwen steepled his fingers and frowned. His expression was as grey as his suit. It was approximated by the looks on the faces of his fellow board members. There were eight of them on the official board of inquiry, and not a friendly one in the lot. Executives. Administrators. Adjusters. How could she convince them? They weren't human beings.

They were expressions of bureaucratic disapproval. Phantoms. She was used to dealing with reality. The intricacies of politicorporate manoeuvring were beyond her.

'This isn't as simple as you seem to believe,' he told her quietly. 'Look at it from our perspective. You freely admit to detonating the engines of, and thereby destroying, an M-Class interstellar freighter. A rather expensive piece of hardware.'

The insurance investigator was possibly the unhappiest member of the board. 'Forty-two million in adjusted dollars. That's minus payload, of course. Engine detonation wouldn't leave anything salvageable, even if we could locate the remains after fifty-seven years.'

Van Leuwen nodded absently before continuing. 'It's not as if we think you're lying. The lifeboat shuttle's flight recorder corroborates some elements of your account. The least controversial ones. That the *Nostromo* set down on LV-426, an unsurveyed and previously unvisited planet, at the time and date specified. That repairs were made. That it resumed its course after a brief layover and was subsequently set for self-destruct and that this, in fact, occurred. That the order for engine overload was provided by you. For reasons unknown.'

'Look, I told you—'

Van Leuwen interrupted, having heard it before. 'It did not, however, contain any entries concerning the hostile alien life-form you *allegedly* picked up during your short stay on the planet's surface.'

'We didn't "pick it up",' she shot back. 'Like I told you, it—'

She broke off, staring at the hollow faces gazing stonily back at her. She was wasting her breath. This wasn't a real board of inquiry. This was a formal wake, a post-interment party. The object here wasn't to ascertain the truth in hopes of vindication, it was to smooth out the rough spots and make the landscape all nice and neat again. And there wasn't a thing she could do about it, she saw now. Her fate had been decided before she'd set foot in the room. The inquiry was a show, the questions a sham. To satisfy the record.

'Then somebody's gotten to it and doctored the recorder. A competent tech could do that in an hour. Who had access to it?'

The representative of the Extrasolar Colonization Administration was a woman on the ungenerous side of fifty. Previously she'd looked bored. Now she just sat in her chair and shook her head slowly.

'Would you just listen to yourself for one minute? Do you really expect us to believe some of the things you've been telling us? Too much hypersleep can do all kinds of funny things to the mind.'

Ripley glared at her, furious at being so helpless. 'You want to hear some funny things?'

Van Leuwen stepped in verbally. 'The analytical team that went over your shuttle centimetre by centimetre found no physical evidence of the creature you describe or anything like it. No damage to the interior of the craft. No etching of metal surfaces that might have been caused by an unknown corrosive substance.'

Ripley had kept control all morning, answering the most inane queries with patience and understanding. The time for being reasonable was at an end, and so was her store of patience.

'That's because I blew it out the airlock!' She subsided a little as this declaration was greeted by the silence of the tomb. 'Like I said.'

The insurance man leaned forward and peered along the desk at the ECA representative. 'Are there any species like this "hostile organism" native to LV-426?'

'No.' The woman exuded confidence. 'It's a rock. No indigenous life bigger than a simple virus. Certainly nothing complex. Not even a flatworm. Never was, never will be.'

Ripley ground her teeth as she struggled to stay calm. 'I told you, it wasn't indigenous.' She tried to meet their eyes, but they were having none of it, so she concentrated on Van Leuwen and the ECA rep. 'There was a signal coming from the surface. The *Nostromo*'s scanner picked it up and woke us from hypersleep, as per standard regulations. When we traced it, we found an alien spacecraft like nothing you or anyone else has ever seen. *That* was on the recorder too.

'The ship was a derelict. Crashed, abandoned . . . we never did find out. We homed in on its beacon. We found the ship's pilot, also like nothing previously encountered. He was dead in his chair with a hole in his chest the size of a welder's tank.'

Maybe the story bothered the ECA rep. Or maybe she was just tired of hearing it for the umpteenth time. Whatever, she felt it was her place to respond.

'To be perfectly frank, we've surveyed over three hundred worlds, and no one's ever reported the existence of a creature, which, using your words'—and she bent to read from her copy of Ripley's formal statement—"gestates in a living human host" and has "concentrated molecular acid for blood." '

Ripley glanced towards Burke, who sat silent and tight-lipped at the far end of the table. He was not a member of the board of inquiry, so he had kept silent throughout the questioning. Not that he could do anything to help her. Everything depended on how her official version of the *Nostromo*'s demise was received. Without the corroborating evidence from the shuttle's flight recorder the board had nothing to go on but her word, and it had been made clear from the start how little weight they'd decided to allot to that. She wondered anew who had doctored the recorder and why. Or maybe it simply had malfunctioned on its own. At this point it didn't much matter. She was tired of playing the game.

'Look, I can see where this is going.' She half smiled, an expression devoid of amusement. This was hardball time, and she was going to finish it out even though she had no chance of winning. 'The whole business with the android—why we followed the beacon in the first place—it all adds up, though I can't prove it.' She looked down the length of the table, and now she did grin. 'Somebody's covering their Ash, and it's been decided that I'm going to take the muck for it. Okay, fine. But there's one thing you can't change, one fact you can't doctor away.

'Those things *exist*. You can wipe me out, but you can't wipe that out. Back on that planet is an alien ship, and on that ship are thousands of eggs. *Thousands*. Do you understand? Do you have any idea what that implies? I suggest you go back there with an expedition and find it, using the flight recorder's data, and find it fast. Find it and deal with it, preferably with an orbital nuke, before one of your survey teams comes back with a little surprise.'

'Thank you, Officer Ripley,' Van Leuwen began, 'that will be—'

'Because just one of those things,' she went on, stepping on him, 'managed to kill my entire crew within twelve hours of hatching.'

The administrator rose. Ripley wasn't the only one in the room who was out of patience. '*Thank* you. That will be all.'

'That's not all!' She stood and glared at him. 'If those things get back here, that *will* be all. Then you can just kiss it goodbye, Jack. Just *kiss it goodbye!*'

The ECA representative turned calmly to the administrator. 'I believe we have enough information on which to base a determination. I think it's time to close this inquest and retire for deliberation.'

Van Leuwen glanced at his fellow board members. He might as well have been looking at mirror images of himself, for all the superficial differences of face and build. They were of one mind.

That was something that could not be openly expressed, however. It would not look good in the record. Above all, everything had to look good in the record.

'Gentlemen, ladies?' Acquiescent nods. He looked back down at the subject under discussion. Dissection was more like it, she thought sourly. 'Officer Ripley, if you'd excuse us, please?'

'Not likely.' Trembling with frustration, she turned to leave the room. As she did so, her eyes fastened on the picture of Dallas that was staring blankly back down from the videoscreen. Captain Dallas. Friend Dallas. Companion Dallas.

Dead Dallas. She strode out angrily.

There was nothing more to do or say. She'd been found guilty, and now they were going to go through the motions of giving her an honest trial. Formalities. The Company and its friends loved their formalities. Nothing wrong with death and tragedy, as long as you could safely suck all the emotion out of it. Then it would be safe to put in the annual report. So the inquest had to be held, emotion translated into sanitized figures in neat columns. A verdict had to be rendered. But not too loudly, lest the neighbours overhear.

None of which really bothered Ripley. The imminent demise of her career didn't bother her. What she couldn't forgive was the blind stupidity being flaunted by the all-powerful in the room she'd left. So they didn't believe her. Given their type of mind-set and the absence of solid evidence, she could understand that. But to ignore her story totally, to refuse to check it out, that she could never forgive. Because there was a lot more at stake than one lousy life, one unspectacular career as a flight transport officer. And they didn't care. It didn't show as a profit or a loss, so they didn't care.

She booted the wall next to Burke as he bought coffee and doughnuts from the vending machine in the hall. The machine thanked him politely as it accepted his credcard. Like practically everything else on Gateway Station, the machine had no odour. Neither did the black liquid it poured. As for the alleged doughnuts, they might once have flown over a wheat field.

'You had them eating out of your hand, kiddo.' Burke was trying to cheer her up. She was grateful for the attempt, even as it failed. But there was no reason to take her anger out on him. Multiple sugars and artificial creamer gave the ersatz coffee some taste.

'They had their minds made up before I even went in there. I've wasted an entire morning. They should've had scripts printed up for everyone to read from, including me. Would've been easier just to recite what they wanted to hear instead of trying to remember the truth.' She glanced at him. 'You know what they think?'

'I can imagine.' He bit into a doughnut.

'They think I'm a headcase.'

'You are a headcase,' he told her cheerfully. 'Have a doughnut. Chocolate or buttermilk?'

She eyed the precooked torus he proffered distastefully. 'You can taste the difference?'

'Not really, but the colours are nice.'

She didn't grin, but she didn't sneer at him, either.

The 'deliberations' didn't take long. No reason why they should, she thought as she reentered the room and resumed her seat. Burke took his place on the far side of the chamber. He started to wink at her, thought better of it, and aborted the gesture. She recognized the eye twitch for what it almost became and was glad he hadn't followed through.

Van Leuwen cleared his throat. He didn't find it necessary to look to his fellow board members for support.

'It is the finding of this board of inquiry that Warrant Officer Ellen Ripley, NOC-14672, has acted with questionable judgment and is therefore declared unfit to hold an ICC licence as a commercial flight officer.'

If any of them expected some sort of reaction from the condemned, they were disappointed. She sat there and stared silently back at them, tight-lipped and defiant. More likely they were relieved. Emotional outbursts would have to be recorded. Van Leuwen continued, unaware that Ripley had reattired him in black cape and hood.

'Said licence is hereby suspended indefinitely, pending review at a future date to be specified later.' He cleared his throat, then his conscience. 'In view of the unusual length of time spent by the defendant in hypersleep and the concomitant indeterminable effects on the human nervous system, no criminal charges will be filed at this time.'

At this time, Ripley thought humourlessly. That was corporatese for 'Keep your mouth shut and stay away from the media and you'll still get to collect your pension.'

'You are released on your own recognizance for a six-month period of psychometric probation, to include monthly review by an approved ICC psychiatric tech and treatment and or medication as may be prescribed.'

It was short, neat, and not at all sweet, and she took it all without a word, until Van Leuwen had finished and departed. Burke saw the look in her eye and tried to restrain her.

'Lay off,' he whispered to her. She threw off his hand and continued up the corridor. 'It's over.'

'Right,' she called back to him as she lengthened her stride. 'So what else can they do to me?'

She caught up with Van Leuwen as he stood waiting for the elevator. 'Why won't you check out LV-426?'

He glanced back at her. 'Ms. Ripley, it wouldn't matter. The decision of the board is final.'

'The heck with the board's decision. We're not talking about me now. We're talking about the next poor souls to find that ship. Just tell me why you won't check it out.'

'Because I don't have to,' he told her brusquely. 'The people who live there checked it out years ago, and they've never reported any "hostile organism" or alien ship. Do you think I'm a complete fool? Did you think the board wouldn't seek some sort of verification, if only to protect ourselves from future inquiries? And by the way, they call it Acheron now.'

Fifty-seven years. Long time. People could accomplish a lot in fifty-seven years. Build, move around, establish new colonies. Ripley struggled with the import of the administrator's words.

'What are you talking about? What people?'

Van Leuwen joined the other passengers in the elevator car. Ripley put an arm between the doors to keep them from closing. The doors' sensors obediently waited for her to remove it.

'Terraformers,' Van Leuwen explained. 'Planetary engineers. Much has happened in that field while you slept, Ripley.

We've made significant advances, great strides. The cosmos is not a hospitable place, but we're changing that. It's what we call a shake-'n'-bake colony. They set up atmosphere processors to make the air breathable. We can do that now, efficiently and economically, as long as we have some kind of resident atmosphere to work with. Hydrogen, argon—methane is best. Acheron is swimming in methane, with a portion of oxygen and sufficient nitrogen for beginning bonding. It's nothing now. The air's barely breathable. But given time, patience, and hard work, there'll be another habitable world out there ready to comfort and succour humanity. At a price, of course. Ours is not a philanthropic institution, though we like to think of what we do as furthering mankind's progress.

'It's a big job. Decades worth. They've already been there more than twenty years. *Peacefully.*'

'Why didn't you tell me?'

'Because it was felt that the information might have biased your testimony. Personally I don't think it would have made a bit of difference. You obviously believe what you believe. But some of my colleagues were of a differing opinion. I doubt it would have changed our decision.'

The doors tried to close, and she slammed them apart. The other passengers began to exhibit signs of annoyance.

'How many colonists?'

Van Leuwen's brow furrowed. 'At last count I'd guess sixty, maybe seventy, families. We've found that people work better when they're not separated from their loved ones. It's more expensive, but it pays for itself in the long run, and it gives the community the feeling of a real colony instead of merely an engineering outpost. It's tough on some of the women and the kids, but when their tour of duty ends, they can retire comfortably. Everyone benefits from the arrangement.'

'Sweet Jesus,' Ripley whispered.

One of the passengers leaned forward, spoke irritably. 'Do you mind?'

Absently she dropped her arm to her side. Freed of their

responsibility, the doors closed quietly. Van Leuwen had already forgotten her, and she him. She was looking instead into her imagination.

Not liking what she saw there.

# II

It was not the best of times, and it certainly was the worst of places. Driven by unearthly meteorological forces, the winds of Acheron hammered unceasingly at the planet's barren surface. They were as old as the rocky globe itself. Without any oceans to compete with they would have scoured the landscape flat eons ago, had not the uneasy forces deep within the basaltic shell continually thrust up new mountains and plateaux. The winds of Acheron were at war with the planet that gave them life.

Heretofore there'd been nothing to interfere with their relentless flow. Nothing to interrupt their sand-filled storms, nothing to push against the gales instead of simply conceding mastery of the air to them—until humans had come to Acheron and claimed it for their own. Not as it was now, a landscape of tortured rock and dust dimly glimpsed through yellowish air, but as it would be once the atmosphere processors had done their work. First the atmosphere itself would be transformed, methane relinquishing its dominance to oxygen and nitrogen. Then the winds would be tamed, and the surface. The final result would be a benign climate whose offspring would take the form of snow and rain and growing things.

That would be the present's legacy to future generations. For now the inhabitants of Acheron ran the processors and struggled to make a dream come true, surviving on a ration of determination, humour, and oversize paycheques. They would not live long enough to see Acheron become a land of milk and honey. Only the Company would live long enough for that. The Company was immortal as none of them could ever be.

The sense of humour common to all pioneers living under difficult conditions was evident throughout the colony, most notably in a steel sign set in concrete pylons outside the last integrated structure:

### HADLEY'S HOPE – Pop. 159
### Welcome to Acheron

Beneath which some local wag had, without official authorization, added in indelible spray paint 'Have a Nice Day.' The winds ignored the request. Airborne particles of sand and grit had corroded much of the steel plate. A new visitor to Acheron, courtesy of the atmosphere processors, had added its own comment with a brown flourish: the first rains had produced the first rust.

Beyond the sign lay the colony itself, a cluster of bunkerlike metal and plasticrete structures joined together by conduits seemingly too fragile to withstand Acheron's winds. They were not as impressive to look upon as was the surrounding terrain with its wind-blasted rock formations and crumbling mountains, but they were almost as solid and a lot more homey. They kept the gales at bay, and the still-thin atmosphere, and protected those who worked within.

High-wheeled tractors and other vehicles crawled down the open roadways between the buildings, emerging from or disappearing into underground garages like so many communal pillbugs. Neon lights flickered fitfully on commercial buildings, advertising the few pitiful, but earnest, entertainments to be had at outrageous prices that were paid without comment. Where large paycheques are found, there are always small businesses operated by men and women with outsize dreams. The company had no interest in running such penny-ante operations itself, but it gladly sold concessions to those who desired to do so.

Beyond the colony complex rose the first of the atmosphere processors. Fusion-powered, it belched a steady storm of cleansed air back into the gaseous envelope that surrounded the planet. Particulate matter and dangerous gases were removed either by burning or by chemical breakdown; oxygen and nitrogen were thrown back into the dim sky. In with the bad air, out with the good. It was not a complicated process, but it was time-consuming and very expensive.

But how much is a world worth? And Acheron was not as bad as some that the Company had invested in. At least it possessed an existing atmosphere capable of modification. Much easier to fine-tune the composition of a world's air than to provide it from scratch. Acheron had weather and near normal gravity. A veritable paradise.

The fiery glow that emanated from the crown of the volcanolike atmosphere processor suggested another realm entirely. None of the symbolism was lost on the colonists. It inspired only additional humour. They hadn't agreed to come to Acheron because of the weather.

There were no soft bodies or pallid, weak faces visible within the colony corridors. Even the children looked tough. Not tough as in mean or bullying, but strong within as well as without. There was no room here for bullies. Cooperation was a lesson learned early. Children grew up faster than their Earthbound counterparts and those who lived on fatter, gentler worlds. They and their parents were a breed unto themselves, self-reliant yet interdependent. They were not unique. Their predecessors had ridden in wagons instead of starships.

It helped to think of oneself as a pioneer. It sounded much better than a numerical job description.

At the centre of this ganglion of men and machines was the tall building known as the control block. It towered above every other artificial structure on Acheron with the exception of the atmosphere processing stations themselves. From the outside it looked spacious. Within, there wasn't a spare square metre to be found. Instrumentation was crowded into corners and sequestered in the crawl spaces beneath the floors and the serviceways above the suspended ceilings. And still there was never enough room. People squeezed a little closer to one another so that the computers and their attendant machines could have more room. Paper piled up in corners despite unceasing efforts to reduce every scrap of necessary information to electronic bytes. Equipment shipped out new from the factory quickly acquired a plethora of homey scratches, dents, and coffee-cup rings.

Two men ran the control block and therefore the colony. One was the operations manager, the other his assistant. They called one another by their first names. Formality was not in vogue on frontier worlds. Insistence on titles and last names and too much supercilious pulling of rank could find a man lost outside without a survival suit or communicator.

Their names were Simpson and Lydecker, and it was a toss-up as to which looked more harried than the other. Both wore the expression of men for whom sleep is a teasing mistress rarely visited. Lydecker looked like an accountant haunted by a major tax deduction misplaced ten years earlier. Simpson was a big, burly type who would have been more comfortable running a truck than a colony. Unfortunately he'd been stuck with brains as well as brawn and hadn't managed to hide it from his employers. The front of his shirt was perpetually sweat-stained. Lydecker confronted him before he could retreat.

'See the weather report for next week?' Simpson was chewing on something fragrant, which stained the inside of his mouth. Probably illegal, Lydecker knew. He said nothing about it. It was Simpson's business, and Simpson was his boss. Besides, he'd been considering borrowing a chew. Small vices were not encouraged on Acheron, but as long as they didn't interfere with a person's work, neither were they held up to ridicule. It was tough enough to keep one's sanity, hard enough to get by.

'What about it?' the operations manager said.

'We're going to have a real Indian summer. Winds should be all the way down to forty knots.'

'Oh, good. I'll break out the inner tubes and the suntan lotion. Heck, I'd settle for just one honest glimpse of the local sun.'

Lydecker shook his head, affecting an air of mock disapproval. 'Never satisfied, are you? Isn't it enough to know it's still up there?'

'I can't help it; I'm greedy. I should shut up and count my blessings, right? You got something else on your mind, Lydecker, or are you just on one of your hour-long coffee breaks?'

'That's me. Goof off every chance I get. I figure my next chance will be in about two years.' He checked a printed readout. 'You remember you sent some wildcatters out to that high plateau out past the Ilium Range a couple days ago?'

'Yeah. Some of our dreamers back home thought there might be some radioactives out that way. So I asked for volunteers, and some guy named Jorden stuck up his mitt. I told 'em to go look if they wanted to. Some others might've taken off in that direction also. What about it?'

'There's a guy on the horn right now. Mom-and-pop survey team. Says he's homing something and wants to know if his claim will be honoured.'

'Everybody's a lawyer these days. Sometimes I think I should've gone in for it myself.'

'What, and ruin your sophisticated image? Besides, there's not much call for lawyers out here. And you make better money.'

'Keep telling me that. It helps.' Simpson shook his head and turned to gaze at a green screen. 'Some honch in a cushy office on Earth says go look at a grid reference in the middle of nowhere, we look. They don't say why, and I don't ask. I don't ask because it takes two weeks to get an answer from back there, and the answer's always "Don't ask." Sometimes I wonder why we bother.'

'I just told you why. For the money.' The assistant operations officer leaned back against a console. 'So what do I tell this guy?'

Simpson turned to stare at a videoscreen that covered most of one wall. It displayed a computer-generated topographical map of the explored portion of Acheron. The map was not very extensive, and the features it illustrated made the worst section of the Kalahari Desert look like Polynesia. Simpson rarely got to see any of Acheron's surface in person. His duties required him to remain close to Operations at all times, and he liked that just fine.

'Tell him,' he informed Lydecker, 'that as far as I'm concerned, if he finds something, it's his. Anybody with the guts to go crawling around out there deserves to keep what he finds.'

The tractor had six wheels, armoured sides, oversize tyres, and a corrosion-proof underbody. It was not completely Acheron-proof, but then, very little of the colony's equipment was. Repeated patching and welding had transformed the once- sleek exterior of the tractor into a collage composed of off-colour metal blotches held together with solder and epoxy sealant. But it kept the wind and sand at bay and climbed steadily forward. That was enough for the people it sheltered.

At the moment it was chugging its way up a gentle slope, the fat tyres kicking up sprays of volcanic dust that the wind was quick to carry away. Eroded sandstone and shale crumbled beneath its weight. A steady westerly gale howled outside its armoured flanks, blasting the pitted windows and light ports in its emotionless, unceasing attempt to blind the vehicle and those within. The determination of those who drove combined with the reliable engine to keep it moving uphill. The engine hummed reassuringly, while the air filters cycled ceaselessly as they fought to keep dust and grit out of the sacrosanct interior.

The machine needed clean air to breathe just as much as did its occupants.

He was not quite as weather-beaten as his vehicle, but Russ Jorden still wore the unmistakable look of someone who'd spent more than his share of time on Acheron. Weathered and wind-blasted. To a lesser degree the same description applied to his wife, Anne, though not to the two children who bounced about in the rear of the big central cabin. Somehow they managed to dart in and around portable sampling equipment and packing cases without getting themselves smashed against the walls. Their ancestors had learned at an early age how to ride something called a horse. The action of the tractor was not very different from the motion one has to cope with atop the spine of that empathetic quadruped, and the children had mastered it almost as soon as they learned how to walk.

Their clothing and faces were smeared with dust despite the nominally inviolable interior of the vehicle. That was a fact of life on Acheron. No matter how tight you tried to seal yourself in, the dust always managed to penetrate vehicles, offices, homes. One of the first colonists had coined a name for this phenomenon that was more descriptive than scientific. 'Particulate osmosis,' he'd called it. Acheronian science. The more imaginative colonists insisted that the dust was sentient, that it hid and waited for doors and windows to open a crack before deliberately rushing inside. Homemakers argued facetiously whether it was faster to wash clothes or scrape them clean.

Russ Jorden wrestled the massive tractor around boulders too big to climb and negotiated a path through narrow crevices in the plateau they were ascending. He was sustained in his efforts by the music of the Locater's steady pinging. It grew louder the nearer they came to the source of the electromagnetic disturbance, but he refused to turn down the volume. Each ping was a melody unto itself, like the chatter of old-time cash registers. His wife monitored the tractor's condition and the life-support systems while her husband drove.

'Look at this fat, juicy, magnetic profile.' Jorden tapped the

small readout on his right. 'And it's mine, mine, mine.
Lydecker says that Simpson said so, and we've got it recorded.
They can't take that away from us now. Not even the Company
can take it away from us. Mine, all mine.'

'Half mine, dear.' His wife glanced over at him and smiled.

'And half mine!' This cheerful desecration of basic
mathematics came from Newt, the Jordens' daughter. She was
six years old going on ten, and she had more energy than both
her parents and the tractor combined. Her father grinned
affectionately without taking his eyes from the driver's console.

'I got too many partners.'

The girl had been playing with her older brother until she'd
finally worn him out. 'Tim's bored, Daddy, and so am I. When
are we going back to town?'

'When we get rich, Newt.'

'You always say that.' She scrambled onto her feet, as agile as
an otter. 'I wanna go back. I wanna play Monster Maze.'

Her brother stuck his face into hers. 'You can play by
yourself this time. You cheat too much.'

'Do not!' She put small fists on unformed hips. 'I'm just the
best, and you're jealous.'

'Am not! You go in places we can't fit.'

'So? That's why I'm the best.'

Their mother spared a moment to glance over from her
bank of monitors and readouts. 'Knock it off. I catch either of
you two playing in the air ducts again, I'll tan your hides. Not
only is it against colony regulations, it's dangerous. What if one
of you missed a step and fell down a vertical shaft?'

'Aw, Mom. Nobody's dumb enough to do that. Besides, all
the kids play it, and nobody's been hurt yet. We're careful.' Her
smile returned. 'An' I'm the best 'cause I can fit places nobody
else can.'

'Like a little worm.' Her brother stuck his tongue out at her.

She duplicated the gesture. 'Nyah, nyah! Jealous, jealous.'
He made a grab for her protruding tongue. She let out a
childish shriek and ducked behind a mobile ore analyzer.

'Look, you two.' There was more affection than anger in Anne Jorden's tone. 'Let's try to calm down for two minutes, okay? We're almost finished up here. We'll head back towards town soon and—'

Russ Jorden had half risen from his seat to stare through the windshield. Childish confrontations temporarily put aside, his wife joined him.

'What is it, Russ?' She put a hand on his shoulder to steady herself as the tractor lurched leftward.

'There's something out there. Clouds parted for just a second, and I *saw* it. I don't know what it is, but it's big. And it's ours. Yours and mine—and the kids'.'

The alien spacecraft dwarfed the tractor as the big six-wheeler trundled to a halt nearby. Twin arches of metallic glass swept skyward in graceful, but somehow disturbing, curves from the stern of the derelict. From a distance they resembled the reaching arms of a prone dead man, locked in advanced rigor mortis. One was shorter than the other, and yet this failed to ruin the symmetry of the ship.

The design was as alien as the composition. It might have been grown instead of built. The slick bulge of the hull still exhibited a peculiar vitreous lustre that the wind-borne grit of Acheron had not completely obliterated.

Jorden locked the tractor's brakes. 'Folks, we have scored big this time. Anne, break out the suits. I wonder if the Hadley Café can synthesize champagne?'

His wife stood where she was, staring out through the tough glass. 'Let's check it out and get back safely before we start celebrating, Russ. Maybe we're not the first to find it.'

'Are you kidding? There's no beacon on this whole plateau. There's no marker outside. Nobody's been here before us. Nobody! She's all ours.' He was heading towards the rear of the cabin as he talked.

Anne still sounded doubtful. 'Hard to believe that anything that big, putting out that kind of resonance, could have sat here for this long without being noticed.'

'Bull.' Jorden was already climbing into his environment suit, flipping catches without hunting for them, closing seal-tights with the ease of long practice. 'You worry too much. I can think of plenty of reasons why it's escaped notice until now.'

'For instance?' Reluctantly she turned from the window and moved to join him in donning her own suit.

'For instance, it's blocked off from the colony's detectors by these mountains, and you know that surveillance satellites are useless in this kind of atmosphere.'

'What about infrared?' She zipped up the front of her suit.

'What infrared? Look at it: dead as a doornail. Probably been sitting here just like that for thousands of years. Even if it got here yesterday, you couldn't pick up any infrared on this part of the planet; new air coming out of the atmosphere processor is too hot.'

'So then how did Operations hit on it?' She was slipping on her equipment, filling up the instrument belt.

He shrugged. 'How the heck should I know? If it's bugging you, you can winkle it out of Lydecker when we get back. The important thing is that we're the ones they picked to check it out. We lucked out.' He turned towards the airlock door. 'C'mon, babe. Let's crack the treasure chest. I'll bet that baby's insides are just crammed with valuable stuff.'

Equally enthusiastic but considerably more self-possessed, Anne Jorden tightened the seals on her own suit. Husband and wife checked each other out: oxygen, tools, lights, energy cells, all in place. When they were ready to leave the tractor, she popped her wind visor and favoured her offspring with a stern gaze.

'You kids stay inside. I mean it.'

'Aw, Mom.' Tim's expression was full of childish disappointment. 'Can't I come too?'

'No, you cannot come too. We'll tell you all about it when we get back.' She closed the airlock door behind her.

Tim immediately ran to the nearest port and pressed his nose against the glass. Outside the tractor, the twilight landscape was illuminated by the helmet beams of his parents.

'I dunno why I can't go too.'

'Because Mommy said so.' Newt was considering what to play next as she pressed her own face against another window. The lights from her parents' helmets grew dim as they advanced towards the strange ship.

Something grabbed her from behind. She squealed and turned to confront her brother.

'Cheater!' he jeered. Then he turned and ran for a place to hide. She followed, yelling back at him.

The bulk of the alien vessel loomed over the two bipeds as they climbed the broken rubble that surrounded it. Wind howled around them. Dust obscured the sun.

'Shouldn't we call in?' Anne stared at the smooth-sided mass.

'Let's wait till we know what to call it in as.' Her husband kicked a chunk of volcanic rock out of his path.

'How about "big weird thing"?'

Russ Jorden turned to face her, surprise showing on his face behind the visor. 'Hey, what's the matter, honey? Nervous?'

'We're preparing to enter a derelict alien vessel of unknown type. You bet I'm nervous.'

He clapped her on the back. 'Just think of all that beautiful money. The ship alone's worth a fortune, even if it's empty. It's a priceless relic. Wonder who built it, where they came from, and why it ended up crashed on this godforsaken lump of gravel?' His voice and expression were full of enthusiasm as he pointed to a dark gash in the ship's side. 'There's a place that's been torn open. Let's check her out.'

They turned towards the opening. As they drew near, Anne Jorden regarded it uneasily. 'I don't think this is the result of damage, Russ. It looks integral with the hull to me. Whoever designed this thing didn't like right angles.'

'I don't care what they liked. We're going *in*.'

A single tear wound its way down Newt Jorden's cheek. She'd been staring out the fore windshield for a long time now.

Finally she stepped down and moved to the driver's chair to shake her sleeping brother. She sniffed and wiped away the tear, not wanting Tim to see her cry.

'Timmy—wake up, Timmy. They've been gone a long time.'

Her brother blinked, removed his feet from the console, and sat up. He glanced unconcernedly at the chronometer set in the control dash, then peered out at the dim, blasted landscape. Despite the tractor's heavy-duty insulation, one could still hear the wind blowing outside when the engine was shut down. Tim sucked on his lower lip.

'It'll be okay, Newt. Dad knows what he's doing.'

At that instant the outside door slammed open, admitting wind, dust, and a tall dark shape. Newt screamed, and Tim scrambled out of the seat as their mother ripped off her visor and threw it aside, heedless of the damage it might do to the delicate instrumentation. Her eyes were wild, and the tendons stood out in her neck as she shoved past her children. She snatched up the dash mike and yelled into the condenser.

'Mayday! Mayday! This is Alpha Kilo Two Four Niner calling Hadley Control. Repeat. This is Alpha Kil . . .'

· Newt barely heard her mother. She had both hands pressed over her mouth as she sucked on stale atmosphere. Behind her, the tractor's filters whined as they fought to strain the particulate-laden air. She was staring out the open door at the ground. Her father lay there, sprawled on his back on the rocks. Somehow her mother had dragged him all the way back from the alien ship.

There was something on his face.

It was flat, heavily ribbed, and had lots of spiderlike chitinous legs. The long, muscular tail was tightly wrapped around the neck of her father's environment suit. More than anything else, the creature resembled a mutated horseshoe crab with a soft exterior. It was pulsing in and out, in and out, like a pump. Like a machine. Except that it was not a machine. It was clearly, obviously, obscenely alive.

Newt began screaming again, and this time she didn't stop.

# III

It was quiet in the apartment except for the blare of the wallscreen. Ripley ignored the simpcom and concentrated instead on the smoke rising from her denicotined cigarette. It formed lazy, hazy patterns in the stagnant air.

Even though it was late in the day, she'd managed to avoid confronting a mirror. Just as well, since her haggard, unkempt appearance could only depress her further. The apartment was in better shape than she was. There were just enough decorative touches to keep it from appearing spartan. None of the touches were what another might call personal. That was understandable. She'd outlived everything that once might have been considered personal. The sink was full of dirty dishes even though the dishwasher sat empty beneath it.

She wore a bathrobe that was ageing as rapidly as its owner. In the adjoining bedroom, sheets and blankets lay in a heap at the base of the mattress. Jones prowled the kitchen, hunting overlooked morsels. He would find none. The kitchen kept itself reasonably antiseptic despite a deliberate lack of cooperation from its owner.

'Hey, Bob!' the wallscreen bleated vapidly. 'I heard that you and the family are heading off for the colonies!'

'Best decision I ever made, Phil,' replied a fatuously grinning nonentity from the opposite side of the wall. 'We'll be starting a new life from scratch in a clean world. No crime, no unemployment . . .'

And the two chiselled performers who were acting out this administration-approved spiel probably lived in an expensive Green Ring on the East Coast, Ripley thought sardonically as she listened to it with half an ear. In Cape Cod condos overlooking Martha's Vineyard or Hilton Head or some other unpolluted, high-priced snob refuge for the fortunate few who knew how to bill and coo and dance, yassuh, dance when imperious corporate chieftains snapped their fingers. None of that for her. No smell of salt, no cool mountain breezes. Inner-city Company dole, and lucky she was to have that much.

She'd find something soon. They just wanted to keep her quiet for a while, until she calmed down. They'd be glad to help her relocate and retrain. After which they'd conveniently forget about her. Which was just dandy keeno fine as far as she was concerned. She wanted no more to do with the Company than the Company wanted to do with her.

If only they hadn't suspended her licence, she'd long since have been out of here and away.

The door buzzed sharply for attention and she jumped. Jones merely glanced up and meowed before trundling off towards the bathroom. He didn't like strangers. Always had been a smart cat.

She put the cigarette (guaranteed to contain no carcinogens, no nicotine, and no tobacco—harmless to your health, or so the warning label on the side of the packet insisted) aside and moved to open the door. She didn't bother to check through the peephole. Hers was a full-security building. Not that after her recent experiences there was anything in an Earthside city that could frighten her.

Carter Burke stood there, wearing his usual apologetic smile. Standing next to him and looking formal was a younger man clad in the severe dress-black uniform of an officer in the Colonial Marines.

'Hi, Ripley.' Burke indicated his companion. 'This is Lieutenant Gorman of the Co—'

The closing door cut his sentence in half. Ripley turned her back on it, but she'd neglected to cut power to the hall speaker. Burke's voice reached her via the concealed membrane.

'Ripley, we have to talk.'

'No, we don't. Get lost, Carter. And take your friend with you.'

'No can do. This is important.'

'Not to me it isn't. Nothing's important to me.'

Burke went silent, but she sensed he hadn't left. She knew him well enough to know that he wouldn't give up easily. The Company rep wasn't demanding, but he was an accomplished wheedler.

As it developed, he didn't have to argue with her. All he had to do was say one sentence.

'We've lost contact with the colony of Acheron.'

A sinking feeling inside as she mulled over the ramifications of that unexpected statement. Well, perhaps not entirely unexpected. She hesitated a moment longer before opening the door. It wasn't a ploy. That much was evident in Burke's expression. Gorman's gaze shifted from one to the other. He was clearly uncomfortable at being ignored, even as he tried not to show it.

She stepped aside. 'Come in.'

Burke surveyed the apartment and gratefully said nothing, shying away from inanities like 'Nice place you have here' when it obviously wasn't. He also forbore from saying, 'You're looking well,' since that also would have constituted an obvious untruth. She could respect him for his restraint. She gestured towards the table.

'Want something? Coffee, tea, spritz?'

'Coffee would be fine,' he replied. Gorman added a nod.

She went into the compact kitchen and dialled up a few cups. Bubbling sounds began to emanate from the processor as she turned back to the den.

'You didn't need to bring the Marines.' She smiled thinly at him. 'I'm past the violent stage. The psych techs said so, and it's right there on my chart.' She waved towards a desk piled high with discs and papers. 'So what's with the escort?'

'I'm here as an official representative of the corps.' Gorman was clearly uneasy and more than willing to let Burke handle the bulk of the conversation. How much did he know, and what had they told him about her? she wondered. Was he disappointed in not encountering some stoned harridan? Not that his opinion of her mattered.

'So you've lost contact.' She feigned indifference. 'So?'

Burke looked down at his slim-line, secured briefcase. 'It has to be checked out. Fast. All communications are down. They've been down too long for the interruption to be due to equipment failure. Acheron's been in business for years. They're experienced people, and they have appropriate backup systems. Maybe they're working on fixing the problem right now. But it's been no-go dead silence for too long. People are getting nervous. Somebody has to go and check it out in person. It's the only way to quiet the nervous Nellies.

'Probably they'll correct the trouble while the ship's on its way out and the whole trip will be a waste of time and money, but it's time to set out.'

He didn't have to elaborate. Ripley had already gotten where he was going and returned. She went into the kitchen and brought out the coffees. While Gorman sipped his cup of brew she began pacing. The den was too small for proper pacing, but she tried, anyway. Burke just waited.

'No,' she said finally. 'There's no way.'

'Hear me out. It's not what you think.'

She stopped in the middle of the floor and stared at him in disbelief. 'Not what I think? Not what I *think*? I don't have to think, Burke. I was reamed, steamed, and dry-cleaned by you guys, and now you want me to go back out *there*? Forget it!'

She was trembling as she spoke. Gorman misinterpreted the reaction as anger, but it was pure fear. She was scared. Gut-scared and trying to mask it with indignation. Burke knew what she was feeling but pressed on, anyway. He had no choice.

'Look,' he began in what he hoped was his best conciliatory

manner, 'we don't know what's going on out there. If their relay satellite's gone out instead of the ground transmitter, the only way to fix it is with a relief team. There are no spacecraft in the colony. If that's the case, then they're all sitting around out there cursing the Company for not getting off its collective butt and sending out a repair crew pronto. If it is the satellite relay, then the relief team won't even have to set foot on the planet itself. But we don't know what the trouble is, and if it's *not* the orbital relay, then I'd like to have you there. As an adviser. That's all.'

Gorman lowered his coffee. 'You wouldn't be going in with the troops. Assuming we even have to go in. I can guarantee your safety.'

She rolled her eyes and glanced at the ceiling.

'These aren't your average city cops or army accompanying us, Ripley,' Burke said forcefully. 'These Colonial Marines are some tough hombres, and they'll be packing state-of-the-art firepower. Man plus machine. There's nothing they can't handle. Right, Lieutenant?'

Gorman allowed himself a slight smile. 'We're trained to deal with the unexpected. We've handled problems on worse worlds than Acheron. Our casualty rate for this kind of operation hovers right around zero. I expect the percentage to improve a little more after this visit.'

If this declaration was intended to impress Ripley, it failed miserably. She looked back to Burke.

'What about you? What's your interest in this?'

'Well, the Company cofinanced the colony in tandem with the Colonial Administration. Sort of an advance against mineral rights and a portion of the long-term developmental profits. We're diversifying, getting into a lot of terraforming. Real estate on a galactic scale. Building better worlds and all that.'

'Yeah, yeah,' she muttered. 'I've seen the commercials.'

'The corporation won't see any substantial profits out of Acheron until terraforming's complete, but a big outfit like that has to consider the long term.' Seeing that this was having no effect on his host, Burke switched to another tack. 'I hear you're working in the cargo docks over Portside?'

Her reply was defensive, as was to be expected. 'That's right. What about it?'

He ignored the challenge. 'Running loaders, forklifts, suspension grates; that sort of thing?'

'It's all I could get. I'm crazy if I'm going to live on charity all my life. Anyway, it keeps my mind off . . . everything. Days off are worse. Too much time to think. I'd rather keep busy.'

'You like that kind of work?'

'Are you trying to be funny?'

He fiddled with the catch on his case. 'Maybe it's not all you can get. What if I said I could get you reinstated as a flight officer? Get you your licence back? And that the Company has agreed to pick up your contract? No more hassles with the commission, no more arguments. The official reprimand comes out of your record. Without a trace. As far as anyone will be concerned, you've been on a leave of absence. Perfectly normal following a long tour of duty. It'll be like nothing happened. Won't even affect your pension rating.'

'What about the ECA and the insurance people?'

'Insurance is settled, over, done with. They're out of it. Since nothing will appear on your record, you won't be considered any more of a risk than you were before your last trip. As far as the ECA is concerned, they'd like to see you go out with the relief team too. It's all taken care of.'

'*If* I go.'

'*If* you go.' He nodded, leaning slightly towards her. He wasn't exactly pleading. It was more like a practised sales pitch. 'It's a second chance, kiddo. Most people who get taken down by a board of inquiry never have the opportunity to come back. If the problem's nothing more than a busted relay satellite, all you have to do is sit in your cubbyhole and read while the techs take care of it. That, and collect your trip pay while you're in hypersleep. By going, you can wipe out all the unpleasantness and put yourself right back up there where you used to be. Full rating, full pension accumulation, the works. I've seen your record. One more long out-trip and you qualify for a captain's certificate.

'And it'll be the best thing in the world for you to face this fear and beat it. You gotta get back on the horse.'

'Spare me, Burke,' she said frostily. 'I've had my psych evaluation for the month.'

His smile slipped a little, but his tone grew more determined. 'Fine. Let's cut the crap, then. I've read your evaluations. You wake up every night, sheets soaking, the same nightmare over and over—'

'No! The answer is no.' She retrieved both coffee cups even though neither was empty. It was another form of dismissal. 'Now please go. I'm sorry. Just go, would you?'

The two men exchanged a look. Gorman's expression was unreadable, but she had the feeling that his attitude had shifted from curious to contemptuous. The heck with him: what did he know? Burke mined a pocket, removed a translucent card, and placed it on the table before heading for the door. He paused in the portal to smile back at her.

'Think about it.'

Then they were gone, leaving her alone with her thoughts. Unpleasant company. Wind. Wind and sand and a moaning sky. The pale disc of an alien sun fluttering like a paper cutout beyond the riven atmosphere. A howling, rising in pitch and intensity, coming closer, until it was right on top of you, smothering you, cutting off your breath.

With a guttural moan Ripley sat straight up in her bed, clutching her chest. She was breathing hard, painfully. Sucking in a particularly deep breath, she glanced around the tiny bedroom. The dim light set in the nightstand illuminated bare walls, a dresser, and a highboy, sheets kicked to the foot of the bed. Jones lay sprawled atop the highboy, the highest point in the room, staring impassively back at her. It was a habit the cat had acquired soon after their return. When they went to bed, he would curl up next to her, only to abandon her soon after she fell asleep in favour of the safety and security of the highboy. He knew the nightmare was on its way and gave it plenty of space.

She used a corner of the sheet to mop the sweat from her forehead and cheeks. Fingers fumbled in the nightstand drawer until they found a cigarette. She flicked the tip and waited for the cylinder to ignite. Something—her head snapped around. Nothing there. Only the soft hum of the clock. There was nothing else in the room. Just Jones and her. Certainly no wind.

Leaning to her left, she pawed through the other nightstand drawer until she'd located the card Burke had left behind. She turned it over in her fingers, then inserted it into a slot in the bedside console. The videoscreen that dominated the far wall immediately flashed the words STAND BY at her. She waited impatiently until Burke's face appeared. He was bleary-eyed and unshaven, having been roused from a sound sleep, but he managed a grin when he saw who was calling.

'Yello? Oh, Ripley. Hi.'

'Burke, just tell me one thing.' She hoped there was enough light in the room for the monitor to pick up her expression as well as her voice. 'That you're going out there to kill them. Not to study. Not to bring back. Just burn them out, clean. Forever.'

He woke up rapidly, she noted. 'That's the plan. If there's anything dangerous walking around out there, we get rid of it. Got a colony to protect. No monkeying around with potentially dangerous organisms. That's Company policy. We find anything lethal, anything at all, we fry it. The scientists can go suck eggs. My word on it.' A long pause and he leaned towards his own pickup, his face looming large on the screen. 'Ripley. Ripley? You still there?'

No more time to think. Maybe it was time to stop thinking and to *do*. 'All right. I'm in.' There, she'd gone and said it. Somehow she'd said it.

He looked like he wanted to reply, to congratulate or thank her. Something. She broke the connection before he could say a word. A thump sounded on the sheets next to her, and she turned to gaze fondly down at Jones. She trailed short nails down his spine, and he primped delightedly, rubbing against her hip and purring.

'And *you*, my dear, are staying right here.'

The cat blinked up at her as he continued to caress her fingers with his back. It was doubtful that he understood either her words or the gist of the previous phone call, but he did not volunteer to accompany her.

*At least one of us still has some sense left*, she thought as she slid back beneath the covers.

# IV

It was an ugly ship. Battered, overused, parts repaired that should have been replaced, too tough and valuable to scrap. Easier for its masters to upgrade it and modify it than build a new one. Its lines were awkward and its engines oversize. A mountain of metal and composites and ceramic, a floating scrap heap, weightless monument to war, it shouldered its way brutally through the mysterious region called hyperspace. Like its human cargo, it was purely functional. Its name was *Sulaco*.

Fourteen dreamers this trip. Eleven engaged in related morphean fantasies, simple and straightforward as the vessel that carried them through the void. Two others more individualistic. A last sleeping under sedation necessary to mute the effects of recurring nightmares. Fourteen dreamers— and one for whom sleep was a superfluous abstraction.

Executive Officer Bishop checked readouts and adjusted controls. The long wait was ended. An alarm sounded throughout the length of the massive military transport. Long dormant machinery, powered down to conserve energy, came back to life. So did long dormant humans as their hypersleep capsules were charged and popped open. Satisfied that his charges had survived their long hibernation, Bishop set about the business of placing *Sulaco* in a low geo-stationary orbit around the colony world of Acheron.

Ripley was the first of the sleepers to awake. Not because she was any more adaptive than her fellow travellers or more used to the effects of hypersleep, but simply because her capsule was first in line for recharge. Sitting up in the enclosed bed, she rubbed briskly at her arms, then started to work on her legs. Burke sat up in the capsule across from her, and the lieutenant—what was his name?—oh, yeah, Gorman, beyond him.

The other capsules contained the *Sulaco*'s military complement: eight men and three women. They were a select group in that they chose to put their lives at risk for the majority of the time they were awake: individuals used to long periods of hypersleep followed by brief, but intense, periods of wakefulness. The kind of people others made room for on a sidewalk or in a bar.

PFC Spunkmeyer was the dropship crew chief, the man responsible along with Pilot-Corporal Ferro for safely conveying his colleagues to the surface of whichever world they happened to be visiting, and then taking them off again in one piece. In a hurry if necessary. He rubbed at his eyes and groaned as he blinked at the hypersleep chamber.

'I'm getting too old for this.' No one paid any attention to this comment, since it was well known (or at least widely rumoured) that Spunkmeyer had enlisted when underage. However, nobody joked about his maturity or lack of it when they were plummeting towards the surface of a new world in the PFC-directed dropship.

Private Drake was rolling out of the capsule next to Spunkmeyer's. He was a little older than Spunkmeyer and a lot uglier. In addition to sharing similarities in appearance with the *Sulaco*, likewise he was built a lot like the old transport. Drake was heavy-duty bad company, with arms like a legendary one-eyed sailor, a nose busted beyond repair by the cosmetic surgeons, and a nasty scar that curled one side of his mouth into a permanent sneer. The scar surgery could have fixed, but Drake hung on to it. It was one medal he was allowed to wear all the time. He wore a tight-fitting floppy cap, which no living soul dared refer to as 'cute'.

Drake was a smartgun operator. He was also skilled in the use of rifles, handguns, grenades, assorted blades, and his teeth.

'They ain't payin' us enough for this,' he mumbled.

'Not enough to have to wake up to your face, Drake.' This from Corporal Dietrich, who was arguably the prettiest of the group except when she opened her mouth.

'Suck vacuum,' Drake told her. He eyed the occupant of another recently opened capsule. 'Hey, Hicks, you look like I feel.'

Hicks was the squad's senior corporal and second in command among the troops after Master Sergeant Apone. He didn't talk much and always seemed to be in the right place at the potentially lethal time, a fact much appreciated by his fellow Marines. He kept his counsel to himself while the others spouted off. When he did speak, what he had to say was usually worth hearing.

Ripley was back on her feet, rubbing the circulation back into her legs and doing standing knee-bends to loosen up stiffened joints. She examined the troopers as they shuffled past her on their way to a bank of lockers. There were no supermen among them, no overly muscled archetypes, but every one of them was lean and hardened. She suspected that the least among them could run all day over the surface of a two-gee world carrying a full equipment pack, fight a running battle while doing so, and then spend the night breaking down and repairing complex computer instrumentation. Brawn and brains aplenty, even if they preferred to talk like common street toughs. The best the contemporary military had to offer. She felt a little safer—but only a little.

Master Sergeant Apone was making his way up the centre aisle, chatting briefly with each of his newly revived soldiers in turn. The sergeant looked as though he could take apart a medium-size truck with his bare hands. As he passed Comtech Corporal Hudson's pallet, the latter voiced a complaint.

'This floor's *freezing*.'

'So were you, ten minutes ago. I never saw such a bunch of old women. Want me to fetch your slippers, Hudson?'

The corporal batted his eyelashes at the sergeant. 'Would you, sir? I'd be ever so grateful!' A few rough chuckles acknowledged Hudson's riposte. Apone smiled to himself as he resumed his walk, chiding his people and urging them to speed it up.

Ripley stayed out of their way as they trudged past. They were a tightly knit bunch, a single fighting organism with eleven heads, and she wasn't a part of their group. She stood outside, isolated. A couple of them nodded to her as they strode past, and there were one or two cursory hellos. That was all she had any right to expect, but it didn't make her feel any more relaxed in their company.

PFC Vasquez just stared as she walked past. Ripley had received warmer inspections from robots. The other smartgun operator didn't blink, didn't smile. Black hair, blacker eyes, thin lips. Attractive if she'd make half an effort.

It required a special talent; a unique combination of strength, mental ability, and reflexes, to operate a smartgun. Ripley waited for the woman to say something. She didn't open her mouth as she passed by. Every one of the troopers looked tough. Drake and Vasquez looked tough *and* mean.

Her counterpart called out to her as she came abreast of his locker. 'Hey, Vasquez, you ever been mistaken for a man?'

'No. Have you?'

Drake proffered an open palm. She slapped it, and his fingers immediately clenched right around her smaller fingers. The pressure increased on both sides—a silent, painful greeting. Both were glad to be out from under hypersleep and alive again.

Finally she whacked him across the face and their hands parted. They laughed, young Dobermans at play. Drake was the stronger but Vasquez was faster, Ripley decided as she watched them. If they had to go down, she resolved to try to keep them on either side of her. It would be the safest place.

Bishop was moving quietly among the group, helping with

massages and a bottle of special postsleep fluid, acting more like a valet than a ship's officer. He appeared older than any of the troopers, including Lieutenant Gorman. As he passed close to Ripley she noticed the alphanumeric code tattooed across the back of his left hand. She stiffened in recognition but said nothing.

'Hey,' Private Frost said to someone out of Ripley's view, 'you take my towel?' Frost was as young as Hudson but better-looking, or so he would insist to anyone who would waste time listening. When it came time for bragging, the two younger troopers usually came out about even. Hudson tended to rely on volume while Frost hunted for the right words.

Spunkmeyer was up near the head of the line and still complaining. 'I need some slack, man. How come they send us straight back out like this? It ain't fair. We got some slack comin', man.'

Hicks murmured softly. 'You just got three weeks. You want to spend your whole life on slack time?'

'I mean breathing, not this frozen stuff. Three weeks in the freezer ain't real off-time.'

'Yeah, Top, what about it?' Dietrich wanted to know.

'You know it ain't up to me.' Apone raised his voice above the griping. 'Awright, let's knock off the jawing. First assembly's in fifteen. I want everybody looking like human beings by then—most of you will have to fake it. Let's shag it.'

Hypersleep wear was stripped off and tossed into the disposal unit. Easier to cremate the remains and provide fresh new attire for the return journey than to try to recycle shorts and tops that had clung to a body for several weeks. The line of lean, naked bodies moved into the shower. High-pressure water jets blasted away accumulated sweat and grime, set nerve endings tingling beneath scoured skin. Through the swirling steam Hudson, Vasquez, and Ferro watched Ripley dry off.

'Who's the freshmeat again?' Vasquez asked the question as she washed cleanser out of her hair.

'She's supposed to be some kinda consultant. Don't know

much about her.' The diminutive Ferro wiped at her belly, which was as flat and muscular as a steel plate, and exaggerated her expression and tone. 'She saw an *alien* once. Or so the skipchat says.'

'Whooah!' Hudson made a face. 'I'm impressed.'

Apone yelled back at them. He was already out in the drying room, towelling off his shoulders. They were as devoid of fat as those of troopers twenty years younger.

'Let's go, let's go. Buncha lazybutts'll run the recyclers dry. C'mon, cycle through. You got to get dirty before you can get clean.'

Informal segregation was the order of the day in the mess room. It was automatic. There was no need for whispered words or little nameplates next to the glasses. Apone and his troopers requisitioned the large table while Ripley, Gorman, Burke, and Bishop sat at the other. Everyone nursed coffee, tea, spritz, or water while they waited for the ship's autochef to deal out eggs and ersatz bacon, toast and hash, condiments, and vitamin supplements.

You could identify each trooper by his or her uniform. No two were exactly alike. This was the result not of specialized identification insignia, but of individual taste. The *Sulaco* was no barracks and Acheron no parade ground. Occasionally Apone would have to chew someone out for a particularly egregious addition, like the time Crowe had showed up with a portrait of his latest girlfriend computer-stencilled across the back of his armour. But for the most part he let the troopers decorate their outfits as they liked.

'Hey, Top,' Hudson chivvied, 'what's the op?'

'Yeah.' Frost blew bubbles in his tea. 'All I know is I get shipping orders and not time to say hello-goodbye to Myrna.'

'Myrna?' Private Wierzbowski raised a bushy eyebrow. 'I thought it was Leina?'

Frost looked momentarily uncertain. 'I think Leina was three months ago. Or six.'

'It's a rescue mission.' Apone sipped his coffee. 'There's

some juicy colonists' daughters we gotta rescue.'

Ferro made a show of looking disappointed. 'Hell, that lets me out.'

'Says who?' Hudson leered at her. She threw sugar at him.

Apone just listened and watched. No reason for him to intervene. He could have quieted them down, could have played it by the book. Instead he left it loose and fair, but only because he knew that his people were the best. He'd walk into a fight with any one of them watching his back and not worry about what he couldn't see, knowing that anything trying to sneak up on him would be taken care of as efficiently as if he had eyes in the back of his head. Let 'em play, let 'em curse ECA and the corps and the Company and him too. When the time came, the playing would stop, and every one of them would be all business.

'Dumb colonists.' Spunkmeyer looked to his plate as food began to put in an appearance. After three weeks asleep he was starving, but not so starving that he couldn't offer the obligatory soldier's culinary comment. 'What's this stuff supposed to be?'

'Eggs, dimwit,' said Ferro.

'I know what an egg is, bubblebrain. I mean this soggy flat yellow stuff on the side.'

'Corn bread, I think.' Wierzbowski fingered his portion and added absently, 'Hey, I wouldn't mind getting me some more a that Arcturan poontang. Remember that time?'

Hicks was sitting on his right side. The corporal glanced up briefly, then looked back to his plate. 'Looks like that new lieutenant's too good to eat with us lowly grunts. Kissing up to the Company rep.'

Wierzbowski stared past the corporal, not caring if anyone should happen to notice the direction of his gaze. 'Yeah.'

'Doesn't matter if he knows his job,' said Crowe.

'The magic word.' Frost hacked at his eggs. 'We'll find out.'

Perhaps it was Gorman's youth that bothered them, even though he was older than half the troopers. More likely it was his appearance: hair neat even after weeks in hypersleep, slack creases sharp and straight, boots gleaming like black metal. He looked too good.

As they ate and muttered and stared, Bishop took the empty seat next to Ripley. She rose pointedly and moved to the far side of the table. The ExO looked wounded.

'I'm sorry you feel that way about synthetics, Ripley.'

She ignored him as she glared down at Burke, her tone accusing. 'You never said anything about there being an android on board! Why not? Don't lie to me, either, Carter. I saw his tattoo outside the showers.'

Burke appeared nonplussed. 'Well, it didn't occur to me. I don't know why you're so upset. It's been Company policy for years to have a synthetic on board every transport. They don't need hypersleep, and it's a lot cheaper than hiring a human pilot to oversee the interstellar jumps. They won't go crazy working a longhaul solo. Nothing special about it.'

'I prefer the term "artificial person" myself,' Bishop interjected softly. 'Is there a problem? Perhaps it's something I can help with.'

'I don't think so.' Burke wiped egg from his lips. 'A synthetic malfunctioned on her last trip out. Some deaths were involved.'

'I'm shocked. Was it long ago?'

'Quite a while, in fact.' Burke made the statement without going into specifics, for which Ripley was grateful.

'Must have been an older model, then.'

'Hyperdine Systems 120-A/2.'

Bending over backwards to be conciliatory, Bishop turned to Ripley. 'Well, that explains it. The old A/2s were always a bit twitchy. That could never happen now, not with the new implanted behavioural inhibitors. Impossible for me to harm or, by omission of action, allow to be harmed a human being. The inhibitors are factory-installed, along with the rest of my cerebral functions. No one can tamper with them. So you see, I'm quite harmless.' He offered her a plate piled high with yellow rectangles. 'More corn bread?'

The plate did not shatter when it struck the far wall as Ripley smacked it out of his hand. Corn bread crumbled as the plate settled to the floor.

'Just stay away from me, Bishop! You got that straight? You keep away from me.'

Wierzbowski observed this byplay in silence, then shrugged and turned back to his food. 'She don't like the corn bread, either.'

Ripley's outburst sparked no more conversation than that as the troopers finished breakfast and retired to the ready room. Ranks of exotic weaponry lined the walls behind them. Some clustered their chairs and started an improvised game of dice. Tough to pick up a floating crap game after you've been unconscious for three weeks, but they tried nonetheless. They straightened lazily as Gorman and Burke entered, but snapped to when Apone barked at them.

'Tench-hut!' The men and women responded as one, arms vertical at their sides, eyes straight ahead, and focused only on what the sergeant might say to them next.

Gorman's eyes flicked over the line. If possible, the troopers were more motionless standing at attention than they had been when frozen in hypersleep. He held them a moment longer before speaking.

'At ease.' The line flexed as muscles were relaxed. 'I'm sorry we didn't have time to brief you before we left Gateway, but—'

'Sir?' said Hudson.

Annoyed, Gorman glanced towards the speaker. Couldn't let him finish his first sentence before starting with the questions. Not that he'd expected anything else. He'd been warned that this bunch might be like that.

'Yes, what is it, Hicks?'

The speaker nodded at the man standing next to him. 'Hudson, sir. He's Hicks.'

'What's the question, soldier?'

'Is this going to be a stand-up fight, sir, or another bug-hunt?'

'If you'd wait a moment, you might find some of your questions anticipated, Hudson. I can understand your impatience and curiosity. There's not a great deal to explain. All we know is that there's still been no contact with the colony. Executive Officer Bishop tried to raise Hadley the instant the *Sulaco* hove within hailing distance of Acheron. He did not obtain a response. The planetary deepspace satellite relay checks out okay, so *that's* not the reason for the lack of contact. We don't know what it is yet.'

'Any ideas?' Crowe asked.

'There is a possibility, just a possibility at this point, mind, that a xenomorph may be involved.'

'A whaat?' said Wierzbowski.

Hicks leaned towards him, whispered softly. 'It's a bug-hunt.' Then louder, to the lieutenant, 'So what are these things, if they're there?'

Gorman nodded to Ripley, who stepped forward. Eleven pairs of eyes locked on her like gun sights: alert, intent, curious, and speculative. They were sizing her up, still unsure whether to class her with Burke and Gorman or somewhere else. They neither cared for her nor disliked her, because they didn't know her yet.

Fine. Leave it at that. She placed a handful of tiny recorder disks on the table before her.

'I've dictated what I know on these. There are some duplicates. You can read them in your rooms or in your suits.'

'I'm a slow reader.' Apone lightened up enough to smile slightly. 'Tease us a bit.'

'Yeah, let's have some previews.' Spunkmeyer leaned back against enough explosive to blow a small hotel apart, snuggling back among the firing tubes and detonators.

'Okay. First off, it's important to understand the organism's life cycle. It's actually two creatures. The first form hatches a spore, a sort of large egg, and attaches itself to its victim. Then it injects an embryo, detaches, and dies. It's essentially a walking reproductive organ. Then the—'

'Sounds like you, Hicks.' Hudson grinned over at the older man, who responded with his usual tolerant smile.

Ripley didn't find it funny. She didn't find anything about the alien funny, but then, she'd seen it. The troopers still weren't convinced she was describing something that existed outside her imagination. She'd have to try to be patient with them. That wasn't going to be easy.

'The embryo, the second form, hosts in the victim's body for several hours. Gestating. Then it'—she had to swallow, fighting a sudden dryness in her throat—'emerges. Moults. Grows rapidly. The adult form advances quickly through a number of intermediate stages until it matures in the form of—'

This time it was Vasquez who interrupted. 'That's all fine, but I only need to know one thing.'

'Yes?'

'Where they are.' She pointed her finger at an empty space between Ripley and the door, cocked her thumb, and blew away an imaginary intruder. Hoots and guffaws of approval came from her colleagues.

'Yo Vasquez!' As always, Drake delighted in his counterpart's demure bloodthirstiness. Her nickname was the Gamin Assassin. It was not misplaced.

She nodded brusquely. 'Anytime. Anywhere.'

'Somebody say "alien"?' Hudson leaned back in his seat, idly fingering a weapon with an especially long and narrow barrel. 'She thought they said "illegal alien" and signed up.'

'Fuck you.' Vasquez threw the comtech a casual finger. He responded by mimicking her tone and attitude as closely as possible.

'Anytime. Anywhere.'

Ripley's tone was as cold as the skin of the *Sulaco*. 'Am I disturbing your conversation, Mr. Hudson? I know most of you are looking at this as just another typical police action. I can assure you it's more than that. I've seen this creature. I've seen what it can do. If you run into it, I can guarantee that you won't do so laughingly.'

Hudson subsided, smirking. Ripley shifted her attention to Vasquez. 'I hope it'll be as easy as you make it out to be, Private. I really do.' Their eyes locked. Neither woman looked away.

Burke broke it up by stepping between them to address the assembled troops. 'That's enough for a preview. I suggest all of you take the time to study the disks Ripley has been kind enough to prepare for you. They contain additional basic information, as well as some highly detailed speculative graphics put together by an advanced imaging computer. I believe you'll find them interesting. I promise they'll hold your attention.' He relinquished the floor to Gorman. The lieutenant was brisk, sounding like a commander even if he didn't quite look like one.

'Thank you Mr. Burke, Ms. Ripley.' His gaze roved over the indifferent faces of his squad. 'Any questions?' A hand waved casually from the back of the group and he sighed resignedly. 'Yes, Hudson?'

The comtech was examining his fingernails. 'How do I get out of this outfit?'

Gorman scowled and forbore from offering the first thought that came to mind. He thanked Ripley again, and gratefully she took a seat.

'All right. I want this operation to go smoothly and by the numbers. I want full DCS and tactical data-base assimilation by oh-eight-thirty.' A few groans rose from the group but nothing in the way of a strong protest. It was no less than what they expected.

'Ordnance loading, weapons strip and checkout, and dropship prep will have seven hours. I want everything and everybody ready to go on time. Let's hit it. You've had three weeks rest.'

# V

The *Sulaco* was a giant metallic seashell drifting in a black sea. Bluish lights flared soundlessly along the flanks of the unlovely hull as she settled into final orbit. On the bridge, Bishop regarded his instruments and readouts unblinkingly. Occasionally he would touch a switch or tap a flurry of commands into the system. For the most part all he had to do was observe while the ship's computers parked the vessel in the desired orbit. The automation that made interstellar navigation possible had reduced man to the status of a last-recourse backup system. Now synthetics like Biship had replaced man. Exploration of the cosmos had become a chauffeured profession.

When the dials and gauges had lined up to his satisfaction, he leaned towards the nearest voice pickup. 'Attention to the bridge. Bishop speaking. This concludes final intraorbital manoeuvring operations. Geosynchronous insertion has been completed. I have adjusted artificial gravity to Acheron norm. Thank you for your cooperation. You may resume work.'

In contrast to the peace and quiet that reigned throughout most of the ship, the cargo loading bay was swarming with activity. Spunkmeyer sat in the roll cage of a big powerloader, a machine that resembled a skeletal mechanical elephant and was much stronger. The waldo gloves in which his hands and feet were inserted picked up the PFC's movements and transferred them to the metal arms and legs of the machine, multiplying his carrying capacity by a factor of several thousand.

He slid the long, reinforced arms into a bulging ordnance rack and lifted out a rack of small tactical missiles. Working with the smooth, effortless movements of his external prosthesis, he swung the load up into the dropship's belly. Clicks and clangs sounded from within as the vessel accepted the offering and automatically secured the missiles in place. Spunkmeyer retreated in search of another load. The powerloader was battered and dirty with grease. Across its back the word *Caterpillar* was faintly visible.

Other troopers drove tow motors or ran loading arms. Occasionally they called to one another, but for the most part the loading and prep operation proceeded without conversation. Also without accident, the members of the squad meshed like the individual gears and wheels of some half-metal, half-organic machine. Despite the close quarters in which they found themselves, and the amount of dangerous machinery in constant motion, no one so much as scraped his neighbour. Hicks watched over it all, checking off one item after another on an electronic manifest, occasionally nodding to himself as one more necessary predrop procedure was satisfactorily completed.

In the armoury Wierzbowski, Drake, and Vasquez were fieldstripping light weapons, their fingers moving with as much precision as the loading machines in the cargo bay. Tiny circuit boards were removed, checked, and blown clean of dust and lint before being reinserted into sleek metal and plastic sculptures of death.

Vasquez removed her heavy smartgun from its rack and locked it into a work stand and lovingly began to run it through the computer-assisted final checkout. The weapon was designed to be worn, not carried. It was equipped with an integral computer lock-and-fire, its own search-and-detection equipment, and was balanced on a precision gimbal that stabilized itself according to its operator's movements. It could do just about everything except pull its own trigger.

Vasquez smiled affectionately as she worked on it. It was a difficult child, a complex child, but it would protect her and her comrades and keep them safe from harm. She lavished more understanding and care on it than she did on any of her colleagues.

Drake understood completely. He also talked to his weapon, albeit silently. None of their fellow troopers found such behaviour abnormal. Everyone knew that all Colonial Marines were slightly unbalanced and that smartgun operators were the strangest of the lot. They tended to treat their weapons as extensions of their own bodies. Unlike their colleagues, gun operation was their principal function. Drake and Vasquez didn't have to worry about mastering communications equipment, piloting a dropship, driving the armoured personnel carrier, or even helping to load the ship for landing. All they were required to do was shoot at things. Death-dealing was their designated specialty.

Both of them loved their work.

Not everyone was as busy as the troopers. Burke had completed his few personal preparations for landing while Gorman was able to leave the actual supervision of final prep to Apone. As they stood off to the side and watched, the Company representative spoke casually to the lieutenant.

'Still nothing from the colony?'

Gorman shook his head and noted something about the loading procedure that induced him to make a notation on his electronic pad. 'Not even a background carrier wave. Dead on all channels.'

'And we're sure about the relay satellite?'

'Bishop insists that he checked it out thoroughly and that it responded perfectly to every command. Says it gave him something to do while we were on final system approach. He ran a standard signal check along the relay back to Earth, and we should get a response in a few days. That'll be the final confirmation, but he felt sure enough of his own check to guarantee the system's performance.'

'Then the problem's down on the surface somewhere.'

Gorman nodded. 'Like we've suspected all along.'

Burke looked thoughtful. 'What about local communications? Community video, operations to tractors, relays between the atmosphere processing stations, and the like?'

The lieutenant shook his head regretfully. 'If anybody's talking to anybody else down there, they're doing it with smoke signals or mirrors. Except for the standard low-end hiss from the local sun, the electromagnetic spectrum's dead as lead.'

The Company rep shrugged. 'Well, we didn't expect to find anything else. Still, there was always hope.'

'There still is. Maybe the colony's taken a mass vow of silence. Maybe all we'll run into is a collective pout.'

'Why would they do something like that?'

'How should I know? Mass religious conversion or something else that demands radio silence.'

'Yeah. Maybe.' Burke wanted to believe Gorman. Gorman wanted to believe Burke. Neither man believed the other for a moment. Whatever had silenced the colony of Acheron hadn't been a matter of choice. People liked to talk, colonists more than most. They wouldn't shut down all communications willingly.

Ripley had been watching the two men. Now she shifted her attention back to the ongoing process of loading and predrop prep. She'd seen military dropships on the newscasts, but this was the first time she'd stood close to one. It made her feel a little safer. Heavily armed and armoured, it looked like a giant black wasp. As she looked on, a six-wheeled armoured personnel carrier was being hoisted into the ship's belly. It was built like an iron ingot, low and squatty, unlovely in profile and purely functional.

Movement on her left made her stumble aside as Frost wheeled a rack of incomprehensible equipment towards her.

'Clear, please,' the trooper said politely.

As she apologized and stepped away she was forced to retreat in another direction in order to get out of Hudson's way.

'Excuse me.' He didn't look at her, concentrating on his lift load of supplies.

Cursing silently to herself, she hunted through the organized confusion until she found Apone. The NCO was chatting with Hicks, both of them studying the corporal's checklist as she approached. She kept quiet until the sergeant acknowledged her presence.

'Something?' he asked curiously.

'Yeah, there's something. I feel like a fifth wheel down here, and I'm sick of doing nothing.'

Apone grinned. 'We're all sick of doing nothing. What about it?'

'Is there anything I can do?'

He scratched the back of his head, eyeing her. 'I don't know. *Is* there anything you can do?'

She turned and pointed. 'I can drive that loader. I've got a class-two dock rating. My latest career move.'

Apone glanced in the direction in which she was pointing. The *Sulaco*'s backup powerloader squatted dormant in its maintenance bay. His people were versatile, but they were soldiers first. Marines, not construction workers. An extra couple of hands would be welcome loading the heavy stuff, especially if they were fashioned of titanium alloy, as were the powerloader's.

'That's no toy.' The scepticism in Apone's voice was matched by that on Hicks's face.

'That's all right,' she replied crisply. 'This isn't Christmas.'

The sergeant pursed his lips. 'Class-two, huh?'

By way of response, she spun on her heel and strode over to the loader, climbed the ladder, and settled into the seat beneath the safety cage. A quick inspection revealed that, as she'd suspected, the loader was little different from the ones she'd operated Portside on Earth. A slightly newer model, maybe. She jabbed at a succession of switches. Motors turned over. A basso whine emanated from the guts of the machine, rising to a steady hum.

Hands and feet slipped into waldo gloves. Like some paralysed dinosaur suddenly shocked back to life, the loader rose on titanium pads. It boomed as she walked it over to the stack of cargo modules. Huge claws extended and dipped, slipping into lifting receptacles beneath the nearest container. She raised it from the top of the pile and swung it back towards the watching men. Her voice rose above the hum of the motors.

'Where you want it?'

Hicks glanced at his sergeant and cocked an eyebrow appreciatively.

Personal preparation proceeded at the same pace as dropship loading but with additional care. Something could go wrong with the APC, or the supplies crammed into it, or with communications or backup, but no soldier would allow anything to go wrong with his or her personal weaponry. Each of them was capable of fighting and winning a small war on his or her own.

First the armour was snapped together and checked for cracks or warps. Then the special combat boots, capable of resisting any combination of weather, corrosion, and teeth. Backpacks that would enable a fragile human being to survive for over a month in a hostile environment without any supplemental aid whatsoever. Harnesses to keep you from bouncing around during a rough drop or while the APC was grinding a path over difficult terrain. Helmets to protect your skull and visors to shield your eyes. Comsets for communicating with the dropship, with the APC, with whichever buddy happened to be guarding your rear.

Fingers flowed smoothly over fastenings and snaps. When everything was done and ready, when all had been checked out and operational, the whole procedure was run again from scratch. And when *that* was over, if you had a minute, you spent it checking out your neighbour's work.

Apone strode back and forth among his people, doing his own unobtrusive checking even though he knew it was unnecessary. He was, however, a firm believer in the for-want-of-a-nail school. Now was the time to spot the overlooked snap, the forgotten catch. Once things turned hairy, regrets were usually fatal.

'Let's move it, girls! On the ready-line. Let's go, let's go. You've slept long enough.'

They formed up and headed for the dropship, chatting excitedly and shuffling along in twos and threes. Apone could have made it pretty if he'd wanted to, formed them up and called cadence, but his people weren't pretty, and he wasn't about to tell them how to walk. The sergeant was pleased to see that their new lieutenant had learned enough by now to keep his mouth shut. They filed into the ship muttering among themselves, no flags flying, no prerecorded bands tootling. Their anthem was a string of well-worn and familiar obscenities passed down from one to the next: defiant words from men and women ready to challenge death. Apone shared them. As all foot soldiers have known for thousands of years, there's nothing noble about dying. Only an irritating finality.

Once inside the dropship, they filed directly into the APC. The carrier would deploy the instant the shuttle craft touched down. It made for a rougher ride, but Colonial Marines do not expect coddling.

As soon as everyone was aboard and the dropship doors secured, a klaxon sounded, signalling depressurization of the *Sulaco*'s cargo bay. Service robots scurried for cover. Warning lights flashed.

The troopers sat in two rows opposite each other, a single aisle running between. Next to the soldiers in their hulking armour, Ripley felt small and vulnerable. In addition to her duty suit she wore only a flight jacket and a communications headset. No one offered her a gun.

Hudson was too juiced up to sit still. The adrenaline was flowing and his eyes were wide. He prowled the aisle, his movements predatory and exaggerated, a cat ready to pounce. As he paced, he kept up a steady stream of psychobabble, unavoidable in the confined space.

'I am *ready*, man. Ready to get it *on*. Check it out. I am the ultimate. State-of-the-art. You *do not* want to mess with me. Hey, Ripley.' She glanced up at him, expressionless. 'Don't worry, little lady. Me and my squad of ultimate killing machines will protect you. Check it out.' He slapped the controls of the servocannon mounted in the overhead gun bay, careful not to hit any of the ready studs.

'Independently targeting particle-beam phalanx gun. Ain't she a cutey? *Vwap!* Fry half a city with this puppy. We got tactical smart missiles, phased-plasma pulse-rifles, RPGs. We got sonic ee-lectronic cannons, we got nukes no flukes, we got knives, sharp sticks—'

Hicks reached up, grabbed Hudson by his battle harness, and yanked him down into an empty seat. His voice was low but it carried.

'Save it.'

'Sure, Hicks.' Hudson sat back, suddenly docile.

Ripley nodded her thanks to the corporal. Young face, old eyes, she thought as she studied him. Seen more than he should have in his time. Probably more than he's wanted to. She didn't mind the quiet that followed Hudson's soliloquy. There was hysteria enough below. She didn't need to listen to any extra. The corporal leaned towards her.

'Don't mind Hudson. Don't mind any of 'em. They're all like that, but in a tight spot there're none better.'

'If he can shoot his gun as well as he does his mouth, maybe it'll take my blood pressure down a notch.'

Hicks grinned. 'Don't worry on that score. Hudson's a comtech, but he's a close-combat specialist, just like everyone else.'

'You too?'

He settled back in his seat: content, self-contained, ready. 'I'm not here because I wanted to be a pastry chef.'

Motors began to throb. The dropship lurched as it was lowered out of the cargo bay on its grapples.

'Hey,' Frost muttered, 'anybody check the locks on this coffin? If they're not tight, we're liable to bounce right out the bottom of the shuttle.'

'Keep cool, sweets,' said Dietrich. 'Checked 'em out myself. We're secure. This six-wheeler goes nowhere until we kiss dirt.' Frost looked relieved.

The dropship's engines rumbled to life. Stomachs lurched as they left the artificial gravity field of the *Sulaco* behind. They were free now, floating slowly away from the big transport. Soon they would be clear and the engines would fire fully. Legs and hands began to float in zero-gee, but their harnesses held them tight to their seats. The floor and walls of the APC quivered as the engines thundered. Gravity returned with a vengeance.

Burke looked like he was on a fishing cruiser off Jamaica. He was grinning eagerly, anxious for the real adventure to begin. 'Here we go!'

Ripley closed her eyes, then opened them almost immediately. Anything was better than staring at the black backsides of her lids. They were like tiny videoscreens alive with wild sparks and floating green blobs. Malign shapes appeared in the blobs. The taut, confident faces of Frost, Crowe, Apone, and Hicks made for more reassuring viewing.

Up in the cockpit, Spunkmeyer and Ferro studied readouts and worked controls. Gees built up within the APC as the dropship's speed increased. A few lips trembled. No one said a word as they plunged towards atmosphere.

Grey limbo below. The dark mantle of clouds that shrouded the surface of Acheron suddenly became something more than a pearlescent sheen to be admired from above. The atmosphere was dense and disturbed, boiling over dry deserts and lifeless rocks, rendering the landscape invisible to everything but sophisticated sensors and imaging equipment.

The dropship bounced through alien jet streams, shuddering and rocking. Ferro's voice sounded icy calm over the open intercom as she shouldered the streamlined craft through the dust-filled gale.

'Switching to DCS ranging. Visibility zero. A real picnic ground. What a bowl of crap.'

'Two-four-oh.' Spunkmeyer was too busy to respond in kind to her complaints. 'Nominal to profile. Picking up some hull ionization.'

Ferro glanced at a readout. 'Bad?'

'Nothing the filters can't handle. Winds two hundred plus.' A screen between them winked to life, displaying a topographic model of the terrain they were overflying. 'Surface ranging on. What'd you expect, Ferro? Tropical beaches?' He nudged a trio of switches. 'Starting to hit thermals. Vertical shift unpredictable. Lotta swirling.'

'Got it.' Ferro thumbed a button. 'Nothing that ain't in our programming. At least the weather hasn't changed down there.' She eyed a readout. 'Rough air ahead.'

The pilot's voice sounded briskly over the APC's intercom system. 'Ferro, here. You all read the profile on this dirtball. Summertime fun it ain't. Stand by for some chop.'

Ripley's eyes flicked rapidly over her companions, crammed tightly together in the confines of the armoured personnel carrier. Hicks lay slumped to one side, asleep in his seat harness. The bouncing seemed not to bother him in the slightest. Most of the other troopers sat quietly, staring straight ahead, their minds mulling over private thoughts. Hudson was talking steadily and silently to himself. His lips moved ceaselessly. Ripley didn't try to read them.

Burke was studying the interior layout of the APC with professional interest. Across from him Gorman sat with his eyes shut tight. His skin was pale, and the sweat stood out on his forehead and neck. His hands were in nonstop motion, rubbing the backs of his knees. Massaging away tenseness—or attempting to dry clamminess, she thought. Maybe it would help him to have someone to talk to.

'How many drops is this for you, Lieutenant?'

His eyes snapped open and he blinked at her. 'Thirty-eight—simulated.'

'How many *combat* drops?' Vasquez asked pointedly.

Gorman tried to reply as though it made no difference. A minor point, and what did it have to do with anything, anyway? 'Well—two. Three, including this one.'

Vasquez and Drake exchanged a glance, said nothing. They didn't have to. Their respective expressions were sufficiently eloquent. Ripley gave Burke an accusing look, and he responded with one of indifferent helplessness, as if to say, 'Hey, I'm a civilian. Got no control over military assignments.'

Which was pure bull, of course, but there was nothing to be gained by arguing about it now. Acheron lay beneath them, Earthside bureaucracy very far away indeed. She chewed her lower lip and tried not to let it bother her. Gorman seemed competent enough. Besides, in any actual confrontation or combat, Apone would run the show. Apone and Hicks.

Cockpit voices continued to reverberate over the intercom. Ferro managed to outgripe Spunkmeyer three to one. In between gripes and complaints they managed to fly the dropship.

'Turning on final approach,' she was saying. 'Coming around to a seven-zero-niner. Terminal guidance locked in.'

'Always knew you were terminal,' said Spunkmeyer. It was an old pilot's joke, and Ferro ignored it.

'Watch your screen. I can't fly this sucker and watch the terrain readouts too. Keep us off the mountains.' A pause, then, 'Where's the beacon?'

'Nothing on relay.' Spunkmeyer's voice was calm. 'Must've gone out along with communications.'

'That's crazy and you know it. Beacons are automatic and individually powered.'

'Okay. *You* find the beacon.'

'I'll settle for somebody waving a lousy flag.' Silence followed. None of the troopers appeared concerned. Ferro and Spunkmeyer had set them down softer than a baby's kiss in worse weather than Acheron's.

'Winds easing. Good kite-flying weather. We'll hold her

steady up here for a while so you kids in back can play with your toys.'

A flurry of motion as the troopers commenced final touchdown preparations. Gorman slipped out of his flight harness and headed up the aisle towards the APC's tactical operations centre. Burke and Ripley followed, leaving the Marines to their work.

The three of them crowded into the bay. Gorman slid behind the control console while Burke took up a stance behind him so he could look over the lieutenant's shoulder. Ripley was pleased to see that there was nothing wrong with Gorman's mechanical skills. He looked relieved to have something to do. His fingers brought readouts and monitor screens to life like an organist extracting notes from stops and keys. Ferro's voice reached them from the cockpit, mildly triumphant.

'Finally got the beacons. Signal is hazy but distinct. And the clouds have cleared enough for us to get some visual. We can see Hadley.'

Gorman spoke towards a pickup. 'How's it look?'

'Just like the brochures,' she said sardonically. 'Vacation spot of the galaxy. Massive construction, dirty. A few lights on, so they've got power somewheres. Can't tell at this distance if they're regular or emergency. Not a lot of 'em. Maybe it's nap time. Give me two weeks in the Antarctic anytime.'

'Spunkmeyer, your impressions?'

'Windy as all get out. They haven't been bombed. Structural integrity looks good, but that's from up here, looking through bad light. Sorry we're too busy to do a ground scan.'

'We'll take care of that in person.' Gorman turned his attention back to the multiple screens. The closer they came to setdown, the more confident he seemed to become. Maybe a fear of heights was his only weakness, Ripley mused. If that proved to be the case, she'd be able to relax.

In addition to the tactical screens there were two small ones for each soldier. All were name-labelled. The upper set relayed the view from the video cams built into the crown of each battle helmet. The lower provided individual bio readouts: EEG, EKG, respiratory rate, circulatory functioning, visual acuity, and so on. Enough information for whoever was monitoring the screens to build up a complete physiological profile of every trooper from the inside out.

Above and to the side of the double set of smaller screens were larger monitors that offered those riding inside the APC a complete wraparound view of the terrain outside. Gorman thumbed controls. Hidden telltales beeped and responded on cue.

'Looking good,' he murmured to himself, as much as to his civilian observers. 'Everybody on line.' Ripley noted that the blood-pressure readouts held remarkably steady. And not one of the soldiers' heart rates rose above seventy-five.

One of the small video monitors displayed static instead of a clear view of the APC's interior. 'Drake, check your camera,' Gorman ordered. 'I'm not getting a picture. Frost, show me Drake. Might be an external break.'

The view on the screen next to Drake's shifted to reveal the helmeted face of the smartgun operator as he whacked himself on the side of the head with a battery pack. His screen snapped into focus instantly.

'That's better. Pan it around a bit.'

Drake complied. 'Learned that one in tech class,' he informed the occupants of the operations bay. 'Got to make sure you hit the left side only or it doesn't work.'

'What happens if you hit the right side?' Ripley asked curiously.

'You overload the internal pressure control, the one that keeps your helmet on your head.' She could see Drake smiling wolfishly into Frost's camera. 'Your eyeballs implode and your brains explode.'

'What brains?' Vasquez let out a snort. Drake promptly leaned forward and tried to smack the right side of her helmet with a battery pack.

Apone quieted them. He knew it didn't matter what was

wrong with Drake's helmet, because the smartgun operator would abandon it the first chance he got. Likewise Vasquez. Drake would appear in his floppy cap and Vasquez in her red bandanna. Nonregulation battle headgear. Both claimed the helmets obstructed the movement of their gun sights, and if that was the way they felt about it, Apone wasn't about to argue with them. They could shave their skulls and fight bald-headed if they wished as long as they shot straight.

'Awright. Fire team A, gear up. Check your backup systems and your power packs. Anybody goes dead when we spread out is liable to end up that way. If some boogeyman doesn't kill you, I will. Let's move. Two minutes.' He glanced to his right. 'Somebody wake up Hicks.'

A few guffaws sounded from the assembled troopers. Ripley had to smile as she let her gaze drop to the biomonitor with the corporal's name above it. The readings indicated a man overwhelmed with boredom. Apone's second in command was deep in REM sleep. Dreaming of balmier climes, no doubt. She wished she could relax like that. Once upon a time she'd been able to. Once this trip was over, maybe she'd be able to again.

The passenger compartment saw a new rush of activity as backpacks were donned and weapons presented. Vasquez and Drake assisted each other in buckling on their complex smartgun harnesses.

The forward-facing viewscreen gave those in the operations bay the same view as Ferro and Spunkmeyer. Directly ahead a metal volcano thrust its perfect cone into the clouds, belching hot gas into the sky. Audio pickups muted the atmosphere processor's thunder.

'How many of those are on Acheron?' Ripley asked Burke.

'That's one of thirty or so. I couldn't give you all the grid references. They're scattered all over the planet. Well, not scattered. Placed, for optimum injection into the atmosphere. Each is fully automated, and their output is controlled from Hadley Operations Central. Their production will be adjusted as the air here becomes more Earth-normal. Eventually they'll shut themselves down. Until that happens, they'll work around the clock for another twenty to thirty years. They're expensive and reliable. We manufacture them, by the way.'

The ship was a drifting mote alongside the massive, rumbling tower. Ripley was impressed. Like everyone else whose work took them out into space, she'd heard about the big terra-forming devices, but she'd never expected to see one in person.

Gorman nudged controls, swinging the main external imager around and down to reveal the silent roofs of the colony. 'Hold at forty,' he commanded Ferro via the console pickup. 'Make a slow circle of the complex. I don't think we'll spot anything from up here, but that's the way the regs say to go, so that's how we'll do it.'

'Can do,' the pilot responded. 'Hang on back there. Might bounce a little while we spiral in. This isn't an atmosphere flyer, remember. It's just a lousy dropship. Tight suborbital manoeu-vring ain't a highlight of its repertoire.'

'Just do as you're told, Corporal.'

'Yes, *sir*.' Ferro added something else too low for her mike to unscramble. Ripley doubted that it was flattering.

They circled in over the town. Nothing moved among the buildings beneath them. The few lights they'd spotted from afar continued to burn. The atmosphere processor roared in the background.

'Everything looks intact,' Burke commented. 'Maybe some kind of plague has everyone on their backs.'

'Maybe.' To Gorman the colony structures looked like the wrecks of ancient freighters littering the ocean floor. 'Okay,' he said sharply to Apone, 'let's do it.'

Back in the passenger bay, the master sergeant rose from his seat and glared at his troops, hanging on to an overhead handgrip as the dropship rocked in Acheron's unceasing gale.

'Awright! You heard the lieutenant. I want a nice clean dispersal this time. Watch the suit in front of you. Anybody trips over anybody else's boots going out gets booted right back up to the ship.'

'Is that a promise?' Crowe looked innocent.

'Hey, Crowe, you want your mommy?' Wierzbowski grinned at his colleague.

'Wish she were here,' the private responded. 'She'd wipe the floor with half you lot.'

They filed towards the front lock, squeezing past operations. Vasquez gave Ripley a nudge as she strolled by. 'You staying in here?'

'You bet.'

'Figures.' The smartgun operator turned away, shifting her attention to the back of Drake's head.

'Set down sixty metres this side of the main telemetry mast.' Gorman swivelled the imager's trakball control. Still no sign of life below. 'Immediate dust-off on my "clear", then find a soft cloud and stay on station.'

'Understood,' said Ferro perfunctorily.

Apone was watching the chronometer built into his suit sleeve. 'Ten seconds, people. Look sharp!'

As the dropship descended to within a hundred and fifty metres of the colony landing pad, its exterior lights flashed on automatically, the powerful beams penetrating a surprising distance into the gloom. The tarmac was damp and freckled with wind-blown garbage, none of which was large enough to upset Ferro's carefully timed touchdown. Hydraulic legs absorbed the shock of contact as tons of metal settled to ground. Seconds later the APC roared out of the cargo bay and away from the compact vessel. Having barely made contact with the surface of Acheron, the dropship's engines thundered, and it crawled back up into the dark sky.

Nothing materialized out of the muck to challenge or confront the personnel carrier as it rumbled up to the first of the silent colony buildings. Spray and mud flew from beneath its solid, armoured wheels. It swerved sharply left so that the crew door would face the town's main entrance. Before the door was half open, Hudson had piled out and hit the ground running. His companions were right behind him. They spread out fast, to cover as much ground as possible without losing sight of one another.

Apone's attention was riveted to the screen of his visor's image intensifier as he scanned the buildings surrounding them. The scanner's internal computer magnified the available light and cleaned up the view as much as it could, resulting in a bright picture that was still luridly tinted and full of contrast. It was enough.

Colony architecture tended to the functional. Beautification of surroundings would come later, when the wind wouldn't ruin all such efforts no matter how modest. Wind whipped trash between the buildings—that detritus that was too heavy to blow away. A chunk of metal rocked on an uneven base, banging mindlessly against a nearby wall, any echo subsumed by the wind. A few neonic lights flickered unsteadily. Gorman's voice sounded crisply over everyone's suit communicator.

'First squad up, on line. Hicks, get your people in a cordon between the entrance and the APC. Watch your rear. Vasquez, take point. Let's move.'

A line of troopers advanced on the main entrylock. No one expected a greeting committee to meet them, any more than they expected to cycle the lock and stroll in without difficulty, but it was still something of a shock to encounter the pair of heavy-duty tractors that were parked nose-to-nose in front of the big door, barring any entry. It implied a conscious effort on the part of those inside to keep something outside.

Vasquez reached the silent machines first and paused to peer inside the operator's cab of the nearest. The controls had been ripped out and strewn around the interior. Impassive, she squeezed between the earthmovers, her tone phlegmatic as she reported back.

'Looks like somebody took a crowbar to the instrumentation.' She reached the main doorway and nodded to her right, where Drake flanked her. Apone arrived, scanned the barrier, and moved to the external door controls. His fingers tried every combination. None of the telltale lights came alive.

'Busted?' Drake inquired.

'Sealed. There's a difference. Hudson, get up here. We need a bypass.'

No funny cracks now as the comtech, all business, put his gun aside and bent to examine the door panel. 'Standard stuff,' he said in less than a minute. Using a tool taken from his work belt, he prised away the protective weather facing and studied the wiring. 'Take two puffs, Sarge.' His fingers deft and deliberate in their movements, despite the wind and cold, he began patching around the ruined circuitry. Apone and the others waited and watched.

'First squad,' the sergeant snapped into his suit pickup, 'assemble on me at the main lock.'

A sign creaked and groaned overhead where it had broken loose from its moorings. The wind howled around them, buffeting nerves more than bodies. Hudson made a connection. Two indicator lights flickered fitfully. Moaning against the dust that had accumulated in its guide rail, the big door slid back on its tracks, travelling in fits and starts, in sync with the blinking lights. Halfway open it jammed. It was more than enough.

Apone motioned Vasquez forward. The muzzle of her smartgun preceding her, she stepped inside. Her companions followed as Gorman's voice crackled in their headsets.

'Second team, move up. Flanking positions, close quarters. How's it look, Sergeant?'

Apone's eyes scanned the interior of the silent structure. 'Clean so far, sir. Nobody home yet.'

'Right. Second team, keep watching behind you as you advance.' The lieutenant spared a moment to glance up and behind him. 'You okay, Ripley?'

She was abruptly aware that she was breathing too fast, as though she'd just finished running a marathon instead of having been standing in one place. She nodded curtly, angry at herself, angry at Gorman for his concern. He returned his attention to the console.

Vasquez and Apone strode down the wide, deserted corridor. A few lights burned blue overhead. Emergency illumination, already beginning to weaken. No telling how long the batteries had been burning. The wind accompanied them partway in, whistling down the metal concourse. Pools of water stained the floor. Farther along, rain dripped through blast holes in the ceiling. Apone tilted his head back so that his helmet camera would simultaneously record the evidence of the firefight and transmit it back to the APC.

'Pulse-rifles,' he murmured, explaining the cause of the ragged holes. 'Somebody's a wild shot.'

In the operations bay, Ripley glanced sharply at Burke. 'People confined to bed don't run around firing pulse-rifles inside their habitat. People with inoperative communications equipment don't go around firing off pulse-rifles. Something else makes them do things like that.' Burke simply shrugged and turned to watch the screens.

Apone made a face at the blast holes. 'Messy.' It was a professional opinion, not an aesthetic one. The master sergeant couldn't abide sloppy work. Of course, these were only colonists, he reminded himself. Engineers, structural technicians, service classifications. No soldiers. Maybe one or two cops. No need for soldiers—until now. And why now? The wind taunted him. He searched the corridor ahead, seeking answers and finding only darkness.

'Move out.'

Vasquez resumed her advance, more machinelike in her movements than any robot. Her smartgun cannon shifted slowly from left to right and back again, covering every inch ahead every few seconds. Her eyes were downcast, intent on the gun's tracking monitor instead of the floor underfoot. Footsteps echoed around and behind her, but ahead it was silent.

Gorman tapped a finger alongside a large red button. 'Quarter and search by twos. Second team, move inside. Hicks, take the upper level. Use your motion trackers. Anybody sees *anything* moving, sing out.'

Someone ventured a couple of lines a capella from Thor's storm-calling song at the end of *Das Rheingold*. It sounded like Hudson, but Ripley couldn't be sure, and no one owned up to the chorus. She tried to watch all the individual camera monitors simultaneously. Every dark corner inside the building was a gateway to Hell, every shadow a lethal threat. She had to fight to keep her breathing steady.

Hicks led his squad up a deserted stairwell to the town's second level. The corridor was a mirror image of the one directly beneath, maybe a little narrower but just as empty. It did offer one benefit: they were pretty well out of the wind.

Standing in the middle of a knot of troops, he unlimbered a small metal box with a glass face. It had delicate insides and, like most marine equipment, a heavily armoured exterior. He aimed it down the hallway and adjusted the controls. A couple of LEDs lit up brightly. The gauges stayed motionless. He panned it slowly from right to left.

'Nothing,' he reported. 'No movement, no signs of life.'

'Move out' was Gorman's disappointed response.

Hicks held the scanner out in front of him while his squad covered him, front, back, and sideways. They passed rooms and offices. Some of the doors stood ajar, others shut tight. The interiors were similar and devoid of surprises.

The farther they went, the more blatant became the evidence of struggle. Furniture was overturned and papers scattered about. Irreplaceable computer storage disks had been trampled underfoot. Personal possessions, shipped at great cost over interstellar distances, had been thrown thoughtlessly aside, smashed and broken. Priceless books of real paper floated soddenly in puddles of water that had leaked from frozen pipes and holes in the ceiling.

'Looks like my room in college.' Burke was trying to be funny. He failed.

Several of the rooms Hicks's squad passed had not just been turned upside down; they'd been burned. Black streaks seared walls of metal and composite. In several offices the triple-paned safety-glass windows had been blown out. Rain and wind gusted through the gaps. Hicks stepped inside one office to lift a half-eaten doughnut from a listing table. A nearby coffee cup overflowed with rainwater. The dark grounds lay scattered across the floor, floating like water mites in the puddles.

Apone's people systematically searched the lower level, moving in pairs that functioned as single organisms. They went through the colonists' modest, compact living quarters one apartment at a time. There wasn't much to see. Hudson kept his eyes on his scanner as he prowled alongside Vasquez, looking up only long enough to take note of a particular stain on one wall. He didn't need sophisticated electronic analysers to tell him what it was: dried blood. Everyone in the APC saw it too. No one said anything.

Hudson's tracker let out a beep, the sound explosively loud in the empty corridor. Vasquez whirled, her gun ready. Tracker and smartgun operator exchanged a glance. Hudson nodded, then walked slowly towards a half-open door that was splintered partway off its frame. Holes produced by pulse-rifle rounds peppered the remnants of the door and the walls framing it.

As the comtech eased out of the way, Vasquez sidled up close to the ruined barrier and kicked it in. She came as close as possible to firing without actually unleashing a stream of destruction on the room's interior.

Dangling from a length of flex conduit, a junction box swung back and forth like a pendulum, driven by the wind that poured in through a broken window. The heavy metal box clacked against the rails of a child's bunk bed as it swung.

Vasquez uttered a guttural sound. 'Motion detectors. I hate 'em.' They both turned back to the hallway.

Ripley was watching the view provided by Hicks's monitor. Suddenly she leaned forward. 'Wait! Tell him to—' Abruptly aware that only Burke and Gorman could hear her, she hurried to plug in her headset jack, patching herself into the intersuit communications net. 'Hicks, this is Ripley. I saw something on your screen. Back up.' He complied, and the picture on his monitor retreated. 'That's it. Now swing left. There!'

The two men who shared the operations bay with her watched as the image provided by the corporal's camera panned until it stabilized on a section of wall full of holes and oddly shaped gouges and depressions. Ripley went cold. She knew what had caused the irregular pattern of destruction.

Hicks ran a glove over the battered metal. 'You seeing this okay? Looks melted.'

'Not melted,' Ripley corrected him. 'Corroded.'

Burke looked over at her, raised an eyebrow. 'Hmmm. Acid for blood.'

'Looks like somebody bagged them one of Ripley's bad guys here.' Hicks sounded less impressed than the Company rep.

Hudson had been making his own inspection of a room on the lower level. Now he beckoned to his companions to join him. 'Hey, if you like that, you're gonna love this.' Ripley and her companions shifted their attention to the view being relayed back to the APC by the voluble private's camera.

He was looking down. His feet framed a gaping hole. As he leaned forward over the edge they could see another hole directly below the first and beyond, dimly illuminated by his helmet light, a section of the maintenance level. Pipes, conduits, wiring—all had been eaten away by the action of some ferocious liquid.

Apone examined the view, turned away. 'Second squad, talk to me. What's your status?'

Hicks's voice replied. 'Just finished our sweep. There's nobody home.'

The master sergeant nodded to himself, spoke to the occupants of the distant APC. 'The place is dead, sir. Dead and deserted. All's quiet on the Hadley front. Whatever happened here, we missed it.'

'Late for the party again.' Drake kicked a lump of corroded

metal aside.

Gorman leaned back and looked thoughtful. 'All right. The area's secured. Let's go in and see what their computer can tell us. First team, head for Operations. You know where that is, Sergeant?'

Apone nudged a sleeve switch. A small map of the Hadley colony appeared on the inside of his helmet visor. 'That tall structure we saw coming in. It's not far, sir. We're on our way.'

'Good. Hudson, when you get there, see if you can bring their CPU on-line. Nothing fancy. We don't want to use it; we just want to talk to it. Hicks, we're coming in. Meet me at the south lock by the uplink tower. Gorman out.'

'Out is right.' Hudson would have spat save for the fact that no suitable target presented itself. 'He's coming in. I feel safer already.'

Vasquez made sure her suit mike was off before agreeing.

The powerful arc lights mounted on the front of the APC illuminated the stained, wind-scoured walls of the colony buildings as the armoured vehicle trundled down the main service street. They passed a couple of smaller vehicles parked in a shielded area. The APC's gleaming metal wheels threw up sheets of dirty water as it rumbled through oversize potholes. Internal shocks absorbed the impact. Wind-blown rain lashed the headlights.

In the driver's compartment, Bishop and Wierzbowski worked smoothly side by side, man and synthetic functioning in perfect harmony. Each respected the other's abilities. Both knew, for example, that Wierzbowski could ignore any advice Bishop gave. Both also knew that the human would probably take it. Wierzbowski squinted through the narrow driver's port and pointed.

'Over there, I think.'

Bishop checked the flashing, brightly coloured map on the screen between them. 'That has to be it. There's no other lock in this area.' He leaned on the wheel, and the heavy machine swung towards a cavernous opening in the wall nearby.

'Yeah, there's Hicks.'

Apone's second in command emerged from the open lock as the armoured personnel carrier ground to a halt. He watched while the crew door cycled and slid aside. A suited Gorman was first down the ramp, followed closely by Burke, Bishop, and Wierzbowski. Burke looked back, searching for the tank's remaining occupant, only to see her hesitate in the portal. She wasn't looking at him. Her attention was focused on the dark entrance leading deep into the colony.

'Ripley?'

Her eyes lowered to meet his. By way of reply, she shook her head sharply from side to side.

'The area's secured.' Burke tried to sound understanding. 'You heard Apone.'

Another negative gesture. Hudson's voice sounded in their headsets.

'Sir, the colony CPU is on-line.'

'Good work, Hudson,' said the lieutenant. 'Those of you in Operations, stand by. We'll be there soon.' He nodded to his companions. 'Let's go.'

# VI

In person the devastation looked much worse than it had on the APC's monitors.

'Looks like your company can write off its share of this colony,' he murmured to Burke.

'The buildings are mostly intact.' The company rep didn't sound concerned. 'The rest's insured.'

'Yeah? What about the colonists?' Ripley asked him.

'We don't know what's happened to them yet.' He sounded slightly irritated by the question.

It was chilly inside the complex. Internal control had failed along with the power, and in any case, the blown-out windows and gaping holes in the walls would have overloaded the equipment quickly, anyway. Ripley found that she was sweating despite her environment suit's best efforts to keep her comfortable. Her eyes were as active as any trooper's as she checked out every hole in the walls and floor, every shadowed corner.

This was where it had all begun. This was the place where it had come from. The alien. There was no doubt in her mind what had happened here. An alien like the one that had caused the destruction of the *Nostromo* and the deaths of all her shipmates had gotten loose in Hadley Colony.

Hicks noticed her nervousness as she scanned the ravaged hallway and the fire-gutted offices and storage rooms. Wordlessly he motioned to Wierzbowski. The trooper nodded imperceptibly, adjusted his stride so that he fell into position on Ripley's right. Hicks slowed down until he was flanking her on the left. Together they formed a protective cordon around her. She noticed the shift and glanced at the corporal. He winked, or at least she thought he might have. It was too fast for her to be certain. Might just have been blinking at something in his eye. Even in the corridor there was enough of a breeze to blow sand and soot around.

Frost emerged from the side corridor just ahead. He beckoned to the new arrivals, speaking to Gorman but looking at Hicks.

'Sir, you should check this out.'

'What is it, Frost?' Gorman was in a hurry to rendezvous with Apone. But the soldier was insistent.

'Easier to show you, sir.'

'Right. It's up this way?' The lieutenant gestured down the corridor. Frost nodded and turned up into darkness, the others following.

He led them into a wing that was completely without power. Their suit lights revealed scenes of destruction worse than anything yet encountered. Ripley found that she was trembling. The APC, safe, solid, heavily armed, and not far off, loomed large in her thoughts. If she ran hard, she'd be back there in a few minutes. And alone once again. No matter how secure the personnel carrier was, she knew she was safer here, surrounded by the soldiers. She kept telling herself that as they advanced.

Frost was gesturing. 'Right ahead here, sir.'

The corridor was blocked. Someone had erected a make-shift barricade of welded pipes and steel plate, extra door panels, ceiling sheathing, and composite flooring. Acid holes and gashes scarred the hastily raised barrier. The metal had been torn and twisted by hideously powerful forces. Just to the right of where Frost was standing the barricade had been ripped open like an old soup can. They squeezed through the narrow opening one at a time.

Lights played over the devastation beyond. 'Anybody know where we are?' Gorman asked.

Burke studied an illuminated company map. 'Medical wing. We're in the right section, and it has the right look.'

They fanned out, the lights from their suits illuminating overturned tables and cabinets, broken chairs and expensive surgical equipment. Smaller medical instruments littered the floor like steel confetti. Additional tables and furniture had been piled, bolted, and welded to the inside of the barricade that once had sealed the wing off from the rest of the complex. Black streaks showed where untended fire had flamed, and the walls were pockmarked with holes from pulse-rifle fire and acid.

Despite the absence of lights, the wing wasn't completely energy-dead. A few isolated instruments and control boards glowed softly with emergency power. Wierzbowski ran a gloved hand over a hole in the wall the size of a basketball.

'Last stand. They threw up that barricade and holed up in here.'

'Makes sense.' Gorman kicked an empty plastic bottle aside. It went clattering across the floor. 'Medical would have the longest-lasting emergency power supply plus its own stock of supplies. This is where I'd come also. No bodies?'

Frost was sweeping the far end of the wing with his light. 'I didn't see any when I came in here, sir, and I don't see any now. Looks like it was a fight.'

'Don't see any of your bad guys, either, Ripley.' Wierzbowski looked up and around. 'Hey, Ripley?' His finger tensed on the pulse-rifle's trigger. 'Where's Ripley?'

'Over here.'

The sound of her voice led them into a second room. Burke examined their new surroundings briefly before pronouncing identification. 'Medical lab. Looks pretty clean. I don't think the fight got this far. I think they lost it in the outer room.'

Wierzbowski's eyes roved the emergency-lit chamber until they found what had attracted Ripley's attention. He muttered something under his breath and walked towards her. So did the others.

At the far side of the lab seven transparent cylinders glowed with violet light. Combined with the fluid, they contained the light served to preserve the organic material within. All seven cylinders were in use.

'It's a still. Somebody makes booze here,' Gorman said. Nobody laughed.

'Stasis tubes. Standard equipment for a colony med lab this size.' Burke approached the glass cylinders.

Seven tubes for seven specimens. Each cylinder held something that looked like a severed hand equipped with too many fingers. The bodies to which the long fingers were attached were flattened and encased in a material like beige leather, thin and translucent. Pseudo-gills drifted lazily in the stasis suspension fluid. There were no visible organs of sight or hearing. A long tail hung from the back of each abomination, trailing freely in the liquid. A couple of the creatures held their tails coiled tightly against their undersides.

Burke spoke to Ripley without taking his eyes off the specimens. 'Are these the same as the one you described in your report?' She nodded without speaking.

Fascinated, the Company rep moved towards one cylinder, leaning forward until his face was almost touching the special glass.

'Watch it, Burke,' Ripley warned him.

As she concluded the warning the creature imprisoned in the tube lunged sharply, slamming against the inner lining of the cylinder. Burke jumped back, startled. From the ventral portion of the flattened handlike body a thin, fleshy projection had emerged. It looked like a tapered section of intestine as it slithered tonguelike over the tube's interior. Eventually it retracted, curling up inside a protective sheath between the gill-like structures. Legs and tail contracted into a resting position.

Hicks glanced emotionlessly at Burke. 'It likes you.'

The Company rep didn't reply as he moved down the line, inspecting each of the cylinders in turn. As he passed a tube he would press his hand against the smooth exterior. Only one of the remaining six specimens reacted to his presence. The others drifted aimlessly in the suspension fluid, their fingers and tails floating freely.

'These are dead,' he said when he'd finished with the last tube. 'There's just two alive. Unless there's a different state they go into, but I doubt it. See, the dead ones have a completely different colour. Faded, like.'

A file folder rested atop each cylinder. By exerting every ounce of self-control she possessed, Ripley was able to remove the file from the top of a tube containing a live face-hugger. Retreating quickly, she opened the folder and began reading with the aid of her suit light. In addition to the printed material the file was overflowing with charts and sonographs. There were a couple of nuclear magnetic resonance image plates, which attempted to show something of the creatures' internal structure. They were badly blurred. All of the lengthy computer printouts had copious notes scribbled freehand in the margins. A physician's handwriting, she decided. They were mostly illegible.

'Anything interesting?' Burke was leaning around the stasis cylinder whose file she was perusing, studying the creature it contained from every possible angle.

'Probably a great deal, but most of it's too technical for me.' She tapped the file. 'Report of the examining physician. Doctor named Ling.'

'Chester O. Ling.' Burke tapped the tube with a fingernail. This time the creature inside failed to respond. 'There were three doctors stationed at Hadley. Ling was a surgeon, I believe. What's he have to say about this little prize here?'

'Removed surgically before embryo implantation could be completed. Standard surgical procedures useless.'

'Wonder why?' Gorman was as interested in the specimen as the rest of them but not to the point of taking his eyes off the rest of the room.

'Body fluids dissolved the instruments as they were applied.
They had to use surgical lasers to both remove and cauterize
the specimen. It was attached to somebody named Marachuk,
John L.' She glanced up at Burke, who shook his head.

'Doesn't ring a bell. Not an administrator or one of the
higher-ups. Must've been a tractor driver or roustabout.'

She looked back down at the report. 'He died during the
procedure. They killed him getting it off.'

Hicks walked over to have a look at the report, peering over
Ripley's shoulder. He didn't have the chance to read it. His
motion tracker emitted an unexpected and startlingly loud
beep.

The four soldiers spun, checking first the entrance to the
lab, moving on to squint at dark corners. Hicks aimed the
tracker back towards the barricade.

'Behind us.' He gestured towards the corridor they'd just left.

'One of us?' Without thinking, Ripley moved closer to the
corporal.

'No way of telling. This baby isn't a precision instrument.
She's made to take a lot of abuse from dumb grunts like me
and still keep on working, but she doesn't render judgments.'

Gorman addressed his headset pickup. 'Apone, we're up in
medical and we've got something. Where are your people?' He
gave his visor map a quick scan. 'Anybody in D-Block?'

'Negative.' All of them could hear the sergeant's filtered
reply. 'We're all over in Operations, as ordered. You want
some company?'

'Not yet. We'll keep you posted.' He nudged the aural pickup
away from his mouth. 'Let's go, Vasquez.'

She nodded tersely and swung the smartgun into the ready
position on its support arm. It locked in place with an
authoritative click. She and Hicks started off in the direction of
the signal source while Frost and Wierzbowski brought up the
rear.

The corporal led them back out into the main corridor and

turned right, into a stainless-steel labyrinth. 'Getting stronger. Definitely not mechanical.' He held the tracker firmly in one hand, cradled his rifle with the other. 'Irregular movement. Where the heck are we, anyway?'

Burke surveyed their surroundings. 'Kitchen. We'll be in among the food-processing equipment if we keep going this way.'

Ripley had slowed until she fell behind Wierzbowski and Frost. Realizing suddenly that there was nothing behind her but darkness, she hurried to catch up to her companions.

Burke's appraisal was confirmed as they advanced and their lights began to bounce off the shiny surfaces of bulky machinery: freezers, cookers, defrosters, and sterilizers. Hicks ignored it all, intent on his tracker.

'It's moving again.'

Vasquez's gaze was cold as she scanned her environment. Plenty of cover in here. Her fingers caressed the smartgun's controls. A long preparation table loomed in their path.

'Which way?'

Hicks hesitated briefly, then nodded towards a complicated array of machinery designed to process freeze-dried meats and vegetables. The soldiers advanced on it, their tread a deliberate, solemn march. Wierzbowski stumbled over a metal cannister and angrily booted it aside, sending it clanging off into the shadows. He kept his balance and his aplomb, but Ripley half climbed the nearest wall.

The corporal's tracker was beeping steadily now, almost humming. The hum rose to a sharp whine. A pile of stockpots suddenly came crashing down off to their right, and a dim shape was faintly glimpsed moving through the shadows behind the preparation counters.

Vasquez pivoted smoothly, her finger already contracting on the trigger. At the same instant Hicks's rifle slammed the heavier barrel upward. Tracer fire ripped into the ceiling, sending droplets of molten metal flying. She whirled and screamed at him.

Ignoring her, he hurried forward into her line of fire and aimed his bright-light under a row of metal cabinets. He stayed like that for what seemed a short eternity before beckoning for Ripley to join him. Her legs wouldn't work, and her feet seemed frozen to the floor. Hicks gestured again, more urgently this time, and she found herself moving forward in a daze.

He was bending over, trying to work his light beneath a high storage locker. She crouched down next to him.

Pinned against the wall by his light like a butterfly on a mounting pin was a tiny, terrified figure. Filthy and staring, the little girl cowered away from the intruders. In one hand she held a plastic food packet that had been half gnawed. The other clutched tight the head of a large doll, holding it by its hair. Of the remainder of the plastic body there was no sign. The child was as emaciated as she was dirty, the skin taut around her small face. She looked far more fragile than the doll's head she carried. Her blond hair was tangled and matted, a garland of steel wool framing her face.

Ripley tried but couldn't hear her breathing.

The girl blinked against the light, the brief gesture sufficient to jump-start Ripley's mind. She extended a hand towards the waif slowly, fingers closed, and smiled at her.

'Come on out,' she said soothingly. 'It's all right. There's nothing to be afraid of here.' She tried to reach farther behind the cabinet.

The girl retreated from the extending fingers, backing away and trembling visibly. She had the look of a rabbit paralysed by oncoming headlights. Ripley's fingers almost reached her. She opened her hand, intending to gently caress the torn blouse.

Like a shot, the girl bolted to her right, scuttling along beneath the cabinetry with incredible agility. Ripley dived forward, scrambling on elbows and knees as she fought to keep the child in view. Outside the cabinets Hicks crabbed frantically sideways until a small gap appeared between two storage lockers. He snapped out a hand, and his fingers locked around a tiny ankle. An instant later he drew it back.

'Ow! Watch it, she bites.'

Ripley reached for the other retreating foot and missed. A second later the girl reached a ventilation duct whose grille had been kicked out. Before Hicks or anyone else could make another grab for her, she'd scrambled inside, wriggling like a fish. Hicks didn't even try to follow. He wouldn't have fit through the narrow opening stark naked, much less clad in his bulky armour.

Ripley dived without thinking, squirming into the duct with her arms held out in front of her, moving with thighs and arms. Her hips barely cleared the opening. The girl was just ahead of her, still moving. As Ripley followed, her breathing loud in the confined tunnel, the child slammed a metal hatch in place ahead of her. With a lunge Ripley reached the barrier and shoved it open before it could be latched from the other side. She cursed as she banged her forehead against the metal overhead.

Shining her light ahead, she forgot the pain. The girl was backed against the far end of a small spherical chamber, one of the colony's ventilation system's pressure-relief bubbles. She was not alone.

Surrounding her were wadded-up blankets and pillows mixed with a haphazard collection of toys, stuffed animals, dolls, cheap jewellery, illustrated books, and empty food packets. There was even a battery-operated disk player muffled by cut-up pillows. The entire array was the result of the girl's foraging through the complex. She'd hauled it back to this place by herself, furnishing her private hideaway according to her own childish plan.

It was more like a nest than a room, Ripley decided.

Somehow this child had survived. Somehow she had coped with and adapted to her devastated environment when all the adults had succumbed. As Ripley struggled with the import of what she was seeing, the girl continued to edge around the back wall. She was heading for another hatch. If the conduit it barred was no bigger in diameter than the cover protecting it, the girl would be out of their grasp. Ripley saw that she could never enter it.

The child turned and dived, and Ripley timed her own lunge to coincide. She managed to get both arms around the girl, locking her in a bear hug. Finding herself trapped, the girl went into a frenzy, kicking and hitting and trying to use her teeth. It was not only frightening, it was horrifying: because, as she fought, the child stayed dead silent. The only noise in the confined space as she struggled in Ripley's grasp was her frantic breathing, and even that was eerily subdued. Only once in her life had Ripley had to try to control someone small who'd fought with similar ferocity, and that was Jones, when she'd had to take him to the vet.

She talked to the child as she kept clear of slashing feet and elbows and small sharp teeth. 'It's okay, it's okay. It's over, you're going to be all right now. It's okay, you're safe.'

Finally the girl ran out of strength, slowing down like a failing motor. She went completely limp in Ripley's arms, almost catatonic, and allowed herself to be rocked back and forth. It was hard to look at the child's face, to meet her traumatized, vacant stare. Lips white and trembling, eyes darting wildly and seeing nothing, she tried to bury herself in the adult's chest, shrinking back from a dark nightmare world only she could see.

Ripley kept rocking the girl back and forth, back and forth, cooing to her in a steady, reassuring voice. As she whispered, she let her gaze roam the chamber until it fell on something lying on the top of the pile of scavenged goods. It was a framed solido of the girl, unmistakable and yet so different. The child in the picture was dressed up and smiling, her hair neat and recently shampooed, a bright ribbon shining in the blonde tresses. Her clothing was immaculate and her skin scrubbed pink. The words beneath the picture were embossed in gold:

*FIRST-GRADE CITIZENSHIP AWARD REBECCA JORDEN*

'Ripley. Ripley?' Hicks's voice, echoing down the air shaft. 'You okay in there?'

'Yes.' Aware they might not have heard her, she raised her voice. 'I'm okay. We're both okay. We're coming out now.'

The girl did not resist as Ripley retraced her crawl feet first, dragging the child by the ankles.

# VII

The girl sat huddled against the back of the chair, hugging her knees to her chest. She looked neither right nor left, nor at any of the adults regarding her curiously. Her attention was focused on a distant point in space. A biomonitor cuff had been strapped to her left arm. Dietrich had been forced to modify it so that it would fit properly around the child's shrunken arm.

Gorman sat nearby while the medtech studied the information the cuff was providing. 'What's her name again?'

Dietrich made a notation on an electronic caduceus pad. 'What?'

'Her name. We got a name, didn't we?'

The medtech nodded absently, absorbed by the readouts. 'Rebecca, I think.'

'Right.' The lieutenant put on his best smile and leaned forward, resting his hands on his knees. 'Now think, Rebecca. Concentrate. You have to try to help us so that we can help you. That's what we're here for, to help you. I want you to take your time and tell us what you remember. Anything at all. Try to start from the beginning.'

The girl didn't move, nor did her expression change. She was unresponsive but not comatose, silent but not mute. A disappointed Gorman sat back and glanced briefly to his left as Ripley entered carrying a steaming coffee mug.

'Where are your parents? You have to try to—'

'Gorman! Give it a rest, would you?'

The lieutenant started to respond sharply. His reply faded to a resigned nod. He rose, shaking his head. 'Total brainlock. Tried everything I could think of except yelling at her, and I'm not about to do that. It could send her over the edge. If she isn't already.'

'She isn't.' Dietrich turned off her portable diagnostic equipment and gently removed her sensor cuff from the girl's unresisting arm. 'Physically she's okay. Borderline malnutrition, but I don't think there's any permanent damage. The wonder of it is that she's alive at all, scrounging unprocessed food packets and freeze-dried powder.' She looked at Ripley. 'You see any vitamin packs in there?'

'I didn't have time for sight-seeing, and she didn't offer to show me around.' She nodded towards the girl.

'Right. Well, she must know about supplements because she's not showing any signs of critical deficiencies. Smart little thing.'

'How is she mentally?' Ripley sipped at her coffee, staring at the waif in the chair. The child's skin was like parchment over the backs of her hands.

'I can't tell for sure, but her motor responses are good. I think it's too early to call it brainlock. I'd say she's on hold.'

'Call it anything you want.' Gorman rose and headed for the exit. 'Whatever it is, we're wasting our time trying to talk to her.' He strode out of the side room and back into Operations to join Burke and Bishop in staring at the colony's central computer terminal. Dietrich headed off in another direction.

For a while Ripley watched the three men, who were intent on the terminals Hudson had resurrected, then knelt alongside the girl. Gently she brushed the child's unkempt hair back out of her eyes. She might have been combing a statue for all the response she elicited. Still smiling, she proffered the steaming cup she was holding.

'Here, try this. If you're not hungry, you must be thirsty. I'll bet it gets cold in that vent bubble, what with the heat off and everything.' She moved the cup around, letting the air carry the warm, aromatic smell of the contents to the girl's nostrils. 'It's just a little instant hot chocolate. Don't you like chocolate?' When the girl didn't react, Ripley wrapped the small hands around the cup, bending the fingers towards each other. Then she tilted hands and cup upward.

Dietrich was correct about the child's motor responses. She drank mechanically and without watching what she was doing. Cocoa spilled down her chin, but most of it went down the small throat and stayed down. Ripley felt vindicated.

Not wanting to overwhelm an obviously shrunken stomach, she pulled the cup away when it was still half full. 'There, wasn't that nice? You can have some more in a minute. I don't know what you've been eating and drinking, and we don't want to make you sick by giving you too much rich stuff too quickly.' She pushed at the blonde tresses again.

'Poor thing. You don't talk much, do you? That's okay by me. You feel like keeping quiet, you keep quiet. I'm kind of the same way. I've found that most people do a lot of talking and they wind up not saying very much. Especially adults when they're talking to children. It's kind of like they enjoy talking at you but not to you. They want you to listen to them all the time, but they don't want to listen to you. I think that's pretty stupid. Just because you're small doesn't mean you don't have some important things to say.' She set the cup aside and dabbed at the brown-stained chin with a cloth. It was easy to feel the ridge of unfinished bone beneath the tightly drawn skin.

'Uh-oh.' She grinned broadly. 'I made a clean spot here. Now I've gone and done it. Guess I'll just have to do the whole thing. Otherwise nothing will match.'

From an open supply packet she withdrew a squeeze bottle full of sterilized water and used it to soak the cloth she was holding. Then she applied the makeshift scrubber firmly to the girl's face, wiping away dirt and accumulated grime in addition to the remaining cocoa spots. Throughout the operation the child sat quietly. But the bright blue eyes shifted and seemed to focus on Ripley for the first time.

She felt a surge of excitement and fought to suppress it.
'Hard to believe there's a little girl under all this.' She made a
show of examining the cloth's surface. 'Enough dirt there to
file a mining claim on.' Bending over, she stared appraisingly
at the newly revealed face. 'Definitely a little girl. And a pretty
one, at that.'

She looked away just long enough to assure herself that no
one from Operations was about to barge in. Any interruption
at this critical moment might undo everything that she'd
worked so hard to accomplish with the aid of a little hot
chocolate and clean water.

No need to worry. Everyone in Operations was still clustered
around the main terminal. Hudson was seated at the console
fingering controls while the others looked on.

A three-dimensional abstract of the colony drifted across the
main screen, lazy geometric outlines tumbling from left to
right, then bottom to top, as Hudson manipulated the
program. The comtech was neither playing nor showing off;
he was hunting something. No rude comments spilled from his
lips now, no casual profanity filled the air. It was work time. If
he cursed at all, it was to himself. The computer knew all the
answers. Finding the right questions was an agonizingly slow
process.

Burke had been inspecting other equipment. Now he shifted
his position for a better view as he whispered to Gorman.

'What's he scanning for?'

'PDTs. Personal data transmitters. Every colonist has one
surgically implanted as soon as they arrive.'

'I know what a PDT is,' Burke replied mildly. 'The Company
manufactures them. I just don't see any point in running a
PDT scan. Surely if there was anyone else left alive in the
complex, we'd have found them by now. Or they'd have found
us.'

'Not necessarily.' Gorman's reply was polite without being
deferential. Technically Burke was along on the expedition as

an observer for the Company, to look after its financial interests. His employer was paying for this little holiday excursion in tandem with the colonial administration, but what authority he had was largely unwritten. He could give advice but not orders. This was a military expedition, and Gorman was in charge. On paper Burke was his equal. The reality was very different.

'Someone could be alive but unable to move. Injured, or maybe trapped inside a damaged building. Sure the scan's a long shot, but procedure demands it. We have to run the check.' He turned to the comtech. 'Everything functioning properly, Hudson?'

'If there's anyone alive within a couple of kilometres of base central, we'll read it out here.' He tapped the screen. 'So far I've got zip except for the kid.'

Wierzbowski offered a comment from the far side of the room. 'Don't PDTs keep broadcasting if the owner dies?'

'Not these new ones.' Dietrich was sorting through her instruments. 'They're partly powered by the body's own electrical field. If the owner fades out, so does the signal. A stiff's electrical capacitance is nil. That's the only drawback to using the body as a battery.'

'No kidding?' Hudson spared the comely medtech a glance. 'How can you tell if somebody's AC or DC?'

'No problem in your case, Hudson.' She snapped her medical satchel shut. 'Clear case of insufficient current.'

It was easier to find another clean cloth than to try to scrub out the first one. Ripley was working on the girl's small hands now, excavating dirt from between the fingers and beneath the nails. Pink skin emerged from behind a mask of dark grime. As she cleaned, she kept up a steady stream of reassuring chatter.

'I don't know how you managed to stay alive with everybody else gone away, but you're one brave kid, Rebecca.'

A sound new to Ripley's ears, barely audible. 'N-newt.'

Ripley tensed and looked away so her excitement wouldn't

show. She kept moving the washcloth as she leaned closer. 'I'm sorry, kid, I didn't hear you. Sometimes my hearing's not so good. What did you say?'

'Newt. My n-name's Newt. That's what everybody calls me. Nobody calls me Rebecca except my brother.'

Ripley was finishing off the second hand. If she didn't respond, the girl might lapse back into silence. At the same time she had to be careful not to say anything that might upset her. Keep it casual and don't ask any questions.

'Well, Newt it is, then. My name's Ripley— and people call me Ripley. You can call me anything you like, though.' When no reply was forthcoming from the girl, Ripley lifted the small hand she'd just finished cleaning and gave it a formal shake.

'Pleased to meet you, Newt.' She pointed at the disembodied doll head that the girl still clutched fiercely in one hand. 'And who is that? Does she have a name? I bet she does. Every doll has a name. When I was your age, I had lots of dolls, and every one of them had a name. Otherwise, how can you tell them apart?'

Newt glanced down at the plastic sphere with its vacant, glassy eyes. 'Casey. She's my only friend.'

'What about me?'

The girl looked at her so sharply that Ripley was taken aback. The assurance in Newt's eyes bespoke a hardness that was anything but childish. Her tone was flat, neutral.

'I don't want you for a friend.'

Ripley tried to conceal her surprise. 'Why not?'

'Because you'll be gone soon, like the others. Like everybody.' She gazed down at the doll head. 'Casey's okay. She'll stay with me. But you'll go away. You'll be dead and you'll leave me alone.'

There was no anger in that childish declamation, no sense of accusation or betrayal. It was delivered coolly and with complete assurance, as though the event had already occurred. It was not a prediction, but rather a statement of fact soon to take place. It chilled Ripley's blood and frightened her more than anything that had happened since the dropship had departed the safety of the orbiting *Sulaco*.

'Oh, Newt. Your mom and dad went away like that, didn't they? You just don't want to talk about it.' The girl nodded, eyes downcast, staring at her knees. Her fingers were white around the doll head. 'They'd be here if they could, honey,' Ripley told her solemnly. 'I know they would.'

'They're dead. That's why they can't come see me anymore. They're dead like everybody else.' This delivered with a cold certainty that was terrifying to see in so small a child.

'Maybe not. How can you be sure?'

Newt raised her eyes and stared straight at Ripley. Small children do not look adults in the eye like that, but Newt was a child in stature only. 'I'm sure. They're dead. They're dead, and soon you'll be dead, and then Casey and I'll be alone again.'

Ripley didn't look away and she didn't smile. She knew this girl could see straight through anything remotely phoney. 'Newt. Look at me, Newt. I'm not going away. I'm not going to leave you and I'm not going to be dead. I promise. I'm going to stay around. I'll be with you as long as you want me to.'

The girl's eyes remained downcast. Ripley could see her struggling with herself, wanting to believe what she'd just heard, trying to believe. After a while she looked up again.

'You promise?'

'Cross my heart.' Ripley performed the childish gesture.

'And hope to die?'

Now Ripley did smile, grimly. 'And hope to die.'

Girl and woman regarded one another. Newt's eyes began to brim, and her lower lip to tremble. Slowly the tension fled from her small body, and the indifferent mask she'd pulled across her face was replaced by something much more natural: the look of a frightened child. She threw both arms around Ripley's neck and began to sob. Ripley could feel the tears streaming down the newly washed cheeks, soaking her own neck. She ignored them, rocking the girl back and forth in her arms, whispering soothing nothings to her.

She closed her own eyes against the tears and the fear and lingering sensation of death that permeated Hadley Operations Central and hoped that the promise she'd just made could be kept.

The breakthrough with the girl was matched by another in Operations as Hudson let out a triumphant whoop. 'Hah! Stop your grinnin' and drop your linen! Found 'em. Give old Hudson a decent machine and he'll turn up your money, your secrets, and your long-lost cousin Jed.' He rewarded the control console with an affectionate whack. 'This baby's been battered, but she can still play ball.'

Gorman leaned over the comtech's shoulder. 'What kind of shape are they in?'

'Unknown. These colonial PDTs are long on signal and short on details. But it looks like all of them.'

'Where?'

'Over at the atmosphere processing station.' Hudson studied the schematic. 'Sublevel C under the south part of the complex.' He tapped the screen. 'This charmer's a sweetheart when it comes to location.'

Everyone in Operations had clustered around the comtech for a look at the monitor. Hudson froze the colony scan and enlarged one portion. In the centre of the processing station's schematic a cluster of glowing blue dots pulsed like deep-sea crustaceans.

Hicks grunted as he stared at the screen. 'Looks like a town meeting.'

'Wonder why they all went over there?' Dietrich mused aloud. 'I thought we'd decided that this was where they made their last stand?'

'Maybe they were able to make a break for it and secure themselves in a better place.' Gorman turned away, brisk and professional. 'Remember, the processing station still has full power. That'd be worth a lot. Let's saddle up and find out.'

'Awright, let's go, girls.' Apone was slipping his pack over his shoulders. Operations became a hive of activity. 'They ain't payin' us by the hour.' He glanced at Hudson. 'How do we get over there?'

The comtech adjusted the screen, reducing the magnification. An overview of the colony appeared on the monitor. 'There's one small service corridor. It's a pretty good hike, Sarge.'

Apone looked to Gorman, waiting for orders. 'I don't know about you, Sergeant,' the lieutenant told him, 'but I'm not fond of long, narrow corridors. And I'd like for everyone to be fresh when we arrive. I'd also like to have the APC's armament backing us up when we go in there.'

'My thoughts exactly, sir.' The sergeant looked relieved. He'd been ready to suggest and argue and was glad that neither was going to be necessary. A couple of the troops nodded and looked satisfied. Gorman might be inexperienced in the field, but at least he wasn't a fool.

Hicks yelled back towards the small ready room. 'Hey, Ripley, we're going for a ride in the country. You coming?'

'We're both coming.' A few looks of surprise greeted her as she led the girl out of the back room. 'This is Newt. Newt, these are my friends. They're your friends too.'

The girl simply nodded, unwilling to extend that privilege beyond Ripley as yet. A couple of the soldiers nodded to the child as they shouldered their equipment. Burke smiled encouragingly at her. Gorman looked surprised.

Newt looked up at her live friend, still clutching the disembodied doll head tightly in her right hand. 'Where are we going?'

'To a safe place. Soon.'

Newt almost smiled.

The atmosphere in the APC during the ride from colony Operations to the processing station was more subdued than it had been when they'd first roared out of the dropship. The universal devastation; the hollow, wounded buildings; and the unmistakable evidence of hard fighting had put a damper on the Marines' initial high spirits.

It was clear that the cause of the colony's interrupted communications with Earth had nothing to do with its relay satellite or base instrumentation. It had to do with Ripley's critter. The colonists had ceased communicating because something had compelled them to do so. If Ripley was to be believed, that something was still hanging around. Undoubtedly the little girl was a storehouse of information on the subject, but no one tried to press questions on her. Dietrich's orders. The child's recovery was still too fragile to jeopardize with traumatizing inquiries. So as they rode along in the APC they had to fill in the gaps in Ripley's library disks with their imaginations. Soldiers have active imaginations.

Wierzbowski drove the personnel carrier across the twilight landscape, traversing a causeway that connected the rest of the colony complex to the atmosphere-processing station a kilometre away. Wind tore at the massive vehicle but could not sway it. The APC was designed for comfortble travel in winds up to three hundred kph. A typical Acheronian gale didn't bother it. Behind it, the dropship had settled to ground at the landing field, awaiting the soldiers' return. Ahead, the conical tower of the massive processing unit glowed with a spectral light as it continued with its business of terraforming Acheron's inhospitable atmosphere.

Ripley and Newt sat side by side just aft of the driver's cab. Wierzbowski kept his attention on the driving. Within the comparative safety of the heavily armoured vehicle the girl gradually grew more voluble. Though there were at least a dozen questions Ripley badly wanted to ask her, she just sat patiently and listened, letting her charge ramble on. Occasionally Newt would offer the answer to an unasked question, anyway. Like now.

'I was best at the game.' She hugged the doll head and stared at the opposite wall. 'I knew the whole maze.'

'The "maze"?' Ripley thought back to where they'd found her. 'You mean the air-duct system?'

'Yeah, you know,' she replied proudly. 'And not just the air

ducts. I could even get into tunnels that were full of wires and
stuff. In the walls, under the floor. I could get into anywhere. I
was the *ace*. I could hide better than anybody. They all said I
was cheating because I was smaller than everybody else, but it
wasn't 'cause I was smaller. I was just smarter, that's all. And
I've got a real good memory. I could remember any place I'd
been before.'

'You're really something, ace.' The girl looked pleased.
Ripley's gaze shifted forward. Through the windshield the
processing station loomed directly ahead.

It was an unbeautiful structure, strictly utilitarian in design.
Its multitude of pipes and chambers and conduits had been
scoured and pitted by decades of wind-blown rock and sand. It
was as efficient as it was ugly. Working around the clock for
years on end, it and its sister stations scattered around the
planet would break down the components of Acheron's
atmosphere, scrub them clean, add to them, and eventually
produce a pleasant biosphere equipped with a balmy, homelike
climate. A great deal of beauty to spring forth from so much
ugliness.

The monolithic metal mass towered over the armoured personnel carrier as Wierzbowski braked to a stop across from the
main entryway. Led by Hicks and Apone, the waiting troopers
deployed in front of the oversize door. Up close to the complex,
the thrum of heavy machinery filled their ears, rising above the
steady whistle of the wind. The well-built machinery continued
to do its job even in the absence of its human masters.

Hudson was first to the entrance and ran his fingers over the
door controls like a locksmith casing his next crack.

'Surprise, chilluns. Everything works.' He thumbed a single
button, and the heavy barrier slid aside to reveal an interior
walkway. Off to the right a concrete ramp led downward.

'Which way, sir?' Apone inquired.

'Take the ramp,' Gorman instructed them from inside the
APC. 'There'll be another at the bottom. Take it down to
C-level.'

'Check.' The sergeant gestured at his troops. 'Drake, take point. The rest of you follow by twos. Let's go.'

Hudson hesitated at the control panel. 'What about the door?'

'There's nobody here. Leave it open.'

They started down the broad ramp into the guts of the station. Light filtered down from above, slanting through floors and catwalks fashioned by steel mesh, bending around conduits ranked side by side like organ pipes. They had their suit lights switched on, anyway. Machinery pounded steadily around them as they descended.

The multiple views provided by their suit cameras bounced and swayed as they walked, making viewing difficult for those watching the monitors inside the APC. Eventually the floor levelled out and the images steadied. Multiple lenses revealed a floor overflowing with heavy cylinders and conduits, stacks of plastic crates, and tall metal bottles.

'B-level.' Gorman addressed the Operations bay pickup. 'They're on the next one down. Try to take it a little slower. It's hard to make anything out when you're moving fast on a downslope.'

Dietrich turned to Frost. 'Maybe he wants us to fly? That way the picture wouldn't bounce.'

'How about if I carry you instead?' Hudson called back to her.

'How about if I throw you over the railing?' she responded. 'Picture would be steady that way, too, until you hit bottom.'

'Shut up back there,' Apone growled as they swung around a turn in the descending rampway. Hudson and the rest obliged.

In the Operations bay Ripley peered over Gorman's right shoulder, and Burke around the other, while Newt tried to squeeze in from behind. Despite all the video wizardry the lieutenant could command, none of the individual suit cameras provided a clear picture of what the troops were seeing.

'Try the low end again,' Burke suggested.

'I did that first thing, Mr. Burke. There's an awful lot of interference down there. The deeper they go, the more junk their signals have to get through, and those suit units don't put out much power. What's an atmosphere-processing station's interior built out of, anyway?'

'Carbon-fibre composites and silica blends up top wherever possible, for strength and lightness. A lot of metallic glass in the partitions. Foundations and sublevels don't have to be so fancy. Concrete and steel floors with a lot of titanium alloy thrown in.'

Gorman was unable to contain his frustration as he fiddled futilely with his instruments. 'If the emergency power was out and the station shut down, I'd be getting clearer reception, but then they'd be advancing with nothing but suit lights to guide them. It's a trade-off.' He shook his head as he studied the blurred images and leaned towards the pickup.

'We're not making that out too well ahead of you. What is it?'

Static garbled Hudson's voice as well as the view provided by his camera. 'You tell me. I only work here.'

The lieutenant looked back at Burke. 'Your people build that?'

The Company rep leaned towards the row of monitors, squinting at the dim images being relayed back from the bowels of the atmosphere-processing station.

'Hell, no.'

'Then you don't know what it is?'

'I've never seen anything like it in my life.'

'Could the colonists have added it?'

Burke continued to stare, finally shook his head. 'If they did, they improvised it. That didn't come out of my station construction manual.'

Something had been added to the latticework of pipes and conduits that crisscrossed the lowest level of the processing station. There was no question that it was the result of design and purpose, not some unknown industrial accident. Visibly damp and lustrous in spots, the peculiar material that had been used to construct the addition resembled a solidified liquid resin or glue. In places light penetrated the material to a depth of several centimetres, revealing a complex internal structure. At other locations the substance was opaque. What little colour it displayed was muted: greens and grays, and here and there a touch of some darker green.

Intricate chambers ranged in size from half a metre in diameter to a dozen metres across, all interconnected by strips of fragile-looking webwork that on closer inspection turned out to be about as fragile as steel cable. Tunnels led off deeper into the maze while peculiar conical pits dead-ended in the floor. So precisely did the added material blend with the existing machinery that it was difficult to tell where human handiwork ended and something of an entirely different nature began. In places the addition almost mimicked existing station equipment, though whether it was imitation with a purpose or merely blind duplication, no one could tell.

The whole gleaming complex extended as far back into C-level as the trooper's cameras could penetrate. Although it filled every available empty space, the epoxylike incrustation did not appear to have in any way impaired the functioning of the station. It continued to rumble on, having its way with Acheron's air, unaffected by the heteromorphic chambering that filled much of its lower level.

Of them all, only Ripley had some idea of what the troopers had stumbled across, and she was momentarily too numb with horrid fascination to explain. She could only stare and remember.

Gorman happened to glance back long enough to catch the expression on her face. 'What is it?'

'I don't know.'

'You know something, which is more than any of the rest of us. Come on, Ripley. Give. Right now I'd pay a hundred credits for an informed guess.'

'I really don't know. I think I've seen something like it once before, but I'm not sure. It's different, somehow. More elaborate and—'

'Let me know when your brain starts working again.' Disappointed, the lieutenant turned back to the mike. 'Proceed with your advance, Sergeant.'

The troopers resumed their march, their suit lights shining on the vitreous walls surrounding them. The deeper they went into the maze, the more it took on the appearance of having been grown or secreted rather than built. The labyrinth looked like the interior of a gigantic organ or bone. Not a human organ, nor a human bone.

Whatever else its purpose, the addition served to concentrate waste heat from the processor's fusion plant. Steam from dripping water formed puddles on the floor and hissed around them. Factory respiration.

'It's opening up a little just ahead.' Hicks panned his camera around. The troop was entering a large, domed chamber. The walls abruptly changed in character and appearance. It was a testimony to their training that not one of the troopers broke down on the spot.

Ripley muttered, 'Oh, God.' Burke mumbled a shocked curse.

Cameras and suit lights illuminated the chamber. Instead of the smooth, curving walls they'd passed earlier, these were rough and uneven. They formed a rugged bas-relief composed of detritus gathered from the town: furniture, wiring, solid and fluid-state components, bits of broken machinery, personal effects, torn clothing, human bones and skulls, all fused together with that omnipresent, translucent, epoxylike resin.

Hudson reached out to run a gloved hand along one wall, casually caressing a cluster of human ribs. He picked at the resinous ooze, barely scratching it.

'Ever see anything like this stuff before?'

'Not me.' Hicks would have spat if he'd had room. 'I'm not a chemist.'

Dietrich was expected to render an opinion and did so. 'Looks like some kind of secreted glue. Your bad guys spit this stuff out or what, Ripley?'

'I—I don't know how it's manufactured, but I've seen it before, on a much smaller scale.'

Gorman pursed his lips, analysis taking over from the initial shock. 'Looks like they ripped apart the colony for building materials.' He indicated the view offered by Hicks's screen. 'There's a whole stack of blank storage disks imbedded there.'

'And portable power cells.' Burke gestured towards another of the individual monitors. 'Expensive stuff. Tore it all apart.'

'And the colonists,' Ripley pointed out, 'when they were done with them.' She turned to look down at the sombre-visaged little girl standing next to her.

'Newt, you'd better go sit up front. Go on.' She nodded and obediently headed for the driver's cab.

The steam on C-level intensified as the troops moved still deeper into the chamber. It was accompanied by a corresponding increase in temperature.

'Hotter'n a furnace in here,' Frost grumbled.

'Yeah,' Hudson agreed sarcastically, 'but it's a *dry* heat.'

Ripley looked to her left. Burke and Gorman stayed intent on the videoscreens. To the lieutenant's left was a small monitor that showed a graphic readout of the station's ground plan.

'They're right under the primary heat exchangers.'

'Yeah.' A fascinated Burke was unable to take his eyes off the view being relayed by Apone's camera. 'Maybe the organisms like the heat. That's why they built—'

'That's not what I mean. Gorman, if your people have to use their weapons in there, they'll rupture the cooling system.'

Burke abruptly realized what Ripley was driving at. 'She's right.'

'So?' asked the lieutenant.

'So,' she continued, 'that releases the freon and/or the water that's been condensed out of the air for cooling purposes.'

'Fine.' He tapped the screens. 'It'll cool everybody off.'

'It'll do more than cool them off.'

'For instance?'

'Fusion containment shuts down.'

'So? *So*?' Why didn't she get to the point? Didn't the woman realize that he was trying to direct a search-and-clear expedition here?

'We're talking thermonuclear explosion.'

That made Gorman sit back and think. He weighed his options. His decision was made easier by the fact that he didn't have any. 'Apone, collect rifle magazines from everybody. We can't have any firing in there.'

Apone wasn't the only one who overheard the order. The troopers eyed one another with a combination of disbelief and dismay.

'Is he crazy?' Wierzbowski clutched his rifle protectively to his ribs, as if daring Gorman to come down and disarm it personally.

Hudson all but growled. 'What're we supposed to use, man? Harsh language?' He spoke into his headset. 'Hey, Lieutenant, you want maybe we should try judo? What if they ain't got any arms?'

'They've got arms,' Ripley assured him tightly.

'You're not going in naked, Hudson,' Gorman told him. 'You've got other weapons you can use.'

'Maybe that wouldn't be such a bad idea,' Dietrich muttered.

'What, using alternates?' Wierzbowski muttered.

'No. Hudson going in naked. No living thing could stand the shock.'

'Screw you, Dietrich,' the comtech shot back.

'Not a chance.' With a sigh the medtech yanked the fully charged magazine from her rifle.

'Flame units only.' Gorman's tone was no-nonsense. 'I want all rifles slung.'

'You heard the lieutenant.' Apone began circulating among them, collecting magazines. 'Pull 'em out.'

One by one the rifles were rendered harmless. Vasquez turned over the power packs for her smartgun with great reluctance. Three of the troopers carried portable incinerator units in addition to their penetration weapons. These were unlimbered, warmed up, and checked. Unnoticed by Apone or any of her colleagues, Vasquez slipped a spare power cell from the back of her pants and slipped it into her smartgun. As soon as the sergeant's eyes and all suit cameras were off them, Drake did likewise. The two smartgun operators exchanged a grim wink.

Hicks had no one to wink at and no smartgun to jimmy with. What he did have was a cylindrical sheath attached to the inner lining of his battle harness. Unzipping his torso armour, he opened the sheath to reveal the gunmetal-grey twin barrels of an antique pump twelve-gauge shotgun with a sawed-off butt stock. As Hudson looked on with professional interest the corporal resealed his armour, clicked back the stock of the well-maintained relic, and chambered a round.

'Where'd you get that, Hicks? When I saw that bulge, I thought you were smuggling liquor, except that'd be out of character for you. Steal it from a museum?'

'Been in my family for a long time. Cute, isn't it?'

'Some family. Can it do anything?'

Hicks showed him a single shell. 'Not your standard military-issue high-velocity armour-piercing round, but you don't want it going off in your face, either.' He kept his voice down. 'I always keep this handy. For close encounters. I don't think it'll penetrate anything far enough to set off any mushrooms.'

'Yeah, real cute.' Hudson favoured the sawed-off with a last admiring look. 'You're a traditionalist, Hicks.'

The corporal smiled thinly. 'It's my tender nature.'

Apone's voice carried back to them from just ahead. 'Let's move. Hicks, since you seem to like it back there, you take rear guard.'

'My pleasure, Sarge.' The corporal rested the old shotgun against his right shoulder, balancing it easily with one hand, his finger light on the heavy trigger. Hudson grinned appreciatively, gave Hicks the high sign, and jogged forward to take up his assigned position near the point.

The air was thick, and their lights were diffused by the roiling steam. Hudson felt as though they were advancing through a steel-and-plastic jungle.

Gorman's voice echoed in his headset. 'Any movement?' The lieutenant sounded faint and far away, even though the comtech knew he was only a couple of levels above and just outside the entrance to the processing station. He kept his eyes on his tracker as he advanced.

'Hudson here, sir. Nothing so far. Zip. The only thing moving around down here is the air.'

He turned a corner and glanced up from the miniature readouts. What he saw made him forget the tracker, forget his rifle, forget everything.

Another encrusted wall lay directly in front of them. It was marred by bulges and ripples and had been sculpted by some unknown, inhuman hand, a teratogenic version of Rodin's *Gates of Hell*. Here were the missing colonists, entombed alive in the same epoxylike resin that had been used to construct the latticework and tunnels, chambers and pits, and had transformed the lowest level of the processing station into something out of a xenopsychotic nightmare.

Each had been cocooned in the wall without regard for human comfort. Arms and legs had been grotesquely twisted, broken when necessary in order to make the unfortunate victim fit properly into the alien scheme and design. Heads lolled at unnatural angles. Many of the bodies had been reduced to desiccated lumps of bone from which the flesh and skin had decayed. Others had been cleaned to the naked bone. They were the fortunate ones who had been granted the gift of death. Every corpse had one thing in common, no matter where it was situated or how it had been placed in the wall: the rib cages had been bent outward, as though the sternum had exploded from behind.

The troopers moved slowly into the embryo chamber. Their expressions were grim. No one said anything. There wasn't one among them who hadn't laughed at death, but this was worse than death. This was obscene.

Dietrich approached the still-intact figure of a woman. The body was ghostly white, drained. The eyelids fluttered and opened as the woman sensed movement, a presence, something. Madness dwelt within. The figure spoke in a hollow, sepulchral voice, a whisper conjured up out of desperation. Trying to hear, Dietrich leaned closer.

'Please—kill me.'

Wide-eyed, the medtech stumbled back. Within the safety of the APC Ripley could only stare helplessly, biting down hard on the knuckles of her left hand. She knew what was coming, knew what prompted the woman's ultimate request, just as she knew that neither she nor anyone else could do anything except comply. The sound of somebody retching came over the Operations bay speakers. Nobody made jokes about that, either.

The woman imprisoned in the wall began to convulse. Somewhere she summoned up the energy to scream, a steady, sawing shriek of mindless agony. Ripley took a step towards the nearest mike, wanting to warn the troopers of what was coming but unable to make her throat work.

It wasn't necessary. They'd studied the research disks she'd prepared for them.

'Flamethrower!' Apone snapped. 'Move!'

Frost handed his incinerator to the sergeant, stepped aside. As Apone took possession, the woman's chest erupted in a spray of blood. From the cavity thus formed, a small fanged skull emerged, hissing viciously.

Apone's finger jerked the trigger of the flamethrower. The two other soldiers who carried similar devices imitated his action. Heat and light filled the chamber, searing the wall and obliterating the screaming horror it contained. Cocoons and their contents melted and ran like translucent taffy. A deafening screeching echoed in their ears as they worked the fire over the entire end of the room. What wasn't carbonized by the intense heat melted. The wall puddled and ran, pooling around their boots like molten plastic. But it didn't smell like plastic. It gave off a thick, organic stench.

Everyone in the chamber was intent on the wall and the flamethrowers. No one saw a section of another wall twitch.

# VIII

The alien had been lying dormant, prone in a pocket that blended in perfectly with the rest of the room. Slowly it emerged from its resting niche. Smoke from burning cocoons and other organic matter billowed roofward, reducing visibility in the chamber to near zero.

Something made Hudson glance briefly at his tracker. His pupils expanded, and he whirled to shout a warning. 'Movement! I've got movement.'

'Position?' inquired Apone sharply.

'Can't lock up. It's too tight in here, and there's too many other bodies.'

An edge crept into the master sergeant's voice. 'Don't tell me that. Talk to me, Hudson. Where is it?'

The comtech struggled to refine the tracker's information. That was the trouble with these field units: they were tough but imprecise.

'Uh, seems to be in front and behind.'

In the Operations bay of the APC, Gorman frantically adjusted gain and sharpness controls on individual monitors. 'We can't see anything back here, Apone. What's going on?'

Ripley knew what was going on. Knew what was coming. She could sense it, even if they couldn't see it, like a wave rushing a black sand beach at night. She found her voice and the mike simultaneously.

'Pull your team out, Gorman. Get them out of there *now*.'

The lieutenant spared her an irritated glare. 'Don't give me orders, lady. I know what I'm doing.'

'Maybe, but you don't know what's being *done*.'

Down on C-level the walls and ceiling of the alien chamber were coming to life. Biomechanical fingers extended talons that could tear metal. Slime-lubricated jaws began to flex, pistoning silently as their owners awoke. Uncertain movements were glimpsed dimly through smoke and steam by the nervous human intruders.

Apone found himself starting to back up. 'Go to infrared. Look sharp, people!' Visors were snapped into place. On their smooth, transparent insides images began to materialize, nightmare silhouettes moving in ghostly silence through the drifting mist.

'Multiple signals,' Hudson declared, 'all around. Closing from all directions.'

Dietrich's nerves snapped, and she whirled to retreat. As she turned, something tall and immensely powerful loomed above the smoke to wrap long arms around her. Limbs like metal bars locked across her chest and contracted. The medtech screamed, and her finger tensed reflexively on the trigger of her flamethrower. A jet of flame engulfed Frost, turning him into a blindly stumbling bipedal torch. His shriek echoed through everyone's headset.

Apone pivoted, unable to see anything in the dense atmosphere and poor light but able to hear entirely too much. The heat from the cooling exchangers on the level above distorted the imaging ability of the troopers' infrared visors.

In the APC, Gorman could only stare as Frost's monitor went to black. At the same time his bioreadouts flattened, hills and valleys signifying life being replaced by grim, straight lines. On the remaining monitor screens, images and outlines bobbed and panned confusedly. Blasts of glowing napalm from the remaining operative flamethrowers combined to overload the light-sensing ability of suit cameras, flaring what images they did provide.

In the midst of chaos and confusion Vasquez and Drake found each other. High-tech harpy nodded knowingly to new-wave neanderthal as she slammed her sequestered magazine back in place.

'Let's rock,' she said curtly.

Standing back to back, they opened up simultaneously with their smartguns, laying down two arcs of fire like welders sealing the skin of a spaceship. In the confined chamber the din from the two heavy weapons was overpowering. To the operators of the smartguns the thunder was a Bach fugue and Grimoire stanthisizer all rolled into one.

Gorman's voice echoed in their ears, barely audible over the roar of battle. 'Who's firing? I ordered a hold on heavy fire!'

Vasquez reached up just long enough to rip away her headset, her eyes and attention riveted on the smartgun's targeting screen. Feet, hands, eyes, and body became extensions of the weapon, all dancing and spinning in unison. Thunder, lightning, smoke, and screams filled the chamber, a little slice of Armageddon on C-level. A great calmness flowed through her.

Surely Heaven couldn't be any better than this.

Ripley flinched as another scream reverberated through the Operations bay speakers. Wierzbowski's suit camera crumbled, followed by the immediate flattening of his biomonitors. Her fingers clenched, the nails digging into the palms. She'd liked Wierzbowski.

What was she doing here, anyway? Why wasn't she back home, poor and unlicensed, but safe in her little apartment, surrounded by Jones and ordinary people and common sense? Why had she voluntarily sought the company of nightmares? Out of altruism? Because she'd suspected all along what had been responsible for the break in communications between Acheron and Earth? Or because she wanted a lousy flight certificate back?

Down in the depths of the processing station, frantic, panicky voices ran into one another on the single personal communications frequency. Headset components sorted sense from the babble. She recognized Hudson's above everyone else's. The comtech's unsophisticated pragmatism shone through the breakdown in tactics.

'Let's get out of here!'

She heard Hicks yelling at someone else. The corporal sounded more frustrated than anything else. 'Not that tunnel, the other one!'

'You sure?' Crowe's picture swung crazily as he ducked something unseen, the view provided by his suit camera a wild blur full of smoke, haze, and biomechanical silhouettes. 'Watch it—behind you. Move, will you!'

Gorman's hands slowed. Something besides button-pushing was required now, and Ripley could see from the ashen expression that had come over the lieutenant's face that he didn't have it.

'Get them out of there!' she screamed at him. 'Do it *now*!'

'Shut up.' He was gulping air like a grouper, studying his readouts. Everything was unravelling, his careful plan of advance coming apart on the remaining monitors too fast for him to think it through. Too fast. 'Just shut up!'

The groan of metal being ripped apart sounded over Crowe's headset pickup as his telemetry went black. Gorman stuttered something incomprehensible, trying to keep control of himself even as he was losing control of the situation.

'Uh, Apone, I want you to lay down a suppressing fire with the incinerators and fall back by squads to the APC. Over.'

The sergeant's distant reply was distorted by static, the roar of the flamethrowers, and the rapid fire stutter of the smartguns.

'Say again? All after incinerators?'

'I said ... ' Gorman repeated his instructions. It didn't matter if anyone heard them. The men and women trapped in the cocoon chamber had time only to react, not to listen.

Only Apone fiddled with his headset, trying to make sense of the garbled orders. Gorman's voice was distorted beyond recognition. The headsets were designed to operate and deliver a clear signal under any conditions, including under water, but there was something happening here that hadn't been anticipated by the communications equipment designers, something that couldn't have been foreseen by anyone because it hadn't been encountered before.

Someone screamed behind the sergeant. Forget Gorman. He switched the headset over to straight intersuit frequency. 'Dietrich? Crowe? Sound off! Wierzbowski, where are you?'

Movement to his left. He whirled and came within a millimetre of blowing Hudson's head off. The comtech's eyes were wild. He was teetering on the edge of sanity and barely recognized the sergeant. No bold assertions now; all false bravado fled. He was terrified out of his skin and made no effort to conceal the fact.

'We're getting juked! We're gonna die in here!'

Apone passed him a rifle magazine. The comtech slapped it home, trying to look every which way at once. 'Feel better?' Apone asked him.

'Yeah, right. Right!' Gratefully the comtech chambered a pulse-rifle round. 'Forget the heat exchanger.' He sensed movement, turned, and fired. The slight recoil imparted by the weapon travelled up his arm to restore a little of his lost confidence.

Off to their right, Vasquez was laying down an uninterrupted field of fire, destroying everything not human that came within a metre of her—be it dead, alive, or part of the processing plant's machinery. She looked out of control. Apone knew better. If she was out of control, they'd all be dead by now.

Hicks ran towards her. Pivoting smoothly, she let loose a long burst from the heavy weapon. The corporal ducked as the smartgun's barrel swung towards his face, stumbling clear as the nightmarish figure stalking him was catapulted backward by Vasquez's blast. Biomechanical fingers had been centimetres from his neck.

Within the APC, Apone's monitor suddenly spun crazily and went dark. Gorman stared at it, as though by doing so he could will it back to life, along with the man it represented.

'I told them to fall back.' His tone was distant, disbelieving. 'They must not have heard the order.'

Ripley shoved her face into his, saw the dazed, baffled expression. 'They're cut off in there! *Do* something!'

He looked up at her slowly. His lips worked, but the mumble they produced was unintelligible. He was shaking his head slightly.

No help from that quarter. The lieutenant was out of it. Burke had backed up against the opposite wall, as though by putting distance between himself and the images on the remaining active monitors he could somehow remove himself from the battle that was raging in the bowels of the processing station.

There was only one thing that would do the surviving soldiers any good now, and that was some kind of immediate help. Gorman wasn't going to do anything about it, and Burke couldn't. So that left Jones's favourite human.

If the cat had been present and capable of taking action on Ripley's behalf, she knew what he would have done: turned the armoured personnel carrier around and driven that sucker at top speed for the landing field. Piled into the dropship, lifted back to the *Sulaco*, slipped into hypersleep, and *gone home*. Not likely anyone in colonial administration would dispute her report this time. Not with a shell-shocked Gorman and half-comatose Burke to back her up. Not with the recordings automatically stored by the APC's computer taken directly from the soldiers' suit cameras to flash in the faces of those smug, content Company representatives.

Get out, go home, get *away*, the voice inside her skull screamed at her. You've got the proof you came for. The colony's kaput, one survivor, the others dead or worse than dead. Go back to Earth and come back with an army next time, not a platoon. Atmosphere fliers for air cover. Heavy weapons. Level the place if they have to, but let 'em do it without you.

There was only one problem with that comforting line of reasoning. Leaving now would mean abandoning Vasquez and Hudson and Hicks and everyone else still alive down in C-level to the tender ministrations of the aliens. If they were lucky, they would die. If they were not, they'd end up cemented into a cocoon wall as replacement for the still-living host colonists they'd mercifully carbonized.

She couldn't do that and live with it. She'd see their faces and hear their screams every time she rested her head on a pillow. If she fled, she'd be swapping the immediate nightmare for hundreds later on. A bad trade. One more time the numbers were against her.

She was terrified of what she had to do, but the anger that had been building inside her at Gorman's ineffectiveness and at the Company for sending her out here with an inexperienced field officer and less than a dozen troops (to save money, no doubt) helped drive her past the paralysed lieutenant towards the APC's cockpit.

The sole survivor of Hadley Colony awaited her with a solemn stare.

'Newt, get in the back and put your seat belt on.'

'You're going after the others, aren't you?'

She paused as she was strapping herself into the driver's chair. 'I have to. There are still people alive down there, and they need help. You understand that, don't you?'

The girl nodded. She understood completely. As Ripley clicked home the latches on the driver's harness, the girl raced back down the aisle.

The warm glow of instruments set in the hold mode greeted Ripley as she turned to the controls. Gorman and Burke might be incapable of reaction, but no such psychological restraints inhibited the APC's movements. She started slapping switches and buttons, grateful now for the time spent during the past year operating all sorts of heavy loading and transport equipment out in Portside. The oversize turbo-charged engine raced reassuringly, and the personnel carrier shook, eager to move out.

The vibration from the engine was enough to shock Gorman back to the real world. He leaned back in his chair and shouted forward. 'Ripley, what are you doing?'

Easy to ignore him, more important to concentrate on the controls. She slammed the massive vehicle into gear. Drive wheels spun on damp ground as the APC lurched towards the gaping entrance to the station.

Smoke was pouring out of the complex. The big armoured wheels skidded slightly on the damp pavement as she wrenched the machine sideways and sent it hurtling down the wide, descending rampway. The ramp accommodated the APC with room to spare. It had been designed to admit big earthmovers and service vehicles. Colonial construction was typically overbuilt. Even so, the roadway was depressed by the weight of the APC's armour, but no cracks appeared in its wake as Ripley sent it racing downward. Her hands hammered the controls of the independently powered wheels as she took out some of her anger on the uncomplaining plastic.

Mist and haze obscured the view provided by the external monitors. She switched to automatic navigation, and the APC kept itself from crashing into the enclosing walls, ranging lasers reading the distance between wheels and obstacles twenty times a second and reporting back to the vehicle's central computer. She maintained speed, knowing that the machine wouldn't let her crash.

Gorman stopped staring at the dimly seen walls rushing by the Operations bay screens, released his suit harness, and stumbled forward, bouncing off the walls as Ripley sent the APC careening wildly around tight corners.

'What are you doing?'

'What's it look like I'm doing?' She didn't turn to face him, absorbed in controlling the carrier.

He put a hand on her shoulder. 'Turn around! That's an order!'

'You can't give me orders, Gorman. I'm a civilian, remember?'

'This is a military expedition under military control. As commanding officer, I am ordering you to turn this vehicle around!'

She gritted her teeth, attention focused on the forward viewscreens. 'Go sit on a grenade, Gorman. I'm busy.'

He reached down and tried to pull her out of the chair. Burke got both arms around him and pulled him off. She would have thanked the Company rep, but she didn't have the time.

They reached C-level and the big wheels screamed as she sent the APC into a mad turn, simultaneously switching off the automatic navigation system and the ranging lasers. The engine revved as they rumbled forward, tearing away pipes and conduits, equipment modules, and chunks of alien encrustation. She glanced at the control console until she located the external instrumentation she wanted: strobe beacon, siren, running lights. She wiped the entire panel with the palm of her right hand.

The exterior of the APC came alive with sodium-arc lights, infrared homing beacons, spinning locater flashers, and the piercing whine of the battle siren. The individual suit monitors were all back in the Operations bay, but she didn't need to see them, zeroing in on the flash of weapons fire just ahead. The lights and roar came from beyond a thick wall of translucent alien resin, the material eerily distributing the light from the guns throughout its substance, giving the cocoon chamber the appearance of a dome pulsing from within.

She nudged the accelerator. The APC smashed through the curving wall like an iron ingot shot from a cannon. Fragments of resin and biomechanical mortar went flying. Huge chunks were crushed beneath the armoured wheels. She wrenched on the wheel, and the personnel carrier pivoted neatly. The rear of the powerful machine swung around and brought down another section of alien wall.

Hicks appeared out of the smoke. He was firing back the way he'd come, holding the big pulse-rifle in one hand while supporting a limping Hudson with the other. Adrenaline, muscle, and determination were all that kept the two men going. Ripley looked away from the windshield and back down the APC's central aisle.

'Burke, they're coming!'

A faint reply as he hollered back towards the cockpit: 'I'm on my way! Hang on.'

The Company rep stumbled to the crew access door, fumbled with unfamiliar controls until the armoured hatch cycled wide. Following in Hicks's and Hudson's footsteps, the two smartgun operators materialized out of the dense mist. They were retreating with precision, side by side, firing and covering the retreat as they fell back on the personnel carrier. As Ripley looked on, Drake's gun went empty. Automatically he snapped the release buckles on the smartgun harness. It sloughed away like an old skin. Before it hit the ground, he'd pulled a flamethrower from his back and had brought it into play. The hollow *whoosh* of napalm mixed with the deep-throated chatter of Vasquez's still operative smartgun.

Hicks reached the APC, put his weapon aside, and all but threw the injured Hudson through the opening. Then he tossed his pulse-rifle after the comtech and cleared the hatch in two strides. Vasquez was still firing as the corporal got both hands under her arms and heaved, pulling her in after him. At the same time she saw a dark, towering silhouette lunge towards Drake from behind, and she changed her field of fire as Hicks was dumping her onto the APC's deck.

A flash of contact lit up an inhuman, frozen grin as the smartgun shells tore apart the alien's thorax. Bright yellow body fluid sprayed in all directions. It splashed across Drake's face and chest. Smoke rose from the staggering body of the smartgun operator as the acid chewed rapidly through flesh and bone. His muscles spasmed, and his flamethrower fired as he toppled backward.

Vasquez and Hicks rolled as a gout of flame slashed through the open crew door, setting portions of the APC's flammable interior ablaze. As Drake fell, Hicks charged the hatch and started to cycle the door. Moving on hands and knees, Vasquez lunged wildly at the opening. The corporal had to leave the controls to grab her. It was a struggle to keep her from plunging outside.

'Drake!' She was screaming, not calm and controlled anymore. 'He's down!'

It took all of Hicks's superior size and strength to wrench her around to face him. 'He's gone! Forget it, Vasquez. He's gone.'

She stared up at him, irrational, her face streaked with soot and grime. 'No. No, he's not! He's . . . '

Hicks looked back at the APC's other occupants. 'Get her away from here. We've got to get this door closed.' Hudson nodded. Together he and Burke dragged the dazed smartgun operator away from the entry hatch. The corporal looked towards the cockpit and raised what was left of his voice. 'Let's go! We're clear back here.'

'Going!' Ripley jammed on the controls and nailed the accelerator. The armoured personnel carrier roared and shuddered as she sent it racing backwards up the ramp.

A storage rack broke free, burying Hudson beneath a pile of equipment. Cursing and flailing, he threw the stuff aside, indifferent to whether it was marked EMERGENCY RATIONS or EXPLOSIVES.

Hicks turned his attention back to the door, fumbled with the controls. It was nearly shut when two sets of long claws suddenly appeared to slam into the metal flange like a pair of power hammers. From her seat Newt let out a primordial child's scream. The sabre-tooth, the giant bear, the boogey-man was at the entrance to the cave, and this time she had no place to hide.

Vasquez stumbled to her feet and joined Hicks and Burke in leaning on the door. Despite their combined efforts, the metal barrier was slowly being wrenched open from the outside. Locks and seals groaned in protest.

Hicks managed to find enough wind to yell at the still numbed Gorman. 'Get on the door!'

The lieutenant heard him and reacted. Reacted by backing away and shaking his head, his eyes wide. Hicks muttered a curse and jammed his shoulder against the latching lever. This freed one hand to pull out the sawed-off twelve-gauge just as a nightmare alien head wedged its way through the opening. Outer jaws parted to reveal the pistonlike inner throat and penetrating teeth. As slime-covered fangs swung towards him, Hicks jammed the muzzle of the shotgun between the gaping demon jaws and pulled the trigger. The explosion of the ancient projectile weapon echoed through the personnel carrier as the shattered skull fell backward, fountaining acid blood. The spray immediately began to eat into the door and deck.

Hicks and Vasquez fell aside, but some of the droplets struck Hudson on the arm. Smoke rose from skin as hissing flesh dissolved. The comtech operator let out a howl and stumbled into the empty seats.

Hicks and Burke slammed the hatch shut and locked it.

Like a runaway comet, the APC rumbled backward up the ramp and slammed into a mass of conduit. Ripley worked on the wheels, spinning the oversize metal rims and ripping free. Sparks showered over the vehicle. In the crew quarters behind her, everyone seemed to be yelling simultaneously. Extinguishers were unbolted and brought into play on the internal fire. Newt stayed out of the way, sitting silently in her seat as panicky adults ran to and fro around her. She was breathing hard but steadily, eyes alert, watching. None of what was happening was new to her. She'd been through it all before.

Something made a soft metallic thump as it landed on the roof.

Gorman had retreated into a corner to the left of the aisle. He was staring blankly at his frantic companions. Consequently he did not see the small gun hatch, against which he was leaning, begin to vibrate. But he felt it when the hatch cover was ripped from its seals. He started to turn, not nearly fast enough, and was snatched through the opening.

There was something at the tip of the alien's tail, something silver-sharp and superfast. It whipped around one leg to bury itself in the lieutenant's shoulder. He screamed. Hicks threw himself into the crew bay fire-control chair and clutched the controls, jabbing contact points and switches with his other hand as the seat motor hummed and swung him around. Brightly coloured telltales came to life on the board, adding no cheer to the beleaguered APC's interior but bringing a smile to the corporal's face.

In response to his actions servomotors whirred and a small turret came to life on the personnel carrier's roof. It spun in a half circle. The alien holding Gorman two-thirds of the way out of the vehicle turned sharply in the direction of the new sound just as twin guns fired in its direction. The heavy shells blew it right off the top of the machine, the impact knocking it clear before the acid in its body began to spill.

Burke dragged the unconscious Gorman back inside while Vasquez hunted for something to plug the opening with.

Trailing fire and smoke, the APC tore up the ramp. Ripley wrestled with the controls as the big vehicle slewed sideways, broadsiding a control room outbuilding. Office furniture and splintered sections of wall exploded in all directions, forming a wake of plastic and composite fibre behind the retreating machine.

Almost clear now, almost out. Another minute or two, and if nothing broke down, they'd be free of the station's confines. Free to . . .

An alien arm arced down right in front of her face to smash the shatterproof windshield. Glistening, slime-coated jaws lunged inside. Ripley threw up both arms to shield her face and leaned away. Once before, she'd been this close to perdition. In the shuttle *Narcissus*, secure in its pilot's seat, luring another alien close so that she could blow it out the airlock. But there was no airlock here, no comforting atmosphere suit enclosing her, no tricks left to pull, and no time to think of any.

She tried to crush the brakes underfoot. The big wheels

locked up at high speed, screeching over the sound of the chaos outside. She felt herself being thrown forward, her head flying towards those gaping jaws. But her seat harness checked her motion and kept her in the chair.

No such restraints secured the alien. Leaning over the windshield, it was clinging awkwardly to the edge of the roof, and not even its inhuman strength could prevent it from being thrown forward. As soon as it landed on the ground she threw the personnel carrier back in gear. It didn't even bump as it trundled over the skeletal body, crushing it beneath its massive weight. Acid squirted over armoured wheels, but the APC's forward movement carried it clear before more than a few inconsequential pits had been eaten in the spinning disks. Their movement was not affected.

Darkness ahead. Clean, welcoming darkness. Not a blank falling over her mind but the darkness of a dimly lit world: the surface of Acheron, framed by the walls of the station. A moment later they were through, rumbling over the connecting causeway towards the landing field.

A noise like bolts dropped in a food processor was coming from the rear of the APC. Occasionally a louder clunk could be heard. It was a sound beyond the soothing effects of lubrication, beyond repair. She fiddled with controls and tried to adjust the noise out of existence, but like her recurring nightmares, it refused early dismissal.

Hicks came forward and, gently but firmly, eased her fingers off the accelerator control. Her face was as white as her knuckles. She blinked, glanced back up at him.

'It's okay,' he assured her, 'we're clear. They're all behind us. I don't think fighting out in the open suits them. Ease up. We're not going much further in this hunk of junk, anyway.'

The grinding noise was overpowering as they slowed. She listened intently as she brought the big vehicle to a halt.

'Don't ask me for an analysis. I'm an operator, not a mechanic.'

Hicks cocked an ear in the direction of the metallic gargling.

'Sounds like a blown transaxle. Maybe two. You're just grinding metal. Actually I'm surprised that the underside of this baby isn't lying back on B-level somewhere. They build these things tough.'

'Not tough enough.' That was Burke's voice, filtering up to them from somewhere in the passenger compartment.

'Nobody expected to have to face anything like these creatures. Ever.' Hicks leaned towards the console and rotated an exterior viewer. The APC looked terrible on the outside, a smoking, acid-scarred hulk. It was supposed to be invulnerable. Now it was scrap.

Ripley spun her seat, glanced at the empty one next to her, and then turned to stare down the aisle that led back through the personnel carrier.

'Newt. Where's Newt?'

A tug on her pants leg. Not hard, so she didn't jump. Newt was squeezed into the tiny space between the driver's seat and the APC's armoured bulkhead. She was trembling and terrified but alert. No catatonia this time, no withdrawal from reality. No reason for an extreme reaction, Ripley knew. Doubtless the girl had been witness to much worse when the aliens had overwhelmed the colony.

Had she been watching the Operations bay monitors when the soldiers had initially penetrated the alien cocoon chamber? Had she seen the face of the woman who had whispered in agony to Dietrich? What if the woman had been . . . ?

But she couldn't have been. If that had been Newt's mother, the girl would be beyond catatonia by now. Gone, withdrawn, and unreachable, perhaps forever.

'You okay?' Sometimes inanities had to be asked. Besides, she wanted, needed, to hear the child respond.

Newt did so with a thumbs-up gesture, still employing selective silence as a defence mechanism. Ripley didn't push her to talk. Keeping quiet while everyone around her was being killed had kept her alive.

'I have to check on the others,' she told the upturned face.

'Will you be all right?'

A nod this time, accompanied by a shy little smile that made Ripley swallow hard. She tried to conceal what she was feeling inside, because this wasn't the time or place to break down. They could do that when they were safely back aboard the *Sulaco*.

'Good, I'll be right back. If you get tired of staying under there, you can come back and join the rest of us, okay?' The smile widened slightly and was followed by a more vigorous nod, but the girl stayed put. She still trusted her own instincts more than she trusted any adult. Ripley wasn't offended. She unbuckled herself and headed back down the aisle.

Hudson was standing off to one side inspecting his arm. The fact that he still had an arm showed that he'd only been lightly misted by the alien acid. He was reliving the last twenty minutes of his life, replaying every second over and over in his mind and not believing what he saw there. She could hear him muttering to himself.

'—I don't believe it. It didn't happen. It didn't happen, man.'

Burke tried to have a look at the injured comtech's arm, more curious than sympathetic. Hudson jerked away from the Company rep.

'I'm all right. Leave it!'

Burke pursed his lips, wanting to see but not willing to push. 'Better let somebody take a look at it. Can't tell what the side effects are. Might be toxic.'

'Yeah? And if it is, I suppose you're going to check stores and break out an antidote in a couple of minutes, right? Dietrich's the medtech.' He swallowed and his anger faded. 'Was our medtech. Stinking bugs.'

Hicks was bending over the motionless Gorman, checking for a pulse. Ripley joined him.

'Anything?' she asked tightly.

'Heartbeat's slow but steady. He's breathing the same way. It's the same with the rest of his vital signs: slowed down but regular. He's alive. If I didn't know better, I'd say he was sleeping, but it ain't sleep. I think he's paralysed.'

Vasquez pushed both of them aside and grabbed the unconscious lieutenant by his collar. She was too furious to cry. 'He's dead is what he is!' She hauled the upper half of Gorman's body upright with one hand and drew back the other in a fist, screaming in his face.

'Wake up, *pendejo*! Wake up. I'm gonna kill you, you useless waste!'

Hicks inserted his bulk between her and the frozen lieutenant. Same soft voice employed, but with a slight edge to it now. Same hard eyes staring into the smartgun operator's face.

'Hold it. Hold it. Back off—right now.'

Their eyes locked. Vasquez continued to hold Gorman half off the deck. Something basic cut its way through her fury. Marine—she was a Marine, and Marines live by basics. The basics in this case were simple. Apone was gone and therefore Hicks was in charge.

'It ain't worth bruising my knuckles,' she finally muttered. She released the lieutenant's collar, and his head bounced off the deck as she turned away, still cursing to herself. Ripley didn't doubt for an instant that if Hicks hadn't intervened, the smartgun operator would have beaten the unconscious Gorman to a pulp.

With Vasquez out of the way Ripley bent over the paralysed officer and opened his tunic. The bloodless purple puncture wound that marred his shoulder had already sealed itself.

'Looks like it stung him or something. Interesting. I didn't know they could do that.'

'Hey!'

The excited shout made Hicks and her turn towards the Operations bay. Hudson was in there. He'd been staring morosely at the biomonitors and videoscreens, and something had caught his eye. Now he beckoned to his remaining companions.

'Look. Crowe and Dietrich aren't dead, man.' He gestured at the bioreadouts, swallowed uneasily. 'They must be like

Gorman. Their signs are real low, but they ain't dead—' His voice trailed off, along with his initial excitement.

If they weren't dead and they were like Hudson, that meant—The comtech started to shake with a mixture of anger and sorrow. He was standing on the thin edge of hysteria. They all were. It clung to them like a psychic leech, hanging on the fringes of their sanity, threatening to invade and take over the instant anyone let down his mental guard.

Ripley knew what those soporific bioreadouts meant. She tried to explain, but she couldn't meet Hudson's eyes as she did so.

'You can't help them.'

'Hey, but if they're still alive—'

'Forget it. Right now they're being cocooned, just like those others. Like the colonists you found in the wall when you went in there. You can't do a damn thing for them. Nobody can. That's the way it is. Just be glad you're here talking about them instead of down there with them. If Dietrich was here, she'd know she couldn't do anything to help you.'

The comtech seemed to sag in on himself. 'This ain't happening.'

Ripley turned away from him. As she did so, her gaze met Vasquez's. It would have been easy for her to say 'I told you so' to the smartgunner. It also would have been superfluous. That one look communicated everything the two women needed to say.

This time it was Vasquez who turned away.

# IX

In the colony medical lab Bishop stood hunched over an ocular probe. Beneath the lens was a stretched slice of one of the dead facehugger parasites, extracted from the specimen in the nearest stasis cylinder. Even in death the biopsied creature looked threatening, lying on its back on the dissection table. The clutching legs looked poised to grab any face that bent too close, the powerful tail ready to propel the creature clear across the room in a single pistoning leap.

The internal structure was as fascinating as the functional exterior, and Bishop was glued to the probe's eyepiece. By combining the probe's resolving power with the versatility of his own artificial eye, he was able to see a great deal that the colonists might have missed.

One of the questions that particularly intrigued him, and which he was anxious to answer, involved the definite possibility of an alien parasite attempting to attach itself to a synthetic like himself. His insides were radically different from those of a purely biological human being. Would a parasite be able to detect the differences before it sprang? If not and it attempted to utilize a synthetic as a host, what might be the probable results of such an enforced union? Would it simply drop off and go searching for another body, or would it mindlessly insert the embryonic seed it carried into an artificial host? If so, would the embryo be able to grow or would it be the more surprised of the couple as it struggled to mature within a body devoid of flesh and blood?

Could a robot be parasitized?

Something made a noise near the doorway. Bishop looked up long enough to see the dropship crew chief roll a pallet full of equipment and supplies into the lab.

'Where you want this stuff?'

'Over there.' Bishop gestured. 'By the end of the bench will do nicely.'

Spunkmeyer began unloading the shipping pallet. 'Need anything else?'

Bishop waved vaguely without taking his gaze from the probe.

'Right. I'll be back in the ship. Buzz me if you need anything.'

Another wave. Spunkmeyer shrugged and turned to leave.

Bishop was a funny sort of bird, the crew chief mused as he wheeled his hand truck down the empty corridors and back out onto the landing tarmac. Funny sort of hybrid, he thought, correcting himself and smiling at the pun. He whistled cheerfully as he snugged his collar higher up around his neck. The wind wasn't blowing too badly, but it was still chilly outside without a full environment suit. Concentrating on a tune also helped to keep his mind off the disaster that had befallen the expedition.

Crowe, Dietrich, old Apone—all gone. Hard to believe, as Hudson kept mumbling over and over to himself. Hard to believe and a shame. He'd known them all; they'd flown together on a number of missions. Though he couldn't say he knew any of them intimately.

He shrugged, even though there was no one around to see the gesture. Death was something they were all used to, an acquaintance each of them fully expected to encounter prior to retirement. Crowe and Dietrich had early appointments, that was all. Nothing to be done about it. But Hicks and the rest had made it out okay. They'd finish their studies and clean up here and be out by tomorrow. That was the plan. A little more study, make a few last recordings, and get out of there. He knew he wasn't the only one looking forward to the moment when the dropship would heave mass and head back to the good ol' *Sulaco*.

His thoughts went back to Bishop again. Maybe there'd been some sort of subtle improvement in the new model synthetics, or maybe it was just Bishop himself, but he found that he rather liked the android. Everybody said that the artificial-intelligence boys had been working hard to improve personality programming for years, even adding a bit of randomness to each new model as it walked off the assembly line. Sure, that was it—Bishop was an individual. You could tell him from another synthetic just by talking to him. And it didn't hurt to have one quiet, courteous companion among all the boastful loudmouths.

As he rolled the hand truck to the top of the dropship's loading ramp, he slipped. Catching his balance, he bent to examine the damp spot. Since there was no depression in which rainwater could pool up, he thought he must have busted a container of Bishop's precious preserving fluid, but there was no tickling, lingering odour of formaldehyde. The shiny stuff clinging to the metal ramp looked more like a thick slime or gel.

He shrugged and straightened. He couldn't remember busting a bottle containing anything like that, and as long as nobody asked him about it, there was no point in worrying. No time for worrying, either. Too much to do so they could get ready to leave.

The wind beat at him. Lousy atmosphere, and yet it was a lot milder than what it had been before the atmosphere processors had started work here. 'Unbreathable,' the presleep briefing had said. Pulling the hand truck in behind him, he hit the switch to retract the ramp and close the door.

Vasquez was pacing the length of the APC. Inactivity in what was still a combat situation was a foreign sensation to her. She wanted a gun in her hands and something to shoot at. She knew the situation called for careful analysis, and it frustrated her because she wasn't the analytical type. Her methods were direct, final, and didn't involve any talk. But she was smart enough to realize that this wasn't your standard operation anymore. Standard operating procedure had been chewed up and spit out by the enemy. Knowing this failed to calm her, however. She wanted to kill something.

Occasionally her fingers would flex as though they were still gripping the controls of her smartgun. Watching her would have made Ripley nervous if she wasn't already as tense as it was possible to be without snapping like the overwound mainspring of an ancient timepiece.

It got to the point where Vasquez knew she could say something or start tearing her hair out. 'All right, we can't blow them up. We can't go down there as a squad; we can't even go back down in the APC because they'll take us apart like a can full of peas. Why not roll some canisters of CN-20 down there? Nerve gas the whole nest? We've got enough on the dropship to make the whole colony uninhabitable.'

Hudson was pleading with his eyes, glancing at each of them in turn. 'Look man, let's just bug out and call it even, okay?' He glanced at the woman standing next to him. 'I'm with Ripley. Let 'em make the whole colony into a playpen if they want to, but we get out now and come back with a warship.'

Vasquez stared at him out of slitted eyes. 'Getting queasy, Hudson?'

'Queasy!' He straightened a little in reaction to the implicit challenge. 'We're in over our heads here. Nobody said we'd run into anything like this. I'll be the first one to volunteer to come back, but when I do, I want the right kind of equipment to deal with the problem. This ain't like mob control, Vasquez. You try kicking some butts here and they'll eat your leg right off.'

Ripley looked at the smartgun operator. 'The nerve gas won't work, anyway. How do we know if it'll affect their biochemistry? Maybe they'll just snort the stuff. The way these things are built, nerve gas might just give them a pleasant high.

I blew one of them out of an airlock with an emergency grapple stuck in its gut, and all it did was slow it down. I had to fry it with my ship's engines.' She leaned back against the wall.

'I say we take off and nuke the entire site from orbit and the whole high plateau where we originally found the ship that brought them here. It's the only way to be sure.'

'Now hold on a second.' Having been silent during the ongoing discussion, Burke abruptly came to life. 'I'm not authorizing that kind of action. That's about as extreme as you can get.'

'You don't think the situation's extreme?' growled Hudson. He toyed with the bandage on his acid-scarred arm and glared hard at the Company representative.

'Of course it's extreme.'

'Then why won't you authorize the use of nukes?' Ripley pressed him. 'You lose the colony and one processing station, but you've still got ninety-five per cent of your terraforming capability unimpaired and operational on the rest of the planet. So why the hesitation?'

Sensing the challenge in her tone, the Company rep backpedalled flawlessly into a conciliatory mode.

'Well, I mean, I know this is an emotional moment. I'm as upset as anybody else. But that doesn't mean we have to resort to snap judgments. We have to move cautiously here. Let's think before we throw out the baby with the bathwater.'

'The baby's dead, Burke, in case you haven't noticed.' Ripley refused to be swayed.

'All I'm saying,' he argued, 'is that it's time to look at the whole situation, if you know what I mean.'

She crossed her arms over her chest. 'No, Burke, what do you mean?'

He thought fast. 'First of all, this installation has a substantial monetary value attached to it. We're talking about an entire colony setup here. Never mind the replacement cost. The investment in transportation alone is enormous, and the process of terraforming Acheron is just starting to show some real progress. It's true that the other atmosphere-processing stations function automatically, but they still require regular maintenance and supervision. Without the means to house and service an appropriate staff locally, that would mean keeping several transports in orbit as floating hotels for the necessary personnel. That involves an ongoing cost you can't begin to imagine.'

'They can bill me,' she told him unsmilingly. 'I got a tab running. What else?'

'For another thing, this is clearly an important species we're dealing with here. We can't just arbitrarily exterminate those who've found their way to this world. The loss to science would be incalculable. We might never encounter them again.'

'Yeah, and that'd be just too bad.' She uncrossed her arms. 'Aren't you forgetting something, Burke? You told me that if we encountered a hostile life-form here, we'd take care of it and forget the scientific concerns. That's why I never liked dealing with administrators: you guys all have selective memories.'

'It just isn't the way to handle things,' he protested.

'Forget it!'

'Yeah, forget it.' Vasquez echoed Ripley's sentiments as well as her words. 'Watch us.'

'Maybe you haven't been keeping up on current events,' Hudson put in, 'but we just got fragged, pal.'

'Look, Burke.' Clearly Ripley was not pleased. 'We had an agreement. I think I've proved my case, made my point, whatever you want to call it. We came here for confirmation of my story and to find out what caused the break in communications between Acheron and Earth. You got your confirmation, the Company's got its explanation, and I've got my vindication. Now it's time to get away from here.'

'I know, I know.' He put an arm over her shoulders, careful not to make it look as if he were being familiar, and turned her away from the others as he lowered his voice. 'But we're dealing with changing scenarios here. You have to be ready to put aside the first reaction that comes to mind, put aside your natural emotions, and know how to take advantage. We've survived here; now we've got to be ready to survive back on Earth.'

'What are you getting at, Burke?'

Either he didn't notice the chill in her eyes or else he chose not to react to it. 'What I'm trying to say is that this thing is *major*, Ripley. I mean, really major. We've never encountered anything like these creatures before, and we might never have the chance to do so again. Their strength and their resourcefulness is unbelievable. You don't just annihilate something like that, not with the kind of potential they imply. You back off until you learn how to handle them, sure, but you don't just blow them away.'

'Wanna bet?'

'You're not thinking rationally. Now, I understand what you're going through. Don't think that I don't. But you've got to put all that aside and look at the larger picture. What's done is done. We can't help the colonists, and we can't do anything for Crowe and Apone and the others, but we can help ourselves. We can learn about these things and make use of them, turn them to our advantage, master them.'

'You don't master something like these aliens. You get out of their way; and if the opportunity presents itself, you blow them to atoms. Don't talk to me about "surviving" back on Earth.'

He took a deep breath. 'Come on, Ripley. These aliens are special in ways we haven't begun to understand. Uniqueness is one thing the cosmos is stingy with. They need to be studied, carefully and under the right conditions, so that we can learn from them. All that went wrong here was that the colonists started studying them without the proper equipment. They didn't know what to expect. We do.'

'Do we? Look what happened to Apone and the rest.'

'They didn't know what they were up against, and they went in a little overconfident. They got caught in a tight spot. That's a mistake we won't make again.'

'You can bet on that.'

'What happened here is tragic, sure, but it won't be repeated. When we come back, we'll be properly equipped. That acid can't eat through everything. We'll take a sample back somehow, have it analysed in company labs. They'll develop a defence, a shield. And we'll figure out a way to immobilize the mature form so it can be manipulated and used. Sure, the aliens are strong, but they're not omnipotent. They're tough but they're not invulnerable. They can be killed by hand weapons as small as pulse-rifles and flamethrowers. That's one thing this expedition *has* proved. You proved it yourself,' he added in a tone of admiration she didn't believe for an instant.

'I'm telling you, Ripley, this is an opportunity few people are given. We can't blow it on an emotional spur-of-the-moment decision. I didn't think you were the type to throw away the chance of a lifetime for something as abstract as a little revenge.'

'It doesn't have anything to do with revenge,' she told him evenly. 'It has to do with survival. Ours.'

'You're still not hearing me.' He dropped his voice to a whisper. 'See, since you're the representative of the company that discovered this species, your percentage of the eventual profits to be derived from the study and concomitant exploitation of them will naturally be some serious money. The fact that the Company once prosecuted you and then had the decision of the prosecuting board overturned doesn't enter into it. Everybody knows that you're the sole survivor of the crew that first encountered these creatures. The law requires that you receive an appropriate royalty. You're going to be richer than you dreamed possible, Ripley.'

She stared silently at him for a long time, as though she were observing an entirely new species of alien just encountered. A particularly loathsome variety at that.

'You son of a . . . .'

He backed off, his expression hardening. The false sense of camaraderie he'd tried to promote was sloughed off like a mask. 'I'm sorry you feel that way. Don't make me pull rank, Ripley.'

'What rank? We've been through all this before.' She nodded down the aisle. 'I believe *Corporal* Hicks has authority here.'

Burke started to laugh at her. Then he saw that she was serious. 'You're kidding. What is this, a joke? Corporal Hicks? Since when was a corporal in charge of anything except his own boots?'

'This operation is under military jurisdiction,' she reminded him quietly. 'That's the way the *Sulaco*'s dispatch orders read. Maybe you didn't bother to read them. I did. That's the way Colonial Administration worded it. You and I, Burke, we're just observers. We're just along for the ride. Apone's dead and Gorman might as well be. Hicks is next in the chain of command.' She peered past the stunned Company rep. 'Right?'

Hicks's reply was matter-of-fact. 'Looks that way.'

Burke's careful corporate self-control was beginning to slip. 'Look, this is a multimillion credit operation. He can't make that kind of decision. Corporals don't authorize nukes. He's just a grunt.' Second thoughts and a hasty glance in the soldier's direction prompted Burke to add a polite, 'No offence.'

'None taken.' Hicks's response was cool and correct. He spoke to his headset pickup. 'Ferro, you been copying all of this?'

'Standing by' came the dropship pilot's reply over their speakers.

'Prepare for dust-off. We're gonna need an immediate evac.'

'Figured as much from what we heard over here. Tough.'

'You don't know the half of it.' Hicks's expression was unchanged as he regarded the tight-lipped Burke. 'You're right about one thing. You can't make a decision like this on the spur of the moment.'

Burke relaxed slightly. 'That's more like it. So what are we going to do?'

'Think it over, like you said we should.' The corporal closed his eyes for about five seconds. 'Okay, I've thought it over. What I think is that we'll take off and nuke the site from orbit. It's the only way to be *sure*.'

He winked. The colour drained from the Company rep's face. He took an angry step in Hicks's direction before realizing that what he was thinking of doing bore no relation to reality. Instead he had to settle for expressing his outrage verbally.

'This is absurd! You seriously can't be thinking of dropping a nuclear device on the colony site.'

'Just a little one,' Hicks assured him calmly, 'but big enough.' He put his hands together, smiled and pushed them apart. '*Whoosh*.'

'I'm telling you for the last time that you don't have the authority to do something like—'

His tirade was interrupted by a loud *clack*: the sound of a pulse-rifle being activated. Vasquez cradled the powerful weapon beneath her right arm. It wasn't pointed in Burke's direction, but then it wasn't exactly aimed away from him, either. Her expression was blank. He knew it wouldn't change if she decided to put a pulse-shell through his chest, either. End of discussion. He sat down heavily in one of the empty seats that lined the wall.

'You're all crazy,' he muttered. 'You know that.'

'Man,' Vasquez told him softly, 'why else would anyone join the Colonial Marines?' She glanced over at the corporal. 'Tell me something, Hicks: Does that mean I can plead insanity for shooting this *mierda*? If I can, I might as well shoot that sorry excuse for a lieutenant while I'm at it. Don't want to waste a good defence.'

'Nobody's shooting anybody,' the corporal informed her firmly. 'We're getting out of here.'

Ripley met his eyes, nodded once, then turned and sat down. She put a reassuring arm around the only conscious nonparticipant in the discussion. Newt leaned against her shoulder.

'We're going home, honey,' she told the girl.

Now that their course of action had been determined, Hicks took a moment to check out the interior of the APC. Between the fire damage and the holes eaten by alien acid, it was clearly a write-off.

'Let's get together what we can carry. Hudson, give me a hand with the lieutenant.'

The comtech eyed the paralysed form of his commanding officer with undisguised distaste. 'How about we just sit him up in Operations and strap him to the chair? He'll feel right at home.'

'No sell. He's still alive, and we've got to get him out of here.'

'Yeah, I know, I know. Just don't keep reminding me.'

'Ripley, you keep an eye on the child. She's sort of taken to you, anyway.'

'The feeling's mutual.' She clasped Newt tightly to her.

'Vasquez, can you cover us until the dropship touches down?'

She smiled at him, showing perfect teeth. 'Can pigs fly?' She tapped the stock of the pulse-rifle.

The corporal turned to face the landing team's last human member. 'You coming?'

'Don't be funny,' Burke grumbled.

'I won't. Not here. This isn't a funny place.' He switched on his headset pickup. 'Bishop, you found anything out?'

The synthetic's voice filled the passenger bay. 'Not much. The equipment here is colonial-style basic. I've gone about as far as I can go with the tools available.'

'It doesn't matter. We're getting out. Pack it up and meet us on the tarmac. Can you make it okay? I don't want to abandon the APC until the dropship's on final approach.'

'No problem. It's been quiet back here.'

'Okay. Don't take anything you can't carry easily. Move it.'

The dropship rose from its place on the concrete pad, fighting the wind as it lifted. Under Ferro's steady hand it hovered, pivoted in midair, and began to move over the colony towards the stalled APC.

'Got you on visual. Wind's let up a little. I'll set her down as close as I can,' Ferro informed them.

'Roger.' Hicks turned to his companions. 'Ready?' Everyone nodded except Burke, who looked sour but said nothing. 'Then let's get out of here.' He cycled the door.

Wind and rain poured in as the ramp extended. They filed rapidly out of the vehicle. The dropship was already in plain sight, edging towards them. Searchlights blazed from its flanks and belly. One illuminated a single human shape striding through the mist towards them.

'Bishop!' Vasquez waved. 'Long time no see.'

He called across to her. 'Didn't work out so good, huh?'

'It stank.' She spat downwind. 'Tell you all about it sometime.'

'Later. After hypersleep. After we've put this place far behind us.'

She nodded, the only one of the waiting group whose attention was not monopolized by the approaching dropship. Her dark eyes continuously scanned the landscape around the personnel carrier. Nearby, Ripley waited, gripping Newt's small hand tightly. Hudson and Hicks carried the still-unconscious Gorman between them.

'Hold it there,' Ferro instructed them. 'Give me a little room. I don't want to come down on top of you.' She thumped her headset pickup. 'It'd be nice if I had a little help up here, Spunkmeyer. Get off the pot.'

The compartment door slid aside behind her. She glanced back over her shoulder, angry and not bothering to hide the fact. 'It's about time. Where the . . .?'

Her eyes widened, and the rest of the accusation trailed away.

It wasn't Spunkmeyer.

The alien barely fitted through the opening. Outer jaws flared to reveal the inner set of teeth. There was a blur of movement and an explosive, organic *whoosh*. Ferro barely had time to scream as she was slammed backward into the control console.

From below, the would-be refugees watched in dismay as the dropship veered wildly to port. Its main engines roared to life, and it accelerated even as it lost altitude. Ripley grabbed Newt and sprinted towards the nearest building.

'Run!'

The dropship clipped a rock formation at the edge of the causeway, slewed left, and struck a basalt ridge. It tumbled, turning completely on its back like a dying dragonfly, struck the tarmac, and exploded. Sections and compartments began to break away from the mainframe, some of them already afire. The body of the ship arced into the air once more, bouncing off the unyielding stone, fire blazing from its engines and superstructure.

Part of an engine module slammed into the APC, setting off its armament. The personnel carrier blew itself to bits as shells and fuel exploded inside it. A flaming Catherine wheel, the remains of the dropship skipped past and rolled into the outskirts of the atmosphere processing station. A tremendous fireball lit the dark sky of Acheron. It faded rapidly.

Emerging from concealment, the stunned survivors stared at the debris in disbelief as their superior firepower and hopes of getting off the planet were simultaneously reduced to charred metal and ash.

'Well, that's *great*!' said a near hysterical Hudson. 'That's just great, man. *Now* what are we supposed to do? We're in some real fine shape now.'

'Are you finished?' Hicks stared hard at the comtech until Hudson looked abashed. Then he glanced at Ripley. 'You okay?'

She nodded and tried to hide her real feelings as she looked down at Newt. She could have spared herself the effort. It was impossible to hide anything from the child. Newt looked calm enough. She was breathing hard, true, but it was from the effort of racing for cover, not from fear. The girl shrugged, sounding remarkably grown-up.

'I guess we're not leaving, right?'

Ripley bit her lip. 'I'm sorry, Newt.'

'You don't have to be sorry. It wasn't your fault.' She stared silently at the flaming wreckage of the dropship.

Hudson was kicking aside rocks, bits of metal, anything smaller than his boot. 'Just tell me what we're supposed to do now. What're we gonna do *now*?'

Burke looked annoyed. 'Maybe we could build a fire and sing songs.'

Hudson took a step towards the Company rep, and Hicks had to intervene.

'We should get back.' Everyone turned to look down at Newt, who was still staring at the burning dropship. 'We should get back 'cause it'll be dark soon. *They* come mostly at night. Mostly.'

'All right.' Hicks nodded in the direction of the ruined APC. It was mostly metal and composites and shouldn't burn much longer. 'The fire's about had it. Let's see what we can find.'

'Scrap metal,' suggested Burke.

'And maybe something more. You coming?'

The Company rep rose from where he'd been sitting. 'I'm sure not staying here.'

'Up to you.' The corporal turned to their synthetic. 'Bishop, see if you can make Operations livable. What I mean is, make sure it's . . . clear.'

The android responded with a gentle smile. 'Take point? I know what that means. I'm expendable, of course.'

'Nobody's expendable.' Hicks started across the tarmac towards the smoking APC. 'Let's move it.'

Day on Acheron was dim twilight; night was darker than the farthest reaches of interstellar space, because not even the stars shone through its dense atmosphere to soften the barren surface with twinkling light. The wind howled around the battered metal buildings of Hadley town, whistling down corridors and rattling broken doors. Sand pattered against cracked windows, a perpetual snare-drum roll. Not a comforting sound to be heard. Inside, everyone waited for the nightmare to come.

Emergency power was sufficient to light Operations and its immediate environs but not much else. There the weary and demoralized survivors gathered to consider their options. Vasquez and Hudson had made one final run to the hulk that was the armoured personnel carrier. Now they set down their prize, a large, scorched, dented packing case. Several similar cases were stacked nearby.

Hicks glanced at the case and tried not to sound too disappointed. He knew what the answer to his question would be but asked it, anyhow. Maybe he was wrong.

'Any ammo?' Vasquez shook her head and slumped into an office chair.

'Everything was stored in the airspace between the APC's walls. It all went up when it caught fire.' She pulled off her sweat-soaked bandanna and wiped a forearm across her hairline. 'Man, what I wouldn't give for some soap and a hot shower.'

Hicks turned towards the table on which reposed their entire weapons inventory.

'This is it, then. Everything we could salvage.' His gaze examined the stock, wishing he could triple it by looking at it. 'We've got four pulse-rifles with about fifty rounds each. Not so good. About fifteen M-40 grenades and two flamethrowers less than half full—one damaged. And we've got four of these robot-sentry units with their scanners and display relays intact.' He approached the stack of packing cases and broke the seal on the nearest. Ripley joined him in inspecting the contents.

Stabilized in packing foam was a squat automatic weapon. Secured in a separate set of boxes next to it was matching video and movement-sensor instrumentation.

'Looks pretty efficient,' she commented.

'They are.' Hicks shut the case. 'Without them I'd say we might as well cut our wrists right now. With them, well, our chances are better than none, anyway. Trouble is we need about a hundred like this one and ten times the ammunition. But I'm grateful for small favours.' He rapped his knuckles on the hard plastic case. 'If these hadn't been packed like this, they would've gone blooey with the rest of the APC.'

'What makes you think we stand a chance, anyway?' Hudson said.

Ripley ignored him. 'How long after we're declared overdue can we expect a rescue?'

Hicks looked thoughtful. He'd been too absorbed with the problems of their immediate survival to think about the possibility of help from outside.

'We should have filed a mission update yesterday. Call it about seventeen days from tonight.'

The comtech whirled and stomped off, waving his arms disconsolately. 'Man, we're not going to make it seventeen *hours*. Those things are going to come in here just like they did before, man. They're going to come in here and get us long before anyone from Earth comes poking around to see what's left of us. And they're gonna find us, too, all sucked out and blown dry like those poor colonists we cremated down on C-level. Like Dietrich and Crowe, man.' He started to sob.

Ripley indicated the silently watching Newt. '*She* survived longer than that with no weapons and no training. The colonists didn't know what hit them. We know what to expect, and we've got more than wrenches and hammers to fight back with. We don't have to clean them out. All we have to do is survive for a couple of weeks. Just keep them away from us and stay alive.'

Hudson laughed bitterly. 'Yeah, no sweat. Just stay alive. Dietrich and Crowe are alive too.'

'We're here, we've got some armaments, and we know what's coming. So you'd better just start dealing with it. Just deal with it, Hudson. Because we need you and I'm tired of your comments.' He gaped at her, but she wasn't through.

'Now get on that central terminal and call up some kind of floor-plan file. Construction blueprints, maintenance schematics, anything that shows the layout of this place. I want to see air ducts, electrical access tunnels, subbasements, water pipes:

every possible way into this wing of the colony. I want to see the guts of this building, Hudson. If they can't reach us, they can't hurt us. They haven't ripped through these walls yet, so maybe that means they can't. This is colony Operations. We're in the most solid structure on the planet, excepting maybe the big atmosphere-processing stations. We're up off the ground, and they haven't shown any signs of being able to climb a sheer wall.'

Hudson hesitated, then straightened slightly, relieved to have something to concentrate on. Hicks nodded his approval to Ripley.

'Aye-firmative,' the comtech told her, a little of his cockiness restored. With it came a dram of confidence. 'I'm on it. You want to know where every plug is in this dump, I'll find it.' He headed for the vacant computer console. Hicks turned to the synthetic.

'You want a job or have you already got something in mind?'

Bishop looked uncertain. This was part of his social programming. An android could never be actually uncertain. 'If you require me for something specific . . .' Hicks shook his head. 'In that case I'll be in Medical. I'd like to continue my research. Perhaps I may stumble across something that will prove useful to us.'

'Fine,' Ripley told him. 'You do that.' She was watching him closely. If Bishop was conscious of this excessive scrutiny, he gave no sign of it as he turned and headed for the lab.

# X

Once Hudson had something to work on, he moved fast. Before long, Ripley, Hicks, and Burke were clustered around the comtech, peering past him at the large flat video display. It illuminated a complex series of charts and mechanical drawings. Newt hopped from one foot to the other, trying to see around the adults' bulk.

Ripley tapped the screen. 'This service tunnel has to be what they're using to move back and forth.'

Hudson studied the readout. 'Yeah, right. It runs from the processing station right into the colony maintenance sublevel, here.' He traced the route with a fingertip. 'That's how they slipped in and surprised the colonists. That's the way I'd come too.'

'All right. There's a fire door at this end. The first thing we do is put one of the remote sentries in the tunnel and seal that door.'

'That won't stop them.' Hicks's gaze roved over the plans. 'Once they've been stopped in the service tunnel, they'll find another way in. We gotta figure on them getting into the complex eventually.'

'That's right. So we put up welded barricades at these intersections'—she pointed to the schematic as she spoke—'and seal these ducts here, and here. Then they can only come at us from these two corridors, and we create a free field of fire for the other two sentry units, here.' She tapped the location, her

370

nail clicking on the hard surface of the illuminated screen. 'Of course, they can always tear the roof off, but I think that'd take them a while. By then our relief should arrive, and we'll be out of here.'

'We'd better be,' Hicks muttered. He studied the layout of Operations intently. 'Otherwise this looks outstanding. Seal the fire door in the tunnel, weld the corridors shut, then all we need is a deck of cards to pass the time.' He straightened and eyed his companions. 'All right, let's move like we got a purpose.'

Hudson half snapped to attention. 'Aye-firmative.'

Next to him Newt copied the gesture and the inflection. 'Aye-firmative.' The comtech looked down at her and smiled before he caught himself. Hopefully no one noticed the transient grin. It would ruin his reputation as an incorrigible hardcase.

Hudson grunted as he set the second heavy sentry gun onto its recoil-absorbing tripod. The weapon was squat, ugly, unencumbered by sights or triggers. Vasquez locked the weapon in place, then snapped on the connectors that led from the firing mechanism to the attached motion sensor. When she was certain the comtech was out of the way, she nudged a single switch marked ACTIVATE. A small green light came to life atop the gun. On the small diagnostic readout set flush in the side, READY flashed yellow, then red.

Both troopers stepped clear. Vasquez picked up a battered wastebasket that had rolled into the corridor and shouted towards the weapon's aural pickup. 'Testing!' Then she threw the empty metal container out into the middle of the corridor.

Both guns swivelled and let loose before the basket hit the floor, reducing the container to dime-size shrapnel. Hudson whooped with delight.

'Take that, suckers!' He lowered his voice as he turned to Vasquez, his eyes rolling. 'Oh, give me a home, where the firepower roams, and the deer and the antelope get shot to hamburger.'

'You always were the sensitive type,' Vasquez told him.

'I know. It shows in my face.' Turning, he put a shoulder against the fire door. 'Give me a hand with this.'

Vasquez helped him roll the heavy steel barrier into place. Then she unpacked the high-intensity portable welding torch she'd brought with her and snapped it alight. Blue flame roared from the muzzle. She turned a dial on the handle, refining the acetylene finger.

'Give me some room, man, or I'm liable to seal your foot to your boot.' Hudson complied, stepping back to watch her. He began to pace, staring down the empty serviceway and listening. He fingered the controls of his headset nervously.

'Hudson here.'

Hicks responded instantly. 'How're you two doing? We're working on the big air duct you located in the plans.'

'A and B sentries are in place and activated. Looks good. Nothing comes up this tunnel they can't pick out.' Vasquez's torch hissed nearby. 'We're sealing the fire door right now.'

'Roger. When you're through, get yourselves back up here.'

'Hey, you think I want a ticket for loitering?'

Hicks smiled to himself. That sounded more like the old Hudson. He nudged the tiny mike away from his lips and adjusted the thick metal plate he was carrying so that it covered the duct opening. Ripley nodded at him and shoved her plate in place. He unlimbered a duplicate of Vasquez's welder and began sealing the plate to the floor.

Behind him, Burke and Newt worked busily, stacking containers of medicine and food in a corner. The aliens hadn't touched the colony's food supplies. More importantly the water-distillation system was still functioning. Since it was self-pressurized, no power was needed to draw it from the taps. They wouldn't starve or go thirsty.

When he'd sealed down two-thirds of the plate, Hicks set the welder aside and extracted a small bracelet from a belt pouch. He flicked a tiny switch set flush with the metal, and a minuscule LED came to life as he handed the circlet to Ripley.

'What is it?'

'Emergency beeper. Military version of the PDTs the colonists had surgically implanted. Doesn't have the range they do, and you wear it outside instead of inside your body, but the idea's the same. With that on I can locate you anywhere near the complex on this.' He tapped the miniature tracker that was built into his battle harness.

She studied it curiously. 'I don't need this.'

'Hey, it's just a precaution. You know.'

She regarded him quizzically for a moment, then shrugged and slipped the bracelet over her wrist. 'Thanks. You wearing one?'

He smiled and looked away. 'Only got one tracker.' He tapped his harness. 'I know where I am. What's next?'

She forgot all about the bracelet as she consulted the hard-copy printout of Hudson's schematic.

Something very strange happened while they worked. They were too busy to notice, and it was left to Newt to point it out.

The wind had died. Stopped utterly. In the unAcheronic stillness outside the colony, a diffuse mist swirled and roiled uncertainly. In two visits to Acheron this was the first time Ripley hadn't heard the wind. It was disquieting.

The absence of wind reduced outside visibility from poor to nonexistent. Fog swirled around Operations, giving the world beyond the triple-paned windows the look of being under water. Nothing moved.

In the service tunnel that connected the buildings of the colony to the processing station and each other, a pair of robot guns sat silently, their motion scanners alert and humming. C gun surveyed the empty corridor, its ARMED light flashing green. Through a hole in the ceiling at the far end of the passageway, fog swirled in. Water condensed on bare metal walls and dripped to the floor. The gun did not fire on the falling drops. It was smarter, more selective than that, able to distinguish between harmless natural phenomena and inimical movement. The water made no attempt to advance, and so the weapon held its fire, waiting patiently for something to kill.

Newt had carried boxes until she'd worn herself out. Ripley carried her from Operations into the medical wing, the small head resting wearily on the woman's shoulder. Occasionally she would try to say something, and Ripley would reply as though she understood. She was hunting for a place where the child could rest quietly and in comparative safety.

The operating theatre was located at the far end of the medical section. Much of its complex equipment sat in recesses in the walls while the rest hung from the ceiling at the tips of extensible arms. A large globe containing lights and additional surgical instrumentation dominated the ceiling. Cabinets and equipment not fastened down had been shoved into a corner to provide room for several folding metal cots.

This was where they would sleep. This was where they would retreat to if the aliens breached the outer defences. The inner redoubt. The keep. The operating room was sealed tighter and had thicker walls than any other part of the colony complex, or so the schematics Hudson had called forth insisted. It looked a lot like an oversize, high-tech vault. If they had to shoot themselves in order to keep from falling alive into the alien's hands, this was where any future rescuers would find the bodies.

But for now it was a safe haven, snug and quiet. Gently Ripley lowered the girl to the nearest cot, smiling down at the upturned face.

'Now you just lie there and have a nap. I have to go help the others, but I'll come in every chance I get to check on you. You deserve a rest. You're exhausted.'

Newt stared up at her. 'I don't want to sleep.'

'You have to, Newt. Everybody has to sometime. You'll feel better after you've had a rest.'

'But I have scary dreams.'

It struck a familiar chord in Ripley, but she managed to feign cheerfulness. 'Everybody has bad dreams, Newt.'

The girl snuggled deeper into the padded cot. 'Not like mine.'

Don't bet on it, child, she thought. Aloud she said, 'I'll bet

Casey doesn't have bad dreams.' She disengaged the doll head from the girl's small fingers and made a show of peering inside. 'Just as I thought: Nothing bad in there. Maybe you could try to be like Casey. Pretend there's nothing in here.' She tapped the girl's forehead, and Newt smiled back.

'You mean, try to make it all empty-like?'

'Yes, empty-like. Like Casey.' She caressed the delicate face, brushing hair back from Newt's forehead. 'If you do that, I'll bet you'll be able to sleep without having any bad dreams.'

She closed the doll head's unblinking eyes and handed it back to its owner. Newt took it, rolling her own eyes as if to say, 'Don't pull that five-year-old stuff on me, lady. I'm six.'

'Ripley, she doesn't have bad dreams, because she's just a piece of plastic.'

'Oh. Sorry, Newt. Well, then, maybe you could pretend you're like her that way. Just made of plastic.'

The girl almost smiled. Almost. 'I'll try.'

'Good girl. Maybe I'll try it myself.'

Newt pulled Casey close up to her neck, looking thoughtful. 'My mommy always said there were no such things as monsters. No real ones. But there *are*.'

Ripley continued to brush isolated strands of blonde hair back from the pale forehead. 'Yes, there are, aren't there?'

'They're as real as you and me. They're not make-believe, and they didn't come out of a book. They're really real, not fake-real like the ones I used to watch on the video. Why do they tell little kids things like that, things that aren't true?' There was a faint tinge of betrayal in her voice.

No lying to this child, Ripley knew. Not that she had the slightest intention of doing so. Newt had experienced too much reality to be fooled by a simple fib. Ripley instinctively sensed that to lie to this girl would be to lose her trust forever.

'Well, some kids can't handle it like you can. The truth, I mean. They're too scared, or their grown-ups think they'll be too scared. Grown-ups have a way of always underestimating little kids' ability to handle the truth. So they try to make things easier for them by making things up.'

'About the monsters. Did one of those things grow inside mommy?'

Ripley found some blankets and began pulling them up around the small body, tucking them tightly around narrow ribs. 'I don't know, Newt. Neither does anybody else. That's the truth. I don't think anybody will ever know.'

The girl considered. 'Isn't that how babies come? I mean, people babies. They grow inside you?'

A chill went down Ripley's spine. 'No, not like that, not like that at all. It's different with people, honey. The way it gets started is different, and the way the baby comes is different. With people the baby and the mother work together. With these aliens the—'

'I understand,' Newt said, interrupting. 'Did you ever have a baby?'

'Yes.' She pushed the blanket up under the child's chin. 'Just once. A little girl.'

'Where is she? Back on Earth?'

'No. She's gone.'

'You mean, dead.'

It wasn't a question. Ripley nodded slowly, trying to remember a small female thing not unlike Newt running and playing, a miracle with dark curls bouncing around her face. Trying to reconcile that memory with the picture of an older woman briefly glimpsed, child and mature lady linked together through time overspent in the stasis of hypersleep. The child's father was a more distant memory still. So much of a life lost and forgotten. Youthful love marred by a lack of common sense, a brief flare of happiness smothered by reality. Divorce. Hypersleep. Time.

She turned away from the bed and reached for a portable space heater. While it wasn't uncomfortable in the operating theatre, it would be more comfortable with the heater on. It looked like a slab of plastic, but when she thumbed the 'on' switch, it emitted a whirr and a faint glow as its integral warming elements came to life. As the heat spread, the operating room became a little less sterile, a shade cosier. Newt blinked sleepily.

'Ripley, I was thinking. Maybe I could do you a favour and fill in for her. Your little girl, I mean. Nothing permanent. Just for a while. You can try it, and if you don't like it, it's okay. I'll understand. No big deal. Whattaya think?'

It took what little remained of Ripley's determination and self-control not to break down in front of the child. She settled for hugging her tightly. She also knew that neither of them might see the light of another dawn. That she might have to turn Newt's face away during a very possible apocalyptic last moment and put the muzzle of a pulse-rifle to those blonde tresses.

'I think it's not the worst idea I've heard all day. Let's talk about it later, okay?'

'Okay.' A shy, hopeful smile.

Ripley switched off the room light and started to rise. A small hand grabbed her arm with desperate force.

'Don't go! Please.'

With great reluctance Ripley disengaged her arm from Newt's grip. 'It'll be all right. I'll be in the other room, right next door. I'm not going to go anywhere else. And don't forget that that's there.' She indicated the miniature video pickup that was imbedded over the doorway. 'You know what that is, don't you?' A small nod in the darkness.

'Uh-huh. It's a securcam.'

'That's right. See, the green light's on. Mr. Hicks and Mr. Hudson checked out all the securcams in this area to make sure all of them were operating properly. It's watching you, and I'll be watching its monitor over in the other room. I'll be able to see you just as clearly in there as I can when I'm right here.'

When Newt still seemed to hesitate, Ripley unsnapped the tracer bracelet Hicks had given her. She slipped it around the girl's smaller wrist, clinching it tight.

'Here. This is for luck. It'll help me keep an eye on you too. Now go to sleep—and don't dream. Okay?'

'I'll try.' The sound of a small body sliding down between clean sheets.

Ripley watched in the dim light from the instruments on standby as the girl turned onto her side, hugging the doll head and gazing through half-lidded eyes at the steadily glowing function light imbedded in the bracelet. The space heater hummed comfortingly as she backed out of the room.

Other half-opened eyes were twitching erratically back and forth. They were the only visible evidence that Lieutenant Gorman was still alive. It was an improvement of sorts. One step further from complete paralysis.

Ripley leaned over the table on which the lieutenant was lying, studying the eye movements and wondering if he could recognize her. 'How is he? I see he's got his eyes open.'

'That might be enough to wear him out.' Bishop looked up from a nearby workbench. He was surrounded by instruments and shining medical equipment. The light of the single high-intensity lamp he was working with threw his features into sharp relief, giving his face a macabre cast.

'Is he in pain?'

'Not according to his bioreadouts. They're hardly conclusive, of course. I'm sure he'll let us know as soon as he regains the use of his larynx. By the way, I've isolated the poison. Interesting stuff. It's a muscle-specific neurotoxin. Affects only the nonvital parts of the system; leaves respiratory and circulatory functions unimpaired. I wonder if the creatures instinctively adjust the dosage for different kinds of potential hosts?'

'I'll ask one of them first chance I get.' As she stared, one eyelid rose all the way before fluttering back down again. 'Either that was an involuntary twitch or else he winked at me. Is he getting better?'

Bishop nodded. 'The toxin seems to be metabolizing. It's powerful, but the body appears capable of breaking it down. It's starting to show up in his urine. Amazing mechanism, the human body. Adaptable. If he continues to flush the poison at a constant rate, he should wake up soon.'

'Let me get this straight, The aliens paralysed the colonists they didn't kill, carried them over to the processing station, and cocooned them to serve as hosts for more of those.' She pointed into the back room where the stasis cylinders held the remaining facehugger specimens.

'Which would mean lots of those parasites, right? One for each colonist. Over a hundred, at least, assuming a mortality rate during the final fight of about a third.'

'Yes, that follows,' Bishop readily agreed.

'But these things, the parasitic facehugger form, come from eggs. So where are all the eggs coming from? When the guy who first found the alien ship reported back to us, he said their were a lot of eggs inside, but he never said how many, and nobody else ever went in after him to look. And not all those eggs may have been viable.

'The thing is, judging from the way the colony here was overwhelmed, I don't think the first aliens had time to haul eggs from that ship back here. That means they had to come from somewhere else.'

'That is the question of the hour.' Bishop swivelled his chair to face her. 'I have been pondering it ceaselessly since the true nature of the disaster here first became apparent to us.'

'Any ideas, bright or otherwise?'

'Without additional solid evidence it is nothing more than a supposition.'

'Go ahead and suppose, then.'

'We could assume a parallel to certain insect forms who have a hivelike organization. An ant or termite colony, for example, is ruled by a single female, a queen, who is the source of new eggs.'

Ripley frowned. Interstellar navigation to entomology was a mental jump she wasn't prepared to make. 'Don't insect queens come from eggs also?'

The synthetic nodded. 'Absolutely.'

'What if there was no queen egg aboard the ship that brought these things here?'

'There's no such thing in a social insect society as a "queen egg," until the workers decide to create one. Ants, bees, termites, all employ essentially the same method. They select an ordinary egg and feed the pupa developing inside a special food high in certain nutrients. Among bees, for example, it is called royal jelly. The chemicals in the jelly act to change the composition of the maturing pupa so that what eventually emerges is an adult queen and not another worker. Theoretically any egg can be used to hatch a queen. Why the insects choose the particular eggs they do is something we still do not know.'

'You're saying that one of those things lays *all* the eggs?'

'Well, not exactly like one we're familiar with. Only if the insect analogy holds up. Assuming it does, there could be other similarities. An alien queen analogous to an ant or termite queen could be much larger physically than the aliens we have so far encountered. A termite queen's abdomen is so bloated with eggs that she can't move by herself at all. She is fed and tended by workers, mated to drones, and defended by highly specialized warriors. She is also quite harmless. On the other hand, a queen bee is far more dangerous than any worker bee because she can sting many times. She is the centre of their lives, quite literally the mother of their society.

'In one respect, at least, we are fortunate that the analogy does not hold up. Ants and bees develop from eggs directly to larvae, pupae, and adults. Each alien embryo requires a live host in which to mature. Otherwise Acheron would be covered with them by now.'

'Funny, but that doesn't reassure me a whole lot. These things are a lot bigger than any ant or termite. Could they be intelligent? Could this hypothetical queen? That's something we never could decide on back on the *Nostromo*. We were too busy trying to keep from getting killed. Not much time for speculation.'

'It's hard to say.' Bishop looked thoughtful. 'There is one thing worth considering, though.'

'What's that?'

'It may have been nothing more than blind instinct, attraction to the heat or whatever, but she did choose, assuming she exists, to incubate her eggs in the one spot in the colony where we couldn't destroy her without destroying ourselves. Beneath the heat exchangers at the processing plant. If that site was chosen from instinct, it means that they may be no brighter than your average termite. If, on the other hand, it was selected on the basis of intelligence, well, then I think we're in very deep trouble indeed.

'That's *if* there's any reality to these suppositions at all. Despite the distance involved, the eggs these aliens hatched from might have been brought down here by the first ones to emerge. There might be no queen involved at all, no complex alien society. Whether by intelligence or instinct, though, we have seen that they cooperate. That's something we don't have to speculate on. We've seen them in action.'

Ripley stood there and considered the ramifications of Bishop's analysis. None of them were encouraging, nor had she expected any to be. She nodded towards the stasis cylinders.

'I want those specimens destroyed as soon as you're done with them. You understand?'

The android glanced towards the two live facehuggers pulsing malevolently in their tubular prisons. He looked unhappy. 'Mr. Burke gave instructions that they were to be kept alive in stasis for return to the Company laboratories. He was very specific.'

The wonder of it was that she went for the intercom instead of the nearest weapon. 'Burke!'

A faint whisper of static failed to mar his reply. 'Yes? That's you, isn't it, Ripley?'

'You bet it's me! Where are you?'

'Scavenging while there's still time. I thought I might learn something on my own, since I just seem to be in everybody's way up there.'

'Meet me in the lab.'

'Now? But I'm still—'

'Now!' She closed the connection and glared at the inoffensive Bishop. 'You come with me.' Obediently he put his work aside and rose to follow her. That was all she was after; to make sure that he'd obey an order if she gave it. It meant he wasn't completely under Burke's sway, Company machine or no Company machine. 'Never mind, forget it.'

'I shall be happy to accompany you if that is what you wish.'

'That's all right. I've decided to handle it on my own. You continue with your research. That's more important than anything else.'

He nodded, looking puzzled, and resumed his seat.

Burke was waiting for her outside the entrance to the lab. His expression was bland. 'This better be important. I think I was onto something, and we may not have much time left.'

'You may not have *any* time left.' He started to protest, and she cut him off with a gesture. 'No, in there.' She gestured at the operating theatre. It ws soundproofed inside, and she could scream at him to her heart's content without drawing everyone else's attention. Burke ought to be grateful for her thoughtfulness. If Vasquez overheard what the Company representative had been planning, she wouldn't waste time arguing with him. She'd put a bullet through him on the spot.

'Bishop tells me you have intentions of taking the live parasites home in your pocket. That true?'

He didn't try to deny it. 'They're harmless in stasis.'

'Those suckers aren't harmless unless they're dead. Don't you understand that yet? I want them killed as soon as Bishop's gotten everything out of them he can.'

'Be reasonable, Ripley.' A ghost of the old, self-assured corporate smile stole over Burke's face. 'Those specimens are worth millions to the Bioweapons Division of the Company. Okay, so we nuke the colony. I'm outvoted on that one. But not on this. Two lousy specimens, Ripley. How much trouble could they cause while secured in stasis? And if you're worried about something happening when we get them back to Earthside labs, don't. We have people who know how to handle things like these.'

'Nobody knows how to handle "things like these." Nobody's ever encountered anything like them. You think it'd be dangerous for some germs to get loose from a weapons lab? Try to imagine what would happen if just one of those parasites got loose in a major city, with its thousands of kilometres of sewers and pipes and glass-fibre channels to hide in.'

'They're not going to get loose. Nothing can break a stasis field.'

'No sale, Burke. There's too much we don't know about these monsters. It's too risky.'

'Come on, I know you're smarter than this.' He was trying to mollify and persuade her at the same time. 'If we play it right, we can both come out of this heroes. Set up for life.'

'Is that the way you really see it?' She eyed him askance. 'Carter Burke, alien smasher? Didn't what happened in C-level of the processing station make any impression on you at all?'

'They went in unprepared and overconfident.' Burke's tone was flat, unemotional. 'They got caught in tight quarters where they couldn't use the proper tactics and weapons. If they'd all used their pulse-rifles and kept their heads and managed to get out without shooting up the heat exchangers, they'd all be here now and we'd be on our way back to the *Sulaco* instead of holed up in Operations like a bunch of frightened rabbits. Sending them in like that was Gorman's decision, not mine. And besides, those were adult aliens they were fighting, not parasites.'

'I didn't hear you object loudly when strategy was being discussed.'

'Who would've listened to me? Don't you remember what Hicks said? What you said? Gorman wouldn't have been any different.' His tone turned sarcastic. 'This is a *military* expedition.'

'Forget the whole idea, Burke. You couldn't pull it off even if

I let you. Just try getting a dangerous organism past ICC quarantine. Section 22350 of the Commerce Code.'

'You've been doing your homework. That's what the code says, all right. But you're forgetting one thing. The code's nothing but words on paper. Paper never stopped a determined man. If I have five minutes alone with the customs inspector on duty when we turn through Gateway Station, we'll get them through. Leave that end of it to me. The ICC can't impound something they don't know anything about.'

'But they *will* know about it, Burke.'

'How? First they'll want to talk to us, then they'll make us walk through a detection tunnel. Big deal. By the time the relief team gets around to inspecting our luggage, I'll have made the necessary arrangements with ship's personnel to set up the stasis tubes somewhere down near the engine or waste-products recycling. We'll pick them up and slip them off the relief ship the same way. Everyone'll be so busy shooting questions at us, they'll have no time for checking cargo.

'Besides, everyone will know we found a devastated colony and that we got out as fast as we could. No one will be looking for us to smuggle anything back in. The Company will back me up on this, Ripley, especially when they see what we've brought them. They'll take good care of you, too, if that's what you're worrying about.'

'I'm sure they'll back you up,' she said. 'I don't doubt that for an instant. Any outfit that would send less than a dozen soldiers out here with an inexperienced goofball like Gorman in charge after hearing my story is capable of anything.'

'You worry too much.'

'Sorry. I like living. I don't like the idea of waking up some morning with an alien monstrosity exploding out of my chest.'

'That's not going to happen.'

'You bet it isn't. Because if you try taking those ugly little teratoids out of here, I'll tell everyone on the rescue ship what you're up to. This time I think people will listen to me. Not that it would ever get that far. All I have to do is tell Vasquez, or

Hicks, or Hudson what you have in mind. They won't wait around for a directive, and they'll use more than angry words. So you might as well give it up, Burke.' She nodded in the direction of the cylinders. 'You're not getting them out of this lab, much less off the surface of this planet.'

'Suppose I can convince the others?'

'You can't, but supposing for a minute that you could, how would you go about convincing them that you're not responsible for the deaths of the one hundred and fifty-seven colonists here?'

Burke's combativeness drained away and he turned pale. 'Now wait a second. What are you talking about?'

'You heard me. The colonists. All those poor, unsuspecting good Company people. Like Newt's family. You said I'd been doing my homework, remember? *You* sent them to that ship, to check out the alien derelict. I just checked it out in the colony log. It's as intact as the plans Hudson called up. Would make interesting reading in court. "Company Directive Six Twelve Nine, dated five thirteen seventy-nine. Proceed to inspect possible electromagnetic emission at coordinates—but I'm not telling you anything you don't already know, am I? Signed Burke, Carter J." ' She was trembling with anger. It was all spilling out of her at once, the frustration and fury at the incompetence and greed that had brought her back to this world of horror.

'You sent them out there, and you didn't even warn them, Burke. You sat through the inquest. You heard my story. Even if you didn't believe everything, you must have believed enough of it to want the coordinates checked out. You must have thought there was something to it or you wouldn't have gone to the trouble of having anyone go out there to look around. Out to the alien ship. You might not have believed, but you suspected. You wondered. Fine. Have it checked out. But checked out carefully by a fully equipped team, not some independent prospector. And warn them of what you suspected. Why didn't you warn them, Burke?'

'Warn them about what?' he protested. He'd heard only her words, hadn't sensed the moral outrage in her voice. That in itself explained a great deal. She was coming to understand Carter J. Burke quite well.

'Look, maybe the thing didn't even exist, right? Maybe there wasn't much to it. All we had to go on was your story, which was a bit much to take at face value.'

'Was it? The *Narcissus*'s recorder was tampered with, Burke. Remember me telling the board of inquiry about that? You wouldn't happen to know what happened to the recorder, would you?'

He ignored the question. 'What do you think would've happened if I'd stuck my neck out and made it into a major security situation?'

'I don't know,' she said tightly. 'Enlighten me.'

'Colonial Administration would've stepped in. That means government officials looking over your shoulder at every turn, paperwork coming out your ears, no freedom of movement at all. Inspectors crawling all over the place looking for an excuse to shut you down and take over in the name of the almighty public interest. No exclusive development rights, nothing. The fact that your story turned out to be right is as much a surprise to me as everyone else.' He shrugged, his manner as blasé as ever. 'It was a bad call, that's all.'

Something finally snapped inside Ripley. Surprising both of them, she grabbed him by the collar and slammed him against the wall.

'*Bad call*? These people are *dead*, Burke! One hundred and fifty-seven of them less one kid, all dead because of your "bad call." That's not counting Apone and the others torn apart or paralysed over there.' She jerked her head in the direction of the processing station.

'Well, they're going to nail your hide to the shed, and I'll be standing there helping to pass out the nails when they do. That's assuming your "bad call" lets any of us get off this chunk of gravel alive. Think about that for a while.' She stepped away from him, shaking with anger.

At least the aliens' motivations were comprehensible.

Burke straightened his back and his shirt, pity in his voice. 'You just can't see the big picture, can you? Your worldview is restricted exclusively to the here and now. You've no interest in what your life could be like tomorrow.'

'Not if it includes you, I don't.'

'I expected more of you, Ripley. I thought you would be smarter than this. I thought I'd be able to count on you when the time came to make the critical decisions.'

'Another bad call on your part, Burke. Sorry to disappoint you.' She spun on her heel and abandoned the observation room, the door closing behind her. Burke followed her with his eyes, his mind a whirl of options.

Breathing hard, she strode towards Operations as the alarm began to sound. It helped to take her mind off the confrontation with Burke. She broke into a run.

# XI

Hudson had the portable tactical console set up next to the colony's main computer terminal. Wires trailed from the console to the computer, a rat's nest of connections that enabled whoever sat behind the tactical board to interface with the colony's remaining functional instrumentation. Hicks looked up as Ripley entered Operations and slapped a switch to kill the alarm. Vasquez and Hudson joined her in clustering around the console.

'They're coming,' he informed them quietly. 'Just thought you'd like to know. They're in the tunnel already.'

Ripley licked her lips as she stared at the console readouts. 'Are we ready for them?'

The corporal shrugged, adjusted a gain control. 'Ready as we can be. Assuming everything we've set up works. Manufacturers' warranties aren't going to be a lot of use to us if something shorts out when it's supposed to be firing, like those sentry guns. They're about all we've got.'

'Don't worry, man, they'll work.' Hudson looked better than at any time since the initial assault on the processing station's lower levels. 'I've set up hundreds of those suckers. Once the ready lights come on, you can leave 'em and forget 'em. I just don't know if they'll be enough.'

'No use worrying about it. We're throwing everything we've got left at them. Either the RSS guns'll stop them or they won't. Depends on how many of them there are.' Hicks thumbed a couple of contact switches. Everything read out on-line and operational. He glanced at the readouts for the motion sensors mounted on A and B guns. They were blinking rapidly, the strobe speeding up until both lights shone steadily. At the same time a crash of heavy gunfire made the floor quiver slightly.

'Guns A and B. Tracking and firing on multiple targets.' He looked up at Hudson. 'You give good firepower.'

The comtech ignored Hicks, watching the multiple readouts. 'Another dozen guns,' he muttered under his breath. 'That's all it would take. If we had another dozen guns . . .'

A steady rumble echoed through the complex as the automatic weapons pounded away beneath them. Twin ammo counters on the console shrank inexorably towards single digits.

'Fifty rounds per gun. How are we going to stop them with only fifty rounds per gun?' Hicks murmured.

'They must all be wall-to-wall down there.' Hudson gestured at the readouts. 'Look at those ammo counters go. It's a shooting gallery down there.'

'What about the acid?' Ripley wondered. 'I know those guns are armoured, but you've seen that stuff at work. It'll eat through anything.'

'As long as the guns keep firing, they ought to be okay,' Hicks told her. 'Those RSS shells have a lot of impact. If it keeps blowing them backward, that'll keep the acid away. It'll spray all over the walls and floor, but the guns should stay clear.'

That certainly seemed to be what was happening in the service tunnel because the robot sentries kept up their steady barrage. Two minutes went by; three. The counter on B gun reached zero, and the thunder below was reduced by half. Its motion sensor continued to flicker on the tactical readout as the empty weapon tracked targets it could no longer fire upon.

'B gun's dry. Twenty left on A.' Hicks watched the counter, his throat dry. 'Ten. Five. That's it.'

A grim silence descended over Operations. It was shattered by a reverberating boom from below. It was repeated at regular intervals like the thunder of a massive gong. Each of them knew what the sound meant.

'They're at the fire door,' Ripley muttered. The booming increased in strength and ferocity. Audible along with the deeper rumble was another new sound: the nerve-racking scrape of claws on steel.

'Think they can break through there?' Ripley thought Hicks looked remarkably calm. Assurance—or resignation?

'One of them ripped a hatch right off the APC when it tried to pull Gorman out, remember?' she reminded him.

Vasquez nodded towards the floor. 'That ain't no hatch down there. It's a Class double-A fire door, three layers of steel alloy with carbon-fibre composite laid between. The door will hold. It's the welds I'm worried about. We didn't have much time. I'd feel better if I'd had a couple bars of chromite solder and a laser instead of a gas torch to work with.'

'And another hour,' Hudson added. 'Why don't you wish for a couple of Katusha Six antipersonnel rockets while you're at it. One of those babies would clean out the whole tunnel.'

The intercom buzzed for attention, startling them. Hicks clicked it on.

'Bishop here. I heard the guns. How are we doing?'

'As well as can be expected. A and B sentries are out of ammo, but they must've done some damage.'

'That's good, because I'm afraid I have some bad news.'

Hudson made a face and leaned back against a cabinet. 'Well, now, that's a switch.'

'What kind of bad news?' Hicks inquired.

'It will be easier to explain and show you at the same time. I'll be right over.'

'We'll be here.' Hicks flipped the intercom off. 'Charming.'

'Hey, no sweat,' said the jaunty comtech. 'We're already in the toilet, so why worry?'

The android arrived quickly and moved to the single high window that overlooked much of the colony complex. The wind had picked back up and blown off the clinging fog.

Visibility was still far from perfect, but it was sufficient to permit them a glimpse of the distant atmosphere-processing station. As they stared, a column of flame unexpectedly jetted skyward from the base of the station. For an instant it was brighter than the steady glow that emanated from the top of the cone itself.

'What was that?' Hudson pressed his face closer to the glass.

'Emergency venting,' Bishop informed him.

Ripley was standing close to the comtech. 'Can the construction contain the overload?'

'Not a chance. Not if the figures I've been monitoring are half accurate, and I have no reason to suppose that they are anything other than completely accurate.'

'What happened?' Hicks spoke as he walked back to the tactical console. 'Did the aliens cause that, monkeying around inside?'

'There's no way to tell. Perhaps. More likely someone hit something vital with a smartgun shell or a blast from a pulse-rifle during the fight on C-level. Or the damage might have been done when the dropship smashed into the base of the complex. The cause is of no import. All that matters is the result, which is not good.'

Ripley started to tap her fingers on the window, thought better of it, and brought her hand back to her side. There might be something out there listening. As she stared, another gush of superheated gas flared from the base of the processing station.

'How long before it blows?'

'There's no way to be sure. One can extrapolate from the available figures but without any degree of certainty. There are too many variables involved that can only be roughly compensated for, and the requisite calculations are complex.'

'How long?' Hicks asked patiently.

The android turned to him. 'Based on the information I've been able to gather, I'm projecting total sysems failure in a little under four hours. The blast radius will be about thirty kilometres. It will be nice and clean. No fallout, of course. About ten megatons.'

'That's very reassuring,' said Hudson dryly.

Hicks sucked air. 'We got problems.'

The comtech unfolded his arms and turned away from his companions. 'I don't believe this,' he said disconsolately. 'Do you believe this? The RSS guns blow a pack of them to bits, the fire door's still holding, and it's all a waste!'

'It's too late to shut the station down? Assuming the instrumentation necessary to do it is still operational?' Ripley stared at the android. 'Not that I'm looking forward to jogging across the tarmac, but if that's the only chance we've got, I'll take a shot at it.'

He smiled regretfully. 'Save your legs. I'm afraid it's too late. The dropship impact, or the guns, or whatever, did too much damage. At this point overload is inevitable.'

'Terrific. So what's the recommended procedure now?'

Vasquez grinned at her. 'Bend over, put your head between your legs, and kiss your ass goodbye.'

Hudson was pacing the floor like a caged cat. 'Oh, man. And I was getting short too! Four more weeks and out. Three of that in hypersleep. Early retirement. Ten years in the Marines and you're out and sitting pretty, they said. Recruiters. Now I'm gonna buy it on this rock. It ain't fair, man!'

Vasquez looked bored. 'Give us a break, Hudson.'

He spun on her. 'That's easy for you to say, Vasquez. You're a lifer. You love mucking around on these alien dirt-balls so you can blow away anything that sticks up bug eyes. Me, I joined for the pension. Ten years and out, take the credit, and buy into a little bar somewhere, hire somebody else to run the joint so I can kick back and jabchat with the customers while the money rolls in.'

The smartgun operator looked back towards the window as another gas jet lit up the mist-shrouded landscape. Her expression was hard. 'You're breaking my heart. Go cross a wire or something.'

'It's simple.' Ripley looked over at Hicks. 'We can't stay here, so we've got to get away. There's only one way to do that. We need the other dropship. The one that's still on the *Sulaco*. Somehow we have to bring it down on remote. There's got to be a way to do that.'

'There *was*. You think I haven't been thinking about that ever since Ferro rolled ours into the station?' Hudson stopped pacing. 'You use a narrow-beam transmitter tuned just for the dropship's controls.'

'I know,' she said impatiently. 'I thought about that, too, but we can't do it that way.'

'Right. The transmitter was on the APC. It's wasted.'

'There's got to be another way to bring that shuttle down, I don't care how. Think of a way. You're the comtech. Think of something.'

'Think of what? We're dead.'

'You can do better than that, Hudson. What about the colony's transmitter? That uplink tower down at the other end of the complex? We could programme it to send that dropship a control frequency. Why can't we use that? It looked like it was intact.'

'The thought had occurred to me earlier.' All eyes turned toward Bishop. 'I've already checked it out. The hardwiring between here and the tower was severed in the fighting between the colonists and the aliens—one more reason why they were unable to communicate with the relay satellite overhead, even if only to leave a warning for anyone who might come to check on them.'

Ripley's mind was spinning like a dynamo, exploring options, considering and disregarding possible solutions until only one was left. 'So what you're saying is that the transmitter itself is still functional but that it can't be utilized from here?'

The android looked thoughtful, finally nodded. 'If it is receiving its share of emergency power, then yes, I don't see why it wouldn't be capable of sending the requisite signals. A lot of power would not be necessary, since all the other channels it would normally be broadcasting are dead.'

'That's it, then.' She scanned her companions' faces. 'Somebody's just going to have to go out there. Take a portable terminal and go out there and plug in manually.'

'Oh, right, right!' said Hudson with mock enthusiasm. 'With those things running around. No way.'

Bishop took a step forward. 'I'll go.' Quiet, matter of fact. As though there was no alternative.'

Ripley gaped at him. 'What?'

He smiled apologetically. 'I'm really the only one present who is qualified to remote-pilot a dropship, anyway. And the outside weather won't bother me the way it would the rest of you. Nor will I be subject to quite the same degree of . . . mental distractions. I'll be able to concentrate on the job.'

'If you aren't accosted by any passing pedestrians,' Ripley pointed out.

'Yes, I will be fine if I am not interrupted.' His smile widened. 'Believe me, I'd prefer not to have to attempt this. I may be synthetic, but I'm not stupid. As nuclear incineration is the sole alternative, however, I am willing to give it a try.'

'All right. Let's get on it. What'll you need?'

'The portable transmitter, of course. And we'll need to check to make sure the antenna is still drawing power. Since we're making an extra-atmospheric broadcast on a narrow beam, the transmitter will have to be realigned as precisely as possible. I will also need some—'

Vasquez interrupted sharply. 'Listen!'

'To what?' Hudson turned a slow circle. 'I don't hear anything.'

'Exactly. It's stopped.'

The smartgun operator was right. The booming and scratching at the fire door had ceased. As they listened, the silence was broken by the high-pitched trill of a motion-sensor alarm. Hicks looked at the tactical console.

'They're into the complex.'

It didn't take long to get together the equipment Bishop

needed. Finding a safe way out for him was another matter entirely. They debated possible exit routes, mixing information from the colony computer with suggestions from the tactical console, and spicing the results with their own heated personal opinions. The result was a consensual route that was the best of an unpromising bunch.

It was presented to Bishop. Android or not, he had that final say. Along with a multitude of other human emotions the new synthetics were also fully programmed for self-preservation. Or as Bishop ventured when the discussion of possible escape paths grew too heated, on the whole he would rather have been in Philadelphia.

There was little to argue about. Everyone agreed that the route selected was the only one that offered half a chance for him to slip out of Operations without drawing unwelcome attention. An uncomfortable silence ensued once this course was agreed upon, until Bishop was ready to depart.

One of the acid holes that was part of the colonists' losing battle with the aliens had formed a suitable gap in the floor of the medical lab. The hole offered access to the maze of subfloor conduits and serviceways. Some of these had been added subsequent to the colony's original construction and tacked on as required by Hadley's industrious inhabitants. It was one of these additions that Bishop was preparing to enter.

The android lowered himself through the opening, sliding and twisting until he was lying on his back, looking up at the others.

'How is it?' Hicks asked him.

Bishop looked back between his feet, then arched his neck to stare straight ahead. The chosen path. 'Dark. Empty. Tight, but I guess I can make it.'

You'd better, Ripley mused silently. 'Ready for the terminal?'

A pair of hands lifted, as if in supplication. 'Pass it down.' She handed him the heavy, compact device.

Turning with an effort, he shoved it into the constricted shaft ahead of him. Fortunately the instrument was sheathed in protective plastic. It would make some noise as it was pushed along the conduit but not as much as metal scraping on metal. He turned on his back and raised his hands a second time.

'Let's have the rest.'

Ripley passed him a small satchel. It contained tools, patch cables and replacement circuit boards, energy bypasses, a service pistol, and a small cutting torch, together with fuel for same. More weight and bulk, but it couldn't be helped. Better to take a little more time reaching the uplink tower than to arrive short of some necessary item.

'You're sure about which way you're going?' Ripley asked him.

'If the updated colony schematic is correct, yes. This duct runs almost out to the uplink assembly. One hundred eighty metres. Say, forty minutes to crawl down there. It would be easier on treads or wheels, but my designers had to go and get sentimental. They gave me legs.' No one laughed.

'After I get there, one hour to patch in and align the antenna. If I get an immediate response, thirty minutes to prep the ship, then about fifty minutes' flight time.'

'Why so long?' Hicks asked him.

'With a pilot on board the dropship it would take half that, but remote-piloting from a portable terminal's going to be damn tricky. The last thing I want to do is rush the descent and maybe lose contact or control. I need the extra time to bring her in slow. Otherwise she's liable to end up like her sister ship.'

Ripley checked her chronometer. 'It's going to be close. You'd better get going.'

'Right. See you soon.' His farewell was full of forced cheerfulness. Entirely for their benefit, Ripley knew. No reason to let it get to her. He was only a synthetic, a near-machine.

She turned away from the hole as Vasquez slid a metal plate over the opening and began spot-welding it in place. There wasn't any maybe about what Bishop had to do. If he failed, they wouldn't have to worry about holding off the aliens. The bonfire that was slowly being ignited inside the processing station would finish them all.

Bishop lay on his back, watching the glow from Vasquez's welder transcribe a circle over his head. It was pretty, and he was sophisticated enough to appreciate beauty, but he was wasting time enjoying it. He rolled onto his belly and began squirming forward, pushing the terminal and the sack of equipment ahead of him. Push, squirm, push, squirm: slow going. The conduit was barely wide enough for his shoulders. Fortunately he was not subject to claustrophobia, any more than he suffered from vertigo or any of the other mental ills mankind was heir to. There was much to be said for artificial intelligence.

In front of him the conduit dwindled towards infinity. This is how a bullet must feel, he mused, lodged in the barrel of a gun. Except that a bullet wasn't burdened with feelings and he was. But only because they'd been programmed into him.

The darkness and loneliness gave him plenty of time for thinking. Moving forward didn't require much mental effort, so he was able to spend the rest considering his condition.

Feelings and programming. Organic tantrums or byte snits? Was there in the last analysis that much difference beween himself and Ripley or, for that matter, any of the other humans? Beyond the fact that he was a pacifist and most of them were warlike, of course. How did a human being acquire its feelings?

Slow programming. A human infant came into the world already preprogrammed by instinct but could be radically reprogrammed by environment, companions, education, and a host of other factors. Bishop knew that his own programming was not affected by environment. What had happened to his earlier relative, then, the one that had gone berserk and caused Ripley to hate him so? A breakdown in programming—or a deliberate bit of malicious reprogramming by some still unidentified human? Why would a human do such a thing?

No matter how sophisticated his own programming or how

much he learned during his allotted term of existence, Bishop knew that the species that had created him would remain forever shrouded in mystery. To a synthetic mankind would always be an enigma, albeit an entertaining and resourceful one.

In contrast to his companions there was nothing mysterious about the aliens. No incomprehensible mysteries to ponder, no double meanings to unravel. You could readily predict how they would act in a given situation. Moreover, a dozen aliens would likely react in the same fashion, whereas a dozen humans might do a dozen completely different and unrelated things, at least half of them illogical. But then, humans were not members of a hive society. At least they chose not to think of themselves as such. Bishop still wasn't sure he agreed.

Not all that much difference between human, alien, and android. All hive cultures. The difference was that the human hive was ruled by chaos brought about by this peculiar thing called individuality. They'd programmed him with it. As a result he was part human. An honorary organic. In some repects he was better than a human being, in others, less. He felt best of all when they acted as though he were one of them.

He checked his chronometer. He'd have to crawl faster or he'd never make it in time.

The robot guns guarding the entrance to Operations opened up, their metallic clatter ringing along the corridors. Ripley picked up her flamethrower and headed for computer central. Vasquez finished welding the floor plate that blocked Bishop's rabbit hole into place with a flourish, put the torch aside, and followed the other woman.

Hicks was staring at the tactical console, mesmerized by the images the video pickups atop the guns were displaying. He barely glanced up long enough to beckon to the two arrivals.

'Have a look at this,' he said quietly.

Ripley forced herself to look. Somehow the fact that they were distant two-dimensional images instead of an immediate reality made it easier. Each time a gun fired, the brief flare from the weapon's muzzle whited out the video, but they could still see clearly enough and often enough to watch the alien horde as it pushed and stumbled up the corridor. Each time one was struck by an RSS shell, the chitinous body would explode, spraying acid blood in all directions. The gaping holes and gouges in the floor and walls stood out sharply. The only thing the acid didn't chew through was other aliens.

Tracer fire lit the swirling mist that poured into the corridor from jagged gashes in the walls as the automatic weapons continued to hammer away at the invaders.

'Twenty metres and closing.' Hicks's attention was drawn to the numerical readouts. 'Fifteen. C and D guns down about fifty per cent.' Ripley checked the safety on her flamethrower to make sure it was off. Vasquez didn't need to check her pulse-rifle. It was part of her.

The readouts flickered steadily. Between the bursts of fire a shrill, inhuman screeching was clearly audible.

'How many?' Ripley asked.

'Can't tell. Lots. Hard to tell how many of them are alive and which are down. They lose arms and legs and keep coming until the guns hit them square.' Hudson's gaze flicked to another readout. 'D gun's down to twenty rounds. Ten.' He swallowed. 'It's out.'

Abruptly all firing ceased as the remaining gun ran out of shells. Smoke and mist obscured the double pickup view from below. Small fires burned where tracers had set flammable material ablaze in the corridor. The floor was littered with twisted and blackened corpses, a biomechanical bone-yard. As they stared at the monitors several bodies collapsed and disappeared as the acid leaking from their limbs chewed a monstrous hole in the floor.

Nothing lunged from the clinging pall of smoke to rip the silent weapons from their mounts. The motion-sensor alarm was silent.

'What's going on?' Hudson fiddled uncertainly with his

instruments. 'What's going on, where are they?'

'I'll be . . .' Ripley exhaled sharply. 'They gave up. They retreated. The guns stopped them. That means they can reason enough to connect cause and effect. They didn't just keep coming mindlessly.'

'Yeah, but check this out.' Hicks tapped the plastic between a pair of readouts. The counter that monitored D gun rested on zero. C gun was down to ten—a few seconds worth of firepower at the previous rate. 'Next time they can walk right up to the door and knock. If only the APC hadn't blown.'

'If the APC hadn't blown, we wouldn't be standing here talking about it. We'd be driving somewhere talking with the turret gun,' Vasquez pointed out sharply.

Only Ripley wasn't discouraged. 'But *they* don't know how far the guns are down. We hurt them. We actually hurt them. Right now they're probably off caucusing somewhere, or whatever it is they do to make group decisions. They'll start looking for another way to get in. That'll take them a while, and when they decide on another approach, they'll be more cautious. They're going to start seeing those sentry guns everywhere.'

'Maybe we got 'em demoralized.' Hudson picked up on her confidence. He had some colour back in his face. 'You were right, Ripley. The ugly monsters aren't invulnerable.'

Hicks looked up from the console and spoke to Vasquez and the comtech. 'I want you two walking the perimeter. Operations to medical. That's about all we can cover. I know we're all strung-out, but try to stay frosty and alert. If Ripley's right, they'll start testing the walls and conduits. We've got to stop any entries before they get out of hand. Pick them off one at a time as they try to get through.'

The two troopers nodded. Hudson abandoned the console, picked up his rifle, and joined Vasquez in heading for the main corridor. Ripley located a half cup of coffee, picked it up, and drained the tepid contents in a single swallow. It tasted lousy but soothed her throat. The corporal watched her, waited until she'd finished.

'How long since you slept? Twenty-four hours?'

Ripley shrugged indifferently. She wasn't surprised by the question. The constant tension had drained her. If she looked half as tired as she felt, it was no wonder that Hicks had expressed concern. Exhaustion threatened to overwhelm her before the aliens did. When she replied, her voice was distant and detached.

'What difference does it make? We're just marking time.'

'That's not what you've been saying.'

She nodded towards the corridor that had swallowed Hudson and Vasquez. 'That was for their benefit. Maybe a little for myself too. We can sleep but *they* won't. They won't slow down and they won't back off until they have what they want, and what they want is us. They'll get us too.'

'Maybe. Maybe not.' He smiled slightly.

She tried to smile back but wasn't sure if she accomplished it or not. Right then she'd have traded a year's flight salary for a hot cup of fresh coffee, but there was no one to trade with, and she was too tired to work on the dispenser. She slung the flamethrower over her shoulder.

'Hicks, I'm not going to wind up like those others. Like the colonists and Dietrich and Crowe. You'll take care of it, won't you, if it comes to that?'

'*If* it comes to that,' he told her softly, 'I'll do us both. Although if we're still here when the processing station blows, it won't be necessary. That'll take care of everything, us and them. Let's see that it doesn't.'

This time he was sure she managed a grin. 'I can't figure you, Hicks. Soldiers aren't supposed to be optimists.'

'Yeah, I know. You're not the first to point it out. I'm a freakin' anomaly.' Turning, he picked something up from behind the tactical console. 'Here, I'd like to introduce you to a close personal friend of mine.'

With the smoothness and ease of long practice he disengaged the pulse-rifle's magazine and set it aside. Then he handed her the weapon.

'M-41A 10-mm pulse-rifle, over and under with a 30-mm pump-action grenade launcher. A real cutie-pie. The Marine's best friend, spouses notwithstanding. Almost jam-proof, self-lubricating, works under water or in a vacuum and can blow a hole through steel plate. All she asks is that you keep her clean and don't slam her around too much and she'll keep you alive.'

Ripley hefted the weapon. It was bulky and awkward, stuffed with recoil-absorbent fibre to counter the push from the high-powered shells it fired. It was much more impressive than her flamethrower. She raised the muzzle and pointed it experimentally at the far wall.

'What do you think?' Hicks asked her. 'Can you handle one?'

She looked back at him, her voice level. 'What do I do?'

He nodded approvingly and handed her the magazine.

No matter how quiet he tried to be, Bishop still made noise as the portable flight terminal and his sack of equipment scraped along the bottom of the conduit. No human being could have maintained the pace he'd kept up since leaving Operations, but that didn't mean he could keep going indefinitely. There were limits even to a synthetic's abilities.

Enhanced vision enabled him to perceive the walls of the pitch-dark tunnel as it continued receding ahead of him. A human would have been totally blinded in the cylindrical duct. At least he didn't have to worry about losing his way. The conduit provided almost a straight shot to the transmitter tower.

An irregular hole appeared in the right-hand wall, admitting a feeble shaft of light. Among the emotions that had been programmed into him was curiosity. He paused to peer through the acid-etched crack. It would be nice to be able to take a bearing in person instead of having to rely exclusively on the computer printout of the service-shaft plans.

Drooling jaws flashed towards his face to slam against the enclosing steel with a vicious scraping sound.

Bishop flattened himself against the far side of the conduit as the echo of the attack rang along the metal. The curve of the wall where the jaws had struck bent slightly inward. Hurriedly he resumed his forward crawl. To his considerable surprise the attack was not repeated, nor could he sense any apparent pursuit.

Maybe the creature had simply sensed motion and had struck blindly. When no reaction had been forthcoming from inside the duct, there was no reason for it to strike again. How did it detect potential hosts? Bishop went through the motions of breathing without actually performing respiration. Nor did he smell of warmth or blood. To a marauding alien an android might seem just like another piece of machinery. So long as one didn't attack or offer resistance, you might be able to walk freely among them. Not that such an excursion appealed to Bishop, since the reactions and motives of the aliens remained unpredictable, but it was a useful bit of information to have acquired. If the hypothesis could be verified, it might offer a means of studying the aliens.

Let someone else study the monsters, he thought. Let someone else seek verification. A bolder model than himself was required. He wanted off Acheron as much for his own sake as for that of the humans he was working with.

He glanced at his chronometer, faintly aglow in the darkness. Still behind schedule. Pale and strained, he tried to move faster.


Ripley had the stock of the big gun snugged up against her cheek. She was doing her best to keep pace with Hicks's instructions, knowing that they didn't have much time, knowing that if she had to use the weapon, she wouldn't be able to ask a second time how something worked. Hicks was as patient with her as possible, considering that he was trying to compress a complete weapons instruction course into a couple of minutes.

The corporal stood close behind her, positioning her arms as he explained how to use the built-in sight. It required a mutual effort to ignore the intimacy of their stance. There a little enough warmth in the devastated colony, little enough humanity to cling to, and this was the first physical, rather than verbal, contact between them.

'Just pull it in real tight,' he was telling her. 'Despite the built-in absorbers, it'll still kick some. That's the price you have to pay for using shells that'll penetrate just about anything.' He indicated a readout built into the side of the stock. 'When this counter reads zero, hit this.' He ran a thumb over a button, and the magazine dropped out, clattering on the floor.

'Usually we're required to recover the used ones: they're expensive. I wouldn't worry about following regs just now.'

'Don't worry,' she told him.

'Just leave it where it falls. Get the other one in quick.' He handed her another magazine, and she struggled to balance the heavy weapon with one hand while loading with the other. 'Just slap it in hard, it likes abuse.' She did so and was rewarded with a sharp click as the magazine snapped home. 'Now charge it.' She tapped another switch. A red telltale sprang to life on the side of the arming mechanism.

Hicks stepped back, eyed her firing stance approvingly. 'That's all there is to it. You're ready for playtime again. Give it another run-through.'

Ripley repeated the procedure: release magazine, check, reload, arm. The gun was awkward physically, comforting mentally. Her hands were trembling from supporting the weight. She lowered the barrel and indicated the metal tube that ran underneath.

'What's this for?'

'That's the grenade launcher. You probably don't want to mess with that. You've got enough to remember already. If you have to use the gun, you want to be able to do it without thinking.'

She stared back at him. 'Look, you started this. Now show me everything. I can handle myself.'

'So I've noticed.'

They ran through sighting procedures again, then grenade loading and firing, a complete course in fifteen minutes. Hicks showed her how to do everything short of breaking down and cleaning the weapon. Satisfied that she'd missed nothing, she left him to ponder the tactical console's readouts as she headed for Medical to check on Newt. Slung from its field straps, her newfound friend bounced comfortingly against her shoulder.

She slowed when she heard footsteps ahead, then relaxed. Despite its great bulk, an alien would make a lot less noise than the lieutenant. Gorman emerged from the doorway, looking weak but sound. Burke was right behind him. He barely glanced at her. That was fine with Ripley. Every time the Company representative opened his mouth, she had an urge to strangle him, but they needed him. They needed every hand they could get, including those stained with blood. Burke was still one of them, a human being.

Though just barely, she thought.

'How do you feel?' she asked Gorman.

The lieutenant leaned against the wall for support and put one hand to his forehead. 'All right, I guess. A little dizzy. One beauty of a hangover. Look, Ripley, I—'

'Forget it.' No time to waste on useless apologies. Besides, what had happened wasn't entirely Gorman's fault. Blame for the fiasco beneath the atmosphere-processing station needed to be apportioned among whoever had been foolish or incompetent enough to have put him in command of the relief team. Gorman's lack of experience aside, no amount of training could have prepared anyone for the actuality of the aliens. How do you organize combat along accepted lines of battle with an enemy that's as dangerous when it's bleeding to death as it is when it's alive? She pushed past him and into the Med lab.

Gorman followed her with his eyes, then turned to head up the corridor. As he did so he encountered Vasquez approaching from the other direction. She regarded him out of cold, slitted eyes. Sweat stained her colourful bandanna and plastered it to her dark hair and skin.

'You still want to kill me?' he said quietly.

Her reply mixed contempt with acceptance. 'It won't be necessary.' She continued past him, striding towards the next checkpoint.

With Gorman and Burke gone, Medical was deserted. She crossed through to the operating theatre where she'd left Newt. The light was dim, but not so weak that she couldn't make out the empty bed. Fear racing through her like a drug, she spun, her eyes frantically scanning the room, until a thought made her bend to look beneath the cot.

She relaxed, the tension draining back out of her. Sure enough, the girl was curled up against the wall, jammed as far back in as she could get. She was fast asleep, Casey clutched tightly in one small hand.

The angelic expression further reassured Ripley, innocent and undisturbed despite the demons that had plagued the child through waking as well as through sleeping hours. Bless the children, she thought, who can sleep anyplace through anything.

Carefully she laid the rifle on the cot. Getting down on hands and knees, she crawled beneath the springs. Without waking the girl she slipped both arms around her. Newt twitched in her sleep, instinctively snuggling her body closer to the adult's comforting warmth. A primal gesture. Ripley turned slightly on her side and sighed.

Newt's face contorted with the externalization of some private, tormented dreamscape. She cried out inarticulately, a vague dream-distorted plea. Ripley rocked her gently.

'There, there. Hush. It's all right. It's all right.'

Several of the high-pressure cooling conduits that encircled the massive atmosphere-processing tower had begun to glow red with excess heat. High-voltage discharges arced around the conical crown and upper latticework, strobing the blighted landscape of Acheron and the silent structures of Hadley town with irregular, intense flashes of light. It would have been obvious to anyone that something was drastically wrong with the station. Damping units fought to contain a reaction that was already out of control. They continued anyway. They were not programmed for futility.

Across from the landing platform a tall metal spire poked towards the clouds. Several parabolic antennae clustered around the top, like birds flocking to a tree in wintertime.

At the base of the tower a solitary figure stood hunched over an open panel, his back facing into the wind.

Bishop had the test-bay cover locked in the open position and had managed to patch the portable terminal console into the tower's instrumentation. Thus far everything had gone as well as anyone dared hope. It hadn't started out that way. He'd arrived late at the tower, having underestimated the length of time it would take him to crawl through the conduit. As if by way of compensation, the preliminary checkout and testing had come off without a hitch, enabling him to make up some of that lost time. Whether he'd made up enough remained to be seen.

His jacket lay draped over the keyboard and monitor of the terminal to shield them from blowing sand and dust. The electronics were far more sensitive to the inclement weather than he was. The last several minutes had seen him typing frenetically, his fingers a blur on the input keys. He accomplished in a minute what would have taken a trained human ten.

Had he been human he might have uttered a small prayer. Perhaps he did anyway. Synthetics have their own secrets. He surveyed the keyboard a last time and muttered to himself.

'Now, if I did it right, and nothing's busted inside . . .' He punched a peripheral function key inscribed with the signal word ENABLE.

Far overhead, the *Sulaco* drifted patiently and silently in the emptiness of space. No busy figures moved through its empty corridors. No machines hummed efficiently as they worked the huge loading bay. Instruments winked on and off silently, maintaining the ship in its geo-stationary orbit above the colony.

A klaxon sounded, though there were none to hear it. Rotating warning lights came to life within the vast cargo hold, though there was no one to witness the interplay of red, blue and green. Hydraulics whined, immensely powerful lifters rumbled along their tracks as the second dropship was trundled out on its overhead rack. Wheels locked in place, and pulleys and levers took over. The shuttle was lowered into the gaping drop bay.

As soon as it was locked in drop position, service booms and automatic decouplers extended from walls and floor to plug into the waiting vessel. Predrop fuelling and final check-out commenced. These were mundane, routine tasks for which human attention was unnecessary. Actually the ship could do the job better without any people around. They would only get in the way and slow down the operation.

Engines were brought on-line, shut down, and restarted. Locks were cycled open and sealed shut. Internal communications flared to life and exchanged numerical sequences with the *Sulaco*'s main computer. A recorded announcement boomed across the vast, open chamber. Procedure required it, even though there was no one present to listen.

'Attention. Attention. Final fuelling operations have begun. Please extinguish all smoking materials.'

Bishop witnessed none of the activity, saw no lights rotating rapidly, heard no warning. He was satisfied nonetheless. The tiny readouts that came alive on the portable guidance console were as eloquent as a Shakespearean sonnet. He knew that the dropship had been prepared and that fuelling was taking place because the console told him so. He'd done more than make contact with the *Sulaco*: he was communicating. He didn't have to be there in person. The portable was his electronic surrogate. It told him everything he needed to know, and what it told him was good.

# XII

She hadn't intended to go to sleep. All she'd wanted was to share a little space, some warmth, and a few moments of quiet with the girl. But her body knew what she needed better than she did. When she relinquished control and allowed it the chance to minister to its own requirements, it took over immediately.

Ripley awoke with a start and just missed banging her head against the underside of the cot. She was wide-awake instantly.

Dim light from the Med lab filtered into the operating room. Checking her watch, she was startled to see that more than an hour had passed. Death could have visited and departed in that much time, but nothing seemed to have changed. No one had come in to wake her, which wasn't surprising. Their minds were occupied with more important matters. The fact that she'd been left alone was in itself a good sign. If the final assault had begun, Hicks or someone else surely would have rousted her out of the warm corner beneath the bed by now.

Gently she disengaged herself from Newt, who slept on, oblivious to adult obsessions with time. Ripley made sure the small jacket was pulled up snugly around the girl's chin before turning to crawl out from beneath the cot. As she turned to roll, she caught another glimpse of the rest of the Med lab—and froze.

The row of stasis cylinders stood just inside the doorway that led towards the rest of Hadley central. Two of them were dark, their tops hinged open, the stasis fields quiescent. Both were empty.

Hardly daring to breathe, she tried to see into every dark corner, under every counter and piece of freestanding equipment. Unable to move, she frantically tried to assess the situation as she nudged the girl sleeping behind her with her left hand.

'Newt,' she whispered. Could the things sense sound waves? They had no visible ears, no obvious organs of hearing, but who could tell how primitive alien senses interpreted their environment? 'Newt, wake up.'

'What?' The girl rolled over and rubbed sleepily at her eyes. 'Ripley? Where are—'

'Shssh!' She put a finger to her lips. 'Don't move. We're in trouble.'

The girl's eyes widened. She responded with a single nod, now as wide-awake and alert as her adult protector. Ripley didn't have to tell her a second time to be quiet. During her solitary nightmare sojourn deep within the conduits and service ducts that honeycombed the colony, the first thing Newt had learned was the survival value of silence. Ripley pointed to the sprung stasis tubes. Newt saw and nodded again. She didn't so much as whimper.

They lay close to each other and listened in the darkness. Listened for sounds of movement, watching for lethal low-slung shapes skittering across the polished floor. The compact space heater hummed efficiently nearby.

Ripley took a deep breath, swallowed, and started to move. Reaching up, she grabbed the springs that lined the underside of the cot and began trying to push it away from the wall. The squeal of metal as the legs scraped across the floor was jarringly loud in the stillness.

When the gap between bed rail and wall was wide enough, she cautiously slid herself up, keeping her back pressed against the wall. With her right hand she reached across the mattress for the pulse-rifle. Her fingers groped among the sheets and blanket.

The pulse-rifle was gone.

Her eyes cleared the rim of the bed. Surely she'd left it lying there in the middle of the mattress! A faint hint of movement caught her attention, and her head snapped around to the left. As it did so, something that was all legs and vileness jumped at her from its perch on the foot of the bed. She uttered a startled, mewling cry of pure terror and ducked back down. Horny talons clutched at her hair as the loathsome shape struck the wall where her head had been a moment earlier. It slid, fighting for a grip while simultaneously searching for the vulnerable face that had shown itself a second ago.

Rolling like mad and digging her bare fingers into the springs, Ripley slammed the cot backward, pinning the teratoid against the wall only centimetres above her face. Its legs twitched and writhed with maniacal ferocity while the muscular tail banged against springs and wall like a demented python. It emitted a shrill, piercing noise, a cross between a squeal and a hiss.

Ripley heaved Newt across the floor and, in a frenzied scramble, rolled out after her. Once clear, she put both hands against the side of the cot and shoved harder against the imprisoned facehugger. Timing her move carefully, she flipped the cot and managed to trap it underneath one of the metal rails.

Clutching Newt close to her, she backed away from the overturned bed. Her eyes were in constant motion, darting from shadow to cupboard, searching out every corner. The whole lab area was fraught with fatal promise. As they retreated, the facehugger, displaying terrifying strength for something so small, shoved the bulk of the bed off its body and scuttled away beneath a bank of cabinets. Its multiple legs were a blur of motion.

Trying to keep to the centre of the room as much as possible, Ripley continued backing towards the doorway. As soon as her back struck the door, she reached up to run a hand over the wall switch. The barrier at her back should have rolled aside. It didn't move. She hit the switch again, then started pounding on it, regardless of the noise she was making. Nothing. Deactivated, broken, it didn't matter. She tried the light switch. Same thing. They were trapped in the darkness.

Trying to keep her eyes on the floor in front of them, she used one fist to pound on the door. Dull thunks resounded from the acoustically dampened material. Naturally the entrance to the operating theatre would be soundproofed. Wouldn't want unexpected screams to unsettle a queasy colonist who happened to be walking past.

Keeping Newt with her, she edged away from the door and around the wall until they were standing behind the big observation window that fronted on the main corridor. Hardly daring to spare a glance away from the threatening floor, she turned and shouted.

'Hey—hey!'

She hammered desperately on the window. No one appeared on the other side of the triple-glazed transparency. A scrabbling noise from the floor made her whirl. Now Newt began to whimper, feeding off the adult's fear. Desperately Ripley stepped out in line with the wall-mounted video surveillance pickup and began waving her arms.

'Hicks! Hicks!'

There was no response, not from the pickup, nor from the empty room on the other side of the glass. The camera didn't pan to focus on her and no curious voice came from its speaker. In frustration Ripley picked up a steel chair and slammed it against the observation window. It bounced off without even scarring the tough material. She kept trying.

Wasting her strength. The window wasn't going to break, and there was no one in the outer lab to witness her frantic efforts. She put the chair aside and struggled to control her breathing as she surveyed the room.

A nearby counter yielded a small, high-beam examination light. Switching it on, she played the narrow beam over the walls. The circle of light whipped over the stasis tubes, past tall assemblies of surgical and anaesthesiological equipment, over flush-mounted storage bins and cabinets and research instrumentation. She could feel Newt shaking next to her as she clung to the tall woman's leg.

'Mommy—Mommmyyyy . . .'

Perversely it helped to steady Ripley. The child was completely dependent on her, and her own obvious fear was only making the girl panic. She swept the beam across the ceiling, brought it back to something. An idea took hold.

Removing her lighter from a jacket pocket, she hastily crumpled together a handful of paper gleaned from the same cabinet that had provided the beam. Moving as slowly as she dared, she boosted Newt up onto the surgical table that occupied the centre of the room, then clambered up after her.

'Mommy—I mean, Ripley—I'm scared.'

'I know, honey,' she replied absently. 'Me too.'

Twisting the paper tightly, she touched the lighter's flame to the top of her improvised torch. It caught instantly, blazing towards the ceiling. She raised her hand and held the fire towards the temperature sensor at the bottom of one of the Med lab's fire-control sprinkler heads. Like much of the self-contained safety equipment that was standard issue for frontier worlds, the sprinkler had its own battery-powered backup power supply. It wasn't affected by whatever had killed the door and the lights.

The flames rapidly consumed her handful of paper, threatening to burn her ungloved skin. She gritted her teeth and held tight to the torch as it illuminated the room, bouncing off the mirror-bright surface of the globular surgical instrument cluster that hung suspended above the operating table.

'Come on, come on,' she muttered tightly.

A red light winked to life on the side of the sprinkler head as the flames from her makeshift torch finally got hot enough to trigger internal sensors. As it was activated, the sensor automatically relayed its information to the other sprinklers set into the ceiling. Water gushed from several dozen outlets, flooding cabinets and floor with an artificial downpour. Simultaneously the Operations complex fire alarm came to life like a waking giant.

In Operations central, Hicks jumped at the sound of the alarm. His gaze darted from the tactical console to the main computer screen. One small section of the floor plan was flashing brightly. He rose and bolted for the exit, shouting into his headset pickup as he ran.

'Vasquez, Hudson, meet me in Medical! We got a fire!' Both troopers abandoned their guard positions and moved to rendezvous with the corporal.

Ripley's clothes clung to her as the sprinklers continued to drench the room and everything in it. The siren continued to hoot wildly. Between its steady howl and the splatter of water on metal and floor, it was impossible to hear anything else.

She tried to see through the heavy spray, wiping water and hair away from her eyes. One elbow banged against the surgical multiglobe and its assortment of cables, high-intensity lights, and tools, setting it swaying. She glanced at it and turned away to resume her inspection of the room. Something made her look a second time.

The something leapt at her face.

Falling water and the shrieking siren drowned out the sound of her scream as she stumbled backward, falling over the table and splashing to the floor, arms flailing, legs kicking wildly. Newt screamed and scrambled clear as Ripley hurled the chittering facehugger away. It slammed into a wall, clung there like an obscene parody of a climbing tarantula, then leapt back at her as though propelled by a steel spring.

Ripley scrambled desperately, pulling equipment down on herself, trying to put something solid between her and the abomination as she retreated. It went over, under, or around everything she heaved in its path, its multijointed legs a frenzy of relentless motion. Claws caught at her boots and it scuttled up her body. She pushed at it again, the feel of the slick leathery hide making her nauseous. The one thing she dared not do was throw up.

It was unbelievably strong. When it had jumped at her from atop the multiglobe, she'd managed to fling it away before it could get a good grip. This time it refused to be dislodged, hung on tight as it ascended her torso. She tried to rip at it, to pull it away, but it avoided her hands as it climbed towards her head with single-minded purpose. Newt screamed abjectly, backing away until she was pressed up against a desk in one corner.

With a last, desperate gesture Ripley slid both hands up her chest until they blocked her face, just as the facehugger arrived. She pushed with all her remaining strength, trying to force it away from her. As she fought, she stumbled blindly, knocking over equipment, sending instruments flying. On the wet floor her feet threatened to slip out from under her. Water continued to pour from the ceiling, flooding the room and blinding her. It also hindered the facehugger's movements somewhat, but it made it impossible for her to get a strong grip on its body or legs.

Newt continued to scream and stare. In consequence she failed to see the crablike legs that appeared above the rim of the desk she was leaning against. But her ability to sense motion had become almost as acute as that of the sentry-gun sensors. Whirling, she jammed the desk against the wall, fear lending strength to her small form. Pinned against the wall, the creature writhed wildly, fighting to free itself with its legs and tail as she leaned against the desk and wailed.

'Ripleyyy!'

The desk bounced and shuddered with the teratoid's struggles. It slipped one leg free, then another. A third, as it began to squeeze itself out of the trap.

'*Ripleeyyy!*'

The facehugger's legs clawed at Ripley's head, trying to reach behind it to interlock even as she whipped her face from side to side. As it fought for an unbreakable grip it extruded the ovipositorlike tubule from its ventral opening. The organ pushed wetly at Ripley's arms, trying to force its way between.

A shape appeared outside the observation window, dim

behind mist-shrouded glass. A hand wiped a clear place. Hicks's face pressed against the glass. His eyes grew wide as he saw what was happening inside. There was no thought of trying to repair the inoperative door mechanism. He stepped back and raised the muzzle of his pulse-rifle.

The heavy shells shattered the triple-paned barrier in several places. The corporal then dived at the resulting spiderweb patterns and exploded into the room in a shower of glittering fragments, a human comet with a glass tail. He hit the floor rolling, his armour grinding through the shards and protecting him from their sharp edges, sliding across to where the facehugger finally got its powerful tail secured around Ripley's throat. It began to choke her and pull itself closer to her face.

Hicks slipped his fingers around the thrashing arachnoidal limbs and pulled with superhuman force. Between the two of them they forced the monstrosity away from her face.

Hudson followed Hicks into the room, stared a moment at Ripley and the corporal as they struggled with the facehugger. Then he spotted Newt leaning against the desk. He shoved her aside, sending her spinning across the damp floor, and, in the same motion, raised his rifle to blast the second parasite to bits before it could crawl free of the desk's imprisoning bulk. Acid splattered, chewing into desk, wall, and floor as the crablike body was blown apart.

Gorman leaned close to Ripley and got both hands around the end of the facehugger's tail. Like a herpetologist removing a boa constrictor from its favourite branch, he unwound it from her throat. She gasped, swallowing air and water and choking spasmodically. But she kept her grip on it as the three of them held it between them.

Hicks blinked against the spray, nodded to his right. 'The corner! Together. Don't let it keep a grip on you.' He glanced over his shoulder towards the watching Hudson. 'Ready?'

'Do it!' The comtech raised his weapon.

The three of them threw the thing into the empty corner. It scrabbled upright in an instant and jumped back at them with demented energy. Hudson's shot caught it in midair, blowing it apart. The heavy downpour from the sprinklers helped to localize the resultant gush of acid. Smoke began to mix with water vapour as the yellow liquid ate into the floor.

Gagging, Ripley fell to her knees. Red streaks like rope burns scarred her throat. As she knelt next to Hicks and Hudson the sprinklers finally shut down. Water dripped from cabinets and equipment, racing away through the holes the acid had eaten in the floor. The fire siren died.

Hicks was staring at the stasis cylinders. 'How did they get out of there? You can't break a stasis field from the inside.' His gaze rose to the security pickup mounted on the far wall. 'I was watching the monitors. Why didn't I see what was going on here?'

'Burke.' It came out as a long wheeze. 'It was Burke.'

It was very quiet in Operations. Everyone's thoughts were racing at breakneck speed, but no one spoke. None of the thoughts were pleasant. Finally Hudson gestured at the subject of all this solemn contemplation and spoke with his usual eloquence.

'I say we grease him right now.'

Burke tried hard not to stare at the menacing muzzle of the comtech's pulse-rifle. One twitch of Hudson's finger and the Company rep knew his head would explode like an over-ripe melon. He managed to maintain an icy calm betrayed only by the isolated beads of sweat that dotted his forehead. The last five minutes had seen him compose and discard half a dozen speeches as he decided it was best to say nothing. Hicks might listen to his arguments, but the wrong word, even the wrong movement, could set any of the others off. In this he was quite correct.

The corporal was pacing back and forth in front of the Company rep's chair. Occasionally he would look down at him and shake his head in disbelief.

'I don't get it. It doesn't make any sense.'

Ripley crossed her arms as she regarded the man-shape in

the chair. In her eyes it had ceased to be human. 'It makes plenty of sense. He wanted an alien, only he couldn't figure out a way to sneak it back through Gateway quarantine. I guaranteed him I'd inform the appropriate authorities if he tried it. That was *my* mistake.'

'Why would he want to try something like that?' Hicks's bemusement was plain on his face.

'For weapons research. Bioweapons. People—and I use the word advisedly—like him do things like that. If it's new and unique, they see a profit in it to the exclusion of everything else.' She shrugged. 'At first I thought he might be different. When I figured otherwise, I made the mistake of not thinking far enough ahead. I'm probably being too hard on myself. I couldn't think beyond what a sane human being might do.'

'I don't get it,' said Vasquez. 'Where's his angle if those things killed you? What's that get him?'

'He had no intention of letting them kill us—right away. Not until we got his toys back to Earth for him. He had it timed just right. Bishop'll have the dropship down pretty soon. By then the facehuggers would've done their job, and Newt and I would be flat-out with nobody knowing the cause. The rest of you would have hauled us unconscious onto the dropship. See, if we were impregnated, parasitized, whatever you want to call it, and then frozen in hypersleep before we woke up, the effects of hypersleep would slow down the embryonic alien's growth just like it does ours. It wouldn't mature during the flight home. Nobody would know what we were carrying, and as long as our vital signs stayed stable, no one would think anything was radically wrong. We'd unload at Gateway, and the first thing the authorities would do is ship us Earthside to a hospital.

'That's where Burke and his Company cronies would step in. They'd claim responsibility, or bribe somebody, and check us into one of their own facilities where they could study us in private. Me and Newt.'

She looked over at the frail figure of the girl sitting nearby.

Newt hugged her knees to her chest and watched the proceedings with sombre eyes. She was all but lost in the adult jacket someone had scrounged for her, scrunched down inside the copious padding and high collar. Her still-damp hair was plastered to her forehead and cheeks.

Hicks stopped pacing to stare at Ripley. 'Wait a minute. *We*'d know about it. Maybe we wouldn't be sure, but we'd sure have it checked out the instant we arrived at the Station. No way would we let anybody ship you Earthside without a complete medical scan.'

Ripley considered this, then nodded. 'The only way it would work is if he sabotaged the sleep capsules for the trip back. With Dietrich gone, each of us would have to put ourselves into hypersleep. He could set his timer to wake him a few days down the road, climb out of his capsule, shut down everybody else's bio-support systems, and jettison the bodies. Then he could make up any story he liked. With most of your squad already killed by the aliens, and the details of the fight over on C-level recorded by your suit scanners and stored in the *Sulaco*'s records, it would be an easy matter to attribute your deaths to the aliens as well.'

'He's *dead*.' Hudson switched his attention from Ripley back to the Company rep. 'You hear that? You're dog meat, pal.'

'This is a totally paranoid delusion.' Burke saw no harm in finally speaking out, convinced that he couldn't hurt himself any more than he already had. 'You saw how strong those things are. I had nothing to do with their escaping.'

'Bullcrap. Nothing's strong enough to force its way out of a stasis tube,' Hicks said evenly.

'I suppose after they climbed out they locked the operating room from the outside, shut down the emergency power to the overhead lights, hid my rifle, and killed the videoscan too.' Ripley looked tired. 'You know, Burke, I don't know which species is worse. You don't see *them* killing each other for a percentage.'

'Let's waste him.' Hicks's expression was unreadable as he

gazed down at the Company rep. 'No offence.'

Ripley shook her head. Inside, the initial rage was giving way to a sickened emptiness. 'Just find someplace to lock him up until it's time to leave.'

'Why?' Hudson was shaking with suppressed anger, his finger taut on the trigger of his rifle.

Ripley glanced at the comtech. 'Because I'd like to take him back. I want people to know what he's done. They need to know what happened to the colony here, and why. I want—'

The lights went out. Hicks turned immediately to the tactical console. The screen still glowed on battery power, but no images flashed across it because the power to the colony's computer had been cut. A quick check of Operations revealed that everything was out: power doors, videoscreens, sensor cameras, the works.

'They cut the power.' Ripley stood motionless in the near blackness.

'What do you mean, *they* cut the power?' Hudson turned a slow circle and started backing towards a wall. 'How could they cut the power, man? They're dumb animals.'

'Who knows what they really are? We don't know enough about them to say that for sure yet.' She picked up the pulse-rifle that Burke had taken and thumbed off the safety. 'Maybe they act like that individually, but they could also have some kind of collective intelligence. Like ants or termites. Bishop talked about that, before he left. Termites build mounds three metres high. Leaf-cutter ants have agriculture. Is that just instinct? What is intelligence, anyway?' She glanced left.

'Stay close, Newt. The rest of you, let's get some trackers going. Come on, get moving. Gorman, keep an eye on Burke.'

Hudson and Vasquez switched on their scanners. The glow of the motion-tracker sensors was comforting in the darkness. Modern technology hadn't failed them completely yet. With the two troopers leading the way, they headed for the corridor. With all power out to Operations, Vasquez had to slide the barrier aside manually.

Ripley's voice sounded behind the smartgun operator. 'Anything?'

'Nothing here.' Vasquez was a shadow against one wall.

She didn't have to put the same question to Hudson because everyone heard the comtech's tracker beep loudly. All eyes turned in his direction.

'There's something. I've got something.' He panned the tracker around. It beeped again, louder this time. 'It's moving. It's *inside* the complex.'

'I don't see anything.' Vasquez's tracker remained silent. 'You're just reading me.'

Hudson's voice cracked slightly. 'No. No! It ain't you. They're inside. Inside the perimeter. They're in *here*.'

'Stay cool, Hudson.' Ripley tried to see to the far end of the corridor. 'Vasquez, you ought to be able to confirm.'

The smartgun operator swung her tracker and her rifle in a wide arc. The last place she pointed both of them was directly behind her. The portable sensor let out a sharp beep.

'Hudson may be right.'

Ripley and Hicks exchanged a glance. At least they wouldn't have to stand around anymore waiting for something to happen.

'It's game time,' the corporal said tightly.

Ripley called to the pair of troopers. 'Get back here, both of you. Fall back to Operations.'

Hudson and Vasquez started to backtrack. The comtech's eyes nervously watched the dark tunnel they were abandoning. The tracker said one thing, his eyes another. Something was wrong.

'This signal's weird. Must be some interference or something. Maybe power arcing unevenly somewhere. There's movement all over the place, but I don't see a thing.'

'Just get back here!' Ripley felt the sweat starting on her forehead, under her arms. Cold, like the pit of her stomach. Hudson turned and broke into a run, reaching the door a moment before Vasquez. Together they pulled it closed and locked the seal-tight.

Once inside, they began sharing out the remnants of their pitifully small armoury. Flamethrowers, grenades, and lastly, a fair distribution of the loaded pulse-rifle magazines. Hudson's tracker continued to beep regularly, rising in a gradual crescendo.

'Movement!' He looked around wildly, saw only the silhouettes of his companions in the shadowed room. 'Signal's clean. Can't be an error.' Picking up the scanner, he panned the business end around the room. 'I've got full range of movement at twenty metres.'

Ripley whispered to Vasquez. 'Seal the door.'

'If I seal the door, how do we get to the dropship?'

'Same way Bishop did. Unless you want to try to walk out.'

'Seventeen metres,' Hudson muttered. Vasquez picked up her handwelder and moved to the door.

Hicks handed one of the flamethrowers to Ripley and began priming the other for himself. 'Let's get these things lit.' A moment later his sprang to life, a small, steady blue flame hissing from the weapon's muzzle like an oversize lighter. Ripley's flared brilliantly as she nudged the button marked IGNITE, which was set in the side of the handgrip.

Sparks showered around Vasquez as she began welding the door to the floor, ceiling and walls. Hudson's tracker was going like mad now, though still not as fast as Ripley's heart.

'They learned,' she said, unable to stand silence. 'Call it instinct or intelligence or group analysis, but they learned. They cut the power and they've avoided the guns. They must have found another way into the complex, something we missed.'

'We didn't miss anything,' Hicks growled.

'Fifteen metres.' Hudson took a step away from the door.

'I don't know how they did it. An acid hole in a duct. Something under the floors that was supposed to be sealed but wasn't. Something the colonists added or modified and didn't bother to insert into the official schematics. We don't know how up-to-date those plans are or when they were last revised to include all structural additions. I don't know, but there has to be something!' She picked up Vasquez's tracker and aimed it at the same direction as Hudson's.

'Twelve metres,' the comtech informed them. 'Man, this is one big signal. Ten metres.'

'They're right on us.' Ripley stared at the door. 'Vasquez, how you coming?'

The smartgun operator didn't reply. Molten droplets singed her skin and landed, smoking, on her suit. She gritted her teeth and tried to hurry the welder along with some choice imprecations.

'Nine metres. Eight.' Hudson announced the last number on a rising inflection and looked around wildly.

'Can't be.' Ripley was insistent, despite the fact that the tracker she was holding offered the same impossible readout. 'That's inside the room.'

'It's right, it's right.' He turned his instrument sideways so she could see the tiny screen and its accompanying telltales. 'Look!'

Ripley fiddled with her own tracker, rolling the fine-tuning controls as Hicks crossed to Hudson's position in a single stride.

'Well, you're not reading it right.'

'I'm not!' The comtech's voice bordered on hysteria. 'I know these little babies, and they don't lie, man. They're too simple to screw up.' He was staring bug-eyed at the flickering readouts. 'Six metres. Five. What the fu—?'

His eyes met Ripley's, and the same realization hit them simultaneously. Both bent their heads back, and they angled the trackers in the same direction. The beeping from both instruments beame a numbing buzz.

Hicks climbed onto a file cabinet. Slinging his rifle over his shoulder and clutching the flamethrower tightly, he raised one of the acoustical ceiling panels and shone his flashlight inside.

It illuminated a vision Dante could not have imagined in his wildest nightmares, nor Poe in the grasp of an uncontrollable delirium.

# XIII

The serviceway between the suspended acoustical ceiling and the metal roof was full of aliens. More aliens than he could quickly count. They clung upside down to pipes and beams, crawling like bats towards his light, glistening metalically. They covered the serviceway as far back as his light could shine.

He didn't need a motion tracker to sense movement behind him. As he snapped light and body around, the beam picked out an alien less than a metre away. It lunged at his face. Ducking wildly, the corporal felt claws capable of rending metal rake across the back of his armour.

As he tumbled back into Operations the army of infiltrating creatures detached en masse from their grips and claw holds. The flimsy suspended ceiling exploded, raining debris and nightmare shapes into the room below. Newt screamed. Hudson opened fire, and Vasquez gave Hicks a hand up as she let go with her flamethrower. Ripley scooped up Newt and stumbled backward. Gorman was at her side in an instant, pumping away with his own rifle. No one had time to notice Burke as the Company rep bolted for the only unblocked corridor, the one that connected Operations to Medical.

Flamethrowers brightened the chaos as they incinerated one attacker after another. Sometimes the burning aliens would stumble into one another, screeching insanely and adding to the confusion and conflagration. They sounded much more like screams of anger than of pain. Acid poured from seared bodies, chewing gaping holes in the floor and adding to the danger.

'Medical!' Ripley was backing up slowly, keeping Newt close to her. 'Get to Medical!' She turned and dashed for the connecting corridor.

The walls blurred around her, but at least the ceiling overhead stayed intact. She was able to concentrate on the corridors ahead. She caught a glimpse of Burke just as the Company rep cleared the heavy door into the lab area and slid it shut behind him. Ripley slammed into it and wrenched at the outside latch, just as it clicked home on the other side.

'Burke! Open the door! Burke, open the door!'

Newt tugged on Ripley's pants as she slipped behind her, pointing down the corridor. 'Look!'

An alien was striding up the passageway towards them. A *big* alien. A shaking Ripley raised her rifle, trying to recall in an instant everything Hicks had taught her about the powerful weapon. She aimed the barrel straight at the middle of the glistening, skeletal chest and squeezed the trigger.

Nothing happened.

A hiss came from the advancing abomination. The outer jaws parted, slime spattering on the floor. Calm, calm, don't lose it, Ripley told herself. She checked the safety. It was off. A glance revealed a full magazine. Newt clung desperately to her leg and began to wail. Ripley's hands were trembling so violently, she nearly dropped the gun.

It was almost on top of them when she remembered that the first high-powered round had to be injected into the breech manually. She did so, jerked convulsively on the trigger. The rifle went off in the thing's face, hurling it backward. She turned away and covered her face as best she could in what had by now become an instinctive defensive gesture. But the energy of the shell impacting on the alien's body at point-blank range had thrown it back with such force that the spraying acid missed them completely.

The dampened recoil was still strong enough to send her

off-balance body stumbling into the locked door. Her sight had been temporarily wiped by the nearness of the explosion, and she blinked furiously, trying to bring her eyes back into focus. Her ears rang with the concussion.

In Operations, Hicks looked up just in time to fire at a leaping outline, the force of the pulse shell hurling his assailant backward into a blazing cabinet. By this time the combined efforts of the flamethrowers had activated the fire-control system, and the overhead sprinkler jets deluged the room. Water cascaded around the corporal, drenched the other soldiers. Some of it penetrated the central colony computer, ruining it for future use. But at least it didn't pool up around their legs. By now there were enough acid holes to drain it off. The fire siren wailed mindlessly, making it difficult for the combatants to hear each other and rendering any thought of unified tactics impossible.

Hudson was screaming at the top of his lungs, his shrill tone audible over the siren's moan. 'Let's go, let's go!'

'Medical!' Hicks yelled to him. He gestured frantically as he retreated towards the corridor. 'Come on!'

As the comtech turned towards him the floor panels erupted under his feet. Clawed arms seized him, powerful triple fingers locking around his ankles and dragging him down. Another towering shape fell on him from behind, and he was gone in seconds, swallowed by the subfloor crawlway. Hicks let loose a rapid-fire burst in the direction of the cavity, hoping he got the comtech as well as his abductors, then turned and ran. Vasquez and Gorman were right behind him, the smart-gun operator laying down a murderous arc of fire as she covered their retreat.

Ripley was fumbling with the door handle when Newt pulled on her arm to attract attention. The girl pointed silently to where the bleeding, half-blown-away alien was trying to rise to advance on them again. Flinching away from the blast and glare, Ripley drilled it a second time. The pulse-rifle's muzzle jerked ceilingward, and Newt covered her ears against the roar. This time the nightmare stayed down.

A voice sounded behind them. 'Hold your fire!' Hicks and the others materialized out of the smoke and dust. They were grime-streaked and soaking wet. She stepped aside, gestured at the door.

'Locked.' It wasn't necessary to explain how. Hicks just nodded.

'Stand clear.' From his belt he removed a cutting torch that was a miniature of the one Vasquez had used earlier to seal first the fire-tunnel door and then the one leading into Operations. It made short work of the lock.

Inhuman shapes appeared at the far end of the corridor. Ripley wondered how they could track their prey so efficiently. They had no visible eyes or ears, no nostrils. Some unknown, special, alien sensing organ? Someday maybe some scientist would dissect one of the monstrosities and produce an answer. Someday after she was long dead, because she had no intention of being around when it was attempted.

Vasquez passed her flamethrower to Gorman and unslung her rifle. From a pouch she extracted several small egg-shaped objects and dumped them into the underslung barrel of the M-41A.

Gorman's eyes widened as he watched her load the grenades. 'Hey, you can't use those in here!' He backed away from her.

'Right. I'm in violation of close-quarter combat regulations ninety-five through ninety-eight. Put me on report.' She aimed the muzzle of the gun at the oncoming horde. '*Fire in the hole!*' She pumped up a round and let fly, turning her head slightly as she did so.

The blast from the grenade staggered Ripley and almost knocked Vasquez off her feet. Ripley was sure that she could see the smartgun operator smiling as the light from the explosion illuminated her battle-streaked face. Hicks wavered, the blue-hot flame of his torch shooting wildly upward for a moment. Then he straightened amd resumed cutting.

The lock fell away from the door a moment later, clattering inside Medical. He reholstered the torch, stood up, and kicked the door open. Molten droplets went flying. Hicks and his companions ignored them. They were used to dodging spraying acid.

He turned just long enough to shout back at Vasquez. 'Thanks a lot! Now I can't hear at all!'

She affected a look of bewilderment that was as genuine and heartfelt as her gentle nature, cupping a hand to one ear. 'Say what?'

They stumbled into the ruined Med lab. Vasquez was the last one through. She turned, slid the heavy door halfway closed behind her, and in rapid succession fired three grenades through the resultant gap. An instant before they went off, she shut the door the rest of the way and ran. The triple boom sounded like a giant gong going off. The heavy metal security door was bent inward off its track.

Ripley had already crossed to the far side of the annex to try the door. This time she wasn't surprised to find it locked. She worked on it as Hicks used his torch to seal the bent door they'd just come through.

In the main lab Burke found himself backing across the dark floor. This time there would be no discussion of hypothetical iniquities, no polite give-and-take. He would be shot on sight. Maybe Hicks would hold off, and Gorman, but they would be unable to restrain Hudson or that crazy Vasquez woman.

Gasping, he crossed to the door that led out into the main complex. If the aliens were wholly preoccupied with his former colleagues, he might have a chance, might pull it off in spite of everything that had gone so dreadfully wrong. He could slip back into the colony proper, away from the fight, and make a roundabout run for the landing field. Bishop was amenable to argument and reason, as any good synthetic ought to be. Maybe he could convince him that everyone else was dead. If he could manage that small semantic feat and disable the android's communicator so that the others couldn't contact him to dispute the assertion, they'd have no choice but to take off immediately. If the directive was delivered with enough force and with no one to counter it, Bishop should comply.

His fingers reached for the door latch, froze without touching the metal. The latch was already turning, seemingly by itself. Almost paralysed with fear, he staggered backward as the door was slowly opened from the *other* side.

The loud crack of a descending stinger was not heard by those in the annex.

Vasquez's grenade party had cleared the corridor long enough for Hicks to get the door sealed. It assured them of a few secure minutes, a holding gesture and no more. Now the corporal backed away from the doorway and readied his rifle for the final confrontation as something whammed against the barrier from outside, dimpling it in the middle. A second crash made metal squeal as the door began to separate from its frame.

Newt tugged insistently at Ripley's hand. Finally the adult took notice, forcing her attention away from the failing door.

'Come on! This way!' Newt was pulling Ripley towards the far wall.

'It won't work, Newt. I could barely fit in your hideaway. The others have armour on, and some of them are bigger. They won't be able to fit in there at all.'

'Not *that* way,' the girl said impatiently. 'There's another.'

Behind a desk an air vent was a dark rectangle againt the wall. Newt expertly unlatched the protective grille and swung it open. She bent to duck inside, but Ripley pulled her back.

She glanced petulantly up at the adult. 'I know where I'm going.'

'I don't doubt that for a minute, Newt. You're just not going first, that's all.'

'I've always gone first before.'

'I wasn't here before, and you didn't have every alien on Acheron chasing you before.' She walked over to Gorman and swapped her rifle for his flamethrower before he could think to protest. Pausing just long enough to tousle Newt's hair affectionately, she dropped to her knees and pushed into the shaft. Darkness unknown confronted her. At the moment it felt like a comforting old friend.

She looked back past her shoulder. 'Get the others. You stay behind me.'

Newt nodded vigorously and disappeared. She was back in seconds, diving into the duct to crowd close to Ripley as the older woman started forward. The girl was followed by Hicks, Gorman, and Vasquez. Between their armour and the big pulse-rifles they were hauling, it was a tight squeeze for the soldiers, but everyone cleared the opening. Vasquez paused long enough to pull the grille shut behind them.

If the tunnel narrowed down ahead or split off into smaller subducts, they'd be trapped, but Ripley wasn't worried. She had a great deal of confidence in Newt. At worst they'd have time to exchange polite farewells before drawing straws, or something similar, to decide who got to deliver the final coup de grace. A glance showed that the girl was right behind her.

Closer than that. Used to moving through the labyrinth of ducts at a much faster pace, Newt was all but crawling up Ripley's legs.

'Come on,' the girl urged her repeatedly, 'crawl faster.'

'I'm doing the best I can. I'm not built for this, Newt. None of us are, and we don't have your experience. You're sure you know where we are?'

'Of course.' The girl's voice was tinged with gentle contempt, as though Ripley had just stated the most obvious thing in the world.

'And you know how to get to the landing field from here?'

'Sure. Keep going. A little farther on and this turns into a bigger tunnel. Then we go left.'

'A bigger duct?' Hicks's voice reverberated from the metal walls as he spoke to Newt. 'Girl, when we get home, I'm going to buy you the biggest doll you ever saw. Or whatever you want.'

'Just a bed will be fine, Mr. Hicks.'

Sure enough, another several minutes of rapid crawling

brought them into the colony's main ventilation duct, right where Newt said it would be. It was spacious enough to allow them to rise from a crawl to a low crouch. Ripley's hands and knees screamed in relief, and their pace increased markedly. She kept banging her head on the low ceiling, but it was such a relief to be off all fours that she hardly noticed the occasional contact.

Despite their increased speed, Newt kept up easily. Where the adults had to bend to clear the top of the duct, she was able to stand and run. Armour clattered and banged in the confined tunnel, but at this point it was agreed that speed was more important than silence. For all they knew, the aliens had poor hearing and located them by smell.

They were coming up on an intersection where two main ducts crossed. Ripley slowed to fire a preventative blast from the flamethrower, methodically searing both passageways.

'Which direction?'

Newt didn't have to think. 'Go right here.' Ripley turned and started up the right-hand tunnel. The new duct was somewhat smaller than the colony main but still larger than the one they'd used to flee Medical.

Behind her and Newt, Hicks was addressing his headset pickup as they scuttled along. 'Bishop, this is Hicks, do you read? Do you read, Bishop? Over.' Silence greeted his initial query, but eventually his persistence was rewarded by a static-distorted but still recognizable voice.

'Yes, I read you. Not very well.'

'Well enough,' Hicks told him. 'It'll get better the closer we come. We're on our way. Taking a route through the colony ductwork. That's why the bad connection. How are things at your end?'

'Good and bad,' the syntheic replied. 'Wind's picked up a lot. But the dropship's on its way. Just reconfirmed drop and release with the *Sulaco*. Estimated time of arrival: sixteen minutes plus. I've got my hands full trying to remote-fly in this wind.' An electronic roar distorted the end of his sentence.

'What was that?' Hicks fiddled with his headset controls. 'Say again, Bishop. Wind?'

'No. The atmosphere-processing station. Emergency venting system is approaching overload. It'll be close, Corporal Hicks. Don't stop for lunch.'

In the darkness the soldier grinned. Not all synthetics were programmed for a sense of humour, and not all those that were knew how to make use of it. Bishop was something else.

'Don't worry. None of us are real hungry right now. We'll make it in time. Stand by out there. Over.'

Preoccupied with his communication, he almost ran over Newt. The girl had halted in the duct. Looking beyond the girl, he saw that Ripley had stopped in front of her.

'What is it, what's wrong?'

'I'm not sure.' Ripley's voice was ghostly in the darkness. 'I could swear I saw—there!'

At the extreme limit of her flashlight Hicks made out a moving, obscene shape. Like a ferret, the alien had somehow managed to flatten its body just enough for it to fit inside the duct. There was additional movement visible beyond the invader.

'Back, go back!' Ripley yelled.

Everyone tried to comply, jamming into each other in the confined tunnel. Behind them the sound of a grating being torn apart echoed through the duct. The grating collapsed with a sharp *spanggg*, and a deadly silhouette flowed through the resultant opening. Vasquez unlimbered her flamethrower and bathed the tunnel behind them in fire. Everyone knew it was a temporary victory. They were trapped.

Vasquez leaned to one side and stared upward. 'Vertical shaft right here. Slick, no handholds.' Her tone was clipped, matter-of-fact. 'Too smooth to try a chimney ascent.'

Hicks broke out his cutting torch, snapped it alight, and began slicing through the wall of the duct. Molten metal spattered his armour as sparks filled the confined tunnel with lurid light. Vasquez's flamethrower roared again, then sputtered out.

'Losing fuel.' From the other direction the column of aliens continued to close on them, their advance slowed by their need to squeeze through the narrow walls.

Hicks had three-quarters of an exit cut in the side of the tunnel when the portable torch flickered and went out. Cursing, he braced his back against the opposite wall of the duct and kicked hard. The metal bent. He kicked again and it gave way. Without pausing to see what lay on the other side, he grabbed his rifle and dived through the opening . . .

. . . to emerge into a narrow serviceway thick with pipes and exposed conduits. Ignoring the still-hot edges of the cavity, he reached back inside to pull Newt to safety. Ripley followed, turned to aid Gorman. He hesitated at the opening long enough to see Vasquez's flamethrower run dry. The smartgun operator dumped it aside and drew her service revolver.

There was movement above her as a grotesque shape dropped down the vertical overhead duct. As the alien landed in the tunnel she rolled clear and let fly with the automatic pistol. The alien tumbled towards her as the small projectiles ripped into its skeletal body. Vasquez snapped her head to one side just in time to avoid the stinger. It buried itself into the metal wall next to her cheek. She kept firing, emptying the pistol into the thrashing form as she kicked at the powerful legs and quivering tail.

A gush of acid finally cut through her armour to sear her thigh. She let out a soft moan of pain.

Gorman froze in the tunnel. He glanced at Ripley. 'They're right behind me. Get going.' Their eyes met for as long as either of them dared spare. Then she turned and raced up the serviceway with Newt in tow. Hicks followed reluctantly, staring back at the opening he'd cut in the ventilation duct. Hoping. Knowing better.

Gorman crawled towards the immobilized smartgun operator. When he reached her, he saw the smoke pouring from the hole in her armour, shut out the gruesome smell of scarred flesh. His fingers locked around her battle harness, and he started dragging her towards the opening.

Too late. The first alien coming from the other direction had already reached and passed the hole Hicks had made. Gorman stopped pulling, leaned forward to look at Vasquez's leg. Where armour, harness, and flesh had been eaten away by the acid, bone gleamed whitely.

Her eyes were glazed when she looked up at him. Her voice was a harsh whisper. 'You always were stupid, Gorman.'

Her fingers seized his in a death grip. A special grip shared by a select few. Gorman returned it as best he was able. Then he handed her a pair of grenades and armed another couple for himself as the aliens closed in on them from both ends of the tunnel. He grinned and raised one of the humming explosives. She barely had enough strength to mimic the gesture.

'Cheers,' he whispered. He couldn't tell if she was grinning back at him because he had closed his eyes, but he had a feeling she was. Something sharp and unyielding stroked his back. He didn't turn to see what it was.

'Cheers,' he whispered feebly. He clicked one of his grenades against one of Vasquez's in the final toast.

Behind them, the serviceway lit up like the sun as Ripley, Newt, and Hicks pounded along full tilt. They were a long way from the opening the corporal had cut in the wall of the duct, but the shock wave from the quadruple explosion was still powerful enough to rock the whole level. Newt kept her balance best and broke out in front of the two adults. It was all Ripley and Hicks could do to keep up with her.

'This way, this way!' she was shouting excitedly. 'Come on, we're almost there!'

'Newt, wait!' Ripley tried to lengthen her stride to catch up to the girl. The sound of her heart was loud in her ears, and her lungs screamed in protest with every step she took. The walls blurred around her. She was dimly aware of Hicks pounding along like a steam engine just behind her. Despite his armour, he probably could have outdistanced her, but he didn't try. Instead he laid back so he could protect against an attack from behind.

Ahead the corridor forked. At the end of the left-hand fork a narrow, angled ventilation chute led upward at a steep forty-five degrees. Newt was standing at its base, gesturing frantically.

'Here! This is where we go up.'

Her body grateful for a respite no matter how temporary, Ripley slowed to a halt as she examined the shaft. It was a steep climb but not a long one. Dim light marked the end of the ascent. From above she could hear the wind booming like air blowing across the lip of a bottle. Narrow climbing ribs dimpled the smooth sides of the shaft.

She looked down to where the chute punched a hole in the floor and disappeared into unknown depths lost in darkness. Nothing stirred down there. Nothing came climbing towards them. They were going to make it.

She put her foot onto the first climbing rib and started up. Newt followed as Hicks emerged from the main corridor behind them.

The girl turned to wave. 'Just up here, Mr Hicks. It's not as far as it looks. I've done it lots of tim—'

Rusted out by seeping water, worn through by the corrosive elements contained in Acheron's undomesticated atmosphere, the rib collapsed beneath her feet. She slipped, managed to catch another rib with one hand. Ripley braced herself against the dangerously slick surface of the chute, turned, and reached back for her. As she did so, she dropped her flashlight, watched it go skittering and bumping down the opening until its comforting glow faded from sight.

She strained until she was sure her arm was separating from her shoulder, her fingers groping for Newt's. No matter how far over she bent, they remained centimetres apart.

'Riiipplleeee . . .'

Newt's grip broke. As she went sliding down the chute Hicks

made a dive for her, laying himself out, flat and indifferent to the coming impact. He slammed into the floor next to the chute, and his fingers dug into the collar of the girl's oversize jacket, holding the material in a death grip.

She slipped out of it.

Her scream reverberated up the chute as she vanished, plummeting down into darkness.

Hicks threw the empty jacket aside and stared at Ripley. Their eyes met for just a second before she released her own grasp and went sliding down the chute after Newt. As she slid, she pushed out with her feet, braking her otherwise uncontrolled descent.

Like the corridor above, the chute forked where it intersected the lower level. Her flashlight gleamed off on her right, and she shifted her weight so she would slide in that direction.

'Newt. Newt!'

A distant wail, plaintive and distorted by distance and intervening metal, floated back to her.

'Mommy—where are you?' Newt was barely audible. Had she taken the other chute?

The shaft bottomed out in a horizontal service tunnel. Her undamaged flashlight lay on the floor, but there was no sign of the girl. As Ripley bent to recover the light the cry reached her again, bouncing off the narrow walls.

'Moommmeee!'

Ripley started down the tunnel in what she hoped was the right direction. The wild slide down the chute had completely disorientated her. Newt's call came again. Fainter? Ripley couldn't tell. She turned a circle, panic growing inside her, her light illuminating only grime and dampness. Every projection contained grinning, slime-lubricated jaws, every hollow was a gaping alien mouth. Then she remembered that she was still wearing her headset. And she remembered something else. Something the corporal had given her that she'd given away in turn.

'Hicks, get down here. I need the locator for that bracelet you gave me.' She cupped her hands to her mouth and shouted down the serviceway. 'Newt! Stay wherever you are. We're coming!'

The girl was in a low, grottolike chamber where the other branch of the chute had dumped her. It was crisscrossed with pipes and plastic conduits and was flooded up to her waist. The only light came from above, through a heavy grating. Maybe Ripley's voice had also, she thought. Using the network of pipes, she started to climb.

A large, bulky object came sliding down the chute. Hicks wouldn't have found the description flattering, but Ripley was immensely relieved to see him no matter how rumpled he looked. The mere presence of another human being in that stygian, haunted tunnel was enough to push back the fear a little way.

He landed on his feet, clutching his rifle in one hand, and unsnapped the emergency location unit from his battle harness. 'I gave *you* that bracelet,' he said accusingly, even as he was switching the tracker on.

'And I gave it to Newt. I figured she'd need it more than I would, and I was right. It's a good thing I did it or we'd never find her in this. You can bawl me out later. Which way?'

He checked the tracker's readout, turned, and started off down the tunnel. It led them into a section of serviceway where the power hadn't been cut. Emergency lights still brightened ceiling and walls. They switched off their lights. Water dripped somewhere nearby. The corporal's gaze rarely strayed from the tracker's screen. He turned left.

'This way. We're getting close.'

The locator led them to a large grate set in the floor—and a voice from below.

'Ripley?'

'It's us, Newt.'

'Here! I'm here, I'm down here.'

Ripley knelt at the edge of the grating, then wrapped her

fingers around the centre bar and pulled. It didn't budge. A quick inspection revealed that it was welded into the floor instead of being latched for easy removal. Peering down, she could just make out Newt's tear-streaked face. The girl reached upward. Her small fingers wriggled between the closely set bars. Ripley gave them a reassuring squeeze.

'Climb down off that pipe, honey. We're going to have to cut through this grate. We'll have you out of there in a minute.'

The girl obediently backed clear, shinnying down the pipe she'd ascended as Hicks fired up his hand torch. Ripley glanced significantly in its direction, then met his eyes as she lowered her voice.

'How much fuel?' She was remembering how Vasquez's flamethrower had run out at a critical moment.

He looked away. 'Enough.' Bending, he began cutting through the first of the bars.

From below Newt could watch sparks shower blindingly as Hicks sliced through the hardened alloy. It was cold in the tunnel, and she was standing in the water again. She bit her lip and fought back tears.

She did not see the glistening apparition rising silently from the water behind her. It would not have mattered if she had. There was nowhere to run to, no safe air duct to duck into. For a moment the alien hovered over her, motionless, dwarfing her tiny form. Only when it moved again did she sense its presence and whirl. She barely had enough time to scream as the shadow engulfed her.

Ripley heard the scream and the brief splashing below and went completely berserk. The grating had been half cut away. She and Hicks wrenched and kicked at it until a portion bent downward. Another kick sent the chunk of crumpled metal tumbling into the water. Heedless of the red-hot edges, Ripley lunged through the opening, her light clutched in one hand, its beam slashing over pipes and conduits.

'Newt! Newt!'

The surface of the dark water reflected the light back up at her. It was placid and still after having swallowed the section of grille. Of the girl there was no sign. All that remained to show that she'd ever been there was Casey. As Ripley looked on helplessly, the doll head sank beneath the oily blackness.

Hicks had to drag her bodily out of the opening. She struggled blindly, trying to rip free of his embrace.

'No, noooo!'

It took all his strength and greater mass to wrestle her away from the opening. 'She's *gone*,' he said intensely. 'There's nothing you or I or anybody else can do now. Let's go!' A glance showed something moving at the far end of the corridor that had led them to the grating. It might be nothing more than his eyes playing tricks on him. Eye tricks on Acheron could prove fatal.

Ripley was sliding rapidly into hysteria, screaming and crying and flailing her arms and legs. He had to lift her clear of the floor to keep her from diving through the gap. A wild plunge into the water-filled darkness below was a short course to suicide.

'No! No! She's still alive! We have to—'

'All right!' Hicks roared. 'She's alive. I believe it. But we gotta get moving. Now! You're not going to be able to catch her that way.' He nodded at the hole in the floor. 'She won't be waiting for you down there, but they will. Look.' He pointed, and she stopped struggling. There was an elevator at the far end of the tunnel.

'If there's emergency power to the lights in this section, then maybe that's functioning too. Let's get out of here. Once we're up top, we can try to think this through where they can't sneak up on us.'

He still had to half drag her to the elevator and push her inside.

The movement he'd detected at the far end of the tunnel coalesced into the advancing outline of an alien. Hicks practically broke the plastic as he jammed a thumb on the 'up' button. The elevator's double doors began to close—not quite fast enough. The creature slammed one huge arm beween them. As both humans looked on in horror, the automatic safety built into the elevator doors buzzed and began to part. The machine could not discriminate between human and alien.

The drooling abomination lunged towards them, and Hicks blew it away, firing his pulse-rifle at point-blank range. Too close. Acid sluiced between the closing doors to splash across his chest as he shielded Ripley with his armour. Fortunately none of the acid struck the elevator cables. The elevator began to ascend, clawing its way towards the surface on lingering emergency power.

Hicks tore at the quick-release catches on the harness as the powerful liquid ate through the composite-fibre armour. His plight was enough to galvanize Ripley out of her panic. She clawed at his straps, trying to help as much as she could. Acid reached his chest and arm, and he yelled, shucking out of the combat armour like an insect shedding its old skin. The smoking plates fell to the floor, and the relentless acid began to eat through the metal underfoot. Acrid fumes filled the air inside the elevator, searing eyes and lungs.

After what seemed like a thousand years, the elevator ground to a halt. Acid ate through the floor and began to drip onto the cables and support wheels.

The doors parted and they stumbled out. This time it was Ripley who had to support Hicks. Smoke continued to rise from his chest, and he was doubled over in agony.

'Come on, you can make it. I thought you were a tough guy.' She inhaled deeply, coughed, and inhaled again. Hicks choked, gritted his teeth, and tried to grin. After the foulness of the tunnels and ductways the less-than-idyllic air of Acheron smelled like perfume. 'Almost there.'

Not far ahead of them the sleek, streamlined shape of Dropship Two was descending erratically towards the landing grid like a dark angel, side-slipping as it fought its way through the powerful wind gusts just above the surface. They could see Bishop, his back to them, standing in the lee of the transmitter tower as he struggled with the portable guidance terminal to bring the dropship in. It sat down hard and slid sideways, coming to a halt near the middle of the landing pad. Except for a bent landing strut, the inelegant touchdown appeared to have left it undamaged.

She yelled. The synthetic turned to see the two of them stumbling out of a doorway in the colony building behind him. Putting the terminal down carefully, he ran to help, getting one powerful arm under Hicks and helping him towards the ship. As they ran, Ripley shouted to the android, her words barely audible over the gale.

'How much time?'

'Plenty!' Bishop looked pleased. He had reason to be. 'Twenty-six minutes.'

'We're not leaving!' She said this as they were staggering up the loading ramp into the warmth and safety of the ship.

Bishop gaped at her. 'What? Why not?'

She studied him carefully, searching for the slightest suggestion of deception in his face and finding none. His question was perfectly understandable under the circumstances. She relaxed a little.

'Tell you in a minute. Let's get Hicks some medical and close this sucker up, and then I'll explain.'

# XIV

Lightning crackled around the upper rim of the failing atmosphere-processing station. Steam blasted from emergency vents. Columns of incandescent gas shot hundreds of metres into the sky as internal compensators struggled futilely to adjust temperature and pressure overloads that were already beyond correction.

Bishop was careful not to drift too close to the station as he guided the dropship towards the upper-level landing platform. As they approached, they passed over the ruined armoured personnel carrier. A shattered, motionless hulk outside the station entryway, the APC had finally stopped smoking. Ripley stared as it slipped past beneath them, a monument to overconfidence and a misplaced faith in the ability of modern technology to conquer any obstacle. Soon it would evaporate along with the station and the rest of Hadley colony.

About a third of the way up the side of the enormous cone that formed the processing station, a narrow landing platform jutted out into the wind. It was designed to accommodate loading skimmers and small atmospheric craft, not something the size of a dropship. Somehow Bishop managed to manoeuvre them in close. The platform groaned under the shuttle's weight. A supporting beam bent dangerously but held.

Ripley finished winding metal tape around the bulky project that had occupied her hands and mind for the past several minutes. She tossed the half-empty tape roll aside and inspected her handiwork. It wasn't a neat job, and it probably violated twenty separate military safety regulations, but she didn't give a damn. She wasn't going on parade, and there was no one around to tell her it was dangerous and impossible.

What she'd done while Bishop was bringing them in close to the station was to secure Hicks's pulse-rifle to the side of a flamethrower. The result was a massive, clumsy siamese weapons package with tremendous and varied firepower. It might even be enough to get her back to the ship alive—if she could carry it.

She turned back to the dropship's armoury and began loading a satchel and her pockets with anything that might kill aliens: grenades; fully charged pulse-rifle magazines; shrapnel clips; and more.

Having programmed the dropship for automatic lift-off should the landing platform show signs of giving way, Bishop made his way aft from the pilot's compartment to help Hicks treat his injuries. The corporal lay sprawled across several flight seats, the contents of a field medical kit strewn around him. Working together, he and Ripley had managed to stanch the bleeding. With the aid of medication his body would heal. The dissolved flesh was already beginning to repair itself. But in order to reduce the pain to a tolerable level, he'd been forced to take several injections. The medication kept him halfway comfortable but blurred his vision and slowed his reactions. The only support he could give to Ripley's mad plan was moral.

Bishop tried to remonstrate. 'Ripley, this isn't a very efficacious idea. I understand how you feel—'

'Do you?' she snapped at him without looking up.

'As a matter of fact, I do. It's part of my programming. It's not sensible to throw one life after another.'

'She's *alive*.' Ripley found an empty pocket and filled it with grenades. 'They brought her here just like they brought all the others, and you know it.'

'It seems the logical thing for them to do, yes. I admit there is no obvious reason for them to deviate from the pattern they have demonstrated thus far. That is not the point. The point is that even if she is here, it is unlikely that you can find her, rescue her, and fight your way back out in time. In seventeen minutes this place will be a cloud of vapour the size of Nebraska.'

She ignored him, her fingers flying as she sealed the overstuffed satchel. 'Hicks, don't let him leave.'

He blinked weakly at her, his face taut with pain. The medication was making his eyes water. 'We ain't going anywhere.' He nodded towards her feet. 'Can you carry that?'

She hefted her hybrid weapon. 'For as long as I have to.' Picking up the satchel, she slung it over one shoulder, then turned and strode to the crew door. She thumbed it open, waiting impatiently for it to cycle. Wind and the roar from the failing atmosphere processor rushed the gap. She stepped to the top of the loading ramp and paused for a last look back.

'See you, Hicks.'

He tried to sit up, failed, and settled for rolling onto his side. One hand held a wad of medicinal gauze tight against his face. 'Dwayne. It's Dwayne.'

She walked back over to grab his hand. 'Ellen.'

That was enough. Hicks nodded, leaned back, and looked satisfied. His voice was a pale shadow of the one she'd come to be familiar with. 'Don't be long, Ellen.'

She swallowed, then turned and exited, not looking back as the hatch closed behind her.

The wind might have blown her off the platform had she not been so heavily equipped. Set in the station wall opposite the dropship were the doors of a large freight elevator. The controls responded instantly to her touch. Plenty of power here. Too much power.

The elevator was empty. She entered and touched the contact switch opposite C-level. The bottom. The seventh level, she thought as the elevator began to descend.

It was slow going. The elevator had been designed to carry massive, sensitive loads, and it would take its time. She stood

with her back pressed against the rear wall, watching bars of
light descend. As the elevator descended into the bowels of the
station the heat grew intense. Steam roared everywhere. She
had difficulty breathing.

The slow pace of the descent allowed her time to remove her
jacket and slip the battle harness she'd appropriated from the
dropship's stores on directly over her undershirt. Sweat
plastered her hair to her neck and forehead as she made a last
check of the weaponry she'd brought with her. A bandolier of
grenades fitted neatly across the front of the harness. She
primed the flamethrower, made sure it was full. Same for the
magazine locked into the underside of the rifle. This time she
remembered to chamber the initial round to activate the load.

Fingers nervously traced the place where marking flares
bulged the thigh pockets of her jumpsuit pants. She fumbled
with an unprimed grenade. It slipped between her fingers and
fell to the floor, bouncing harmlessly. Trembling, she
recovered it and slid it back into a pocket. Despite all of Hicks's
detailed instructions, she was acutely aware that she didn't
know anything about grenades and flares and such.

Worst of all was the fact that for the first time since they'd
landed on Acheron she was alone. Completely and utterly
alone. She didn't have much time to think about it because the
elevator motors were slowing.

The elevator hit bottom with a gentle bump. The safety cage
enclosing the lift retracted. She raised the awkward double
muzzle of rifle and flamethrower as the doors parted.

An empty corridor lay before her. In addition to the
illumination provided by the emergency lighting, faint reddish
glows came from behind thick metal bulges. Steam hissed from
broken pipes. Sparks flared from overloaded, damaged
circuits. Couplings groaned while stressed machinery throbbed
and whined. Somewhere in the distance a massive mechanical
arm or piston was going *ka-rank, ka-rank*.

Her gaze darted left, then right. Her knuckles were white
above the dual weapon she carried. She had no flexible battle

visor to help her, though in the presence of so much excess heat its infrared-imaging sensors wouldn't have been of much use, anyway. She stepped out into the corridor, into a scene designed by Piranesi, decorated by Dante.

She was struck by the aliens' presence as soon as she turned the first bend in the walkway. Epoxy-like material covered conduits and pipes, flowing smoothly up into the overhead walkways to blend machinery and resin together, creating a single chamber. She had Hicks's locator taped to the top of the flamethrower, and she looked at it as often as she dared. It was still functioning, still homing in on its single target.

A voice echoed along the corridor, startling her. It was calm and efficient and artificial.

'Attention. Emergency. All personnel must evacuate immediately. You now have fourteen minutes to reach minimum safe distance.'

The locator continued to track; range and direction spelled out lucidly by its LED display.

As she advanced, she blinked sweat out of her eyes. Steam swirled around her, making it difficult to see more than a short distance in any direction. Flashing emergency lights lit an intersecting passageway just ahead.

Movement. She whirled, and the flamethrower belched napalm, incinerating an imaginary demon. Nothing there. Would the blast of heat from her weapon be noticed? No time to worry about maybes now. She resumed her march, trying not to shake as she concentrated on the locator's readouts.

She entered the lower level.

In the inner chambers now. The walls around her subsumed skeletal shapes, the bodies of the unfortunate colonists who had been brought here to serve as helpless hosts for embryonic aliens. Their resin-encrusted figures gleamed like insects frozen in amber. The locator's signal strengthened, leading her off to the left. She had to bend to clear a low overhang.

At each turning point or intersection she was careful to ignite a timed flare and place it on the floor behind her. It would be easy to get lost in the maze without the markers to help her find her way back. One passageway was so narrow, she had to turn sideways to slip through it. Her eyes touched upon one tormented face after another, each entombed colonist caught in a rictus of agony.

Something grabbed her. Her knees sagged, and the breath went out of her before she could even scream. But the hand was human. It was attached to an imprisoned body, surmounted by a face. A familiar face. Carter Burke.

'Ripley.' The moan was barely human. 'Help me. I can feel it inside. It's moving . . .'

She stared at him, beyond horror now. No one deserved this.

'Here.' His fingers clutched convulsively around the grenade she handed him. She primed it and hurried on. The voice of the station boomed around her. There was a rising note of mechanical urgency in its tone.

'You now have eleven minutes to reach minimum safe distance.'

According to the locator, she was all but on top of the target. Behind her the grenade went off, the concussion nearly knocking her off her feet. It was answered by a second, more forceful, eruption from deep within the station itself. A siren began to wail, and the whole installation shuddered. The locator led her around a corner. She tensed in anticipation. The locator's range finder read out zero.

Newt's tracer bracelet lay on the tunnel floor, the metal fabric shredded. The glow from its sender module was a bright, cheerless green. Ripley sagged against a wall.

It was all over. All over.

Newt's eyes fluttered open, and she became aware of her surroundings. She had been cocooned in a pillarlike structure at the edge of a cluster of ovoid shapes: alien eggs. She recognized them right away. Before they'd been carried off or killed, the last desperate adult colonists had managed to acquire a few for study.

But those had all been empty, open at the tops. These were sealed.

Somehow the egg nearest her prison became aware of her stirrings. It quivered and then began to open, an obscene flower. Something damp and leathery stirred within. Transfixed by terror, Newt stared as jointed, arachnid legs appeared over the lip of the ovoid. They emerged one at a time. She knew what was going to happen next, and she reacted the only way she could, the only way she knew how—she screamed.

Ripley heard, turned towards the sound, and broke into a run.

With horrible fascination Newt watched as the facehugger climbed out of the egg. It paused for a moment on the rim, gathering its strength and taking its bearings. Then it turned towards her. Ripley came pounding into the chamber as it poised to leap. Her finger tensed on the pulse-rifle's trigger. The single shell tore the crouching creature apart.

The flash from the muzzle illuminated the figure of a mature alien standing nearby. It spun and charged the intruder just in time for twin bursts from the rifle to catapult it backward. Ripley advanced on the corpse, firing again and again, a murderous expression on her face. The alien jerked onto its back, and she finished it with the flamethrower.

While it burned, she ran to Newt. The resinous material of the girl's cocoon hadn't hardened completely yet, and Ripley was able to loosen it enough for Newt to crawl free.

'Here.' Ripley turned her back to the girl and bent her knees. 'Climb aboard.' Newt clambered up onto the adult's hips and locked her hands around Ripley's neck. Her voice was weak.

'I knew you'd come.'

'So long as I could still breathe. Okay, we're getting out of here. I want you to hang on, Newt. Hang on real tight. I'm not going to be able to hold you, because I've got to be able to use the guns.'

She didn't see the nod, but she felt it against her back. 'I understand. Don't worry. I won't let go.'

Ripley sensed movement off to their right. She ignored it as she blasted the eggs with the flamethrower. Only then did she turn it on the advancing aliens. One almost reached her, a living fireball, and she blew it apart with two bursts from the rifle. Ducking beneath a glistening cylindrical mass, she retreated. A piercing shriek filled the air, rising above the pounding of failing machinery, the wail of the emergency siren and the screech of attacking aliens.

She'd have seen it earlier if she'd looked up instead of straight ahead when she'd entered the egg chamber. It was just as well that she hadn't because, despite her determination, she might have faltered. A gigantic silhouette in the ruddy mist, the alien queen glowered above her egg cache like a great, gleaming insectoid Buddha. The fanged skull was horror incarnate. Six limbs, two legs and four taloned arms, were folded grotesquely over a distended abdomen. Swollen with eggs, it comprised a vast, tubular sac that was suspended from the latticework of pipes and conduits by a weblike membrane, as though an endless coil of intestine had been draped along the supporting machinery.

Ripley realized she'd passed right beneath part of the sac a moment earlier.

Inside the abdominal container countless eggs churned towards a pulsating ovipositor in a vile, organic assembly line. There they emerged, glistening and wet, to be picked up by tiny drones. These miniature versions of the alien warriors scuttled back and forth as they attended to the needs of both eggs and queen. They ignored the staring human in their midst as they concentrated with single-minded intensity on the task of transferring newly deposited eggs to a place of safety.

Ripley remembered how Vasquez had done it as she pumped the slide on the grenade launcher: pumped and fired four times. The grenades punched deep into the flimsy egg sac and exploded, blowing it to shreds. Eggs and tons of noisome, gelatinous material spilled over the floor of the chamber. The queen went berserk, screeching like a psychotic locomotive. Ripley laid about with the flamethrower, methodically igniting everything in sight as she retreated. Eggs shrivelled in the inferno, and the figures of warriors and drones vanished amid frenzied thrashing.

The queen towered above the carnage, struggling in the flames. Two warriors closed in on Ripley. The pulse-rifle clicked empty. Smoothly she ejected the magazine, slammed another one home, and held the trigger down. Her attackers vanished in the homicidal hail of fire.

It didn't matter if it moved or not. She blasted everything that didn't look wholly mechanical as she ran for the elevator, setting fire to equipment and destroying controls and instrumentation together with attacking aliens. Sweat and steam half blinded her, but the flares she'd dropped to mark her path shone brightly, jewels set among the devastation. Sirens howled around her, and the station rocked with internal convulsions.

She almost ran past one flare, skidded to a halt, and turned towards it. She staggered on as if in a dream, her lungs straining no longer. Her body was so pumped up, she felt as though she were flying across the metal floor.

Behind her, the queen detached from the ruined egg sac, ripping it away from her abdomen. Rising on legs the size of temple pillars, she lumbered forward, crushing machinery, cocoons, drones, and anything else in her path.

Ripley used the flamethrower to sterilize the corridor ahead, letting loose incinerating blasts at regular intervals, firing down side corridors before she crossed them to keep from being surprised. By the time she and Newt reached the freight elevator, the weapon's tank was empty.

The elevator she'd used for the descent had been demolished by falling debris. She hit the call button on its companion and was rewarded by the whine of a healthy motor as the second metal cage commenced its slow fall from the upper levels. An enraged shriek made her turn. A distant, glistening shape like a runaway crane was trying to batter its way through intervening pipes and conduits to reach them. The queen's skull scraped the ceiling.

She checked the pulse-rifle. The magazine was empty, and she was out of refills, having spent shells profligately while rescuing Newt. No more grenades, either. She tossed the useless dual weapon aside, glad to be rid of the weight.

The cage's descent was too slow. There was a service ladder set inside the wall next to the twin elevator shafts, and she scrambled up the first rungs. Newt was as light as a feather on her back.

As she dived into the stairwell a powerful black arm shot through the doorway like a piston. Razor-sharp talons slammed into the floor centimetres from her legs, digging into the metal.

Which way now? She was no longer fearful, had no time to panic. Too many other things to concentrate on. She was too busy to be terrified.

There: an open stairwell leading to the station's upper levels. It rocked and shuddered as the huge installation began tearing itself to bits beneath her. Behind her, the floor buckled as something incredibly powerful threw itself insanely against the metal wall. Talons and jaws pierced the thick alloy plates.

'You now have two minutes to reach minimum safety distance,' the sad voice of the station informed any who might be listening.

Ripley fell, banging one knee against the metal stairs. Pain forced her to pause. As she caught her breath the sound of the elevator motors starting up made her look back down through the open latticework of the building. The elevator cage had begun to ascend. She could hear the overloaded cables groaning in the open shaft.

She resumed her heavenward flight, the stairwell becoming a mad blur around her. There was only one reason why the elevator would resume its ascent.

At last they reached the doorway that led out onto the upper-level landing platform. With Newt still somehow clinging to her, Ripley slammed the door open and stumbled out into the wind and smoke.

The dropship was gone.

'*Bishop!*' The wind carried her scream away as she scanned the sky. 'Bishop!' Newt sobbed against her back.

A whine made her turn as the straining elevator slowly rose into view. She backed away from the door until she was leaning against the narrow railing that encircled the landing platform. It was ten levels to the hard ground below. The skin of the heaving processing station was as smooth as glass. They couldn't go up and they couldn't go down. They couldn't even dive into an air duct.

The platform shook as an explosion ripped through the bowels of the station. Metal beams buckled, nearly throwing her off her feet. With a shriek of rending steel a nearby cooling tower collapsed, keeling over like a slain sequoia. The explosions didn't stop after the first one this time. They began to sequence as backup safety systems failed to contain the expanding reaction. On the other side of the doorway the elevator ground to a halt. The safety cage enclosing the cargo bay began to part.

She whispered to Newt. 'Close your eyes, baby.' The girl nodded solemnly, knowing what Ripley intended as she put one leg over the railing. They would hit the ground together, quick and clean.

She was just about to step off into open air when the dropship rose into view almost beneath them, its hovering thrusters roaring. She hadn't heard it approach because of the howling wind. The ship's loading boom was extended, a single, long metal strut reaching towards them like the finger of God. How Bishop held the vessel steady in the rippling gale Ripley didn't know—and didn't care. Behind her, she could just hear the voice of the station. It, like the installation it served, had almost run out of time.

'You now have thirty seconds to reach . . .'

She jumped onto the loading boom and hung on as it retracted into the dropship's cargo bay. An instant later a tremendous explosion tore through the station. The resultant

wind shear slammed the hovering craft sideways. Extended
landing legs ripped into a complex of platform, wall, and
conduit. Metal squealed against metal, the entanglement
threatening to drag the ship downward.

Inside the hold Ripley threw heself into a flight seat, cradling
Newt against her as she strapped both of them in. Glancing up
the aisle, she could just see into the cockpit where Bishop was
fighting the controls. As they retracted, the sound of the
landing legs pulling free echoed through the little vessel. She
slammed home the latches on her seat harness, wrapped both
arms tightly around Newt.

'Punch it, Bishop!'

The entire lower level of the station vanished in an
expanding fireball. The ground heaved, earth and metal
vapourizing as the dropship erupted skyward. Its engines fired
hard, and the resultant gees slammed Ripley and Newt back in
their seat. No comfortable, gradual climb to orbit this time.
Bishop had the engines open full throttle as the dropship
clawed its way through the blighted atmosphere. Ripley's back
protested even as she mentally urged Bishop to increase the
velocity.

As they left blue for black, the clouds lit up from beneath. A
bubble of white-hot gas burst through the troposphere. The
shock wave from the thermonuclear explosion rattled the ship
but didn't damage it, and they continued to climb towards high
orbit.

Within the metal bottle Ripley and Newt stared out of a
viewport, watching as the blinding flare dissipated behind
them. Then Newt slumped against Ripley's shoulder and
began to cry quietly. Ripley rocked her and stroked her hair.

'It's okay, baby. We made it. It's over.'

Ahead of them the great, ungainly bulk of the *Sulaco* hung in
geo-synchronous orbit, awaiting the arrival of its smaller
offspring. On Bishop's command the dropship rose until
docking grapples snapped home, lifting them into the cargo
bay. The outer lock doors cycled shut. Automatic warning

lights swept the dark, deserted chamber, and a warning horn ceased hooting. Excess engine heat was vented as the cavernous hold filled with air.

Within the ship Bishop stood behind Ripley while she knelt beside the comatose Hicks. She glanced questioningly at the android.

'I gave him another shot for the pain. He kept insisting that he didn't need it, but he didn't fight the injection. Strange thing, pain. Stranger to me still, this peculiar inner need of certain types of human to pretend that it doesn't exist. Many are the times I'm glad I'm synthetic.'

'We need to get him to the *Sulaco*'s medical ward,' she replied, rising. 'If you can get his arms, I'll take his feet.'

Bishop smiled. 'He is resting comfortably now. It will be better for him if we jostle him as little as possible. And you are tired. For that matter, *I'm* tired. It'll be easier if we get a stretcher.'

Ripley hesitated, looking down at Hicks, then nodded. 'You're right, of course.'

Picking up Newt, she preceded the android down the aisle leading to the extended loading ramp. They could have a self-propelling stretcher back for Hicks in a few minutes. Bishop continued to talk.

'I'm sorry if I gave you a scare when you emerged onto the landing platform and saw the ship missing, but the site had simply become too unstable. I was afraid I'd lose the ship if I remained docked. It was simpler and safer to hover a short distance away. Close to the ground, the wind is not as strong. I had a monitor on the exit all the time so that I'd know when you arrived.'

'Wish I'd known that at the time.'

'I know. I had to circle and hope that things didn't get too rough to take you off. In the absence of human direction I had to use my own judgment, according to my programming. I'm sorry if I didn't handle it the best way.'

They were halfway down the loading ramp. She paused and put a hand on his shoulder, stared evenly into artificial eyes.

'You did okay, Bishop.'

'Well, thanks, I—' He stopped in mid-sentence, his attention focused on something glimpsed out of the corner of one eye. Nothing, really. An innocuous drop of liquid had splashed onto the ramp next to his shoe. Condensate from the skin of the dropship.

The droplet began to hiss as it started to eat into the metal ramp. Acid.

Something sharp and glistening burst from the centre of his chest, spraying Ripley with milky android internal fluid. An alien stinger, queen-size, driving straight through him from behind. Bishop thrashed, uttering meaningless machine noises and clutching the protruding point of the spear as it slowly lifted him off the landing ramp.

The queen had concealed herself among the landing mechanism inside one strut bay. The atmospheric plates that normally sealed the bay flush with the rest of the dropship's skin had been bent aside or ripped away. She'd blended in perfectly with the rest of the heavy machinery until she began to emerge.

Seizing Bishop in two huge hands, she ripped him apart and flung the two halves aside. Rotating warning lights flashed on her shining dark limbs as she slowly descended to the deck, still smoking where Ripley had half fried her. Acid dripped from minor wounds that were healing rapidly. Sextuple limbs unfolded in unhuman geometries.

Breaking out of her paralysis, Ripley lowered Newt to the deck without taking her eyes off the descending nightmare.

'Go!'

Newt bolted for the nearest cluster of packing crates and equipment. The alien dropped to the deck and pivoted in the direction of the movement. Ripley backed clear, waving her arms and shouting, making faces, jumping up and down—doing anything and everything she could think of to draw the monster's attention away from the fleeing child.

Her decoying action was successful. The giant whirled,

moving much too quickly for anything so huge, and sprang as Ripley sprinted for the oversize internal storage door that dominated the far end of the cargo hold. Massive feet boomed on the deck behind her.

She cleared the door and flailed at the 'close' switch. The barrier whirred as it complied with the command, moving much faster than the doors of the now vanished station. An echoing *whang* reverberated through the storage room as the alien struck the solid wall an instant too late.

Ripley didn't have time to stand around to see if the door would hold. She moved rapidly among bulky, dark shapes, searching for a particular one.

Outside, the queen's attention was drawn from the stubborn barrier to visible movement. A network of trenchike service channels protected by heavy metal grillework underlaid the cargo bay deck like the tributaries of a river system. The channels were just deep enough for Newt to enter. She'd dropped through one service opening and had begun crawling, scurrying towards the other end of the cargo bay like a burrowing rabbit.

The alien tracked the movement. Talons swooped, ripped up a section of grillework just behind the frantic child. Newt tried to move faster, scrambling desperately as another piece of grille disappeared right at her heels. The next to go would be directly above her.

The alien paused in mid-reach at the sound of the heavy storage room door grinding open behind her. In the opening stood a massive, articulated silhouette.

Riding two tons of hardened steel, Ripley strode out in the powerloader. Her hands were inside waldo gloves while her feet rested in similar receptacles attached to the floor controls of the safety cab. Wearing the loader like high-tech armour, she advanced on the watching queen. The loader's ponderous feet boomed against the deck plates. Ripley's face was a mask of maternal fury devoid of fear.

'Get away from her, *you!*'

The queen emitted an inhuman screech and leapt at the oncoming machine.

Ripley threw her arm in a movement not normally associated with the activities of powerloaders or similar devices, but the elegant machine reacted perfectly. One massive hydraulic arm slammed into the alien's skull and threw it back against the wall. The queen reacted instantly and charged again, only to crash into a backhand that literally landed like a ton. She fell backward into a pile of heavy loading equipment.

'Come on!' Ripley wore a frenzied, distorted smile. 'Come on!'

Tail lashing with rage, the queen charged the loader a third time. Four biomechanical arms swung at the loader's two. The great stinger stabbed at the flanks and underside of the loader, glancing harmlessly off solid metal. Ripley parried and struck with sweeping blows of the steel tines, backing up the loader, then advancing, pivoting to keep the machine's arms between her and the queen. The battle moved across the deck, demolishing packing crates, portable instrumentation, small machinery, everything in the path of the fight. The cargo bay echoed with the nightmarish sounds of two dragons battling to the death.

Getting the two powerful mechanical hands around a pair of alien arms, Ripley clenched her own fingers tight inside the waldoes, crushing both biomechanical limbs. The queen writhed with outrage, the talons of her other hands coming within inches of penetrating the safety cage to tear the tiny human apart. Ripley raised her arms, lifting the queen off the deck. The loader's engine groaned as it protested against the excessive weight. Hind legs ripped at the machine, denting the safety cage protecting its operator. The alien skull inclined towards her, and the outer jaws began to part. Ripley clung grimly to her controls.

The inner striking teeth exploded towards her. She ducked, and they slammed into the seat cushion behind her in an explosion of gelatinous drool. Yellow acid foamed over the hydraulic arms, crawling towards the safety cage. The queen tore at high-pressure hoses. Purple fluid sprayed in all directions, machine blood mixing with alien blood.

As it lost hydraulic pressure on one side the loader crumpled and fell over. The queen immediately rolled to get on top of it, avoiding the crushing metal arms, trying to find a way to penetrate the safety cage. Ripley hit a switch on the loader's console, and its cutting torch came to life, the intense blue flame firing straight into the alien's face. It screamed and drew back, dragging the loader with it. As she fell and the world was turned upside down around her, Ripley's safety harness kept her secured to the driver's seat.

Together machine, biomechanoid, and human rolled into the rectangular pit of the loading dock. The loader landed on top of the alien, crushing part of its torso and pinning it beneath its great weight. Acid began to seep in a steady flow from the badly damaged body.

Ripley's eyes widened as she fought with the loader's controls. The dripping acid spread out over the airlock doors and began to smoke as it started eating its way through the superstrong alloy. Beyond the outer dock lay void.

As the first tiny holes appeared, she struggled to unstrap herself from the driver's seat. Air began to leave the *Sulaco* as the insatiable emptiness of space sucked at the ship. A rising wind tore at Ripley as she stumbled clear of the loader. Jumping a puddle of smoking acid, she grabbed at the bottom rungs of the ladder that was built into the wall of the airlock. One hand slapped the inner door's emergency override. Above, the heavy inner airlock doors began rumbling towards each other like steel jaws. She climbed wildly.

Beneath her, the first holes widened, were joined by others as the acid did its work. The flow of escaping air around her increased in volume, slowing her ascent.

Newt had emerged from the network of subfloor channels to hide among a forest of gas cylinders. When the powerloader, Ripley, and the alien had tumbled into the airlock, she'd slipped out for a better look.

Now the suction from below pulled her legs out from under her and dragged her, kicking and screaming, across the smooth deck. Bishop, or rather his upper half, saw her coming. He grabbed a support stanchion with one hand. With the other he reached out, and thanks to perfect synthetic timing, just managed to get his fingers entwined in the girl's belt as she slid by. She hung there in his grasp, floating in the intensifying gale like a Newt-flag as the wind sucked at her.

Ripley's head emerged above deck level. As she tried to kick up and out with her right leg, something caressed her left ankle and latched hold. An experimental tug almost tore Ripley's arms from their sockets. Desperately she threw both arms around the ladder's upper rung, which was mounted a foot away on the deck. The inner airlock doors continued rumbling towards one another. If she didn't pull herself clear or drop back down within a couple of seconds, she'd end up looking just like Bishop.

Below, the acid-weakened outer lock doors groaned. A portion of the inner reinforcing collapsed. The interlocked powerloader and alien queen settled a few centimetres. Ripley felt her arm giving way as she was dragged down, but it was her shoe that came away first. Her leg was free.

Summoning strength from unknown depths, she dragged herself onto the deck just as the inner airlock doors slammed shut. Beneath her, the alien queen uttered another scream of rage and exerted all her incomprehensible strength. The heavy loader squealed as she began to push it aside.

It was half off when the outer doors, honeycombed by acid, fell apart, sending chunks of metal, bubbles of acid, the queen, and the powerloader spilling out into space. Ripley rose and stumbled to the nearest viewport. The queen's efforts were enough to propel her clear of the *Sulaco*'s artificial gravity field. Still screaming and tearing at the powerloader, the queen tumbled slowly back towards the inhospitable world she'd recently fled.

Ripley stared as her nemesis faded to a dot, then a dim point, and was at last swallowed by the rolling clouds. Within the cargo bay turbulent air eddied and settled as the *Sulaco*'s cyclers worked to replenish the atmosphere that had been lost.

Bishop was still holding Newt with one hand. His bisected torso trailed artificial inner organs and sparking conduits. His eyelids fluttered, and his head sometimes jerked unpredictably, bumping against the deck. His internal regulators had managed to shut off the flow of android blood, fighting a holding action against the massive injury. White encrustation sparkled along the edge of the tear.

He managed a small, grim smile as he eyed the approaching Ripley. 'Not bad for a human.' He regained control of his eyelids long enough to give her an unmistakable wink.

Ripley stumbled over to Newt. The girl looked dazed.

'Mommy—mommy?'

'Right here, baby. I'm right here.' Sweeping the girl up in her arms, she hugged her as hard as she could. Then she headed towards the *Sulaco*'s crew quarters.

Around them, the big ship's systems hummed reassuringly. She found her way up to Medical and returned to the cargo hold with a stretcher in tow. Bishop assured her that he could wait. With the stretcher's aid she gently loaded the sleeping Hicks and trundled him back to the hospital ward. His expression was peaceful, content. He'd missed the whole thing, luxuriating in the effects of the injection Bishop had given him.

As for the android, he lay on the deck, his hands crossed over his chest and his eyes closed. She couldn't tell if he was dead or sleeping. Better minds than hers would determine that once they got back to Earth.

In sleep Hicks's face lost much of its macho Marine toughness. He looked much like any other man. Handsomer though, and certainly more tired. Except that he wasn't like any other man. If it hadn't been for him, she'd be dead, Newt would be dead, all dead. Only the *Sulaco* would have lived on, an empty receptacle awaiting the return of humans who would never come.

She thought of waking him, decided against it. In a little while, when she was sure that his vital signs were stabilized and the repairs to his acid-scarred flesh well under way, she'd place him in one of the empty, waiting hypersleep capsules.

She turned to inspect the sleeping chamber. Three capsules to prep. If he still lived, Bishop wouldn't need one. The synthetic would probably have found hypersleep confining.

Newt looked up at her. She held two of Ripley's fingers as they strode together up the corridor.

'Are we going to sleep now?'

'That's right, Newt.'

'Can we dream?'

Ripley gazed down at the bright, upturned face and smiled. 'Yes, honey. I think we both can.'

# ALIEN³

Novelization by Alan Dean Foster
Based on a screenplay by
David Giler & Walter Hill and Larry Ferguson
Story by Vincent Ward

With thanks to Insight Computers
of Tempe, Arizona
for their wonderful computers.

ADF

# I

Bad dreams.

Funny thing about nightmares. They're like a chronically recurring disease. Mental malaria. Just when you think you've got them licked they hit you all over again, sneaking up on you when you're unprepared, when you're completely relaxed and least expect them. Not a damn thing you can do about it, either. Not a damn thing. Can't take any pills or potions, can't ask for a retroactive injection. The only cure is good sound sleep, and that just feeds the infection.

So you try not to sleep. But in deep space you don't have any choice. Avoid the cryonic chambers and the boredom on a deep-space transport will kill you. Or even worse, you'll survive, dazed and mumbling after the sacrifice of ten, twenty, thirty years of useless consciousness. A lifetime wasted gazing at gauges, seeking enlightenment in the unvarying glare of readouts of limited colours. You can read, and watch the vid, and exercise, and think of what might have been had you opted to slay the boredom with deep sleep. Not many professions where it's considered desirable to sleep on the job. Not a bad deal at all. Pay's good, and you have the chance to observe social and technological advance from a unique perspective. Postponing death does not equate with but rather mimics immortality.

Except for the nightmares. They're the inescapable downside to serving on a deep-space vessel. Normal cure is to wake up. But you can't wake up in deep sleep. The machines won't let you. It's their job to keep you under, slow down your body functions, delay awareness. Only, the engineers haven't figured out yet how to slow down dreams and their bastard cousin the nightmare. So along with your respiration and circulation your unconscious musings are similarly drawn out, lengthened, extended. A single dream can last a year, two. Or a single nightmare.

Under certain circumstances being bored to death might be the preferable alternative. But you've got no options in deep sleep. The cold, the regulated atmosphere, the needles that poke and probe according to the preset medical programmes, rule your body, if not your life. When you lie down in deep sleep you surrender volition to the care of mechanicals, trusting in them, relying on them. And why not? Over the decades they've proven themselves a helluva lot more reliable than the people who designed them. Machines bear no grudges, engage in no animosity. The judgments they render are based solely on observation and analysis. Emotion is something they're not required to quantify, much less act upon.

The machine that was the *Sulaco* was doing its job. The four sleepers on board alternately dreamt and rested, speeding along their preprogrammed course coddled by the best technology civilization could devise. It kept them alive, regulated their vitals, treated momentary blips in their systems. Ripley, Hicks, Newt, even Bishop, though what was left of Bishop was easy to maintain. He was used to being turned on and off. Of the four he was the only one who didn't dream, didn't have nightmares. It was something he regretted. It seemed like such a waste of time, to sleep but not to dream. However, the designers of the advanced android series to which he belonged would have regarded dreaming as an expensive frivolity, and therefore did not apply themselves to the resolution of the problem.

Naturally no one thought to inquire of the androids what they thought of the situation.

After Bishop, who technically was part of the ship and not the crew and therefore did not count, Hicks was the worst off of the sleepers. Not because his nightmares were any more severe than those of his companions, but because the injuries he had recently suffered did not lend themselves to extended neglect. He needed the attention of a modern, full-service medical facility, of which the closest example lay another two years travel time and an enormous distance away.

Ripley had done what she could for him, leaving final diagnosis and prescription to the efficient judgment of the *Sulaco*'s medical instrumentation, but as none of the ship's medical personnel had survived the trouble on Acheron, his treatment was perforce minimal. A couple of years locked in deep sleep were not conducive to rapid healing. There was little she'd been able to do except watch him slide into protective unconsciousness and hope.

While the ship did its best his body laboured to repair the damage. Slowing down his vitals helped because that likewise slowed down the spread of potential infection, but about the internal injuries he'd suffered, the ship could do nothing. He'd survived this long on determination, living off his reserves. Now he needed surgery.

Something was moving in the sleep chamber that was not a part of the ship, though in the sense that it too was wholly driven by programming it was not so very different from the cold, indifferent corridors it stalked. A single imperative inspired its relentless search, drove it mindlessly onward. Not food, for it was not hungry and did not eat. Not sex, for it had none. It was motivated solely and completely by the desire to procreate. Though organic, it was as much a machine as the computers that guided the ship, though it was possessed of a determination quite foreign to them.

More than any other terrestrial creature it resembled a horseshoe crab with a flexible tail. It advanced across the smooth floor of the sleep chamber on articulated legs fashioned of an unusually carbon-rich chiton. Its physiology was simple, straightforward, and designed to carry out but one biological function and to do that better than any comparable construction known. No machine could have done better.

Guided by senses that were a unique combination of the primitive and sophisticated, driven by an embedded imperative unequalled in any other living being, it scuttled determinedly across the chamber.

Scaling the smooth flank of the cryonic cylinder was a simple matter for something so superbly engineered. The top of the chamber was fashioned of transparent metallic glass. Within slept a small organic shape; half-formed, blonde, innocent save for her nightmares, which were as sophisticated and frequently more extensive than those of the adults sleeping nearby. Eyes closed, oblivious to the horror which explored the thin dome enclosing her, she slept on.

She was not dreaming. Presently the nightmare was concrete and very real. Far better that she remained unaware of its existence.

Impatiently the thing explored the sleep cylinder, beginning at one end and working methodically up to the head. The cylinder was tight, triple-sealed, in many ways more secure than the hull of the *Sulaco* itself. Though anxious, the creature was incapable of frustration. The prospect of imminent fulfilment of its biological imperative only excited it and drove it to greater efforts. The extensible tube which protruded from its ventral side probed the unyielding transparency which shielded the helpless body on the unreachable cushions, proximity to its quarry driving the creature into a frenzy of activity.

Sliding to one side, it eventually located the nearly imperceptible line which separated the transparent dome of the cylinder from its metal base. Tiny claws drove into the minuscule crack as the incredibly powerful tail secured a purchase on the instrumentation at the head of the cylinder. The creature exerted tremendous leverage, its small body quivering with the effort. Seals were strained. The thing's effort was unforgiving, its reserves of strength inconceivable.

The lower edge of the transparent dome snapped, the metallic glass splitting parallel to the floor. A sliver of the clear material, sharp as a surgical instrument, drove straight through the creature's body. Frigid air erupted from the cylinder until an internal emergency seal restored its atmospheric integrity.

Prone on her bed of uneasy dreams Newt moaned softly, her head turning to one side, eyes moving beneath closed lids. But she did not wake up. The cylinder's integrity had been restored just in time to save her life.

Emitting periodic, unearthly shrieks the mortally wounded crawler flung itself across the room, legs and tail flailing spasmodically at the transparent sliver which pierced its body. It landed atop the cylinder in which reposed the motionless Hicks, its legs convulsively gripping the crest of the dome. Shuddering, quivering, it clawed at the metallic glass while acidic body fluids pumped from the wound. They ate into the glass, into the metal base of the cylinder, into and through the floor. Smoke began to rise from somewhere beneath the deck, filling the chamber.

Around the room, throughout the ship, telltales winked to life, warning lights began to flash and Klaxons to sound. There was no one awake to hear them, but that did not affect the *Sulaco*'s reaction. It was doing its job, complying with its programming. Meanwhile smoke continued to billow from the ragged aperture in the floor. Atop Hicks's cylinder the crawler humped obscenely as it continued to bleed destruction.

A female voice, calm and serenely artificial, echoed unheard within the chamber. 'Attention. Explosive gases are accumulating within the cryogenic compartment. Explosive gases are accumulating within the cryogenic compartment.'

Flush-mounted fans began to hum within the ceiling, inhaling the swirling, thickening gas. Acid continued to drip from the now motionless, dead crawler.

Beneath the floor something exploded. Bright, actinic light flared, to be followed by a spurt of sharp yellow flame. Darker smoke began to mix with the thinner gases that now filled the chamber. The overhead lights flickered uncertainly.

The exhaust fans stopped.

'Fire in cryogenic compartment,' the unperturbed female voice declared in the tone of something with nothing to lose. 'Fire in cryogenic compartment.'

A nozzle emerged from the ceiling, rotating like a miniature cannon. It halted, focusing on the flames and gas emerging from the hole in the floor. Liquid bubbled at its tip, gushed in the direction of the blaze. For an instant the flames were subdued.

Sparks erupted from the base of the nozzle. The burgeoning stream died, dribbling ineffectively from the powerhead.

'Fire suppression system inactivated. Fire suppression system inactivated. Exhaust system inactivated. Exhaust system inactivated. Fire and explosive gases in cryogenic chamber.'

Motors hummed to life. The four functioning cryonic cylinders rose from their cradles on hydraulic supports. Their telltales winking, they began to move to the far side of the room. Some smoke and intensifying flame obscured but did not slow their passage. Still pierced through by the chunk of metallic glass, the dead crawler slid off the moving coffin and fell to the floor.

'All personnel report to EEV,' the voice insisted, its tone unchanged. 'Precautionary evacuation in one minute.'

Moving in single file the cryonic cylinders entered a transport tube, travelled at high speed through the bowels of the ship until they emerged in the starboard lock, there to be loaded by automatic handlers into the waiting Emergency Escape Vehicle. They were its only occupants. Behind the transparent faceplate, Newt twitched in her sleep.

Lights flashed, motors hummed. the voice spoke even though there were none to hear. 'All EEVs will be jettisoned in ten seconds. Nine . . . .'

Interior locks slammed shut, externals opened wide. The voice continued its countdown.

At 'zero' two things happened with inimical simultaneity: ten EEVs, nine of them empty, were ejected from the ship, and the proportion of escaping gases within the damaged cryonic chamber interacted critically with the flames that were emerging from the acid-leached hole in the floor. For a brief eruptive instant the entire fore port side of the *Sulaco* blazed in fiery imitation of the distant stars.

Half the fleeing EEVs were severely jolted by the explosion. Two began tumbling, completely out of control. One embarked upon a short, curving path which brought it back in a wide, sweeping arc to the ship from which it had been ejected. It did not slow as it neared its storage pod. Instead it slammed at full acceleration into the side of the transport. A second, larger explosion rocked the great vessel. Wounded, it lurched onward through emptiness, periodically emitting irregular bursts of light and heat while littering the immaculate void with molten, shredded sections of its irrevocably damaged self.

On board the escape craft containing the four cryonic cylinders, telltales were flashing, circuits flickering and sparking. The EEV's smaller, less sophisticated computers struggled to isolate, minimize, and contain the damage that had been caused by the last-second explosion. The vehicle had not been hulled, but the concussion had damaged sensitive instrumentation.

It sought status clarification from the mother ship and when none was forthcoming, instigated a scan of its immediate surroundings. Halfway through the hasty survey the requisite instrumentation failed but it was quickly rejuvenated via a backup system. The *Sulaco* had been journeying far off the beaten photonic path, its mission having carried it to the fringes of human exploration. It had not travelled long upon its homeward path when overcome by disaster. Mankind's presence in this section of space was marked but intermittent, his installations far apart and few between.

The EEV's guiding computer found something. Undesirable,

not a primary choice. But under existing conditions it was the only choice. The ship could not estimate how long it could continue to function given the serious nature of the damage it had suffered. Its primary task was the preservation of the human life it bore. A course was chosen and set. Still sputtering, striving mightily to repair itself, the compact vessel's drive throbbed to life.

Fiorina wasn't an impressive world, and in appearance even less inviting, but it was the only one in the Neroid Sector with an active beacon. The EEV's data banks locked in on the steady signal. Twice the damaged navigation system lost the beam, but continued on the proscribed course anyway. Twice the signal was recovered. Information on Fiorina was scarce and dated, as befitted its isolation and peculiar status.

'Fiorina "Fury" 361,' the readout stated. 'Outer veil mineral ore refinery. Maximum security work-correctional facility.' The words meant nothing to the ship's computer. They would have meant much to its passengers, but they were not in position or condition to read anything. 'Additional information requested?' the computer flashed plaintively. When the proper button was not immediately pressed, the screen obediently blanked.

Days later the EEV plunged towards the grey, roiling atmosphere of its destination. There was nothing inviting about the dark clouds that obscured the planetary surface. No glimpse of blue or green showed through them, no indication of life. But the catalogue indicated the presence of a human installation, and the communications beacon threw its unvarying pulse into emptiness with becoming steadiness.

On-board systems continued to fail with discouraging regularity. The EEV's computer strained to keep the craft under control as one backup after another kicked in. Clouds the colour of coal dust raced past the unoccupied ports as atmospheric lightning flashed threateningly off the chilled, sealed coffins within.

The computer experienced no strain as it tried to bring the

EEV down safely. There was no extra urgency in its efforts. It would have functioned identically had the sky been clear and the winds gentle, had its own internal systems been functioning optimally instead of flaring and failing with progressive regularity.

The craft's landing gear had not responded to the drop command and there was neither time nor power to try a second approach. Given the jumbled, precipitous nature of the landscape immediately surrounding the beacon and formal landing site, the computer opted to try for a touchdown on the relatively smooth sand beach.

When additional power was requested, it developed that it did not exist. The computer tried. That was its job. But the EEV fell far short of the beach, slamming into the sea at too acute an angle.

Within the compartment, braces and bulkheads struggled to absorb the impact. Metal and carbon composites groaned, buffeted by forces they were never intended to withstand. Support struts cracked or bent, walls twisted. The computer concentrated all its efforts on trying to ensure that the four cylinders in its care remained intact. The crisis left little time for much else. About itself the computer cared nothing. Self-care was not a function with which it had been equipped.

The surface of Fiorina was as barren as its sky, a riot of grey-black stone scoured by howling winds. A few twisted, contorted growths clung to protected hollows in the rock. Driving rain agitated the surface of dank, cold pools.

The inanimate shapes of heavy machinery dotted the mournful landscape. Loaders, transports, and immense excavators and lifters rested where they had been abandoned, too massive and expensive to evacuate from the incredibly rich site which had once demanded their presence. Three immense burrowing excavators sat facing the wind like a trio of gigantic carnivorous worms, their drilling snouts quiescent, their operator compartments dark and deserted. Smaller machines and vehicles clustered in groups like so many starving parasites, as if waiting for one of the larger machines to grind to life so they might eagerly gather crumbs from its flanks.

Below the site dark breakers smashed methodically into a beach of gleaming black sand, expending their energy on a lifeless shore. No elegant arthropods skittered across the surface of that shadowy bay, no birds darted down on skilled, questing wings to probe the broken edges of the incoming waves for small, edible things.

There were fish in the waters, though. Strange, elongated creatures with bulging eyes and small, sharp teeth. The human transients who called Fiorina home engaged in occasional arguments as to their true nature, but as these people were not the sort for whom a lengthy discussion of the nature of parallel evolution was the preferred mode of entertainment, they tended to accept the fact that the ocean-going creatures, whatever their peculiar taxonomy, were edible, and let it go at that. Fresh victuals of any kind were scarce. Better perhaps not to peer too deeply into the origins of whatever ended up in the cookpot, so long as it was palatable.

The man walking along the beach was thoughtful and in no particular hurry. His intelligent face was preoccupied, his expression noncommittal. Light plastic attire protected his perfectly bald head from the wind and rain. Occasionally he kicked in irritation at the alien insects which swarmed around his feet, seeking a way past the slick, treated plastic. While Fiorina's visitors occasionally sought to harvest the dubious bounty of its difficult waters, the more primitive native life-forms were not above trying to feast on the visitors.

He strolled silently past abandoned derricks and fossilized cranes, wholly intent on his thoughts. He did not smile. His attitude was dominated by a quiet resignation born not of determination but indifference, as though he cared little about what happened today, or whether there was a tomorrow. In any event he found far more pleasure in gazing inward. His all too familiar surroundings gave him little pleasure.

A sound caused him to look up. He blinked, wiping cold

drizzle from his face mask. The distant roar drew his gaze to a point in the sky. Without warning a lowering cloud gave violent birth to a sliver of descending metal. It glowed softly and the air around it screamed as it fell.

He gazed at the place where it had struck the ocean, pausing before resuming his walk.

Halfway up the beach he checked his chronometer, then turned and began to retrace his steps. Occasionally he glanced out to sea. Seeing nothing, he expected to find nothing. So the limp form which appeared on the sand ahead of him was a surprise. He increased his pace slightly and bent over the body as wavelets lapped around his feet. For the first time his blood began to race slightly. The body was that of a woman, and she was still alive. He rolled her over onto her back.

Stared down into Ripley's unconscious, salt-streaked face.

He looked up, but the beach still belonged to him alone. Him, and this utterly unexpected new arrival. Leaving her to go for help would mean delaying treatment which might save her life, not to mention exposing her to the small but still enthusiastic predators which inhabited parts of Fiorina.

Lifting her beneath her arms, he heaved once and managed to get her torso around his shoulders. Legs straining, he lifted. With the woman on his shoulders and back he headed slowly towards the weather lock from which he'd emerged earlier.

Inside he paused to catch his breath, then continued on towards the bug wash. Three prisoners who'd been working outside were busy delousing, naked beneath the hot, steady spray that mixed water with disinfectant. As medical officer, Clemens carried a certain amount of authority. He used it now.

'Listen up!' The men turned to regard him curiously. Clemens interacted infrequently with the prisoners except for those who sought him out for sick call. Their initial indifference vanished as soon as they spotted the body hanging from his shoulders. 'An EEV's come down.' They exchanged glances. 'Don't just stand there,' he snapped, trying to divert their attention from his burden. 'Get out on the beach. There may be others. And notify Andrews.'

They hesitated, then began to move. As they exited the wash and began grabbing at their clothes, they stared at the woman Clemens carried. He didn't dare set her down.

# II

Andrews didn't like working the Communicator. Every use went down in his permanent record. Deep-space communication was expensive and he was expected to make use of the device only when absolutely and unavoidably necessary. It might develop that his judgment would not agree with that of some slick-assed bonehead back at headquarters, in which case his accumulated pay might be docked, or he might be denied a promotion. All without a chance to defend himself, because by the time he made it out of the hellhole that was Fiorina and back home, the cretin who'd docked him would probably be long since dead or retired.

Hell, why was he worrying? Everyone he'd ever known would be dead by the time he got back home. That didn't render him any less anxious to make that oft-anticipated journey.

So he did his rotten job as best he could and hoped that his rotten employers would eventually take note of his skill and professionalism and offer early retirement, except that now a rotten, unforeseen difficulty had arisen with the sole intent of complicating his life. Andrews harboured an intense dislike for the unforeseen. One of the few compensations of his job was its unremitting predictability.

Until now. And it compelled him to make use of the Communicator. Angrily he hammered the keys.

FURY 361—CLASS C PRISON UNIT–IRIS 12037154.

REPORT EEV UNIT 2650 CRASH
OCCUPANTS  –  BISHOP MODEL ANDROID,
                          INACTIVE HICKS, CPL.—ES
                          MARINES—L55321—DOA RIPLEY,
                          LT.—CO SVC.—B515617—
                          SURVIVOR UNIDENTIFIED
                          JUVENILE FEMALE—DOA
REQUEST EMERG. EVAC. SOONEST POSSIBLE—
AWAIT RESPONSE SUPT. ANDREWS M51021.
[Time delay transmis 1844—Fiorina]

Clemens had dragged the woman out of the water and had
hustled her up to the facility as quickly as possible. So quickly
that her condition and not her gender had dominated their
thoughts. Reflection would come later, and with it the
problems Andrews envisioned.

As for the EEV itself, they'd used the mutated oxen to winch
it ashore. Any of the mine vehicles could have done the job
quicker and easier, but those which had been abandoned
outside had long since given up the ghost of active function,
and those within the complex were too valuable to the
inhabitants to risk exposing to the weather, even assuming the
men could have safely hoisted an appropriate vehicle outside.
Simpler to use the oxen, unaccustomed as they were to the
task. But they performed effectively, save for one that
collapsed subsequently and died, doubtless from having been
subjected to the unfamiliar strain of actual work.

Once within reach of the mine's sole remaining operational
external crane, it was easy enough to secure the badly damaged
escape craft to the bracing and lower it inside. Andrews was
there when the men went in, soon to emerge and declare that
the woman hadn't come alone, that there were others.

The superintendent wasn't pleased. More complications,
more holes in his placid daily routine. More decisions to make.
He didn't like making decisions. There was always the danger
of making a wrong one.

The marine corporal was dead, likewise the unfortunate

child. The android didn't matter. Andrews was somewhat relieved. Only the woman to deal with, then, and just as well. She presented complications enough.

One of the men informed him that the Communicator was holding an on-line message. Leaving the EEV and its contents in the care of others, the superintendent made his way back to his office. He was a big man in his late forties, muscular, powerful, determined. He had to be all of that and more or he'd never have been assigned to Fiorina.

The reply was as terse as his original communication.

TO: FURY 361—CLASS C PRISON UNIT 1237154
FROM: NETWORK CONCOM 01500—WEYLAND-YUTANI MESSAGE RECEIVED.

Well, now, that was profound. Andrews stared at the readout screen but nothing else was forthcoming. No suggestions, no requests for additional information, no elegant corporate explication. No criticism, no praise. Somehow he'd expected more.

He could send another message requesting more data, except that the powers-that-be were likely to deem it extraneous and dock his pay for the cost. They'd responded, hadn't they? Even if they hadn't exactly replied. There was nothing he could do but deal with the situation as best he saw fit . . . and wait.

Another dream. No sense of time in dreams, no temporal spaciousness. People see all sorts of things in dreams, both intensely realistic and wholly imaginary. Rarely do they see clocks.

The twin-barrelled flamethrower was heavy in her hands as she cautiously approached the cryonic cylinders. A quick check revealed all three occupants untouched, undisturbed. Bishop, quiescent in fragments. Newt ethereal in her perfect childish beauty, so foreign to the place and time in which she unwillingly found herself. Hicks peaceful, unmarred. She felt herself hesitating as she drew near, but his dome remained shut, his eyes closed.

A sound and she whirled, flipping a switch on the weapon's ribs even as her finger convulsed on the trigger. The device emitted a plastic click. That was all. Frantically she tried again. A short, reluctant burst of flame emerged a few inches from one of the barrels, died.

Panicky, she inspected the weapon, checking the fill levels, the trigger, those leads that were visible. Everything seemed functional. It ought to work, it had to work . . . .

Something nearby, close. She dreamt herself retreating, backing up cautiously, seeking the protection of a solid wall as she fumbled with the flamethrower. It was near. She knew it too well to think otherwise. Her fingers wrestled with the balky device. She'd found the trouble, she was sure. A minute more, that was all she needed. Recharge this, rest, then ready to fire. Half a minute. She happened to glance downward.

The alien's tail was between her legs.

She spun screaming, right into its waiting arms, and tried to bring the flamethrower to bear. A hand clutched; horribly elegant, incredibly powerful fingers crushed the weapon in the middle, collapsing the twin barrels, the other arm trapping her. She pummelled the shiny, glistening thorax with her fists. Useless the gesture, useless everything now.

It spun her around and shoved her across the nearest cryonic pod. Shoved again. Her face was pressed tight to the cool, inorganic glass. Beneath her, Hicks opened his eyes and smiled again. And again.

She screamed.

The infirmary was compact and nearly empty. It abutted a much larger medical facility designed to handle dozens of patients a day. Those miners, prospective patients, were long gone from Fiorina. They had accomplished their task years ago, extracting the valuable ore from the ground and then following it back home. Only the prisoners remained, and they had no need of such extensive facilities.

So the larger unit had been gutted of salvageable material

and the smaller semi-surgery turned over to the prison. Cheaper that way. Less room to heat, less energy required, money saved. Where prisoners were concerned that was always the best way.

Not that they'd been left with nothing. Supplies and equipment were more than ample for the installation's needs. The Company could afford to be generous. Besides, shipping even worthwhile material offworld was expensive. Better to leave some of it, the lesser quality stuff, and gain credit for concomitant compassion. The good publicity was worth more than the equipment.

Besides the facility there was Clemens. Like some of the supplies he was too good for Fiorina, though it would have been difficult to convince anyone familiar with his case of that. Nor would he have raised much in the way of objections. But the prisoners were lucky to have him, and they knew it. Most of them were not stupid. Merely unpleasant. It was a combination which in some men gave rise to captains of industry and pillars of government. In others it led merely to defeat and degradation. When this situation was directed inward the sufferers were treated or incarcerated on places like Earth.

When it erupted outward to encompass the innocent it led elsewhere. To Fiorina, for example. Clemens was only one of many who'd realized too late that his personal path diverged from the normal run of humanity to lead instead to this place.

The woman was trying to say something. Her lips were moving and she was straining upward, though whether pushing against or away from something he was unable to tell. Leaning close, he put his ear to her mouth. Sounds emerged, bubbling and gurgling, as if rising towards the surface from deep within.

He straightened and turned her head to one side, holding it firmly but gently. Gagging, choking, she vomited forth a stream of dark salt water. The heaving ended quickly and she subsided, still unconscious but resting quietly now; still, easy. He eased her head back onto the pillow, gazing solemnly at her masklike visage. Her features were delicate, almost girlish despite her age. There was about her the air of someone who had spent too much time as a tourist in hell.

Well, being dumped out of a ship via EEV and then awakened and revived from deep sleep by a crash into the sea would be enough to mark anyone, he told himself.

The infirmary door hissed softly as it slid back to admit Andrews and Aaron. Clemens wasn't crazy about either the superintendent or his number two. At the same time he was quite aware that Andrews wasn't in love with the facility's sole medical technician either. Though in status he might be a notch above the general population, Clemens was still a prisoner serving sentence, a fact neither of the two men ever let him forget. Not that he was likely to. Many things were difficult to accomplish on Fiorina, but forgetting was impossible.

They halted by the side of the bed and stared down at its motionless occupant. Andrews grunted at nothing in particular.

'What's her status, Mr. Clemens?'

The technician sat back slightly, glanced up at the man who for all practical purposes served as Fiorina's lord and master.

'She's alive.'

Andrews's expression tightened and he favoured the tech with a sardonic smile. 'Thank you, Mr. Clemens. That's very helpful. And while I suppose I wouldn't, or shouldn't, want it to be otherwise, it also does mean that we have a problem, doesn't it?'

'Not to worry, sir. I think we can pull her through. There's no internal bleeding, nothing broken, not even a serious sprain. I think she'll make a complete recovery.'

'Which, as you know, Mr. Clemens, is precisely what concerns me.' He stared appraisingly at the woman in the bed. 'I wish she hadn't come here. I wish she wasn't here now.'

'Without wishing to sound disrespectful, sir, I have this feeling that she'd eagerly concur with you. Based on what I was told about her landing and having seen for myself the current condition of her EEV, I'm of the opinion that she didn't have a whole hell of a lot of choice in the matter. Any idea where they're from? What ship?'

'No,' Andrews muttered. 'I notified Weyland-Y.'

'They answer?' Clemens was holding Ripley's wrist, ostensibly to check her pulse.

'If you can call it that. They acknowledged receipt of my message. That's all. Guess they're not feeling real talkative.'

'Understandable, if they had an interest in the ship that was lost. Probably running around like mad trying to decide what your report signifies.' The mental image of confounded Company nabobs pleased him.

'Let me know if there's any change in her condition.'

'Like if she should conveniently expire?'

Andrews glared at him. 'I'm already upset enough over this as it is, Clemens. Be smart. Don't make it worse. And don't make me start thinking of it and you in the same breath. There's no need for excessive morbidity. It may surprise you to learn that I hope she lives. Though if she regains consciousness she may think otherwise. Let's go,' he told his factotum. The two men departed.

The woman moaned softly, her head shifting nervously from side to side. Physical reaction, Clemens wondered, or side effects of the medication he'd hastily and hopefully dumped into her system? He sat watching her, endlessly grateful for the opportunity to relax in her orbit, for the chance simply to be close to her, study her, smell her. He'd all but forgotten what it was like to be in a woman's presence. The memories returned rapidly, jolted by her appearance. Beneath the bruises and strain she was quite beautiful, he thought. More, much more, than he'd had any right to expect.

She moaned again. Not the medication, he decided, or pain from her injuries. She was dreaming. No harm there. After all, a few dreams couldn't hurt her.

The dimly lit assembly hall was four storeys high. Men hung

from the second floor railing, murmuring softly to each other, some smoking various combinations of plant and chemical. The upper levels were deserted. Like most of the Fiorina mine, it was designed to accommodate far more than the couple of dozen men presently gathered together in its cavernous depths.

They had assembled at the superintendent's request. All twenty-five of them. Hard, lean, bald, young and not so young, and those for whom youth was but a fading warm memory. Andrews sat confronting them, his second-in-command Aaron nearby. Clemens stood some distance away from both prisoners and jailers, as befitted his peculiar status.

Two jailers, twenty-five prisoners. They could have jumped the superintendent and his assistant at any time, overpowered them with comparative ease. To what end? Revolt would only give them control of the installation they already ran. There was nowhere to escape to, no better place on Fiorina that they were forbidden to visit. When the next supply ship arrived and ascertained the situation, it would simply decline to drop supplies and would file a report. Heavily armed troops would follow, the revolutionaries would be dealt with, and all who had participated and survived would find their sentences extended.

The small pleasures that might be gained from defiance of authority were not worth another month on Fiorina, much less another year or two. The most obdurate prisoners realized as much. So there were no revolts, no challenges to Andrews's authority. Survival on and, more importantly, escape from Fiorina depended on doing what was expected of one. The prisoners might not be content, but they were pacific.

Aaron surveyed the murmuring crowd, raised his voice impatiently. 'All right, all right. Let's pull it together, get it going. Right? Right. If you please, Mr. Dillon.'

Dillon stepped forward. He was a leader among the imprisoned and not merely because of his size and strength. The wire rimless glasses he wore were far more an affectation, a concession to tradition, than a necessity. He preferred them to contacts, and of course the Company could hardly be expected to expend time and money to provide a prisoner with transplants. That suited Dillon fine. The glasses were antiques, a family heirloom which had somehow survived the generations intact. They served his requirements adequately.

The single dreadlock that hung from his otherwise naked pate swung slowly as he walked. It took a lot of time and effort to keep the hirsute decoration free of Fiorina's persistent bugs, but he tolerated the limited discomfort in order to maintain the small statement of individuality.

He cleared his throat distinctly. 'Give us strength, O Lord, to endure. We recognize that we are poor sinners in the hands of an angry God. Let the circle be unbroken . . . until the day. Amen.' It was a brief invocation. It was enough. Upon its conclusion the body of prisoners raised their right fists, lowered them silently. The gesture was one of acceptance and resignation, not defiance. On Fiorina defiance bought you nothing except the ostracism of your companions and possibly an early grave.

Because if you got too far out of line Andrews could and would exile you from the installation, with comparative impunity. There was no one around to object, to check on him, to evaluate the correctness of his actions. No independent board of inquiry to follow up a prisoner's death. Andrews proposed, Andrews imposed. It would have been intolerable save for the fact that while the superintendent was a hard man, he was also fair. The prisoners considered themselves fortunate at that. It could easily have been otherwise.

He surveyed his charges. He knew each of them intimately, far better than he would have liked to, had he been given the option. He knew their individual strengths and weaknesses, distastes and peccadilloes, the details of their case histories. Some of them were scum, others merely fatally antisocial, and there was a broad range in between. He cleared his throat importantly.

'Thank you, gentlemen. There's been a lot of talk about what happened early this morning, most of it frivolous. So you can consider this a rumour control session.

'Here are the facts. As some of you know, a 337 model EEV crash-landed here at 0600 on the morning watch. There was one survivor, two dead, and a droid that was smashed beyond hope of repair.' He paused briefly to let that sink in.

'The survivor is a woman.'

The mumbling began. Andrews listened, watched intently, trying to note the extent of reactions. It wasn't bad . . . yet.

One of the prisoners leaned over the upper railing. Morse was in his late twenties but looked older. Fiorina aged its unwilling citizens quickly. He sported a large number of gold-anodized teeth, a consequence of certain antisocial activities. The gold colour was a cosmetic choice. He seemed jumpy, his normal condition.

'I just want to say that when I arrived here I took a vow of celibacy. That means no women. No sex of any kind.' His agitated stare swept the assembly. 'We all took the vow. Now, let me say that I, for one, do not appreciate Company policy allowing her to freely intermingle . . .'

As he droned on, Aaron whispered to his superior. 'Cheeky bastard, ain't he, sir?'

Finally Dillon stepped in front of his fellow prisoner, his resonant voice soft but firm. 'What brother means to say is that we view the presence of any outsider, especially a woman, as a violation of the harmony, a potential break of the spiritual unity that gets us through each day and keeps us sane. You hear what I say, Superintendent? You take my meaning?'

Andrews met Dillon's gaze unflinchingly. 'Believe me, we are well aware of your feelings in this matter. I assure you, all of you, that everything will be done to accommodate your concerns and that this business will be rectified as soon as possible. I think that's in everyone's best interest.' Murmurs rose from the crowd.

'You will be pleased to know that I have already requested a rescue team. Hopefully, they will be here inside of a week to evacuate her ASAP.' Someone in the middle spoke up. 'A week, Superintendent? Nobody can get here that fast. Not from anywhere.'

Andrews eyed the man. 'Apparently there's a ship in transit to Motinea. She's been in the programme for months. This is an emergency. There are rules even the Company has to comply with. I'm sure they'll contact her, kick at least a pilot out of deep sleep, and divert her our way to make the pickup. And that will put an end to that.'

He knew no such thing, of course, but it was the logical course of action for the Company to take and he felt a certain confidence in presupposing. If the ship bound for Motinea didn't divert, then he'd deal with the situation as required. One potential crisis at a time.

He glanced up at Clemens. 'Have you had enough time to make an evaluation?'

The tech crossed his arms diffidently across his chest. 'Sort of. Best I can manage, with what we have here.'

'Never mind the complaints. What's her medical status?'

Clemens was well aware that every eye in the room was suddenly focused on him, but he didn't acknowledge them, keeping his attention on the superintendent. 'She doesn't seem too badly damaged. Mostly just bruised and banged up. One of her ribs may be broken. If so it's only a stress fracture. What is potentially more dangerous is that she came out of deep sleep too abruptly.' He paused to collect his thoughts.

'Look, I'm just a general tech and even I can see that she's going to need specialist attention. Somebody gets whacked out of deep sleep early, without the appropriate biophysical prep, and there can be all kinds of problems. Unpredictable side effects, latent respiratory and circulatory complications, cellular disruptions that sometimes don't manifest themselves for days or weeks – stuff I wouldn't begin to know how to diagnose, much less properly treat. For her sake I hope that rescue ship carries full medical facilities.'

'Will she live?' Andrews asked him.

The tech shook his head in quiet wonder. The superintendent was good at hearing only what he wanted to hear.

'Assuming nothing shows up later, I think she'll be fine. But don't quote me on that. Especially to a registered physician.'

'What're you afraid of?' Someone sniggered behind him. 'Bein' accused of malpractice?' Inclement laughter rose from some in the group.

Andrews stepped on it quickly, before Clemens or anyone else could reply. 'Look, none of us here is naive. It's in everybody's best interests if the woman doesn't come out of the infirmary until the rescue team arrives. And certainly not without an escort. Out of sight, out of mind, right?' No one chose to comment one way or the other. 'So we should all stick to our set routines and not get unduly agitated. Correct? All right.' He rose. 'Thank you, gentlemen.'

No one moved. Dillon turned and spoke softly. 'Okay.'

The assemblage began to break up, the men to return to their daily tasks. Andrews was not miffed by the slight. It was a small gesture by the prisoners, and he was willing to allow small gestures. It let some of the pressure off, mitigated their need to attempt big ones.

The meeting had gone as well as could have been expected. He felt he'd dealt with the situation properly, putting a stop to rumour and speculation before it could get out of hand. Aaron at his side, he headed back to his office.

A more informative response from the Company would have been helpful, however.

Clemens found his exit blocked by Dillon. 'Something on your mind?'

The big man looked concerned. 'Pill pusher. You should be careful of this woman.'

Clemens smiled. 'She's not in any condition to cause much trouble. Don't we owe all God's children a fighting chance?'

'We don't know whose child she is.' The two men stared at each other a moment longer. Then Dillon moved aside to let the tech pass. His gaze followed Clemens until he stepped through the portal leading to tunnel D.

The woman lay motionless on the bed, for a change not moaning, not dreaming. Clemens checked the IV pack taped to her arm. Without knowing the specifics of her condition he'd been forced to treat her for general debilitation. In addition to glucose and sucrose the pack contained a broad range of tolerant antibiotics in solution, REM-sleep modifiers, and painkillers. The tough ID tag she'd been wearing had been damaged in the crash, so he'd been forced to treat her without the crucial information it contained. He'd monitored her carefully for any signs of rejection and was relieved when none manifested themselves. At least she wasn't allergic to anything he'd pumped into her system so far.

He was gratified to see that the armpack was nearly empty. That meant her body was making good use of the rehab solution. The readouts on the VS checker as he passed it over her chest and skull stayed green. Thus encouraged, he slipped a capsule into the injector and turned her arm slightly to expose more of the tricep.

Her eyes snapped open as if she'd only been faking sleep. Startled by the speed of her reaction, he hesitated. She indicated the device in his hand.

'What's that?'

'General site injector.'

'I can see that. You know what I mean.'

He smiled slightly. 'A light cocktail of my own devising. Sort of an eye-opener. Adrenaline, some selected designer endorphins, a couple of mystery proteins. For flavour. I think your body's recovered sufficiently to metabolize them. Five minutes after they've dispersed through your system you'll feel a lot better than you do now.'

She continued to eye him warily. 'Are you a doctor?'

He shrugged and looked away momentarily, as if the question made him uncomfortable. 'General med tech. I've only got a 3-C rating. But I'm the best you're going to find around here.' He leaned forward, eyes narrowing as he inspected her hair appraisingly. 'I really ought to shave your head. Should've done it right away but I was busy with more important things.'

This admission caused Ripley to sit bolt upright in the bed, clutching the sheet protectively to her neck.

'Take it easy. I'm no murderer. Though you'll find them here.'

'Why do you have to shave my head?'

'Microscopic parasites. Carnivorous arthropods. They're endemic to Fiorina. Fortunately they don't find humans particularly tasty ... except for the keratin in our hair. For some reason they don't have the same appetite for fingernails. Wrong consistency, maybe. We just call 'em lice, and to hell with scientific nomenclature.'

'Can't you use some kind of spray, or prophylactic shampoo, something?' Her eyes remained fixed on the razor.

'Oh, the Company tried that when they were starting up the mine, but these little suckers are tough. Anything'd have to be to make a success of it on this world. Turned out that anything strong enough to dent the parasites raised blisters on the skin. Bad enough on the scalp. Damn sight worse lower down. Shaving turned out to be a simpler, cheaper, and more effective solution. Some of the guys hang on to a little hair out of spite and fight the bugs as best they can. Eyebrows, for example. You wouldn't think anybody would give a damn about something as ephemeral as eyebrows. But dense hair, that's out of the question. Try to live with the lice and they'll drive you crazy, crawling around, eating, itching—'

'All right, all right,' Ripley replied quickly. 'I get the picture.'

'I'll give you an electric razor for downstairs. When you're feeling better you can attend to that. The infirmary's about the most sterile room in the installation, so you should be okay for a while, but the little buggers'll find you eventually. They're too small to screen out. Just shave and they won't bother you.' She hesitated, thoughtful, then nodded understandingly.

'My name is Clemens. I'm the chief medical officer here at

Fury 361.'

Her brows knitted. 'That doesn't sound like a mine designation.'

'Mine's what it used to be. Last of the worthwhile ore was dug out, refined, and shipped offworld some time ago. Weyland-Yutani had this huge facility cost that forced them to abandon, so to recoup a few credits they lease the operative part of it for a maximum-security prison. Everybody benefits. Society is separated from its most undesirable undesirables and the Company gets free caretakers. Everybody benefits, except those of us who are sent here.' He gestured with the injector. 'Do you mind? This is just sort of a stabilizer.'

She was feeling safe enough now to let him approach as she turned her attention to examining her surroundings. 'How did I get here?'

'You crash-landed in an EEV. Nobody knows what happened to your mothership or what caused you to be ejected. If Harry Andrews – he's the superintendent here – knows, he isn't saying.

'Whatever catastrophe caused you to be ejected also must have damaged the landing controls on the EEV because you smacked into the bay pretty hard. We hauled it back here. I haven't been inside myself, but if the exterior's any indication of the kind of internal damage she suffered, you're damn lucky to be alive, much less more or less in one piece.'

She swallowed. 'What about the others?'

'Yeah, I was kind of wondering about that myself. Where's the rest of the crew? Did they get off on other EEVs?'

'There is no "rest of the crew," ' she informed him tersely. 'It's a long story, one I don't feel much like telling right now. I mean what about those who were in the EEV with me? How many were there?'

'Two. Three if you count the android.' He paused. 'I'm afraid they didn't make it.'

'What?' It wasn't sinking in.

'They didn't survive.'

She considered for a long moment, then shook her head brusquely. 'I want to go to the ship. I have to see for myself.' She started to sit up and he put a restraining hand on her shoulder.

'Hey, hang on. As your doctor, I have to tell you that you're in no condition for that.'

'You're not a doctor, remember?' She slipped out of the other side of the bed and stood waiting expectantly, quite naked. 'You want to get me some clothes, or should I go like this?'

Clemens took his time deciding, not entirely displeased by the opportunity to view her vertically. 'Given the nature of our indigenous population, I would strongly suggest clothes.' Rising, he opened a locker on the far side of the infirmary and began sorting through the contents.

'Keep in mind as you gambol through our little wonderland that the prison population here is strictly male and none of them have seen a woman in years. Neither have I, for that matter.'

She waited, hand on hip, giving him the calculating eye. 'Yeah, but I don't have to worry about you, because you're a not-doctor, remember?'

He grinned in spite of himself.

# III

Clemens noted how her eyes darted to and fro as he led her through the corridors and along the walkways. Like those of a nervous child ... or sophisticated predator. She missed nothing. The slightest sound drew her instant attention. Their feet made little noise on the worn metal. The garb he'd scavenged for her was a little small, but she didn't seem to mind.

'I've no idea how long you were in deep sleep, but coming out of it the way you did can be a helluva jolt to the system. Just so you don't panic if I look at you crossways, you should know that I'm still monitoring you for possible delayed side effects. So let's steady on as we go, Ripley.'

She looked at him sharply. 'How do you know my name?'

'It's stencilled on the back of your shorts.' He smiled apologetically. 'We also found your ID tag. It was so mangled the computer could hardly read it, but we got that much off it. Unfortunately, most of your personal medical info was scrambled. I had to guess a lot.'

Ripley rolled her shoulders forward experimentally, let her head roll from side to side. 'Feels like you did a pretty good job. Thanks.'

To his immense surprise he found that he was slightly embarrassed. 'Hey, any jerk can slap on an armpack.'

She grinned. 'I don't think so. It takes a specially qualified jerk.'

The work crew was being as careful as possible with the hulk of the EEV as they eased it onto hastily raised blocks. The old crane groaned with the effort. There hadn't been much call for its use since the mine had been shut down, and temporary reactivation for the purpose of manipulating the emergency vehicle had been a touchy process. But the machinery was responding adequately. Cables sang as the craft was gently lowered.

It had attracted its share of stares when it had first been hauled inside the complex. Ripley drew rather more as she and Clemens approached. She did a much better job of pretending not to notice than the prisoners did of trying not to look.

'Just what kind of place is this work prison?' she asked her guide as they started up a ramp towards the battered lifeship.

Clemens stayed close. 'Used to be a mine cum refinery. Mostly platinum-group minerals. Naturally the raw ore was refined on the spot. Much cheaper than shipping it offworld for processing elsewhere. I understand there was a considerable rise in the price of platinum about the time the ore body here was located. Otherwise it wouldn't have been worth the Company's while to go to the expense of setting up a facility this size this far from any point of consumption. It was a rich lode, highly concentrated.'

'And now?' She had stopped outside the EEV and was inspecting the damaged hull.

'Weyland-Yutani's got it on hold. Interstellar commodities trading isn't exactly my specialty and I don't know that anybody here gets their jollies from following the relevant rises and falls in raw materials prices. I think I heard that a drop in the price of the refined metal was accompanied by less need for the stuff.

'So most of the equipment here's been mothballed. Not worth the expense of moving it, not worth enough as salvage. There's still ore in the ground and if the price goes up I'm sure the Company would reopen. That means we'd probably get moved. Wouldn't do to have felons associating with nice, moral miners. Not that anybody would mind being shifted off this rock. The change would be sweet and it's pretty hard to conceive of anyplace else being worse.

'So we're just caretakers, just a custodial staff. Keeps things from freezing up in case the price of the ore or the need for it goes back up. Works out well for the government and the Company.'

'I'd think you'd go crazy after a year or so in a place like this.'

Clemens had to laugh. 'That's what they said some of us were before we were sent here. But I don't think we are, at least not the majority of us. The isolation isn't nearly so trying if you can learn to think of yourself as a contemplative penitent instead of an incarcerated felon.'

'Any women ever been here?'

'Sorry, Lieutenant Ripley. This is a double Y chromosome facility. Strictly male.'

She nodded, then turned and bent to crawl through what remained of the battered air lock. Clemens let her forge a path, then followed.

The battered exterior of the craft was pristine compared to what she encountered inside. Walls were crumpled and bent, readouts and consoles smashed, equipment strewn haphazardly across the deck. The thick smell of salt water permeated everything. She paused, astonished that anything or anyone could have survived intact, much less her own fragile form.

'Where are the bodies?'

Clemens was equally taken with the extent of the destruction, marvelling that Ripley had suffered no more damage than she had.

'We have a morgue. Mining's the kind of enterprise that demands one. We've put your friends in there until the investigative team arrives, probably in a week's time.'

'There was an android . . . .'

Clemens made a face. 'Disconnected and discombobulated. There were pieces of him all over the place. What's left was thrown in the trash. The corporal was impaled by a support beam straight through the chest. Even if he'd been conscious he'd never have known what hit him. As it was he probably never came out of deep sleep long enough to hurt.'

'The girl?' She was holding a lot in, Clemens saw. He had no idea how much.

'She drowned in her cryotube. I don't imagine she was conscious when it happened. If anything, she went out more quietly than the corporal. I'm sorry.'

Ripley digested this quietly. Then her shoulders began to shake and the tears came. That was all. No yelling, no screaming, no violent railing at an unfair, uncaring universe. Little Newt. Newt, who'd never had a chance. At least she was free. Wiping at her eyes, Ripley turned to survey the remains of the little girl's cryotube. The faceplate was broken, which was understandable.

Abruptly she frowned. The metal below the faceplate was strangely discoloured. She leaned forward and ran her fingers over the stain.

Clemens looked on curiously. 'What is it?'

Ripley rose, the emotion of the moment transformed into something else. There was no concern in her voice now, none of the tenderness he'd noted previously.

'Where is she?'

'I told you, the morgue. Don't you remember?' He eyed her with concern, worried that she might be having a reaction to something from the armpack. 'You're disoriented. Half your system still thinks it's in deep sleep.'

She whirled on him so suddenly that he started. 'I want to see what's left of her body.'

'What do you mean, what's left? The body's intact.'

'Is it? I want to see it. I need to see for myself.'

He frowned but held off questioning her. There was something in her expression . . . One thing was clear: there would be no denying her access. Not that there was any reason to. He had the feeling her desire to view the corpse had nothing to do with nostalgia. Difficult on short acquaintance to figure what she was really like, but excessively morbid she wasn't.

The circular stairwell was narrow and slippery, but cut time off the long hike from the storage chamber where the EEV had been secured. Clemens was unable to contain his curiosity any longer.

'Any particular reason you're so insistent?'

'I have to make sure how she died,' she replied evenly. 'That it wasn't something else.'

'Something else?' Under different circumstances Clemens might have been insulted. 'I hate to be repetitious about a sensitive subject, but it's quite clear that her cylinder was breached and that she drowned.' He considered. 'Was she your daughter?'

'No,' Ripley replied evenly, 'she wasn't my daughter. My daughter died a long time ago.'

As she spoke her eyes avoided his. But of course she was still weak and had to concentrate on the narrow, spiralling steps.

'Then why this need?'

Instead of answering directly she said, 'Even though we weren't related, she was very close to me. You think I *want* to see her the way you've described her? I'd much rather remember her as she was. I wouldn't ask to do this if it wasn't damned important to me.'

He started to reply, then stopped himself. Already he knew that Ripley wasn't the sort of person you could force a reply from. If she was going to tell him anything it would come in her own good time.

He unlocked the entrance and preceded her inside. A bottom drawer responded to his official key code and slid open on silent rollers. She moved up to stand alongside him and together they gazed down at the peaceful, tiny body.

'Give me a moment. Please.'

Clemens nodded and walked across the room to fiddle with a readout. Occasionally he turned to watch as his companion examined the little girl's corpse. Despite the emotions that had to be tearing through her, she was efficient and thorough. When he thought a decent amount of time had passed, he rejoined her.

'Okay?' He expected a nod, perhaps a last sigh. He most definitely did not expect what she finally said.

'No. We need an autopsy.'

'You're joking.' He gaped at her.

'No way. You think I'd joke about something like this? We have to make sure how she died.' Ripley's eyes were steel-hard.

'I told you: she drowned.' He started to slide the body drawer back, only to have her intervene.

'I'm not so sure.' She took a deep breath. 'I want you to cut her open.'

He stared at her in disbelief. 'Listen to me. I think you're disoriented. Half your system's still in cryosleep.'

'Look,' she said in a thoroughly no-nonsense tone, 'I have a very good reason for asking this and I want you to do it.'

'Would you care to share this reason?' He was very composed.

She hesitated. 'Isn't it enough that I'm asking?'

'No, it is not. "Request of close personal friend" won't cut it with Company inspectors. You've got to do better than that.' He stood waiting, impatient.

'All right,' she said finally. 'Risk of possible contagion.'

'What kind of "contagion"?' he snapped.

She was clearly reaching. 'I'm not the doctor. You are.'

He shook his head. 'You'll have to do better than that.'

'Cholera.' She eyed him squarely. Her determination was remarkable.

'You can't be serious. There hasn't been a case reported in two hundred years. C'mon, tell me another. Never turn down a good laugh in this place. Smallpox, maybe? Dengue fever?'

'I am telling you. Cholera. I was part of the combat team that nuked Acheron. They were experimenting with all kinds of mutated bacterial and viral strains in what was supposed to be a safe, closed environment. Maybe you know about some of the

Company's interests. The infection got loose and . . . spread. It was particularly virulent and there was no effective antidote. Nor could the infection be contained, though the people there tried.'

'So they nuked the place? Seems like a pretty extreme prescription. Of course, we don't hear much out here, but it seems to me we would have heard about that.'

'Really? I guess you don't work for the same Company I do. Or maybe you did hear. Your superintendent doesn't strike me as an especially loquacious kind of guy. He may know all about it and just decided there was no reason to pass the information along.'

'Yeah.' She had him confused, Clemens had to confess. And curious. Was Andrews hiding that particular piece of news? It wasn't as if he was obligated to keep the prisoners conversant with current events.

But cholera? Mutated strain or not, it still seemed like a pretty thin story. Of course, if she was telling the truth and the little girl's corpse was infected with something they might not be able to combat . . .

Or maybe it was a half-truth. Maybe there was a risk of some kind of infection and the cholera story was the only cover she'd been able to think up on short notice. Obviously she thought she had her reasons. She *was* military. What the hell did he know about it?

She was standing silently, watching him, waiting.

*What the hell*, he thought.

'As you wish.'

Compared to the morgue the rest of the petrified, neglected complex was as bright and cheerful as an alpine meadow at high spring. Stainless steel cabinets lined one wall, bar codes taped to several. The tough laminated tile floor was chipped and cracked. Easy enough to repair, except that they didn't have the equipment or the necessary skills, and nobody cared anyway.

The gleaming cream-white table in the centre of the room

was bare beneath the overhead lights. A masked and gowned Clemens bent over the prepped corpse of the little girl and commenced the initial incision with the scalpel, pausing to wipe at his brow. It had been a long time since he'd done anything like this and not only was he badly out of practice, he wasn't at all sure why he was doing it now.

A saw sliced silently and efficiently through the undersized rib cage.

'You're sure you want to go through with this?' he asked the staring Ripley. She ignored him, watching silently, her heart cold, emotions stored safely away where they wouldn't interfere. He shrugged and continued with the incision.

Placing both gloved hands in the opening he'd made, knuckles against knuckles, he took a deep breath and pulled apart, prying open and exposing the chest cavity. Concentrating, he peered inward, occasionally bending close and looking sideways for a different view. Eventually he straightened and relaxed his fingers.

'We have nothing unusual. Everything's where it's supposed to be. Nothing missing. No sign of disease, no unusual discolouration, no sign of contagion. I paid particular attention to the lungs. If anything, they appear abnormally healthy. Flooded with fluid, as I suspected. I'm sure analysis will show Fiorinian sea water. Kind of an odd physical state for cholera, hmmm?'

He made a final cross-lateral cut, inspected within, then glanced up. 'Still nothing. Satisfied?'

She turned away.

'Now, since I'm not entirely stupid, do you want to tell me what you're really looking for?'

Before she could reply, the far door was thrown open. The two sombre figures who entered ignored it as it smashed into the interior wall.

Andrews's expression was even less convivial than usual.

'Mr. Clemens.'

'Superintendent.' Clemens's reply was correct but not

deferential. Ripley observed the unspoken byplay between the two with interest. 'I don't believe you've met Lieutenant Ripley.'

She suspected that the burly super's appraising glance lasted rather longer than he intended. His attention shifted to the operating table, then back to his med tech.

'What's going on here, Mr. Clemens?'

'Yeah, right sir,' Aaron chipped in, a verbal as well as physical echo of his boss. 'What's going on, Mr. Clemens?'

'First, Lieutenant Ripley is feeling much better, I'm happy to say. As you can see, physically she's doing quite well.' Andrews didn't rise to the bait. Mildly disappointed, Clemens continued. 'Second, in the interests of public health and security, I'm conducting an autopsy on the deceased child.'

'Without my authority?' The superintendent all but growled.

The tech replied matter-of-factly, not at all intimidated. 'There didn't seem to be time.'

Andrews's brows lifted slightly. 'Don't give me that, Clemens. That's one thing we have in surplus on Fiorina.'

'What I mean is that the lieutenant was concerned about the possible presence in the body of a mutated infectious organism.'

The superintendent glanced questioningly at the silent Ripley. 'Is that true?'

She nodded, offering no further explanation.

'It's turned out all right,' Clemens interjected. 'The body is perfectly normal and shows no signs of contagion. I was certain,' he finished dryly, 'that you'd want me to follow up on this as promptly as possible. Hence my desire to begin immediately.'

You could almost see the thoughts dancing in Andrews's brain, Ripley thought. Fermenting.

'All right,' he said finally, 'but it might be helpful if Lieutenant Ripley didn't parade around in front of the prisoners, as I am told she did in the last hour. Semimonastic vows notwithstanding. Nothing personal, you understand,

Lieutenant. The suggestion is made as much for your protection as for my peace of mind.'

'I quite understand,' she murmured, half smiling.

'I'm sure that you do.' He turned back to the med tech. 'It might also be helpful if you kept me informed as to any change in her physical status. I'm expected to keep the official log updated on this sort of thing. Or would that be asking too much?'

Ripley took a step forward. 'We have to cremate the bodies.'

Andrews frowned at her. 'Nonsense. We'll keep the bodies on ice until a rescue team arrives. There are forms that will need to be filled out. I don't have that kind of jurisdictional leeway.'

'Cremate . . . that's a good one, sir,' Aaron sniggered, always eager to please.

'Look, I'm not making an arbitrary request here,' Ripley told him, 'and it has nothing to do with . . . personal feelings. There is a public health issue at stake.' She eyed Clemens expectantly.

*What on earth is troubling her so*? he found himself wondering. Aloud he said, 'Lieutenant Ripley feels that the possibility of a communicable infection still exists.'

The superintendent's gaze narrowed suspiciously. 'I thought you said there was no sign of disease.'

'What I said was that as far as I was concerned the body was clean and showed no sign of contagion. You know how sophisticated the facilities I have at my disposal are, and what an outstanding reputation I maintain in the interworld medical profession.' Andrews grunted understandingly.

'Just because I pronounce the body clean doesn't mean that it necessarily is. It would appear that the child drowned plain and simple, though without the proper forensics tests it's impossible to be absolutely certain. At the risk of contradicting my own analysis I think it would be unwise to tolerate even the possibility of a mutated virus getting loose within the installation. I don't think the members of the rescue team would look kindly on such a development upon their arrival, either. It might make them rather standoffish, and we do treasure our occasional visits, don't we?

'Not to mention which a preventable outbreak of something the Marines had to nuke Acheron to destroy would look very bad on your report, wouldn't it? Assuming you were still alive to care.'

Andrews now looked distinctly unhappy. 'Freezing the body should take care of any viruses present.'

'Not necessarily,' Ripley told him.

'How do you know it wouldn't?'

'We're talking complex bioengineered mutations here. How do you know that it would?'

The superintendent cursed under his breath, his troubled expression deepening. 'There are at present twenty-five prisoners in this facility. They are caretakers second. All are double Y chromos—former career criminals, thieves, rapists, murderers, arsonists, child molesters, drug dealers . . . scum.' He paused to let the litany sink in.

'But scum that have taken on religion. It may make them appear and sound mellow, but I, for one, don't think it makes them any less dangerous. However, I value its meliorating effect. So I try not to offend their convictions. They appreciate my tolerance and I'm rewarded with a greater amount of peace and quiet than you'd expect to find in a situation like this.

'I don't want to disturb the established order. I don't want ripples in the water. And I most especially don't want a woman walking around giving them ideas and stirring up memories which they have conveniently managed to bury in their respective pasts.'

'Yes,' Ripley agreed. 'Obviously, as you've said, for my own personal safety. In addition to which, despite what you seem to think, I'm not entirely oblivious to the potential problems my temporary presence here creates for you.'

'Exactly.' Andrews was clearly pleased by her apparent desire to cooperate. Or in other words, to make life as easy as possible for him. He glanced back at the med tech. 'I will leave the details of the cremation to you, Mr. Clemens.' He turned to leave.

'Just one thing, Superintendent.'

Andrews halted. 'Yes?'

'When I'm done, will you be wanting a time and circumstances report? For the official log, of course.'

Andrews pursed his lips thoughtfully. 'That won't be necessary, Mr. Clemens. Just 'com me. I'll take care of the rest.'

'As you say, Superintendent.' Clemens grinned thinly.

# IV

Meat. Some of it familiar, some not. Dull rust red struck through with flashes of bright crimson. Small carcasses dangling from old hooks. Huge slabs tipped with protuberant suggestions of amputated limbs, outlined in frozen fat.

Nearby, chickens and cattle, oblivious to their eventual fate. A lone sheep. Live meat.

Most of the abattoir was empty. It had been built to handle the daily needs of hundreds of technicians, miners, and refining personnel. It was far larger than the caretaker prisoners required. They could have left more space between supplies, but the vast rear of the huge chamber, with its echoes of draining blood and slicing and chopping, was a place they preferred to avoid. Too many animate ghosts lingered there, seeking form among milling molecules of tainted air.

The two men wrestled with the cart between them, on which rested the unwieldy carcass of a dead ox. Frank tried to guide it while Murphy goosed forward motion out of the rechargeable electric motor. The motor sputtered and sparked complainingly. When it finally burned out they would simply activate another cart. There were no repair techs among the prison population.

Frank wore the look of the permanently doomed. His much younger companion was not nearly so devastated of aspect. Only Murphy's eyes revealed the furtive nature of someone who'd been on the run and on the wrong side of the law since he'd been old enough to contemplate the notion of working without sticking to a regular job. Much easier to appropriate the earnings of others, preferably but not necessarily without their knowledge. Sometimes he'd been caught, other times not.

The last time had been one too many, and he'd been sent to serve out his sentence on welcoming, exotic Fiorina.

Murphy touched a switch and the cart dumped the clumsy bulk onto the deeply stained floor. Frank was ready with the chains. Together they fastened them around the dead animal's hind legs and began to winch it off the tiles. It went up slowly, in quivering, uneven jerks. The thin but surprisingly strong alloyed links rattled under the load.

'Well, at least Christmas came early.' Frank struggled with the load, breathing hard.

'How's that?' Murphy asked him.

'Any dead ox is a good ox.'

'God, ain't it right. Smelly bastards, all covered with lice. Rather eat 'em than clean 'em.'

Frank looked towards the stalls. 'Only three more of the buggers left, then we're done with the pillocks. God, I hate hosing these brutes down. Always get shit on my boots.'

Murphy was sucking on his lower lip, his thoughts elsewhere. 'Speakin' of hosing down, Frank . . .'

'Yeah?'

Memories glistened in the other man's voice, haunted his face. They were less than pleasant. 'I mean, if you got a chance . . . just supposing . . . what would you say to her?'

His companion frowned. 'What do you mean, if I got a chance?'

'You know. If you got a chance.' Murphy was breathing harder now.

Frank considered. 'Just casual, you mean?'

'Yeah. If she just came along by herself, like, without Andrews or Clemens hangin' with her. How would you put it to her? You know, if you ran into her in the mess hall or something.'

The other man's eyes glittered. 'No problem. Never had any problem with the ladies. I'd say, "Good day, my dear, how's it going? Anything I could do to be of service?" Then I'd give her the look. You know—up and down. Give her a wink, nasty smile, she'd get the picture.'

'Right,' said Murphy sarcastically. 'And she'd smile back and say, "Kiss my ass, you horny old fucker." '

'I'd be happy to kiss her ass. Be happy to kiss her anywhere she wants.'

'Yeah.' Murphy's expression darkened unpleasantly. 'But treat 'em mean, keep 'em keen . . . right, Frank?'

The older man nodded knowingly. 'Treat the queens like whores and the whores like queens. Can't go wrong.'

Together they heaved on the chains until the carcass was properly positioned. Frank locked the hoist and they stepped back, letting the dead animal swing in its harness.

Contemplative silence separated the two men for a long moment. Then Frank uttered a casual obscenity. 'Frank?'

'Yeah?'

'What do you think killed Babe?' He nodded at the carcass.

Frank shrugged. 'Beats me. Just keeled over. Heart attack, maybe.'

Murphy spoke from the other side. 'How could it have been a heart attack? How old was she?'

'Charts say eleven. In the prime. Tough luck for her, good for us. You know the super won't let us kill any of the animals for meat except on special occasions. So me, I look on this as a bonus for work well done. Chop her up. Later we'll throw her in the stew. Animal this size ought to last for a while. Make the dehys taste like real food.'

'Yeah!' Murphy could taste it now, ladled over hot loaves of the self-rising, self-cooking bread from the stores.

Something on the cart caught his attention. Whatever it was, it had been pancaked, flattened beneath the massive bulk of the dead animal. Still discernible was a small, disclike body, a thick, flexible tail, and multiple spidery arms, now crushed and broken. A look of distaste on his face, he picked it up by the tail, the splintered arms dangling towards the floor.

'What's this?'

Frank leaned over for a look, shrugged indifferently. 'Dunno. What am I, a xenologist? Looks like some jellyfish from the beach.'

The other man sniffed. The thing had no odour. 'Right.'

He tossed it casually aside.

The leadworks was a kind of liquid hell, a place of fire and simmering heat waves, where both vision and objects wavered as if uncertain of outline. Like much of the rest of the mining facility it had been abandoned largely intact. The difference was that it gave the prisoners something to do, leadworking being considerably less complex than, say, platinum wire production or heavy machinery maintenance. Fiorina's inhabitants were encouraged to make use of the facility, not only to occupy and amuse themselves but also to replace certain equipment as it broke down.

Presently the automatic extruders were drawing molten lead from the glowing cauldron into thin tubes which would be used to replace those in an older part of the facility's plant.

The prisoners on duty watched, alternately fascinated and bored by the largely automated procedure. Not only was the leadworks a popular place to work because it offered opportunities for reaction, but also because it was one of the consistently warmest spots in the complex.

'You goin'?' The man who spoke checked two of the simple readouts on the monitoring console. As always, they were well within allowable parameters.

His companion frowned. 'Haven't decided. It's nothin' to do with us.'

'Be a break in routine, though.'

'Still, I dunno.'

A third man turned from the searing cauldron and pushed his protective goggles up onto his forehead. 'Dillon gonna be there?'

Even as he ventured the query the towering prisoner in question appeared, striding down the metal catwalk towards them.

'Shut it down,' he said simply when he reached them. The first prisoner obediently flipped a switch and the cauldron immediately began to cool.

'What's the story, man?' asked the man with the goggles, blinking particles from his eyes.

'Yeah,' said the prisoner in the middle. 'We been talkin' about it, but we ain't been able to decide.'

'It's been decided,' Dillon informed him. He let his gaze rest on each of them in turn. 'We're all goin'. Maybe we didn't know these people, but we show our respect. They wanna burn bodies, that's fine by us, long as it isn't one of us.' Having imparted this information, he turned to leave.

The three men followed, the one with the goggles slipping them down around his neck. 'Ain't had a funeral in a long time.'

'That's right,' agreed his companion soberly. 'I've been kind of missing the service. It's so much like a passage, you know? Off this place.'

'Amen to that, brother,' said the first man, increasing his stride to keep pace with the taller Dillon.

The old smelter creaked and groaned as it was juiced to life. The immense chamber had been cut and blasted out of the solid rock directly above the ore body, then lined where necessary with heat-reflective shielding. Monitors and controls lined the walkways and railings. Cranes and other heavy tracked equipment rested silently where they had been parked by the departing miners. In the shadows thrown by the reduced lighting they resembled Mesozoic fossils escaped from some distant museum.

Flames began to flicker around the bevelled edges of the holding pit. They heightened the stark figures of the two prisoners who stood on a crane suspended over the abyss. A pair of nylon sacks hung between them. Their limp contents caused them to sag noticeably in the middle.

Ripley gazed up at the men and their burden, her hands tightening on the rail that separated her from the artificial hell below. Clemens stood next to her, wanting to say something and, as always, failing to find the right words. Having used up all the consolation in his body a number of years ago, he now discovered there was none left for the single forlorn woman standing beside him.

Aaron was there too, and Dillon, and a number of the other prisoners. Despite the fact that the dead man had in fact been something of a government enforcer, none of them smiled or ventured sarcastic remarks. Death was too familiar a companion to all of them, and had been too much of a daily presence in their lives, to be treated with disrespect.

Andrews harrumphed importantly and opened the thin book he carried. 'We commit this child and this man to your keeping, O Lord. Their bodies have been taken from the shadows of our nights. They have been released from all darkness and pain. Do not let their souls wander the void, but take them into the company of those who have preceded them.'

In the control centre below, the prisoner called Troy listened via 'com to the proceedings on the catwalk overhead. When Andrews reached the designated place in the eulogy the prisoner tech began adjusting controls. Telltales shifted from yellow to green. A deep whine sounded behind him, rose to complaining pitch, and died. Other lights flashed ready.

Below the catwalk white-hot flame filled the smelting pit. It roared efficiently, impressively in the semi-darkness. No mountain of ore waited to greet the fire, no crowd of technicians stood ready to fine-tune the process of reducing tons of rubble to slag. The flames seared the sides of the pit and nothing more.

Tears ran slowly down Ripley's cheeks as she stared at the controlled conflagration. She was silent in her sorrow and remembrance, making no noise, issuing no sounds. There were only the tears. Clemens looked on sympathetically. He wanted to take her in his arms, hold her, comfort her. But there were others present, Andrews among them. He stayed where he was.

'The child and the man have gone beyond our world,' Andrews droned on. 'Their bodies may lie broken, but their souls are forever eternal and everlasting.'

'We who suffer ask the question: Why?' Eyes shifted from the superintendent to Dillon. 'Why are the innocent punished? Why the sacrifice? Why the pain?' 'There are no promises,' the big prisoner intoned solemnly. 'There is no certainty. Only that some will be called. That some will be saved.'

Up on the crane the rising heat from the furnace finally became too much for the men stationed there. They rocked several times and heaved their burden into the pit, beating a hasty retreat for cooler climes. The sacks fell, tumbling a few times, before being swallowed by the inferno. There was a brief, slightly higher flicker of flame near the edge of the pit as the bags and their contents were instantly incinerated.

Ripley staggered slightly and clutched at Clemens's arm. He was startled but held his ground, giving her the support she needed. The rest of the men looked on. There was no envy in their expressions; only sympathy. Dillon took no notice. He was still reciting.

'But these departed spirits will never know the hardships, the grief and pain which lie ahead for those of us who remain. So we commit these bodies to the void with a glad heart. For within each seed there is the promise of a flower, and within each death, no matter how small, there is always a new life. A new beginning.'

There was movement in the abattoir, a stirring amid the dangling carcasses and balletic wraiths of frozen air. The massive corpse of the ox twitched, then began to dance crazily in its chains.

There was no one to witness the gut swelling and expanding until the dead skin was taut as that of a crazed dirigible. No one to see it burst under the pressure, sending bits of flesh and fat flying. Internal organs, liver and stomach, coils of ropy intestines tumbled to the floor. And something else.

A head lifted, struggling upward with spasmodic, instinctive confidence. The compact nightmare turned a slow circle, scanning its surroundings. Hunting. Awkwardly at first but with astonishingly rapid assurance it began to move, searching. It found the air duct and inspected it briefly before vanishing within.

From the time it had emerged from the belly of the ox until its studied disappearance, less than a minute had elapsed.

Upon concluding his speech Dillon bowed his head. The other prisoners did likewise. Ripley glanced at them, then back to the pit where the fires were being electronically banked. She reached up and scratched at her hair, then one ear. A moment later again. This time she looked down at her fingers.

They were coated with what looked like dark, motile dust.

Disgusted, she frantically wiped them clean against her borrowed jumpsuit, looked up to find Clemens eying her knowingly.

'I warned you.'

'Okay, I'm convinced. Now what do I do about it?'

'You can live with it,' he told her, 'or . . . ' He rubbed his naked pate and smiled regretfully.

Her expression twisted. 'There's no other way?'

He shook his head. 'If there was we'd have found it by now. Not that there's been much impetus to do so. Vanity's one of the first casualties of assignment to Fiorina. You might as well be comfortable. It'll grow back after you leave, and if you don't do anything in the meantime the bugs'll eat the stuff right down to the roots anyway. They may be tiny, but they have large appetites and lousy table manners. Believe me, you'll look worse if you try to ignore it, and you'll scratch yourself silly.'

She slumped. 'All right. Which way to the beauty parlour?'

The tech was apologetic. 'I'm afraid you're talking to it.'

The line of shower stalls was stark and sterile, pale white beneath the overheads. Presently all were deserted save one. As the hot, chemically treated water cascaded down her body, Ripley studied herself in the mirror that formed part of one wall.

Strange to be without hair. It was such a slight, ephemeral part of one's body. The only aspect of one's appearance that could be altered easily and at will. She felt herself physically diminished somehow, a queen suddenly bereft of her crown. Yet it would grow back. Clemens had assured her of that. The prisoners had to shave themselves regularly. There was nothing about the bugs or the air that rendered the condition permanent.

She soaped her bare scalp. It was a strange sensation and she felt chilled despite the roaring hot water. The old mining and smelting facility might be short of many things, but water wasn't one of them. The big desalinization plant down on the bay had been built to provide water for all installation functions and its full complement of personnel as well. Even at minimal operational levels it provided more than enough water for the prisoners to waste.

She shut her eyes and stepped back under the full force of the heavy spray. As far as she was concerned the past ten thousand years of human civilization had produced three really important inventions: speech, writing, and indoor plumbing.

Outside the stalls, old death and new problems awaited, though the latter seemed insignificant compared to what she'd already been through. Clemens and Andrews and the rest didn't, couldn't, understand that, nor did she feel it incumbent upon herself to elaborate for them.

After what she'd endured, the prospect of being forced to spend a few weeks in the company of some hardened criminals was about as daunting as a walk in the park.

The prisoners had their meals in what had been the

supervisors' mess when the mine had been in operation. The room still exceeded their modest requirements. But while the facility was impressive despite having been stripped of its original expensive decor, the food was something else again. Still, complaints were infrequent and mild. If not precisely of gourmet quality, at least there was plenty of it. While not wishing to pamper its indentured caretakers, neither did the Company wish them to starve.

Within certain prescribed and well known temporal parameters the men could eat when they wished. Thanks to the extra space they tended to cluster in small groups. A few chose to eat alone. Their solitude was always respected. In Fiorina's restricted environment enforced conversation was threatening conversation.

Dillon picked up his preheated tray and scanned the room. Men were chatting, consuming, pretending they had lives. As always, the superintendent and his assistant ate in the same hall as the prisoners, though off to one side. Wordlessly he homed in on a table occupied by three men displaying particularly absorbed expressions. No, not absorbed, he corrected himself. Sullen.

Well, that was hardly a unique situation on Fiorina. Nevertheless, he was curious.

Golic glanced up as the new arrival's bulk shadowed the table, looked away quickly. His eyes met those of his friends Boggs and Rains. The three of them concentrated on their bland meals with preternatural intensity as Dillon slid into the empty seat. They did not object to his presence, but neither did they welcome him.

The four ate in silence. Dillon watched them closely, and they were conscious of his watching them, and still no one said anything.

Finally the big man had had enough. Pausing with his spoon halfway to his mouth, he settled on Boggs.

'Okay. This is eating time, interacting time. Not contemplation seminar. Lotta talk goin' round that we got some disharmony here. One of you guys want to tell me what the problem is?'

Boggs looked away. Golic concentrated on his mash. Dillon did not raise his voice but his impatience was evident nonetheless.

'Speak to me, brothers. You all know me and so you know that I can be persistent. I sense that you are troubled and I wish only to help.' He placed a massive, powerful fist gently on the table next to his tray. 'Unburden your spirits. Tell me what's the matter.'

Rains hesitated, then put down his fork and pushed his tray towards the centre of the table. 'All right, you want to know what's wrong? I'll tell you what's wrong. I've learned how to get along here. I never thought that I would but I have. I don't mind the dark, I don't mind the bugs, I don't mind the isolation or all the talk of ghosts in the machinery. But I mind Golic.' He waved at the individual in question, who blissfully continued scarfing down his food.

Dillon turned to Boggs. 'That the way you feel about it?'

Boggs continued to stir his food nervously, finally looked up. 'I ain't one to start something or cause trouble. I just want to get along and serve my time like everybody else.'

The big man leaned forward and the table creaked slightly beneath his weight. 'I asked you if that's the way you feel about it.'

'All right, yeah. Yeah. Hey, the man is crazy. I don't care what Clemens or the "official" reports say. He's nuts. If he wasn't like this when he got here then he is now. The planet or the place or both have made him like that. He's running on smoke drive, and he smells bad. I ain't goin' outside with him anymore. Not to the beach, not to check the shafts, not nowhere. And ain't nobody can make me,' he finished belligerently. 'I know my rights.'

'Your rights?' Dillon smiled thinly. 'Yes, of course. Your rights.' He glanced to his left. 'You got anything to say for yourself?'

Golic looked up, particles of food clinging to his thick lips, and grinned idiotically. He essayed an indifferent shrug before returning to his meal.

Dillon regarded the other two steadily. 'Because Golic doesn't like to talk doesn't mean he's crazy. Just nonverbal. Frankly, from everything I've seen he manages to express what he's feeling as well as anybody else. There are no orators here.'

'Get to the point,' Boggs mumbled unhappily.

'The point is that he's going with you. He's part of your work team and until further notice or unless he does something more threatening than keep his mouth shut, that's the way it stays. You all have a job to do. Take it from me, you will learn not to mind Golic or his little idiosyncrasies. He's nothing more than another poor, miserable, suffering son of a bitch like you and me. Which means he's no crazier than any of the rest of us.'

'Except he smells worse,' Rains snapped disgustedly.

'And he's crazy,' Boggs added, unrepentant.

Dillon straightened in his seat. 'Look, you're making far too much out of this. I've seen it before. It happens when there isn't a whole helluva lot else to do. You start picking on the food, then the bugs, then each other. Golic's different, that's all. No better and no worse than the rest of us.'

'He stinks,' Rains muttered.

Dillon shot the other man a cautionary look. 'None of us is a walking bouquet down here. Knock this shit off. You have a job to do. The three of you. It's a good job.'

'Didn't ask for it,' Boggs muttered.

'Nobody asks for anything here. You take what's given to you and make the best of it. That way lies survival. For you and for everybody else. This ain't like some Earthside prison. You riot here and no citizen media comes runnin' to listen to your complaints. You just get a lot more uncomfortable. Or you die.' Boggs shuffled his feet uneasily.

'Now, listen to me. There's others who'd be willing to take on foraging duty. But in case you ain't noticed, Andrews ain't in a

very accommodating mood right now. I wouldn't be asking
him about switching assignments and changing rosters.' The
big man smiled encouragingly. 'Hey, you get to work at your
own speed, and you're out of sight of the superintendent and
his toady. Maybe you'll get lucky, find some good stuff you can
try and keep to yourselves.'

'Fat chance of that.' Rains was still bitter, but less so. Dillon
had reminded him of possibilities.

'That's better,' said the big man. 'Just keep your mind on
your work and you won't even notice Golic. You are foragers.
You know what that entails. Hunting for overlooked provisions
and useful equipment. As we all know from previous
scavenging expeditions, Weyland-Yutani's noble, upstanding
miners had the useful habit of appropriating their employers'
supplies and hoarding them in little private storerooms and
cubbies they cut out of the rock in the hopes they could
smuggle some of the stuff out and sell it on the open market.
They were trying to supplement their incomes. We're
interested in supplementing our lives.

'I don't want to hear anymore objections and I don't want to
discuss it further. There's tougher duty needs doing if you
insist on pressing the matter. You are to do this to help your
fellow prisoners. You are to do this to prove your loyalty to me.
And I don't want to hear another word about poor Golic.'

'Yeah, but—' Rains started to argue. He broke off before he
could get started, staring. Boggs looked up. So did Golic.
Dillon turned slowly.

Ripley stood in the doorway, surveying the mess hall, which
had gone completely silent at her entrance. Her eyes saw
everything, met no one's. Stepping over to the food line she
studied the identical trays distastefully. The prisoner on
serving duty gaped at her unashamedly, his manipulator
dangling limp from one hand. Taking a chunk of cornbread
from a large plastic basket, she turned and let her gaze rove
through the room one more time, until it settled on Dillon.

Andrews and his assistant were as absorbed in the silent

tableau as the prisoners. The superintendent watched thoughtfully as the lieutenant walked over to the big man's table and stopped. His knowing expression was resigned as he turned back to his food.

'As I thought, Mr. Aaron. As I thought.'

His second-in-command frowned, still gazing across the room at Ripley. 'You called it, sir. What now?'

Andrews sighed. 'Nothing. For now. Eat your food.' He picked up a fork and dug into the steaming brown mass in the centre of his tray.

Ripley stood opposite Dillon, behind Boggs. The four men picked at their meals, resolutely indifferent to her presence.

'Thanks for your words at the funeral. They helped. I didn't think I could react like that anymore to anything as futile as words, but I was wrong. I just want you to know that I appreciated it.'

The big man gazed fixedly at his plate, shovelling in food with a single-minded determination that was impressive to behold. When she didn't move away he finally looked up.

'You shouldn't be here. Not just on Fiorina . . . you didn't have much choice about that. But in this room. With us. You ought to stay in the infirmary, where you belong. Out of the way.'

She bit off a piece of cornbread, chewed reflectively. For something with a dehy base it was almost tasty.

'I got hungry.'

'Clemens could've brought you something.'

'I got bored.'

Frustrated, he put down his fork and glanced up at her. 'I don't know why you're doing this. There's worse things than bein' bored. I don't know why you're talking to me. You don't wanna know me, Lieutenant. I am a murderer and a rapist. Of women.'

'Really.' Her eyebrows, which she had thinned but not shaved completely, rose. 'I guess I must make you nervous.'

Boggs's fork halted halfway to his mouth. Rains frowned,

and Golic just kept eating, ignoring the byplay completely. Dillon hesitated a moment, then a slow smile spread across his hardened face. He nodded and Ripley took the remaining empty chair.

'Do you have any faith, sister?'

'In what?' She gnawed on the cornbread.

'In anything.'

She didn't have to pause to consider. 'Not much.'

He raised a hand and waved, the expansive gesture encompassing the mess hall and its inhabitants. 'We got lots of faith here. Not much else, it's true, but that we got. It doesn't take up much space, the Company and the government can't take it away from us, and every man watches over his own personal store of the stuff. It's not only useful in a place like this, it's damn necessary. Otherwise you despair and in despairing you lose your soul. The government can take away your freedom but not your soul.

'On Earth, in a place like this, it would be different. But this ain't Earth. It ain't even the Sol system. Out here people react differently. Free people and prisoners alike. We're less than free but more than dead. One of the things that keeps us that way is our faith. We have lots, Lieutenant. Enough even for you.'

'I got the feeling that women weren't allowed in your faith.'

'Why? Because we're all men here? That's a consequence of our population, not our philosophy. If women were sent they'd be invited in. Incarceration doesn't discriminate as to gender. Reason there ain't no women in the faith is that we never had any sent here. But we tolerate anyone. Not much reason to exclude somebody when they're already excluded from everything else by the simple fact of being sent here. We even tolerate the intolerable.' His smile widened.

'Thank you,' she replied dryly.

He noted her tone. 'Hey, that's just a statement of principle. Nothing personal. We got a good place here to wait. Up to now, no temptation.'

She leaned back in the chair. 'I guess if you can take this place for longer than a year without going crazy, you can take anybody.'

Dillon was eating again, enjoying the meal. 'Fiorina's as good a place to wait as any other. No surprises. More freedom of movement than you'd have on an inhabited world. Andrews doesn't worry about us going too far from the installation because there's no place to go. It's hard out there. Not much to eat, rotten weather. No company. We're all long-termers here, though not everyone's a lifer. Everyone knows everyone else, what they're like, who can be depended on and who needs a little extra help to make it.' He chewed and swallowed.

'There's worse places to serve out your time. I ain't been there, but I've heard of 'em. All things considered, Fiorina suits me just fine. No temptation here.'

Ripley gave him a sideways look. 'What exactly are you waiting for?'

The big man didn't miss a beat. Or a forkful. 'We are waiting,' he told her in all seriousness, 'for God to return and raise his servants to redemption.'

She frowned. 'I think you're in for a long wait.'

# V

Later Clemens showed her the assembly hall, pointing out inconsequentials he thought she might find of interest. Eventually they sat, alone in the spacious room. Prisoner Martin quietly swept up nearby.

'How much of the story of this place do you know?'

'What you've told me. What Andrews said. A little that I heard from some of the prisoners.'

'Yeah, I saw you talking to Dillon.' He poured himself a short whiskey from the metal flask he carried. The distant ceiling loomed above them, four storeys high.

'It's pretty interesting, from a psychosocial point of view. Dillon and the rest of them got religion, so to speak, about five years ago.'

'What kind of religion?'

Clemens sipped at his liquor. 'I don't know. Hard to say. Some sort of millenarian apocalyptic Christian fundamentalist brew.'

'Ummmm.'

'Exactly. The point is that when the Company wanted to close down this facility, Dillon and the rest of the converts wanted to stay. The Company knows a good thing when it sees it. So they were allowed to remain as custodians, with two minders and a medical officer.' He gestured at the deserted assembly hall. 'And here we are.'

'It's not so bad. Nobody checks on us, nobody bothers us.

Regular supply drops from passing ships take care of the essentials. Anything we can scavenge we're allowed to make use of, and the company pays the men minimal caretaker wages while they do their time, which is a damn sight better than what a prisoner earns doing prison work Earthside.

For comfort the men have view-and-read chips and their private religion. There's plenty to eat, even if it does tend to get monotonous; the water's decent, and so long as you shave regular, the bugs don't bother you. There are few inimical native life-forms and they can't get into the installation. If the weather was better, it would almost be pleasant.'

She looked thoughtful as she sipped at her drink. 'What about you? How did you happen to get this great assignment?'

He held his cup between his fingers, twirling it back and forth, side to side. 'I know you'll find this hard to believe, but it's actually much nicer than my previous posting. I like being left alone. I like being ignored. This is a good place for that. Unless somebody needs attention or gets hurt, which happens a lot less than you might think, my time here is pretty much my own. I can sit and read, watch a viewer, explore the complex, or go into a holding room and scream my head off.' He smiled winningly. 'It's a helluva lot better than having some sadistic guard or whiny prisoner always on your case.' He gestured at her bald pate.

'How do you like your haircut?'

She ran her fingers delicately across her naked skull. 'Feels weird. Like the hair's still there but when you reach for it, there's nothing.'

He nodded. 'Like someone who's lost a leg and thinks he can still feel his foot. The body's a funny thing, and the mind's a heck of a lot funnier.' He drained his glass, looked into her eyes.

'Now that I've gone out on a limb for you with Andrews over the cremation, damaging my already less than perfect relationship with the good man, and briefed you on the humdrum history of Fury 161, how about you telling me what you were looking for in that dead girl? And why was it necessary to cremate the bodies?' She started to reply and he raised his hand, palm towards her.

'Please, no more about nasty germs. Andrews was right. Cold storage would have been enough to render them harmless. But that wasn't good enough for you. I want to know why.'

She nodded, set her cup aside, and turned back to him. 'First I have to know something else.'

He shrugged. 'Name it.'

'Are you attracted to me?'

His gaze narrowed. As he was wondering how to respond, he heard his own voice answering, as though his lips and tongue had abruptly chosen to operate independent of his brain. Which was not, he reflected in mild astonishment, necessarily a bad thing.

'In what way?'

'In that way.'

The universe, it appeared, was still full of wonders, even if Fiorina's perpetual cloud cover tended to obscure them. 'You are rather direct. Speaking to someone afflicted with a penchant for solitude, as I have already mentioned, I find that more than a little disconcerting.'

'Sorry. It's the only way I know how to be. I've been out here a long time.'

'Yes,' he murmured. 'So have I.'

'I don't have time for subterfuges. I don't have time for much of anything except what's really important. I've had to learn that.'

He refilled both cups, picked up his own, and swirled the contents, studying the uninformative eddies which appeared in the liquid.

The fan blades were each twice the size of a man. They had to be, to suck air from the surface and draw it down into the condensers which scrubbed, cleaned, and purified Fiorina's dusty atmosphere before pumping the result into shafts and structures. Even so, they were imperfect. Fiorina's atmosphere was simply too dirty.

There were ten fans, one to a shaft. Eight were silent. The remaining pair roared at half speed, supplying air to the installation's western quadrant.

Murphy sang through the respiratory mask that covered his nose and mouth, filtering out surface particles before they were drawn off by the fan. Carbon deposits tended to accumulate on the ductway walls. He burned them off with his laser, watched as the fan sucked them away from his feet and into the filters. It wasn't the best job to have, nor the worst. He took his time and did the best he could. Not because he gave a damn or anticipated the imminent arrival of Company inspectors, but because when he finished with the ducts they'd give him something else to do. Might as well go about the cleaning as thoroughly as possible so it would kill as much time as possible.

He was off tune but enthusiastic.

Abruptly he stopped singing. A large deposit had accumulated in the recess off to his left. Damn storage areas were like that, always catching large debris that the surface filters missed. He knelt and extended the handle of the push broom, winkling the object out. It moved freely, not at all like a clump of mucky carbon.

It was flat and flexible. At first he thought it was an old uniform, but when he had it out in the main duct he saw that it was some kind of animal skin. It was dark and shiny, more like metal foil than flesh. Funny stuff.

Stretching it out on the floor he saw that it was big enough to enclose two men, or a young calf. What the hell . . .?

Then he knew. There were a few large native animals on Fiorina; poor, dirt-hugging primitive things with feeble nervous systems and slow response times. Obviously one had somehow stumbled into an air intake and, unable to get out again, had perished for lack of food and water. It couldn't use the ladders, and the roaring fan constituted an impenetrable barrier. He poked at the empty skin. This desiccated husk was all that remained of the unfortunate visitor. No telling how long it had lain in the recess, ignored and unnoticed.

The skin looked awfully fresh to have contained an old, long since dried-out corpse. The bugs, he reminded himself. The bugs would make short work of any flesh that came their way. It was interesting. He hadn't known that the bugs would eat bone.

Or maybe there'd been no bones to dispose of. Maybe it had been a ... what was the word? An invertebrate, yeah. Something without bones. Wasn't Fiorina home to those too? He'd have to look it up, or better yet, ask Clemens. The medic would know. He'd bundle the skin up and take it to the infirmary. Maybe he'd made a discovery of some kind, found the skin of a new type of animal. It would look good on his record.

Meanwhile he wasn't getting any work done.

Turning, he burned off a couple of deposits clinging to the lower right-hand curve of the duct. That's when he heard the noise. Frowning, he shut off the laser and flicked on the safety as he turned to look behind him. He'd about decided that his imagination was starting to get to him when he heard it again — a kind of wet, lapping sound.

There was a slightly larger recess a few metres down the duct, a sometime storage area for supplies and tools. It should be empty now, cleaned out, the supplies stocked elsewhere and the tools salvaged by the departing maintenance personnel. But the gurgling noise grew louder the nearer he crept.

He had to bend to see inside. Wishing he had a light, he squinted in the reflected glow from the duct. There was something moving, an indistinct bulk in the darkness. The creature that had shed its skin? If so and he could bring it out alive he was sure to receive an official company commendation. Maybe his unanticipated contribution to the moribund state of Fiorinan science would be worth a couple of months off his sentence.

His eyes grew accustomed to the weak illumination. He could see it more clearly now, make out a head on a neck. It sensed his presence and turned towards him.

He froze, unable to move. His eyes widened.

Liquid emerged suddenly in a tight, concentrated stream from the unformed monster's mouth, striking the paralysed prisoner square in the face. Gas hissed as flesh melted on contact with the highly caustic fluid. Murphy stumbled backward, screaming and clawing at his disintegrating face.

Smoke pouring through his clutching fingers, he staggered away from the recess, bouncing off first one wall then the other. He had no thought of where he was going, or where he was. He thought of nothing save the pain. He did not think of the fan.

When he stumbled into the huge blades they shredded him instantly, sending blood and ragged chunks of flesh splattering against the metalwork of the duct. It would have taken some time for his erstwhile friends to have found him if his skull hadn't been caught just right between one blade and the casing. Fouled, the safeties took over and shut down the mechanism. The motor stopped and the blades ground to a halt. Down the main corridor a previously quiet fan automatically picked up the slack.

Then it was quiet again in the side shaft except for the distant, barely audible noise which emerged from the old storage recess, a perverse mewling hiss there was no longer anyone present to overhear.

Clemens's quarters were luxurious compared to those of the other prisoners. He had more space and, as the facility's medical technician, access to certain amenities denied his fellow Fiorinans. But the room was comfortable only by comparison. It would not have passed muster on the most isolated outpost on Earth.

Still, he was aware of his unique position, and as grateful as he could be under the circumstances. Recently those circumstances had become a great deal better than normal.

Ripley shifted beneath the bedsheets of the cot, stretching and blinking at the ceiling. Clemens stood across the floor, near the built-ins. A narcostick smoked between his lips as he poured something dark and potent from a canister into a glass. For the first time she saw him with his official cowl down. The imprinted code on the back of his shaven skull was clearly visible.

Turning, he saw her looking at him and gestured with the container.

'Sorry I can't offer you a drink, but you're on medication.'

She squinted. 'What is it this time?'

'It would surprise you.'

'I don't doubt it.' She smiled. 'You've already surprised me.'

'Thanks.' He held the glass up to the light. 'The medical instrumentation the Company left behind is rudimentary, but sophisticated enough in its way. Since we can't always rely on supply drops I have to be able to synthesize quite a range of medications. The programme that synthesizes rubbing alcohol doesn't take much adjusting to turn out something considerably more palatable.' He sipped at the contents of the glass, looking pleased with himself.

'A small hobby, but a rewarding one.'

'Does Andrews know?' she asked him.

'I don't think so. I sure as hell haven't told him. If he knew, he'd order me to stop. Say it was bad for morale and dangerous if the other men knew I could do it. I couldn't disagree with him there. But until he does find out, I'll go on happily rearranging ethyl molecules and their stimulating relations to suit my own personal needs.' He held the canister over an open tumbler. 'Don't worry. I'll save you some. For later.'

'That's thoughtful of you.'

'Don't mention it. When I was in school recombinant synthetic chemistry was one of my better subjects.' He hesitated. 'Speaking of thoughtfulness, while I am deeply appreciative of your attentions, I also realize that they manifested themselves at just the right moment to deflect my last question. In the best possible way, of course. I wouldn't want you to think for a minute that I'd have had it any other way. But the damn thing has a grip on me and won't let loose.'

She stared up at him, his glass held delicately in one hand. 'You're spoiling the mood.'

'That's not my intention. But I'm still a medical officer and one does have a job to do, and frankly, the more effort you put into avoiding the issue, the more curious I am to find out why. What were you looking for in the girl? Why were you so insistent on having the bodies cremated?'

'I get it. Now that I'm in your bed, you think I owe you an answer.'

He replied patiently. 'Trying to get me mad isn't going to work either. No, you owe me an answer because it's my job to get one and because I stuck my neck out for you to give you what you wanted. Being in my bed has nothing to do with it.' He smiled thinly. 'Your nonresponsiveness in this matter is likely to complicate our future relationship no end.'

She sighed resignedly and turned onto her side. 'It's really nothing. Can't we just leave it at that? When I was in deep sleep I had a real bad dream.' She shut her eyes against the gruesome memory. 'I don't want to talk about it. I just had to be sure what killed her.'

She looked back up at the medic. 'You have no idea what my recent life has been like or what I've been through. It would make your wildest nightmares seem like the fuzzy musings of an innocent five-year-old. I know that I'll never forget any of it. Never! But that doesn't keep me from trying. So if I seem a little irrational or unreasonably insistent about certain things, try to indulge me. Believe me, I need that. I need someone to be concerned about me for a change. As far as Newt . . . as far as the girl is concerned, I made a mistake.'

His thumb caressed the side of the small glass he held as he nodded slowly, tight-lipped and understanding. 'Yes, possibly.'

She continued to stare at him. 'Maybe I've made another mistake.'

'How's that?'

'Fraternizing with the prisoners. Physical contact. That's against the rules, isn't it?'

'Definitely. Who was the lucky fellow?'

'You, dummy.'

Clemens eyed her uncertainly. 'I'm not a prisoner.'

She gestured. 'Then what about the code on the back of your head?'

His hand went reflexively to the back of his skull. 'I suppose that does demand an explanation. But I don't think this is the moment for it. Sorry. We are rather spoiling things, aren't we?' The intercom buzzed for attention. He looked apologetic as he moved to acknowledge the call.

'Got to respond. I'm not allowed the luxury of refusing calls. This isn't Sorbonne Centrale.' He flicked on the two-way. A thin, poorly reproduced voice filtered through.

'Clemens?'

The medic shot her a resigned look. 'Yes, Mr. Aaron.'

'Andrews wants you to report to Vent Shaft Seventeen in the Second Quadrant. ASAP. We've had an accident.'

Suddenly involved, he turned to make certain the omnidirectional mike built into the unit got a good dose of his reply. 'Something serious?'

'Yeah, you could call it that,' the assistant told him. 'One of the prisoners on work detail got diced.' The unit clicked off abruptly.

'Damn.' Clemens drained his glass and set it down on the console, turning back to his guest. 'I'm sorry. I have to go. Official duties.'

Ripley tensed slightly, fingering the glass. 'I was just starting to enjoy the conversation. As opposed to other things.'

'How do you think I feel?' he muttered as he popped a closet and began removing clothes.

'Maybe I should come along.'

He glanced back at her. 'Better that you don't. It's one thing if I'm seen as treating you as part of my regular rounds. If everyone starts noticing us together all the time with you looking decidedly healthy, it might inspire questions. And talk. Among these guys, the less talk the better.'

'I understand. I don't like it, but I understand.'

He stepped into work trousers. 'Those are the two things you have to do to survive on Fiorina. Also, I don't think your presence would be appreciated by Superintendent Andrews. Wait here and take it easy.' He smiled reassuringly. 'I'll be back.'

She said nothing further, looking distinctly unhappy.

There wasn't much to examine. Hell, Clemens thought as he surveyed the carnage inside the air duct, there wasn't much to bury. Cause of death was a foregone conclusion. There were as many stains on the motionless fan as on the walls.

It didn't make a lot of sense. Men regularly stepped on or brushed against ragged metal edges and cut themselves, or fell off catwalks, or injured themselves trying to body surf in the choppy bay, but they knew intimately the potential dangers of the mothballed mine and studiously avoided them. The giant fan was a threat impossible to dismiss or overlook.

Which didn't necessarily mean the unfortunate and now deceased Murphy was innocent of fooling around. He could have been running, or sliding on the slick ductwork, or just teasing the blades with his broom. He must have slipped, or had part of his clothing caught up in the works. They'd never know, of course. No reason to assign two men to duct cleaning duty. Murphy had been working alone.

Aaron was evidently of similar mind. The assistant was staring grimly at the fan. 'He was a nutter. I gave him the assignment. I should've known better, should've sent somebody else, or at least paired him up with someone a little more stable.' Behind them prisoner Jude continued to mop up.

Andrews was quietly furious. Not because Murphy was dead, but because of the circumstances. They would not reflect favourably on him. Besides which it would mean more paperwork.

'No apologies, Mr. Aaron. It wasn't your fault. From the look of it, it wasn't anybody's fault except perhaps Mr. Murphy's, and he paid for it.' He looked to his medic. 'Your observations, Mr. Clemens?'

The tech shrugged. 'Not really much to say, is there? Cause of death is unarguably obvious. I doubt he felt any discomfort. I'm sure it was instantaneous.'

'No shit.' Aaron surveyed the widely scattered human debris with unconcealed distaste.

'I am trying to concoct a scenario,' the superintendent continued. 'For the report, you understand. I find it difficult to believe that he simply stumbled into so blatant a danger, one in whose proximity he had spent some time working. Perhaps he was pulled in?'

Clemens pursed his lips. 'Possible. I'm neither physicist nor mechanic—'

'None of us are, Mr. Clemens,' Andrews reminded him. 'I am not asking you to render judgment, but simply to offer your opinion on the matter.'

The medic nodded. 'A sudden rush of air might do it, I would imagine. Power surge resulting in exceptional suction. Only—'

'Right,' Aaron said quickly. 'Almost happened to me once, in the main quadrant. Four years ago. I always tell people, keep an eye out for the fans. They're so damn big and solid and steady, you don't think of the unexpected happening in their vicinity.' He shook his head steadily. 'Doesn't matter how much I talk. Nobody listens.'

'That's fine,' Clemens agreed, 'except that before I came down I checked the programming, and the fan was blowing. A power surge should've sent him spinning *up* the duct, not flying into the blades.'

Aaron's gaze narrowed, then he shrugged mentally. Let the superintendent and the medic work it out. It was their responsibility. Meant nothing to him. He'd offered his reasoning, done the best he could. He was sorry for Murphy, but what the hell. Accidents happened.

Clemens strolled up the duct tunnel, studying the walls. The bloodstains diminished gradually.

There was a large recess in the left side of the tunnel and he knelt to peer inside. It was a typical ancillary storage chamber, long since cleaned out. As he started to rise and move on, something caught his eye and caused him to hesitate.

It looked like a spill. Not blood. Some kind of chemical discolouration. The normally smooth metal surface was badly pitted.

Andrews had moved up silently to stand nearby. Now he joined the medic in studying the recess. 'What's that?'

Clemens straightened. 'I really don't know. I just thought it looked funny. Probably been like that ever since the ductwork was installed.' His indifference was somewhat forced and the superintendent picked up on it immediately, pinning the medic with his gaze. Clemens looked away.

'I want to see you in my quarters in, say, thirty minutes,' he said evenly. 'If you please, Mr. Clemens.'

He turned towards the rest of the search party, which was busy gathering up the remains of the dead man. 'Right. This isn't where I want to spend the rest of my day. Let's finish up and get out so Mr. Troy can restart the unit and we can all get back to normal.' He began shepherding the men towards the exit.

Clemens lingered. As soon as he was certain Andrews was fully occupied with concluding the grisly cleanup, the medic returned to his examination of the damaged metal.

It was quiet as a tomb inside the EEV. Shattered consoles clung like pinned arachnids to the walls. Equipment lay where it had fallen from braces or spilled from cabinets. The pilot's chair swung at an angle on its support shaft, like a drunken glove.

A single light illuminated the chaotic interior. Ripley was working inside the burst bulkhead, alternating the laser cutter with less intrusive tools. A protective composite plate peeled away reluctantly to reveal a sealed panel beneath. Gratified, she went to work on the panel clips, using a special tool to remove them one at a time. The panel itself was clearly labelled.

FLIGHT RECORDER
DO NOT BREAK SEAL
OFFICIAL AUTHORIZATION REQUIRED ISA 445

As soon as the last clip was snapped off she removed the panel and set it aside. Beneath, a smooth-surfaced black box sat snug inside a double-walled, specially cushioned compartment. The compartment was dry and clean, with no lingering smell or dampness to suggest that it had been violated by the intrusive salt water of the bay.

The latch on the side released smoothly and the box face slid aside, revealing readouts and flush-mounted buttons beneath the protective shield. She thumbed one and several telltales lit up instantly. Touching it again, she watched as they shut down.

The box slipped freely out of its compartment. She set it gently on the deck, next to the light, and let her gaze once more rove the devastated interior of the emergency vehicle, trying to remember, trying to forget.

Something moved behind her, scrabbling against the torn and broken superstructure. She whirled, panicky, as her eyes detected movement in the darkness.

'Damn!' she cried, slumping. 'You *trying* to scare the life out of me?'

Clemens paused in the cramped entrance, an incongruously boyish grin on his face. 'Sorry, but the doorbell isn't working.' Straining, he stepped into the chamber. 'You know, wandering about without an escort is really going to piss Superintendent Andrews off. Whatever you're up to, putting yourself on his bad side isn't going to help.'

'Screw him. What about the accident?' Her tone was intent, her expression earnest.

'Very bad, I'm afraid.' He leaned against some dangling wiring, backed off hastily when it threatened to come down around him. 'One of the prisoners has been killed.'

She looked concerned. 'How?'

'It wasn't pretty. Sure you want to know?'

She made a small noise. 'If you're worried about me fainting on you, you've got the wrong lady.'

'I thought as much. Just giving you the option. It happened in one of the operational air shafts.' He shook his head at the memory. 'Poor silly bastard backed into a working two-metre high-speed fan. Splattered him all over the place. We had to scrape him off the walls.'

'I get the picture. It happens.'

'Not here it doesn't. Andrews is ticked. It means he has to file a report.'

'By communications beam?'

'No. No need for the expense. I imagine it'll go out with the next ship.'

'Then what's he worried about? Nobody'll read it for months.'

'You'd have to know the superintendent to understand. He takes everything personal.'

'Too bad for him, especially considering his current employment.'

Clemens nodded, looking thoughtful. 'I found something at the accident site, just a bit away from where it happened. A mark, a burn on the floor. Discoloured, blistered metal. It looked a lot like what you found on the girl's cryotube.'

She just stared at him, her gaze unblinking, uninformative, her expression unfathomable.

'Look, I'm on your side,' the medic insisted when she remained silent. 'Whatever it is you're involved in or trying to do, I want to help. But I'd like to know what's going on, or at least what you think is going on. Otherwise I'm not going to be able to be of much use to you. Maybe you can do whatever it is you're trying to do alone. I can't make you talk to me. I just think that I can help, make it easier for you. I have access to equipment. You don't. I have some knowledge that you don't. I won't interfere and I'll rely entirely on your judgment. I have to, since I don't have a clue as to what you're up to.'

She paused, considering, while he watched her hopefully. 'I hardly know you. Why should I trust you?'

He forced himself to ignore the hurt, knowing there was nothing personal in the query. 'No reason. Only that without somebody's help it's going to be hard for you, whatever it is you're trying to do. I hardly know you, either, but I'm willing to follow your lead.'

'Why? Why should you? By your own admission you don't have any idea what's going on, what's at stake.'

He smiled encouragingly. 'Maybe I think I know you a little better than you think you know me.'

'You're crazy.'

'Is that a hindrance to what you're doing?'

She smiled in spite of herself. 'Probably just the opposite. All right.' She slid the black box out where he could see it clearly. 'I need to know what happened here in the EEV, why we were ejected from our ship while still in deep sleep. If you really want to be helpful, find me a computer with audio and sensory interpretation capabilities so I can access this flight recorder.'

Clemens looked doubtful. 'We don't have anything like that here. The Company salvaged all the sophisticated cybernetics. Everything they left us is either basic program and response or strictly ROM.' He smiled sardonically. 'I imagine they didn't want a bunch of dumb prisoners messing with their expensive machinery.'

'What about Bishop?'

'Bishop?' He frowned.

'The droid that crashed with me.'

'He was checked and discarded as useless.'

'Let me be the judge of that.' A note of concern entered her voice. 'His components haven't been cannibalized or compacted, have they?'

'I told you: nobody here's smart enough to do the first, and there wasn't any reason to waste the energy to carry out the latter. What's left of him's in fewer pieces than the prisoner who got killed, but not many. Don't tell me you think you can get some use out of him?'

'All right, I won't tell you. Where is he?'

Clemens looked resigned. 'I'll point you in the proper direction, but I'm afraid I can't join you. I have an appointment. Watch your step, okay?'

She was unfazed. 'If I wasn't in the habit of doing so, I'd be dead now twenty times over.'

# VI

The candleworks was more than a hobby. While the installation's sealed, self-contained fusion plant generated more than enough energy to light the entire facility should anyone think it necessary, it provided nothing in the way of portable energy. Rechargeable lights were a scarce and precious commodity. After all, the Company techs whose responsibility it had been to decide what was salvaged and what was left behind had logically assumed that the prisoners wouldn't want to go wandering about the surface of Fiorina at night. Within the installation the fusion plant would provide all the illumination they wanted. And since fusion plants simply did not fail, there was no need to consider, nor were substantial provisions made for, backup.

But there were supplies, secreted by miners or forgotten by the evacuation techs, down in the shafts from which millions of tons of ore had been extracted. Supplies which could make life for prisoners and staff alike a little easier. There was plenty of time to hunt them out. All that was wanting was portable illumination.

The candleworks solved that, in addition to giving the inhabitants of Fiorina something different to do. There was plenty of the special wax in storage. One of those bulk supplies not worth the expense of shipping it offworld, it had originally been used to make test moulds for new equipment. A computer-guided laser Cadcam would model the part and etch the wax, which would then be filled with plastic or carbon composite, and hey presto—instant replacement part. No machinery necessary, no long drawn-out work with lathes and cutters. Afterwards the special wax could be melted down and used again.

The prisoners had no need for replacement parts. What equipment was necessary for their survival was self-contained and functioned just fine without their attentions. So they made candles.

They flickered brightly, cheeringly, throughout the works, dangling in bunches from the ceiling, flashing in lead moulds the prisoners had made for themselves. The industrial wax of an advanced civilization served perfectly well to mimic the efforts of a technology thousands of years old.

Prisoner Gregor was helping Golic, Boggs, and Rains stuff the special extra-dense illumination candles into their oversized backpacks. The inclusion of a few carefully chosen impurities helped such candles hold their shape and burn for a very long time. They had no choice but to make use of them, since Andrews would hardly allow use of the installation's irreplaceable portable lights for frivolous activities.

Not that the men really minded. The technology might be primitive, but there was no significant difference in the quality of the illumination provided by the candles and that supplied by their precious few rechargeable fuel cells. Light was light. And there were plenty of candles.

Golic alternated between shoving the squat tapers into his pack and food into his mouth. Particles spilled from his lips, fell into his pack. Rains eyed him with distaste.

'There you are.' Gregor hefted one of the bulky packs. 'This'll top you off. Golic, don't fidget about. What's all this damn food you've got in here? It's not properly wrapped.' The subject of his query smiled blankly and continued to stuff food into his mouth.

Boggs eyed him with disgust. 'What the hell does he ever do right?'

Rains snorted. 'Eat. He's got that down pretty good.'

Dillon and prisoner Junior appeared in the doorway.

'Hey, Golic,' the bigger man murmured.

The prisoner thus questioned glanced up and replied through his half-masticated mouthful. 'Yeah?'

'Light a candle for Murphy, will you?'

Food spilled from his lips as Golic smiled reassuringly. 'Right. I'll light a thousand.' He was suddenly wistful. 'He was a special friend. He never complained about me, not once. I loved him. Did his head really get split into a million pieces? That's what they're saying.'

Dillon helped them slip into the bulky backpacks, giving each man a slap on the shoulder after checking out his individual harness.

'Watch yourselves down there. You've got adequate maps. Use 'em. You find anything that's too big to bring back, make damn good and sure you mark its location so a follow-up team can find it. I remember four years ago a bunch of guys dug out some miner's personal cache of canned goods. Enough to sweeten the kitchen for months. Didn't mark it right and we never did find the place again. Maybe you three'll get lucky.'

Boggs made a rude noise and there were chuckles all around. 'That's me. Always feeling lucky.'

'Right, then.' Dillon stepped aside. 'Get goin', don't come back till you find something worthwhile, and watch out for those hundred-metre dropshafts.'

The big man watched them disappear into the access tunnel, watched until distance and curves smothered their lights. Then he and Junior turned and ambled off in the direction of the assembly hall. He had work of his own to attend to.

Andrews's quarters were spacious, if furnished in Spartan style. As superintendent, he'd been given the chambers, which had been the former province of the mine chief. He had plenty of room to spread out, but insufficient furniture to fill the considerable space. Not being a man of much imagination or inclined to delusions of grandeur, he'd sealed most of the rooms and confined himself to three, one each for hygiene, sleeping, and meeting with visitors.

It was the latter activity which occupied him now, as he sat across the modest desk from his single medic. Clemens presented a problem. Technically he was a prisoner and could be treated just like the others. But no one, the superintendent included, disputed his unique status. Less than a free man but higher than an indentured custodian, he earned more than any of the other prisoners. More importantly, they relied on him for services no one else could render. So did Andrews and Aaron.

Clemens was also a cut above the rest of the prison population intellectually. Given the dearth of sparkling conversation available on Fiorina, Andrews valued that ability almost as much as the man's medical talents. Talking with Aaron was about as stimulating as speaking into the log.

But he had to be careful. It wouldn't do for Clemens, any more than for any other prisoner, to acquire too high an opinion of himself. When they met, the two men spun cautious verbs around one another, word waltzing as delicately as a pair of weathered rattlesnakes. Clemens was continually pushing the envelope of independence and Andrews sealing it up again.

The pot dipped over the medic's cup, pouring tea. 'Sugar?'

'Thank you,' Clemens replied. The superintendent passed the plastic container and watched while his guest ladled out white granules.

'Milk?'

'Yes, please.'

Andrews slid the can across the table and leaned forward intently as Clemens lightened the heavy black liquid.

'Listen to me, you piece of shit,' the superintendent informed his guest fraternally, 'you screw with me one more time and I'll cut you in half.'

The medic eased the container of milk aside, picked up his

tea, and began to stir it quietly. In the dead silence that ensued, the sound of the spoon ticking methodically against the interior of the ceramic cup seemed as loud and deliberate as a hammer slamming into an anvil.

'I'm not sure I understand,' he said finally.

Andrews sat back in his chair, his eyes cutting into his guest. 'At 0700 hours I received a reply to my report from the Network. I may point out that to the best of my knowledge this is the first high-level, priority communication this installation has ever received. Even when Fiorina was a working, functioning mining and refining operation it was never so honoured. You know why?'

Clemens sipped his tea. 'High-level priority communications have to go through subspace to beat the time problem. That costs plenty.'

Andrews was nodding. 'More than you or I'll ever see.'

'So why rail at me?'

'It's this woman.' Andrews was clearly troubled. 'They want her looked after. No, more than looked after. They made it very clear they consider her to be of the highest priority. In fact, the communication managed to convey the impression that the rest of the operation here could vanish into a black hole so long as we made sure the woman was alive and in good health when the rescue team arrives.'

'Why?'

'I was hoping you could tell me.' The superintendent gazed at him intently.

Clemens carefully set his empty cup down on the table. 'I see that it's time to be perfectly frank with you, sir.' Andrews leaned forward eagerly.

The medic smiled apologetically. 'I don't know a damn thing.'

There was a pause as Andrews's expression darkened. 'I'm glad you find this funny, Clemens. I'm pleased you find it amusing. I wish I could say the same. You know what a communication like this does?'

'Puts your ass in a sling?' Clemens said pleasantly.

'Puts everyone's ass in a sling. We screw up here, this woman gets hurt or anything, there'll be hell to pay.'

'Then we shouldn't have any trouble arranging compensation, since we all live there now.'

'Be as clever as you want. I don't think the urge will be as strong if something untoward happens and some sentences are extended.'

Clemens stiffened slightly. 'They're that concerned?'

'I'd show you the actual communication if it wouldn't violate policy. Take my word for it.'

'I don't understand what all the fuss is about,' Clemens said honestly. 'Sure she's been through a great deal, but others have survived deep-space tragedies. Why is the Company so interested in her?'

'I have no idea.' Andrews placed his interlocked fingers in front of him. 'Why'd you let her out of the infirmary? It's all related to this accident with Murphy somehow. I'd bet my pension on it.' He slapped both hands down on the desk. 'This is what happens when one of these dumb sons of bitches walks around with a hard-on. Why couldn't you have kept her bottled up and out of sight?'

'There was no reason to. She was healthy, ambulatory, and wanted out. I didn't have either the reason or the authority to restrain her.' Clemens's studied savoir faire was beginning to weaken. 'I'm a doctor. Not a jailer.'

The superintendent's expression twisted. 'Don't hand me that. We both know exactly what you are.'

Clemens rose and started for the door. Andrews's fingers unlocked and this time he smacked the table with a heavy fist. 'Sit down! I haven't dismissed you yet.'

The medic replied without turning, struggling to keep himself under control. 'I was under the impression I was here at your invitation, not official order. Presently I think it might be better if I left. At the moment I find you very unpleasant to be around. If I remain I might say or do something regrettable.'

'You might?' Andrews affected mock dismay. 'Isn't that lovely. Consider this, Mr. Clemens. How would you like me to have you exposed? Though they are a matter of public record elsewhere, up till now the details of your life have been your own here on Fiorina. This personal privilege has facilitated your work with the prisoners, has indeed given you a certain awkward but nonetheless very real status among them. That is easily revoked. If that were to occur I expect that your life here would become rather less pleasant.' He paused to let everything sink in before continuing.

'What, no witty riposte? No clever jibe? Do I take your silence to mean that you would prefer not to have your dirty little past made part of the general conversation here? Of course, it needn't stop there. Perhaps you'd like me to explain the details of your sordid history to your patient and new friend Lieutenant Ripley? For her personal edification, of course. Strictly in the interests of helping her to allot her remaining time here appropriately.

'No? Then sit the hell down.'

Wordlessly, Clemens turned and resumed his seat. He looked suddenly older, like a man who'd recently lost something precious and had no hope of recovering it.

Andrews regarded his guest thoughtfully. 'I've always been straight with you. I think that's good policy, especially in an environment like we have here. So you won't be particularly upset or surprised when I say that I don't like you.'

'No,' Clemens murmured in a soft, flat voice. 'I'm not surprised.'

'I don't like you,' the superintendent repeated. 'You're unpredictable, insolent, possibly dangerous. You have a certain amount of education and are undeniably intelligent, which makes you more of a threat than the average prisoner. You question everything and spend too much time alone. Always a bad sign. I've survived in this business a long time and I speak from experience. I know what to look for. Your typical incarceree will revolt, sometimes even kill, but it's always the quiet, smart ones who cause the really serious problems.' He went silent for a moment, considering.

'But you were assigned to this posting and I have to live with that. I just want you to know that if I didn't need a medical officer I wouldn't let you within light-years of this operation.'

'I'm very grateful.'

'How about trying something new, Clemens? Something really different. Try keeping your sarcasms to yourself.' He squirmed slightly in his chair. 'Now, I'm going to ask you one more time. As your intellectual equal. As someone you respect if not like. As the individual ultimately responsible for the safety and well-being of every man in this facility, yourself included. Is there anything I should know?'

'About what?'

Andrews silently counted to five before smiling. 'About the woman. Don't toy with me anymore. I think that I've made my position clear, personally as well as professionally.'

'Why should I know anything other than the self-evident about her?'

'Because you spend every second you can with her. And I have my suspicions that not all of your concerns are medical in nature. You are far too solicitous of her needs. It doesn't fit your personality profile. You just said yourself that she's fit and able to get around fine on her own. D'you think I'm blind? Do you think I'd have been given this post if I wasn't capable of picking up on the slightest deviations from the norm?' He muttered to himself. 'Deviates' deviations.'

Clemens sighed. 'What do you want to know?'

'That's better.' Andrews nodded approvingly. 'Has she said anything to you? Not about herself personally. I don't give a damn about that. Wallow in mutual reminiscence all you want, I don't care. I mean professionally. About where she's come from. What her mission was, or is. Most particularly, what the hell was she doing in an EEV with a busted droid, a drowned six-year-old kid, and a dead corporal, and where the hell is the rest of her ship's crew? For that matter, where the hell is her ship?'

'She told me she was part of a combat team that came to grief. The last she remembers was going into deep sleep. At that time the marine was alive and the girl's cryotube was functioning normally. It's been my assumption all along that the girl was drowned and the marine killed in the crash of the EEV.

'I assume beyond that it's all classified. I haven't pressed her for more. She does carry marine lieutenant rank, you know.'

'That's all?' Andrews persisted.

Clemens studied his empty teacup. 'Yes.'

'Nothing more?'

'No.'

'You're sure?'

The medic looked up and met the older man's eyes evenly. 'Very sure.'

Andrews's gaze dropped to his hands and he spoke through clenched teeth. It was obvious there was more, something the medic wasn't telling him, but short of physical coercion there wasn't a damned thing he could do about it. And physical coercion wouldn't work with someone like Clemens, whose inherent stubbornness would keep him from admitting that he had no pride left to defend.

'Get out of here.'

Clemens rose wordlessly and started a second time for the door.

'One more thing.' The medic paused, looked back to find the superintendent watching him closely. 'I take comfort in the daily routine here. So do you. There's a great deal of reassurance to be found in codified monotony. I'm not going to let it be broken. Systematic repetition of familiar tasks is the best and safest narcotic. I'm not going to allow the animals to become agitated. Not by a woman, not by accidents. Not by you.'

'Whatever you say,' Clemens replied agreeably.

'Don't go getting any funny ideas. Independent action is a valueless concept on Fiorina. Don't think too much. It'll damage your standing in our little community, especially with me, and you'll only end up hurting yourself. You'll do better to keep your long-term goals in mind at all times.

'Your loyalties are to this operation, and to your employer. Not to strangers, or to some misguided notions you may happen to erect on the foundation of your own boredom. She will be gone soon and we will still be here. You and I, Dillon and Aaron and all the rest. Everything will be as it was before the EEV crashed. Don't jeopardize your enviable situation for a temporary abstraction. Do you understand?'

'Yes. Your point is quite clear. Even to someone like me.'

Andrews continued to brood uneasily. 'I don't want trouble with our employers. I don't want trouble of any kind. I get paid to see that trouble doesn't happen. Our presence here is ... frowned upon by certain social elements back on Earth. Until the accident we hadn't suffered a death from other than natural causes since the day this group took over caretaking duties from its predecessors. I am aware that it could not have been prevented but it still looks bad in the records. I don't like looking bad, Mr. Clemens.' He squinted up at the medic. 'You take my meaning?'

'Perfectly, sir.'

Andrews continued. 'Rescue and resupply will be here soon enough. Meanwhile, you keep an eye on the lieutenant and if you observe anything, ah, potentially disruptive, I know that I can rely on you to notify me of it immediately. Right?'

Clemens nodded briskly. 'Right.'

Though only partially mollified, the other man could think of nothing more to say. 'Very well, then. We understand one another. Good night, Mr. Clemens.'

'Good night, Superintendent.' He shut the door quietly behind him.

The wind of Fiorina rose and fell, dropping occasionally to querulous zephyrs or rising to tornadic shrieks, but it never stopped. It blew steadily off the bay, carrying the pungent odour of salt water to the outer sections of the installation. Sometimes storms and currents dredged odours more alien from the depths of the sea and sent them spiralling down through the air shafts, slipping through the scrubbers to remind the men that the world they occupied was foreign to the inhabitants of distant Earth, and would kill them if it could.

They went outside but rarely, preferring the familiar surroundings of the immense installation to the oppressive spaciousness of the sullen landscape. There was nothing to look at except the dark waves that broke on the black sand beach, nothing to remind them of the world they had once known. That was fortunate. Such memories were more painful than any degree of toil.

The water was cold and home to tiny, disgusting creatures that bit. Sometimes a few of the men chose to go fishing, but only for physical and not spiritual nourishment. Inside the facility it was warm and dry. The wind was no more than distant, discordant music, to be ignored. Sometimes it was necessary to go outside. These excursions were invariably brief, and attended to with as much haste as possible, moving from one refuge to another as quickly as possible.

In contrast, the figure picking through the sheltered mountain of debris was doing so with deliberation and care. Ripley paced the surface of the immense pit, her eyes fixed on its irregular surface. The original excavation had been filled in with discarded, broken equipment. She wrestled her way past monumental components, punctured storage tanks, worn-out drill bits the size of small trucks, brightly coloured vines of old wiring and corroded tubes.

Wind whipped around outside and she clutched at the neck of the suit Clemens had found for her. The ruined mechanical landscape had seemed endless and the cold was still penetrating her muscles, slowing her and interfering with her perceptions.

Not to the extent, however, that she failed to see the expensive silvery filaments protruding from a smaller pimple of recently discarded trash. Kneeling, she began tearing at the refuse, heaving ruined equipment and bags of garbage aside to reveal . . .

Bishop.

Or, more accurately, what was left of him. The android components were scattered amid the rest of the junk and she had to dig and sort for another hour before she was certain she'd salvaged absolutely everything that might be of use.

She made a preliminary attempt to correctly position the parts. Not only was the result unencouraging, it was downright pitiful. Most of the face and lower jaw was missing, crushed beyond recognition in the EEV or lost somewhere within the mass of trash outside. Portions of the neck, left shoulder, and back had somehow survived intact. In addition there were sensitive related components which had spilled or been torn free from the exterior shell.

Grim-faced and alone, she began carefully packing them into the sack she'd brought with her.

That's when the arm coiled around her neck and the hands grabbed hard at her shoulders. Another hand appeared, clutching feverishly between her legs, fondling roughly. A man materialized in front of her. He was grinning, but there was no humour in his expression.

With a cry she broke free of the arms restraining her. The startled prisoner just gaped as her fist landed in his face and her foot between his thighs. As he crumpled, prisoner Junior appeared and wrapped his thick arms around her, lifting her off the ground to the encouraging sniggers of his companions, throwing her spread-eagled across a corroded pipe. The other men closed in, their body odour obliterating the smell of salt, their eyes glittering.

'Knock it off.'

Gregor turned, his gaze narrowing as he isolated a silhouette, close. Dillon.

Gregor forced a grin. 'Jump in the saddle, man. You wanna go first?'

Dillon's voice was low, ominous. 'I said knock it off.'

With his weight resting on the gasping Ripley, Junior snarled back over his shoulder. 'Hey, what's it to you, man?'

'It's wrong.'

'Fuck you.'

Dillon moved then, deceptively fast. The two men in back went down hard. Junior whirled and brought a huge fist around like a scythe, only to have his opponent weave, gut-punch him, and snatch up a metal bar. Junior staggered and tried to dodge, but the bar connected with the side of his skull. The second blow was harder, and he dropped like stone.

The others cowered and Dillon whacked them again, just to keep them thinking. Then he turned to Ripley, his expression solemn.

'You okay?'

She straightened, still breathing hard. 'Yeah. Nothing hurt but my feelings.'

'Take off,' he said to her. He indicated his fellow prisoners. 'I've got to reeducate some of the brothers. We're gonna discuss some matters of the spirit.'

She nodded, hefted her bag of Bishop, and started back. As she passed the men on the ground Gregor glanced up at her. She punched him squarely in the mouth. Feeling better, she resumed her course.

# VII

There is night, which is dark. There is the obdurate emptiness of dreams, whose lights are only imaginary. Beyond all is the void, illuminated however faintly by a million trillion nuclear furnaces.

True darkness, the utter absence of light, the place where a stray photon is as impotent as an atomic anomaly, lies only deep within the earth. 'In caverns measureless to man' as the old stanza rhythmically declaims. Or in those cracks and crevices man creates in order to extract the wealth of planets.

A tiny but in and of itself impressive portion of one corner of Fiorina was honeycombed with such excavations, intersecting and crisscrossing like the components of a vast unseen puzzle, their overall pattern discernible only in the records the miners had left behind.

Boggs held his wax-impregnated torch high, waved it around as Rains lit a candle. To such men the darkness was nothing to be feared. It was merely an absence of light. It was also warm within the tunnels, almost oppressively warm.

Rains placed the long-burning taper on the floor, next to the wall. Behind them a line of identical flames stretched off into the distance, delineating the trail they'd taken and the route back to the occupied portion of the complex.

Golic sat down, resting his back against a door set in the solid rock. There was a sign on the door, battered and worn by machinery and time.

TOXIC WASTE DISPOSAL
THIS SPACE HERMETICALLY SEALED
ACCESS TO UNAUTHORIZED PERSONNEL
PROHIBITED

That was just fine with the explorers. They had no wish to be suitably authorized.

Rains had unfolded the chart at his feet and crouched, studying the lines and shafts by the light of his torch. The map was no simple matter of vertical and horizontal lines. There were old shafts and comparatively recent ones, fill-ins and reopenings, angle cuts and reduced diameter accessways to accommodate specialized machinery only. Not to mention the thousands of intersecting air ducts. Different colours signified different things.

Numerous earlier expeditions had given the prisoners some idea of what to expect, but there was always the chance that each new team would run into something unexpected. A scrambled byte in the storage units could shift an abyssal shaft ten metres out of line, or into a different tunnel. The chart was a tentative guide at best. So they advanced carefully, putting their faith in their own senses and not in dated printouts.

Boggs leaned close. 'How many?' Though he spoke softly, his voice still echoed down the smooth-walled passage.

Rains checked the chart against his portable datapack. 'This makes a hundred and eighty-six.'

His companion grunted. 'I say we call it a vacation and start back.'

'No can do.' Rains gestured at the seemingly endless length of tunnel that lay before them. 'We've at least got to check out the rest of this stretch or Dillon'll pound us.'

'What he don't know won't irritate him. I won't tell. How about you, Golic?' The third member of the trio was digging through his backpack. Hearing his name he looked up, frowned, and uttered a low, vaguely inquisitive sound. 'That's what I thought.'

Golic approached an ancient cigarette machine. Kicking the

lock off, he yanked open the door and began loading packs of preserved narcosticks into his duffel. Naturally he chewed as he worked.

On the surface the noise would have been far less noticeable, but in the restricted surroundings and total silence of the tunnel the third man's rumbling maceration resounded like a large, improperly lubricated piece of machinery. Boggs grumbled.

'Can't you chew with your mouth closed? Or better yet, swallow that crap you're eating whole? I'm trying to figure how big this compartment is so we can decide if it's legit toxic storage or some miner's private stock, and I can't think with all the goddamn noise you're making.'

Rains rustled the chart disapprovingly. 'Just because we're away from the others doesn't mean we should ignore the precepts. You're not supposed to swear.'

Boggs's mouth tightened. 'Sorry.' He stared daggers at Golic, who quite naturally ignored them. Finally he gave up and rose to squint down the tunnel. 'We've circled this entire section once. That's all anyone could ask. How many candles, again?' There was no reply from the floor. 'Rains, how many candles?'

His companion wasn't listening. Instead he was scratching himself furiously, an intense nervous reaction that had nothing whatsoever to do with the bugs, who didn't live in the shafts anyway. It was so uncharacteristic, so atypical, that it even managed the daunting task of drawing Golic's attention away from his food. Boggs found himself staring fixedly back the way they'd come.

One by one, the candles which traced their path back to the surface were going out.

'What the shit is doing that?'

Golic pursed his lips, wiping food crumbs from his mouth with the back of one hand. 'You're not supposed to swear.'

'Shut up.' Not fear—there was nothing to fear in the tunnels—but concern had crept into Boggs's voice. 'It's okay to say "shit." It's not against God.'

'How do you know?' Golic muttered with almost childlike curiosity.

'Because I asked him the last time we talked and he said it was okay. Now shut up.'

'Dillon'll scream if we don't come back with anything,' Golic pointed out. The mystery was making him positively voluble. Boggs decided he preferred it when the other man did nothing but eat.

'Let him scream.' He waited while Rains lit another torch. Reluctantly, Golic repacked his remaining food and rose. All three stared back down the tunnel, back the way they'd come. Whatever was snuffing out the candles remained invisible.

'Must be a breeze from one of the vent shafts. Backwash from the nearest circulating unit. Or maybe a storm on the surface. You know what those sudden downdraughts can do. Damn! If all the candles go out, how're we going to know where we are?'

'We've still got the chart.' Rains fingered the sturdy printout.

'You want to rely on that to get us back?'

'Hey, I didn't say that. It's just that we're not lost. Only inconvenienced.'

'Well, I don't wanna be inconvenienced, and I don't wanna be stuck down here any longer than absolutely necessary.'

'Neither do I.' Rains sighed resignedly. 'You know what that means. Somebody will have to go back and relight 'em.'

'Unless you just want to call it quits now?' Boggs asked hopefully.

Rains managed a grin. 'Huh-huh. We finish this tunnel, then we can go back.'

'Have it your way.' Boggs crossed his arms and succeeded in projecting the air of a man intending to go nowhere fast. 'It's your call; you get to do the work.'

'Fair enough. Guess I'm nominated.'

Boggs gestured at Golic. 'Give him your torch.'

The other man was reluctant. 'That just leaves us here with the one.'

'There's nothing wrong with it.' Boggs waved the light around to illustrate his point. 'And we have the rest of the candles. Besides, Rains'll be right back. Won't you, buddy?'

'Quick as I can. Shouldn't take too long.'

'Right, then.'

Reluctantly, Golic passed the taller man his light. Together, he and Boggs watched as their companion moved off up the line of candles, pausing to relight each one as he came to it. Each rested where it had been set on the floor. There was nothing to indicate what had extinguished them.

Just a sudden downdraught, Rains told himself. Had to be. Boggs's voice reverberated down the passageway, faint with increasing distance.

'Hey, Rains, watch your step!' They'd marked the couple of vertical shafts they'd passed, but still, if the other man rushed himself in the darkness, disaster was never very far away.

Rains appreciated the caution. You live in close quarters with a very few people for a comparatively long time, you learn to rely on one another. Not that Boggs had reason to worry. Rains advanced with admirable care.

Ahead of him another candle went out and he frowned. There was no hint of a breeze, nothing to suggest the presence of the hypothesized downdraught. What else could be extinguishing the tapers? Very few living things were known to spend much time in the tunnels. There was a kind of primitive large insect that was big enough to knock over a candle, but why a whole row? He shook his head dolefully though there was no one near to observe the gesture. The insect wouldn't move this fast.

Then what?

The tapers he'd reignited burned reassuringly behind him. He straightened. There were no mystical forces at work here. Raising the torch, he aimed it up the tunnel, saw nothing.

Kneeling, he relit the next candle and started towards the next in line. As he did so the light of his torch bounced off the walls, off smooth-cut rock. Off something angular and massive.

It moved.

Very fast, oh, so very fast. Shards of reflection like chromed glass inlaid in adamantine black metal. It made an incongruously soft gurgling sound as it sprang soundlessly towards him. He was unable to identify it, had never seen anything like it, except perhaps in some especially bad dreams half remembered from childhood.

In an instant it was upon him, and at that moment he would gratefully have sought comfort in his worst nightmares.

A hundred metres down the tunnel Golic and Boggs listened to their companion's single echoing shriek. Cold sweat broke out the back of Boggs's neck and hands. Horribly, the scream did not cut off sharply, but instead faded away slowly and gradually like a high-pitched whistle receding into the distance.

Suddenly panicked, Boggs grabbed up the remaining light and took off running, down the passageway, away from the scream. Golic charged after him.

Boggs wouldn't have guessed that he could still move so fast. For a few moments he actually put some distance between them. Then his lack of wind began to tell and he slowed, the torch he clutched making mad shadows on the walls, ceiling, floor. By the time Golic ran him down he was completely exhausted and equally disoriented. Only by sheer good luck had they avoided stumbling into an open sampler pit or down a connecting shaft.

Staggering slightly, he grabbed the other man's arm and spun him around.

Golic gaped in dumb terror. 'Didn't you hear it? It was Rains! Oh, God, it was Rains.'

'Yeah.' Boggs fought to get his breath. 'I heard it. He's hurt himself.' Prying the torch from the other man's trembling fingers he played it up and down the deserted passageway. 'We've got to help him.'

'Help him?' Golic's eyes were wide. 'You help him. I wanna get out of here!'

'Take it easy. So do I, so do I. First we've got to figure out where we are.'

'Isn't that a candle?'

Turning, Boggs advanced a few cautious steps. Sure enough, the line of flickering tapers was clearly visible, stretching off into the distance.

'Damn. We must've cut through an accessway. We ran in a circle. We're back—'

He stopped, steadying the light on the far wall. A figure was leaning there, still as anything to be found in cold storage.

Rains.

Staring not back at them but at nothing. His eyes were wide open and immobile as frozen jelly. The expression on his face was not a fit thing for men to look upon. The rest of him was . . . the rest of him was . . .

Boggs felt a hot alkaline rush in his throat and doubled over, retching violently. The torch fell from his suddenly weakened fingers and Golic knelt to pick it up. As he rose he happened to glance ceilingward.

There was something up there. Something on the ceiling. It was big and black and fast and its face was a vision of pure hell. As he stared openmouthed it leaned down, hanging like a gigantic bat from its clawed hind legs, and enveloped Boggs's head in a pair of hands with fingers like articulated cables. Boggs inhaled sharply, gagging on his own vomit.

With an abrupt, convulsive twist the arachnoid horror jerked Boggs's head right off his shoulders, as cleanly as Golic would have removed a loose bolt from its screw. But not as neatly. Blood fountained from the headless torso, splattering the creature, Rains's body, the staring Golic. It broke his paralysis but in the process also snapped something inside his head.

With ghastly indifference the gargoyle tossed Boggs's decapitated skull to the floor and turned slowly to confront the remaining bipedal life-form. Its teeth gleamed like the platinum ingots which had been torn from Fiorina's bowels.

Howling as if all the legions of the damned were after him, Golic whirled and tore down the tunnel. He didn't look where he was going and he didn't think about what he'd seen, and most of all he didn't look back. He didn't dare look back.

If he did, he knew he might see something.

Bishop's remains had been carefully laid out on the worktable. Bright overhead lights illuminated each component. Tools rested in their holders, ready to be called upon. The profusion of torn hair-thin fibre-optic cables were staggering.

Some Ripley had simply tied off as best she could. Her experience did not extend to making repairs on the microscopic level. She'd spent a lot of time wiring the parts together as best she could, sealing and taping, making the obvious connection and hoping nothing absolutely critical lay beyond her limited talent for improvisation.

She wiped her eyes and studied her handiwork. It looked promising, but that meant nothing. Theroetically it stood a chance of working, but then theoretically she shouldn't be in the fix she was in.

No way to know without trying it. She tested the vital connections, then touched a switch. Something sizzled briefly, making her jerk back in the chair. She adjusted a connection, tried the switch again. This time there was no extraneous flash.

Carefully she slipped one bundle of fibre-optic filaments into what she hoped was still a functional self-sorting contact socket. A red digital readout on the test unit nearby immediately went from zero to between seven and eight. As she threw another switch the numbers wavered but held steady.

The android's remaining intact eye blinked. Ripley leaned forward. 'Verbal interaction command. Run self-test sequence.' Then she wondered why she was whispering.

Within the battered artificial skull something whined. Other telltales on the test unit winked encouragingly. A garbled burbling emerged from the artificial larynx and the collagenic lips parted slightly.

Anxiously she reached into the open throat, her fingers working inside. The burbling resolved itself as the single eye fixed on her face.

'Ripley.'

She took a deep breath. She had visual, cognition, coordination, and memory. The external ears looked pretty good, but that signified nothing. All that mattered was the condition of the internal circuits.

'Hello, Bishop.' She was surprised at the warmth in her tone. After all, it wasn't as if she were addressinig a human being. 'Please render a preliminary condition report.'

There was a pause, following which, astonishingly, the single eye performed an eloquent roll in its socket. 'Lousy. Motor functions are gone, extracranial peripherals nonresponsive, prospects for carrying out programmed functions nil. Minimal sensory facilities barely operative. Not an optimistic self-diagnosis, I'm afraid.'

'I'm sorry to hear that,' she told him honestly. 'I wish it could be otherwise.'

'Not as much as I do.'

'Can you feel anything?'

'Yes. My legs hurt.'

Her lips tightened. 'I'm sorry that—'

'It's okay. Pain simulation is only data, which from the rest of my present condition I infer is probably inaccurate. Confirm?'

'I'm afraid so.' She managed a weak smile. 'I'm afraid that your legs, like most of the rest of you, has gone the way of all flesh.'

'Too bad. Hate to see all that quality work lost. Not that it matters in the scheme of things. After all, I'm just a glorified toaster. How are you? I like your new haircut. Reminds me of me before my accessories were installed. Not quite as shiny, though.'

'I see that your sense of humour's still intact.'

The eye blinked. 'Like I said, basic mental functions are still operative. Humour occupies a very small portion of my RAM-interpretive capacity.'

'I'd disagree.' Her smile faded. 'I need your help.'

A gurgle emerged from between the artificial lips. 'Don't

expect anything extensive.'

'It doesn't involve a lot of analysis. More straightforward probing. Where I am right now they don't have much in the way of intrusive capability. What I need to know is can you access the data bank on an EEV flight recorder?'

'No problem. Why?'

'You'll find out faster from the recorder than I could explain. Then you can tell me.'

The eye swivelled. 'I can just see it. You'll have to use a direct cranial jump, since my auxiliary appendages are gone.'

'I know. I'm all set . . . I hope.'

'Go ahead and plug in, then.'

She picked up the filament running from the black box and leaned forward towards the disembodied skull. 'I've never done this before. It won't hurt or anything?'

'On the contrary, I'm hoping it'll make me feel better.'

She nodded and gently inserted the filament into one of several receptacles in the back of his head, wiggling it slightly to make sure the fit was tight.

'That tickles.' She jerked her fingers back. 'Just kidding,' the android told her with a reassuring smile. 'Hang on.' His eyes closed and the remnants of his forehead wrinkled in concentration. It was, she knew admiringly, nothing more than a redundant bit of cosmetic programming, but it was encouraging to see that something besides the android's basics still functioned.

'I'm home,' Bishop murmured several minutes later. 'Took longer than I thought. I had to run the probe around some damaged sectors.'

'I tested the recorder when I first found it. It checked out okay.'

'It is. The damaged sectors are in me. What do you want to know?'

'Everything.'

'McNary Flight Recorder, model OV-122, serial number FR-3664874, installed—'

560 ALAN DEAN FOSTER

'Are all your language intuition circuits gone? You know what I mean. From the time it was emergency activated. What happened on the *Sulaco*? Why were the cryotubes ejected?'

A new voice emerged from the android's larynx. It was female and mechanical. 'Explosive gasses present in the cryogenic compartment. Fire in the cryogenic compartment. All personnel report to evacuation stations.' Bishop's voice returned. 'There are a large number of repeats without significant deviation in content. Do you wish to hear them all?'

Ripley rubbed her chin, thinking hard. 'No, that's sufficient for now. Explosive gases? Where did they come from? And what started the fire?' When no response was forthcoming she became alarmed. 'Bishop? Can you hear me?'

There was gurgling, then the android's silky faux voice. 'Sorry. This is harder than I thought it would be. Powering up and functioning are weakening already damaged sectors. I keep losing memory and response capability. I don't know how much longer I can keep this up. You'd better keep your questions brief.'

'Don't null out on me yet, Bishop,' she said anxiously. 'I was asking you about the report of fire.'

'Fire . . .—*crackle*—*. . .yes. It was electrical, in the subflooring of the cryogenics compartment. Presence of a catalyst combined with damaged materials to produce the explosive gas. Ventilation failed completely. Result was immediately life-threatening. Hence ship's decision to evacuate. EEV detected evidence of explosion on board subsequent to evacuation, with concomitant damage to EEV controls. That's why our landing here was less than perfect. Present status of *Sulaco* unknown. Further details of flight from *Sulaco* to present position available.'

'Skip 'em. Did sensors detect any motile life-forms on the *Sulaco* prior to emergency separation?'

Silence. Then, 'It's very dark here, Ripley. Inside. I'm not used to being dark. Even as we speak portions of me are shutting down. Reasoning is growing difficult and I'm having to fall back on pure logic. I don't like that. It's too stark. Not anything like what I was designed for. I'm not what I used to be.'

'Just a little longer, Bishop,' she urged him. She tried tweaking the power up but it did nothing more than make his eye widen slightly and she hastily returned to prescribed levels. 'You know what I'm asking. Does the flight recorder indicate the presence of anything on the *Sulaco* besides the four survivors of Acheron? Was there an alien on board? Bishop!'

Nothing. She fine-tuned instrumentation, nudged controls. The eye rolled.

'Back off. I'm still here. So are the answers. It's just taking longer and longer to bring the two together. To answer your question. Yes.'

Ripley took a deep breath. The workroom seemed to close in around her, the walls to inch a little nearer. Not that she'd felt safe within the infirmary. For a long while now she hadn't felt safe anywhere.

'Is it still on the *Sulaco* or did it come down with us on the EEV?'

'It was with us all the way.'

Her tone tightened. 'Does the Company know?'

'The Company knows everything that happened on the ship, from the time it left Earth for Acheron until now, provided it's still intact somewhere out there. It all goes into the central computer and gets fed back to the Network.'

A feeling of deadly déjà vu settled over her. She'd battled the Company on this once before, had seen how it had reacted. Any common sense or humanity that faceless organization possessed was subsumed in an all-encompassing, overpowering greed. Back on Earth individuals might grow old and die, to be replaced with new personnel, new directors. But the Company was immortal. It would go on and on. Somehow she doubted that time had wrought any significant changes in its policies, not to mention its corporate morals. In any event, she couldn't take that chance.

'Do they still want an alien?'

'I don't know. Hidden corporate imperatives were not a vital part of my programming. At least, I don't think they were. I can't be sure. I'm not feeling very well.'

'Do me a favour, Bishop; take a look around and see.'

She waited while he searched. 'Sorry,' he said finally. 'There's nothing there now. That doesn't mean there never was. I am no longer capable of accessing the sectors where such information would ordinarily be stored. I wish I could help you more but in my present condition I'm really not good for much.'

'Bull. Your identity programme's still intact.' She leaned forward and fondly touched the base of the decapitated skull. 'There's still a lot of Bishop in there. I'll save your programme. I've got plenty of storage capacity available here. If I ever get out of this I'll make sure you come with me. They can wire you up again.'

'How are you going to save my identity? Copy it into standard chip-ROM? I know what that's like. No sensory input, no tactile output. Blind, deaf, dumb, and immobile. Humans call it limbo. Know what we androids call it? Gumbo. Electronic gumbo. No, thanks. I'd rather go null than nuts.'

'You won't go nuts, Bishop. You're too tough for that.'

'Am I? I'm only as tough as my body and my programming. The former's gone and the latter's fading fast. I'd rather be an intact memory than a desiccated reality. I'm tired. Everything's slipping away. Do me a favour and just disconnect. It's possible I could be reworked, installed in a new body, but there'd be omphalotic damage, maybe identity loss as well. I'd never be top of the line again. I'd rather not have to deal with that. Do you understand what it means, to look forward only to being less than you were? No, thanks. I'd rather be nothing.'

She hesitated. 'You're sure?'

'Do it for me, Ripley. You owe me.'

'I don't owe you anything, Bishop. You're just a machine.'

'I saved you and the girl on Acheron. Do it for me . . . as a friend.'

Reluctantly, she nodded. The eye winked a last time, then closed peacefully. There was no reaction, no twitching or jerking when she pulled the filaments. Once more the head lay motionless on the worktable.

'Sorry, Bishop, but you're like an old calculator. Friendly and comfortable. If you can be repaired, I'm going to see to it that that comes to pass. If not, well, sleep peacefully wherever it is that androids sleep, and try not to dream. If things work out, I'll get back to you later.'

Her gaze lifted and she found herself staring at the far wall. A single halo hung there. It showed a small thatched cottage nestled amid green trees and hedges. A crystalline blue-green stream flowed past the front of the cottage and clouds scudded by overhead. As she watched, the sky darkened and a brilliant sunset appeared above the house.

Her fingers fumbled along the tabletop until they closed around a precision extractor. Flung with all the considerable force of which she was capable and accelerated by her cry of outrage and frustration, it made a most satisfying noise as it reduced the impossibly bucolic simulation to glittering fragments.

Most of the blood on Golic's jacket and face had dried to a thick, glutinous consistency, but some was still liquid enough to drip onto the mess hall table. He ate quietly, spooning up the crispy cereal. Once, he paused to add some sugar from a bowl. He stared straight at the dish but did not see it. What he saw now was very private and wholly internalized.

The day cook, whose name was Eric, entered with a load of plates. As he started towards the first table he caught sight of Golic and stopped. And stared. Fortunately the plates were unbreakable. It was hard to get things like new plates on Fiorina.

'Golic?' he finally murmured. The prisoner at the table continued to eat and did not look up.

The sound of the crashing dishes brought others in: Dillon,

Andrews, Aaron, Morse, and a prisoner named Arthur. They joined the stupefied cook in staring at the apparition seated alone at the table.

Golic finally noticed all the attention. He looked up and smiled.

Blankly.

Ripley was sitting alone in the rear of the infirmary when they brought him in. She watched silently as Dillon, Andrews, Aaron, and Clemens walked the straitjacketed Golic over to a bed and eased him down. His face and hair were spotted with matted blood, his eyes in constant motion as they repeatedly checked the ventilator covers, the ceiling, the door.

Clemens did his best to clean him up, using soft towels, mild solvent, and disinfectant. Golic looked to be in much worse shape than he actually was. Physically, anyway. It was left to Andrews, Aaron, and Dillon to tie him to the cot. His mouth remained unrestrained.

'Go ahead, don't listen to me. Don't believe me. It doesn't matter. Nothing matters anymore. You pious assholes are all gonna die. The Beast has risen and it feeds on human flesh. Nobody can stop it. The time has come.' He turned away from the superintendent, staring straight ahead. 'I saw it. It looked at me. It had no eyes, but it looked at me.'

'What about Boggs and Rains?' Dillon asked evenly. 'Where are they? What's happened to them?'

Golic blinked, regarded his interrogators unrepentantly. 'I didn't do it. Back in the tunnel. They never had a chance, not a chance. There was nothing I could do but save myself. The dragon did it. Slaughtered 'em like pigs. It wasn't me. Why do I get blamed for everything? Nobody can stop it.' He began to laugh and cry simultaneously. 'Not a chance, no, no, not a chance!' Clemens was working on the back of his head now.

Andrews studied the quivering remains of what had once been a human being. Not much of a human being, true, but human nonetheless. He was not pleased, but neither was he angry. There was nothing here to get angry at.

'Stark raving mad. I'm not saying it was anyone's fault, but he should have been chained up. Figuratively speaking, of course.' The superintendent glanced at his medic. 'Sedated. You didn't see this coming, Mr. Clemens?'

'You know me, sir. I don't diagnose. I only prescribe.' Clemens had almost finished his cleaning. Golic looked better, but only if you avoided his eyes.

'Yes, of course. Precognitive psychology isn't your speciality, is it? If anyone should have taken note, it was me.'

'Don't blame yourself, sir,' said Aaron.

'I'm not. Merely verbalizing certain regrets. Sometimes insanity lurks quiet and unseen beneath the surface of a man, awaiting only the proper stimulus for it to burst forth. Like certain desert seeds that propagate only once every ten or eleven years, when the rains are heavy enough.' He sighed. 'I would very much like to see a normal, gentle rain again.'

'Well, you called it right, sir,' Aaron continued. 'He's mad as a fuckin' hatter.'

'I do so delight in the manner in which you enliven your everyday conversation with pithy anachronisms, Mr. Aaron.' Andrews looked to his trustee. 'He seems to be calming down a little. Permanent tranquillization is an expensive proposition and its use would have to be justified in the record. Let's try keeping him separated from the rest for a while, Mr. Dillon, and see if it has a salutary effect. I don't want him causing panic. Clemens, sedate this poor idiot sufficiently so that he won't be danger to himself or to anyone else. Mr. Dillon, I'll rely on you to keep an eye on him after he's released. Hopefully he will improve. It would make things simpler.'

'Very well, Superintendent. But no full sedation until we know about the other brothers.'

'You ain't gonna get anything out of that.' Aaron gestured disgustedly at the straitjacket's trembling inhabitant.

'We have to try.' Dillon leaned close, searching his fellow prisoner's face. 'Pull yourself together, man. Talk to me. Where are the brothers? Where are Rains and Boggs?'

Golick licked his lips. They were badly chewed and still bled slightly despite Clemens's efficient ministrations. 'Rains?' he whispered, his brow furrowing with the effort of trying to remember. 'Boggs?' Suddenly his eyes widened afresh and he looked up sharply, as if seeing them for the first time. 'I didn't do it! It wasn't me. It was . . . it was . . . ' He started sobbing again, bawling and babbling hysterically.

Andrews looked on, shaking his head sadly. 'Hopeless. Mr. Aaron's right. You're not going to get anything out of him for a while, if ever. We're not going to wait until we do.'

Dillon straightened. 'It's your call, Superintendent.'

'We'll have to send out a search party. Sensible people who aren't afraid of the dark or each other. I'm afraid we have to assume that there is a very good chance this simple bastard has murdered them.' He hesitated. 'If you are at all familiar with his record, then you know that such a scenario is not beyond the realm of possibility.'

'You don't know that, sir,' said Dillon. 'He never lied to me. He's crazy. He's a fool. But he's not a liar.'

'You are well-meaning, Mr. Dillon, but overly generous to a fellow prisoner.' Andrews fought back the sarcasm which sprang immediately to mind. 'Personally I'd consider Golic a poor vessel for your trust.'

Dillon's lips tightened. 'I'm not naive, sire. I know enough about him to want to keep an eye on him as much as help him.'

'Good. I don't want any more people vanishing because of his ravings.'

Ripley rose and approached the group. All eyes turned to regard her.

'There's a chance he's telling the truth.' Clemens gaped at her. She ignored him. 'I need to talk to him about this dragon.'

Andrews's reply was crisp. 'You're not talking to anyone, Lieutenant. I am not interested in your opinions because you are not in full possession of the facts.' He gestured towards Golic. 'This man is a convicted multiple murderer, known for particularly brutal and ghastly crimes.'

'I didn't do it!' the man in the straitjacket burbled helplessly.

Andrews looked around. 'Isn't that right, Mr. Dillon?'

'Yeah,' Dillon agreed reluctantly, 'that part's right.'

Ripley gazed hard at the superintendent. 'I need to talk to you. It's important.'

The older man considered thoughtfully. 'When I have finished with my official duties I'll be quite pleased to have a little chat. Yes?'

She looked as if she wanted to say something further, but simply nodded.

# VIII

Aaron took charge of the water pitcher, making sure the glasses were filled. He needn't have bothered. Once Ripley started talking, no one noticed irrelevant details such as thirst.

She explained carefully and in detail, leaving nothing out, from the time the original alien eggs had been discovered in the hold of the gigantic ship of still unknown origin on Acheron, to the destruction of the original crew of the *Nostromo* and Ripley's subsequent escape, to the later devastating encounter on Acheron and her flight from there in the company of her now dead companions.

Her ability to recall every relevant incident and detail might have struck an observer as prodigious, but remembering was not her problem. What tormented her daily was her inability to forget.

It was quiet in the superintendent's quarters for quite a while after she finished. Ripley downed half her glass of purified water, watching his face.

He laced his fingers over his belly. 'Let me see if I have this correct, Lieutenant. What you say we're dealing with here is an eight-foot-tall carnivorous insect of some kind with acidic body fluids, and that it arrived on your spaceship.'

'We don't know that it's an insect,' she corrected him. 'That's the simplest and most obvious analog, but nobody knows for sure. They don't lend themselves to easy taxonomic study. It's hard to dissect something that dissolves your instruments after it's dead and tries to eat or impregnate you while it's alive. The colony on Acheron devoted itself frantically to such studies. It didn't matter. The creatures wiped them out before they could learn anything. Unfortunately, their records were destroyed when the base fusion plant went critical. We know a little about them, just enough to make a few generalizations.

'About all we can say with a reasonable degree of assurance is that they have a biosocial system crudely analogous to the social insects of Earth, like the ants and the bees and so forth. Beyond that, nobody knows anything. Their intelligence level is certainly much greater than that of any social arthropod, though at this point it's hard to say whether they're capable of higher reasoning as we know it. I'm almost certain they can communicate by smell. They may have additional perceptive capabilities we know nothing about.

'They're incredibly quick, strong, and tough. I personally watched one survive quite well in deep interstellar vacuum until I could fry it with an EEV's engines.'

'And it kills on sight and is generally unpleasant,' Andrews finished for her. 'So you claim. And of course you expect me to accept this entire fantastic story solely on your word.'

'Right, sir,' said Aaron quickly, 'that's a beauty. Never heard anything like it, sir.'

'No, I don't expect you to accept it,' Ripley replied softly. 'I've dealt with people like you before.'

Andrews replied without umbrage. 'I'll ignore that. Assuming for the moment that I accept the gist of what you've said, what would you suggest we do? Compose our wills and wait to be eaten?'

'For some people that might not be a bad idea, but it doesn't work for me. These things can be fought. They can be killed. What kind of weapons have you got?'

Andrews unlocked his fingers and looked unhappy. 'This is a prison. Even though there's nowhere for anyone to escape to on Fiorina, it's not a good idea to allow prisoners access to firearms. Someone might get the idea they could use them to take over the supply shuttle, or some similar crackbrained idea. Removing weapons removes the temptations to steal and use them.'

'No weapons of any kind?'

'Sorry. This is a modern, civilized prison facility. We're on the honour system. The men here, though extreme cases, are doing more than just paying their debts to society. They're functioning as active caretakers. The Company feels that the presence of weapons would intimidate them, to the detriment of their work. Why do you think there are only two supervisors here, myself and Aaron? If not for the system, we couldn't control this bunch with twenty supervisors and a complete arsenal.' He paused thoughtfully.

'There are some large carving knives in the abattoir, a few more in the mess hall and kitchen. Some fire axes scattered about. Nothing terribly formidable.'

Ripley slumped in her chair, muttering disconsolately. 'Then we're fucked.'

'No, you're fucked,' the superintendent replied calmly. 'Confined to the infirmary. Quarantined.'

She gaped at him. 'But why?'

'Because you've been a problem ever since you showed up here, and I don't want that problem compounded. It's my responsibility to deal with this now, whatever it is, and I'll rest easier knowing where you are at all times. The men are going to be nervous enough as it is. Having you floating around at your leisure poking into places you shouldn't will be anything but a stabilizing influence.'

'You can't do this. I've done nothing wrong.'

'I didn't say that you had. I'm confining you for your own safety. I'm in charge here and I'm exercising my discretion as installation superintendent. Feel free to file an official complaint with a board of inquiry when you get back.' He smiled paternally.

'You'll have it all to yourself, Lieutenant. I think you'll be safe from any large nasty beasts while you're there. Right? Yes, that's a good girl. Mr. Aaron will escort you.'

Ripley rose. 'You're making a bad decision.'

'Somehow I think I'll manage to live with it. Aaron, after escorting the lieutenant to her new quarters, get going on organizing a search party. Fast. Right now all we have to go on is that babbling Golic. Boggs and Rains may only be injured and waiting for help.'

'Right, sir.'

'You're all wrong on this, Andrews,' Ripley told him. 'All wrong. You're not going to find anybody alive in those tunnels.'

'We'll see.' He followed her with his eyes as his assistant guided her out.

She sat on the cot, sullen and angry. Clemens stood nearby, eyeing her. Aaron's voice sounding over the intercom system made her look up.

'Let's all report to the mess hall. Mr. Andrews wants a meeting. Mess hall, right away, gang.' A subtle electronic hum punctuated the second-in-command's brief announcement.

Ripley looked over at the medical officer. 'Isn't there any way off Fiorina? An emergency service shuttle? Some damned way to escape?'

Clemens shook his head. 'This is a prison now, remember? There's no way out. Our supply ship comes once every six months.'

'That's it?' She slumped.

'No reason to panic. They are sending someone to pick you up and investigate this whole mess. Quite soon, I gather.'

'Really? What's soon?'

'I don't know.' Clemens was clearly bothered by something other than the unfortunate Murphy's death. 'No one's ever been in a hurry to get here before. It's always the other way 'round. Diverting a ship from its regular run is difficult, not to mention expensive as hell. Do you want to tell me what you and Andrews talked about?'

She looked away. 'No, I don't. You'd just think I was crazy.' Her attention wandered to the far corner where the catatonic Golic stood staring blankly at the wall. He looked a lot better since Clemens had cleaned him up.

'That's a bit uncharitable,' the med tech murmured. 'How are you feeling?'

Ripley licked her lips. 'Not so hot. Nauseous, sick to my stomach. And pissed off.'

He straightened, nodding to himself. 'Shock's starting to set in. Not unexpected, given what you've been through recently. It's a wonder you're not over there sharing a blank wall with Golic.' Walking over, he gave her a cursory examination, then headed for a cabinet, popped the catch, and began fumbling with the contents.

'I'd best give you another cocktail.'

She saw him working with the injector. 'No. I need to stay alert.' Her eyes instinctively considered possible entrances: the air vents, the doorways. But her vision was hazy, her thoughts dulled.

Clemens came towards her, holding the injector in one hand. 'Look at you. Call that alert? You're practically falling over. The body's a hell of an efficient machine, but it's still just a machine. Ask too much of it and you risk overload.'

She shoved back a sleeve. 'Don't lecture me. I know when I'm pushing things. Just give me the stuff.'

The figure in the corner was mumbling aloud. 'I don't know why people blame me for things. Weird, isn't it? It's not like I'm perfect or something but, sweet William, I don't see where some people come off always blaming others for life's little problems.'

Clemens smiled. 'That's quite profound. Thank you, Golic.' He filled the injector, checking the level.

As she sat there waiting to receive the medication she happened to glance in Golic's direction and was surprised to see him grinning back at her. His expression was inhuman, devoid of thought—a pure idiot's delight. She looked away distastefully, her mind on matters of greater import.

'Are you married?' the straitjacketed hulk asked unexpectedly.

Ripley started. 'Me?'

'You should get married.' Golic was utterly serious. 'Have kids . . . pretty girl. I know lots of 'em. Back home. They always like me. You're gonna die too.' He began to whistle to himself.

'Are you?' Clemens inquired.

'What?'

'Married.'

'Why?'

'Just curious.'

'No.' He came towards her, the injector hanging from his fingers. 'How about levelling with me?'

He hesitated. 'Could you be a little more specific?'

'When I asked you how you got assigned here you avoided the question. When I asked you about the prison ID tattoo on the back of your head you ducked me again.'

Clemens looked away. 'It's a long sad story. A bit melodramatic, I'm afraid.'

'So entertain me.' She crossed her arms over her chest and settled back on the cot.

'Well, my problem was that I was smart. Very smart. I knew everything, you see. I was brilliant and therefore thought I could get away with anything. And for a while I did.

'I was right out of med school, during which time I had managed the extraordinary accomplishment of finishing in the top five per cent of my class despite having acquired what I confidently believed to be a tolerable addiction to Midaphine. Do you know that particular pharmaceutical?'

Ripley shook her head slowly.

'Oh, it's a lovely chain of peptides and such, it is. Makes you feel like you're invincible without compromising your judgment. It does demand that you maintain a certain level in your bloodstream, though. Clever fellow that I was, I had no trouble appropriating adequate supplies from whatever facility I happened to be working in at the time.

'I was considered most promising, a physician-to-be of exceptional gifts and stamina, insightful and caring. No one suspected that my primary patient was always myself.

'It happened during my first residency. The centre was delighted to have me. I did the work of two, never complained, was almost always correct in my diagnosis and prescriptions. I did a thirty-six-hour stretch in an ER, went out, got high as an orbital shuttle, was crawling into bed to lose myself in the sensation of floating all night, when the 'com buzzed.

'A pressure unit had blown on the centre's fuel station. Everyone they could get hold of was called in to help. Thirty seriously injured but only a few had to be sent to intensive care. The rest just needed quick but rote attention. Nothing complicated. Nothing a halfway competent intern couldn't have managed. I figured I'd take care of it myself and then hiphead it back home before anyone noticed that I was awfully bright and cheery for someone who'd just been yanked out of the sack at three in the morning.' He paused a moment to gather his thoughts.

'Eleven of the thirty died when I prescribed the wrong dosage of painkiller. Such a small thing. Such a simple thing. Any fool could've handled it. Any fool. That's Midaphine for you. Hardly ever affects your judgment. Only once in a while.'

'I'm sorry,' she said softly.

'Don't be.' His expression was unforgiving. 'No one else was. I got seven years in prison, lifetime probation, and my licence permanently reduced to a 3-C, with severe restrictions on what and where I could practise. While in prison I kicked my wonderful habit. Didn't matter. Too many relatives around who remembered their dead. I never had a chance of getting the restrictions revised. I embarrassed my profession, and the examiners delighted in making an example of me. After that you can imagine how many outfits were eager to employ someone with my professional qualifications. So here I am.'

'I'm still sorry.'

'For me? Or about what happened? If it's the latter, so am I.

About the prison sentence and subsequent restrictions, no. I deserved it. I deserved everything that's happened to me. I wiped out eleven lives. Casually, with a dumb smile on my face. I'm sure that the people I killed had promising careers as well. I destroyed eleven families. And while I can't ever forget, I've learned to live with it. That's one positive thing about being assigned to a place like this. It helps you learn how to live with things that you've done.'

'Did you serve time here?'

'Yes, and I got to know this motley crew quite well. So when they stayed, I stayed. Nobody else would employ me.' He moved to give her the injection. 'So, will you trust me with an injector?'

As he was leaning towards her the alien hit the floor behind him as silently as it fell from the ceiling, landing in a supportive crouch and straining to its full height. It was astonishing and appalling how something that size could move so quietly. She saw it come erect, towering over the smiling medic, metallic incisors gleaming in the pale overhead light.

Even as she fought to make her paralysed vocal cords function, part of her noted that it was slightly different in appearance from every alien type she had encountered previously. The head was fuller, the body more massive. The more subtle physical discrepancies registered as brief, observational tics in the frozen instant of horror.

Clemens leaned towards her, suddenly more than merely concerned. 'Hey, what's wrong? You look like you're having trouble breathing. I can—'

The alien ripped his head off and flung it aside. Still she didn't scream. She wanted to. She tried. But she couldn't. Her diaphragm pushed air but no sound.

It shoved Clemens's spurting corpse aside and gazed down at her. If only it had eyes, a part of her thought, instead of visual perceptors as yet unstudied. No matter how horrible or bloodshot, at least you could connect with an eye. The windows of the soul, she'd read somewhere.

The alien had no eyes and, quite likely, no soul.

She started to shiver. She'd run from them before, and fought them before, but in the enclosed confines of the tomblike infirmary there was nowhere to run and nothing to fight with. It was all over. A part of her was glad. At least there would be no more nightmares, no more waking up screaming in strange beds. There would be peace.

'Hey, you, get over here!' Golic suddenly shouted. 'Lemme loose. I can help you. We can kill all these assholes.'

The Boschian vision turned slowly to regard the prisoner. Then it looked once more at the immobile woman on the bed. With a singular leap it flung itself at the ceiling, cablelike fingers grasping the edge of the gaping air duct through which it had arrived, and was gone. Skittering sounds echoed from above, quickly fading into the distance.

Ripley didn't move. Nothing had happened. The beast hadn't touched her. But then, she understood virtually nothing about them. Something about her had put it off. Perhaps they wouldn't attack the unhealthy. Or maybe it had been something in Golic's manner.

Though still alive, she wasn't sure whether to be grateful or not.

# IX

Andrews stood before his charges in the mess hall, silently surveying their expectant, curious faces while Dillon prepared to give his traditional invocation. Aaron sat nearby, wondering what his boss had on his mind.

'All rise, all pray. Blessed is the Lord.' The prisoners complied, striking reverent attitudes. Dillon continued.

'Give us the strength, O Lord, to endure. We recognize we are poor sinners in the hands of an angry God. Let the circle be unbroken, until the day. Amen.' Each prisoner raised his fist, then took a seat.

As Dillon surveyed them his formerly beatific expression twisting with appalling suddenness.

'What the fuck is happening here? What is this bullshit that's coming down? We got murder! We got rape! We got brothers in trouble! I don't want no more bullshit around here! We got problems, we stand together.'

Andrews let the silence that followed Dillon's outburst linger until he was confident he had everyone's attention. He cleared his throat ceremoniously.

'Yes, thank you, Mr. Dillon,' he began in his usual no-nonsense tone. 'All right. Once again this is rumour control. Here are the facts.'

'At 0400 hours prisoner Murphy, through carelessness and probably a good dose of stupidity on his part, was found dead in Vent shaft Seventeen. From the information gathered on the spot it would appear that he was standing too close to the ventilator fan when a strong downdraught struck, and was consequently sucked or blown into the blades. Medical officer Clemens acted as coroner on the occasion and his official report is as straightforward as you might expect as to cause of death.'

Several of the prisoners murmured under their breath. Andrews eyed them until they were quiet once more.

He began to pace as he spoke. 'Not long thereafter prisoners Boggs, Rains, and Golic left on a routine forage and scavenge mission into the shafts. They were well equipped and presumably knew what they were about.'

'I can confirm that,' Dillon put in.

Andrews acknowledged the big man's comment with a glance, resumed his declamation. 'At about 0700 hours prisoner Golic reappeared in a deranged state. He was covered with blood and babbling nonsense. Presently he is physically restrained and receiving medical treatment in the infirmary. Prisoners Boggs and Rains are still missing. We are forced to consider the possibility that they have met with foul play at the hands of prisoner Golic.' He paused to let that sink in.

'The history of the prisoner in question is not incompatible with such a suspicion. While no one is sent here who has not first been treated and cleared by Rehabilitation Central on Earth, not every programme of treatment is perfect or everlasting.'

'I heard that,' said Dillon.

'Just so. However, until prisoners Rains and Boggs, or their bodies, are located and the reason for their absence resolved, any conclusions are necessarily premature. They may be sitting in one of the tunnels, injured and unable to move, waiting for help to arrive. Or they may have gotten lost trying to find their way out. Obviously there is an urgent need to organize and send out a search party. Volunteers will be appreciated and the offer appropriately noted in your records.' He stopped in front of the north wall, which had been fashioned of locally poured lead.

'I think it's fair to say that our smoothly running facility has suddenly developed a few problems. It is no cause for panic or alarm and in fact is to be occasionally expected in a situation like this. Whatever the eventual resolution of this particular unfortunate incident I think that I may safely say a return to normal operations can be anticipated within a very short while.

'In the meantime we must all keep our wits about us and pull together for the next few days, until the rescue team arrives to pick up Lieutenant Ripley. I may even go so far as to say that her unplanned arrival here, while creating some problems of its own, has likewise caused the Company to divert a ship to Fiorina. That means the possibility of obtaining extra supplies and perhaps a few luxuries well ahead of schedule. It is something to look forward to. So we should all be looking to the days ahead with anticipation.'

The door to his right slammed open to admit Ripley. Out of breath and anxious, she ignored the stares of everyone present.

'It's here! It got Clemens!' She was glancing around wildly, her eyes inspecting the dark corners and distant corridors of the assembly hall.

The veins bulged in Andrews's neck. 'Lieutenant, I've had about enough of you. Stop this raving at once! Stop it! You're spreading panic unnecessarily and without proof, and I won't have it, you hear me? I won't have it!'

She glared at him. 'I'm telling you, it's here!'

'And I'm telling you, get control of yourself, Lieutenant!' He looked sharply to his right. 'Mr. Aaron, get that foolish woman under control at once. Get her back to the infirmary!'

'Yes, sir.' Aaron took a step towards Ripley. Her expression made him hesitate. She looked no less physically capable than the average prisoner.

As he considered what to do next the lights suddenly flickered wildly. Prisoners shouted, ran into one another, looked around in confusion. Andrews shook his head dolefully.

'I won't have this kind of nonsense in my facility. Do you all hear me? I will not put up with it.' A faint scraping noise caused him to glance upward.

The alien reached down and nipped the superintendent off

the floor as neatly as a spider trapping a fly. In an instant both predator and prey were gone. In the ensuing hysteria only Ripley and prisoner Morse actually saw the monster drag the quiescent form of Andrews into an open air shaft.

Ripley took up a seat in a corner and lit a narcostick. She found herself remembering Clemens. Her expression hardened. Clemens: better not to think of him, just as she'd learned to quickly forget other men with whom she'd formed attachments, only to have them snatched away and destroyed by other representatives of the seemingly indestructive alien horde.

Except that they were not indestructible. They could be killed. And so long as she was alive, that seemed to be her destiny. To wipe them out, to eliminate them from the face of the universe. It was a calling she would gladly, oh, so gladly, have bequeathed to another.

Why her? It was a question she had pondered on more than one occasion. Why should she have been singled out? No, she reflected, that wasn't right. Nothing was singling her out. Fate hadn't chosen her to deal with a lifetime of horror and devastation. Others had confronted the aliens and perished. Only she continued to suffer because only she continued to survive.

It was a destiny she could abandon at any time. The infirmary was well stocked, its contents clearly labelled. A single, simple injection could wipe away all the pain and the terror. Easy enough to put an end to it. Except that she was a survivor. Perhaps that was her task in life, simply to survive. No, fate hadn't singled her out for special mistreatment. She wasn't responsible for the fact that she was tougher than anyone else. It was just something she'd have to learn to live with.

Another man gone. One she hadn't been especially fond of this time. She regretted it nonetheless. Andrews was human, and if nothing else deserved to die a decent death.

The alien had left dead silence in the wake of its astonishingly swift attack. In its aftermath the men had resumed sitting or standing, each staring into the distance, at his neighbour, or inwardly. As usual it was left to Dillon to kneel and begin the prayer.

'We have been given a sign, brothers. How we deal with it will determine our fates.'

'Amen,' several of the prisoners chorused. The comments of several others were fortunately unintelligible.

Dillon continued. 'We give thanks, O Lord, your wrath has come and the time is near that we be judged. The apocalypse is upon us. Let us be ready. Let your mercy be just.'

Near the back of the hall the prisoners had begun to whisper to one another, Dillon's prayer notwithstanding.

'It was big,' prisoner David muttered. 'I mean, *big*. And fast.'

'I saw it, asshole.' Kevin was gazing intently at the place on the ceiling from which the alien had hung. 'I was there. Y'think I'm blind?'

'Yeah, but I mean it was big.' So intent were they on the memory of what had just happened that they even forgot to stare at Ripley.

Prisoner William rose and surveyed his comrades. 'Okay, so what do we do now, mates?' A couple of the men looked at one another but no one said anything. 'Well, who's in charge? I mean, we need to get organized here, right?'

Aaron swallowed, glanced around the room. 'I guess I'm next in line.'

Morse rolled his eyes ceilingward. 'Eighty-five's gonna be in charge. Jesus, give me a break!'

'Don't call me that!' Aaron glared at the prisoner who'd spoken. 'Not now, not ever!' Rising, he advanced to confront them.

'Look, no way I can replace Andrews. I'm not even gonna pretend that I can. You guys didn't appreciate him. I know he was a hardass sometimes, but he was the best man I ever worked with.'

Dillon was less than impressed. 'I don't want to hear that shit.' His gaze shifted from the assistant to the lanky figure seated on the far side of the hall. 'What about you? You're an officer. How about showing us a little leadership?'

Ripley glanced briefly in his direction, took a puff on her narcostick, and looked away.

Williams broke the ensuing silence, gesturing at Dillon. 'You take over. You run things here anyway.'

The bigger man shook his head quickly. 'No fuckin' way. I ain't the command type. I just take care of my own.'

'Well, what's the fuckin' beast want?' The discouraged Williams inquired aloud. 'Is the fucker gonna try and get us all?'

The narcostick eased from Ripley's lips. 'Yeah.'

'Well, isn't that sweet?' Morse growled sarcastically. 'How do we stop it?'

Disgusted, Ripley tossed the remains of her narcostick aside and rose to confront the group.

'We don't have any weapons, right? No smart guns, no pulse rifles, nothing?'

Aaron nodded reluctantly. 'Right.'

She looked thoughtful. 'I haven't seen one exactly like this before. It's bigger, its legs are different. The other ones were afraid of fire, or at least respectful of it. Not much else.'

She let her gaze roam the hall. 'Can we seal off this area?'

'No chance,' Aaron told her. 'The developed mine complex is ten miles square. There's six hundred air ducts that access the surface. This goddamn place is big.'

'What about video? We could try to locate it that way. I see monitors everywhere.'

Again the assistant superintendent shook his head. 'Internal video system hasn't worked in years. No reason to keep an expensive hih-tech system just to monitor a lousy twenty-five caretaker prisoners who aren't going anywhere anyhow. Fact is, nothin' much works here anymore. We got a lot of technology, but no way to fix it.'

'What eight-five's tryin' to tell you—' Morse started to say.

'Don't call me that!' Aaron snapped.

The prisoner ignored him. '—is that we got no entertainment centres, no climate control, no viewscreens, no surveillance, no freezers, no fuckin' ice cream, no guns, no rubbers, no women. All we got here is shit.'

'Shut up,' Dillon said warningly.

'What the hell are we even talkin' to her for?' Morse continued. 'She's the one that brought the fucker here. Let's run her head through the wall.'

Ripley shrugged ever so slightly. 'Sounds good to me.'

Dillon walked over to confront Morse. 'I won't say it again,' he said softly. 'Keep your mouth shut.'

Morse considered, then dropped his gaze and backed off. For the time being.

The assistant super eyed Ripley. 'All right. What do we do now?'

She was aware that not just the three men at the table but the majority of the prisoners were watching her, waiting.

'On Acheron we tried to seal ourselves off and establish a defensive perimeter. It worked, but only for a little while. These things always find a way in. First I need to see, not hear, what our exact physical situation is.'

'It's fucked,' Morse growled, but under his breath.

Aaron nodded. 'Come with me.' He looked to Dillon. 'Sorry, but you know the regs.'

The big man blinked slowly by way of acknowledgment. 'Just don't be too long, okay?'

Aaron tried to grin, failed. 'Look at it this way: no work detail today.'

Dillon let his gaze sweep the upper level of the library. 'Then why is it I don't feel relaxed?'

They moved along the main passageway, Aaron holding the schematic map, Ripley shifting her attention from the printout to the corridor and walls. There was overhead light, but dim.

Morse was wrong. Some of the complex's basic life support system still functioned.

She tapped the plastic sheet. 'What's this?'

'Access serviceway. Connects the infirmary to the mess hall.'

'Maybe we can go in, flush it out.'

He stayed close. 'Come on. There's miles and miles of tunnels down there.'

She traced lines on the sheet. 'It won't go far. It'll nest in this area right around here, in one of the smaller passageways or air shafts.'

His expression twisted. 'Nest? don't you mean "rest"?'

She glanced over at him. 'I mean what I say. Just don't ask me for details. If we can kill or immobilize it, remind me and I'll explain. Otherwise you don't want to know.'

He held her stare a moment longer, then dropped his eyes back to the map. 'How do you know that?'

'It's like a lion. It sticks close to the zebras.'

'We don't have any zebras here.'

She halted and gave him a look.

'Oh, right,' he said, subdued. 'But running around down there in the dark? You gotta be kiddin'. We got no overheads once you get out of the main shaft here.'

'How about flashlights?'

'Sure. We got six thousand of them. And rechargeable batteries. But no bulbs. Somebody forgot that little detail. I told ya, nothin' works.'

'What about torches? Do we have the capability of making fire? Most humans have enjoyed that privilege since the Stone Age.'

The old vertical shaft stretched up and down into darkness, the ladder welded to its interior filthy with carboniferous grime and accumulated gunk. Damp air ascended languidly from the black depths, thick in Ripley's nostrils as she leaned out of the corridor and aimed her torch downward. No bottom was visible, nor had she expected to see one.

They'd started in through the tunnel where Murphy had been killed, past the huge ventilator blades, which Aaron had shut down prior to their departure. She sniffed, wrinkled her nose. The rising air was more than damp; it was pungent with rotting vegetation and the sharp tang of recycled chemicals.

'What's down there?'

Aaron crowded close behind her. 'Air and water purification and recirculation.'

'Which explains the stink. Fusion?'

'Yeah, but sealed away. Everything operates on automatic. A couple of techs from the supply ship run a status check every six months.' He grinned. 'You don't think they'd trust the maintenance details of a functioning fusion plant to the delicate ministrations of a bunch of prisoners and a couple of prison administrators with general degrees, do you?'

She didn't smile back. 'Nothing the Company does would surprise me.' Holding on to the edge of the opening she aimed the torch upward, played the light over the smooth metal walls. 'What's upstairs?'

'Low-tech stuff. Storage chambers, most of 'em empty now. Cleaned out when Weyland-Yutani closed down the mine. Service accessways. Power and water conduits. All the tunnels and shafts are bigger than they need to be. With all the drilling and cording equipment at hand the engineers were able to make it easy on themselves. They built everything oversized.' He paused. 'You think it might have gone up there somewhere?'

'It would naturally choose a large, comfortable chamber for a nest, and it likes to keep above its . . . prey. Drop down from above rather than come up from below. Also, the upper levels are closer to the prison habitat. That's where it'll expect us to be holed up. If we're lucky we might be able to come up behind it. If we're unlucky . . .'

'Yeah?' Aaron prompted.

'We might be able to come up behind it.' She swung out onto the ladder and began climbing.

Not only was the ladder thick with encrusted grime, but the moist air rising from below had stimulated the growth of local algae and other microorganisms. The rungs were slippery and uneven. She made sure to grip the side of the ladder firmly with her free hand as she ascended.

The shaft intersected one or more cross-corridors approximately every three metres. At each level she shoved her torch inside, illuminating each tunnel for a respectable distance before resuming her ascent.

While he was trying to watch Ripley, Aaron's concentration slipped along with his foot. Behind him Dillon quickly looped his left arm around the ladder and caught the flailing ankle with his other hand, shoving the assistant super's boot back onto the nearest rung.

'You all right up there?' he inquired in a terse whisper.

'Fine,' Aaron replied, albeit a little shakily. 'Just keep that torch out of my ass.'

'Funny you should mention that,' the big man replied in the half darkness. 'I've spent years dreaming of doing just that.'

'Save it for another time, okay?' Aaron hurried himself, not wanting Ripley to get dangerously far ahead.

'One thing more, man,' Dillon murmured.

The assistant superintendent glanced back down. 'What now?'

'Anytime you want to trade places, you let me know.'

'In your dreams.' Despite their circumstances each man mustered a fraternal grin of understanding. Then they resumed climbing, the brief feeling of camaraderie swept away in the desperation and anxiety of their situation.

Ripley glanced down, wondering what they were talking about. It was good that they could manage to smile under such conditions. She wished she could share in their amusement, but knew she could not. She was much too conscious of what might lie ahead of them. Inhaling resignedly, she ascended the next step and aimed her light into still another opening.

Straight into the face of the creature.

If her fingers hadn't contracted in terror she surely would have fallen off the ladder as she screamed. Reflexively she swung her torch. It struck the horror square atop the gleaming black head . . . which crumbled into pieces on contact.

'What . . . what is it?' Aaron was yelling below her.

She ignored him as she fought to regain her equilibrium. Only then did she pull herself up the ladder and step off into the tunnel.

Together the three stared at the collapsed, dried-out husk of the adult alien.

'Ugly sucker, ain't it?' Dillon volunteered.

Ripley knelt to examine the cast-off shell. Her fingers trembled slightly as she touched it, then steadied. It was perfectly harmless, a shadow of an enigma. There was nothing there. The skull where her torch had struck had been empty inside. Experimentally she gave the remainder of the shell a light push and the massive, streamlined form tumbled over onto its side. She straightened.

'What is it?' Aaron asked her. He prodded the husk with his foot.

'It's shed its skin, moulted somehow.' She looked sharply up the tunnel. 'This is a new one. I've never seen this before. Not at this stage of development.'

'What's it mean?' Dillon muttered.

'Can't say. No precedent. One thing we can be sure of, though. It's bigger now.'

'How much bigger?' Aaron joined her in peering up the dark passageway.

'That depends,' Ripley murmured.

'On what?'

'On what it's become.' She started forward, holding her light out in front of her as she pushed her way past him.

Something inside her urged her on, making her increase rather than slow the pace. She hardly paused long enough to shine her torch down the side passages that branched off the main tunnel. The discovery of the alien husk had charged her with the same sort of relentless determination that had enabled her to survive the devastation of Acheron. Determination, and a growing anger. She found herself thinking of Jonesy. No one wonder she and the cat had survived the *Nostromo*. Curiosity and a talent for survival were two of the skills they'd shared.

Jonesy was gone now, a victim of the time distortions made necessary by space travel. No more cat-nightmares for him. Only she was left to deal with life, and all the memories.

'Slow up.' Aaron had to break into a jog to catch up with her. He held up the map, then gestured ahead. 'Almost there.'

She looked at him. 'I hope this was worth the climb. What happened to all the damn lifts in this place?'

'You kidding? Deactivated when the installation was closed down. Why should a bunch of prisoners need to be in this sector anyway?' He started forward, taking the lead.

They walked another hundred metres before the tunnel opened up into a much larger passageway, one wide and high enough to accommodate vehicles as well as men. The assistant superintendent stopped next to the far wall, holding his torch out to illuminate a sign welded to the metal.

TOXIC WASTE STORAGE
THIS CHAMBER HERMETICALLY SECURED
NO ACCESS WITHOUT AUTHORIZATION
*rating B-8 or Higher Required*

'Well, well. What do we have here?' For the first time in days Ripley allowed herself to feel a twinge of hope.

'There's more than a dozen of these scattered around the facility.' Aaron was bending to study the detailed inscription below the plate. 'This is the closest one to our living quarters.' He tapped the wall with his torch and sparks dribbled to the floor.

'They were gonna shove a lot of heavy-duty waste in here. Refining by-products, that sort of thing. Some of these are full and permanently sealed, others partially filled. Cheaper, easier, and safer than stuffing the junk into drums and dumping it out in space.

'This one's never been used. Maybe because it's so close to the habitat areas. Or maybe they just never got around to it, closed up shop before they needed the room. I've been inside. It's clean as a whistle in there.'

Ripley studied the wall. 'What's the access like?'

'Pretty much what you'd expect for a storage facility carrying this rating.' He led her around to the front.

The door was scratched and filthy, but still impressive. She noted the almost invisible seams at the corners. 'This is the only way in or out?'

Aaron nodded. 'That's right. I checked the stats before we came down. Entrance is just big enough for a small loader-transporter with driver and cargo. Ceiling, walls, and floor are six feet thick, solid ceramocarbide steel. So's the door. All controls and active components are external, or embedded in the matrix itself.'

'Let's make sure we've got this right. You get something in there and close the door, no way it can get out?'

Aaron grunted confidently. 'Right. No fuckin' way. That sucker is tight. According to the specs it'll hold a perfect vacuum. Nothin' bigger than a neutrino could slip through. That ceramocarbide stuff even dissipates lasers. You'd need a controlled nuclear explosion to cut your way in.'

'You sure this thing is still operational?'

He indicated a nearby control box. 'Why don't you find out?'

She moved forward and broke the thin seal that covered the enclosure. The lid flipped down, exposing several controls. She studied them for a moment, then thumbed a large green button.

The immense door didn't so much slide aside as appear to vanish silently into the wall. She cycled it again, admiring the smooth play of forces that could shift so much mass with such speed and ease. The prisoners were similarly impressed. The efficiency of the long-dormant technology lifted their spirits considerably.

Beyond the open barrier was a slick-walled, empty chamber. An ephemeral coating of dust covered the floor. It would accommodate several full-grown aliens with ease.

'Let me see the map.' Aaron handed her the sheet and her index finger drew patterns on the plastic. 'We're here?' He leaned close and nodded. 'Administration's here, assembly hall up this corridor?'

'You got it. Fast, too,' he added admiringly.

'I owe the fact that I'm still alive to an understanding of spatial relationships.' She tapped the sheet. 'If we can get it to chase us down these passageways, here and here, then close these off one at a time, we might get it inside.' The three of them stared into the storage chamber.

Dillon looked back at her. 'Lemme get this straight. You wanna burn it down and outta the pipes, force it here, slam the door, and trap its ass?'

She spoke without looking up from the map. 'Ummm.'

'And you're looking for help from us Y-chromo boys.'

'You got something better to do?'

'Why should we put our asses on the line for you?'

She finally glanced up at him, her eyes steely. 'Your asses are already on the line. The only question is what you're going to do about it.'

# X

Accompanied by prisoner David, Aaron showed Ripley through the vast storage chamber. When they reached the section where the drums were stored, he paused and pointed.

'This is where we keep it. I don't know what this shit's called.'

'Quinitricetyline,' David supplied helpfully.

'I knew that,' the assistant superintendent grumbled as he checked his notepad. 'Okay. I'm off to work out the section assignments with Dillon for the paintbrush team. David, you get these drums organized, ready to move.' He turned and headed in the direction of the main corridor.

'Right, Eight-five,' David called after him.

'Don't call me that!' Aaron vanished into the darkness of the distant corridor.

Ripley examined the drums. They were slightly corroded and obviously hadn't been touched in some time, but otherwise appeared intact.

'What's this "Eight-five" thing?'

David put gloved hands on the nearest container. 'Lot of the prisoners used to call him that. We got his personnel charts out of the computer a few years ago. It's his IQ.' He grinned as he started to roll the drum.

Ripley stood and watched. 'He seems to have a lot of faith in this stuff. What's your opinion?'

The prisoner positioned the drum for loading. 'Hell, I'm just a dumb watchman, like the rest of the guys here. But I did see a drum of this crap fall into a beachhead bunker once. Blast put a tug in dry dock for seventeen weeks. Great stuff.'

In another part of the storage chamber prisoners Troy and Arthur sorted through the mass of discarded electronics components. Troy shoved a glass bead into the cylinder he was holding, thumbed the switch, then disgustedly wrenched the bead free and began hunting for another.

'Goddamn it. One fucking bulb in two thousand works.'

His companion looked up from his own search. 'Hey, it could be a lot worse. We mighta got the paintbrush detail.' He tried a bead in his own tube, hit the switch. To his astonishment and delight, it lit.

The two men filled the air duct with little room to spare, slathering the interior surface with the pungent qui-nitricetyline.

'This shit smells awful,' Prisoner Kevin announced for the hundredth time. His companion barely deigned to reply.

'I've told you already; don't breathe it.'

'Why not?'

'Fuckin' fumes.'

'I'm in a fuckin' pipe with it. How can I keep from breathing it?'

Outside the toxic waste storage chamber other men were dumping buckets of the QTC and spreading it around as best they could, with brooms and mops and, where those were lacking, with their booted feet.

In the corridor Dillon was waiting with Ripley. Everything was proceeding according to plan, though whether the plan would proceed according to plan remained to be seen.

He glanced towards her, analysed the expression on her face. Not that he was particularly sensitive, but he'd seen a lot of life.

'You miss the doc, right?'

'I didn't know him very well,' she muttered by way of reply.

'I thought you two got real close.'

Now she looked over at him. 'I guess you've been looking through some keyholes.'

Dillon smiled. 'That's what I thought.'

The nausea didn't slip up on her; it attacked hard and fast, overwhelming her equilibrium, forcing her to lean against the wall for support as she gagged and coughed. Dillon moved to support her but she shoved him away, fighting for air. He eyed her with sudden concern.

'You okay?'

She took a deep breath and nodded.

'Whatever you say. But you don't look okay to me, sister.'

Aaron surveyed the convicts who'd accompanied him—some nearby, others on the walkway above. All carried primed emergency flares which would ignite on hard contact.

'Okay, listen up.' All eyes turned to regard him attentively. 'Don't light this fire till I give you the signal. This is the signal.' He raised his arm. 'You guys got it? Think you can remember that?'

They were all intent on him. So intent that the man nearest the vertical air duct dropped the flare he'd been holding. He clutched it, missed, and held his breath as it slid to the ledge near his feet.

His companion hadn't noticed. Straining, he knelt to retrieve it, let out a sigh of relief. . .

As the alien appeared behind the grate on which the flare lay poised precariously, and reached for him.

The man managed to scream, the flare flipping from his fingers to fall to the ground below.

Where it flowered brightly.

Aaron heard and saw the explosion simultaneously. His eyes widened. 'No, goddamn it! Wait for the fucking signal! Shit!'

Then he saw the alien and forgot about the flames.

They spread as rapidly as the desperate planners had hoped, shooting down QTC-painted corridors, licking up air vents, frying soaked floors and walkways. In her own corridor Ripley heard the approaching flames and pressed herself against unpainted ground as the air vents overhead caught. A convict nearby wasn't as fast. He screamed as heat ignited his clothing.

Morse rolled wildly away from the licking flames, in time to see the alien scuttle past overhead.

'It's over here! Hey, it's here!' No one had the inclination or ability to respond to his alarm.

It was impossible to keep track of half of what was happening. Injured men flung themselves from burning railings or dropped from the hot ceiling. Prisoner Eric saw the fire reaching for him and darted at the last possible instant into the safety of an uncoated service pipe, barely squeezing through in time to avoid the blast of fire that seared the bottoms of his feet. Another man died as the alien emerged from a steaming ventilation duct to land directly on him.

Running like mad, Aaron and one of the convicts raced for the waste disposal chamber, trying to stay ahead of the flames. The assistant superintendent made it; his companion wasn't quite so fast . . . or as lucky. The fire engulfed but did not stop him.

As they stumbled into the storage chamber junction, Ripley, Dillon, and prisoner Junior managed to knock the burning man to the floor and beat at the flames on his back. Aaron fought to catch his breath. As he did so a scuttling sound overhead caught his attention. With unexpected presence of mind he grabbed a QTC-soaked mop and jabbed it into the nearby flames. Holding the makeshift torch aloft, he jammed it into the gaping overhead duct port. The scuttling noise faded.

The prisoner died in Junior's arms, his mouth working without producing words. Junior rose and charged into the smoke and fire, screaming.

'Come and get me, chino! Come and get me!'

In the main access corridor smoke inhalation toppled another man. The last thing he saw as he went down was the alien rising before him, silhouetted by the flames and incredible heat. He tried to scream too, but failed.

Junior turned a corner and skidded to a halt. As he did so the alien whirled.

'Run, run!' The grieving prisoner charged past the monster, which gave chase without hesitation.

They all converged near the entrance to the toxic storage facility; Ripley and Dillon, Aaron and Morse, the other surviving prisoners. As the alien turned to confront them they emulated Aaron's example, lighting mops and heaving the makeshift missiles at the beast. Junior took the opportunity to move up close behind it.

'Here! Take a shot, fucker!'

Where quarry was concerned the alien once again demonstrated its inclination to choose proximity over proliferation. Whirling, it pounced on Junior. The two tumbled backward . . . into the storage chamber.

Struggling to ward off the intense heat, Dillon continued to extinguish flaming companions. When the last man was merely smouldering, he turned and tried to penetrate the flames to reach the back wall.

Ripley reached the control box and fumbled for the red button as Aaron jammed still another flaming mop into the entrance. A moment later Dillon managed to activate the sprinkler system.

Junior uttered a last, faint, hopeless cry as the heavy door slammed shut in front of him, sealing off the storage chamber. At the same time the showers opened up. Exhausted, terrified men, all with varying degrees of smoke or burn damage, hovered motionless in the corridor as the water poured down.

A noise from behind the door then, a distant skittering sound. Things that were not hands exploring, not-fingers scraping at their surroundings. The trapped alien was hunting, searching, for a way out. Gradually the noise ceased.

A couple of the survivors looked at one another as if about to burst into cheers. Ripley anticipated them curtly.

'It's not over.'

One of the men retorted angrily, 'Bullshit. It's inside, the door worked. We've got it.'

'What are you talking about?' Aaron challenged her. 'We got the bastard trapped, just like you planned it.'

Ripley didn't even look at him. She didn't have to explain herself because the silence was suddenly rocked by an ear-splitting concussion. A few of the men winced and a couple turned to run.

The rest gaped in amazement at the door, in which a huge convex dent had suddenly appeared. The echo of contact continued to cannonade along the multiple corridors. Before it had faded entirely a second thunderous boom reverberated through the antechamber and a second bulge appeared in the door.

'Son of a bitch,' Aaron muttered aloud, 'that's a ceramocarbide door.'

Dillon wasn't listening to him. A survivor of another kind, he was watching Ripley. She hadn't moved, so neither did he. If she started running he'd follow close on her heels, without any intention of stopping.

But she continued to hold her ground as a third dent manifested itself. His ears rang. *This is a lady I wish I'd known before*, he mused silently. *A lady who could change a man, alter the course and direction of his life. She could have changed mine. But that was before. Too late now. Been too late for a long time.*

No more concussive vibrations rattled his eardrums. No fourth bulge appeared in the barrier. Dead silence ruled the corridor. Gradually everyone's attention shifted from that no longer perfect but still intact doorway back to the single woman in their midst.

When she slowly sat down and closed her eyes, back against one wall, the unified sigh of relief that filled the room was like the last failing breeze that marks the passing of a recent storm.

# XI

The survivors gathered in the assembly hall, reduced in number but expanded in spirit. Dillon stood before them, waiting to make sure all were present. Only then did he begin.

'Rejoice, brothers! Even for those who have fallen this is a time of rejoicing. Even as we mourn their passing we salute their courage. Because of their sacrifice, we live, and who is to say which of us, the living or the dead, has the better deal?

'Of one thing we are certain: they have their reward. They are in a far better place because there can be no worse one. They will live forever. Rejoice. Those who are dead but go on, freed of their restraints, free from the excoriations of a thoughtless society. It abandoned them, and now they have abandoned it. They have moved up. They have moved higher. Rejoice and give thanks!'

The men bowed their heads and began to murmur softly to themselves.

Ripley and Aaron watched from the gallery above. Eventually the assistant superintendent glanced over at his companion. Both had spent time in the showers. They were far from refreshed, but at least they were clean. Ripley had delighted in the hot, pounding spray, knowing that this time she could enjoy it without having to keep a wary eye on the sealtight or the vents.

'What do you think of this?' He indicated the ragged, makeshift assemblage below.

She'd been listening with only half a mind, the rest of her thoughts elsewhere. 'Not much. I guess if they take pleasure in it. . .'

'You got it right there. Fuckers are crazy. But it keeps 'em quiet. The super and I were in agreement on that. Andrews always said it was a good thing Dillon and his meatballs were hung up on this holy roller crap. Makes 'em more docile.'

She glanced back at him. 'You're not the religious type.'

'Me? Shit, no. I got a job.' He looked thoughtful. 'I figure rescue team gets here in four, five days. Six, tops. They open the door, go in there with smart guns, and kill the bastard. Right?'

'Have you heard anything from them?' Her tone was non-committal.

'Naw.' He was feeling pretty good about the situation. And about himself. Out of this mess there was sure to come some good things.

'We only got a "message received." No details. Later we got something that said you were top priority. Again, no explanation. They don't cut us in on much. We're the ass-end of the totem pole out here.'

'Look,' she began guardedly, 'if the Company wants to take the thing back—'

'Take it back? Are you kiddin'? They aren't lunatics, you know. They'll kill it right away.' He frowned at her, then shrugged mentally. Sometimes he thought he understood this unusual woman perfectly, and then she'd throw him a complete curve.

Well, it wasn't his business to understand her; only to keep her alive. That was what Weyland-Yutani wanted. With Andrews gone and the alien safely contained, he was beginning to see some possibilities in the situation. Not only was he now the one in charge, it would be up to him to greet and explain things to the Company representative. He could render himself, as well as recent events, memorable in the eyes of his superiors. There might be a bonus in it for him or, even better, early retirement from Fiorina. It was not too much to hope for.

Besides, after years of toadying to Andrews and after what he'd been through the past couple of days, he'd earned whatever came his way.

'Hey, you're really concerned about this, aren't you? Why? What's there to be worried about? The damn thing's locked up where it can't get at us.'

'It's not the alien. It's the Company. I've gone around with them on this twice before.' She turned to him. 'They've coveted one of these things ever since my original crewmates discovered them. For bioweapons research. They don't understand what they're dealing with, and I don't care how much data they've accumulated on it. I'm concerned that they might want to try and take this one back.'

He gaped at her, and she found his honest disbelief reassuring. For the moment, at least, she was not without allies.

'Take it back? You mean alive? To Earth?'

She nodded.

'You've got to be kidding.'

'Look into my eyes, Aaron. This isn't a real humorous subject with me.'

'Shit, you mean it. That's insane. They gotta kill it.'

Ripley smiled tightly. 'Right. So I take it that we're agreed on this point?'

'You're damn right,' he said fervently.

He was with her, then, she mused. For now. The Company had a way of swaying people, inducing them to reassess their positions. Not to mention their values.

The infirmary was quiet. Peace had returned to the installation, if not to some of its inhabitants. Concerned that in Clemens's absence certain of the prisoners whose presence on Fiorina stemmed at least in part from their personal misapplication of certain proscribed pharmaceuticals might attempt to liberate them or their chemical cousins from their designated repository, Aaron sent Morse to keep an eye on them, as well as on the infirmary's sole occupant.

Morse sat on one of the cots, perusing a viewer. He was not one of those despondent over the dearth of entertainment material available on Fiorina, since he'd never been much of one for casual diversions. He was a man of action, or had been in his younger, more active days. Now he was a spieler, dealing in reminiscences.

Despite the fact that they'd known each other and had worked side by side for years, Golic had offered no greeting at his arrival, nor a single word since. Now the hulking prisoner finally turned his face away from the wall, his arms still buried inside the archaic restraining jacket.

'Hey, Morse.'

The older man looked up from his viewer. 'So you can still talk. Big deal. You never had nothin' to say anyhow.'

'C'mon, brother. Let me out of this thing.'

Morse grinned unpleasantly. 'Oh, so now that you're all wrapped up like a holiday roast suddenly I'm a "brother"? Don't give me any shit.'

'Come on, man, it hurts.'

'Sorry.' Morse turned back to his viewer. 'Aaron says to let you go, I'll let you go. Until then you stay tied up. I don't wanna get in no trouble. Not with a Company ship coming.'

'I didn't do nothing. I mean, I understand I was a little crazy for a while. Shit, who wouldn't be after what I saw? But I'm okay now. The doc fixed me. Just ask him.'

'Can't do that. The doc bought it. You heard.'

'Oh, yeah. That's right. I remember now. Too bad. He was a good guy, even if he did slap me in this.'

'Don't talk to me.' Morse made a disgusted face.

Golic continued to plead. 'What'd I do? Just tell me, what'd I do?'

Morse sighed and set the viewer aside, eyeing his fellow prisoner. 'I dunno, but I'll tell you what I'm going to do. I'm gonna guard your ass just like I was ordered.'

Golic sniffed derisively. 'You afraid of that pissant Aaron?'

'No, I aint, even if he is the unofficial superintendent now. I just don't want no trouble with Dillon, and if you're smart, which I doubt, neither do you.'

The bigger man sniffed glumly. 'All I did was tell about the dragon. About what it did to Boggs and Rains. Nobody believed me, but I wasn't lying. I should be the last one to be tied up. It ain't fair? You know what I'm sayin' is true. You saw it.'

Morse remembered. 'Fuckin'-A I saw it! It was big. And fast. Man, it was fast. And ug-ly.' He shuddered slightly. 'There's cleaner ways to die.'

'Hey, that's right.' Golic struggled futilely against his restraints. 'Let me loose, man. You got to let me loose. What if it gets in here? I couldn't even run. I'd be dead meat.'

'You'd be dead meat anyway. I saw enough to know that. But it doesn't matter because it ain't gonna get in here.' He smiled proudly. 'We got it trapped. Me and the others. Locked up tight. I'll bet it's good and mad. The Company'll deal with it when the ship gets here.'

'That's right,' Golic agreed readily. 'And the way I hear it, they'll be here soon. So what's the big deal? Why should I have to hang around like this? By the time the ship shows orbit my arms'll be dead. I'll need surgery, and all for nothin'. Come on, man. You know they ain't gonna take me offworld for no surgery, and we may not get a new medic for months. I'll have to suffer all that time, and it'll all be your fault.'

'Hey, lay off. I didn't put you in that.'

'No, but you're keepin' me in it, and the guy that gave the order's dead now. Aaron doesn't give a shit. He's too busy trying to make that lady lieutenant. Has he even asked about me?'

'Well, no,' Morse admitted guardedly.

'See?' Golic's face was full of pathetic eagerness. 'I won't cause you no trouble, Morse. I'll lay low until the ship gets here. Aaron won't even know I'm around. Come on, lemme loose. I'm hungry. What's the big deal? Didn't I always give you free ciggies before anybody else?'

'Well . . . yeah.'

'You're my friend. I love you.'

'Yeah, I love you too.' Morse hesitated, then cursed softly. 'Fuck it, why not? Nobody deserves to be tied up like an animal all day. Not even a big dumb schmuck like you. But you're gonna behave yourself. No fuckin' around or I'll get nothin' but shit.'

'Sure, Morse. Anything you say.' He turned to present his back and Morse began undoing the seals on the straps. 'No problem. Trust me, buddy. I'd do it for you.'

'Yeah, but I ain't crazy enough to get myself in a sack like this. They know I'm sane,' the other man said.

'C'mon, don't make fun of me. Do I sound like I'm crazy? Course not. It's just that everybody likes to make fun of me because I like to eat all the time.'

'It's not that you like to eat, it's your table manners, man.' Morse guffawed at his own humour as he undid the strap. 'That's got it.'

'Gimmie a hand, willya? My arms are so numb I can't move 'em.'

'Shit. Bad enough they ask me to keep an eye on you, now I gotta play nursemaid too.' He reached up and pulled the jacket off Golic. The bigger man helped as best he could.

'Where they got it?'

'Up in the nearest waste tank on Level Five. Man, did we get that sucker nailed down! I mean tight.' He fairly preened. 'Fuckin' marines couldn't do it, but we did.'

Golic was swinging his arms. Back and forth across his expansive chest, then up and around in ever-widening circles, getting the circulation back.

'But it's still alive?'

'Yeah. Too bad. You oughta see the dents it put in the door. Ceramocarbide door, man!' He shook his head wonderingly. 'One tough-ass organism. But we got it.'

'I gotta see it again.' The big man's gaze was focused on a point beyond Morse, on something visible only to Golic. His expression was impassive, unwavering. 'Got to see it again. He's my friend.'

Morse took a sudden, wary step backward. 'What the fuck you talkin' about?' His gaze whipped to the infirmary entrance.

Golic calmly ripped a small fire extinguisher off the nearby wall and the other man's eyes widened. He made a leap for the door . . . too slow. The extinguisher came down once, a second time, and Morse crumpled like a misplaced intention.

Golic looked down at him thoughtfully, his face full of idiot sadness, his tone apologetic. 'Sorry, brother, but I had a feeling you wouldn't understand. No more ciggies for you, mate.'

Silently he stepped over the unconscious form and exited the room.

# XII

Aaron fussed with the deep-space communicator. He was checked out on the equipment—it was a requirement of his rating—but he hadn't had occasion to make use of it since his assignment to Fiorina. Andrews had always handled things on the rare occasions when expensive near instantaneous communication between the installation and headquarters had been required. He was both pleased and relieved when the readouts cleared for use, indicating that contact with the necessary relays had been established.

Ripley hovered over him as he worked the keyboard. She offered no suggestions, for which he felt an obscure but nonetheless real gratitude. The message appeared on the main screen as he transmitted, each letter representing an impressive amount of sending power. Fortunately, with the fusion plant operating as efficiently as ever, there was no dearth of the necessary energy. As to the cost, another matter entirely, he opted to ignore that until and unless the Company should indicate otherwise.

FURY 361—CLASS C PRISON UNIT, FIORINA
REPORT DEATH OF SUPT. ANDREWS, MEDICAL OFFICER CLEMENS, EIGHT PRISONERS. NAMES TO FOLLOW...

When he'd finished the list he glanced back up at her. 'Okay, we got the first part. All nice and formal, the way the Company likes it. Now what do I say?'

'Tell them what happened. That the alien arrived on the EEV and escaped into the complex, that it was hunting down the local population one man at a time until we devised a plan of action, and that we've trapped it.'

'Right.' He turned back to the keyboard, hesitated. 'What do we call it? Just "the alien"?'

'That'd probably do for the Company. They'd know what you were referring to. Technically it's a xenomorph.'

'Right.' He hesitated. 'How do you spell it?'

'Here.' She elbowed him aside impatiently and leaned over the keyboard. 'With your permission?'

'Go ahead,' he said expansively. Impressed, he watched as her fingers flew over the keys.

HAVE TRAPPED XENOMORPH. REQUEST PERMISSION TO TERMINATE.

Aaron frowned up at her as she stood back from the board. 'That was a waste. We can't kill it. We don't have any weapons here, remember?'

Ripley ignored him, concentrating on the lambent screen. 'We don't have to tell them that.'

'Then why ask?' He was obviously confused, and she was in no hurry to enlighten him. Just then there were more important things on her mind.

Sure enough, letters began to appear on the readout. She smiled humourlessly. They weren't wasting any time replying, no doubt for fear that in the absence of a ready response she might simply proceed.

TO FURY 361—CLASS C PRISON UNIT
FROM NETWORK COMCON WEYLAND-YUTANI
MESSAGE RECEIVED

Aaron leaned back in the chair and rubbed his forehead tiredly. 'See? That's all they ever tell us. Treat us like shit, like we're not worth the expense of sending a few extra words.'

'Wait,' she told him.

He blinked. Subsequent to the expected official acknowledgment, letters continued to appear on the screen.

RESCUE UNIT TO ARRIVE YOUR ORBIT 1200
HOURS. STAND BY TO RECEIVE. PERMISSION DENIED
TO TERMINATE XENOMORPH. AVOID CONTACT
UNTIL RESCUE TEAM ARRIVES. REPEAT IMPERA-
TIVE—PERMISSION DENIED.

There was more, in the same vein, but Ripley had seen
enough. 'Shit.' She turned away, chewing her lower lip
thoughtfully. 'I knew it.'

Aaron's gaze narrowed as he tried to divide his attention
between Ripley and the screen. 'What do you mean, you knew
it? It doesn't mean anything. They know we don't have any
weapons.'

'Then why the "imperative"? Why the anxious insistence that
we don't do something they must realize we're not capable of
doing?'

He shrugged uncomprehendingly. 'I guess they don't want
to take any chances.'

'That's right,' she murmured tightly. 'They don't want to
take any chances.'

'Hey,' he said, suddenly alarmed, 'you're not thinking of
countermanding Company policy, are you?'

Now she did smile. 'Who, me? Perish the thought.'

The vestibule outside the toxic storage chamber was dimly
illuminated, but the inadequate light did not trouble the three
prisoners on duty. There was nothing in the shafts and tunnels
that could harm them, and no noise from within. The three
dents stood out clearly in the heavy door. They had not been
expanded, nor had they been joined by a fourth.

One man leaned casually against the wall, cleaning the dirt
from under his nails with a thin sliver of plastic. His companion
sat on the hard, cold floor, conversing softly.

'And I say the thing's gotta be dead by now.' The speaker
had sandy hair flecked with grey at the temples and a large,
curving nose that in another age and time would have given
him the aspect of a Lebanese merchant.

'How you figure that?' the other man asked.

'You heard the boss. Nothin' can get in or out of that box.' He jerked a thumb in the direction of the storage chamber. 'Not even gases.'

'Yeah. So?'

The first man tapped the side of his head with a finger. 'Think, stupid. If gas can't get out, that means air can't get in. The sucker's been in there long enough already to use up all the air twice over.'

The other glanced at the dented door. 'Well, maybe.'

'What d'you mean, maybe? It's big. That means it uses a lot of air. A lot more than a human.'

'We don't know that.' His companion wore the sombre air of the unconvinced. 'It ain't human. Maybe it uses less air. Or maybe it can hibernate or somethin'.'

'Maybe you oughta go in and check on how it's doin'.' The nail-cleaner looked up from his work with a bored expression. 'Hey, did you hear something?'

The other man suddenly looked to his right, into the dim light of the main tunnel.

'What's the matter?' His companion was grinning. 'The boogeyman out there?'

'No, dammit, I heard something.' Footsteps then, clear and coming closer.

'Shit.' The nail-cleaner moved away from the wall, staring.

A figure hove into view, hands clasped behind its back. The two men relaxed. There was some uneasy laughter.

'Dammit, Golic.' The man resumed his seat on the floor. 'You might've let us know it was you. Whistled or something.'

'Yeah,' said his companion. He waved at the chamber. 'I don't think it can whistle.'

'I'll remember,' the big man told them. His expression was distant and he swayed slightly from side to side.

'Hey, you okay, man? You look weird,' said the nail-cleaner.

His companion chuckled. 'He always looks weird.'

'It's okay,' Golic muttered. 'Let's go. Off and on. I gotta get in there.' He nodded towards the chamber.

The two men on the floor exchanged a puzzled glance, one carefully slipping his nail cleaner into a pocket. He was watching the new arrival closely.

'What the hell's he talking' about?' the theory-spinner wondered.

'Fucker's crazy,' his companion declared with conviction.

'What you want here, man? When did they let you out of the infirmary, anyway?'

'It's all right.' Golic's face shone with beatific determination. 'I just need to go in there and see the Beast. We got a lot of shit to talk over,' he added, as if that explained everything. 'I gotta go in there. You understand.'

'No, I don't understand. But I do know one thing. Neither you nor anyone else is goin' in there, dickhead. Big motherfucker'd eat you alive. Plus, you let that fucker out, and you can kiss our collective ass good-bye. Don't you know nothin', brother?'

'You wanna commit suicide,' declared his companion, 'go jump down a mine shaft. But you're not doin' it here. The super'd have our butts.' He started towards the intruder.

'The Superintendent is dead,' Golic announced solemnly as he brought out the club he'd been holding behind his back and used it to smash the skull of the man coming towards him.

'What the fuck? . . . Get him—!'

Golic was much faster and far more agile than they imagined, but then this time he was driven by something a good deal more powerful than a simple lust for food. The two men went down beneath the club, their heads and faces bloodied. It was all over very quickly. Golic didn't pause to see if his companions were still alive because he didn't really care. All that mattered to him now was the obsession which had taken complete control of his mind, his emotions, his very being.

He regarded the two bodies sprawled at his feet. 'I didn't really want to do that. I'll talk to your mothers. I'll explain it.'

Dropping the club, he walked up to the door and ran his fingers over the dented alloy. Pressing one ear to the smooth surface, he listened intently. No sound, no scraping, nothing. He giggled softly and moved to the control box, studying it thoughtfully for a long moment, much as a child would examine a complex new toy.

Chuckling to himself, he began fiddling with the controls, running his fingers playfully over the buttons until one clicked home. Deep within the surrounding ceramocarbide, mechanisms whined, metal brushed against metal. The door started to slide aside.

Only to halt as one of the big dents banged up against the jamb.

Frowning, Golic put his body into the narrow gap and pushed against the reluctant barrier, straining with his bulk. Motors hummed in confusion. The door opened a little wider, then stopped completely. The whirr of the motor died. Silence reigned once more.

His body blocking the opening, Golic turned to peer into the blackness within. 'Okay, I'm here. It's done. Just tell me what you want. Just tell me what to do, brother.' He smiled.

The darkness ahead was silent as a tomb. Nothing moved within.

'Let's get this straight. I'm with you all the way. I just want to do my job. You just gotta tell me what to do next.'

Though it lingered in the still air for quite some time, the two unconscious, bleeding men sprawled on the floor did not hear the singular high-pitched scream.

Dillon relaxed on his cot, engaged in his thousandth or ten thousandth game of solitaire. Idly he turned over another card and fingered his one long dreadlock as he spoke to the woman who stood before him.

'You're tellin' me they're comin' to take this thing away?'

'They'll try,' Ripley assured him. 'They don't want to kill it.'

'Why? It don't make no sense.'

'I agree completely, but they'll try anyway. I've gone around with them on this before. They look on the alien as a potential source of new bioproducts, perhaps even a weapons system.'

Dillon chuckled, a deep, rich sound. But he was clearly disturbed at the idea. 'Man, they're crazy.'

'They won't listen. They think they know everything. That because nothing on Earth can touch them, this thing can't either. But it doesn't care how much power, how many politicians the Company controls. They try to take it back for study and it'll take over. The risk is too great. We've got to figure out some way to finish it off before they get here.'

'From what you're tellin' me they ain't gonna like that much.'

'I don't give a damn what they think. I know better than anyone, better than any of their so-called specialists, what these things can do. Sure you can build a cell that'll hold one. We've proven that here. But these things are patient. And they'll exploit the slimmest opportunity. Make one slip with them and it's all over. That doesn't mean a lot here, or on an isolated little outcolony like Acheron. But if these things ever get loose on Earth, it'll make Armageddon seem like a school picnic.'

The big man fingered his dreadlock as he puffed away on his relaxer. 'Sister, I lost a lot of the faithful trappin' the motherfucker. Men I'd known and lived with for some long, hard years. There weren't many of us here to begin with and I'm gonna to miss them.' He looked up. 'Me and my brothers ain't gonna be the ones goin' in there and hittin' it with a stick.

'Why do we have to kill it anyway, if the Company's coming for it? Let them worry about it.'

She held her temper. 'I told you. They're going to try to take it back to Earth.'

He shrugged indifferently. 'What's wrong with that?'

'It'll destroy them. They can't control it. I told you, it'll kill them all. Everyone.'

He lay on his back, eying the ceiling and puffing contentedly. 'Like I said, what's wrong with that?'

Footsteps came pounding down the corridor outside the big

man's room. He sat up curiously as Ripley turned.

Morse halted, breathing hard. His gaze darted from one to the other. Clearly he hadn't expected to find Ripley there. 'Hey, Dillon!'

The big man removed the smoker from his lips. 'You're interrupting a private discussion, brother.'

Morse glanced anew at Ripley, then back to his fellow prisoner. 'Put it on hold. I think we got a very large fucking problem, mate.'

Aaron was no medical tech, but it didn't take a doctor to see how the two men had been killed. Their heads had been bashed in. That wasn't the alien's technique. The bloody club lying nearby only confirmed his suspicions. As for the one who'd killed them, he hadn't profited by his deed. Golic's mutilated corpse lay nearby.

Aaron rose to join the others in gazing numbly at the gap in the toxic storage chamber's doorway. Dillon had stuck a torch inside, confirmed that it was empty.

'This cuts it,' the acting superintendent muttered angrily. 'Miserable son of a bitch let it loose. Crazy fucker. Got what he deserved, by God. Now what the fuck are we gonna do? Andrews was right. We should've kept the dumb shithead chained up or sedated. Stupid-ass rehab "experts".' He paused, eying Ripley with some concern. 'What's the matter? Side effects again?'

She was leaning against the wall for support, sucking air in long, awkward gasps and holding her stomach with her other hand.

'Piss on her,' Morse growled. 'The fuckin' thing's loose out there.' He looked around wildly. 'Now what the fuck are we gonna do?'

'I just said that,' Aaron growled. 'You're the dumb prick that let Golic go. You miserable little shit, you've killed all of us!'

For a man of undistinguished physique he packed an impressive punch. Morse went down hard, blood streaming from his nose. As the acting superintendent loomed over him he was grabbed from behind. Dillon easily lifted him off the floor and set him aside. Aaron glared back at the big man, panting.

'Cut that shit out,' Dillon warned him.

'Watch yourself, Dillon! I'm still in charge here.'

'I ain't disputing it. But you don't be doin' that. You get me? You don't be beating on the brothers. That's my job.'

They regarded each other a moment longer. Then Aaron took a deep breath and looked away, back down at the cringing Morse. 'Then tell your fuckin' bozo to shape up. All this shit is his fault!'

Dillon ignored both of them as he turned to Ripley. 'What do you think? We took care of it once. We still got a chance?'

She was still leaning against the wall, breathing hard, her expression twisted. Her head was killing her. When she finally looked up her face was knotted with pain and nausea.

'I need . . . I need to get to the EEV.'

'Yeah, sure, but first we got to decide what to do about the creature.'

'No.' She shook her head sharply, her eyes watering slightly. 'EEV first . . . now.'

Aaron watched her anxiously. 'Yeah, okay. No problem. Whatever you say. But why?'

'The neuroscanner. I need to use one of the scanners that are built into every cryotube. I don't know if you've got anything similar in the infirmary but it wouldn't matter if you did. Clemens is gone, and I only know how to operate the instrumentation on the EEV. If it's still functional.' She winced, bending forward and clutching at her belly.

Dillon took a step towards her, beating Aaron to her side. This time she didn't object to the hands that helped steady her. She leaned against the big man for support until her breathing slowed.

'What the hell's wrong with you? You don't look so good.'

'Side effects from medication Clemens was giving her,' Aaron told him. His gaze narrowed uncertainly. 'I think.'

'Who gives a shit what's wrong with her?' Morse snapped. 'What are *we* gonna do?'

Aaron glared at him. 'You want to hit your back again, you little dork? Shut the fuck up and quit causin' panic.'

Morse didn't back off. 'Panic! You're so goddam dumb, you couldn't spell it. Don't tell me about panic! We ought to panic! We're screwed!'

'Yeah! And whose fault is it?'

'Both of you, shut up!' Dillon roared.

For a moment there was silence as each man glared at his neighbour but did not speak. Eventually Aaron shrugged.

'Okay, I'm out of ideas. What do we do?'

'What about the beach?' Morse opined hopefully.

'Right,' the acting superintendent responded sarcastically. 'The sun won't be up for another week, and when it's down it's forty below zero outside. The rescue team is ten hours away, so that makes a lot of sense.'

'Wonderful,' Morse grumbled as Ripley turned and wandered off. 'So you just want us to stay here and let this fuckin' beast eat us for lunch.'

'Get everybody that's still left together,' Dillon told him abruptly. 'Get 'em to the assembly hall. Lieutenant, you can—' He looked around, puzzled. 'Where'd she go?'

Within the vast unloading bay the Emergency Escape Vehicle rested where it had been left, undisturbed and looking lonely in the flickering industrial gloom. Footsteps echoed along walkways, precise and finite in the metal-walled pit. Faint illumination preceded feet, lighting the way through the semi-darkness.

Ripley stripped down in the cramped quarters, carefully setting her clothes aside. Naked, she sat down opposite a small keyboard. Several attempts were required before it flickered to life.

Her fingers worked the keyboard. She paused, played the keys again, then sat staring thoughtfully at the information displayed on the small screen. Rising, she left the readout and turned to the cryotube that had conveyed her to Fiorina.

It was an effort to squeeze back inside, and when she turned to work on the keyboard her hand barely reached.

'You need some help?'

She stared at Aaron's sudden appearance.

'Hey, didn't mean to scare you. Look, you shouldn't be wandering around alone.'

'I've heard that one before. Do me a favour. Run the keyboard. I can't reach over and see what I'm doing.'

He nodded and took the seat as she settled back into the tube. 'What do you want me to do?'

'Very little, I hope. The procedure's pretty straightforward. You ready?' she asked, not turning her head to face him.

He gazed at the screen, willing but baffled by the multiple options and instructions. 'I guess so. What do I do now?'

'Ignore the technospeak. There's an option menu at the bottom.'

His eyes dropped and he found himself nodding. 'I see it. What next?'

'Hit either $B$ or $C$. What's $C$?'

He studied the glowing print. 'Display biofunctions.'

'That's it.'

On his command the screen was replaced by another, no less complicated than its predecessor. 'Okay, now I've got a whole page of new turkeytalk.'

'Same procedure. Menu at the bottom. There should be a $V$ command, for visual display. Hit it.'

He complied, glancing back towards the cylinder.

Within the claustrophobic confines of the tube a small motor began to hum. Ripley shifted uncomfortably on the cushioned pallet, feeling very much like a bug under a microscope. Her surroundings suddenly pressed close around her, the wall and ceiling of the EEV threatened to collapse and pin her forever in place. She concentrated on keeping her heartbeat regular, her breathing steady as she closed her eyes. It helped, a little.

The display monitor in front of Aaron flickered. The

incomprehensible technical information vanished, to be replaced by an in-depth medical percep scan of the inside of Ripley's head.

'Okay,' he told her, 'we're hot. I'm looking at your brain. The scanner's also printing a lot of information next to the image, and there's all sorts of option switches at the bottom of the screen.'

'They're to make the scan system-specific,' she heard herself telling him. 'You know—nervous system, circulatory. Like that. Let's keep it as general as possible. Leave everything alone.'

'No problem there.' He stared in fascination at the screen. 'What am I supposed to be looking for? I don't know how to read this stuff.'

'Ignore the printouts and concentrate on the visuals,' she told him. 'Where is it now?'

'Moving down your neck. Am I supposed to see something?'

'If it's there, you'll know it when you see it.'

'Okay, but it all looks normal to me so far. Of course, I'm not Clemens.'

'Don't worry about it,' she told him. 'You won't have to be.'

She could hear the soft whine of the scanner as it moved down her body, sliding smoothly on its hidden track somewhere deep within the instrument-packed cryotube. Even though there was no actual physical contact between her and the instrument, she found herself twitching slightly at its perceived presence. Whoever said there was no link between imagination and physicality had never spent any time in cryogenic deep sleep.

'Upper chest now,' Aaron was saying. 'I can see the tops of your lungs. Heart coming into view.'

Despite her determination she found herself tensing uncontrollably. The muscles of her right forearm began to twitch spasmodically. The acting superintendent's voice buzzed in her ears, a lethal drone.

'Full chest view, at least according to what it says here. Heart and lungs seem to be functioning normally. Moving down.'

The twitching stopped, her breathing eased. 'Are you sure?'

'Hey, I don't see anything. If you'd give me an idea what I'm supposed to be looking for . . . maybe I missed it.'

'No.' Her mind was working furiously. 'No, you didn't miss it.'

'How do we get some enhancement?'

'Try *B*.'

He complied, to no avail. 'Nothing.' He tried again, muttering to himself. 'I gotta get a better angle.'

The instrumentation hummed. Suddenly he paused. 'Holy shit—' He broke off, eyes bulging as he leaned towards the screen.

'What?' she demanded. 'What is it?'

'I don't know how to tell you this. I think you got one inside you.'

He stared at the screen in disbelief. The embryonic creature was definitely kin to the monster that had destroyed the men . . . and yet it was also distinctively, subtly different.

It wasn't fair, she thought. She'd known, she'd more than suspected, for days. Then her chest scan had come through clean, giving her hope. Now this, the ultimate morbid revelation. Still, it wasn't a shock.

Now that her suspicions were confirmed she felt oddly liberated. The future was no longer in doubt. She could proceed, confident in the knowledge that she was taking the right course. The only course.

"What's it look like?'

'Fucking horrible,' Aaron told her, at once repelled and fascinated by what he was seeing. 'Like one of them, only small. Maybe a little different.'

'Maybe? Are you sure?'

'I'm not sure of anything. I didn't hang around to take pictures of the big one.'

'Keyboard,' she told him. 'Hit the pause button.'

'Already did. The scanner's stopped moving.'

'Now move the screen. I've got to take a look.'

The acting superintendent hesitated, looking towards the

cryotube and its recumbent occupant. 'I don't think you want to.'

'It's my choice. Do it.'

His lips tightened. 'Okay. If you think you're ready.'

'I didn't say I was ready. Just do it.'

He adjusted the viewscreen, waiting while she took a long, unblinking look.

'Okay. That's enough.' Aaron instantly deactivated the scanner.

'I'm sorry,' he murmured as gently as he could. 'I don't know what to say. Anything I can do—'

'Yeah.' She started struggling against the confines of the tube. 'Help me get out of here.' Her arms were extended upward, reaching towards him.

# XIII

The assembly hall looked emptier than ever with its reduced population of prisoners. The men muttered and argued among themselves as Dillon's fist slammed into the transparent window on the wall. Reaching in, he ripped free the loosely secured fire axe within and turned to hold it over his head.

'Give us strength, O Lord, to endure. Until the day. Amen.'

Fists rose into the air. The men were uncertain, but determined. Dillon surveyed them intently.

'It's loose. It's out there. A rescue team is on the way with the guns and shit. Right now there isn't anyplace that's real safe. I say we stay here. No overhead vent shafts. If it comes in, it's gotta be through the door. We post a guard to let us know if it's comin'. In any case, lay low. Be ready and stay right, in case your time comes.'

'Bullshit, man,' said prisoner David. 'We'll all be trapped in here like rats.'

Dillon glared at him. 'Most of you got blades stashed away. Get 'em out.'

'Right.' William grunted. 'You think we're gonna stab that motherfucker to death?'

'I don't think shit,' Dillon told him. 'Maybe you can hurt it while you're checkin' out. It's something. You got any better ideas?'

William did not. Nor did anyone else.

'I'm tellin' you,' Dillon continued, 'until that rescue team gets here, we're in the shit. Get prepared.'

'I ain't stayin' here.' William was already backing away. 'You can bet on it.'

Dillon turned, spat to his left. 'Suit yourself.'

Aaron tapped out the necessary code, then ran his thumb over the identiprint. The inner door which protected central communications slid aside, telltales coming to life on the board, the screen clearing obediently as the system awaited input.

'Okay,' he told the woman hovering nearby, 'what do you want to send?'

'You got a line back to the Network?'

His brows furrowed as he checked the readouts. 'Yeah, it's up. What do you want to say?'

'I want to tell them the whole place has gone toxic. I think they'll buy it. There's enough refining waste lying around to make it believable.'

He gaped at her. 'Are you kidding? Tell them that and they won't come here. Not until they can run and check out the results of a remote inspection, anyway. The rescue team'll turn back.'

'Exactly.'

'What are you talking about? We're like dead fish in a market waiting here. Our only hope is that they arrive in time to kill this fucker before it gets the rest of us. And maybe they can do something for you. You think of that? You're so sure this thing can beat anything they've got, but you don't know that for a fact. Maybe they can freeze you, do some kind of operation.

'You said that they've been accumulating information on it. You think they'd be coming to try and take one back if they didn't think they could contain it? Hell, we contained it and we weren't even ready for it. They'll be all set up to try a capture. They got the technology.'

She remained adamant. 'All the Company's got is greed for brains. I know. I've dealt with them and I've dealt with the aliens and frankly I'm not so sure that in the long run the

Company isn't the greater threat. I can't take the chance. All I know for certain is that if one of these things gets off this planet it'll kill everything. That's what it's designed to do: kill and multiply.

'We can't let the Company come here. They'll do everything in their power to take it back with them.' She made a disgusted noise. 'For profit.'

'Fuck you. I'm sorry as hell you got this thing inside you, lady, but I want to get rescued. I guess I've got more confidence in the Company than you. As it happens, I don't think you're looking at the situation rationally, and I suppose you've got plenty of reasons not to. But that doesn't mean I have to see things the same way, and I don't.

'I don't give a shit about these meatball prisoners. They can kill the thing or avoid it and howl holy hosannas to the heavens until they drop dead, but I got a wife and kid. Married real young so that despite the time distortions we'd still have quality time together when I finished my tour here. I was set to go back on the next rotation. Because of all this I can maybe claim extenuating hazards and go back with the rescue ship. I'll collect full-term pay and probably a bonus. If that happens you could say that your xenomorph's done me a favour.'

'I'm sorry. Look, I know this is hard for you,' she told him, trying to keep a rein on her temper, 'but I've got to send a message back. There's a hell of a lot more at stake here than your personal visions of happy suburban retirement. If the alien gets loose on Earth your sappy fantasies won't be worth crap.'

'I'll put my trust in the Company,' he said firmly.

'Dammit, Aaron, I need the code!'

He leaned back in the seat. 'Sorry, mum. It's classified. Can't expect me to violate the regs, can you?'

She knew she didn't have much time and she was starting to lose it. Here she was, dealing with the Company attitude again—that closed, restricted corporate world where ethics and morals were conveniently masked by regulations.

'Look, shithead, you can screw your precious regulations. It's got to be done. Give it to me!'

'No fuckin' way, lady. You don't get the code out of me without killing me first.'

She bent towards him, then forced herself to ease off. Once again she found herself tired beyond imagining. Why was she driving herself like this? She didn't owe anybody anything, least of all the representatives of the Company. If they took the alien on board their ship and it killed all of them, what was that to her?

'Nothing personal, you understand,' he was saying even as he was watching her carefully, alert for any sudden moves. He didn't think she posed him any real danger, but in the short time that he'd seen her operate he'd learned enough to know that it would be dangerous to underestimate her. 'I think you're okay.'

'Thanks.' Her tone was flat, dulled.

'So that's settled. We're working together again.' He was inordinately pleased. 'Got any ideas?'

She turned and he tensed momentarily, but she kept going past him to the service counter and drew herself a glass of water. Her thirst was constant and not due to tension and nerves. Her body was supplying fluids for more than one.

'The worker-warrior won't kill me,' she told him as she halted nearby.

His eyebrows rose. 'Oh, yeah? Why not?'

She sipped at the glass. 'It can't nail me without risking the health of the embryonic queen. And while I know that one of them can reproduce others of its kind, it may not be able to produce more than a single queen. Not enough of the right genetic material or something. I don't know that for a fact, but the proof is that it hasn't tried to kill me so far.'

'You really want to bet this thing's that smart?'

'Smarts may not have anything to do with it. It may be pure instinct. Damage the host and you risk premature damage to the unborn queen. It makes sense.' She met his gaze. 'It could've killed me twice already, but it didn't. It knows what I'm carrying.' She rubbed her chin thoughtfully.

'I'm going to find it,' she announced suddenly. 'We'll see how smart it is.'

He gaped at her. 'You're gonna go look for it?'

'Yeah. I got a pretty good idea where it is. It's just up there in the attic.'

He frowned. 'What attic? We don't have an attic.'

'It's a metaphor.' She finished the water.

'Oh.' He was staring at her.

'Wanna come?'

He shook his head. She smiled, put the glass back in its holder, and turned to exit the communications room. Aaron followed her with his eyes.

'Fuck me,' he murmured to no one in particular.

# XIV

The access corridor was empty. Pausing, she jammed the torch she'd been carrying into a seam in the wall, studying the line of aged, rusting pipes nearby. Grabbing the nearest, she braced herself and yanked hard. The metal snapped and bent towards her. A second yank broke it free. Satisfied, she continued on.

The infirmary seemed more deserted than ever. She paused for a look around, half expecting to see Clemens bent over his workstation, glancing up to grin in her direction. The computer was dark and silent, the chair empty.

It was hard to pull herself up into the overhead air duct while manipulating both the five-foot length of pipe and the flashlight, but she managed. The duct was dark and empty. Adjusting the battered flashlight for wide beam, she flashed it behind her before starting off in the opposite direction.

Exactly how long or how far she crawled before she started calling, she didn't know; only that the faint light from the infirmary had long since faded behind her. Her shouts were muted at first, then louder as fear gave way to anger. Her fate was inevitable. She just had to know. She had to see that thing face-to-face.

'Come on! I know you're here!' She advanced on hands and knees. 'Come on. Just do what you do.'

The air vent bent sharply to the left. She kept moving, alternately muttering and shouting. 'Come on, you shithead. Where are you when I need you?'

Her knees were getting raw when she finally paused, listening intently. A noise? Or her own imagination, working overtime?

'Shit.' She resumed her awkward, uncomfortable advance, turning another corner.

It opened into an alcove large enough to allow her to stand. Gratefully she climbed to her feet, stretching. The alcove was home to a decrepit, rusting water purification unit consisting of a thousand-gallon tank and a maze of neglected pipes.

Behind the tank the ventilation duct stretched off before her, an endless, difficult-to-negotiate tube of darkness. As she stared a fresh wave of nausea overcame her and she leaned against the tank for support.

As she did so an alien tail flicked out and knocked the flashlight from her fingers.

It landed on the concrete floor, spinning but staying lit. Ripley whirled, a feeling of desperation creeping up her spine.

The alien peered out at her from within the network of pipes and conduits where it had been resting. It regarded her.

'You fucker,' she muttered as she gathered her strength. Then she rammed the metal pipe directly into its thorax.

With an echoing roar it exploded from behind the maze, metal pipes giving way like straws. Fully aroused and alert, it crouched directly in front of her, thick gelatinous saliva dripping from its outer jaws.

She held her ground, straightening. 'Come on, fucker. Kill me!' When it didn't react she slammed at it again with the pipe.

With a roar it reached out and slapped the pipe away, stood glaring at her. Sweat pouring down her face, she continued to stare back.

Then it whirled and bolted into the darkness. She slumped, gazing after it.

'Bastard.'

Dillon found the lieutenant in the assembly hall, seated by herself in the huge, deeply shadowed room. She sat with her head in her hands, utterly exhausted, utterly alone. The fire axe dangling from his right hand, he walked over and halted nearby. She must have been aware of his presence, but did nothing to acknowledge it.

Ordinarily he would have respected her silence and moved on, but conditions had passed beyond ordinary.

'You okay?' She didn't reply, didn't look up.

'What are you doin' out here? You're supposed to be lyin' low like everybody else. What happens if that thing shows up?'

Her head rose. 'It's not going to kill me.'

'Why not?'

'Because I've got one of them inside of me. The big one won't kill its own.'

Dillon stared at her. 'Bullshit.'

'Look, I saw it an hour ago. I stood right next to it. I could've been lunch, but it wouldn't touch me. It ran away. It won't kill its future.'

'How do you know this thing's inside you?'

'I saw it on the cat-scan. It's a queen. It can make thousands like the one that's running around out there.'

'You mean like a queen bee?'

'Or ant. But, it's just an analogy. These creatures aren't insects. They just have a crudely analogous social structure. We don't know a great deal about them. As you may have noticed, they don't make for an easy study.'

'How do you know it's a queen?' he found himself asking.

'For one thing, the shape of the skull is very distinct. It's backed by a large, upsweeping frill. The beginnings of that were clearly visible in the scanner images. For another, the gestation period for the warrior-worker analogs is quite short, in some cases only a day or so. They mature through their different stages with incredible speed.' She looked rueful. 'Very effective survival trait.

'If this was an ordinary worker it would have come out by now, emerging through the sternum region. Also, it's gestating in the uterine cavity instead of the chest. Since a queen is a much more complex organism it apparently requires both more space and time to mature. Otherwise I'd be dead by now.

'I've seen how they work. It's not very pretty. When full grown this thing is enormous, much bigger than the one we've been fighting here. It's definitely going to be a queen, an egg layer. Millions of eggs. It's not going to be anything like the one that's out there running around loose.' Her voice fell. 'Like I said, nobody's had any experience with a larval queen. I don't know how long a gestation period it requires, except that it's self-evidently a lot longer than an ordinary worker.'

He gazed down at her. 'Still sounds like bullshit to me. If you got this thing inside you, how'd it get there?'

She was staring down at her hands. 'While I was in deep sleep. I guess the horrible dream I had wasn't exactly a dream. I got raped, though I don't know that that's a wholly accurate term. Rape is an act of premeditated violence. This was an act of procreation, even if my participation wasn't voluntary. We would call it rape, but I doubt that the creature would. It would probably find the concept ... well, alien.' She looked thoughtful, thinking back.

'The one that got loose on my first ship, the *Nostromo*, was making preparations to reproduce itself, but it wasn't a queen either. At least some of them must be hermaphroditic. Self-fertilizing, so that even one isolated individual can perpetuate the species. A warrior-worker is capable of producing eggs, but only slowly, one at a time, until it can develop a queen to take over the job. That's how this one was able to start a queen inside me. At least, that's the best scenario I can come up with. I'm no xenologist.'

She hesitated. 'Great, huh? I get to be mother of the mother of the apocalypse. I can't do what I should. So you've got to help. You've got to kill me.'

He took a step backward. 'What the fuck you talkin' about?'

'You don't get it, do you? I'm finished. I'm dead the minute it's born because I'll no longer be necessary to its continued survival. I've seen it happen. That I can live with, if it's not too strict a contradiction in terms. I've been ready to die ever since

I encountered the first one of these things. But I will be damned if I'm going to let those idiots from Weyland-Yutani take it back to Earth. They just might succeed, and that would be it for the rest of mankind. Maybe for all life on the planet. I don't see why these things wouldn't be able to reproduce in any animal of a size larger than, say, a cat.

'It has to die, and in order for that to happen somebody's got to kill me. You up to it?'

'You don't have to worry about that.'

'It's kind of funny, in a way. I've done so much killing lately and now I find I can't manage just one more. Maybe because I've had to concentrate so hard on surviving. So you've got to help me.' She met his gaze unwaveringly.

'Just do it. No speeches.' She turned her back on him. 'Come on,' she urged him, 'do it! You're supposed to be a killer . . . kill me. Come on, Dillon. Push yourself. Look back. I think you can do it, you big, ugly son of a bitch.'

He studied her slim form, the pale neck and slumped shoulders. A single well-directed blow would do it, cut through her spinal cord and vertebrae quick and clean. Death would be almost instantaneous. Then he could turn his attention to her belly, to the monstrous organism growing inside. Drag the corpse to the smelter and dump it all in the furnace. It would all be over and done with in a couple of minutes. He raised the axe.

The muscles in his face and arms tightened convulsively and the axe made a faint whooshing sound as it cut through the stale air. He brought it down and around full force . . . to slam into the wall next to her head. She jerked at the impact, then blinked and whirled on him.

'What the hell is this? You're not doing me any favours.'

'I don't like losin' a fight, not to nobody, not to nothin'. The big one out there's already killed half my guys, got the other half scared shitless. As long as it's alive, you're not saving any universe.'

'What's wrong? I thought you were a killer.'

'I want to get this thing and I need you to do it. If it won't kill you, then maybe that helps us fight it.' She stared at him helplessly. 'Otherwise, fuck you. Go kill yourself.'

'We knock its ass off, then you'll kill me?'

'No problem. Quick, painless, easy.' He reached up to tear the axe out of the wall.

The remaining men had assembled in the main hall. Aaron stood off to one side, sipping something from a tumbler. Dillon and Ripley stood side by side in the centre, confronting the others.

'This is the choice,' the big man was telling them. 'You die sitting here on your ass, or maybe you die out there. But at least we take a shot at killing it. We owe it one. It's fucked us over. Maybe we get even for the others. Now, how do you want it?'

Morse eyed him in disbelief. 'What the fuck are you talkin' about?'

'Killin' that big motherfucker.'

Aaron took a step forward, suddenly uneasy. 'Hold it. There's a rescue team on the way. Why don't we just sit it out?'

Ripley eyed him narrowly. 'Rescue team for who?'

'For us.'

'Bullshit,' she snapped. 'All they want's the beast. You know that.'

'I don't give a damn what they want. They aren't gonna kill us.'

'I'm not so sure. You don't know the Company the way I do.'

'Come on. They're gonna get us out of here, take us home.'

'They ain't gonna take *us* home,' Dillon observed.

'That still doesn't mean we should go and fight it,' Morse whined. 'Jesus Christ, give me a break.'

Aaron shook his head slowly. 'You guys got to be fucking nuts. I got a wife. I got a kid. I'm going home.'

Dillon's expression was hard, unyielding, and his tone smacked of unpleasant reality. 'Get real. Nobody gives a shit about you, Eight-five. You are not one of us. You are not a believer. You are just a Company man.'

'That's right,' Aaron told him. 'I'm a Company man and not some fucking criminal. You keep telling me how dumb I am, but I'm smart enough not to have a life sentence on this rock, and I'm smart enough to wait for some firepower to show up before we get out and fight this thing.'

'Right. Okay. You just sit here on your ass. It's fine.'

Morse's head jerked. 'How about if I sit here on my ass?'

'No problem,' Dillon assured him. 'I forgot. You're the guy that's got a deal with God to live forever. And the rest of you pussies can sit out too. Me and her'—he indicated Ripley— 'we'll do all the fighting.'

Morse hesitated, found some of the others gazing at him. He licked his lower lip. 'Okay. I'm with you. I want it to die. I hate the fucker. It killed my friends, too. But why can't we wait a few hours and have the fuckin' company techs with guns on our side? Why the shit do we have to make some fucking suicide run?'

'Because they won't kill it,' Ripley informed him. 'They may kill you just for having seen it, but they won't kill *it*.'

'That's crazy.' Aaron was shaking his head again. 'Just horseshit. They won't kill us.'

'Think not?' She grinned wolfishly. 'The first time they heard about this thing it was crew expendable. The second time they sent some marines: they were expendable. What makes you think they're gonna care about a bunch of double-Y chromos at the back end of space? Do you really think they're gonna let you interfere with advanced Company weapons research? They think you're crud, all of you. They don't give a damn about one friend of yours that died. Not one.' There was silence when she'd finished. Then someone in the back spoke up.

'You got some kind of plan?'

Dillon studied his companions, his colleagues in hell. 'This is a refinery as well as a mine, isn't it? The thing's afraid of fire ain't it? All we have to do is get the fuckin' beast into the big mould, pour hot metal on it.'

He kicked a stool across the floor. 'You're all gonna die. Only question is when. This is as good a place to take your first step to heaven as any. It's ours. It ain't much, but it's ours. Only question in life is how you check out. Now, you want it on your feet, or on your knees beggin'? I ain't much for beggin'. Nobody never gave me nothin'. So I say, fuck it. Let's fight.'

The men looked at one another, each waiting for someone else to break the silence that ensued. When it finally happened, the responses came fast and confident.

'Yeah, okay. I'm in.'

'Why not? We ain't got nothin' to lose.'

'Yeah . . . okay . . . right . . . I'm in.'

A voice rose higher. 'Let's kick its fuckin' ass.'

Someone else smiled. 'You hold it, I'll kick it.'

'Fuck it,' snapped Morse finally. 'Let's go for it.'

Somehow they got some of the lights on in the corridors. It wasn't a question of power; the central fusion plant provided plenty of that. But there were terminals and switches and controls that hadn't been maintained for years in the damp climate of Fiorina. So some corridors and access ways had light while others continued to dwell in darkness.

Ripley surveyed the moulding chamber thoughtfully as Dillon and prisoner Troy crowded close. Troy was the most technically oriented of the survivors, having enjoyed a brief career as a successful engineer before having the misfortune to find his wife and superior in the sack together. He'd murdered both of them, with all the technical skill he'd been able to muster. Faint howls of temporary insanity had bought him a ticket to Fiorina.

Now he demonstrated how the controls worked, which instruments were critical to the chamber's operation. Ripley watched and listened, uncertain.

'When was the last time you used this thing?'

'We fired it up five, six years ago. Routine maintenance check. That was the last time.'

She pursed her lips. 'Are you sure the piston's working?'

It was Dillon who replied. 'Nothin's for sure. Includin' you.'

'All I can say is that the indicators are all positive.' Troy shrugged helplessly. 'It's the best we've got.'

'Remember,' Dillon reminded them both, 'we trap it here first. We hit the release, start the piston, then the piston will shove the motherfucker right into the mould. This is a high-tech cold-stamp facility. End of his ass. End of story.'

Ripley eyed him. 'What if someone screws up?'

'Then we're fucked,' Dillon informed her calmly. 'We've got one chance. One shot at this, that's all. You'll never have time to reset. Remember, when you hit the release, for a few seconds you're gonna be trapped in here with that fucking thing.'

She nodded. 'I'll do it. You guys don't drop the ball, I won't.'

Dillon studied her closely. 'Sister, you'd better be right about that thing not wanting you. Because if it wants out, that's how it's gonna go. Right through you.'

She just stared back. 'Save you some work, wouldn't it?' Troy blinked at her, but there was no time for questions.

'Where you gonna be?' she asked the big man.

'I'll be around.'

'What about the others? Where are they?'

'Praying.'

The survivors spread out, working their way through the corridors, head-butting the walls to pump themselves up, cursing and whooping. They no longer cared if the monster heard them. Indeed, they wanted it to hear them.

Torchlight gleamed off access ways and tunnels, throwing nervous but excited faces into sharp relief. Prisoner Gregor peered out of an alcove to see his buddy William deep in prayer.

'Hey Willie? You believe in this heaven shit?'

The other man looked up. 'I dunno.'

ALAN DEAN FOSTER

'Me neither.'

'Fuck it. What else we gonna believe in? Bit late, now we're stuck here.'

'Yeah, ain't that the truth? Well, hey, what the fuck, right?' He laughed heartily and they both listened to the echoes as they boomed back and forth down the corridor, amplified and distorted.

Morse heard them all: distant reverberations of nervous laughter, of terror and near hysteria. He pressed the switch that would activate the door he'd been assigned to monitor. It whined . . . and jammed partway open. Swallowing nervously, he leaned through the gap.

'Hey, guys? Hold it, hold it. I don't know about this shit. Maybe we should rethink this. I mean, my fuckin' door ain't workin' right. Guys?'

There was no response from down the corridor.

Farther up, Gregor turned to face his companion. 'What the fuck's he saying?'

'Shit, I dunno,' said William with a shrug.


Prisoner Kevin held the long-burning flare out in front of him as he felt his way along the corridor wall. There was another man behind him, and behind him another, and so on for a substantial length of the tunnel. None were in sight now, though, and his nerves were jumping like bowstrings.

'Hey, you hear something?' he murmured to anyone who might happen to be within earshot. 'I heard Morse. Sounded kinda—'

The scream silenced him. It was so near it was painful. His legs kept moving him forward, as though momentary mental paralysis had yet to reach the lower half of his body.

Ahead, the alien was dismembering a friend of his named Vincent, who no longer had anything to scream with. He hesitated only briefly.

'Come and get me, you fucker!'

Obligingly, the monster dropped the piece of Vincent it was

holding and charged.

Kevin had been something of an athlete in his day. Those memories returned with a rush as he tore back up the corridor. Couple years back there wasn't a man he'd met he couldn't outrun. But he wasn't racing a man now. The inhuman apparition was closing fast, even as he accelerated to a sprint. The slower he became, the faster his hellacious pursuer closed.

He all but threw himself at the switch, whirling as he did so, his back slamming into the corridor wall, his chest heaving like a bellows. The steel door it controlled slammed shut.

Something crashed into it a bare second after it sealed, making a huge dent in the middle. He slumped slightly and somehow found the wind to gasp aloud, 'Door C9 . . . closed!'

At the other end of the recently traversed passageway prisoner Jude appeared, no mop in hand now. Instead he held his own flare aloft, illuminating the corridor.

'Yoo-hoo. Hey, fuckface, come and get me. Take your best shot.'

Confounded by the unyielding door, the alien pivoted at the sound and rushed in its direction. Jude took off running, not as fast as Kevin but with a bigger head start. The alien closed fast. Once again, seconds were the difference. The closing doorway separated it from its prey.

On the other side of the barrier Jude struggled to regain his wind. 'Over in the east wing: door B7. Safe.'

An instant later an alien foreleg smashed through the small glass window set in the steel. Screaming, Jude scrabbled backward along the wall, away from the clutching, frantic claws.

Dillon stood alone in the corridor he'd chosen to patrol and muttered to himself, 'It's started.'

'It's in tunnel B,' Morse was yelling as he ran down his own private passageway. 'Must be heading over to channel A!'

At an intersection, William nearly ran over Gregor as the two men joined up. 'I heard it,' Gregor muttered. 'Channel E, dammit.'

'Did you say B?'

'No, E.'

William frowned as he ran. 'We're supposed to stay—'

'Move your fucking ass!' In no mood to debate what their theoretical relative positions ought to have been, Gregor accelerated wordlessly. William trailed in his wake.

In a side corridor Jude linked up with Kevin, and they glanced knowingly at the other. 'You too?'

'Yeah.' Kevin was fighting for air.

'Okay. Over to E. Everybody.'

Kevin made a face, trying to remember. 'Where the fuck's E?'

His companion gestured impatiently. 'This way. Get a fuckin' move-on.'

David was still alone, and he didn't relish the continuing solitude. According to plan, he should have linked up with someone else by now. He did, however, find what remained of Vincent. It slowed but did not halt him.

'Kevin? Gregor? Morse? I found Vincent.' There was no response. He kept moving, unwilling to stop for anyone or anything. 'Let's shut this fucker down.' The section of tunnel directly ahead was darker than the one he'd just vacated, but at least it was empty.

In the main corridor Dillon glanced at Troy. 'Help them.'

The other prisoner nodded and headed into the maze of corridors, hefting his map.

Prisoner Eric stood nearby, his gaze shifting constantly from Dillon to Ripley. He chewed his lower lip, then his fingernails.

She studied the monitor panel. It showed Gregor going one way, Morse the other. Her expression twisted.

'Where the fuck is he going? Why don't they stick to the plan?'

'You're immune,' Dillon reminded her. 'They're not.'

'Well, what the hell are they doin'?'

Dillon's attention was focused on the dimly lit far end of the corridor. 'Improvising.'

She rested her hand on the main piston control, saw Eric staring at her. He was sweating profusely.

David stumbled through the darkened corridor, holding his flare aloft and trying to penetrate the blackness ahead.

'Here, kitty, kitty, kitty. Here—' He broke off. The alien was clearly visible at the far end, pounding ineffectually on the door through which Jude had recently vanished.

He cocked his arm as the alien turned. 'Here, pussycat. Playtime!' He heaved the hissing flare. The alien was already coming towards him before the flare struck the floor.

Turning, he raced at high speed back the way he'd come. The distance to the next barrier was relatively short and he felt confident he'd make it. Sure enough, he was through in plenty of time. His hand came down hard on the close button. The door slipped downward . . . and stopped.

His eyes widened and he made a soft mewling noise as he stumbled backward, one faltering step at a time.

As he stared, the door continued to descend in halting jerks. He quivered as the alien slammed full speed into the door. Metal buckled but continued to descend in its uneven, herky-jerky fashion.

An alien paw punched through the gap and made a grab at David's leg. Screaming, he leapt onto a ledge in the corridor wall. The hand continued to flail around, hunting for him, as the door jerked down, down. At the last instant the foreleg withdrew.

There was silence in the corridor.

It took him a long moment to find his voice and when he did, what emerged was little more than a terrified whimper.

'Door 3, channel F. Shut . . . I hope.'

Morse didn't hear him as he continued to stumble blindly down his own corridor. 'Kevin? Gregor? Where the fuck are you? Where is everybody? K, L, M, all locked and secured.' He glanced at a plate set into the wall. 'I'm back in A.'

In a side passageway Gregor was likewise counting panels. 'Channel V secure. Channel P holding.'

Behind him William struggled to keep pace. 'Did you say P or D?' he shouted. 'For fuck's sake—'

Gregor turned without stopping. 'Shut the fuck up! Move!'

Unsure of his position, Kevin discovered that he'd doubled back on himself. 'Shit. I'm in R. That's safe. That's safe. Isn't it?'

Jude overheard, raised his voice so his companion could hear. 'You forgot, man. R leads back into F. I'm moving through F right now. Gonna shut it down.'

Disoriented, Troy halted at an intersection. He'd moved too fast, ignoring the map and trusting to memory. Now he found himself appraising the multiple tunnels uncertainly.

'Channel F? Where the fuck—There ain't no fuckin' Channel F.'

He moved forward, hesitated, and chose the corridor to his immediate right, instead.

That corridor, however, was already occupied by another frustrated inhabitant.

Dillon and Ripley heard the distant screams. As usual, the screams didn't last for very long.

'Morse?' Dillon called out. 'Kevin, Gregor?'

Ripley strained to see past him. 'What's going on back there?'

The big man glanced tensely back at her. 'All they have to do is run down the damn corridors.' He hefted his axe and started forward. 'Stay here.'

The side corridor from which they expected their visitor remained deserted. No alien. No people. Only distant, echoing voices, some distinctly panicky.

Behind him, Eric voiced his thoughts aloud. 'Where in hell is it?' Dillon just glanced at him.

Sucking up his courage, David moved back to the door and peered through the small window. The corridor beyond was empty. He raised his voice.

'I've lost him. Don't know where the fucking thing is. Not

gonna open the door. I think it went up in the fucking air vent.'
He turned slowly to inspect the single air vent in the tunnel
above him.

He was right.

Ripley waited until the last of the echoes faded to silence.
Eric had been moving forward, his eyes harbingers of
imminent collapse. If someone didn't do something he was
going to break and take off running. There was nowhere to
run to. She moved towards him, caught his gaze, trying to stare
him down, to transfer some of her own confidence into him.

Dillon had disappeared down the side corridor. It didn't take
him long to find Troy's remains. After a quick look around he
retreated back the way he'd come.

Morse and Jude had finally linked up. They ran along side
by side . . . until Jude slipped and went down hard. His fingers
fumbled at the warm, sticky mess which had tripped him up.

'For fuck's sake . . . yuck.'

When Jude lifted it towards the flare for a better look, Morse
recoiled in horror. Then he got a good look at what he'd
picked up, and they screamed in unison.

Ripley listened intently, momentarily forgetting Eric. The
screams were close now—immediate, not echoes. Suddenly the
prisoner whirled and rushed back towards the piston control.
She ran after him . . .

As the alien appeared, racing across the corridor.

Eric's fingers started to convulse on the control and she
barely had time to grab his hand.

'Wait! It's not in position yet!' With an effort of will she
managed to block him from releasing the piston.

That was all it took. Defeated mentally as well as physically,
he slumped back, exhausted and trembling.

Kevin moved slowly through the corridor. He was getting
close to the piston alcove now, as safe a place as any. He'd done
everything that had been asked of him. They couldn't ask for
more, not now.

Something made him look up. The alien positioned in the

vent above didn't bother to drop. Instead it reached down and snatched him up as easily as if it had been fishing for a frog. Blood splattered.

At the far end of the passageway Dillon appeared. Spotting Kevin's jerking legs he rushed forward and threw both arms around the twitching knees. It was something the alien wasn't prepared for and the two men dropped.

Ripley saw Dillon drag the wounded prisoner into the main corridor. With a glance at the useless Eric she started forward to help.

Blood spurted from the injured man's neck. Whipping off her jacket, she wrapped it around the wound as tightly as she could. The blood slowed, but not enough. Dillon held the man close, murmuring.

'No death, only—'

There was no time to finish the prayer. The alien emerged from the side access. Ripley rose and started backing away.

'Leave the body. Draw it in.'

Dillon nodded and joined her, the two of them retreating towards the control alcove.

The alien watched. They were moving slowly, with nowhere to retreat to. There was still life in the damaged figure on the floor. The alien jumped forward to finish the job.

Spinning, Ripley made a slashing gesture in Eric's direction. Eric erupted from his hiding place and slammed his hand down on the control.

The piston shot forward, sweeping up both Kevin's body and that of the alien, shunting them towards the gap which led to the furnace. Heat and howling air filled the corridor.

But the alien had vanished.

Sweating, Ripley took a step forward. 'Where the hell's it gone?'

'Shit!' Dillon tried to peer around the machinery. 'It must be behind the fucking piston.'

'Behind it?' She gaped at him.

'Seal the doors,' he bellowed. 'We gotta get it back!' They

exchanged a glance, then took off in opposite directions.

'Jude, Morse!' Dillon pounded down the corridor he'd chosen, searching for survivors. Meanwhile Ripley went in search of Eric and William. Found them, too, all mixed up together and no longer worrying. About anything. She continued on.

Morse was creeping now, no longer running. Hearing a noise, he paused to check the side access way from which it had come, exhaled at the sight of nothing. He began retracing his steps, keeping his eyes forward.

Until he bumped into something soft and animate.

'What the—!'

It was Jude. Equally startled, the other man whirled, displaying the scissors he carried like a weapon. Simultaneously relieved and furious, Morse grabbed the twin blades and angled them upward.

'Not like this. Like this, moron.' He whacked the other man on the side of the head. Jude blinked, nodded, and started off in the other direction.

Dillon was back in the main corridor, yelling. 'Jude, Jude!' The other man heard him, hesitated.

The alien was right behind him.

He ran like hell, towards Dillon, who urged him on.

'Don't look back. As fast you fucking can!'

Jude came on, trying, trying for his life. But he wasn't Kevin, or Gregor. The alien caught him. Blood exploded against the door that Dillon desperately sent slamming shut.

In the next corridor Ripley heard, growled to herself. Time was ticking away as the piston continued its inexorable and currently useless slide forward.

Gregor screamed for help, but there was no one around to hear him. He raced blindly down the passageway, ricocheting off the corners like a pinball until he slammed into Morse, running hard the other way. Nervous, then half laughing, they picked themselves up, staring in relief at one another.

Until the alien flashed past and smashed into Gregor in

midlaugh, tearing him apart.

Blood and pulp showering his face and torso, Morse fought to scramble away, screaming for mercy to something that neither understood nor cared about his desperation. He could only stare as the creature methodically eviscerated Gregor's corpse. Then he crawled frantically.

He bumped into something unyielding and his head whipped around. Feet. His head tilted back. Ripley's feet.

She threw the flare she was holding at the alien as it tried to duck into an air vent. The burning magnesium alloy forced it to drop Gregor's ravaged body.

'Come on, you bastard!'

As Morse looked on in fascination, the alien, instead of rushing forward to decapitate the lieutenant, coiled up against the far wall. She advanced, ignoring its cringing and spitting.

'Come on. I got what you want. Follow me. I want to show you something. Come on, damn you!'

The alien's tail flicked out and lashed at her. Not hard enough to kill; just enough to fend her off.

At that moment Dillon arrived in the doorway, staring. She whirled on him. 'Get back! Don't get in the way!'

The alien resumed its attack posture, turning to face the newcomer. Desperately Ripley inserted herself between it and Dillon, who suddenly realized not only what was happening but what she was trying to do.

Moving up behind, he grabbed her and held her tight.

The alien went berserk, but kept its distance as the two humans retreated, Ripley tight in Dillon's grasp.

It followed them into the main corridor, keeping the distance between them constant, waiting. Dillon glanced towards the waiting mould, called out.

'In here, stupid!'

The alien hesitated, then leapt to the ceiling and scuttled over the doorjamb.

'Shut it!' Ripley said frantically. 'Now!'

Dillon didn't need to be told. He activated the door in front

of her. It slammed tight, imprisoned them both in the main
corridor with the creature.

Morse appeared behind it, saw what was happening. 'Get
out! Get the fuck out now!'

Ripley yelled back at him. 'Close the door!' The other man
hesitated. As he did so, the alien turned towards him. 'Now!'

Morse jerked forward and hit the switch. The door rammed
down, sealing them off from his position. A moment later the
piston appeared, continuing on its cleansing passage and
obscuring them from view.

He turned and ran back the way he'd come.

Within the main corridor the piston crunched into the alien,
knocking it backward. Forgetting now about the two humans, it
turned and sought to squeeze a leg past the heavy barrier.
There was no room, no space at all. The piston continued to
force it towards the mould.

Dillon and Ripley were already there. End of the line.
Nowhere else to go.

Morse scrambled up the ladder which led to the crane cab,
wondering if he remembered enough to activate it. He'd have
to. There was no time to consult manuals, and no one left to
ask.

The massive landing craft disdained the use of the mine's
ill-maintained landing port. Instead it set down on the gravel
outside, the backwash of its manoeuvring engines sending dirt
and rocks flying. Moments later heavily armed men and
women were rushing towards the facility's main entrance.

From within the lock Aaron watched them disembark, a
broad smile on his face. They had smart guns and armour
piercers, thermoseeking rails and rapid-fire handguns. They
knew what they'd be up against and they'd come prepared. He
straightened his uniform as best as he could and prepared to
pop the lock.

'I knew they'd make it.' He raised his voice. 'Hey, over here!
This way!' He started to activate the lock mechanism.

He never got the chance. The door exploded inward, six commandos and two medical officers rushing through even before the dust had settled. All business, the commandos spread out to cover the lock area. Aaron moved forward, thinking as he did so the captain in their midst was a dead ringer for the dead android that had been on the lieutenant's lifeboat.

'Right, sir,' he announced as he stopped in front of the officer and snapped off a crisp salute. 'Warder Aaron, 137512.'

The captain ignored him. 'Where is Lieutenant Ripley? Is she still alive?'

A little miffed at the indifference but still eager to be of help, Aaron replied quickly. 'Right, sir. If she's alive, she's in the mould. They're all in the leadworks with the beast, sir. Absolute madness. Wouldn't wait. I tried to tell 'em—'

The officer cut him off abruptly. 'You've seen this beast?'

'Right, sir. Horrible. Unbelievable. She's got one inside her.'

'We know that.' He nodded tersely in the direction of the commandos. 'We'll take over now. Show us where you last saw her.'

Aaron nodded, eagerly led them into the depths of the complex.

Ripley and Dillon continued retreating into the mould until there was ceramic alloy at their backs and nowhere else to stand. A grinding of gears caught her attention and her head jerked back. Overhead she could see machinery moving as the refinery responded inexorably to its programmed sequence.

'Climb,' she told her companion. 'It's our only chance!'

'What about you?' Dillon spoke as the alien entered the back part of the mould, forced along by the massive piston.

'It won't kill me.'

'Bullshit! There's gonna be ten tons of hot metal in here!'

'Good! I keep telling you I want to die.'

'Yeah, but I don't—'

Soon the alien would be on top of them. 'Now's your chance,' Ripley shouted. 'Get going!'

He hesitated, then grabbed her. 'I'm taking you with me!' He shoved her bodily upward.

Despite her resistance he managed to climb. Seeing that he wasn't going to go without her she reluctantly started to follow suit, moving in front of him up the side of the mould. The alien turned away from the piston, spotted them, and followed.

At the top of the mould Ripley secured herself on the edge and reached down to help Dillon. The pursuing alien's inner jaws shot out, reaching. Dillon kicked down, slashing with the fire axe.

Ripley continued her ascent as Dillon fought off the pursuit. More noise drew her attention to the now functioning gantry crane. She could see Morse inside, cursing and hammering at the controls.

The Company squad appeared on the crest of the observation platform, their leader taking in all of what was happening below at a glance. Morse saw them shouting at him, ignored them as he frantically worked controls.

The container of now molten alloy bubbled as it was tipped.

'Don't do it!' the captain of the new arrivals shouted. 'No!'

The alien was very close now, but not quite close enough. Not quite. White-hot liquid metal poured past Ripley and Dillon, a torrent of intense heat that forced both of them to cover their faces with their hands. The metallic cascade struck the alien and knocked it screeching back into the mould, sweeping it away as flames leaped in all directions.

High above, Morse stood and stared down through the window of the crane, his expression a mask of satisfaction.

'Eat shit, you miserable fucker!'

Dillon joined Ripley on the edge of the mould, both of them staring downward as they shielded their faces against the heat rising from the pool of bubbling metal. Suddenly her attention was drawn by movement across the way.

'They're here!' She clutched desperately at her companion. 'Keep your promise!'

Dillon stared at her. 'You mean it.'

'Yes! I've got it inside me! Quit fucking around!'

Uncertainly, he put his hands around her throat.

She stared at him angrily. 'Do it!'

His fingers tightened. A little pressure, a twist, and her neck would snap. That was all it would take. A moment of effort, of exertion. It wasn't as if he didn't know how, as if he hadn't done it before, a long time ago.

'I can't!' The denial emerged from his throat half cry, half croak. 'I can't do it!' He looked at her almost pleadingly.

His expression turned to one of horror as he turned around, only to confront the burning and smoking alien. Resigned, he allowed himself to be pulled into its embrace, the two of them vanishing beneath the roiling surface of the molten metal. Ripley looked on in astonishment, at once repelled and fascinated. An instant later the curving alien skull reappeared. Dripping molten metal, it began to haul itself out of the mould.

Looking around wildly, she spotted the emergency chain. It was old and corroded, as might be the controls it activated. Not that it mattered. There was nothing else. She wrenched on it.

Water erupted from the large bore quencher that hung over the lip of the mould. She found herself tangled up in the chain, unable to get loose. The torrent of water drenched her, sweeping her around in tight spirals. But the chain would not let her go.

The cold water struck the alien and its hot metal coat. The head exploded first, then the rest of the body. Then the mould, vomiting chunks of supercooled metal and steam. Morse was thrown to the floor of the crane's cab as it rocked on its supports, while the commando unit ducked reflexively for cover.

Warm water and rapidly cooling metal rained down on the chamber.

When the deluge ended, the commando team resumed its approach. But not before Ripley had swung herself up onto the crane platform, Morse reaching out to help her.

Once aboard, she leaned against the guard rail and gazed

down into the furnace. Time again to be sick. The attacks of nausea and pain were coming more rapidly now.

She spotted the Company men coming up the stairs from below, heading for the crane. Aaron was in the forefront. She tried to escape but had no place to go.

'Don't come any closer,' she shouted. 'Stay where you are.'

Aaron halted. 'Wait. They're here to help.'

She stared at him, pitying the poor simpleton. He had no idea what the stakes were, or what was likely to happen to him when the Company finally obtained what it was after. Except that that was not going to happen.

Another wave of nausea swept over her and she staggered against the railing. As she straightened, a figure stepped out from behind the heavily armed commandos. She gaped, uncertain at first of what she was seeing. It was a face she knew.

'Bishop?' she heard herself mumbling uncertainly.

He stopped, the others crowding close behind him, waiting for orders. The figure indicated they should relax. Then he turned to her, smiling reassuringly.

'I just want to help you. We're all on the same side.'

'No more bullshit!' she snapped. Weak as she was, it took an effort to make the exclamation sound convincing. 'I just felt the damn thing move.'

As everyone present watched, she stepped farther out on the gantry platform. Something smacked into her lungs and she winced, never taking her eyes off the figure before her.

It was Bishop. No, not Bishop, but a perfect duplicate of him. A completely in control, perfect down to the pores on his chin double of the sadly dismembered and cybernetically deceased Bishop. *Bishop II*, she told herself numbly. *Bishop Redux. Bishop to pawn four; Bishop takes Queen.*

*Not as long as this lady's alive*, she thought determinedly.

'You know who I am,' the figure said.

'Yeah. A droid. Same model as Bishop. Sent by the fucking Company.'

'I'm not the Bishop android. I designed it. I'm the prototype, so naturally I modelled its features after my own. I'm very human. I was sent here to show you a friendly face, and to demonstrate how important you are to us. To me. I've been involved with this project from the beginning. You mean a lot to me, Lieutenant Ripley. To a great many people. Please come down.

'I just want to help you. We have everything here to help you, Ripley.' He gazed anxiously up at her. Now she recognized the outfits two of Bishop II's companions wore: they were biomedical technicians. It made her think of Clemens.

'Fuck you. I know all about "friendly" Company faces. The last one I saw belonged to an asshole named Burke.'

The man's smile faded. 'Mr. Burke proved to be a poor choice to accompany your previous mission, an individual rather more interested in his own personal aggrandisement than in good Company policy. I assure you it was a mistake that will not be repeated. That is why I am here now instead of some inexperienced, overly ambitious underling.'

'And you, of course, have no personal ambitions.'

'I only want to help you.'

'You're a liar,' she said quietly. 'You don't give a shit about me or anyone else. You just want to take it back. These things have acid for blood where you Company people just have money. I don't see a lot of difference.'

Bishop II studied the floor for a moment before again raising his eyes to the solitary figure atop the crane platform. 'You have plenty of reasons to be wary, but unfortunately not much time. We just want to take you home. We don't care anymore what happens to it. We know what you've been through. You've shown great courage.'

'Bullshit!'

'You're wrong. We want to help.'

'What does that mean?'

'We want to take the thing out of you.'

'And keep it?'